The
Robot
Novels

By Isaac Asimov
Published by Ballantine Books:

THE CLASSIC FOUNDATION SERIES:
    Foundation
    Foundation and Empire
    Second Foundation
    Foundation's Edge
    Foundation and Earth

THE GALACTIC EMPIRE NOVELS:
    The Stars, Like Dust
    The Currents of Space
    Pebble in the Sky

THE ROBOT NOVELS:
    The Caves of Steel
    The Naked Sun
    The Robots of Dawn
    Robots and Empire

I, ROBOT

THE GODS THEMSELVES

THE END OF ETERNITY

THE BICENTENNIAL MAN and Other Stories

NIGHTFALL and Other Stories

NINE TOMORROWS

THE MARTIAN WAY and Other Stories

THE WINDS OF CHANGE and Other Stories

THE EARLY ASIMOV—Book One

THE EARLY ASIMOV—Book Two

THE LUCKY STARR ADVENTURES:
Writing as Paul French:
    David Starr—Space Ranger
    Lucky Starr and the Pirates of the Asteroids
    Lucky Starr and the Oceans of Venus
    Lucky Starr and the Big Sun of Mercury
    Lucky Starr and the Moons of Jupiter
    Lucky Starr and the Rings of Saturn

The Robot Novels

The Caves of Steel
The Naked Sun
The Robots of Dawn

Isaac Asimov

A Del Rey Book

Ballantine Books • New York

A Del Rey Book
Published by Ballantine Books

Library of Congress Catalog Card Number: 88-91946
ISBN: 345-33119-2

This edition published by arrangement with Doubleday & Co., Inc.

Manufactured in the United States of America

Cover design by Richard Aquan
Cover art by Michael Whelan
Text design by Holly Johnson

First Ballantine Books Trade Edition: October 1988
10 9 8 7 6 5 4 3 2 1

Contents

A Bit About Lije Baley and R. Daneel . . .

The three books in the volume you are now holding were not planned as a trilogy; I am not good at forethoughtful literary schemes. Each book I write is an immediate challenge to be completed without any thought for the future. I never deliberately work out the plot on one book in such a way as to lay the groundwork for an already planned second book. Instead, if I decide on a second book, I find I have to reread the first and try to extract from it something on which I can hang the second.

Thus, when I wrote *The Caves of Steel* in 1953, it was, as far as I knew, a single book destined to stand by itself. Why not? My three earlier novels (*Pebble in the Sky; The Stars, Like Dust;* and *The Currents of Space*) were all one-shots. I have never to this day written another story about Joseph Schwartz or Biron Farrill or Rik. To be sure, those three early novels are lumped together as "The Empire Novels," but that is a unity of setting and not one of plot and character.

The situation changed with *The Caves of Steel* for two reasons. First, the book did better than any book I had written up to that time. I like to think that I am impervious to the success or failure of a book, that my only interest is in *writing* it. "What happens to a book after I finish writing it," I like to say, "is the publisher's worry, not mine."

I suppose, though, that that will only go so far. The success of *The Caves of Steel* did not go totally unnoticed by me. At that time I was busy with a totally unconnected novel, *The End of Eternity*, but I found myself planning to return to the dramatis personae of *The Caves of Steel* at the very first chance.

That's where the second reason came in. It wasn't just the novel's success. I had, in the course of writing *The Caves of Steel*, become very pleased with the two characters I had created, Elijah Baley and R. Daneel Olivaw. I wanted to encounter them again!

The only way to encounter them was to write another book, and so I did—*The Naked Sun*. It was perfectly clear to me that I was going to follow the formula of the first book. There was going to be a murder before the start of the book (I hate revelling in gore and violence and I like my murders off-stage) and again Elijah would find himself stuck with both a criminal puzzle and a political problem.

So far, so good, but I'm not master of my books. I think up an ending which strikes me as good. I then think up a beginning and at once begin to write. Everything that goes between the beginning and the ending is made up as I go along, and sometimes the intermediate details surprise me. No, let me be honest, the intermediate details *always* surprise me.

In the case of *The Naked Sun*, the biggest surprise was the introduction of a new character—Gladia Delmarre. I admit that I had to have a suspect and the nature of the plot made it necessary that the suspect be feminine, but how on Earth did it come about that I fell in love with her? For fall in love I did!

And once I was in love with her, it became impossible to leave Elijah unmoved, so although the ending was precisely what I had planned it to be when I started the book, I found myself inserting a small detail that left me in tears.

Now I was in a terrible fix. I had to bring back Elijah Baley and R. Daneel *and Gladia, too*. I couldn't leave the love story unfinished for it was breaking my heart.

Except that I *did* leave it unfinished. *The Naked Sun* was published in 1957, and in 1958 I began a third book, but it didn't work. I quit—the only time I ever abandoned a novel and returned the advance. That particular failure came just at a time when I was switching my main effort to nonfiction. Perhaps it was my intense drive to write nonfiction that deflected my novel-writing abilities to the point of failure. Or perhaps it was my failure at the third Elijah Baley novel that helped turn me to nonfiction. I honestly can't say, but for a quarter of a century, the trilogy remained unfinished and I tried not to think about what I had done.

Then things changed. In 1981, Doubleday lost patience with me and told me that I had to write another *Foundation* book, and added another zero to my usual advance in order to explain the necessity more clearly.

I like to say that I am impervious to money, but I suppose I am a *wee* bit pervious, especially when I'm a champion at feeling guilt. Doubleday was very eloquent concerning their loyalty in publishing every darn thing I gave them to publish even when the project in question couldn't possibly make any money at all, and how I did owe them a *little* loyalty in return.

So I wrote *Foundation's Edge* and to my utter astonishment it was a bestseller.

Well! Apparently, I could still write novels, even the kind of novels I wrote when I was a callow lad. At once, my guilt at having abandoned Elijah, Daneel, and Gladia rose as high as my nostrils and began to choke me. If that's the way things are, I thought, let's try the third robot novel again.

I did, and it turned out to be *The Robots of Dawn*. I planned it to be twice as long as the earlier books because that's the way Doubleday wanted it, and in so doing I had room to deal with Elijah and Gladia in considerable detail, which delighted me.

Again I found it necessary to introduce a new character, a second robot, R. Giskard Reventlov. And that, in turn, made it necessary to continue the story, for when I was through with the book, it turned out I wasn't through with him. Hence the fourth book in the series, *Robots and Empire*, which is not part of the trilogy, for it takes place two hundred years later, after Elijah Baley has left this mortal vale. However, Gladia is still alive and so are the two robots, Daneel and Giskard. Elijah remains a pervasive influence in the new book, but the patient Daneel finally has the chance to be the hero.

Robots and Empire was first published in September, 1985, and is available in paperback from Del Rey. If you like this trilogy, you'll like the fourth book, too. (I like to say that I scorn promoting my books. I'm a writer, not a peddler, I say.—But surely a *little* promotion, now and then, can't hurt, can it?)

The Caves of Steel

Contents

Conversation with a Commissioner

Lije Baley had just reached his desk when he became aware of R. Sammy watching him expectantly.

The dour lines of his long face hardened. "What do you want?"

"The boss wants you, Lije. Right away. Soon as you come in."

"All right."

R. Sammy stood there blankly.

Baley said, "I said, all right. Go away!"

R. Sammy turned on his heel and left to go about his duties. Baley wondered irritably why those same duties couldn't be done by a man.

He paused to examine the contents of his tobacco pouch and make a mental calculation. At two pipefuls a day, he could stretch it to next quota day.

Then he stepped out from behind his railing (he'd rated a railed corner two years ago) and walked the length of the common room.

Simpson looked up from a merc-pool file as he passed. "Boss wants you, Lije."

"I know. R. Sammy told me."

A closely coded tape reeled out of the merc-pool's vitals as the small instrument searched and analyzed its "memory" for the desired information stored in the tiny vibration pattern of the gleaming mercury surface within.

"I'd kick R. Sammy's behind if I weren't afraid I'd break a leg," said Simpson. "I saw Vince Barrett the other day."

"Oh?"

"He was looking for his job back. Or any job in the Department. The poor kid's desperate, but what could I tell him. R. Sammy's doing his job and that's all. The kid has to work a delivery tread on the yeast farms now. He was a bright boy, too. Everyone liked him."

Baley shrugged and said in a manner stiffer than he intended or felt, "It's a thing we're all living through."

The boss rated a private office. It said JULIUS ENDERBY on the clouded glass. Nice letters. Carefully etched into the fabric of the glass. Underneath, it said COMMISSIONER OF POLICE, CITY OF NEW YORK.

Baley stepped in and said, "You want to see me, Commissioner?"

Enderby looked up. He wore spectacles because his eyes were sensitive and couldn't take the usual contact lenses. It was only after one got used to the sight of them that one could take in the rest of the face, which was quite undistinguished. Baley had a strong notion that the Commissioner valued his glasses for the personality they lent him and suspected that his eyeballs weren't as sensitive as all that.

The Commissioner looked definitely nervous. He straightened his cuffs, leaned back, and said, too heartily, "Sit down, Lije. Sit down."

Baley sat down stiffly and waited.

Enderby said, "How's Jessie? And the boy?"

"Fine," said Baley, hollowly. "Just fine. And your family?"

"Fine," echoed Enderby. "Just fine."

It had been a false start.

Baley thought: Something's wrong with his face.

Aloud, he said, "Commissioner, I wish you wouldn't send R. Sammy out after me."

"Well, you know how I feel about those things, Lije. But he's been put here and I've got to use him for something."

"It's uncomfortable, Commissioner. He tells me you want me and then he stands there. You know what I mean. I have to tell him to go or he just keeps on standing there."

"Oh, that's my fault, Lije. I gave him the message to deliver and forgot to tell him specifically to get back to his job when he was through."

Baley sighed. The fine wrinkles about his intensely brown eyes grew more pronounced. "Anyway, you wanted to see me."

"Yes, Lije," said the Commissioner, "but not for anything easy."

He stood up, turned away, and walked to the wall behind his desk. He touched an inconspicuous contact switch and a section of the wall grew transparent.

Baley blinked at the unexpected insurge of grayish light.

The Commissioner smiled. "I had this arranged specially last year, Lije. I don't think I've showed it to you before. Come over here and take a look. In the old days, all rooms had things like this. They were called 'windows.' Did you know that?"

Baley knew that very well, having viewed many historical novels.

"I've heard of them," he said.

"Come here."

Baley squirmed a bit, but did as he was told. There was something indecent about the exposure of the privacy of a room to the outside world. Sometimes the Commissioner carried his affectation of Medievalism to a rather foolish extreme.

Like his glasses, Baley thought.

That was it! That was what made him look wrong!

Baley said, "Pardon me, Commissioner, but you're wearing new glasses, aren't you?"

The Commissioner stared at him in mild surprise, took off his glasses, looked at them and then at Baley. Without his glasses, his round face seemed rounder and his chin a trifle more pronounced. He looked vaguer, too, as his eyes failed to focus properly.

He said, "Yes."

He put his glasses back on his nose, then added with real anger, "I broke my old ones three days ago. What with one thing or another I wasn't able to replace them till this morning. Lije, those three days were hell."

"On account of the glasses?"

"And other things, too. I'm getting to that."

He turned to the window and so did Baley. With mild shock, Baley realized it was raining. For a minute, he was lost in the spectacle of water dropping from the sky, while the Commissioner exuded a kind of pride as though the phenomenon were a matter of his own arranging.

"This is the third time this month I've watched it rain. Quite a sight, don't you think?"

Against his will, Baley had to admit to himself that it was impressive. In his forty-two years he had rarely seen rain, or any of the phenomena of nature, for that matter.

He said, "It always seems a waste for all that water to come down on the city. It should restrict itself to the reservoirs."

"Lije," said the Commissioner, "you're a modernist. That's your trouble. In Medieval times, people lived in the open. I don't mean on the farms only. I mean in the cities, too. Even in New York. When it rained, they didn't think of it as waste. They gloried in it. They lived close to nature. It's healthier, better. The troubles of modern life come from being divorced from nature. Read up on the Coal Century, sometimes."

Baley had. He had heard many people moaning about the invention of the atomic pile. He moaned about it himself when things went wrong, or when he got tired. Moaning like that was a built-in facet of human nature. Back in the Coal Century, people moaned about the invention of the steam engine. In one of Shakespeare's plays, a character moaned about the invention of gunpowder. A thousand years in the future, they'd be moaning about the invention of the positronic brain.

The hell with it.

He said grimly, "Look, Julius." (It wasn't his habit to get friendly with the Commissioner during office hours, however many "Lijes" the Commissioner threw at him, but something special seemed called for here.) "Look, Julius, you're talking about everything except what I came in here for, and it's worrying me. What is it?"

The Commissioner said, "I'll get to it, Lije. Let me do it my way. It's—it's trouble."

"Sure. What isn't on this planet? More trouble with the R's?"

"In a way, yes. Lije. I stand here and wonder how much more trouble the old world can take. When I put in this window, I wasn't just letting in the sky once in a while. I let in the City. I look at it and I wonder what will become of it in another century."

Baley felt repelled by the other's sentimentality, but he found himself staring outward in fascination. Even dimmed by the weather, the City was a tremendous thing to see. The Police Department was in the upper levels of City Hall, and City Hall reached high. From the Commissioner's window, the neighboring towers fell short and the tops were visible. They were so many fingers, groping upward. Their walls were blank, featureless. They were the outer shells of human hives.

"In a way," said the Commissioner, "I'm sorry it's raining. We can't see Spacetown."

Baley looked westward, but it was as the Commissioner said. The horizon closed down. New York's towers grew misty and came to an end against blank whiteness.

"I know what Spacetown is like," said Baley.

"I like the picture from here," said the Commissioner. "It can just be made out in the gap between the two Brunswick Sectors. Low domes spread out. It's the difference between us and the Spacers. We reach high and crowd close. With them, each family has a dome for itself. One family: one house. And land between each dome. Have you ever spoken to any of the Spacers, Lije?"

"A few times. About a month ago, I spoke to one right here on your intercom," Baley said, patiently.

"Yes, I remember. But then, I'm just getting philosophical. We and they. Different ways of life."

Baley's stomach was beginning to constrict a little. The more devious the Commissioner's approach, the deadlier he thought might be the conclusion.

He said, "All right. But what's so surprising about it? You can't spread eight billion people over Earth in little domes. They've got space on their worlds, so let them live their way."

The Commissioner walked to his chair and sat down. His eyes looked unblinkingly at Baley, shrunken a bit by the concave lenses in his spectacles. He said, "Not everyone is that tolerant about differences in culture. Either among us or among the Spacers."

"All right. So what?"

"So three days ago, a Spacer died."

Now it was coming. The corners of Baley's thin lips raised a trifle, but the effect upon his long, sad face was unnoticeable. He said, "Too bad. Something contagious, I hope. A virus. A cold, perhaps."

The Commissioner looked startled. "What are you talking about?"

Baley didn't care to explain. The precision with which the Spacers had bred disease out of their societies was well known. The care with which they avoided, as far as possible, contact with disease-riddled Earthmen was even better known. But then, sarcasm was lost on the Commissioner.

Baley said, "I'm just talking. What did he die of?" He turned back to the window.

The Commissioner said, "He died of a missing chest. Someone had used a blaster on him."

Baley's back grew rigid. He said, without turning, "What are you talking about?"

"I'm talking about murder," said the Commissioner, softly. "You're a plain-clothes man. You know what murder is."

And now Baley turned. "But a Spacer! Three days ago?"

"Yes."

"But who did it? How?"

"The Spacers say it was an Earthman."

"It can't be."

"Why not? You don't like the Spacers. I don't. Who on Earth does? Someone didn't like them a little too much, that's all."

"Sure, but——"

"There was the fire at the Los Angeles factories. There was the Berlin R-smashing. There were the riots in Shanghai."

"All right."

"It all points to rising discontent. Maybe to some sort of organization."

Baley said, "Commissioner, I don't get this. Are you testing me for some reason?"

"What?" The Commissioner looked honestly bewildered.

Baley watched him. "Three days ago a Spacer was murdered and the Spacers think the murderer is an Earthman. Till now," his finger tapped the desk, "nothing's come out. Is that right? Commissioner, that's unbelievable. Jehoshaphat, Commissioner, a thing like this would blow New York off the face of the planet if it really happened."

The Commissioner shook his head. "It's not as simple as that. Look, Lije, I've been out three days. I've been in conference with the Mayor. I've been out to Spacetown. I've been down in Washington, talking to the Terrestrial Bureau of Investigation."

"Oh? And what do the Terries have to say?"

"They say it's our baby. It's inside city limits. Spacetown is under New York jurisdiction."

"But *with* extraterritorial rights."

"I know. I'm coming to that." The Commissioner's eyes fell away from Baley's flinty stare. He seemed to regard himself as having been suddenly demoted to the position of Baley's underling, and Baley behaved as though he accepted the fact.

"The Spacers can run the show," said Baley.

"Wait a minute, Lije," pleaded the Commissioner. "Don't rush me. I'm trying to talk this over, friend to friend. I want you to know my position. I was there when the news broke. I had an appointment with him—with Roj Nemennuh Sarton."

"The victim?"

"The victim." The Commissioner groaned. "Five minutes more and I, myself, would have discovered the body. What a shock that would have been. As it was, it was brutal, brutal. They met me and told me. It started a three-day nightmare, Lije. That on top of having everything blur on me and having no time to replace my glasses for days. *That* won't happen again, at least. I've ordered three pairs."

Baley considered the picture he conjured up of the event. He could see the tall, fair figures of the Spacers approaching the Commissioner with the news and breaking it to him in their unvarnished emotionless way. Julius would remove his glasses and polish them. Inevitably, under the impact of the event, he would drop them, then look down at the broken remnants with a quiver of his soft, full lips. Baley was quite certain that, for five minutes anyway, the Commissioner was much more disturbed over his glasses than over the murder.

The Commissioner was saying, "It's a devil of a position. As you say, the Spacers have extraterritorial rights. They *can* insist on their own investigation, make whatever report they wish to their home governments. The Outer Worlds could use this as an excuse to pile on indemnity charges. You know how *that* would sit with the population."

"It would be political suicide for the White House to agree to pay."

"And another kind of suicide not to pay."

"You don't have to draw a picture," said Baley. He had been a small boy when the gleaming cruisers from outer space last sent down their soldiers into Washington, New York, and Moscow to collect what they claimed was theirs.

"Then you see. Pay or not pay, it's trouble. The only way out is to find the murderer on our own and hand him over to the Spacers. It's up to us."

"Why not give it to the TBI? Even if it is our jurisdiction from a legalistic viewpoint, there's the question of interstellar relations——"

"The TBI won't touch it. This is *hot* and it's in our lap." For a moment, he lifted his head and gazed keenly at his subordinate. "And it's not good, Lije. Every one of us stands the chance of being out of a job."

Baley said, "Replace us all? Nuts. The trained men to do it with don't exist."

"R's," said the Commissioner. "*They* exist."

"What?"

"R. Sammy is just a beginning. He runs errands. Others can patrol the expressways. Damn it, man, I know the Spacers better than you do, and I know what they're doing. There are R's that can do your work and mine. We can be declassified. Don't think differently. And at our age, to hit the labor pool . . ."

Baley said, gruffly, "All right."

The Commissioner looked abashed. "Sorry, Lije."

Baley nodded and tried not to think of his father. The Commissioner knew the story, of course.

Baley said, "When did all this replacement business come up?"

"Look, you're being naïve, Lije. It's been happening all along. It's been happening for twenty-five years, ever since the Spacers came. You know that. It's just beginning to reach higher, that's all. If we muff this case, it's a big, long step toward the point where we can stop looking forward to collecting our pension-tab booklets. On the other hand, Lije, if we handle the matter well, it can shove that point far into the future. And it would be a particular break for you."

"For me?" said Baley.

"You'll be the operative in charge, Lije."

"I don't rate it, Commissioner. I'm a C-5, that's all."

"You want a C-6 rating, don't you?"

Did he? Baley knew the privileges a C-6 rating carried. A seat on the expressway in the rush hour, not just from ten to four. Higher up on the list-of-choice at the Section kitchens. Maybe even a chance at a better apartment and a quota ticket to the Solarium levels for Jessie.

"I want it," he said. "Sure. Why wouldn't I? But what would I get if I couldn't break the case?"

"Why wouldn't you break it, Lije?" the Commissioner wheedled. "You're a good man. You're one of the best we have."

"But there are half a dozen men with higher ratings in my department section. Why should they be passed over?"

Baley did not say out loud, though his bearing implied it strongly, that the Commissioner did not move outside protocol in this fashion except in cases of wild emergency.

The Commissioner folded his hands. "Two reasons. You're not just another detective to me, Lije. We're friends, too. I'm not forgetting we were in college together. Sometimes it may look as though I have forgotten, but that's the fault of rating. I'm Commissioner, and you know what that means. But I'm still your friend and this is a tremendous chance for the right person. I want you to have it."

"That's one reason," said Baley, without warmth.

"The second reason is that I think you're my friend. I need a favor."

"What sort of favor?"

"I want you to take on a Spacer partner in this deal. That was the condition the Spacers made. They've agreed not to report the murder; they've agreed to leave the investigation in our hands. In return, they insist one of their own agents be in on the deal, the whole deal."

"It sounds like they don't trust us altogether."

"Surely you see their point. If this is mishandled, a number of them will be in trouble with their own governments. I'll give them the benefit of the doubt, Lije. I'm willing to believe they mean well."

"I'm sure they do, Commissioner. That's the trouble with them."

The Commissioner looked blank at that, but went on. "Are you willing to take on a Spacer partner, Lije?"

"You're asking that as a favor?"

"Yes, I'm asking you to take the job with all the conditions the Spacers have set up."

"I'll take a Spacer partner, Commissioner."

"Thanks, Lije. He'll have to live with you."

"Oh, now, hold on."

"I know. I know. But you've got a large apartment, Lije. Three rooms. Only one child. You can put him up. He'll be no trouble. No trouble at all. And it's necessary."

"Jessie won't like it. I know that."

"You tell Jessie," the Commissioner was earnest, so earnest that his eyes seemed to bore holes through the glass discs blocking his stare, "that's if you do this for me, I'll do what I can when this is all over to jump you a grade. C-7, Lije. C-7!"

"All right, Commissioner, it's a deal."

Baley half rose from his chair, caught the look on Enderby's face, and sat down again.

"There's something else?"

Slowly, the Commissioner nodded. "One more item."

"Which is?"

"The name of your partner."

"What difference does that make?"

"The Spacers," said the Commissioner, "have peculiar ways. The partner they're supplying isn't—isn't . . ."

Baley's eyes opened wide. "Just a minute!"

"You've got to, Lije. You've *got* to. There's no way out."

"Stay at my apartment? A thing like that?"

"As a friend, please!"

"No. *No!*"

"Lije, I can't trust anyone else in this. Do I have to spell it out for you? We've *got* to work with the Spacers. We've got to succeed, if we're to keep the indemnity ships away from Earth. But we can't succeed just any old way. You'll be partnered with one of their R's. If *he* breaks the case, if he can report that we're incompetent, we're ruined, anyway. We, as a department. You see that, don't you? So you've got a delicate job on your hands. You've got to work with him, but see to it that *you* solve the case and not he. Understand?'

"You mean co-operate with him 100 per cent, except that I cut his throat? Pat him on the back with a knife in my hand?"

"What else can we do? There's no other way out."

Lije Baley stood irresolute. "I don't know what Jessie will say."

"I'll talk to her, if you want me to."

"No, Commissioner." He drew a deep, sighing breath. "What's my partner's name?"

"R. Daneel Olivaw."

Baley said, sadly, "This isn't a time for euphemism, Commissioner. I'm taking the job, so let's use his full name. *Robot* Daneel Olivaw."

Round Trip on an Expressway

There was the usual, entirely normal crowd on the expressway: the standees on the lower level and those with seat privileges above. A continuous trickle of humanity filtered off the expressway, across the decelerating strips to localways or into the stationaries that led under arches or over bridges into the endless mazes of the City Sections. Another trickle, just as continuous, worked inward from the other side, across the accelerating strips and onto the expressway.

There were the infinite lights: the luminous walls and ceilings that seemed to drip cool, even phosphorescence; the flashing advertisements screaming for attention; the harsh, steady gleam of the "light-worms" that directed THIS WAY TO JERSEY SECTIONS, FOLLOW ARROWS TO EAST RIVER SHUTTLE, UPPER LEVEL FOR ALL WAYS TO LONG ISLAND SECTIONS.

Most of all there was the noise that was inseparable from life: the sound of millions talking, laughing, coughing, calling, humming, breathing.

No directions anywhere to Spacetown, thought Baley.

He stepped from strip to strip with ease of the lifetime's practice. Children learned to "hop the strips" as soon as they learned to walk. Baley scarcely felt the jerk of acceleration as his velocity increased with each step. He was not even aware that he leaned forward against the force. In thirty seconds he had reached the final sixty-mile-an-hour strip and could step aboard the railed and glassed-in moving platform that was the expressway.

No directions to Spacetown, he thought.

No need for directions. If you've business there, you know the way. If you don't know the way, you've no business there. When Spacetown was first established some twenty-five years earlier, there was a strong tendency to make a showplace out of it. The hordes of the City herded in that direction.

The Spacers put a stop to that. Politely (they were always polite), but without any compromise with tact, they put up a force barrier between themselves and the City. They established a combination Immigration Service and Customs Inspection. If you had business, you identified yourself, allowed yourself to be searched, and submitted to a medical examination and a routine disinfection.

It gave rise to dissatisfaction. Naturally. More dissatisfaction than it deserved. Enough dissatisfaction to put a serious spoke in the program of modernization. Baley remembered the Barrier Riots. He had been part of the mob that had suspended itself from the rails of the expressways, crowded onto the seats in disregard of rating privileges, run recklessly along and across the strips at the risk of a broken body, and remained just outside the Spacetown barrier for two days, shouting slogans and destroying City property out of sheer frustration.

Baley could still sing the chants of the time if he put his mind to it. There was "Man Was Born on Mother Earth, Do You Hear?" to an old folk tune with the gibberish refrain, "Hinky-dinky-parley-voo."

> *"Man was born on Mother Earth, do you hear?*
> *Earth's the world that gave him birth, do you hear?*
> *Spacer, get you off the face*
> *Of Mother Earth and into space.*
> *Dirty Spacer, do you hear?*

There were hundreds of verses. A few were witty, most were stupid, many were obscene. Every one, however, ended with "Dirty Spacer, do you hear?" Dirty, dirty. It was the futile throwing back in the face of the Spacers their most keenly felt insult: their insistence on considering the natives of Earth as disgustingly diseased.

The Spacers didn't leave, of course. It wasn't even necessary for them to bring any of their offensive weapons into play. Earth's outmoded fleet had long since learned that it was suicide to venture near any Outer World ship. Earth planes that had ventured over the Spacetown area in the very early days of its establishment had simply disappeared. At the most, a shredded wing tip might tumble down to Earth.

And no mob could be so maddened as to forget the effect of the subetheric hand disruptors used on Earthmen in the wars of a century ago.

So the Spacers sat behind their barrier, which itself was the product of their own advanced science, and that no method existed on Earth of breaking. They just waited stolidly on the other side of the barrier until the City quieted the mob with somno vapor and retch gas. The below-level penitentiaries rattled afterward with ringleaders, malcontents, and people who had been picked up simply because they were nearest at hand. After a while they were all set free.

After a proper interval, the Spacers eased their restrictions. The barrier was removed and the City Police entrusted with the protection of Spacetown's isolation. Most important of all, the medical examination was more unobtrusive.

Now, thought Baley, things might take a reverse trend. If the Spacers seriously thought that an Earthman had entered Spacetown and committed murder, the barrier might go up again. It would be bad.

He lifted himself onto the expressway platform, made his way through the standees to the tight spiral ramp that led to the upper level, and there sat down. He didn't put his rating ticket in his hatband till they passed the last of the Hudson Sections. A C-5 had no seat rights east of the Hudson and west of Long Island, and although there was ample seating available at the moment, one of the way guards would have automatically ousted him. People were increasingly petty about rating privileges and, in all honesty, Baley lumped himself in with "people."

The air made the characteristic whistling noise as if frictioned off the curved windshields set up above the back of every seat. It made talking a chore, but it was no bar to thinking when you were used to it.

Most Earthmen were Medievalists in one way or another. It was an easy thing to be when it meant looking back to a time when Earth was *the* world and not just one of fifty. The misfit one of fifty at that. Baley's head snapped to the right at the sound of a female shriek. A woman had dropped her handbag; he saw it for an instant a pastel pink blob against the dull gray of the strips. A passenger hurrying from the expressway must inadvertently have kicked it in the direction of deceleration and now the owner was whirling away from her property.

A corner of Baley's mouth quirked. She might catch up with it, if she were clever enough to hurry to a strip that moved slower still and if other feet did not kick it this way or that. He would never know whether she would or not. The scene was half a mile to the rear, already.

Chances were she wouldn't. It had been calculated that, on the average, something was dropped on the strips every three minutes somewhere in the City and not recovered. The Lost and Found Department was a huge proposition. It was just one more complication of modern life.

Baley thought: It was simpler once. Everything was simpler. That's what makes Medievalists.

Medievalism took different forms. To the unimaginative Julius Enderby, it meant the adoption of archaisms. Spectacles! Windows!

To Baley, it was a study of history. Particularly the history of folkways.

The City now! New York City in which he lived and had his being. Larger than any City but Los Angeles. More populous than any but Shanghai. It was only three centuries old.

To be sure, something had existed in the same geographic area before then that had been *called* New York City. That primitive gathering of population had existed for three thousand years, not three hundred, but it hadn't been a *City*.

There were no Cities then. There were just huddles of dwelling places large and small, open to the air. They were something like the Spacers' Domes, only much different, of course. These huddles (the largest barely reaching ten million in population and most never reached one million) were scattered all over Earth by the thousands. By modern standards, they had been completely inefficient, economically.

Efficiency had been forced on Earth with increasing population. Two billion people, three billion, even five billion could be supported by the planet by progressive lowering of the standard of living. When the population reaches eight billion, however, semistarvation becomes too much like the real thing. A radical change had to take place in man's culture, particularly when it turned out that the Outer Worlds (which had merely been Earth's colonies a thousand years before) were tremendously serious in their immigration restrictions.

The radical change had been the gradual formation of the Cities over a thousand years of Earth's history. Efficiency implied bigness. Even in Medieval times that had been realized, perhaps unconsciously. Home industry gave way to factories and factories to continental industries.

Think of the inefficiency of a hundred thousand houses for a hundred thousand families as compared with a hundred-thousand-unit Section; a book-film collection in each house as compared with a Section film concentrate; independent video for each family as compared with video-piping systems.

For that matter, take the simple folly of endless duplication of kitchens and bathrooms as compared with the thoroughly efficient diners and shower rooms made possible by City culture.

More and more the villages, towns, and "cities" of Earth died and were swallowed by the Cities. Even the early prospects of atomic war only slowed the trend. With the invention of the force shield, the trend became a headlong race.

City culture meant optimum distribution of food, increasing utilization of yeasts and hydroponics. New York City spread over two thousand square miles and at the last census its population was well over twenty million. There were some eight hundred Cities on Earth, average population, ten million.

Each City became a semiautonomous unit, economically all but self-sufficient. It could roof itself in, gird itself about, burrow itself under. It became a steel cave, a tremendous, self-contained cave of steel and concrete.

It could lay itself out scientifically. At the center was the enormous complex of administrative offices. In careful orientation to one another and to the whole were the large residential Sections connected and interlaced by the expressway and the local ways. Toward the outskirts were the factories, the hydroponic plants, the yeast-culture vats, the power plants. Through all the melee were the water pipes and sewage ducts, schools, prisons and shops, power lines and communication beams.

There was no doubt about it: the City was the culmination of man's mastery over the environment. Not space travel, not the fifty colonized worlds that were now so haughtily independent, but the City.

Practically none of Earth's population lived outside the Cities. Outside was the wilderness, the open sky that few men could face with anything like equanimity. To be sure, the open space was necessary. It held the water that men must have, the coal and the wood that were the ultimate raw materials for plastics and for the eternally growing yeasts. (Petroleum had long since gone, but oil-rich strains of yeast were an adequate substitute.) The land between the Cities still held the mines, and was still used to a larger extent than most men realized for growing food and grazing stock. It was inefficient, but beef, pork, and grain always found a luxury market and could be used for export purposes.

But few humans were required to run the mines and ranches, to exploit the farms and pipe the water, and these supervised at long distance. Robots did the work better and required less.

Robots! That was the one huge irony. It was on Earth that the positronic brain was invented and on Earth that robots had first been put to productive use.

Not on the Outer Worlds. Of course, the Outer Worlds always acted as though robots had been born of their culture.

In a way, of course, the culmination of robot economy had taken place on the Outer Worlds. Here on Earth, robots had always been

restricted to the mines and farmlands. Only in the last quarter century, under the urgings of the Spacers, had robots filtered their slow
way into the Cities.

The Cities were good. Everyone but the Medievalists knew that
there was no substitute, no reasonable substitute. The only trouble
was that they wouldn't stay good. Earth's population was still rising.
Some day, with all that the Cities could do, the available calories per
person would simply fall below subsistence level.

It was all the worse because of the existence of the Spacers, the
descendants of the early emigrants from Earth, living in luxury on
their underpopulated robot-ridden worlds out in space. They were
coolly determined to keep the comfort that grew out of the emptiness
of their worlds and for that purpose they kept their birth rate down
and immigrants from teeming Earth out. And this——

Spacetown coming up!

A nudge at Baley's unconscious warned him that he was approaching the Newark Section. If he stayed where he was much longer, he'd
find himself speeding southwestward to the Trenton Section turning
of the way, through the heart of the warm and musty-odored yeast
country.

It was a matter of timing. It took so long to shinny down the ramp,
so long to squirm through the grunting standees, so long to slip along
the railing and out an opening, so long to hop across the decelerating
strips.

When he was done, he was precisely at the off-shooting of the proper
stationary. At no time did he time his steps consciously. If he had, he
would probably have missed.

Baley found himself in unusual semi-isolation. Only a policeman
was with him inside the stationary and, except for the whirring of the
expressway, there was an almost uncomfortable silence.

The policeman approached, and Baley flashed his badge impatiently. The policeman lifted his hand in permission to pass on.

The passage narrowed and curved sharply three or four times. That
was obviously purposeful. Mobs of Earthmen couldn't gather in it with
any degree of comfort and direct charges were impossible.

Baley was thankful that the arrangements were for him to meet his
partner this side of Spacetown. He didn't like the thought of a medical
examination any better for its reputed politeness.

A Spacer was standing at the point where a series of doors marked
the openings to the open air and the domes of Spacetown. He was
dressed in the Earth fashion, trousers tight at the waist, loose at the
ankle, and color-striped down the seam of each leg. He wore an ordinary Textron shirt, open collar, seam-zipped, and ruffled at the wrist,
but he was a Spacer. There was something about the way he stood,
the way he held his head, the calm and unemotional lines of his broad

high-cheekboned face, the careful set of his short, bronze hair lying
flatly backward and without a part, that marked him off from the native Earthman.

Baley approached woodenly and said in a monotone, "I am Plain-
clothes Man Elijah Baley, Police Department, City of New York, Rating C-5."

He showed his credentials and went on, "I have been instructed to
meet R. Daneel Olivaw at Spacetown Approachway." He looked at
his watch. "I am a little early. May I request the announcement of my
presence?"

He felt more than a little cold inside. He was used, after a fashion,
to the Earth-model robots. The Spacer models would be different. He
had never met one, but there was nothing more common on Earth
than the horrid whispered stories about the tremendous and formidable robots that worked in superhuman fashion on the far-off, glittering Outer Worlds. He found himself gritting his teeth.

The Spacer, who had listened politely, said, "It will not be necessary. I have been waiting for you."

Baley's hand went up automatically, then dropped. So did his long
chin, looking longer in the process. He didn't quite manage to say
anything. The words froze.

The Spacer said, "I shall introduce myself. I am R. Daneel Olivaw."

"Yes? Am I making a mistake? I thought the first initial——"

"Quite so. I am a robot. Were you not told?"

"I was told." Baley put a damp hand to his hair and smoothed it
back unnecessarily. Then he held it out. "I'm sorry, Mr. Olivaw. I
don't know what I was thinking of. Good day. I am Elijah Baley, your
partner."

"Good." The robot's hand closed on his with a smoothly increasing
pressure that reached a comfortably friendly peak, then declined. "Yet
I seem to detect disturbance. May I ask that you be frank with me? It
is best to have as many relevant facts as possible in a relationship such
as ours. And it is customary on my world for partners to call one
another by the familiar name. I trust that that is not counter to your
own customs."

"It's just, you see, that you don't look like a robot," said Baley,
desperately.

"And that disturbs you?"

"It shouldn't, I suppose, Da—Daneel. Are they all like you on your
world?"

"There are individual differences, Elijah, as with men."

"Our own robots . . . Well, you can tell they're robots, you understand. You look like a Spacer."

"Oh, I see. You expected a rather crude model and were surprised.
Yet it is only logical that our people use a robot of pronounced hu-

manoid characteristics in this case if we expected to avoid unpleasantness. Is that not so?"

It was certainly so. An obvious robot roaming the City would be in quick trouble.

Baley said, "Yes."

"Then let us leave now, Elijah."

They made their way back to the expressway. R. Daneel caught the purpose of the accelerating strips and maneuvered along them with a quick proficiency. Baley, who had begun by moderating his speed, ended by hastening it in annoyance.

The robot kept pace. He showed no awareness of any difficulty. Baley wondered if R. Daneel were not deliberately moving slower than he might. He reached the endless cars of expressway and scrambled aboard with what amounted to outright recklessness. The robot followed easily.

Baley was red. He swallowed twice and said, "I'll stay down here with you."

"Down here?" The robot, apparently oblivious to both the noise and the rhythmic swaying of the platform, said, "Is my information wrong? I was told that a rating of C-5 entitled one to a seat on the upper level under certain conditions."

"You're right. I can go up there, but you can't."

"Why can I not go up with you?"

"It takes a C-5, Daneel."

"I am aware of that."

"You're not a C-5." Talking was difficult. The hiss of frictioning air was louder on the less shielded lower level and Baley was understandably anxious to keep his voice low.

R. Daneel said, "Why should I not be a C-5? I am your partner and, consequently, of equal rank. I was given this."

From an inner shirt pocket he produced a rectangular credential card, quite genuine. The name given was Daneel Olivaw, without the all-important initial. The rating was C-5.

"Come on up," said Baley, woodenly.

Baley looked straight ahead, once seated, angry with himself, very conscious of the robot sitting next to him. He had been caught twice. First he had not recognized R. Daneel as a robot; secondly, he had not guessed the logic that demanded R. Daneel be given a C-5 rating.

The trouble was, of course, that he was not the plain-clothes man of popular myth. He was not incapable of surprise, imperturbable of appearance, infinite of adaptability, and lightning of mental grasp. He had never supposed he was, but he had never regretted the lack before.

What made him regret it was that, to all appearances, R. Daneel Olivaw *was* that very myth, embodied.

He had to be. He was a robot.

Baley began to find excuses for himself. He was accustomed to the robots like R. Sammy at the office. He had expected the creature with a skin of a hard and glossy plastic, nearly dead white in color. He had expected an expression fixed at an unreal level of inane good humor. He had expected jerky, faintly uncertain motions.

R. Daneel was none of it.

Baley risked a quick glance at the robot. R. Daneel turned simultaneously to meet his eyes and nod gravely. His lips had moved naturally when he had spoken and did not simply remain parted as those of Earth robots did. There had been glimpses of an articulating tongue.

Baley thought: Why does he have to sit there so calmly? This must be something completely new to him. Noise, lights, crowds!

Baley got up, brushed past R. Daneel, and said, "Follow me!"

Off the expressway, down the decelerating strips.

Baley thought: Good Lord, what do I tell Jessie, anyway?

The coming of the robot had rattled that thought out of his head, but it was coming back with sickening urgency now that they were heading down the localway that led into the very jaws of the Lower Bronx Section.

He said, "This is all one building, you know, Daneel; everything you see, the whole City. Twenty million people live in it. The expressways go continuously, night and day, at sixty miles an hour. There are two hundred and fifty miles of it altogether and hundreds of miles of localways."

Any minute now, Baley thought, I'll be figuring out how many tons of yeast product New York eats per day and how many cubic feet of water we drink and how many megawatts of power the atomic piles deliver per hour.

Daneel said, "I was informed of this and other similar data in my briefing."

Baley thought: Well, that covers the food, drink, and power situation, too, I suppose. Why try to impress a robot?

They were at East 182nd Street and in not more than two hundred yards they would be at the elevator banks that fed those steel and concrete layers of apartments that included his own.

He was on the point of saying, "This way," when he was stopped by a knot of people gathering outside the brilliantly lighted force door of one of the many retail departments that lined the ground levels solidly in this Section.

He asked of the nearest person in an automatic tone of authority, "What's going on?"

The man he addressed, who was standing on tiptoe, said, "Damned if I know, I just got here."

Someone else said, excitedly, "They got those lousy R's in there. I

think maybe they'll throw them out here. Boy, I'd like to take them
apart."

Baley looked nervously at Daneel, but, if the latter caught the significance of the words or even heard them, he did not show it by any
outward sign.

Baley plunged into the crowd. "Let me through. Let me through.
Police!"

They made way. Baley caught words behind him.

". . . take them apart. Nut by nut. Split them down the seams slow-
like . . ." And someone else laughed.

Baley turned a little cold. The City was the acme of efficiency, but
it made demands of its inhabitants. It asked them to live in a tight
routine and order their lives under a strict and scientific control. Occasionally, built-up inhibitions exploded.

He remembered the Barrier Riots.

Reasons for anti-robot rioting certainly existed. Men who found
themselves faced with the prospect of the desperate minimum involved in declassification, after half a lifetime of effort, could not decide coldbloodedly that individual robots were not to blame. Individual
robots could at least be struck at.

One could not strike at something called "governmental policy" or
at a slogan like "Higher production with robot labor."

The government called it growing pains. It shook its collective head
sorrowfully and assured everyone that after a necessary period of adjustment, a new and better life would exist for all.

But the Medievalist movement expanded along with the declassification process. Men grew desperate and the border between bitter
frustration and wild destruction is sometimes easily crossed.

At this moment, minutes could be separating the pent-up hostility
of the crowd from a flashing orgy of blood and smash.

Baley writhed his way desperately to the force door.

   # Incident at a Shoe Counter

The interior of the store was emptier than the street outside. The
manager, with commendable foresight, had thrown the force door early
in the game, preventing potential troublemakers from entering. It also
kept the principals in the argument from leaving, but that was minor.

Baley got through the force door by using his officer's neutralizer. Unexpectedly, he found R. Daneel still behind him. The robot was pocketing a neutralizer of his own, a slim one, smaller and neater than the standard police model.

The manager ran to them instantly, talking loudly. "Officers, my clerks have been assigned me by the City. I am perfectly within my rights."

There were three robots standing rodlike at the rear of the department. Six humans were standing near the force door. They were all women.

"All right, now," said Baley crisply. "What's going on? What's all the fuss about?"

One of the women said, shrilly, "I came in for shoes. Why can't I have a decent clerk? Ain't I respectable?" Her clothing, especially her hat, were just sufficiently extreme to make it more than a rhetorical question. The angry flush that covered her face masked imperfectly her overdone makeup.

The manager said, "I'll wait on her myself if I have to, but I can't wait on all of them, Officer. There's nothing wrong with my men. They're registered clerks. I have their spec charts and guarantee slips—"

"Spec charts," screamed the woman. She laughed shrilly, turning to the rest. "Listen to him. He calls them men! What's the matter with you anyway? They ain't men. They're robots!" She stretched out the syllables. "And I tell you what they do, in case you don't know. They steal jobs from men. That's why the government always protects them. They work for nothin' and, on account o' that, families gotta live out in the barracks and eat raw yeast mush. Decent hard-working families. We'd smash up all the ro-bots, if I was boss. I tell you that!"

The others talked confusedly and there was always the growing rumble from the crowd just beyond the force door.

Baley was conscious, brutally conscious, of R. Daneel Olivaw standing at his elbow. He looked at the clerks. They were Earth-made, and even on that scale, relatively inexpensive models. They were just robots made to know a few simple things. They would know all the style numbers, their prices, the sizes available in each. They could keep track of stock fluctuations, probably better than humans could, since they would have no outside interests. They could compute the proper orders for the next week. They could measure the customer's foot.

In themselves, harmless. As a group, incredibly dangerous.

Baley could sympathize with the woman more deeply than he would have believed possible the day before. No, two hours before. He could feel R. Daneel's nearness and he wondered if R. Daneel could not replace an ordinary plain-clothes man C-5. He could see the barracks, as he thought that. He could taste the yeast mush. He could remember his father.

His father had been a nuclear physicist, with a rating that had put him in the top percentile of the City. There had been an accident at the power plant and his father had borne the blame. He had been declassified. Baley did not know the details; it had happened when he was a year old.

But he remembered the barracks of his childhood; the grinding communal existence just this side of the edge of bearability. He remembered his mother not at all; she had not survived long. His father he recalled well, a sodden man, morose and lost, speaking sometimes of his past in hoarse, broken sentences.

His father died, still declassified, when Lije was eight. Young Baley and his two older sisters moved into the Section orphanage. Children's Level, they called it. His mother's brother, Uncle Boris, was himself too poor to prevent that.

So it continued hard. And it was hard going through school, with no father-derived status privileges to smooth the way.

And now he had to stand in the middle of a growing riot and beat down men and women who, after all, only feared declassification for themselves and those they loved, as he himself did.

Tonelessly, he said to the woman who had already spoken, "Let's not have any trouble, lady. The clerks aren't doing you any harm."

"Sure they ain't done me no harm," sopranoed the woman. "They ain't gonna, either. Think I'll let their cold, greasy fingers touch me? I came in here expecting to get treated like a human being. I'm a citizen. I got a right to have human beings wait on me. And listen, I got two kids waiting for supper. They can't go to the Section kitchen without me, like they was orphans. I gotta get out of here."

"Well, now," said Baley, feeling his temper slipping, "if you had let yourself be waited on, you'd have been out of here by now. You're just making trouble for nothing. Come on now."

"Well!" The woman registered shock. "Maybe you think you can talk to me like I was dirt. Maybe it's time the guv'min' reelized robots ain't the only things on Earth. I'm a hard-working woman and I've got rights." She went on and on and on.

Baley felt harassed and caught. The situation was out of hand. Even if the woman would consent to be waited on, the waiting crowd was ugly enough for anything.

There must be a hundred crammed outside the display window now. In the few minutes since the plain-clothes men had entered the store, the crowd had doubled.

"What is the usual procedure in such a case?" asked R. Daneel Olivaw, suddenly.

Baley nearly jumped. He said, "This is an unusual case in the first place."

"What is the law?"

"The R's have been duly assigned here. They're registered clerks. There's nothing illegal about that."

They were speaking in whispers. Baley tried to look official and threatening. Olivaw's expression, as always, meant nothing at all.

"In that case," said R. Daneel, "order the woman to let herself be waited on or to leave."

Baley lifted a corner of his lip briefly. "It's a mob we have to deal with, not a woman. There's nothing to do but call a riot squad."

"It should not be necessary for citizens to require more than one officer of the law to direct what should be done," said Daneel.

He turned his broad face to the store manager. "Open the force door, sir."

Baley's arm shot forward to seize R. Daneel's shoulder, swing him about. He arrested the motion. If, at this moment, two law men quarreled openly, it would mean the end of all chance for a peaceful solution.

The manager protested, looked at Baley. Baley did not meet his eye. R. Daneel said, unmoved, "I order you with the authority of the law."

The manager bleated, "I'll hold the City responsible for any damage to the goods or fixtures. I serve notice that I'm doing this under orders."

The barrier went down; men and women crowded in. There was a happy roar from them. They sensed victory.

Baley had heard of similar riots. He had even witnessed one. He had seen robots being lifted backward from straining arm to straining arm. Men yanked and twisted at the metal mimicry of men. They used hammers, force knives, needle guns. They finally reduced the miserable objects to shredded metal and wire. Expensive positronic brains, the most intricate creation of the human mind, were thrown from hand to hand like footballs and mashed to uselessness in a trifle of time.

Then, with the genius of destruction so merrily let loose, the mobs turned on anything else that could be taken apart.

The robot clerks could have no knowledge of any of this, but they squealed as the crowd flooded inward and lifted their arms before their faces as though in a primitive effort at hiding. The woman who had started the fuss, frightened at seeing it grow suddenly so far beyond what she had expected, gasped, "Here, now. Here, now."

Her hat was shoved down over her face and her voice became only a meaningless shrillness.

The manager was shrieking, "Stop them, Officer. Stop them!"

R. Daneel spoke. Without apparent effort, his voice was suddenly decibels higher than a human's voice had a right to be. Of course, thought Baley for the tenth time, he's not——

R. Daneel said, "The next man who moves will be shot."

Someone well in the back yelled, "Get him!"

But for a moment, no one moved.

R. Daneel stepped nimbly upon a chair and from that to the top of a Transtex display case. The colored fluorescence gleaming through the slits of polarized molecular film turned his cool, smooth face into something unearthly.

Unearthly, thought Baley.

The tableau held as R. Daneel waited, a quietly formidable person.

R. Daneel said crisply, "You are saying, This man is holding a neuronic whip, or a tickler. If we all rush forward, we will bear him down and at most one or two of us will be hurt and even they will recover. Meanwhile, we will do just as we wish and to space with law and order."

His voice was neither harsh nor angry, but it carried authority. It had the tone of confident command. He went on, "You are mistaken. What I hold is not a neuronic whip, nor is it a tickler. It is a blaster and very deadly. I will use it and I will not aim over your heads. I will kill many of you before you seize me, perhaps most of you. I am serious. I look serious, do I not?"

There was motion at the outskirts, but the crowd no longer grew. If newcomers still stopped out of curiosity, others were hurrying away. Those nearest R. Daneel were holding their breath, trying desperately not to sway forward in response to the mass pressure of the bodies behind them.

The woman with the hat broke the spell. In a sudden whirlpool of sobbing, she yelled, "He's gonna kill us. I ain't done nothing. Oh, lemme outta here."

She turned, but faced an immovable wall of crammed men and women. She sank to her knees. The backward motion in the silent crowd grew more pronounced.

R. Daneel jumped down from the display counter and said, "I will now walk to the door. I will shoot the man or woman who touches me. When I reach the door, I will shoot any man or woman who is not moving about his business. This woman here——"

"No, no," yelled the woman with the hat, "I tell ya I didn't do nothing. I didn't mean no harm. I don't want no shoes. I just wanta go home."

"This woman here," went on Daneel, "will remain. She will be waited on."

He stepped forward.

The mob faced him dumbly. Baley closed his eyes. It wasn't his fault, he thought desperately. There'll be murder done and the worst mess in the world, but *they* forced a robot on me as a partner. *They* gave him equal status.

It wouldn't do. He didn't believe himself. He might have stopped R. Daneel at the start. He had let R. Daneel take responsibility, instead, and had felt a cowardly relief. When he tried to tell himself that R. Daneel's personality simply dominated the situation, he was filled with a sudden self-loathing. A *robot* dominating . . .

There was no unusual noise, no shouting and cursing, no groans, no yells. He opened his eyes.

They were dispersing.

The manager of the store was cooling down, adjusting his twisted jacket, smoothing his hair, muttering angry threats at the vanishing crowd.

The smooth, fading whistle of a squad car came to a halt just outside. Baley thought: Sure, when it's all over.

The manager plucked his sleeve. "Let's have no more trouble, Officer."

Baley said, "There won't be any trouble."

It was easy to get rid of the squad-car police. They had come in response to reports of a crowd in the street. They knew no details and could see for themselves that the street was clear. R. Daneel stepped aside and showed no sign of interest as Baley explained to the men in the squad car, minimizing the event and completely burying R. Daneel's part in it.

Afterward, he pulled R. Daneel to one side, against the steel and concrete of one of the building shafts.

"Listen," he said, "I'm not trying to steal your show, you understand."

"Steal my show? Is it one of your Earth idioms?"

"I didn't report your part in this."

"I do not know all your customs. On my world, a complete report is usual, but perhaps it is not so on your world. In any case, a civil rebellion was averted. That is the important thing, is it not?"

"Is it? Now you look here." Baley tried to sound as forceful as possible under the necessity of speaking in an angry whisper. "Don't you ever do it again."

"Never again insist on the observance of law? If I am not to do that, what then is my purpose?"

"Don't ever threaten a human being with a blaster again."

"I would not have fired under any circumstances, Elijah, as you know very well. I am incapable of hurting a human. But, as you see, I did not have to fire. I did not expect to have to."

"That was the purest luck, your not having to fire. Don't take that kind of chance again. I could have pulled the grandstand stunt you did——"

"Grandstand stunt? What is that?"

"Never mind. Get the sense from what I'm saying. I could have pulled a blaster on the crowd myself. I had the blaster to do it with. But it isn't the kind of gamble I am justified in taking, or you, either. It was safer to call squad cars to the scene than to try one-man heroics."

R. Daneel considered. He shook his head. "I think you are wrong, partner Elijah. My briefing on human characteristics here among the people of Earth includes the information that, unlike the men of the Outer Worlds, they are trained from birth to accept authority. Apparently this is the result of your way of living. One man, representing authority firmly enough, was quite sufficient, as I proved. Your own desire for a squad car was only an expression, really, of your almost instinctive wish for superior authority to take responsibility out of your hands. On my own world, I admit that what I did would have been most unjustified."

Baley's long face was red with anger. "If they had recognized you as a robot——"

"I was sure they wouldn't."

"In any case, remember that you *are* a robot. Nothing more than a robot. Just a robot. Like those clerks in the shoe store."

"But this is obvious."

"And you're *not* human." Baley felt himself being driven into cruelty against his will.

R. Daneel seemed to consider that. He said, "The division between human and robot is perhaps not as significant as that between intelligence and nonintelligence."

"Maybe on your world," said Baley, "but not on Earth."

He looked at his watch and could scarcely make out that he was an hour and a quarter late. His throat was dry and raw with the thought that R. Daneel had won the first round, had won when he himself had stood by helpless.

He thought of the youngster, Vince Barrett, the teen-ager whom R. Sammy had replaced. And of himself, Elijah Baley, whom R. Daneel *could* replace. Jehoshaphat, at least his father had been thrown out because of an accident that had done damage, that had killed people. Maybe it *was* his fault. Baley didn't know. Suppose he had been eased out to make room for a mechanical physicist. Just for that. For no other reason. Nothing he could do about it.

He said, curtly, "Let's go now. I've got to get you home."

R. Daneel said, "You see, it is not proper to make any distinction of lesser meaning than the fact of intel——"

Baley's voice rose. "All *right*. The subject is closed. Jessie is waiting

for us." He walked in the direction of the nearest intrasection
communo-tube. "I'd better call and tell her we're on our way up."

"Jessie?"

"My wife."

Jehoshaphat, thought Baley, I'm in a fine mood to face Jessie.

 **Introduction
to a Family**

It had been her name that had first made Elijah Baley really conscious
of Jessie. He had met her at the Section Christmas party back in '02,
over a bowl of punch. He had just finished his schooling, just taken
his first job with the City, just moved into the Section. He was living
in one of the bachelor alcoves of Common Room 122A. Not bad for
a bachelor alcove.

She was handing out the punch. "I'm Jessie," she said. "Jessie Na-
vodny. I don't know you."

"Baley," he said, "Lije Baley. I've just moved into the Section."

He took his glass of punch and smiled mechanically. She impressed
him as a cheerful and friendly person, so he stayed near her. He was
new and it is a lonely feeling to be at a party where you find yourself
watching people standing about in cliques of which you aren't a part.
Later, when enough alcohol had trickled down throats, it might be
better.

Meanwhile, he remained at the punch bowl, watching the folks come
and go and sipping thoughtfully.

"I helped make the punch." The girl's voice broke in upon him. "I
can guarantee it. Do you want more?"

Baley realized his little glass was empty. He smiled and said, "Yes."

The girl's face was oval and not precisely pretty, mostly because of
a slightly overlarge nose. Her dress was demure and she wore her light
brown hair in a series of ringlets over her forehead.

She joined him in the next punch and he felt better.

"Jessie," he said, feeling the name with his tongue. "It's nice. Do
you mind if I use it when I'm talking to you?"

"Certainly. If you want to. Do you know what it's short for?"

"Jessica?"

"You'll never guess."

"I can't think of anything else."

She laughed and said archly, "My full name is Jezebel."

That was when his interest flared. He put his punch glass down and said, intently, "No, really?"

"Honestly. I'm not kidding. Jezebel. It's my real-for-true name on all my records. My parents liked the sound of it."

She was quite proud of it, even though there was never a less likely Jezebel in the world.

Baley said, seriously, "My name is Elijah, you know. My full name, I mean."

It didn't register with her.

He said, "Elijah was Jezebel's great enemy."

"He was?"

"Why, sure. In the Bible."

"Oh? I didn't know that. Now isn't that *funny*? I hope that doesn't mean you'll have to be my enemy in real life."

From the very beginning there was no question of that. It was the coincidence of the names at first that made her more than just a pleasant girl at the punch bowl. But afterward he had grown to find her cheerful, tender-hearted, and, finally, even pretty. He appreciated her cheerfulness particularly. His own sardonic view of life needed the antidote.

But Jessie never seemed to mind his long grave face.

"Oh, goodness," she said, "what if you do look like an awful lemon? I know you're not really, and I guess if you were always grinning away like clockwork, the way I do, we'd just explode when we got together. You stay the way you are, Lije, and keep me from floating away."

And she kept Lije Baley from sinking down. He applied for a small Couples apartment and got a contingent admission pending marriage. He showed it to her and said, "Will you fix it so I can get out of Bachelor's, Jessie? I don't like it there."

Maybe it wasn't the most romantic proposal in the world, but Jessie liked it.

Baley could only remember one occasion on which Jessie's habitual cheer deserted her completely and that, too, had involved her name. It was in their first year of marriage, and their baby had not yet come. In fact, it had been the very month in which Bentley was conceived. (Their I.Q. rating, Genetic Values status, and his position in the Department entitled him to two children, of which the first might be conceived during the first year.) Maybe, as Baley thought back upon it, Bentley's beginnings might explain part of her unusual skittishness.

Jessie had been drooping a bit because of Baley's consistent overtime.

She said, "It's embarrassing to eat alone at the kitchen every night."

Baley was tired and out of sorts. He said, "Why should it be? You can meet some nice single fellows there."

And of course she promptly fired up. "Do you think I can't make an impression on them, Lije Baley?"

Maybe it was just because he was tired; maybe because Julius Enderby, a classmate of his, had moved up another notch on the C-scale rating while he himself had not. Maybe it was simply because he was a little tired of having her try to act up to the name she bore when she was nothing of the sort and never could be anything of the sort.

In any case, he said bitingly, "I suppose you can, but I don't think you'll try. I wish you'd forget your name and be yourself."

"I'll be just what I please."

"Trying to be Jezebel won't get you anywhere. If you must know the truth, the name doesn't mean what you think, anyway. The Jezebel of the Bible was a faithful wife and a good one according to her lights. She had no lovers that we know of, cut no high jinks, and took no moral liberties at all."

Jessie stared angrily at him. "That's isn't so. I've heard the phrase, 'a painted Jezebel.' I know what that means."

"Maybe you think you do, but listen. After Jezebel's husband, king Ahab died, her son, Jehoram, became king. One of the captains of his army, Jehu, rebelled against him and assassinated him. Jehu then rode to Jezreel where the old queen-mother, Jezebel, was residing. Jezebel heard of his coming and knew that he could only mean to kill her. In her pride and courage, she painted her face and dressed herself in her best clothes so that she could meet him as a haughty and defiant queen. He had her thrown from the window of the palace and killed, but she made a good end, according to my notions. And that's what people refer to when they speak of 'a painted Jezebel,' whether they know it or not."

The next evening Jessie said in a small voice, "I've been reading the Bible, Lije."

"What?" For a moment, Baley was honestly bewildered.

"The parts about Jezebel."

"Oh! Jessie, I'm sorry if I hurt your feelings. I was being childish."

"No. No." She pushed his hand from her waist and sat on the couch, cool and upright, with a definite space between them. "It's good to know the truth. I don't want to be fooled by not knowing. So I read about her. She *was* a wicked woman, Lije."

"Well, her enemies wrote those chapters. We don't know her side."

"She killed all the prophets of the Lord she could lay her hands on."

"So they say she did." Baley felt about in his pocket for a stick of chewing gum. (In later years he abandoned that habit because Jessie said that with his long face and sad, brown eyes, it made him look like an old cow stuck with an unpleasant wad of grass it couldn't swallow and wouldn't spit out.) He said, "If you want her side, I could think of some arguments for you. She valued the religion of her ancestors who had been in the land long before the Hebrews came. The Hebrews had their own God, and what's more, it was an exclusive God. They weren't content to worship Him themselves; they wanted everyone in reach to worship Him as well.

"Jezebel was a conservative, sticking to the old beliefs against the new ones. After all, if the new beliefs had a higher moral content, the old ones were more emotionally satisfying. The fact that she killed priests just marks her as a child of her times. It was the usual method of proselytization in those days. If you read I Kings, you must remember that Elijah (*my* namesake this time) had a contest with 850 prophets of Baal to see which could bring down fire from heaven. Elijah won and promptly ordered the crowd of onlookers to kill the 850 Baalites. And they did."

Jessie bit her lip. "What about Naboth's vineyard, Lije. Here was this Naboth not bothering anybody, except that he refused to sell the King his vineyard. So Jezebel arranged to have people perjure themselves and say that Naboth had committed blasphemy or something."

"He was supposed to have 'blasphemed God and the king,' " said Baley.

"Yes. So they confiscated his property after they executed him."

"That was wrong. Of course, in modern times, Naboth would have been handled quite easily. If the City wanted his property or even if one of the Medieval nations had wanted his property, the courts would have ordered him off, had him removed by force if necessary, and paid him whatever they considered a fair price. King Ahab didn't have that way out. Still, Jezebel's solution was wrong. The only excuse for her is that Ahab was sick and unhappy over the situation and she felt that her love for her husband came ahead of Naboth's welfare. I keep telling you, she was the model of a faithful wi——"

Jessie flung herself away from him, red-faced and angry. "I think you're mean and spiteful."

He looked at her with complete dismay. "What have I done? What's the matter with you?"

She left the apartment without answering and spent the evening and half the night at the subetheric video levels, traveling petulantly from showing to showing and using up a two-month supply of her quota allowance (and her husband's, to boot).

When she came back to a still wakeful Lije Baley, she had nothing further to say to him.

It occurred to Baley later, much later, that he had utterly smashed an important part of Jessie's life. Her name had signified something intriguingly wicked to her. It was a delightful makeweight for her prim, overrespectable past. It gave her an aroma of licentiousness, and she adored that.

But it was gone. She never mentioned her full name again, not to

Lije, not to her friends, and maybe, for all Baley knew, not even to herself. She was Jessie and took to signing her name so.

As the days passed she began speaking to him again, and after a week or so their relationship was on the old footing and, with all subsequent quarrels, nothing ever reached that one bad spot of intensity.

Only once was there even an indirect reference to the matter. It was in her eighth month of pregnancy. She had left her own position as dietitian's assistant in Section Kitchen A-23 and with unaccustomed time on her hands was amusing herself in speculation and preparation for the baby's birth.

She said, one evening, "What about Bentley?"

"Pardon me, dear?" said Baley, looking up from a sheaf of work he had brought home with him. (With an additional mouth soon to feed and Jessie's pay stopped and his own promotions to the nonclerical levels as far off, seemingly, as ever, extra work was necessary.)

"I mean if the baby's a boy. What about Bentley as a name?"

Baley pulled down the corners of his mouth. "Bentley Baley? Don't you think the names are too similar?"

"I don't know. It has a swing, I think. Besides, the child can always pick out a middle name to suit himself when he gets older."

"Well, it's all right with me."

"Are you sure? I mean . . . Maybe you wanted him to be named Elijah?"

"And be called Junior? I don't think that's a good idea. He can name his son Elijah, if he wants to."

Then Jessie said, "There's just one thing," and stopped.

After an interval, he looked up. "What one thing?"

She did not quite meet his eye, but she said, forcefully enough, "Bentley isn't a Bible name, is it?"

"No," said Baley. "I'm quite sure it isn't."

"All right then. I don't want any Bible names."

And that was the only harking back that took place from that time to the day when Elijah Baley was coming home with Robot Daneel Olivaw, when he had been married for more than eighteen years and when his son Bentley Baley (middle name still unchosen) was past sixteen.

Baley paused before the large double door on which there glowed in large letters PERSONAL—MEN. In smaller letters were written SUBSECTIONS 1A—1E. In still smaller letters, just above the key slit, it stated: "In case of loss of key, communicate at once with 27-101-51."

A man inched past them, inserted an aluminum sliver into the key slit, and walked in. He closed the door behind him, making no attempt to hold it open for Baley. Had he done so, Baley would have been seriously offended. By strong custom men disregarded one another's

presence entirely either within or just outside the Personals. Baley
remembered one of the more interesting marital confidences to have
been Jessie's telling him that the situation was quite different at Wom-
en's Personals.

She was always saying, "I met Josephine Greely at Personal and she
said . . ."

It was one of the penalties of civic advancement that when the
Baleys were granted permission for the activation of the small wash-
bowl in their bedroom, Jessie's social life suffered.

Baley said, without completely masking his embarrassment, "Please
wait out here, Daneel."

"Do you intend washing?" asked R. Daneel.

Baley squirmed and thought: Damned robot! If they were briefing
him on everything under steel, why didn't they teach him manners?
I'll be responsible if he ever says anything like this to anyone else.

He said, "I'll shower. It gets crowded evenings. I'll lose time then.
If I get it done now we'll have the whole evening before us."

R. Daneel's face maintained its repose. "Is it part of the social custom that I wait outside?"

Baley's embarrassment deepened. "Why need you go in for—for no
purpose."

"Oh, I understand you. Yes, of course. Nevertheless, Elijah, my
hands grow dirty, too, and I will wash them."

He indicated his palms, holding them out before him. They were
pink and plump with proper creases. They bore every mark of excellent workmanship and were as clean as need be.

Baley said, "We have a washbasin in the apartment, you know." He
said it casually. Snobbery would be lost on a robot.

"Thank you for your kindness. On the whole, however, I think it
would be preferable to make use of this place. If I am to live with you
men of Earth, it is best that I adopt as many of your customs and
attitudes as I can."

"Come on in, then."

The bright cheerfulness of the interior was a sharp contrast to the
busy utilitarianism of most of the rest of the City, but this time the
effect was lost on Baley's consciousness.

He whispered to Daneel, "I may take up to half an hour or so. Wait
for me." He started away, then returned to add, "And listen, don't
talk to anybody and don't look at anybody. Not a word, not a glance!
It's a custom."

He looked hurriedly about to make certain that his own small conversation had not been noted, was not being met by shocked glances.
Nobody, fortunately, was in the antecorridor, and after all it *was* only
the antecorridor.

He hurried down it, feeling vaguely dirty, past the common chambers to the private stalls. It had been five years now since he had been awarded one—large enough to contain a shower, a small laundry, and other necessities. It even had a small projector that could be keyed in for the new films.

"A home away from home," he had joked when it was first made available to him. But now, he often wondered how he would bear the adjustment back to the more Spartan existence of the common chambers if his stall privileges were ever canceled.

He pressed the button that activated the laundry and the smooth face of the meter lighted.

R. Daneel was waiting patiently when Baley returned with a scrubbed body, clean underwear, a freshened shirt, and, generally, a feeling of greater comfort.

"No trouble?" Baley asked, when they were well outside the door and able to talk.

"None at all, Elijah," said R. Daneel.

Jessie was at the door, smiling nervously. Baley kissed her.

"Jessie," he mumbled, "this is my new partner, Daneel Olivaw."

Jessie held out a hand, which R. Daneel took and released. She turned to her husband, then looked timidly at R. Daneel.

She said, "Won't you sit down, Mr. Olivaw? I must talk to my husband on family matters. It'll just take a minute. I hope you won't mind."

Her hand was on Baley's sleeve. He followed her into the next room.

She said, in a hurried whisper, "You aren't hurt, are you? I've been so worried ever since the broadcast."

"What broadcast?"

"It came through nearly an hour ago. About the riot at the shoe counter. They said two plain-clothes men stopped it. I knew you were coming home with a partner and this was right in our subsection and right when you were coming home and I thought they were making it better than it was and you were——"

"*Please*, Jessie. You see I'm perfectly all right."

Jessie caught hold of herself with an effort. She said, shakily, "Your partner isn't from your division, is he?"

"No," replied Baley miserably. "He's—a complete stranger."

"How do I treat him?"

"Like anybody else. He's just my partner, that's all."

He said it so unconvincingly, that Jessie's quick eyes narrowed. "What's wrong?"

"Nothing. Come, let's go back into the living room. I'll begin to look queer."

Lije Baley felt a little uncertain about the apartment now. Until this very moment, he had felt no qualms. In fact, he had always been proud of it. It had three large rooms; the living room, for instance, was an ample fifteen by eighteen. There was a closet in each room. One of the main ventilation ducts passed directly by. It meant a little rumbling noise on rare occasions, but, on the other hand, assured first-rate temperature control and well-conditioned air. Nor was it too far from either Personal, which was a prime convenience.

But with the creature from worlds beyond space sitting in the midst of it, Baley was suddenly uncertain. The apartment seemed mean and cramped.

Jessie said, with a gaiety that was slightly synthetic, "Have you and Mr. Olivaw eaten, Lije?"

"As a matter of fact," said Baley, quickly, "Daneel will not be eating with us. I'll eat, though."

Jessie accepted the situation without trouble. With food supplies so narrowly controlled and rationing tighter than ever, it was good form to refuse another's hospitality.

She said, "I hope you won't mind our eating, Mr. Olivaw. Lije, Bentley, and I generally eat at the Community kitchen. It's much more convenient and there's more variety, you see, and just between you and me, bigger helpings, too. But then, Lije and I *do* have permission to eat in our apartment three times a week if we want to—Lije is quite successful at the Bureau and we have very nice status—and I thought that just for this occasion, if you wanted to join us, we would have a little private feast of our own, though I do think that people who overdo their privacy privileges are just a bit antisocial, you know."

R. Daneel listened politely.

Baley said, with an undercover "shushing" wiggle of his fingers, "Jessie, I'm hungry."

R. Daneel said, "Would I be breaking a custom, Mrs. Baley, if I addressed you by your given name?"

"Why, no, of course not." Jessie folded a table out of the wall and plugged the plate warmer into the central depression on the table top. "You just go right ahead and call me Jessie all you feel like—uh—Daneel." She giggled.

Baley felt savage. The situation was getting rapidly more uncomfortable. Jessie thought R. Daneel was a man. The thing would be someone to boast of and talk about in Women's Personal. He was good-looking in a wooden way, too, and Jessie was pleased with his deference. Anyone could see that.

Baley wondered about R. Daneel's impression of Jessie. She hadn't changed much in eighteen years, or at least not to Lije Baley. She was heavier, of course, and her figure had lost much of its youthful vigor. There were lines at the angles of the mouth and a trace of heaviness about her cheeks. Her hair was more conservatively styled and dimmer brown than it had once been.

But that's all beside the point, thought Baley, somberly. On the Outer Worlds the women were tall and as slim and regal as the men. Or, at least, the book-films had them so and that must be the kind of woman R. Daneel was used to.

But R. Daneel seemed quite unperturbed by Jessie's conversation, her appearance, or her appropriation of his name. He said, 'Are you sure that is proper? The name, Jessie, seems to be a diminutive. Perhaps its use is restricted to members of your immediate circle and I would be more proper if I used your full given name."

Jessie, who was breaking open the insulating wrapper surrounding the dinner ration, bent her head over the task in sudden concentration.

"Just Jessie," she said, tightly. "Everyone calls me that. There's nothing else."

The door opened and a youngster entered cautiously. His eyes found R. Daneel almost at once.

"Dad?" said the boy, uncertainly.

"My son, Bentley," said Baley, in a low voice. "This is Mr. Olivaw, Ben."

"He's your partner, huh, Dad? How d'ya do, Mr. Olivaw." Ben's eyes grew large and luminous. "Say, Dad, what happened down in the shoe place? The newscast said——"

"Don't ask any questions now, Ben," interposed Baley sharply.

Bentley's face fell and he looked toward his mother, who motioned him to a seat.

"Did you do what I told you, Bentley?" she asked, when he sat down. Her hands moved caressingly over his hair. It was as dark as his father's and he was going to have his father's height, but all the rest of him was hers. He had Jessie's oval face, her hazel eyes, her lighthearted way of looking at life.

"Sure, Mom," said Bentley, hitching himself forward a bit to look into the double dish from which savory vapors were already rising. "What we got to eat? Not zymoveal again, Mom? Huh, Mom?"

"There's nothing wrong with zymoveal," said Jessie, her lips pressing together. "Now, you just can eat what's put in front of you and let's not have any comments."

It was quite obvious they *were* having zymoveal.

Baley took his own seat. He himself would have preferred something other than zymoveal, with its sharp flavor and definite aftertaste, but Jessie had explained her problem before this.

"Well, I just can't, Lije," she had said. "I live right here on these levels all day and I can't make enemies or life wouldn't be bearable.

They know I used to be assistant dietitian and if I just walked off with steak or chicken every other week when there's hardly anyone else on the floor that has private eating privileges even on Sunday, they'd say it was pull or friends in the prep room. It would be talk, talk, talk, and I wouldn't be able to put my nose out the door or visit Personal in peace. As it is, zymoveal and protoveg are very good. They're well-balanced nourishment with no waste and, as a matter of fact, they're full of vitamins and minerals and everything anyone needs and we can have all the chicken we want when we eat in Community on the chicken Tuesdays."

Baley gave in easily. It was as Jessie said; the first problem of living is to minimize friction with the crowds that surround you on all sides. Bentley was a little harder to convince.

On this occasion, he said, "Gee, Mom, why can't I use Dad's ticket and eat in Community myself? I'd just as soon."

Jessie shook her head in annoyance and said, "I'm surprised at you, Bentley. What would people say if they saw you eating by yourself as though your own family weren't good enough for you or had thrown you out of the apartment?"

"Well, gosh, it's none of people's business."

Baley said, with a nervous edge in his voice, "Do as your mother tells you, Bentley."

Bentley shrugged, unhappily.

R. Daneel said, suddenly, from the other side of the room, "Have I the family's permission to view these book-films during your meal?"

"Oh sure," said Bentley, slipping away from the table, a look of instant interest upon his face. "They're mine. I got them from the library on special school permit. I'll get you my viewer. It's a pretty good one. Dad gave it to me for my last birthday."

He brought it to R. Daneel and said, "Are you interested in robots, Mr. Olivaw?"

Baley dropped his spoon and bent to pick it up.

R. Daneel said, "Yes, Bentley. I am quite interested."

"Then you'll like these. They're all about robots. I've got to write an essay on them for school, so I'm doing research. It's quite a complicated subject," he said importantly. "I'm against them myself."

"Sit down, Bentley," said Baley, desperately, "and don't bother Mr. Olivaw."

"He's not bothering me, Elijah. I'd like to talk to you about the problem, Bentley, another time. Your father and I will be very busy tonight."

"Thanks, Mr. Olivaw." Bentley took his seat, with a look of distaste in his mother's direction, broke off a portion of the crumbly pink zymoveal with his fork.

Baley thought: Busy tonight?

Then, with a resounding shock, he remembered his job. He thought of a Spacer lying dead in Spacetown and realized that for hours he had been so involved with his own dilemma that he had forgotten the cold fact of murder.

 # Analysis of a Murder

Jessie said good-bye to them. She was wearing a formal hat and a little jacket of keratofiber as she said, "I hope you'll excuse me, Mr. Olivaw. I know you have a great deal to discuss with Lije."

She pushed her son ahead of her as she opened the door.

"When will you be back, Jessie?" asked Baley.

She paused. "When do you want me to be back?"

"Well . . . No use staying out all night. Why don't you come back your usual time? Midnight or so." He looked doubtfully at R. Daneel.

R. Daneel nodded. "I regret having to drive you from your home."

"Don't worry about *that*, Mr. Olivaw. You're not driving me out at all. This is my usual evening out with the girls anyway. Come on, Ben."

The youngster was rebellious. "Aw, why the dickens do I have to go, anyway. I'm not going to bother them. Nuts!"

"Now, do as I say."

"Well, why can't I go to the etherics along with you?"

"Because I'm going with some friends and you've got other things——" The door closed behind them.

And now the moment had come. Baley had put it off in his mind. He had thought: First let's meet the robot and see what he's like. Then it was: Let's get him home. And then: Let's eat.

But now it was all over and there was no room for further delay. It was down at last to the question of murder, of interstellar complications, of possible raises in ratings, of possible disgrace. And he had no way of even beginning except to turn to the robot for help.

His fingernails moved aimlessly on the table, which had not been returned to its wall recess.

R. Daneel said, "How secure are we against being overheard?"

Baley looked up, surprised. "No one would listen to what's proceeding in another man's apartment."

"It is not your custom to eavesdrop?"

"It just isn't done, Daneel. You might as well suppose they'd—I don't know—that they'd look in your plate while you're eating."

"Or that they would commit murder?"

"What?"

"It is against your customs to kill, is it not, Elijah?"

Baley felt anger rising. "See here, if we're going to be partners, don't try to imitate Spacer arrogance. There's no room for it in you, R. Daneel." He could not resist emphasizing the "R."

"I am sorry if I have hurt your feelings, Elijah. My intention was only to indicate that, since human beings are occasionally capable of murder in defiance of custom, they may be able to violate custom for the smaller impropriety of eavesdropping."

"The apartment is adequately insulated," said Baley, still frowning. "You haven't heard anything from the apartments on any side of us, have you? Well, they won't hear us, either. Besides, why should anyone think anything of importance is going on here?"

"Let us not underestimate the enemy."

Baley shrugged. "Let's get started. My information is sketchy, so I can spread out my hand without much trouble. I know that a man named Roj Nemennuh Sarton, a citizen of the planet Aurora, and a resident of Spacetown, has been murdered by person or persons unknown. I understand that it is the opinion of the Spacers that this is not an isolated event. Am I right?"

"You are quite right, Elijah."

"They tie it up with recent attempts to sabotage the Spacer-sponsored project of converting us to an integrated human/robot society on the model of the Outer Worlds, and assume the murder was the product of a well-organized terrorist group."

"Yes."

"All right. Then to begin with, is this Spacer assumption necessarily true? Why can't the murder have been the work of an isolated fanatic? This is strong anti-robot sentiment on Earth, but there are no organized parties advocating violence of this sort."

"Not openly, perhaps. No."

"Even a secret organization dedicated to the destruction of robots and robot factories would have the common sense to realize that the worst thing they could do would be to murder a Spacer. It seems much more likely to have been the work of an unbalanced mind."

R. Daneel listened carefully, then said, "I think the weight of probability is against the 'fanatic' theory. The person killed was too well chosen and the time of the murder too appropriate for anything but deliberate planning on the part of an organized group."

"Well, then, you've got more information than I have. Spill it!"

"Your phraseology is obscure, but I think I understand. I will have to explain some of the background to you. As seen from Spacetown, Elijah, relations with Earth are unsatisfactory."

"Tough," muttered Baley.

"I have been told that when Spacetown was first established, it was taken for granted by most of our people that Earth would be willing to adopt the integrated society that has worked so well on the Outer Worlds. Even after the first riots, we thought that it was only a matter of your people getting over the first shock of novelty.

"That has not proven to be the case. Even with the cooperation of the Terrestrial government and of most of the various City governments, resistance has been continuous and progress has been very slow. Naturally, this has been a matter of great concern to our people."

"Out of altruism, I suppose," said Baley.

"Not entirely," said R. Daneel, "although it is good of you to attribute worthy motives to them. It is our common belief that a healthy and modernized Earth would be of great benefit to the whole Galaxy. At least, it is the common belief among our people at Spacetown. I must admit that there are strong elements opposed to them on the Outer Worlds."

"What? Disagreements among the Spacers?"

"Certainly. There are some who think that a modernized Earth will be a dangerous and an imperialistic Earth. This is particularly true among the populations of those older worlds which are closer to Earth and have greater reason to remember the first few centuries of interstellar travel when their worlds were controlled, politically and economically, by Earth."

Baley sighed. "Ancient history. Are they really worried? Are they still kicking at us for things that happened a thousand years ago?"

"Humans," said R. Daneel, "have their own peculiar makeup. They are not as reasonable, in many ways, as we robots, since their circuits are not as preplanned. I am told this, too, has its advantages."

"Perhaps it may," said Baley, dryly.

"You are in a better position to know," said R. Daneel. "In any case, continuing failure on Earth has strengthened the Nationalist parties on the Outer Worlds. They say that it is obvious that Earthmen are different from Spacers and cannot be fitted into the same traditions. They say that if we imposed robots on Earth by superior force, we would be loosing destruction on the Galaxy. One thing they never forget, you see, is that Earth's population is eight billions, while the total population of the fifty Outer Worlds combined is scarcely more than five and a half billions. Our people here, particularly Dr. Sarton——"

"He was a doctor?"

"A Doctor of Sociology, specializing in robotics, and a very brilliant man."

"I see. Go on."

"As I said, Dr. Sarton and the others realized that Spacetown and all it meant would not exist much longer if such sentiments on the Outer Worlds were allowed to grow by feeding on our continued failure. Dr. Sarton felt that the time had come to make a supreme effort to understand the psychology of the Earthman. It is easy to say that the Earth people are innately conservative and to speak tritely of 'the unchanging Earth' and 'the inscrutable Terrestrial mind,' but that is only evading the problem.

"Dr. Sarton said it was ignorance speaking and that we could not dismiss the Earthman with a proverb or a bromide. He said the Spacers who were trying to remake Earth must abandon the isolation of Spacetown and mingle with Earthmen. They must live as they, think as they, be as they."

Baley said, "The Spacers? Impossible."

"You are quite right," said R. Daneel. "Despite his views, Dr. Sarton himself could not have brought himself to enter any of the Cities, and he knew it. He would have been unable to bear the hugeness and the crowds. Even if he had been forced inside at the point of a blaster, the externals would have weighed him down so that he could never have penetrated the inner truths for which he sought."

"What about the way they're always worrying about disease?" demanded Baley. "Don't forget that. I don't think there's one of them that would risk entering a City on that account alone."

"There is that, too. Disease in the Earthly sense is unknown on the Outer Worlds and the fear of the unknown is always morbid. Dr. Sarton appreciated all of this, but, nevertheless, he insisted on the necessity of growing to know the Earthman and his way of life intimately."

"He seems to have worked himself into a corner."

"Not quite. The objections to entering the City hold for the human Spacers. Robot Spacers are another thing entirely."

Baley thought: I keep forgetting, damn it. Aloud, he said, "Oh?"

"Yes," said R. Daneel. "We are more flexible, naturally. At least in this respect. We can be designed for adaptation to an Earthly life. By being built into a particularly close similarity to the human externals, we could be accepted by Earthmen and allowed a closer view of their life."

"And you yourself——" began Baley in sudden enlightenment.

"Am just such a robot. For a year, Dr. Sarton had been working upon the design and construction of such robots. I was the first of his robots and so far the only one. Unfortunately, my education is not yet complete. I have been hurried into my role prematurely as a result of the murder."

"Then not all Spacer robots are like you? I mean, some look more like robots and less like humans. Right?"

"Why, naturally. The outward appearance is dependent on a robot's function. My own function requires a very manlike appearance, and I have it. Others are different, although all are humanoid. Certainly they are more humanoid than the distressingly primitive robots I saw at the shoe counter. Are all your robots like that?"

"More or less," said Baley. "You don't approve?"

"Of course not. It is difficult to accept a gross parody of the human form as an intellectual equal. Can your factories do no better?"

"I'm sure they can, Daneel. I think we just prefer to know when we're dealing with a robot and when we're not." He stared directly into the robot's eyes as he said that. They were bright and moist, as a human's would be, but it seemed to Baley that their gaze was steady and did not flicker slightly from point to point as a man's would.

R. Daneel said, "I am hopeful that in time I will grow to understand that point of view."

For a moment, Baley thought there was sarcasm in the sentence, then dismissed the possibility.

"In any case," said R. Daneel, "Dr. Sarton saw clearly the fact that it was a case for C/Fe."

"See fee? What's that?"

"Just the chemical symbols for the elements carbon and iron, Elijah. Carbon is the basis of human life and iron of robot life. It becomes easy to speak of C/Fe when you wish to express a culture that combines the best of the two on an equal but parallel basis."

"See fee. Do you write it with a hyphen? Or how?"

"No, Elijah. A diagonal line between the two is the accepted way. It symbolizes neither one nor the other, but a mixture of the two, without priority."

Against his will, Baley found himself interested. Formal education on Earth included virtually no information on Outer World history or sociology after the Great Rebellion that made them independent of the mother planet. The popular book-film romances, to be sure, had their stock Outer World characters: the visiting tycoon, choleric and eccentric; the beautiful heiress, invariably smitten by the Earthman's charms and drowning disdain in love; the arrogant Spacer rival, wicked and forever beaten. These were worthless pictures, since they denied even the most elementary and well-known truths: that Spacers never entered Cities and Spacer women virtually never visited Earth.

For the first time in his life, Baley was stirred by an odd curiosity. What was Spacer life really like?

He brought his mind back to the issue at hand with something of an effort. He said, "I think I get what you're driving at. Your Dr. Sarton was attacking the problem of Earth's conversion to C/Fe from a new and promising angle. Our conservative groups or Medievalists, as they call themselves, were perturbed. They were afraid he might succeed. So they killed him. That's the motivation that makes it an organized plot and not an isolated outrage. Right?"

"I would put it about like that, Elijah. Yes."

Baley whistled thoughtfully under his breath. His long fingers tapped lightly against the table. Then he shook his head. "It won't wash. It won't wash at all."

"Pardon me. I do not understand you."

"I'm trying to get the picture. An Earthman walks into Spacetown, walks up to Dr. Sarton, blasts him, and walks out. I just don't see it. Surely the entrance to Spacetown is guarded."

R. Daneel nodded. "I think it is safe to say that no Earthman can possibly have passed through the entrance illegally."

"Then where does that leave you?"

"It would leave us in a confusing position, Elijah, if the entrance were the only way of reaching Spacetown from New York City."

Baley watched his partner thoughtfully. "I don't get you. It's the only connection between the two."

"Directly between the two, yes." R. Daneel waited a moment, then said, "You do not follow me. Is that not so?"

"That *is* so. I don't get you at all."

"Well, if it will not offend you, I will try to explain myself. May I have a piece of paper and a writer? Thank you. Look here, partner Elijah, I will draw a big circle and label it 'New York City.' Now, tangent to it, I will draw a small circle and label it 'Spacetown.' Here, where they touch, I draw an arrowhead and label it 'Barrier.' Now do you see no other connection?"

Baley said, "Of course not. There is no other connection."

"In a way," said the robot, "I am glad to hear you say this. It is in accordance with what I have been taught about Terrestrial ways of thinking. The barrier is the only *direct* connection. But both the City and Spacetown are open to the countryside in all directions. It is possible for a Terrestrial to leave the City at any of numerous exits and strike out cross country to Spacetown, where no barrier will stop him."

The tip of Baley's tongue touched his upper lip and for a moment stayed there. Then he said, "Cross country?"

"Yes."

"Cross *country*! Alone?"

"Why not?"

"Walking?"

"Undoubtedly walking. Walking would offer the least chance of detection. The murder took place early in the working day and the trip was undoubtedly negotiated in the hours before dawn."

"Impossible! There isn't a man in the City who would do it. Leave the City? Alone?"

"Ordinarily, it would seem unlikely. Yes. We Spacers know that. It is why we guard only the entrance. Even in the Great Riot, your people attacked only at the barrier that then protected the entrance. Not one left the City."

"Well, then?"

"But now we are dealing with an unusual situation. It is not the blind attack of a mob following the line of least resistance, but the organized attempt of a small group to strike, deliberately, at the unguarded point. It explains why, as you say, a Terrestrial could enter Spacetown, walk up to his victim, kill him, and walk away. The man attacked through a complete blind spot on our part."

Baley shook his head. "It's too unlikely. Have your people done anything to check that theory?"

"Yes, we have. Your Commissioner of Police was present almost at the time of the murder——"

"I know. He told me so."

"That, Elijah, is another example of the timeliness of the murder. Your Commissioner has co-operated with Dr. Sarton in the past and he was the Earthman with whom Dr. Sarton planned to make initial arrangements concerning the infiltration of your city by R's such as myself. The appointment for that morning was to concern that. The murder, of course, stopped those plans, at least temporarily, and the fact that it happened when your own Commissioner of Police was actually within Spacetown made the entire situation more difficult and embarrassing for Earth, and for our own people, too.

"But that is not what I started to say. Your Commissioner was present. We said to him, 'The man must have come cross country.' Like you, he said, 'Impossible,' or perhaps, 'Unthinkable.' He was quite disturbed, of course, and perhaps that may have made it difficult for him to see the essential point. Nevertheless, we forced him to begin checking that possibility almost at once."

Baley thought of the Commissioner's broken glasses and, even in the middle of somber thoughts, a corner of his mouth twitched. Poor Julius! Yes, he *would* be disturbed. Of course, there would be no way for Enderby to have explained the situation to the lofty Spacers, who looked upon physical disability as a peculiarly disgusting attribute to the non-genetically selected Earthmen. At least, he couldn't without losing face, and face was valuable to Police Commissioner Julius Enderby. Well, Earthmen had to stick together in some respects. The robot would never find out about Enderby's nearsightedness from Baley.

R. Daneel continued, "One by one, the various exit points from the City were investigated. Do you know how many there are, Elijah?"

Baley shook his head, then hazarded, "Twenty?"

"Five hundred and two."

"What?"

"Originally, there were many more. Five hundred and two are all
that remain functional. Your City represents a slow growth, Elijah. It
was once open to the sky and people crossed from City to country
freely."

"Of course. I know that."

"Well, when it was first enclosed, there were many exits left. Five
hundred and two still remain. The rest are built over or blocked up.
We are not counting, of course, the entrance points for air freight."

"Well, what of the exit points?"

"It was hopeless. They are unguarded. We could find no official who
was in charge or who considered them under his jurisdiction. It seemed
as though no one even knew they existed. A man could have walked
out of any of them at any time and returned at will. He would never
have been detected."

"Anything else? The weapon was gone, I suppose."

"Oh, yes."

"Any clues of any sort?"

"None. We have investigated the grounds surrounding Spacetown
thoroughly. The robots on the truck farms were quite useless as possible witnesses. They are little more than automatic farm machinery,
scarcely humanoid. And there were no humans."

"Uh-huh. What next?"

"Having failed, so far, at one end, Spacetown, we will work at the
other, New York City. It will be our duty to track down all possible
subversive groups, to sift all dissident organizations——"

"How much time do you intend to spend?" interrupted Baley.

"As little as possible, as much as necessary."

"Well," said Baley, thoughtfully, "I wish you had another partner
in this mess."

"I do not," said R. Daneel. "The Commissioner spoke very highly
of your loyalty and ability."

"It was nice of him," said Baley sardonically. He thought: Poor Julius. I'm on his conscience and he tries hard.

"We didn't rely entirely on him," said R. Daneel. "We checked your
records. You have expressed yourself openly against the use of robots
in your department."

"Oh? Do you object?"

"Not at all. Your opinions are, obviously, your own. But it made it
necessary for us to check your psychological profile very closely. We
know that, although you dislike R's intensely, you *will* work with one
if you conceive it to be your duty. You have an extraordinarily high
loyalty aptitude and a respect for legitimate authority. It is what we
need. Commissioner Enderby judged you well."

"You have no personal resentment toward my anti-robot sentiments?"

R. Daneel said, "If they do not prevent you from working with me and helping me do what is required of me, how can they matter?"

Baley felt stopped. He said, belligerently, "Well, then, if I pass the test, how about you? What makes you a detective?"

"I do not understand you."

"You were designed as an information-gathering machine. A man-imitation to record the facts of human life for the Spacers."

"That is a good beginning for an investigator, is it not? To be an information-gathering machine?"

"A beginning, maybe. But it's not all there is, by a long shot."

"To be sure, there has been a final adjustment of my circuits."

"I'd be curious to hear the details of that, Daneel."

"That is easy enough. A particularly strong drive has been inserted into my motivation banks; a desire for justice."

"*Justice!*" cried Baley. The irony faded from his face and was replaced by a look of the most earnest distrust.

But R. Daneel turned swiftly in his chair and stared at the door. "Someone is out there."

Someone was. The door opened and Jessie, pale and thin-lipped, walked in.

Baley was startled. "Why, Jessie! Is anything wrong?"

She stood there, eyes not meeting his. "I'm sorry. I had to . . ." Her voice trailed off.

"Where's Bentley?"

"He's to stay the night in the Youth Hall."

Baley said, "Why? I didn't tell you to do that."

"You said your partner would stay the night. I felt he would need Bentley's room."

R. Daneel said, "There was no necessity, Jessie."

Jessie lifted her eyes to R. Daneel's face, staring at it earnestly.

Baley looked at his fingertips, sick at what might follow somehow unable to interpose. The momentary silence pressed thickly on his eardrums and then, far away, as though through folds of plastex, he heard his wife say, "I think you are a robot, Daneel."

And R. Daneel replied, in a voice as calm as ever, "I am."

Whispers in a Bedroom

On the uppermost levels of some of the wealthiest subsections of the City are the natural Solariums, where a partition of quartz with a movable metal shield excludes the air but lets in the sunlight. There the wives and daughters of the City's highest administrators and executives may tan themselves. There a unique thing happens every evening.

Night falls.

In the rest of the City (including the UV-Solariums, where the millions, in strict sequence of allotted time, may occasionally expose themselves to the artificial wavelengths of arc lights) there are only the arbitrary cycles of hours.

The business of the City might easily continue in three eight-hour or four six-hour shifts, by "day" and "night" alike. Light and work could easily proceed endlessly. There are always civic reformers who periodically suggest such a thing in the interest of economy and efficiency.

The notion is never accepted.

Much of the earlier habits of Earthly society have been given up in the interest of that same economy and efficiency: space, privacy, even much of free will. They are the products of civilization, however, and not more than ten thousand years old.

The adjustment of sleep to night, however, is as old as man: a million years. The habit is not easy to give up. Although the evening is unseen, apartment lights dim as the hours of darkness pass and the City's pulse sinks. Though no one can tell noon from midnight by any cosmic phenomenon along the enclosed avenues of the City, mankind follows the mute partitionings of the hour hand.

The expressways empty, the noise of life sinks, the moving mob among the colossal alleys melt away; New York City lies in Earth's unnoticed shadow, and its population sleeps.

Elijah Baley did not sleep. He lay in bed and there was no light in his apartment, but that was as far as it went.

Jessie lay next to him, motionless in the darkness. He had not felt nor heard her move.

On the other side of the wall sat, stood, lay (Baley wondered which) R. Daneel Olivaw.

Baley whispered, "Jessie!" Then again, "Jessie!"

The dark figure beside him stirred slightly under the sheet. "What do you want?"

"Jessie, don't make it worse for me."

"You might have told me."

"How could I? I was planning to, when I could think of a way. Jehoshaphat, Jessie— "

"Sh!"

Baley's voice returned to its whisper. "How did you find out? Won't you tell me?"

Jessie turned toward him. He could sense her eyes looking through the darkness at him.

"Lije." Her voice was scarcely more than a stirring of air. "Can he hear us? That thing?"

"Not if we whisper."

"How do you know? Maybe he has special ears to pick up tiny sounds. Spacer robots can do all sorts of things."

Baley knew that. The prorobot propaganda was forever stressing the miraculous feats of the Spacer robots, their endurance, their extra senses, their service to humanity in a hundred novel ways. Personally, he thought that approach defeated itself. Earthmen hated the robots all the more for their superiority.

He whispered, "Not Daneel. They made him human-type on purpose. They wanted him to be accepted as a human being, so he must have only human senses."

"How do you know?"

"If he had extra senses, there would be too much danger of his giving himself away as non-human by accident. He would do too much, know too much."

"Well, maybe."

Silence fell again.

A minute passed and Baley tried a second time. "Jessie, if you'll just let things be until——until . . . Look, dear, it's unfair of you to be angry."

"Angry? Oh, Lije, you fool. I'm not angry. I'm scared; I'm scared clean to death."

She made a gulping sound and clutched at the neck of his pajamas. For a while, they clung together, and Baley's growing sense of injury evaporated into a troubled concern.

"Why, Jessie? There's nothing to be worried about. He's harmless. I swear he is."

"Can't you get rid of him, Lije?"

"You know I can't. It's Department business. How can I?"

"What kind of business, Lije? Tell me."

"Now, Jessie, I'm surprised at you." He groped for her cheek in the darkness and patted it. It was wet. Using his pajama sleeve, he carefully wiped her eyes.

"Now, look," he said tenderly, "you're being a baby."

"Tell them at the Department to have someone else do it, whatever it is. Please, Lije."

Baley's voice hardened a bit. "Jessie, you've been a policeman's wife long enough to know an assignment is an assignment."

"Well, why did it have to be you?"

"Julius Enderby——"

She stiffened in his arms. "I might have known. Why can't you tell Julius Enderby to have someone else do the dirty work just once. You stand for too much, Lije, and this is just——"

"All right, all right," he said, soothingly.

She subsided, quivering.

Baley thought: She'll never understand.

Julius Enderby had been a fighting word with them since their engagement. Enderby had been two classes ahead of Baley at the City School of Administrative Studies. They had been friends. When Baley had taken his battery of aptitude tests and neuroanalysis and found himself in line for the police force, he found Enderby there ahead of him. Enderby had already moved into the plain-clothes division.

Baley followed Enderby, but at a continually greater distance. It was no one's fault, precisely. Baley was capable enough, efficient enough, but he lacked something that Enderby had. Enderby fit the administrative machine perfectly. He was one of those persons who was born for a hierarchy, who was just naturally comfortable in a bureaucracy.

The Commissioner wasn't a great brain, and Baley knew it. He had his childish peculiarities, his intermittent rash of ostentatious Medievalism, for instance. But he was smooth with others; he offended no one; he took orders gracefully; he gave them with the proper mixture of gentleness and firmness. He even got along with the Spacers. He was perhaps overobsequious to them (Baley himself could never have dealt with them for half a day without getting into a state of bristle; he was sure of that, even though he had never really spoken to a Spacer), but they trusted him, and that made him extremely useful to the City.

So, in a Civil Service where smooth and sociable performance was more useful than an individualistic competence, Enderby went up the scale quickly, and was at the Commissioner level when Baley himself was nothing more than a C-5. Baley did not resent the contrast, though he was human enough to regret it. Enderby did not forget their earlier friendship and, in his queer way, tried to make up for his success by doing what he could for Baley.

The assignment of partnership with R. Daneel was an example of it. It was tough and unpleasant, but there was no question that it carried within it the germs of tremendous advance. The Commissioner might have given the chance to someone else. His own talk, that morning, of needing a favor masked but did not hide that fact.

Jessie never saw things that way. On similar occasions in the past, she had said, "It's your silly loyalty index. I'm so tired of hearing everyone praise you for being so full of a sense of duty. Think of yourself once in a while. I notice the ones on top don't bring up the topic of their *own* loyalty index."

Baley lay in bed in a state of stiff wakefulness, letting Jessie calm down. He had to *think*. He had to be certain of his suspicions. Little things chased one another and fitted together in his mind. Slowly they were building into a pattern.

He felt the mattress give as Jessie stirred.

"Lije?" Her lips were at his ear.

"What?"

"Why don't you resign?"

"Don't be crazy."

"Why not?" She was suddenly almost eager. "You can get rid of that horrible robot that way. Just walk in and tell Enderby you're through."

Baley said coldly, "I can't resign in the middle of an important case. I can't throw the whole thing down the disposal tube just anytime I feel like it. A trick like that means declassification for cause."

"Even so. You can work your way up again. You can do it, Lije. There are a dozen places where you'd fit into Service."

"Civil Service doesn't take men who are declassified for cause. Manual labor is the only thing I can do; the only thing you could do. Bentley would lose all inherited status. For God's sake, Jessie, you don't know what it's like."

"I've read about it. I'm not afraid of it," she mumbled.

"You're crazy. You're plain crazy." Baley could feel himself trembling. There was a familiar, flashing picture of his father in his mind's eye. His father, moldering away toward death.

Jessie sighed heavily.

Baley's mind turned savagely away from her. In desperation, it returned to the pattern it was constructing.

He said, tightly, "Jessie, you've got to tell me. How did you find out Daneel was a robot? What made you decide that?"

She began, "Well . . ." and just ran down. It was the third time she had begun to explain and failed.

He crushed her hand in his, willing her to speak. "Please, Jessie. What's frightening you?"

She said, "I just guessed he was a robot, Lije."

He said, "There wasn't anything to make you guess that, Jessie. You didn't think he was a robot before you left, now did you?"

"No-o, but I got to thinking . . ."

"Come on, Jessie. What was it?"

"Well . . . Look, Lije, the girls were talking in the Personal. You know how they are. Just talking about everything."

Women! thought Baley.

"Anyway," said Jessie. "The rumor is all over town. It must be."

"All over town?" Baley felt a quick and savage touch of triumph, or nearly that. Another piece in place!

"It was the way they sounded. They said there was talk about a Spacer robot loose in the city. He was supposed to look just like a man and to be working with the police. They even asked *me* about it. They laughed and said, 'Does your Lije know anything about it, Jessie?' and I laughed, and said, 'Don't be silly!'

"Then we went to the etherics and I got to thinking about your new partner. Do you remember those pictures you brought home, the ones Julius Enderby took in Spacetown, to show me what Spacers looked like? Well, I got to thinking that's what your partner looked like. It just came to me that that's what he looked like and I said to myself, Oh, my God, someone must've recognized him in the shoe department and he's with Lije and I just said I had a headache and I ran——"

Baley said, "Now, Jessie, stop, stop. Get hold of yourself. Now why are you afraid? You're not afraid of Daneel himself. You faced up to him when you came home. You faced up to him fine. So——"

He stopped speaking. He sat up in bed, eyes uselessly wide in the darkness.

He felt his wife move against his side. His hand leaped, found her lips and pressed against them. She heaved against his grip, her hands grasping his wrist and wrenching, but he leaned down against her the more heavily.

Then, suddenly, he released her. She whimpered.

He said, huskily, "Sorry, Jessie, I was listening."

He was getting out of bed, pulling warm Plastofilm over the soles of his feet.

"Lije, where are you going? Don't leave me."

"It's all right. I'm just going to the door."

The Plastofilm made a soft, shuffling noise as he circled the bed. He cracked the door to the living room and waited a long moment. Nothing happened. It was so quiet, he could hear the thin whistle of Jessie's breath from their bed. He could hear the dull rhythm of blood in his ears.

Baley's hand crept through the opening of the door, snaking out to the spot he needed no light to find. His fingers closed upon the knob that controlled the ceiling illumination. He exerted the smallest pressure he could and the ceiling gleamed dimly, so dimly that the lower half of the living room remained in semidusk.

He saw enough, however. The main door was closed and the living room lay lifeless and quiet.

He turned the knob back into the off position and moved back to bed.

It was all he needed. The pieces fit. The pattern was complete.

Jessie pleaded with him. "Lije, what's wrong?"

"Nothing's wrong, Jessie. Everything's all right. He's not here."

"The robot? Do you mean he's gone? For good?"

"No, no. He'll be back. And before he does, answer my question."

"What question?"

"What are you afraid of?"

Jessie said nothing.

Baley grew more insistent. "You said you were scared to death."

"Of him."

"No, we went through that. You weren't afraid of him and besides, you know quite well a robot cannot hurt a human being."

Her words came slowly. "I thought if everyone knew he was a robot there might be a riot. We'd be killed."

"Why kill us?"

"You know what riots are like."

"They don't even know where the robot is, do they?"

"They might find out."

"And that's what you're afraid of, a riot?"

"Well——"

"Sh!" He pressed Jessie down to the pillow.

Then he put his lips to her ear. "He's come back. Now listen and don't say a word. Everything's fine. He'll be gone in the morning and he won't be back. There'll be no riot, nothing."

He was almost contented as he said that, almost completely contented. He felt he could sleep.

He thought again. No riot, nothing. And no declassification.

And just before he actually fell asleep, he thought: Not even a murder investigation. Not even that. The whole thing's solved. . . .

He slept.

7. Excursion into Spacetown

Police Commissioner Julius Enderby polished his glasses with exquisite care and placed them upon the bridge of his nose.

Baley thought: It's a good trick. Keeps you busy while you're thinking what to say, and it doesn't cost money the way lighting up a pipe does.

And because the thought had entered his mind, he drew out his pipe and dipped into his pinched store of rough-cut. One of the few luxury crops still grown on Earth was tobacco, and its end was visibly approaching. Prices had gone up, never down, in Baley's lifetime; quotas down, never up.

Enderby, having adjusted his glasses, felt for the switch at one end of his desk and flicked his door into one-way transparency for a moment. "Where is he now, by the way?"

"He told me he wanted to be shown through the Department, and I let Jack Tobin do the honors." Baley lit his pipe and tightened its baffle carefully. The Commissioner, like most non-indulgers, was petty about tobacco smoke.

"I hope you didn't tell him Daneel was a robot."

"Of course I didn't."

The Commissioner did not relax. One hand remained aimlessly busy with the automatic calendar on his desk.

"How is it?" he asked, without looking at Baley.

"Middling rough."

"I'm sorry, Lije."

Baley said, firmly, "You might have warned me that he looked completely human."

The Commissioner looked surprised. "I didn't?" Then, with sudden petulance, "Damn it, you should have known. I wouldn't have asked you to have him stay at your house if he looked like R. Sammy. Now would I?"

"I know, Commissioner, but I'd never seen a robot like that and you had. I didn't even know such things were possible. I just wished you'd mentioned it, that's all."

"Look, Lije, I'm sorry. I should have told you. You're right. It's just that this job, this whole deal, has me so on edge that half the time I'm just snapping at people for no reason. He, I mean this Daneel thing, is a new-type robot. It's still in the experimental stage."

"So he explained himself."

"Oh. Well, that's it, then."

52

Baley tensed a little. This was it, now. He said, casualy, teeth clenched on pipestem, "R. Daneel has arranged a trip to Spacetown for me."

"To Spacetown!" Enderby looked up with instant indignation.

"Yes. It's the logical next move, Commissioner. I'd like to see the scene of the crime, ask a few questions."

Enderby shook his head decidedly. "I don't think that's a good idea, Lije. We've gone over the ground. I doubt there's anything new to be learned. And they're strange people. Kid gloves! They got to be handled with kid gloves. You don't have the experience."

He put a plump hand to his forehead and added, with unexpected fervor, "I hate them."

Baley inserted hostility into his voice. "Damn it, the robot came here and I should go there. It's bad enough sharing a front seat with a robot; I hate to take a back seat. Of course, if you don't think I'm capable of running this investigation, Commissioner——"

"It isn't that, Lije. It's not you, it's the Spacers. You don't know what they're like."

Baley deepened his frown. "Well, then, Commissioner, suppose you come along." His right hand rested on his knee, and two of his fingers crossed automatically as he said that.

The Commissioner's eyes widened. "No. Lije. I won't go there. Don't ask me to." He seemed visibly to catch hold of his runaway words. More quietly, he said, with an unconvincing smile, "Lots of work here, you know. I'm days behind."

Baley regarded him thoughtfully. "I tell you what, then. Why not get into it by trimension later on. Just for a while, you understand. In case I need help."

"Well, yes. I suppose I can do that." He sounded unenthusiastic.

"Good." Baley looked at the wall clock, nodded, and got up. "I'll be in touch with you."

Baley looked back as he left the office, keeping the door open for part of an additional second. He saw the Commissioner's head begin bending down toward the crook of one elbow as it rested on the desk. The plain-clothes man could almost swear he heard a sob.

Jehoshaphat! he thought, in outright shock.

He paused in the common room and sat on the corner of a nearby desk, ignoring its occupant, who looked up, murmured a casual greeting, and returned to his work.

Baley unclipped the baffle from the bowl of the pipe and blew into it. He inverted the pipe itself over the desk's small ash vacuum and let the powdery white tobacco ash vanish. He looked regretfully at the empty pipe, readjusted the baffle and put it away. Another pipeful gone forever!

He reconsidered what had just taken place. In one way, Enderby had not surprised him. He had expected resistance to any attempt on his own part to enter Spacetown. He had heard the Commissioner talk often enough about the difficulties of dealing with Spacers, about the dangers of allowing any but experienced negotiators to have anything to do with them, even over trifles.

He had not expected, however, to have the Commissioner give in so easily. He had supposed, at the very least, that Enderby would have insisted on accompanying him. The pressure of other work was meaningless in the face of the importance of this problem.

And that was not what Baley wanted. He wanted exactly what he had gotten. He wanted the Commissioner to be present by trimensional personification so that he could witness the proceedings from a point of safety.

Safety was the key word. Baley would need a witness that could not be put out of the way immediately. He needed that much as the minimum guarantee of his own safety.

The Commissioner had agreed to that at once. Baley remembered the parting sob, or ghost of one, and thought: Jehoshaphat, the man's into this past his depth.

A cheerful, slurring voice sounded just at Baley's shoulder and Baley started.

"What the devil do you want?" he demanded savagely.

The smile on R. Sammy's face remained foolishly fixed. "Jack says to tell you Daneel is ready, Lije."

"All right. Now get out of here."

He frowned at the robot's departing back. There was nothing so irritating as having that clumsy metal contraption forever making free with your front name. He'd complained about that when R. Sammy first arrived and the Commissioner had shrugged his shoulders and said, "You can't have it both ways, Lije. The public insists that City robots be built with a strong friendship circuit. All right, then. He is drawn to you. He calls you the friendliest name he knows."

Friendship circuit! No robot built, of any type, could possibly hurt a human being. That was the First Law of Robotics:

"A robot may not injure a human being, or, through inaction, allow a human being to come to harm."

No positronic brain was ever built without that injunction driven so deeply into its basic circuits that no conceivable derangement could displace it. There was no need for specialized friendship circuits.

Yet the Commissioner was right. The Earthman's distrust for robots was something quite irrational and friendship circuits had to be incorporated, just as all robots had to be made smiling. On Earth, at any rate.

R. Daneel, now, never smiled.

Sighing, Baley rose to his feet. He thought: Spacetown, next stop—or, maybe, last stop!

The police forces of the City, as well as certain high officials, could still make use of individual squad cars along the corridors of the City and even along the ancient underground motorways that were barred to foot traffic. There were perennial demands on the part of the Liberals that these motorways be converted to children's playgrounds, to new shopping areas, or to expressway or localway extensions.

The strong pleas of "Civic safety!" remained unvanquished, however. In cases of fires too large to be handled by local devices, in cases of massive breakdowns in power lines or ventilators, most of all in cases of serious riot, there had to be some means whereby the forces of the City could be mobilized at the stricken point in a hurry. No substitute for the motorways existed or could exist.

Baley had traveled along a motorway several times before in his life, but its indecent emptiness always depressed him. It seemed a million miles from the warm, living pulsation of the City. It stretched out like a blind and hollow worm before his eyes as he sat at the controls of the squad car. It opened continuously into new stretches as he moved around this gentle curve or that. Behind him, he knew without looking, another blind and hollow worm continually contracted and closed. The motorway was well lit, but lighting was meaningless in the silence and emptiness.

R. Daneel did nothing to break the silence or fill that emptiness. He looked straight ahead, as unimpressed by the empty motorway as by the bulging expressway.

In one sounding moment, to the tune of a wild whine of the squad car's siren, they popped out of the motorway and curved gradually into the vehicular lane of a City corridor.

The vehicular lanes were still conscientiously marked down each major corridor in reverence for one vestigial portion of the past. There were no vehicles any longer, except for squad cars, fire engines, and maintenance trucks, and pedestrians used the lanes in complete self-assurance. They scattered in indignant hurry before the advance of Baley's squealing car.

Baley, himself, drew a freer breath as noise surged in about him, but it was an interval only. In less than two hundred yards they turned into the subdued corridors that led into Spacetown Entrance.

They were expected. The guards obviously knew R. Daneel by sight and, although themselves human, nodded to him without the least self-consciousness.

One approached Baley and saluted with perfect, if frigid, military courtesy. He was tall and grave, though not the perfect specimen of Spacer physique that R. Daneel was.

He said, "Your identification card, if you please, sir."

It was inspected quickly but thoroughly. Baley noticed that the guard wore flesh-colored gloves and had an all but unnoticeable filter in each nostril.

The guard saluted again and returned the card. He said, "There is a small Men's Personal here which we would be pleased to have you use if you wish to shower."

It was in Baley's mind to deny the necessity, but R. Daneel plucked gently at his sleeve, as the guard stepped back to his place.

R. Daneel said, "It is customary, partner Elijah, for City dwellers to shower before entering Spacetown. I tell you this since I know you have no desire, through lack of information on this matter, to render yourself or ourselves uncomfortable. It is also advisable for you to attend to any matters of personal hygiene you may think advisable. There will be no facilities within Spacetown for that purpose."

"No facilities!" said Baley, strenuously. "But that's impossible."

"I mean, of course," said R. Daneel, "none for use by City dwellers."

Baley's face filled with a clearly hostile astonishment.

R. Daneel said, "I regret the situation, but it is a matter of custom."

Wordlessly, Baley entered the Personal. He felt, rather than saw, R. Daneel entering behind him.

He thought: Checking on me? Making sure I wash the City dust off myself?

For a furious moment, he reveled in the thought of the shock he was preparing for Spacetown. It seemed to him suddenly minor that he might, in effect, be pointing a blaster at his own chest.

The Personal was small, but it was well appointed and antiseptic in its cleanliness. There was a trace of sharpness in the air. Baley sniffed at it, momentarily puzzled.

Then he thought: Ozone! They've got ultraviolet radiation flooding the place.

A little sign blinked on and off several times, then remained steadily lit. It said, "Visitor will please remove all clothing, including shoes, and place in the receptacle below."

Baley acquiesced. He unhitched his blaster and blaster strap and recircled it about his naked waist. It felt heavy and uncomfortable.

The receptacle closed and his clothing was gone. The lighted sign blanked out. A new sign flashed ahead.

It said: "Visitor will please tend to personal needs, then make use of the shower indicated by arrow."

Baley felt like a machine tool being shaped by long-distance force edges on an assembly line.

His first act upon entering the small shower cubicle was to draw up the moisture-proof flap on his blaster holster and clip it down firmly all about. He knew by long-standing test that he could still draw and use it in less than five seconds.

There was no knob or hook on which to hang his blaster. There was not even a visible shower head. He placed it in a corner away from the cubicle's entrance door.

Another sign flashed: "Visitor will please hold arms directly out from his body and stand in the central circle with feet in the indicated positions."

As he placed his feet in the small depressions allowed for them, the sign blanked out. As it did so, a stinging, foaming spray hit him from ceiling, floor, and four walls. He felt the water welling up even beneath the soles of his feet. For a full minute it lasted, his skin reddening under the combined force of the heat and pressure and his lungs gasping for air in the warm dampness. There followed another minute of cool, low-pressure spray, and then finally a minute of warm air that left him dry and refreshed.

He picked up his blaster and blaster strap and found that they, too, were dry and warm. He strapped them on and stepped out of the cubicle in time to see R. Daneel emerge from a neighboring shower. Of course! R. Daneel was not a City dweller, but he had accumulated City dust.

Quite automatically, Baley looked away. Then, with the thought, that, after all, R. Daneel's customs were not City customs, he forced his unwilling eyes back for one moment. His lips quirked in a tiny smile. R. Daneel's resemblance to humanity was not restricted to his face and hands but had been carried out with painstaking accuracy over the entire body.

Baley stepped forward in the direction he had been traveling continuously since entering the Personal. He found his clothes awaiting for him, neatly folded. They had a warm, clean odor to them.

A sign said, "Visitor will please resume his clothing and place his hand in the indicated depression."

Baley did so. He felt a definite tingling in the ball of his middle finger as he laid it down upon the clean, milky surface. He lifted his hand hastily and found a little drop of blood oozing out. As he watched, it stopped flowing.

He shook it off and pinched the finger. No more blood was flowing even then.

Obviously, they were analyzing his blood. He felt a definite pang of anxiety. His own yearly routine examination by Department doctors, he felt sure, was not carried on with the thoroughness or, perhaps, with the knowledge of these cold robot-makers from outer space. He was not sure he wanted too probing an inquiry into the state of his health.

The time of waiting seemed long to Baley, but when the light flashed again, it said simply, "Visitor will proceed."

Baley drew a long breath of relief. He walked onward and stepped through an archway. Two metal rods closed in before him and, written in luminous air, were the words: "Visitor is warned to proceed no further."

"What the devil—" called out Baley, forgetting in his anger the fact that he was still in the Personal.

R. Daneel's voice was in his ear. "The sniffers have detected a power source, I imagine. Are you carrying your blaster, Elijah?"

Baley whirled, his face a deep crimson. He tried twice, then managed to croak out, "A police officer has his blaster on him or in easy reach at all times, on duty and off."

It was the first time he had spoken in a Personal, proper, since he was ten years old. That had been in his uncle Boris's presence and had merely been an automatic complaint when he stubbed his toe. Uncle Boris had beaten him well when he reached home and had lectured him strongly on the necessities of public decency.

R. Daneel said, "No visitor may be armed. It is our custom, Elijah. Even your Commissioner leaves his blaster behind on all visits."

Under almost any other circumstances, Baley would have turned on his heel and walked away, away from Spacetown and away from that robot. Now, however, he was almost mad with desire to go through with his exact plan and have his revenge to the brim in that way.

This, he thought, was the unobtrusive medical examination that had replaced the more detailed one of the early days. He could well understand, he could understand to overflowing, the indignation and anger that had led to the Barrier Riots of his youth.

In black anger, Baley unhitched his blaster belt. R. Daneel took it from him and placed it within a recess in the wall. A thin metal plate slithered across it.

"If you put your thumb in the depression," said R. Daneel, "only your thumb will open it later on."

Baley felt undressed, far more so, in fact, than he had felt in the shower. He stepped across the point at which the rods had lately barred him, and, finally, out of the Personal.

He was back in a corridor again, but there was an element of strangeness about it. Up ahead, the light had an unfamiliar quality to it. He felt a whiff of air against his face and, automatically, he thought a squad car had passed.

R. Daneel must have read his uneasiness in his face. He said, "You are essentially in open air now, Elijah. It is unconditioned."

Baley felt faintly sick. How could the Spacers be so rigidly careful of a human body, merely because it came from the City, and then breathe the dirty air of the open fields? He tightened his nostrils, as though by pulling them together he could the more effectively screen the ingoing air.

R. Daneel said, "I believe you will find that open air is not deleterious to human health."

"All right," said Baley, faintly.

The air currents hit annoyingly against his face. They were gentle enough, but they were erratic. That bothered him.

Worse came. The corridor opened into blueness and as they approached its end, strong white light washed down. Baley had seen sunlight. He had been in a natural Solarium once in the line of duty. But there, protecting glass had enclosed the place and the sun's own image had been refracted into a generalized glow. Here, all was open.

Automatically, he looked up at the sun, then turned away. His dazzled eyes blinked and watered.

A Spacer was approaching. A moment of misgiving struck Baley.

R. Daneel, however, stepped forward to greet the approaching man with a handshake. The Spacer turned to Baley and said, "Won't you come with me, sir? I am Dr. Han Fastolfe."

Things were better inside one of the domes. Baley found himself goggling at the size of the rooms and the way in which space was so carelessly distributed, but was thankful for the feel of the conditioned air.

Fastolfe said, sitting down and crossing his long legs, "I'm assuming that you prefer conditioning to unobstructed wind."

He seemed friendly enough. There were fine wrinkles on his forehead and a certain flabbiness to the skin below his eyes and just under his chin. His hair was thinning, but showed no signs of gray. His large ears stood away from his head, giving him a humorous and homely appearance that comforted Baley.

Early that morning, Baley had looked once again at those pictures of Spacetown that Enderby had taken. R. Daneel had just arranged the Spacetown appointment and Baley was absorbing the notion that he was to meet Spacers in the flesh. Somehow that was considerably different from speaking to them across the miles of carrier wave, as he had done on several occasions before.

The Spacers in those pictures had been, generally speaking, like those that were occasionally featured in the book-films: tall, red-headed, grave, coldly handsome. Like R. Daneel Olivaw, for instance.

R. Daneel named the Spacers for Baley and when Baley suddenly pointed and said in surprise, "That isn't you, is it?" R. Daneel answered, "No, Elijah, that is my designer, Dr. Sarton."

He said it unemotionally.

"You were made in your maker's image?" asked Baley, sardonically, but there was no answer to that and, in truth, Baley scarcely expected one. The Bible, as he knew, circulated only to the most limited extent on the Outer Worlds.

And now Baley looked at Han Fastolfe, a man who deviated very noticeably from the Spacer norm in looks, and the Earthman felt a pronounced gratitude for that fact.

"Won't you accept food?" asked Fastolfe.

He indicated the table that separated himself and R. Daneel from the Earthman. It bore nothing but a bowl of varicolored spheroids. Baley felt vaguely startled. He had taken them for table decorations.

R. Daneel explained. "These are the fruits of natural plant life grown on Aurora. I suggest you try this kind. It is called an apple and is reputed to be pleasant."

Fastolfe smiled. "R. Daneel does not know this by personal experience, of course, but he is quite right."

Baley brought an apple to his mouth. Its surface was red and green. It was cool to the touch and had a faint but pleasant odor. With an effort, he bit into it and the unexpected tartness of the pulpy contents hurt his teeth.

He chewed it gingerly. City dwellers ate natural food, of course, whenever rations allowed it. He himself had eaten natural meat and bread often. But such food had always been processed in some way. It had been cooked or ground, blended or compounded. Fruit, now, properly speaking, should come in the form of sauce or preserve. What he was holding now must have come straight from the dirt of a planet's soil.

He thought: I hope they've washed it at least.

Again he wondered at the spottiness of Spacer notions concerning cleanliness.

Fastolfe said, "Let me introduce myself a bit more specifically. I am in charge of the investigation of the murder of Dr. Sarton at the Spacetown end as Commissioner Enderby is at the City end. If I can help you in any way, I stand ready to do so. We are as eager for a quiet solution of the affair and prevention of future incidents of the sort as any of you City men can be."

"Thank you, Dr. Fastolfe," said Baley. "Your attitude is appreciated."

So much, he thought, for the amenities. He bit into the center of the apple and hard, dark little ovoids popped into his mouth. He spat automatically. They flew out and fell to the ground. One would have struck Fastolfe's leg had not the Spacer moved it hastily.

Baley reddened, started to bend.

Fastolfe said, pleasantly, "It is quite all right, Mr. Baley. Just leave them, please."

Baley straightened again. He put the apple down gingerly. He had the uncomfortable feeling that once he was gone, the lost little objects would be found and picked up by suction; the bowl of fruit would be burnt or discarded far from Spacetown; the very room they were sitting in would be sprayed with viricide.

He covered his embarrassment with brusqueness. He said, "I would like to ask permission to have Commissioner Enderby join our conference by trimensional personification."

Fastolfe's eyebrows raised. "Certainly, if you wish it. Daneel, would you make the connection?"

Baley sat in stiff discomfort until the shiny surface of the large parallelepiped in one corner of the room dissolved away to show Commissioner Julius Enderby and part of his desk. At that moment, the discomfort eased and Baley felt nothing short of love for that familiar figure, and a longing to be safely back in the office with him or anywhere in the City, for that matter. Even in the least prepossessing portion of the Jersey yeast-vat districts.

Now that he had his witness, Baley saw no reason for delay. He said, "I believe I have penetrated the mystery surrounding the death of Dr. Sarton."

Out of the corner of his eye, he saw Enderby springing to his feet and grabbing wildly (and successfully) at his flying spectacles. By standing, the Commissioner thrust his head out of limits of the trimensic receiver and was forced to sit down again, red-faced and speechless.

In a much quieter way, Dr. Fastolfe, head inclined to one side, was startled. Only R. Daneel was unmoved.

"Do you mean," said Fastolfe, "that you know the murderer?"

"No," said Baley, "I mean there was no murder."

"What!" screamed Enderby.

"One moment, Commissioner Enderby," said Fastolfe, raising a hand. His eyes held Baley's and he said, "Do you mean that Dr. Sarton is alive?"

"Yes, sir, and I believe I know where he is."

"Where?"

"Right there," said Baley, and pointed firmly at R. Daneel Olivaw.

Debate over a Robot

At the moment, Baley was most conscious of the thud of his own pulse. He seemed to be living in a moment of suspended time. R. Daneel's expression was, as always, empty of emotion. Han Fastolfe wore a look of well-bred astonishment on his face and nothing more.

It was Commissioner Julius Enderby's reaction that most concerned Baley, however. The trimensic receiver out of which his face stared did not allow of perfect reproduction. There was always that tiny flicker and that not-quite-ideal resolution. Through that imperfection and through the further masking of the Commissioner's spectacles, Enderby's eyes were unreadable.

Baley thought: Don't go to pieces on me, Julius. I need you.

He didn't really think Fastolfe would act in haste or under emotional impulse. He had read somewhere once that Spacers had no religion, but substituted, instead, a cold and phlegmatic intellectualism raised to the heights of a philosophy. He believed that and counted on it. They would make a point of acting slowly and then only on the basis of reason.

If he were alone among them and had said what he had said, he was certain that he would never have returned to the City. Cold reason would have dictated that. The Spacers' plans were more to them, many times over, than the life of a City dweller. There would be some excuse made to Julius Enderby. Maybe they would present his corpse to the Commissioner, shake their heads, and speak of an Earthman conspiracy having struck again. The Commissioner would believe them. It was the way he was built. If he hated Spacers, it was a hatred based on fear. He wouldn't dare disbelieve them.

That was why he had to be an actual witness of events, a witness, moreover, safely out of reach of the Spacers' calculated safety measures.

The Commissioner said, chokingly, "Lije, you're all wrong, I saw Dr. Sarton's corpse."

"You saw the charred remnants of something you were told was Dr. Sarton's corpse," retorted Baley, boldly. He thought grimly of the Commissioner's broken glasses. That had been an unexpected favor for the Spacers.

"No, no, Lije. I knew Dr. Sarton well and his head was undamaged. It was he." The Commissioner put his hand to his glasses uneasily, as though he, too, remembered, and added, "I looked at him closely, very closely."

"How about this one, Commissioner?" asked Baley, pointing to R. Daneel again. "Doesn't he resemble Dr. Sarton?"

"Yes, the way a statue would."

"An expressionless attitude can be assumed, Commissioner. Suppose that were a robot you had seen blasted to death. You say you looked closely. Did you look closely enough to see whether the charred surface at the edge of the blast was really decomposed organic tissue or a deliberately introduced layer of carbonization over fused metal."

The Commissioner looked revolted. He said, "You're being ridiculous."

Baley turned to the Spacer. "Are you willing to have the body exhumed for examination, Dr. Fastolfe?"

Dr. Fastolfe smiled. "Ordinarily, I would have no objection, Mr. Baley, but I'm afraid we do not bury our dead. Cremation is a universal custom among us."

"Very convenient," said Baley.

"Tell me, Mr. Baley," said Dr. Fastolfe, "just how did you arrive at this very extraordinary conclusion of yours?"

Baley thought: He isn't giving up. He'll brazen it out, if he can.

He said, "It wasn't difficult. There's more to imitating a robot than just putting on a frozen expression and adopting a stilted style of conversation. The trouble with you men of the Outer Worlds is that you're too used to robots. You've gotten to accept them almost as human beings. You've grown blind to the differences. On Earth, it's different. We're very conscious of what a robot is.

"Now in the first place, R. Daneel is too good a human to be a robot. My first impression of him was that he was a Spacer. It was quite an effort for me to adjust myself to his statement that he was a robot. And of course, the reason for that was that he *was* a Spacer and *wasn't* a robot."

R. Daneel interrupted, without any sign of self-consciousness at being himself so intimately the topic of debate. He said, "As I told you, partner Elijah, I was designed to take a temporary place in a human society. The resemblance to humanity is purposeful."

"Even," said Baley, "down to the painstaking duplication of those portions of the body, which, in the ordinary course of events, would always be covered by clothes? Even to the duplication of organs which, in a robot, would have no conceivable function?"

Enderby said suddenly, "How did you find that out?"

Baley reddened. "I couldn't help noticing in the—in the Personal."

Enderby looked shocked.

Fastolfe said, "Surely you understand that a resemblance must be complete if it is to be useful. For our purposes, half measures are as bad as nothing at all."

Baley asked abruptly, "May I smoke?"

Three pipefuls in one day was a ridiculous extravagance, but he was riding a rolling torrent of recklessness and needed the release of tobacco. After all, he was talking back to Spacers. He was going to force their lies down their own throats.

Fastolfe said, "I'm sorry, but I'd prefer that you didn't."

It was a "preference" that had the force of a command. Baley felt that. He thrust back the pipe, the bowl of which he had already taken into his hand in anticipation of automatic permission.

Of course not, he thought bitterly. Enderby didn't warn me, because he doesn't smoke himself, but it's obvious. It follows. They don't smoke on their hygienic Outer Worlds, or drink, or have any human vices. No wonder they accept robots in their damned—what did R. Daneel call it—C/Fe society? No wonder R. Daneel can play the robot as well as he does. They're all robots out there to begin with.

He said, "The too complete resemblance is just one point out of a number. There was a near riot in my section as I was taking *him* home." (He had to point. He could not bring himself to say either R. Daneel or Dr. Sarton.) "It was he that stopped the trouble and he did it by pointing a blaster at the potential rioters."

"Good Lord," said Enderby, energetically, "the report stated that it was you——"

"I know, Commissioner," said Baley. "The report was based on information that I gave. I didn't want to have it on the record that a robot had threatened to blast men and women."

"No, no. Of course not." Enderby was quite obviously horrified. He leaned forward to look at something that was out of range of the trimensic receiver.

Baley could guess what it was. The Commissioner was checking the power gauge to see if the transmitter were tapped.

"Is that a point in your argument?" asked Fastolfe.

"It certainly is. The First Law of Robotics states that a robot cannot harm a human being."

"But R. Daneel did no harm."

"True. He even stated afterward that he wouldn't have fired under any circumstances. Still, no robot I ever heard of could have violated the spirit of the First Law to the extent of threatening to blast a man, even if he really had no intention to do so."

"I see. Are you a robotics expert, Mr. Baley?"

"No, sir. But I've had a course in general robotics and in positronic analysis. I'm not completely ignorant."

"That's nice," said Fastolfe, agreeably, "but you see, I *am* a robotics expert, and I assure you that the essence of the robot mind lies in a completely literal interpretation of the universe. It recognizes no spirit in the First Law, only the letter. The simple models you have on Earth may have their First Law so overlaid with additional safeguards that, to be sure, they may well be incapable of threatening a human. An advanced model such as R. Daneel is another matter. If I gather the situation correctly, Daneel's threat was necessary to prevent a riot. It was intended then to prevent harm to human beings. He was obeying the First Law, not defying it."

Baley squirmed inwardly, but maintained a tight external calm. It would go hard, but he would match this Spacer at his own game.

He said, "You may counter each point separately, but they add up just the same. Last evening in our discussion of the so-called murder, this alleged robot claimed that he had been converted into a detective by the installation of a new drive into his positronic circuits. A drive, if you please, for justice."

"I'll vouch for that," said Fastolfe. "It was done to him three days ago under my own supervision."

"A drive for *justice*? Justice, Dr. Fastolfe, is an abstraction. Only a human being can use the term."

"If you define 'justice' in such a way that it is an abstraction, if you say that it is the rendering of each man his due, that it is adhering to the right, or anything of the sort, I grant you your argument, Mr. Baley. A human understanding of abstractions cannot be built into a positronic brain in the present state of our knowledge."

"You admit that, then—as an expert in robotics?"

"Certainly. The question is, what did R. Daneel mean by using the term 'justice'?"

"From the context of our own conversation, he meant what you and I and any human being would mean, but what no robot could mean."

"Why don't you ask him, Mr. Baley, to define the term?"

Baley felt a certain loss of confidence. He turned to R. Daneel. "Well?"

"Yes, Elijah?"

"What is your definition of justice?"

"Justice, Elijah, is that which exists when all the laws are enforced."

Fastolfe nodded. "A good definition, Mr. Baley, for a robot. The desire to see all laws enforced has been built into R. Daneel, now. Justice is a very concrete term to him since it is based on law enforcement, which is in turn based upon the existence of specific and definite laws. There is nothing abstract about it. A human being can recognize the fact that, on the basis of an abstract moral code, some laws may be bad ones and their enforcement unjust. What do you say, R. Daneel?"

"An unjust law," said R. Daneel evenly, "is a contradiction in terms."

"To a robot it is, Mr. Baley. So you see, you mustn't confuse your justice and R. Daneel's."

Baley turned to R. Daneel sharply and said, "You left my apartment last night."

R. Daneel replied, "I did. If my leaving disturbed your sleep, I am sorry."

"Where did you go?"

"To the Men's Personal."

For a moment, Baley was staggered. It was the answer he had already decided was the truth, but he had not expected it to be the answer R. Daneel would give. He felt a little more of his certainty oozing away, yet he held firmly on his track. The Commissioner was watching, his lensed eyes flicking from one to the other as they spoke. Baley *couldn't* back down now, no matter what sophistries they used against him. He had to hold to his point.

He said, "On reaching my section, *he* insisted on entering Personal with me. His excuse was a poor one. During the night, he left to visit Personal again as he has just admitted. If he were a man, I'd say he had every reason and right to do so. Obviously. As a robot, however, the trip was meaningless. The conclusion can only be that he is a man."

Fastolfe nodded. He seemed not in the least put out. He said, "This is most interesting. Suppose we ask Daneel why he made his trip to Personal last night."

Commissioner Enderby leaned forward. "Please, Dr. Fastolfe," he muttered, "it is not proper to——"

"You need not be concerned, Commissioner," said Fastolfe, his thin lips curving back in something that looked like a smile but wasn't, "I'm certain that Daneel's answer will not offend your sensibilities or those of Mr. Baley. Won't you tell us, Daneel?"

R. Daneel said, "Elijah's wife, Jessie, left the apartment last night on friendly terms with me. It was quite obvious that she had no reason for thinking me to be other than human. She returned to the apartment knowing I was a robot. The obvious conclusion is that the information to that effect exists outside the apartment. It followed that my conversation with Elijah last night had been overheard. In no other way could the secret of my true nature have become common knowledge.

"Elijah told me that the apartments were well insulated. We spoke together in low voices. Ordinary eavesdropping would not do. Still, it was known that Elijah is a policeman. If a conspiracy exists within the City sufficiently well organized to have planned the murder of Dr. Sarton, they may well have been aware that Elijah had been placed in charge of the murder investigation. It would fall within the realm of possibility then, even of probability, that his apartment had been spy-beamed.

"I searched the apartment as well as I could after Elijah and Jessie had gone to bed, but could find no transmitter. This complicated matters. A focused duo-beam could do the trick even in the absence of a transmitter, but that requires rather elaborate equipment.

"Analysis of the situation led to the following conclusion. The one place where a City dweller can do almost anything without being disturbed or questioned is in the Personals. He could even set up a duo-beam. The custom of absolute privacy in the Personals is very strong and other men would not even look at him. The Section Personal is quite close to Elijah's apartment, so that the distance factor is not important. A suitcase model could be used. I went to the Personal to investigate."

"And what did you find?" asked Baley quickly.

"Nothing, Elijah. No sign of a duo-beam."

Dr. Fastolfe said, "Well, Mr. Baley, does this sound reasonable to you?"

But Baley's uncertainty was gone, now. He said, "Reasonable as far as it goes, perhaps, but it stops short of perfection by a hell of a way. What *he* doesn't know is that my wife told me where she got the information and *when*. She learned he was a robot shortly after she left the house. Even then, a rumor had been circulating for hours. So the fact that he was a robot could not have leaked out through spying on our last evening's conversation."

"Nevertheless," said Dr. Fastolfe, "his action last night of going to the Personal stands explained, I think."

"But something is brought up that is *not* explained," retorted Baley, heatedly. "Where, when, and how was the leak? How did the news get about that there was a Spacer robot in the City? As far as I know, only two of us knew about the deal, Commissioner Enderby and myself, and we told no one.—Commissioner, did anyone else in the Department know?"

"No," said Enderby, anxiously. "Not even the Mayor. Only we, and Dr. Fastolfe."

"And *he*," added Baley, pointing.

"I?" asked R. Daneel.

"Why not?"

"I was with you at all times, Elijah."

"You were *not*," cried Baley, fiercely. "I was in Personal for half an hour or more before we went to my apartment. During that time, we two were completely out of contact with one another. It was then that you got in touch with your group in the City."

"What group?" asked Fastolfe.

And "What group?" echoed Commissioner Enderby almost simultaneously.

Baley rose from his chair and turned to the trimensic receiver. "Commissioner, I want you to listen closely to this. Tell me if it doesn't all fall into a pattern. A murder is reported and by a curious coincidence it happens just as you are entering Spacetown to keep an appointment with the murdered man. You are shown the corpse of something supposed to be human, but the corpse has since been disposed of and is not available for close examination.

"The Spacers insist an Earthman did the killing, even though the only way they can make such an accusation stick is to suppose that a City man had left the City and cut cross country to Spacetown alone and at night. You know damn well how unlikely that is.

"Next they send a supposed robot into the City; in fact, they *insist* on sending him. The first thing the robot does is to threaten a crowd of human beings with a blaster. The second is to set in motion the rumor that there is a Spacer robot in the City. In fact, the rumor is so specific that Jessie told me it was known that he was working with the police. That means that before long it will be known that it was the robot who handled that blaster. Maybe even now the rumor is spreading across the yeast-vat country and down the Long Island hydroponic plants that there's a killer robot on the loose."

"This is impossible. Impossible!" groaned Enderby.

"No, it isn't. It's exactly what's happening, Commissioner. Don't you see it? There's a conspiracy in the City, all right, but it's run from Spacetown. The Spacers *want* to be able to report a murder. They *want* riots. They *want* an assault on Spacetown. The worse things get, the better the incident—and Spacer ships come down and occupy the Cities of Earth."

Fastolfe said, mildly, "We had an excuse in the Barrier Riots of twenty-five years ago."

"You weren't ready then. You are now." Baley's heart was pounding madly.

"This is quite a complicated plot you're attributing to us, Mr. Baley. If we wanted to occupy Earth, we could do so in much simpler fashion."

"Maybe not, Dr. Fastolfe. Your so-called robot told me that public opinion concerning Earth is by no means unified on your Outer Worlds. I think he was telling the truth at that time, anyway. Maybe an outright occupation wouldn't sit well with the people at home. Maybe an incident is an absolute necessity. A good shocking incident."

"Like a murder, eh? Is that it? You'll admit it would have to be a pretended murder. You won't suggest, I hope, that we'd really kill one of ourselves for the sake of an incident."

"You built a robot to look like Dr. Sarton, blasted the robot, and showed the remains to Commissioner Enderby."

"And then," said Dr. Fastolfe, "having used R. Daneel to impersonate Dr. Sarton in the false murder, we have to use Dr. Sarton to impersonate R. Daneel in the false investigation of the false murder."

"Exactly. I am telling you this in the presence of a witness who is not here in the flesh and whom you cannot blast out of existence and who is important enough to be believed by the City government and by Washington itself. We will be prepared for you and we know what your intentions are. If necessary, our government will report directly to your people, expose the situation for exactly what it is. I doubt if this sort of interstellar rape will be tolerated."

Fastolfe shook his head. "Please, Mr. Baley, you are being unreasonable. Really, you have the most astonishing notions. Suppose now, just quietly suppose, that R. Daneel is really R. Daneel. Suppose he is actually a robot. Wouldn't it follow that the corpse Commissioner Enderby saw was really Dr. Sarton? It would be scarcely reasonable to believe that the corpse were still another robot. Commissioner Enderby witnessed R. Daneel under construction and can vouch for the fact that only one existed."

"If it comes to that," said Baley, stubbornly, "the Commissioner is not a robotics expert. You might have had a dozen such robots."

"Stick to the point, Mr. Baley. What if R. Daneel is really R. Daneel? Would not the entire structure of your reasoning fall to the ground? Would you have any further basis for your belief in this completely melodramatic and implausible interstellar plot you have constructed?"

"*If* he is a robot! I say he is human."

"Yet you haven't really investigated the problem, Mr. Baley," said Fastolfe. "To differentiate a robot, even a very humanoid robot, from a human being, it isn't necessary to make elaborately shaky deductions from little things he says and does. For instance, have you tried sticking a pin into R. Daneel?"

"What?" Baley's mouth fell open.

"It's a simple experiment. There are others perhaps not quite so simple. His skin and hair look real, but have you tried looking at them under adequate magnification. Then again, he seems to breathe, particularly when he is using air to talk, but have you noticed that his breathing is irregular, that minutes may go by during which he has no breath at all. You might even have trapped some of his expired air and measured the carbon dioxide content. You might have tried to draw a sample of blood. You might have tried to detect a pulse in his wrist, or a heartbeat under his shirt. Do you see what I mean, Mr. Baley?"

"That's just talk," said Baley, uneasily. "I'm not going to be bluffed. I might have tried any of those things, but do you suppose this alleged robot would have let me bring a hypodermic to him, or a stethoscope or a microscope?"

"Of course. I see your point," said Fastolfe. He looked at R. Daneel and gestured slightly.

R. Daneel touched the cuff of his right shirt sleeve and the diamagnetic seam fell apart the entire length of his arm. A smooth, sinewy, and apparently entirely human limb lay exposed. Its short, bronze hairs, both in quantity and distribution, were exactly what one would expect of a human being.

Baley said, "So?"

R. Daneel pinched the ball of his right middle finger with the thumb and forefinger of his left hand. Exactly what the details of the manipulation that followed were, Baley could not see.

But, just as the fabric of the sleeve had fallen in two when the diamagnetic field of its seam had been interrupted, so now the arm itself fell in two.

There, under a thin layer of fleshlike material, was the dull blue gray of stainless steel rods, cords, and joints.

"Would you care to examine Daneel's workings more closely, Mr. Baley?" asked Dr. Fastolfe politely.

Baley could scarcely hear the remark for the buzzing in his ears and for the sudden jarring of the Commissioner's high-pitched and hysterical laughter.

Elucidation by a Spacer

The minutes passed and the buzzing grew louder and drowned out the laughter. The dome and all it contained wavered and Baley's time sense wavered, too.

At least, he found himself sitting in an unchanged position but with a definite feeling of lost time. The Commissioner was gone; the trimensic receiver was milky and opaque; and R. Daneel sat at his side, pinching up the skin of Baley's bared upper arm. Baley could see, just beneath the skin, the small thin darkness of a hyposliver. It vanished as he watched, soaking and spreading away into the intercellular fluid, from that into the blood stream and the neighboring cells, from that into all the cells of his body.

His grip on reality heightened.

"Do you feel better, partner Elijah?" asked R. Daneel.

Baley did. He rolled down his sleeve and looked about. Dr. Fastolfe sat where he had been, a small smile softening the homeliness of his face.

Baley said, "Did I black out?"

Dr. Fastolfe said, "In a way, yes. You received a sizable shock, I'm afraid."

It came back to Baley quite clearly. He seized R. Daneel's nearer arm quickly, forcing up the sleeve as far as it would go, exposing the wrist. The robot's flesh felt soft to his fingers, but underneath was the hardness of something more than bone.

R. Daneel let his arm rest easily in the plain-clothes man's grip. Baley stared at it, pinching the skin along the median line. Was there a faint seam?

It was logical, of course, that there should be. A robot, covered with synthetic skin, and deliberately made to look human, could not be repaired in the ordinary fashion. A chest plate could not be unriveted for the purpose. A skull could not be hinged up and outward. Instead, the various parts of the mechanical body would have to be put together along a line of micromagnetic fields. An arm, a head, an entire body, must fall in two at the proper touch, then come together again at a contrary touch.

Baley looked up. "Where's the Commissioner?" he mumbled, hot with mortification.

"Pressing business," said Dr. Fastolfe. "I encouraged him to leave, I'm afraid. I assured him we would take care of you."

"You've taken care of me quite nicely already, thank you," said Baley, grimly. "I think our business is done."

He lifted himself erect on tired joints. He felt an old man, very suddenly. Too old to start over again. He needed no deep insight to foresee that future.

The Commissioner would be half frightened and half furious. He would face Baley whitely, taking his glasses off to wipe them every fifteen seconds. His soft voice (Julius Enderby almost never shouted) would explain carefully that the Spacers had been mortally offended.

"You *can't* talk to Spacers that way, Lije. They won't take it." (Baley could hear Enderby's voice very plainly down to the finest shade of intonation.) "I warned you. No saying how much damage you've done. I can see your point, mind you. I see what you were trying to do. If they were Earthmen, it would be different. I'd say yes, chance it. Run the risk. Smoke them out. But *Spacers!* You might have told me, Lije. You might have consulted me. I know them. I know them inside and out."

And what would Baley be able to say? That Enderby was exactly the man he couldn't tell. That the project was one of tremendous risk and Enderby a man of tremendous caution. That it had been Enderby himself who had pointed up the supreme dangers of either outright

failure or of the wrong kind of success. That the one way of defeating
declassification was to show that guilt lay in Spacetown itself. . . .

Enderby would say, "There'll have to be a report on this, Lije.
There'll be all sorts of repercussions. I know the Spacers. They'll demand your removal from the case, and it'll have to be that way. You
understand that, Lije, don't you? I'll try to make it easy on you. You
can count on that. I'll protect you as far as I can, Lije."

Baley knew that would be exactly true. The Commissioner would
protect him, but only as far as he could, not to the point, for instance,
of infuriating further an angry Mayor.

He could hear the Mayor, too. "Damn it, Enderby, what *is* all this?
Why wasn't I consulted? Who's running the City? Why was an unauthorized robot allowed inside the City? And just what the devil did
this Baley . . ."

If it came to a choice between Baley's future in the Department
and the Commissioner's own, what possible result could Baley expect?
He could find no reasonable way of blaming Enderby.

The least he could expect was demotion, and that was bad enough.
The mere act of living in a modern City insured the bare possibility
of existence, even for those entirely declassified. How bare that possibility was he knew only too well.

It was the addition of status that brought the little things: a more
comfortable seat here, a better cut of meat there, a shorter wait in
line at the other place. To the philosophical mind, these items might
seem scarcely worth any great trouble to acquire.

Yet no one, however philosophical, could give up those privileges,
once acquired, without a pang. That was the point.

What a trifling addition to the convenience of the apartment an
activated washbasin was when for thirty years previously the trip to
Personal had been an automatic and unregarded one. How useless it
was even as a device to prove "status" when it was considered the
height of ill form to parade "status." Yet were the washbasin to be
deactivated, how humiliating and unbearable would each added trip
to Personal be! How yearningly attractive the memory of the bedroom
shave! How filled with a sense of lost luxury!

It was fashionable for modern political writers to look back with a
smug disapproval at the "fiscalism" of Medieval times, when economy
was based on money. The competitive struggle for existence, they
said, was brutal. No truly complex society could be maintained because of the strains introduced by the eternal "fight-for-the-buck."
(Scholars had varying interpretations of the word "buck," but there
was no dispute over the meaning as a whole.)

By contrast, modern "civism" was praised highly as efficient and
enlightened.

Maybe so. There were historical novels both in the romantic and

the sensational tradition, and the Medievalists thought "fiscalism" had
bred such things as individualism and initiative.

Baley wouldn't commit himself, but now he wondered sickly if ever
a man fought harder for that buck, whatever it was, or felt its loss
more deeply, than a City dweller fought to keep from losing his Sunday night option on a chicken drumstick—a real-flesh drumstick from
a once-living bird.

Baley thought: Not me so much. There's Jessie and Ben.

Dr. Fastolfe's voice broke in upon his thoughts. "Mr. Baley, do you
hear me?"

Baley blinked. "Yes?" How long had he been standing there like a
frozen fool?

"Won't you sit down, sir? Having taken care of the matter on your
mind, you may now be interested in some films we have taken of the
scene of the crime and of the events immediately following."

"No, thank you. I have business in the City."

"Surely the case of Dr. Sarton comes first."

"Not with me. I imagine I'm off the case already." Suddenly, he
boiled over. "Damn it, if you could prove R. Daneel was a robot, why
didn't you do it at once? Why did you make such a farce of it all?"

"My dear Mr. Baley, I was very interested in your deductions. As
for being off the case, I doubt it. Before the Commissioner left, I made
a special point of asking that you be retained. I believe he will co-
operate."

Baley sat down, not entirely voluntarily. He said, sharply, "Why?"

Dr. Fastolfe crossed his legs and sighed. "Mr. Baley, in general I
have met two kinds of City dwellers, rioters and politicians. Your Commissioner is useful to us, but he is a politician. He tells us what we
want to hear. He *handles* us, if you know what I mean. Now you come
here and boldly accused us of tremendous crimes and tried to prove
your case. I enjoyed the process. I found it a hopeful development."

"How hopeful?" asked Baley sardonically.

"Hopeful enough. You are someone I can deal with frankly. Last
night, Mr. Baley, R. Daneel reported to me by shielded subether. Some
things about you interested me very much. For instance, there was
the point concerning the nature of the book-films in your apartment."

"What about them?"

"A good many dealt with historical and archaeological subjects. It
makes it appear that you are interested in human society and that you
know a little about its evolution."

"Even policemen can spend their free time on book-films, if they so
choose."

"Quite. I'm glad of your choice in viewing matter. It will help me
in what I am trying to do. In the first place, I want to explain, or try
to, the exclusivism of the men of the Outer Worlds. We live here in

Spacetown; we don't enter the City; we mingle with you City dwellers only in a very rigidly limited fashion. We breathe the open air, but when we do, we wear filters. I sit here now with filters in my nostrils, gloves on my hands, and a fixed determination to come no closer to you than I can help. Why do you suppose that is?"

Baley said, "There's no point in guessing." Let *him* talk now.

"If you guessed as some of your people do, you would say that it was because we despised the men of Earth and refused to lose caste by allowing their shadow to fall upon us. That is not so. The true answer is really quite obvious. The medical examination you went through, as well as the cleansing procedures, were not matters of ritual. They were dictated by necessity."

"Disease?"

"Yes, disease. My dear Mr. Baley, the Earthmen who colonized the Outer Worlds found themselves on planets entirely free of Terrestrial bacteria and viruses. They brought their own, of course, but they also brought with them the latest medical and microbiological techniques. They had a small community of micro-organisms to deal with and no intermediate hosts. There were no mosquitoes to spread malaria, no snails to spread schistosomiasis. Disease agents were wiped out and symbiotic bacteria allowed to grow. Gradually, the Outer Worlds became disease-free. Naturally, as time went on, entrance requirements for immigrant Earthmen were made more and more rigorous, since less and less could the Outer Worlds endure the possible introduction of disease."

"You've never been sick, Dr. Fastolfe?"

"Not with a parasitic disease, Mr. Baley. We are all liable to degenerative diseases such as atheroschlerosis, of course, but I have never had what you would call a cold. If I were to contract one, I might die of it. I've built up no resistance to it whatsoever. That's what's wrong with us here in Spacetown. Those of us who come here run a definite risk. Earth is riddled with diseases to which we have no defense, no *natural* defense. You yourself are carrying the germs of almost every known disease. You are not aware of it, since you keep them all under control at almost all times through the antibodies your body has developed over the years. I, myself, lack the antibodies. Do you wonder that I come no closer to you? Believe me, Mr. Baley, I act aloof only in self-defense."

Baley said, "If this is so, why isn't the fact made known on Earth? I mean, that it is not just queasiness on your part, but a defense against an actual physical danger."

The Spacer shook his head. "We are few, Mr. Baley, and are disliked as foreigners anyway. We maintain our own safety on the basis of a rather shaky prestige as a superior class of being. We cannot afford to lose face by admitting that we are *afraid* to approach an Earthman.

Not at least until there is a better understanding between Earthmen and Spacers."

"There won't be, on present terms. It's your supposed superiority that we—they hate you for."

"It is a dilemma. Don't think we aren't aware of it."

"Does the Commissioner know of this?"

"We have never explained it to him flatly, as I have just done to you. He may guess it, however. He is quite an intelligent man."

"If he guessed it, he might have told me," Baley said reflectively.

Dr. Fastolfe lifted his eyebrows. "If he had, then you wouldn't have considered the possibility of R. Daneel being a human Spacer. Is that it?"

Baley shrugged slightly, tossing the matter to one side.

But Dr. Fastolfe went on, "That's quite true, you know. Putting the psychological difficulties to one side, the terrible effect of the noise and crowds upon us, the fact remains that for one of us to enter the City is the equivalent of a death sentence. It is why Dr. Sarton initiated his project of humanoid robots. They were substitute men, designed to enter the City instead of us——"

"Yes. R. Daneel explained this to me."

"Do you disapprove?"

"Look," said Baley, "since we're talking to one another so freely, let me ask a question in simple words. Why have you Spacers come to Earth anyway? Why don't you leave us alone?"

Dr. Fastolfe said, with obvious surprise, "Are you *satisfied* with life on earth?"

"We get along."

"Yes, but for how long will that continue? Your population goes up continuously; the available calories meet the needs only as a result of greater and greater effort. Earth is in a blind alley, man."

"We get along," repeated Baley stubbornly.

"Barely. A City like New York must spend every ounce of effort getting water in and waste out. The nuclear power plants are kept going by uranium supplies that are constantly more difficult to obtain even from the other planets of the system, and the supply needed goes up steadily. The life of the City depends every moment on the arrival of wood pulp for the yeast vats and minerals for the hydroponic plants. Air must be circulated unceasingly. The balance is a very delicate one in a hundred directions, and growing more delicate each year. What would happen to New York if the tremendous flow of input and outgo were to be interrupted for even a single hour?"

"It never has been."

"Which is not security for the future. In primitive times, individual population centers were virtually self-supporting, living on the produce of neighboring farms. Nothing but immediate disaster, a flood or a pestilence or crop failure, could harm them. As the centers grew and technology improved, localized disasters could be overcome by drawing on help from distant centers, but at the cost of making ever larger areas interdependent. In Medieval times, the open cities, even the largest, could subsist on food stores and on emergency supplies of all sorts for a week at least. When New York first became a City, it could have lived on itself for a day. Now it cannot do so for an hour. A disaster that would have been uncomfortable ten thousand years ago, merely serious a thousand years ago, and acute a hundred years ago would now be surely fatal."

Baley moved restlessly in his chair. "I've heard all this before. The Medievalists want an end to Cities. They want us to get back to the soil and to natural agriculture. Well, they're mad; we can't. There are too many of us and you can't go backward in history, only forward. Of course, if emigration to the Outer Worlds were not restricted——"

"You know why it must be restricted."

"Then what is there to do? You're tapping a dead power line."

"What about emigration to new worlds? There are a hundred billion stars in the Galaxy. It is estimated that there are a hundred million planets that are inhabitable or can be made inhabitable."

"That's ridiculous."

"Why?" asked Dr. Fastolfe, with vehemence. "Why is the suggestion ridiculous? Earthmen have colonized planets in the past. Over thirty of the fifty Outer Worlds, including my native Aurora, were directly colonized by Earthmen. Is colonization no longer possible?"

"Well . . ."

"No answer? Let me suggest that if it *is* no longer possible, it is because of the development of City culture on Earth. Before the Cities, human life on Earth wasn't so specialized that they couldn't break loose and start all over on a raw world. They did it thirty times. But now, Earthmen are all so coddled, so enwombed in their imprisoning caves of steel that they are caught forever. You, Mr. Baley, won't even believe that a City dweller is capable of crossing country to get to Spacetown. Crossing space to get to a new world must represent impossibility squared to you. Civism is ruining Earth, sir."

Baley said angrily, "And if it does? How does it concern you people? It's our problem. We'll solve it. If not, it's our own particular road to hell."

"Better your own road to hell than another's road to heaven, eh? I know how you must feel. It is not pleasant to listen to the preaching of a stranger. Yet I wish your people could preach to us, for we, too, have a problem, one that is quite analogous to yours."

Baley smiled crookedly. "Overpopulation?"

"Analogous, not identical. Ours is underpopulation. How old would you say I was?"

The Earthman considered for a moment and then deliberately over-estimated. "Sixty, I'd say."

"A hundred and sixty, you should say."

"What!"

"A hundred and sixty-three next birthday, to be exact. There's no trick to that. I'm using the Standard Earth year as the unit. If I'm fortunate, if I take care of myself, most of all, if I catch no disease on Earth, I may double that age. Men on Aurora have been known to live over three hundred and fifty years. And life expectancy is still increasing."

Baley looked to R. Daneel (who throughout the conversation had been listening in stolid silence), as though he were seeking confirmation.

He said, "How is that possible?"

"In an underpopulated society, it is practical to concentrate study on gerontology, to do research on the aging process. In a world such as yours, a lengthened life expectancy would be disastrous. You couldn't afford the resulting rise in population. On Aurora, there is room for tricentenarians. Then, of course, a long life becomes doubly and triply precious.

"If you were to die now, you would lose perhaps forty years of your life, probably less. If I were to die, I would lose a hundred fifty years, probably more. In a culture such as ours, then, individual life is of prime importance. Our birth rate is low and population increase is rigidly controlled. We maintain a definite robot/man ratio designed to maintain the individual in the greatest comfort. Logically, developing children are carefully screened for physical and mental defects before being allowed to mature."

Baley interrupted. "You mean you kill them if they don't——"

"If they don't measure up. Quite painlessly, I assure you. The notion shocks you, just as the Earthman's uncontrolled breeding shocks us."

"We're controlled, Dr. Fastolfe. Each family is allowed so many children."

Dr. Fastolfe smiled tolerantly. "So many of any kind of children; not so many *healthy* children. And even so, there are many illegitimates and your population increases."

"Who's to judge which children should live?"

"That's rather complicated and not to be answered in a sentence. Someday we may talk it out in detail."

"Well, where's your problem? You sound satisfied with your society."

"It is stable. That's the trouble. It is too stable."

Baley said, "Nothing pleases you. Our civilization is at the ragged edge of chaos, according to you, and your own is too stable."

"It is possible to be too stable. No Outer World has colonized a new planet in two and half centuries. There is no prospect for colonization in the future. Our lives in the Outer Worlds are too long to risk and too comfortable to upset."

"I don't know about that, Dr. Fastolfe. You've come to Earth. You risk disease."

"Yes, I do. There are some of us, Mr. Baley, who feel that the future of the human race is even worth the possible loss of an extended lifetime. Too few of us, I am sorry to say."

"All right. We're coming to the point. How is Spacetown helping matters?"

"In trying to introduce robots here on Earth, we're doing our best to upset the balance of your City economy."

"That's your way of helping?" Baley's lips quivered. "You mean you're creating a growing group of displaced and declassified men on purpose?"

"Not out of cruelty or callousness, believe me. A group of displaced men, as you call them, are what we need to serve as a nucleus for colonization. Your ancient America was discovered by ships fitted out with men from the prisons. Don't you see that the City's womb has failed the displaced man. He has nothing to lose and worlds to gain by leaving Earth."

"But it isn't working."

"No, it isn't," said Dr. Fastolfe, sadly. "There is something wrong. The resentment of the Earthman for the robot blocks things. Yet those very robots can accompany humans, smooth the difficulties of initial adjustment to a raw world, make colonization practical."

"Then what? More Outer Worlds?"

"No. The Outer Worlds were established before Civism had spread over Earth, before the Cities. The new colonies will be built by humans who have the City background plus the beginnings of a C/Fe culture. It will be a synthesis, a cross-breeding. As it stands now, Earth's own structure must go ricketing down in the near future, the Outer Worlds will slowly degenerate and decay in a somewhat further future, but the new colonies will be a new and healthy strain, combining the best of both cultures. By their reaction upon the older worlds, including Earth, we ourselves may gain new life."

"I don't know. It's all misty, Dr. Fastolfe."

"It's a dream, yes. Think about it." Abruptly the Spacer rose to his feet. "I have spent more time with you than I intended. In fact, more time than our health ordinances allow. You will excuse me?"

•   •   •   •

Baley and R. Daneel left the dome. Sunlight, at a different angle, somewhat yellower, washed down upon them once again. In Baley, there was a vague wonder whether sunlight might not seem different on another world. Less harsh and brazen perhaps. More acceptable.

Another world? The ugly Spacer with the prominent ears had filled his mind with queer imaginings. Did the doctors of Aurora once look at the child Fastolfe and wonder if he ought to be allowed to mature? Wasn't he too ugly? Or did their criteria include physical appearance at all? When did ugliness become a deformity and what deformities . . .

But when the sunlight vanished and they entered the first door that led to the Personal, the mood became harder to maintain.

Baley shook his head with exasperation. It was all ridiculous. Forcing Earthmen to emigrate, to set up a new society! It was nonsense! What were these Spacers *really* after?

He thought about it and came to no conclusion.

Slowly, their squad car rolled down the vehicular lane. Reality was surging all about Baley. His blaster was a warm and comfortable weight against his hip. The noise and vibrant life of the City was just as warm, just as comfortable.

For a moment, as the City closed in, his nose tingled to a slight and fugitive pungence.

He thought wonderingly: the City smells.

He thought of the twenty million human beings crammed into the steel walls of the great cave and for the first time in his life he smelled with nostrils that had been washed clean by outdoor air.

He thought: Would it be different on another world? Less people and more air—cleaner?

But the afternoon roar of the City was all around them, the smell faded and was gone, and he felt a little ashamed of himself.

He let the drive rod in slowly and tapped a larger share of the beamed power. The squad car accelerated sharply as it slanted down into the empty motorway.

"Daneel," he said.

"Yes, Elijah."

"Why was Dr. Fastolfe telling me all he did?"

"It seems probable to me, Elijah, that he wished to impress you with the importance of the investigation. We are not here just to solve a murder, but to save Spacetown and with it, the future of the human race."

Baley said dryly, "I think he'd have been better off if he'd let me see the scene of the crime and interview the men who first found the body."

"I doubt if you could have added anything, Elijah. We have been quite thorough."

"Have you? You've got nothing. Not a clue. Not a suspect."

"No, you are right. The answer must be in the City. To be accurate, though, we did have one suspect."

"What? You said nothing of this before."

"I did not feel it to be necessary, Elijah. Surely it is obvious to you that one suspect automatically existed."

"Who? In the devil's name, who?"

"The one Earthman who was on the scene. Commissioner Julius Enderby."

 ## Afternoon of a Plain-clothes Man

The squad car veered to one side, halted against the impersonal concrete wall of the motorway. With the humming of its motor stopped, the silence was dead and thick.

Baley looked at the robot next to him and said in an incongruously quiet voice, "What?"

Time stretched while Baley waited for an answer. A small and lonesome vibration rose and reached a minor peak, then faded. It was the sound of another squad car, boring its way past them on some unknown errand, perhaps a mile away. Or else it was a fire car hurrying along toward its own appointment with combustion.

A detached portion of Baley's mind wondered if any one man any longer knew all the motorways that twisted about in New York City's bowels. At no time in the day or night could the entire motorway system be completely empty, and yet there must be individual passages that no man had entered in years. With sudden, devastating clarity, he remembered a short story he had viewed as a youngster.

It concerned the motorways of London and began, quietly enough, with a murder. The murderer fled toward a prearranged hideout in the corner of the motorway in whose dust his own shoeprints had been the only disturbance for a century. In that abandoned hole, he could wait in complete safety till the search died.

But he took a wrong turning and in the silence and loneness of those twisting corridors he swore a mad and blaspheming oath that, in spite of the Trinity and all the saints, he would yet reach his haven.

From that time on, no turning was right. He wandered through an unending maze from the Brighton Sector on the Channel to Norwich and from Coventry to Canterbury. He burrowed endlessly beneath the great City of London from end to end of its sprawl across the southeastern corner of Medieval England. His clothes were rags and his shoes ribbons, his strength wore down but never left him. He was tired, tired, but unable to stop. He could only go on and on with only wrong turnings ahead of him.

Sometimes he heard the sound of passing cars, but they were always in the next corridor, and however fast he rushed (for he would gladly have given himself up by then) the corridors he reached were always empty. Sometimes he saw an exit far ahead that would lead to the City's life and breath, but it always glimmered further away as he approached until he would turn—and it would be gone.

Occasionally, Londoners on official business through the underground would see a misty figure limping silently toward them, a semitransparent arm lifted in pleading, a mouth open and moving, but soundless. As it approached, it would waver and vanish.

It was a story that had lost the attributes of ordinary fiction and had entered the realm of folklore. The "Wandering Londoner" had become a familiar phrase to all the world.

In the depths of New York City, Baley remembered the story and stirred uneasily.

R. Daneel spoke and there was a small echo to his voice. He said, "We may be overheard."

"Down here? Not a chance. Now what about the Commissioner?"

"He was on the scene, Elijah. He is a City dweller. He was inevitably a suspect."

"Was! Is he still a suspect?"

"No. His innocence was quickly established. For one thing, there was no blaster in his possession. There could not very well be one. He had entered Spacetown in the usual fashion; that was quite certain; and, as you know, blasters are removed as a matter of course."

"Was the murder weapon found at all, by the way?"

"No, Elijah. Every blaster in Spacetown was checked and none had been fired for weeks. A check of the radiation chambers was quite conclusive."

"Then whoever had committed the murder had either hidden the weapon so well——"

"It could not have been hidden anywhere in Spacetown. We were quite thorough."

Baley said impatiently, "I'm trying to consider all possibilities. It was either hidden or it was carried away by the murderer when he left."

"Exactly."

"And if you admit only the second possibility, then the Commissioner is cleared."

"Yes. As a precaution, of course, he was cerebroanalyzed."

"What?"

"By cerebroanalysis, I mean the interpretation of the electromagnetic fields of the living brain cells."

"Oh," said Baley, unenlightened. "And what does that tell you?"

"It gives us information concerning the temperamental and emotional makeup of an individual. In the case of Commissioner Enderby, it told us that he was incapable of killing Dr. Sarton. Quite incapable."

"No," agreed Baley. "He isn't the type. I could have told you that."

"It is better to have objective information. Naturally, all our people in Spacetown allowed themselves to be cerebroanalyzed as well."

"All incapable, I suppose."

"No question. It is why we know that the murderer must be a City dweller."

"Well, then, all we have to do is pass the whole City under your cute little process."

"It would not be very practical, Elijah. There might be millions temporarily capable of the deed."

"Millions," grunted Baley, thinking of the crowds of that long ago day who had screamed at the dirty Spacers, and of the threatening and slobbering crowds outside the shoe store the night before.

He thought: Poor Julius. A suspect!

He could hear the Commissioner's voice describing the period after the discovery of the body: "It was brutal, brutal." No wonder he broke his glasses in shock and dismay. No wonder he did not want to return to Spacetown. "I hate them," he had ground out between his teeth.

Poor Julius. The man who could handle Spacers. The man whose greatest value to the City lay in his ability to get along with them. How much did that contribute to his rapid promotions?

No wonder the Commissioner had wanted Baley to take over. Good old loyal, closed-mouth Baley. College chum! He would keep quiet if he found out about that little incident. Baley wondered how cerebroanalysis was carried out. He imagined huge electrodes, busy pantographs skidding inklines across graphed paper, self-adjusting gears clicking into place now and then.

Poor Julius! If his state of mind were as appalled as it almost had a right to be, he might already be seeing himself at the end of his career with a forced letter of resignation in the hands of the Mayor.

The squad car slanted up into the sublevels of City Hall.

It was 14:30 when Baley arrived back at his desk. The Commissioner was out. R. Sammy, grinning, did not know where the Commissioner was.

Baley spent some time thinking. The fact that he was hungry didn't register.

At 15:20 R. Sammy came to his desk and said, "The Commissioner is in now, Lije."

Baley said, "Thanks."

For once he listened to R. Sammy without being annoyed. R. Sammy, after all, was a kind of relation to R. Daneel, and R. Daneel obviously wasn't a person—or thing, rather—to get annoyed with. Baley wondered how it would be on a new planet with men and robots starting even in a City culture. He considered the situation quite dispassionately.

The Commissioner was going through some documents as Baley entered, stopping occasionally to make notations.

He said, "That was a fairly giant-size blooper you pulled out in Spacetown."

It flooded back strongly. The verbal duel with Fastolfe . . .

His long face took on a lugubrious expression of chagrin. "I'll admit I did, Commissioner. I'm sorry."

Enderby looked up. His expression was keen through his glasses. He seemed more himself than at any time these thirty hours. He said, "No real matter. Fastolfe didn't seem to mind, so we'll forget it. Unpredictable, these Spacers. You don't deserve your luck, Lije. Next time you talk it over with me before you make like a one-man subether hero."

Baley nodded. The whole thing rolled off his shoulders. He had tried a grandstand stunt and it hadn't worked. Okay. He was a little surprised that he could be so casual about it, but there it was.

He said, "Look, Commissioner. I want to have a two-man apartment assigned to Daneel and myself. I'm not taking him home tonight."

"What's all this?"

"The news is out that he's a robot. Remember? Maybe nothing will happen, but if there is a riot, I don't want my family in the middle of it."

"Nonsense, Lije. I've had the thing checked. There's no such rumor in the City."

"Jessie got the story somewhere, Commissioner."

"Well, there's no organized rumor. Nothing dangerous. I've been checking this ever since I got off the trimensic at Fastolfe's dome. It was why I left. I had to track it down, naturally, and fast. Anyway, here are the reports. See for yourself. There's Doris Gillid's report. She went through a dozen Women's Personals in different parts of the City. You know Doris. She's a competent girl. Well, nothing showed. Nothing showed anywhere."

"Then how did Jessie get the rumor, Commissioner?"

"It can be explained. R. Daneel made a show of himself in the shoe store. Did he really pull a blaster, Lije, or were you stretching it a little?"

"He really pulled one. Pointed it, too."

Commissioner Enderby shook his head. "All right. Someone recognized him. As a robot, I mean."

"Hold on," said Baley, indignantly. "You can't tell him for a robot."

"Why not?"

"Could you? I couldn't."

"What does that prove? We're no experts. Suppose there was a technician out of the Westchester robot factories in the crowd. A professional. A man who has spent his life building and designing robots. He notices something queer about R. Daneel. Maybe in the way he talks or holds himself. He speculates about it. Maybe he tells his wife. She tells a few friends. Then it dies. It's too improbable. People don't believe it. Only it got to Jessie before it died."

"Maybe," said Baley, doubtfully. "But how about an assignment to a bachelor room for two, anyway?"

The Commissioner shrugged, lifted the intercom. After a while, he said, "Section Q—27 is all they can do. It's not a very good neighborhood."

"It'll do," said Baley.

"Where's R. Daneel now, by the way?"

"He's at our record files. He's trying to collect information on Medievalist agitators."

"Good Lord, there are millions."

"I know, but it keeps him happy."

Baley was nearly at the door, when he turned, half on impulse, and said, "Commissioner, did Dr. Sarton ever talk to you about Spacetown's program? I mean, about introducing the C/Fe culture?"

"The what?"

"Introducing robots."

"Occasionally." The Commissioner's tone was not one of any particular interest.

"Did he ever explain what Spacetown's point was?"

"Oh, improve health, raise the standard of living. The usual talk; it didn't impress me. Oh, I agreed with him. I nodded my head and all that. What could I do? It's just a matter of humoring them and hoping they'll keep within reason in their notions. Maybe someday . . ."

Baley waited but he didn't say what maybe-someday might bring.

Baley said, "Did he ever mention anything about emigration?"

"Emigration! Never. Letting an Earthman into a Outer World is like finding a diamond asteroid in the rings of Saturn."

"I mean emigration to new worlds."

But the Commissioner answered that one with a simple stare of incredulousness.

Baley chewed that for a moment, then said with sudden bluntness, "What's cerebroanalysis, Commissioner? Ever heard of it?"

The Commissioner's round face didn't pucker; his eyes didn't blink. He said evenly, "No, what's it supposed to be?"

"Nothing. Just picked it up."

He left the office and at his desk continued thinking. Certainly, the Commissioner wasn't *that* good an actor. Well, then . . .

At 16:05 Baley called Jessie and told her he wouldn't be home that night or probably any night for a while. It took a while after that to disengage her.

"Lije, is there trouble? Are you in danger?"

A policeman is always in a certain amount of danger, he explained lightly. It didn't satisfy her. "Where will you be staying?"

He didn't tell her. "If you're going to be lonely tonight," he said, "stay at your mother's." He broke connections abruptly, which was probably just as well.

At 16:20 he made a call to Washington. It took a certain length of time to reach the man he wanted and an almost equally long time to convince him he ought to make an air trip to New York the next day. By 16:40, he had succeeded.

At 16:55 the Commissioner left, passing him with an uncertain smile. The day shift left en masse. The sparser population that filled the offices in the evening and through the night made its way in and greeted him in varied tones of surprise.

R. Daneel came to his desk with a sheaf of papers.

"And those are?" asked Baley.

"A list of men and women who might belong to a Medievalist organization."

"How many does the list include?"

"Over a million," said R. Daneel. "These are just part of them."

"Do you expect to check them all, Daneel?"

"Obviously that would be impractical, Elijah."

"You see, Daneel, almost all Earthmen are Medievalists in one way or another. The Commissioner, Jessie, myself. Look at the Commissioner's——" (He almost said, "spectacles," then remembered that Earthmen must stick together and that the Commissioner's face must be protected in the figurative as well as the literal sense.) He concluded, lamely, "eye ornaments."

"Yes," said R. Daneel, "I had noticed them, but thought it indelicate, perhaps, to refer to them. I have not seen such ornaments on other City dwellers."

"It is a very old-fashioned sort of thing."

"Does it serve a purpose of any sort?"

Baley said, abruptly, "How did you get your list?"

"It was a machine that did it for me. Apparently, one sets it for a particular type of offense and it does the rest. I let it scan all disorderly conduct cases involving robots over the past twenty-five years. Another machine scanned all City newspapers over an equal period for the names of those involved in unfavorable statements concerning robots or men of the Outer Worlds. It is amazing what can be done in three hours. The machine even eliminated the names of nonsurvivors from the lists."

"You are amazed? Surely you've got computers on the Outer Worlds?"

"Of many sorts, certainly. Very advanced ones. Still, none are as massive and complex as the ones here. You must remember, of course, that even the largest Outer World scarcely has the population of one of your Cities and extreme complexity is not necessary."

Baley said, "Have you ever been on Aurora?"

"No," said R. Daneel, "I was assembled here on Earth."

"Then how do you know about Outer World computers?"

"But surely that is obvious, partner Elijah. My data store is drawn from that of the late Dr. Sarton. You may take it for granted that it is rich in factual material concerning the Outer Worlds."

"I see. Can you eat, Daneel?"

"I am nuclear-powered. I had thought you were aware of that."

"I'm perfectly aware of it. I didn't ask you if you needed to eat. I asked if you could eat. If you could put food in your mouth, chew it, and swallow it. I should think that would be an important item in seeming to be a man."

"I see your point. Yes, I can perform the mechanical operations of chewing and swallowing. My capacity is, of course, quite limited, and I would have to remove the ingested material from what you might call my stomach sooner or later."

"All right. You can regurgitate, or whatever you do, in the quiet of our room tonight. The point is that I'm hungry. I've missed lunch, damn it, and I want you with me when I eat. And you can't sit there and *not* eat without attracting attention. So if you can eat, that's what I want to hear. Let's go!"

Section kitchens were the same all over the City. What's more, Baley had been in Washington, Toronto, Los Angeles, London, and Budapest in the way of business, and they had been the same there, too. Perhaps it had been different in Medieval times when languages had varied and dietaries as well. Nowadays, yeast products were just the same from Shanghai to Tashkent and from Winnipeg to Buenos Aires; and English might not be the "English" of Shakespeare or Churchill, but it was the final potpourri that was current over all the continents and, with some modification, on the Outer Worlds as well.

But language and dietary aside, there were the deeper similarities.

There was always that particular odor, undefinable but completely characteristic of "kitchen." There was the waiting triple line moving slowly in, converging at the door and splitting up again, right, left, center. There was the rumble of humanity, speaking and moving, and the sharper clatter of plastic on plastic. There was the gleam of simulated wood, highly polished, highlights on glass, long tables, the touch of steam in the air.

Baley inched slowly forward as the line moved (with all possible staggering of meal hours, a wait of at least ten minutes was almost unavoidable) and said to R. Daneel in sudden curiosity, "Can you smile?"

R. Daneel, who had been gazing at the interior of the kitchen with cool absorption, said, "I beg your pardon, Elijah."

"I'm just wondering, Daneel. Can you smile?" He spoke in a casual whisper.

R. Daneel smiled. The gesture was sudden and surprising. His lips curled back and the skin about either end folded. Only the mouth smiled, however. The rest of the robot's face was untouched.

Baley shook his head. "Don't bother, R. Daneel. It doesn't do a thing for you."

They were at the entrance. Person after person thrust his metal food tab through the appropriate slot and had it scanned. Click—click—click—

Someone once calculated that a smoothly running kitchen could allow the entrance of two hundred persons a minute, the tags of each one being fully scanned to prevent kitchen-jumping, meal-jumping, and ration-stretching. They had also calculated how long a waiting line was necessary for maximum efficiency and how much time was lost when any one person required special treatment.

It was therefore always a calamity to interrupt that smooth click—click by stepping to the manual window, as Baley and R. Daneel did, in order to thrust a special-permit pass at the official in charge.

Jessie, filled with the knowledge of an assistant dietitian, had explained it once to Baley.

"It upsets things completely," she said. "It throws off consumption figures and inventory estimates. It means special checks. You have to match slips with all the different Section kitchens to make sure the balance isn't too unbalanced, if you know what I mean. There's a separate balance sheet to be made out each week. Then if anything goes wrong and you're overdrawn, it's always your fault. It's never the fault of the City Government for passing out special tickets to everybody and his kid sister. Oh, no. And when we have to say that free choice is suspended for the meal, don't the people in line make a fuss. It's always the fault of the people behind the counter. . . ."

Baley had the story in the fullest detail and so he quite understood the dry and poisonous look he received from the woman behind the window. She made a few hurried notes. Home Section, occupations, reason for meal displacement ("official business," a very irritating reason indeed, but quite irrefutable). Then she folded the slip with firm motions of her fingers and pushed it into a slot. A computer seized it, devoured the contents, and digested the information.

She turned to R. Daneel.

Baley let her have the worst. He said, "My friend is out-of-City."

The woman looked finally and completely outraged. She said, "Home City, please."

Baley intercepted the ball for Daneel once again. "All records are to be credited to the Police Department. No details necessary. Official business."

The woman brought down a pad of slips with a jerk of her arm and filled in the necessary matter in dark-light code with practiced pressings of the first two fingers of her right hand.

She said, "How long will you be eating here?"

"Till further notice," said Baley.

"Press fingers here," she said, inverting the information blank.

Baley had a short qualm as R. Daneel's even fingers with their glistening nails pressed downward. Surely, they wouldn't have forgotten to supply him with fingerprints.

The woman took the blank away and fed it into the all-consuming machine at her elbow. It belched nothing back and Baley breathed more easily.

She gave them little metal tags that were in the bright red that meant "temporary."

She said, "No free choices. We're short this week. Take table DF."

They made their way toward DF.

R. Daneel said, "I am under the impression that most of your people eat in kitchens such as these regularly."

"Yes. Of course, it's rather gruesome eating in a strange kitchen. There's no one about whom you know. In your own kitchen, it's quite different. You have your own seat which you occupy all the time. You're with your family, your friends. Especially when you're young, mealtimes are the bright spot of the day." Baley smiled in brief reminiscence.

Table DF was apparently among those reserved for transients. Those already seated watched their plates uneasily and did not talk with one another. They looked with sneaking envy at the laughing crowds at the other tables.

There is no one so uncomfortable, thought Baley, as the man eating out-of-Section. Be it ever so humble, the old saying went, there's no place like home-kitchen. Even the food tastes better, no matter how many chemists are ready to swear it to be no different from the food in Johannesburg.

He sat down on a stool and R. Daneel sat down next to him.

"No free choice," said Baley, with a wave of his fingers, "so just close the switch there and wait."

It took two minutes. A disc slid back in the table top and a dish lifted.

"Mashed potatoes, zymoveal sauce, and stewed apricots. Oh, well," said Baley.

A fork and two slices of whole yeast bread appeared in a recess just in front of the low railing that went down the long center of the table.

R. Daneel said in a low voice, "You may help yourself to my serving, if you wish."

For a moment, Baley was scandalized. Then he remembered and mumbled, "That's bad manners. Go on. Eat."

Baley ate industriously but without the relaxation that allows complete enjoyment. Carefully, he flicked an occasional glance at R. Daneel. The robot ate with precise motions of his jaws. Too precise. It didn't look quite natural.

Strange! Now that Baley knew for a fact that R. Daneel was in truth a robot, all sorts of little items showed up clearly. For instance, there was no movement of an Adam's apple when R. Daneel swallowed.

Yet he didn't much mind so much. Was he getting used to the creature? Suppose people started afresh on a new world (how that ran through his mind ever since Dr. Fastolfe had put it there); suppose Bentley, for instance, were to leave Earth; could he get so he didn't mind working and living alongside robots? Why not? The Spacers themselves did it.

R. Daneel said, "Elijah, is it bad manners to watch another man while he is eating?"

"If you mean stare directly at him, of course. That's only common sense, isn't it? A man has a right to his privacy. Ordinary conversation is entirely in order, but you don't peer at a man while he's swallowing."

"I see. Why is it then that I count eight people watching us closely, very closely."

Baley put down his fork. He looked about as though he were searching for the salt-pinch dispenser. "I see nothing out of the ordinary."

But he said it without conviction. The mob of diners was only a vast conglomeration of chaos to him. And when R. Daneel turned his impersonal brown eyes upon him, Baley suspected uncomfortably that those were not eyes he saw, but scanners capable of noting, with photographic accuracy and in split seconds of time, the entire panorama.

"I am quite certain," said R. Daneel, calmly.

"Well, then, what of it? It's crude behavior, but what does it prove?"

"I cannot say, Elijah, but is it coincidence that six of the watchers were in the crowd outside the shoe store last night?"

 ## Escape Along the Strips

Baley's grip tightened convulsively on his fork.

"Are you sure?" he asked automatically, and as he said it, he realized the uselessness of the question. You don't ask a computer if it is sure of the answer it disgorges; not even a computer with arms and legs.

R. Daneel said, "Quite!"

"Are they close to us?"

"Not very. They are scattered."

"All right, then." Baley returned to his meal, his fork moving mechanically. Behind the frown on his long face, his mind worked furiously.

Suppose the incident last night had been organized by a group of anti-robot fanatics, that it had not been the spontaneous trouble it had seemed. Such a group of agitators could easily include men who had studied robots with the intensity born of deep opposition. One of them might have recognized R. Daneel for what he was. (The Commissioner had suggested that, in a way. Damn it, there were surprising depths to that man.)

It worked itself out logically. Granting they had been unable to act in an organized manner on the spur of last evening's moment, they would still have been able to plan for the future. If they could recognize a robot such as R. Daneel, they could certainly realize that Baley himself was a police officer. A police officer in the unusual company of a humanoid robot would very likely be a responsible man in the organization. (With the wisdom of hindsight, Baley followed the line of reasoning with no trouble at all.)

It followed then that observers at City Hall (or perhaps agents within City Hall) would be bound to spot Baley, R. Daneel, or both before too long a time had passed. That they had done so within twenty-four hours was not surprising. They might have done so in less time if so much of Baley's day had not been spent in Spacetown and along the motorway.

R. Daneel had finished his meal. He sat quietly waiting, his perfect hands resting lightly on the end of the table.

"Had we not better do something?" he asked.

"We're safe here in the kitchen," said Baley. "Now leave this to me. Please."

Baley looked about him cautiously and it was as though he saw a kitchen for the first time.

People! Thousands of them. What was the capacity of an average kitchen? He had once seen the figure. Two thousand two hundred, he thought. This one was larger than average.

Suppose the cry, "Robot," were sent out into the air. Suppose it were tossed among the thousands like a . . .

He was at a loss for a comparison, but it didn't matter. It wouldn't happen.

A spontaneous riot could flare anywhere, in the kitchens as easily as in the corridors or in the elevators. More easily, perhaps. There was a lack of inhibition at mealtimes, a sense of horseplay that could degenerate into something more serious at a trifle.

But a planned riot would be different. Here in the kitchen, the planners would themselves be trapped in a large and mob-filled room. Once the dishes went flying and the tables cracking there would be no easy way to escape. Hundreds would certainly die and they themselves might easily be among them.

No, a safe riot would have to be planned in the avenues of the City, in some relatively narrow passageway. Panic and hysteria would travel slowly along the constriction and there would be time for the quick, prepared fadeaway along the side passage or the unobtrusive step onto an escalating localway that would move them to a higher level and disappearance.

Baley felt trapped. There were probably others waiting outside. Baley and R. Daneel were to be followed to a proper point and the fuse would be set off.

R. Daneel said, "Why not arrest them?"

"That would only start the trouble sooner. You know their faces, don't you? You won't forget?"

"I'm not capable of forgetting."

"Then we'll nab them another time. For now, we'll break their net. Follow me. Do exactly as I do."

He rose, turned his dish carefully upside down, centering it on the movable disc from below which it had risen. He put his fork back in its recess. R. Daneel, watching, matched his action. The dishes and utensils dropped out of sight.

R. Daneel said, "They are getting up, too."

"All right. It's my feeling they won't get too close. Not here."

The two moved into line now, drifting toward an exit where the

click—click—click of the tags sounded ritualistically, each click recording the expenditure of a ration unit.

Baley looked back through the steamy haze and the noise and, with
incongruous sharpness, thought of a visit to the City Zoo with Ben
six or seven years ago. No, eight, because Ben had just passed his
eighth birthday then. (Jehoshaphat! Where did the time go?)

It had been Ben's first visit and he had been excited. After all, he
had never actually seen a cat or a dog before. Then, on top of that,
there was the bird cage! Even Baley himself, who had seen it a dozen
times before, was not immune to its fascination.

There is something about the first sight of living objects hurtling
through air that is incomparably startling. It was feeding time in the
sparrow cage and an attendant was dumping cracked oats into a long
trough (human beings had grown used to yeast substitutes, but animals, more conservative in their way, insisted on real grain).

The sparrows flocked down in what seemed like hundreds. Wing to
wing, with an ear-splitting twitter, they lined the trough. . . .

That was it; that was the picture that came to Baley's mind as he
looked back at the kitchen he was leaving. Sparrows at the trough.
The thought repelled him.

He thought: Jehoshaphat, there must be a better way.

But what better way? What was wrong with this way? It had never
bothered him before.

He said abruptly to R. Daneel, "Ready, Daneel?"

"I am ready, Elijah."

They left the kitchen and escape was now clearly and flatly up to
Baley.

There is a game that youngsters know called "running the strips." Its
rules vary in trivial fashion from City to City, but its essentials are
eternal. A boy from San Francisco can join the game in Cairo with no
trouble.

Its object is to get from point A to point B via the City's rapid transit
system in such a way that the "leader" manages to lose as many of
his followers as possible. A leader who arrives at the destination alone
is skillful indeed, as is a follower who refuses to be shaken.

The game is usually conducted during the evening rush hour when
the increased density of the commuters makes it at once more hazard-
ous and more complicated. The leader sets off, running up and down
the accelerating strips. He does his best to do the unexpected, remaining standing on a given strip as long as possible, then leaping off suddenly in either direction. He will run quickly through several strips,
then remain waiting once more.

Pity the follower who incautiously careens forward one strip too far.
Before he has caught his mistake, unless he is extraordinarily nimble,

he has driven past the leader or fallen behind. The clever leader will compound the error by moving quickly in the appropriate direction.

A move designed to increase the complexity of the task tenfold involves boarding the localways or the expressways themselves, and hurtling off the other side. It is bad form to avoid them completely and also bad form to linger on them.

The attraction of the game is not easy for an adult to understand, particularly for an adult who has never himself been a teen-age strip-runner. The players are roughly treated by legitimate travelers into whose path they find themselves inevitably flying. They are persecuted bitterly by the police and punished by their parents. They are denounced in the schools and on the subetherics. No year passes without its four or five teen-agers killed at the game, its dozens hurt, its cases of innocent bystanders meeting tragedy of varying degree.

Yet nothing can be done to wipe out the strip-running gangs. The greater the danger, the more the strip-runners have that most valuable of all prizes, honor in the eyes of their fellows. A successful one may well swagger; a well-known leader is cock-of-the-walk.

Elijah Baley, for instance, remembered with satisfaction even now that he had been a strip-runner once. He had led a gang of twenty from the Concourse Sector to the borders of Queens, crossing three expressways. In two tireless and relentless hours, he had shaken off some of the most agile followers of the Bronx, and arrived at the destination point alone. They talked about that run for months.

Baley was in his forties now, of course. He hadn't run the strips for over twenty years, but he remembered some of the tricks. What he had lost in agility, he made up in another respect. He was a policeman. No one but another policeman as experienced as himself could possibly know the City as well, know where almost every metal-bordered alley began and ended.

He walked away from the kitchen briskly, but not too rapidly. Each moment he expected the cry of "Robot, robot" to ring out behind him. That initial set of moments was the riskiest. He counted the steps until he felt the first accelerating strip moving under him.

He stopped for a moment, while R. Daneel moved smoothly up beside him.

"Are they still behind us, Daneel?" asked Baley in a whisper.

"Yes. They're moving closer."

"That won't last," said Baley confidently. He looked at the strips stretching to either side, with their human cargo whipping to his left more and more rapidly as their distance from him increased. He had felt the strips beneath his feet many times a day almost all the days of his life, but he had not bent his knees in anticipation of running them in seven thousand days and more. He felt the old familiar thrill and his breath grew more rapid.

He quite forgot the one time he had caught Ben at the game. He had lectured him interminably and threatened to have him put under police surveillance.

Lightly, quickly, at double the "safe" rate, he went up the strips. He leaned forward sharply against the acceleration. The local way was humming past. For a moment, it looked as though he would mount, but suddenly he was fading backward, backward, dodging through the crowd to the left and right as it thickened on the slower strips.

He stopped, and let himself be carried along at a mere fifteen miles an hour.

"How many are with us, Daneel?"

"Only one, Elijah." The robot was at his side, unruffled, unbreathing.

"He must have been a good one in his day, too, but he won't last either."

Full of self-confidence, he felt a half-remembered sensation of his younger days. It consisted partly of the feeling of immersion in a mystic rite to which others did not belong, partly of the purely physical sensation of wind against hair and face, partly of a tenuous sense of danger.

"They call this the side shuffle," he said to R. Daneel in a low voice.

His long stride ate distance, but he moved along a single strip, dodging the legitimate crowd with a minimum of effort. He kept it up, moving always closer to the strip's edge, until the steady movement of his head through the crowd must have been hypnotic in its constant velocity—as it was intended to be.

And then, without a break in his step, he shifted two inches sideways and was on the adjoining strip. He felt an aching in his thigh muscles as he kept his balance.

He whipped through a cluster of commuters and was on the forty-five-mile strip.

"How is it now, Daneel?" he asked.

"He is still with us," was the calm answer.

Baley's lips tightened. There was nothing for it but to use the moving platforms themselves, and that really required coordination; more, perhaps, than he still retained.

He looked about quickly. Exactly where were they now? B-22d Street flashed by. He made rapid calculations and was off. Up the remaining strips, smoothly and steadily, a swing onto the localway platform.

The impersonal faces of men and women, calloused with the ennui of way-riding, were jolted into something like indignation as Baley and R. Daneel clambered aboard and squeezed through the railings.

"Hey, now," called a woman shrilly, clutching at her hat.

"Sorry," said Baley, breathlessly.

He forced his way through the standees and with a wriggle was off

on the other side. At the last moment, a jostled passenger thumped
his back in anger. He went staggering.

Desperately he tried to regain his footing. He lurched across a strip
boundary and the sudden change in velocity forced him to his knees
and then over to his side.

He had the sudden, panicky vision of men colliding with him and
bowling over, of a spreading confusion on the strips, one of the dreaded
"man-jams" that would not fail to put dozens in the hospital with
broken limbs.

But R. Daneel's arm was under his back. He felt himself lifted with
more than a man's strength.

"Thanks," gasped Baley, and there was no time for more.

Off he went and down the decelerating strips in a complicated pattern so designed that his feet met the V-joint strips of an expressway
at the exact point of crossover. Without the loss of rhythm, he was
accelerating again, then up and over an expressway.

"Is he with us, Daneel?"

"Not one in sight, Elijah."

"Good. But what a strip-runner you would have been, Daneel!—
Oops, now, now!"

Off into another localway in a whirl and down the strips with a
clatter to a doorway, large and official in appearance. A guard rose to
his feet.

Baley flashed his identification. "Official business."

They were inside.

"Power plant," said Baley, curtly. "This breaks our tracks completely."

He had been in power plants before, including this one. Familiarity
did not lessen his feelings of uncomfortable awe. The feeling was
heightened by the haunting thought that once his father had been
high in the hierarchy of a plant such as this. That is, before . . .

There was the surrounding hum of the tremendous generators hidden in the central well of the plant, the faint sharpness of ozone in
the air, the grim and silent threat of the red lines that marked the
limits beyond which no one could pass without protective clothing.

Somewhere in the plant (Baley had no idea exactly where) a pound
of fissionable material was consumed each day. Every so often, the
radioactive fission products, the so-called "hot ash," were forced by
air pressure through leaden pipes to distant caverns ten miles out in
the ocean and a half mile below the ocean floor. Baley sometimes
wondered what would happen when the caverns were filled.

He said to R. Daneel with sudden gruffness, "Stay away from the
red lines." Then, he bethought himself and added sheepishly, "But I
suppose it doesn't matter to you."

"Is it a question of radioactivity?" asked Daneel.

"Yes."

"Then it does matter to me. Gamma radiation destroys the delicate balance of a positronic brain. It would affect me much sooner than it would affect you."

"You mean it would *kill* you?"

"I would require a new positronic brain. Since no two can be alike, I would be a new individual. The Daneel you now speak to would be, in a manner of speaking, dead."

Baley looked at the other doubtfully. "I never knew that.—Up these ramps."

"The point isn't stressed. Spacetown wishes to convince Earthmen of the usefulness of such as myself, not of our weaknesses."

"Then why tell me?"

R. Daneel turned his eyes full on his human companion. "You are my partner, Elijah. It is well that you know my weaknesses and short-comings."

Baley cleared his throat and had nothing more to say on the subject.

"Out in this direction," he said a moment later, "and we're a quarter mile from our apartment."

It was a grim, lower-class apartment. One small room and two beds. Two fold-in chairs and a closet. A built-in subetheric screen that allowed no manual adjustment, and would be working only at stated hours, but *would* be working then. No washbasin, not even an unactivated one, and no facilities for cooking or even boiling water. A small trash-disposal pipe was in one corner of the room, an ugly, unadorned, unpleasantly functional object.

Baley shrugged. "This is it. I guess we can stand it."

R. Daneel walked to the trash-disposal pipe. His shirt unseamed at a touch, revealing a smooth and, to all appearances, well-muscled chest.

"What are you doing?" asked Baley.

"Getting rid of the food I ingested. If I were to leave it, it would putrefy and I would become an object of distaste."

R. Daneel placed two fingers carefully under one nipple and pushed in a definite pattern of pressure. His chest opened longitudinally. R. Daneel reached in and from a welter of gleaming metal withdrew a thin, translucent sac, partly distended. He opened it while Baley watched with a kind of horror.

R. Daneel hesitated. He said, "The food is perfectly clean. I do not salivate or chew. It was drawn in through the gullet by suction, you know. It is edible."

"That's all right," said Baley, gently. "I'm not hungry. You just get rid of it."

R. Daneel's food sac was of fluorocarbon plastic, Baley decided. At least the food did not cling to it. It came out smoothly and was placed little by little into the pipe. A waste of good food at that, he thought.

He sat down on one bed and removed his shirt. He said, "I suggest an early start tomorrow."

"For a specific reason?"

"The location of this apartment isn't known to our friends yet. Or at least I hope not. If we leave early, we are that much safer. Once in City Hall, we will have to decide whether our partnership is any longer practical."

"You think it is perhaps not?"

Baley shrugged and said dourly, "We can't go through this sort of thing every day."

"But it seems to me——"

R. Daneel was interrupted by the sharp scarlet sliver of the door signal.

Baley rose silently to his feet and unlimbered his blaster. The door signal flashed once more.

He moved silently to the door, put his thumb on the blaster contact while he threw the switch that activated the one-way transparency patch. It wasn't a good view-patch; it was small and had a distorting effect, but it was quite good enough to show Baley's youngster, Ben, outside the door.

Baley acted quickly. He flung the door open, snatched brutally at Ben's wrist as the boy raised his hand to signal a third time, and pulled him in.

The look of fright and bewilderment faded only slowly from Ben's eyes as he leaned breathlessly against the wall toward which he had been hurled. He rubbed his wrist.

"Dad!" he said in grieved tones. "You didn't have to grab me like that."

Baley was staring through the view-patch of the once-again-closed door. As nearly as he could tell, the corridor was empty.

"Did you see anyone out there, Ben?"

"No. Gee, Dad, I just came to see if you were all right."

"Why shouldn't I be all right?"

"I don't know. It was Mom. She was crying and all like that. She said I had to find you. If I didn't go, she said she would go herself, and then she didn't know what would happen. She made me go, Dad."

Baley said, "How did you find me? Did your mother know where I was?"

"No, she didn't. I called up your office."

"And they told you?"

Ben looked startled at his father's vehemence. He said, in a low voice, "Sure. Weren't they supposed to?"

Baley and Daneel looked at one another.

Baley rose heavily to his feet. He said, "Where's your mother now, Ben? At the apartment?"

"No, we went to Grandma's for dinner and stayed there. I'm supposed to go back there now. I mean, as long as you're all right, Dad."

"You'll stay here. Daneel, did you notice the exact location of the floor communo?"

The robot said, "Yes. Do you intend leaving the room to use it?"

"I've got to. I've got to get in touch with Jessie."

"Might I suggest that it would be more logical to let Bentley do that. It is a form of risk and he is less valuable."

Baley stared. "Why you——"

He thought: Jehoshaphat, what am I getting angry about?

He went on more calmly, "You don't understand, Daneel. Among us, it is not customary for a man to send his young son into possible danger, even if it is logical to do so."

"Danger!" squeaked Ben in a sort of horrified pleasure. "What's going on, Dad? Huh, Dad?"

"Nothing, Ben. Now, this isn't any of your business. Understand? Get ready for bed. I want you in bed when I get back. You hear me?"

"Aw, gosh. You could tell a fellow. I won't say anything."

"In bed!"

"Gosh!"

Baley hitched his jacket back as he stood at the floor communo, so that his blaster butt was ready for snatching. He spoke his personal number into the mouthpiece and waited while a computer fifteen miles away checked it to make sure the call was permissible. It was a very short wait that was involved, since a plain-clothes man had no limit on the number of his business calls. He spoke the code number of his mother-in-law's apartment.

The small screen at the base of the instrument lit up, and her face looked out at him.

He said, in a low voice, "Mother, put on Jessie."

Jessie must have been waiting for him. She was on at once. Baley looked at her face and then darkened the screen deliberately.

"All right, Jessie. Ben's here. Now, what's the matter?" His eyes roved from side to side continuously, watching.

"Are you all right? You aren't in trouble?"

"I'm obviously all right, Jessie. Now stop it."

"Oh, Lije, I've been so worried."

"What about?" he asked tightly.

"You know. Your friend."

"What about him?"

"I told you last night. There'll be trouble."

"Now, that's nonsense. I'm keeping Ben with me for tonight and you go to bed. Good-by, dear."

He broke the connections and waited for two breaths before starting back. His face was gray with apprehension and fear.

Ben was standing in the middle of the room when Baley returned. One of his contact lenses was neatly pocketed in a little suction cup. The other was still in his eye.

Ben said, "Gosh, Dad, isn't there any water in this place? Mr. Olivaw says I can't go to the Personal."

"He's right. You can't. Put that thing back in your eye, Ben. It won't hurt you to sleep with them for one night."

"All right." Ben put it back, put away his suction cup and climbed into bed. "Boy, what a mattress!"

Baley said to R. Daneel, "I suppose you won't mind sitting up."

"Of course not. I was interested, by the way, in the queer glass Bentley wears close to his eye. Do all Earthmen wear them?"

"No. Just some," said Baley, absently. "I don't, for instance."

"For what reason is it worn?"

Baley was too absorbed with his own thoughts to answer. His own uneasy thoughts.

The lights were out.

Baley remained wakeful. He was dimly aware of Ben's breathing as it turned deep and regular and became a bit rough. When he turned his head, he grew somehow conscious of R. Daneel, sitting in a chair with grave immobility, face turned toward the door.

Then he fell asleep, and when he slept, he dreamed.

He dreamed Jessie was falling into the fission chamber of a nuclear power plant, falling and falling. She held out her arms to him, shrieking, but he could only stand frozenly just outside a scarlet line and watch her distorted figure turn as it fell, growing smaller until it was only a dot.

He could only watch her, in the dream, knowing that it was he, himself, who had pushed her.

12. Words from an Expert

Elijah Baley looked up as Commissioner Julius Enderby entered the office. He nodded wearily.

The Commissioner looked at the clock and grunted, "Don't tell me you've been here all night!"

Baley said, "I won't."

The Commissioner said in a low voice, "Any trouble last night?"

Baley shook his head.

The Commissioner said, "I've been thinking that I could be minimizing the possibility of riots. If there's anything to——"

Baley said tightly, "For God's sake, Commissioner, if anything happened, I'd tell you. There was no trouble of any sort."

"All right." The Commissioner moved away, passing beyond the door that marked off the unusual privacy that became his exalted position.

Baley looked after him and thought: *He* must have slept last night.

Baley bent to the routine report he was trying to write as a cover-up for the real activities of the last two days, but the words he had tapped out by finger touched blurred and danced. Slowly, he became aware of an object standing by his desk.

He lifted his head. "What do you want?"

It was R. Sammy. Baley thought: Julius's private flunky. It pays to be a Commissioner.

R. Sammy said through his fatuous grin, "The Commissioner wants to see you, Lije. He says right away."

Baley waved his hand. "He just saw me. Tell him I'll be in later."

R. Sammy said, "He says right away."

"All right. All right. Go away."

The robot backed away, saying, "The Commissioner wants to see you right away, Lije. He says right away."

"Jehoshaphat," said Baley between his teeth. "I'm going. I'm going." He got up from his desk, headed for the office, and R. Sammy was silent.

Baley said as he entered, "Damn it, Commissioner, *don't* send that thing after me, will you?"

But the Commissioner only said, "Sit down, Lije. Sit down."

Baley sat down and stared. Perhaps he had done old Julius an injustice. Perhaps the man hadn't slept after all. He looked fairly beat.

The Commissioner was tapping the paper before him. "There's a record of a call you made to a Dr. Gerrigel at Washington by insulated beam."

"That's right, Commissioner."

"There's no record of the conversation, naturally, since it was insulated. What's it all about?"

"I'm after background information."

"He's a roboticist, isn't he?"

"That's right."

The Commissioner put out a lower lip and suddenly looked like a child about to pout. "But what's the point? What kind of information are you after?"

"I'm not sure, Commissioner. I just have a feeling that in a case like this, information on robots might help." Baley clamped his mouth shut after that. He wasn't going to be specific, and that was that.

"I wouldn't, Lije. I wouldn't. I don't think it's wise."

"What's your objection, Commissioner?"

"The fewer people who know about all this, the better."

"I'll tell him as little as I can. Naturally."

"I still don't think it's wise."

Baley was feeling just sufficiently wretched to lose patience.

He said, "Are you ordering me not to see him?"

"No. No. You do as you see fit. You're heading this investigation. Only . . ."

"Only what?"

The Commissioner shook his head. "Nothing.—Where is *he?* You know who I mean."

Baley did. He said, "Daneel's still at the files."

The Commissioner paused a long moment, then said, "We're not making much progress, you know."

"We're not making any so far. Still, things may change."

"All right, then," said the Commissioner, but he didn't look as though he really thought it were all right.

R. Daneel was at Baley's desk, when the latter returned.

"Well, and what have *you* got?" Baley asked gruffly.

"I have completed my first, rather hasty, search through the files, partner Elijah, and I have located two of the people who tried to track us last night and who, moreover, were at the shoe store during the former incident."

"Let's see."

R. Daneel placed the small, stamp-size cards before Baley. They were mottled with the small dots that served as code. The robot also produced a portable decoder and placed one of the cards into an appropriate slot. The dots possessed electrical conduction properties different from that of the card as a whole. The electric field passing through the card was therefore distorted in a highly specific manner and in response to that specification the three-by-six screen above the decoder was filled with words. Words which, uncoded, would have filled several sheets of standard size report paper. Words, moreover, which could not possibly be interpreted by anyone not in possession of an official police decoder.

Baley read through the materials stolidly. The first person was Francis Clousarr, age thirty-three at time of arrest two years before; cause of arrest, inciting to riot; employee at New York Yeast; home address, so-and-so; parentage, so-and-so; hair, eyes, distinguishing marks, educational history, employment history, psychoanalytic profile, physical profile, data here, data there, and finally reference to tri-photo in the rogues' gallery.

"You checked the photograph?" asked Baley.

"Yes, Elijah."

The second person was Gerhard Paul. Baley glanced at the material on that card and said, "This is all no good."

R. Daneel said, "I am sure that cannot be so. If there is an organization of Earthmen who are capable of the crime we are investigating, these are members. Is that not an obvious likelihood? Should they then not be questioned?"

"We'd get nothing out of them."

"They were there, both at the shoe store and in the kitchen. They cannot deny it."

"Just being there's no crime. Besides which, they *can* deny it. They can just say they weren't there. It's as simple as that. How can we prove they're lying?"

"I saw them."

"That's no proof," said Baley, savagely. "No court, if it ever came to that, would believe you could remember two faces in a blur of a million."

"It is obvious that I can."

"Sure. Tell them what you are. As soon as you do that, you're no witness. Your kind have no status in any court of law on Earth."

R. Daneel said, "I take it, then, that you have changed your mind."

"What do you mean?"

"Yesterday, in the kitchen, you said there was no need to arrest them. You said that as long as I remembered their faces, we could arrest them at any time."

"Well, I didn't think it through," said Baley. "I was crazy. It can't be done."

"Not even for psychological reasons? They would not know we have no legal proof of their complicity in conspiracy."

Baley said, tensely, "Look, I am expecting Dr. Gerrigel of Washington in half an hour. Do you mind waiting till he's been here and gone? Do you mind?"

"I will wait," said R. Daneel.

Anthony Gerrigel was a precise and very polite man of middle height, who looked far from being one of the most erudite roboticists on Earth. He was nearly twenty minutes late, it turned out, and quite apologetic about it. Baley, white with anger born of apprehension, shrugged off the apologies gracelessly. He checked his reservation on Conference Room D, repeated his instructions that they were not to be disturbed on any account for an hour, and led Dr. Gerrigel and R. Daneel down the corridor, up a ramp, and through a door that led to one of the spy-beam-insulated chambers.

Baley checked the walls carefully before sitting down, listening to the soft burr of the pulsometer in his hand, waiting for any fading of the steady sound which would indicate a break, even a small one, in the insulation. He turned it on the ceiling, floor, and, with particular care, on the door. There was no break.

Dr. Gerrigel smiled a little. He looked like a man who never smiled more than a little. He was dressed with a neatness that could only be described as fussy. His iron-gray hair was smoothed carefully back and his face looked pink and freshly washed. He sat with a posture of prim stiffness as though repeated maternal advice in his younger years concerning the desirability of good posture had rigidified his spine forever.

He said to Baley, "You make this all seem very formidable."

"It's quite important, Doctor. I need information about robots that only you can give me, perhaps. Anything we say here, of course, is top secret and the City will expect you to forget it all when you leave." Baley looked at his watch.

The little smile on the roboticist's face winked away. He said, "Let me explain why I am late." The matter obviously weighed upon him. "I decided not to go by air. I get airsick."

"That's too bad," said Baley. He put away the pulsometer, after checking its standard settings to make last-minute certain that there was nothing wrong with *it*, and sat down.

"Or at least not exactly airsick, but nervous. A mild agoraphobia. It's nothing particularly abnormal, but there it is. So I took the expressways."

Baley felt a sudden sharp interest. "Agoraphobia?"

"I make it sound worse than it is," the roboticist said at once. "It's just the feeling you get in a plane. Have you ever been in one, Mr. Baley?"

"Several times."

"Then you must know what I mean. It's that feeling of being surrounded by nothing; of being separated from—from empty air by a mere inch of metal. It's very uncomfortable."

"So you took the expressway?"

"Yes."

"All the way from Washington to New York?"

"Oh, I've done it before. Since they built the Baltimore-Philadelphia tunnel, it's quite simple."

So it was. Baley had never made the trip himself, but he was perfectly aware that it was possible. Washington, Baltimore, Philadelphia, and New York had grown, in the last two centuries, to the point where all nearly touched. The Four-City Area was almost the official name for the entire stretch of coast, and there were a considerable number of people who favored administrational consolidation and the formation of a single super-City. Baley disagreed with that, himself. New York City itself was almost too large to be handled by a centralized government. A larger City, with over fifty million population, would break down under its own weight.

"The trouble was," Dr. Gerrigel was saying, "that I missed a connection in Chester Sector, Philadelphia, and lost time. That, and a little difficulty in getting a transient room assignment, ended by making me late."

"Don't worry about that, Doctor. What you say, though, is interesting. In view of your dislike for planes, what would you say to going outside City limits on foot, Dr. Gerrigel?"

"For what reason?" He looked startled and more than a little apprehensive.

"It's just a rhetorical question. I'm not suggesting that you really should. I want to know how the notion strikes you, that's all."

"It strikes me very unpleasantly."

"Suppose you had to leave the City at night and walk cross country for half a mile or more."

"I—I don't think I could be persuaded to."

"No matter how important the necessity?"

"If it were to save my life or the lives of my family, I might try. . . ." He looked embarrassed. "May I ask the point of these questions, Mr. Baley?"

"I'll tell you. A serious crime has been committed, a particularly disturbing murder. I'm not at liberty to give you the details. There is a story, however, that the murderer, in order to commit the crime, did just what we were discussing; he crossed open country at night and alone. I was just wondering what kind of man could do that."

Dr. Gerrigel shuddered. "No one I know. Certainly not I. Of course, among millions I suppose you could find a few hardy individuals."

"But you wouldn't say it was a very likely thing for a human being to do?"

"No. Certainly, not likely."

"In fact, if there's any other explanation for the crime, any other *conceivable* explanation, it should be considered."

Dr. Gerrigel looked more uncomfortable than ever as he sat bolt upright with his well-kept hands precisely folded in his lap. "Do you have an alternate explanation in mind?"

"Yes. It occurs to me that a robot, for instance, would have no difficulty at all in crossing open country."

Dr. Gerrigel stood up. "Oh, my dear sir!"

"What's wrong?"

"You mean a robot may have committed the crime?"

"Why not?"

"Murder? Of a human being?"

"Yes. Please sit down, Doctor."

The roboticist did as he was told. He said, "Mr. Baley, there are two acts involved: walking cross country, and murder. A human being could commit the latter easily, but would find difficulty in doing the former. A robot could do the former easily, but the latter act would be completely impossible. If you're going to replace an unlikely theory by an impossible one——"

"Impossible is a hell of a strong word, Doctor."

"You've heard of the First Law of Robotics, Mr. Baley?"

"Sure. I can even quote it: A robot may not injure a human being, or, through inaction, allow a human being to come to harm." Baley suddenly pointed a finger at the roboticist and went on, "Why can't a robot be built without the First Law? What's so sacred about it?"

Dr. Gerrigel looked startled, then tittered, "Oh, Mr. Baley."

"Well, what's the answer?"

"Surely, Mr. Baley, if you even know a little about robotics, you must know the gigantic task involved, both mathematically and electronically, in building a positronic brain."

"I have an idea," said Baley. He remembered well his visit to a robot factory once in the way of business. He had seen their library of bookfilms, long ones, each of which contained the mathematical analysis of a single type of positronic brain. It took more than an hour for the average such film to be viewed at standard scanning speed, condensed though its symbolisms were. And no two brains were alike, even when prepared according to the most rigid specifications. That, Baley understood, was a consequence of Heisenberg's Uncertainty Principle. This meant that each film had to be supplemented by appendices involving possible variations.

Oh, it was a job, all right. Baley wouldn't deny that.

Dr. Gerrigel said, "Well, then, you must understand that a design for a new type of positronic brain, even one where only minor innovations are involved, is not the matter of a night's work. It usually involves the entire research staff of a moderately sized factory and takes anywhere up to a year of time. Even this large expenditure of work would not be nearly enough if it were not that the basic theory of such circuits has already been standardized and may be used as a foundation for further elaboration. The standard basic theory involved the Three Laws of Robotics: the First Law, which you've quoted; the Second Law which states, 'A robot must obey the orders given by human beings except where such orders would conflict with the First Law,' and the Third Law, which states, 'A robot must protect its own existence as long as such protection does not conflict with the First or Second Law.' Do you understand?"

R. Daneel, who, to all appearances, had been following the conversation with close attention, broke in. "If you will excuse me, Elijah, I would like to see if I follow Dr. Gerrigel. What you imply, sir, is that any attempt to build a robot, the working of whose positronic brain is not oriented about the Three Laws, would require first the setting up of a new basic theory and that this, in turn, would take many years."

The roboticist looked very gratified. "That is exactly what I mean, Mr. . . ."

Baley waited a moment, then carefully introduced R. Daneel: "This is Daneel Olivaw, Dr. Gerrigel."

"Good day, Mr. Olivaw." Dr. Gerrigel extended his hand and shook Daneel's. He went on, "It is my estimation that it would take fifty years to develop the basic theory of a non-Asenion positronic brain— that is, one in which the basic assumptions of the Three Laws are disallowed—and bring it to the point where robots similar to modern models could be constructed."

"And this has never been done?" asked Baley. "I mean, Doctor, that we've been building robots for several thousand years. In all that time, hasn't anybody or any group had fifty years to spare?"

"Certainly," said the roboticist, "but it is not the sort of work that anyone would care to do."

"I find that hard to believe. Human curiosity will undertake anything."

"It hasn't undertaken the non-Asenion robot. The human race, Mr. Baley, has a strong Frankenstein complex."

"A what?"

"That's a popular name derived from a Medieval novel describing a robot that turned on its creator. I never read the novel myself. But that's beside the point. What I wish to say is that robots without the First Law are simply not built."

"And no theory for it even exists?"

"Not to my knowledge, and my knowledge," he smiled self-consciously, "is rather extensive."

"And a robot with the First Law built in could not kill a man?"

"Never. Unless such killing were completely accidental or unless it were necessary to save the lives of two or more men. In either case, the positronic potential built up would ruin the brain past recovery."

"All right," said Baley. "All this represents the situation on Earth. Right?"

"Yes. Certainly."

"What about the Outer Worlds?"

Some of Dr. Gerrigel's self-assurance seemed to ooze away. "Oh dear, Mr. Baley, I couldn't say of my own knowledge, but I'm sure that if non-Asenion positronic brains were ever designed or if the mathematical theory were worked out, we'd hear of it."

"Would we? Well, let me follow up another thought in my mind, Dr. Gerrigel. I hope you don't mind."

"No. Not at all." He looked helplessly first at Baley, then at R. Daneel. "After all, if it is as important as you say, I'm glad to do all I can."

"Thank you, Doctor. My question is, why humanoid robots? I mean that I've been taking them for granted all my life, but now it occurs to me that I don't know the reason for their existence. Why should a robot have a head and four limbs? Why should he look more or less like a man?"

"You mean, why shouldn't he be built functionally, like any other machine?"

"Right," said Baley. "Why not?"

Dr. Gerrigel smiled a little. "Really, Mr. Baley, you were born too late. The early literature of robotics is riddled with a discussion of that very matter and the polemics involved were something frightful. If you would like a very good reference to the disputations among the functionalists and anti-functionalists, I can recommend Hanford's *History of Robotics*. Mathematics is kept to a minimum. I think you'd find it very interesting."

"I'll look it up," said Baley, patiently. "Meanwhile, could you give me an idea?"

"The decision was made on the basis of economics. Look here, Mr. Baley, if you were supervising a farm, would you care to build a tractor with a positronic brain, a reaper, a harrow, a milker, an automobile, and so on, each with a positronic brain; or would you rather have ordinary unbrained machinery with a single positronic robot to run them all. I warn you that the second alternative represents only a fiftieth or a hundredth the expense."

"But why the human form?"

"Because the human form is the most successful generalized form in all nature. We are not a specialized animal, Mr. Baley, except for our nervous system and a few odd items. If you want a design capable of doing a great many widely various things, all fairly well, you could do no better than to imitate the human form. Besides that, our entire technology is based on the human form. An automobile, for instance, has its controls so made as to be grasped and manipulated most easily by human hands and feet of a certain size and shape, attached to the body by limbs of a certain length and joints of a certain type. Even such simple objects as chairs and tables or knives and forks are designed to meet the requirements of human measurements and manner of working. It is easier to have robots imitate the human shape than to redesign radically the very philosophy of our tools."

"I see. That makes sense. Now isn't it true, Doctor, that the roboticists of the Outer World manufacture robots that are much more humanoid than our own?"

"I believe that is true."

"Could they manufacture a robot so humanoid that it would pass for human under ordinary conditions?"

Dr. Gerrigel lifted his eyebrows and considered that. "I think they could, Mr. Baley. It would be terribly expensive. I doubt that the return could be profitable."

"Do you suppose," went on Baley, relentlessly, "that they could make a robot that would fool *you* into thinking it was a human?"

The roboticist tittered. "Oh, my dear Mr. Baley. I doubt that. Really. There's more to a robot than just his appear——"

Dr. Gerrigel froze in the middle of the word. Slowly, he turned to R. Daneel, and his pink face went very pale.

"Oh, dear me," he whispered. "Oh, dear me."

He reached out one hand and touched R. Daneel's cheek gingerly. R. Daneel did not move away but gazed at the roboticist calmly.

"Dear me," said Dr. Gerrigel, with what was almost a sob in his voice, "you *are* a robot."

"It took you a long time to realize that," said Baley, dryly.

"I wasn't expecting it. I never saw one like this. Outer World manufacture?"

"Yes," said Baley.

"It's obvious now. The way he holds himself. The manner of his speaking. It is not a perfect imitation, Mr. Baley."

"It's pretty good, though, isn't it?"

"Oh, it's marvelous. I doubt that anyone could recognize the imposture at sight. I am very grateful to you for having me brought face to face with him. May I examine him?" The roboticist was on his feet, eager.

Baley put out a hand. "Please, Doctor. In a moment. First, the matter of the murder, you know."

"Is that real, then?" Dr. Gerrigel was bitterly disappointed and showed it. "I thought perhaps that was just a device to keep my mind engaged and to see how long I could be fooled by——"

"It is not a device, Dr. Gerrigel. Tell me, now, in constructing a robot as humanoid as this one, with the deliberate purpose of having it pass as human, is it not necessary to make its brain possess properties as close to that of the human brain as possible?"

"Certainly."

"Very well. Could not such a humanoid brain lack the First Law? Perhaps it is left out accidentally. You say the theory is unknown. The very fact that it is unknown means that the constructors might set up a brain without the First Law. They would not know what to avoid."

Dr. Gerrigel was shaking his head vigorously. "No. No. Impossible."

"Are you sure? We can test the Second Law, of course—Daneel, let me have your blaster."

Baley's eyes never left the robot. His own hand, well to one side, gripped his own blaster tightly.

R. Daneel said calmly, "Here it is, Elijah," and held it out, butt first.

Baley said, "A plain-clothes man must never abandon his blaster, but a robot has no choice but to obey a human."

"Except, Mr. Baley," said Dr. Gerrigel, "when obedience involves breaking the First Law."

"Do you know, Doctor, that Daneel drew his blaster on an unarmed group of men and women and threatened to shoot?"

"But I did not shoot," said Daneel.

"Granted, but the threat was unusual in itself, wasn't it, Doctor?"

Dr. Gerrigel bit his lip. "I'd need to know the exact circumstances to judge. It sounds unusual."

"Consider this, then. R. Daneel was on the scene at the time of the murder, and if you omit the possibility of an Earthman having moved across open country, carrying a weapon with him, Daneel and Daneel alone of all the persons on the scene could have hidden the weapon."

"Hidden the weapon?" asked Dr. Gerrigel.

"Let me explain. The blaster that did the killing was not found. The scene of the murder was searched minutely and it was not found. Yet it could not have vanished like smoke. There is only one place it could have been, only one place they would not have thought to look."

"Where, Elijah?" asked R. Daneel.

Baley brought his blaster into view, held its barrel firmly in the robot's direction.

"In your food sac," he said. "In your food sac, Daneel!"

 # Shift to the Machine

"That is not so," said R. Daneel, quietly.

"Yes? We'll let the Doctor decide. Dr. Gerrigel?"

"Mr. Baley?" The roboticist, whose glance had been alternating wildly between the plain-clothes man and the robot as they spoke, let it come to rest upon the human being.

"I've asked you here for an authoritative analysis of this robot. I can arrange to have you use the laboratories of the City Bureau of Standards. If you need any piece of equipment they don't have, I'll get it for you. What I want is a quick and definite answer and hang the expense and trouble."

Baley rose. His words had emerged calmly enough, but he felt a rising hysteria behind them. At the moment, he felt that if he could only seize Dr. Gerrigel by the throat and choke the necessary statements out of him, he would forego all science.

He said, "Well, Dr. Gerrigel?"

Dr. Gerrigel tittered nervously and said, "My dear Mr. Baley, I won't need a laboratory."

"Why not?" asked Baley apprehensively. He stood there, muscles tense, feeling himself twitch.

"It's not difficult to test the First Law. I've never had to, you understand, but it's simple enough."

Baley pulled air in through his mouth and let it out slowly. He said, "Would you explain what you mean? Are you saying that you can test him here?"

"Yes, of course. Look, Mr. Baley, I'll give you an analogy. If I were a Doctor of Medicine and had to test a patient's blood sugar, I'd need a chemical laboratory. If I needed to measure his basal metabolic rate, or test his cortical function, or check his genes to pinpoint a congenital malfunction, I'd need elaborate equipment. On the other hand, I could check whether he were blind by merely passing my hand before his eyes and I could test whether he were dead by merely feeling his pulse.

"What I'm getting at is that the more important and fundamental the property being tested, the simpler the needed equipment. It's the same in a robot. The First Law is fundamental. It affects everything. If it were absent, the robot could not react properly in two dozen obvious ways."

As he spoke, he took out a flat, black object which expanded into a small book-viewer. He inserted a well-worn spool into the receptacle.

110

He then took out a stop watch and a series of white, plastic slivers that fitted together to form something that looked like a slide rule with three independent movable scales. The notations upon it struck no chord of familiarity to Baley.

Dr. Gerrigel tapped his book-viewer and smiled a little, as though the prospect of a bit of field work cheered him.

He said, "It's my *Handbook* of Robotics. I never go anywhere without it. It's part of my clothes." He giggled self-consciously.

He put the eyepiece of the viewer to his eyes and his finger dealt delicately with the controls. The viewer whirred and stopped, whirred and stopped.

"Built-in index," the roboticist said, proudly, his voice a little muffled because of the way in which the viewer covered his mouth. "I constructed it myself. It saves a great deal of time. But then, that's not the point now, is it? Let's see. Umm, won't you move your chair near me, Daneel?"

R. Daneel did so. During the roboticist's preparations, he had watched closely and unemotionally.

Baley shifted his blaster.

What followed confused and disappointed him. Dr. Gerrigel proceeded to ask questions and perform actions that seemed without meaning, punctuated by references to his triple slide rule and occasionally to the viewer.

At one time, he asked, "If I have two cousins, five years apart in age, and the younger is a girl, what sex is the older?"

Daneel answered (inevitably, Baley thought), "It is impossible to say on the information given."

To which Dr. Gerrigel's only response, aside from a glance at his stop watch, was to extend his right hand as far as he could sideways and to say, "Would you touch the tip of my middle finger with the tip of the third finger of your left hand?"

Daneel did that promptly and easily.

In fifteen minutes, not more, Dr. Gerrigel was finished. He used his slide rule for a last silent calculation, then disassembled it with a series of snaps. He put away his stop watch, withdrew the *Handbook* from the viewer, and collapsed the latter.

"Is that all?" said Baley, frowning.

"That's all."

"But it's ridiculous. You've asked nothing that pertains to the First Law."

"Oh, my dear Mr. Baley, when a doctor hits your knee with a little rubber mallet and it jerks, don't you accept the fact that it gives information concerning the presence or absence of some degenerative nerve disease? When he looks closely at your eyes and considers the reaction of your iris to light, are you surprised that he can tell you something concerning your possible addiction to the use of certain alkaloids?"

Baley said, "Well, then? What's your decision?"

"Daneel is fully equipped with the First Law!" The roboticist jerked his head in a sharp affirmative.

"You can't be right," said Baley huskily.

Baley would not have thought that Dr. Gerrigel could stiffen into a rigidity that was greater than his usual position. He did so, however, visibly. The man's eyes grew narrow and hard.

"Are you teaching me my job?"

"I don't mean you're incompetent," said Baley. He put out a large, pleading hand. "But couldn't you be mistaken? You've said yourself nobody knows anything about the theory of non-Asenion robots. A blind man could read by using Braille or a sound-scriber. Suppose you didn't know that Braille or sound-scribing existed. Couldn't you, in all honesty, say that a man had eyes because he knew the contents of a certain book-film, and be mistaken?"

"Yes," the roboticist grew genial again, "I see your point. But still a blind man could not read by use of his eyes and it is that which I .was testing, if I may continue the analogy. Take my word for it, regardless of what a non-Asenion robot could or could not do, it is certain that R. Daneel is equipped with First Law."

"Couldn't he have falsified his answers?" Baley was floundering, and he knew it.

"Of course not. That is the difference between a robot and a man. A human brain, or any mammalian brain, cannot be completely analyzed by any mathematical discipline now known. No response can therefore be counted upon as a certainty. The robot brain is completely analyzable, or it could not be constructed. We know exactly what the responses to given stimuli must be. No robot can truly falsify answers. The thing you call falsification just doesn't exist in the robot's mental horizon."

"Then let's get down to cases. R. Daneel did point a blaster at a crowd of human beings. I saw that. I was there. Granted that he didn't shoot, wouldn't the First Law still have forced him into a kind of neurosis? It didn't, you know. He was perfectly normal afterward."

"Not at all," said R. Daneel, suddenly. "Partner Elijah, would you look at the blaster that you took from me?"

Baley looked down upon the blaster he held cradled in his left hand.

"Break open the charge chamber," urged R. Daneel. "Inspect it."

Baley weighed his chances, then slowly put his own blaster on the table beside him. With a quick movement, he opened the robot's blaster.

"It's empty," he said, blankly.

"There is no charge in it," agreed R. Daneel. "If you will look closer, you will see that there has never been a charge in it. The blaster has no ignition bud and cannot be used."

Baley said, "You held an uncharged blaster on the crowd?"

"I had to have a blaster or fail in my role as plain-clothes man," said R. Daneel. "Yet to carry a charged and usable blaster might have made it possible for me to hurt a human being by accident, a thing which is, of course, unthinkable. I would have explained this at the time, but you were angry and would not listen."

Baley stared bleakly at the useless blaster in his hand and said in a low voice, "I think that's all, Dr. Gerrigel. Thank you for helping out."

Baley sent out for lunch, but when it came (yeast-nut cake and a rather extravagant slice of fried chicken on cracker) he could only stare at it.

Round and round went the currents of his mind. The lines of his long face were etched in deep gloom.

He was living in an unreal world, a cruel, topsy-turvy world.

How had it happened? The immediate past stretched behind him like a misty improbable dream dating back to the moment he had stepped into Julius Enderby's office and found himself suddenly immersed in a nightmare of murder and robotics.

Jehoshaphat! It had begun only fifty hours before.

Persistently, he had sought the solution in Spacetown. Twice he had accused R. Daneel, once as a human being in disguise, and once as an admitted and actual robot, each time as a murderer. Twice the accusation had been bent back and broken.

He was being driven back. Against his will he was forced to turn his thoughts into the City, and since last night he dared not. Certain questions battered at his conscious mind, but he would not listen; he felt he could not. If he heard them, he couldn't help but answer them and, oh God, he didn't want to face the answers.

"Lije! Lije!" A hand shook Baley's shoulder roughly.

Baley stirred and said, "What's up, Phil?"

Philip Norris, Plain-clothes man C-5, sat down, put his hands on his knees, and leaned forward, peering at Baley's face. "What happened to you? Been living on knockout drops lately? You were sitting there with your eyes open and, near as I could make out, you were dead."

He rubbed his thinning, pale blond hair, and his close-set eyes appraised Baley's cooling lunch greedily. "Chicken!" he said. "It's getting so you can't get it without a doctor's prescription."

"Take some," said Baley, listlessly.

Decorum won out and Norris said, "Oh, well, I'm going out to eat in a minute. You keep it.—Say, what's doing with the Commish?"

"What?"

Norris attempted a casual attitude, but his hands were restless. He said, "Go on. You know what I mean. You've been living with him ever since he got back. What's up? A promotion in the works?"

Baley frowned and felt reality return somewhat at the touch of office politics. Norris had approximately his own seniority and he was bound to watch most assiduously for any sign of official preference in Baley's direction.

Baley said, "No promotion. Believe me. It's nothing. Nothing, and if it's the Commissioner you're wanting, I wish I could give him to you. Jehoshaphat! Take him!"

Norris said, "Don't get me wrong. I don't care if you get promoted. I just mean that if you've got any pull with the Commish, how about using it for the kid?"

"What kid?"

There was no need of any answer to that. Vincent Barrett, the youngster who had been moved out of his job to make room for R. Sammy, was shuffling up from an unnoticed corner of the room. A skull cap turned restlessly in his hands and the skin over his high cheekbones moved as he tried to smile.

"Hello, Mr. Baley."

"Oh, hello, Vince. How're you doing?"

"Not so good, Mr. Baley."

He was looking about hungrily. Baley thought: He looks lost, half dead—declassified.

Then, savagely, his lips almost moving with the force of his emotion, he thought: But what does he want from me?

He said, "I'm sorry, kid." What else was there to say?

"I keep thinking——maybe something has turned up."

Norris moved in close and spoke into Baley's ear. "Someone's got to stop this sort of thing. They're going to move out Chen-low now."

"What?"

"Haven't you heard?"

"No, I haven't. Damn it, he's a C–3. He's got ten years behind him."

"I grant that. But a machine with legs can do his work. Who's next?"

Young Vince Barrett was oblivious to the whispers. He said out of the depths of his own thinking, "Mr. Baley?"

"Yes, Vince?"

"You know what they say? They say Lyrane Millane, the subetherics dancer, is really a robot."

"That's silly."

"Is it? They say they can make robots look just like humans; with a special plastic skin, sort of."

Baley thought guiltily of R. Daneel and found no words. He shook his head.

The boy said, "Do you suppose anyone will mind if I just walk around. It makes me feel better to see the old place."

"Go ahead, kid."

The youngster wandered off. Baley and Norris watched him go. Norris said, "It looks as though the Medievalists are right."

"You mean back to the soil? Is that it, Phil?"

"*No.* I mean about the robots. Back to the soil. Huh! Old Earth has an unlimited future. We don't need robots, that's all."

Baley muttered, "Eight billion people and the uranium running out! What's unlimited about it?"

"What if the uranium does run out. We'll import it. Or we'll discover other nuclear processes. There's no way you can stop mankind, Lije. You've got to be optimistic about it and have faith in the old human brain. Our greatest resource is ingenuity and we'll never run out of that, Lije."

He was fairly started now. He went on, "For one thing, we can use sunpower and that's good for billions of years. We can build space stations inside Mercury's orbit to act as energy accumulators. We'll transmit energy to Earth by direct beam."

This project was not new to Baley. The speculative fringe of science had been playing with the notion for a hundred and fifty years at least. What was holding it up was the impossibility so far of projecting a beam tight enough to reach fifty million miles without dispersal to uselessness. Baley said as much.

Norris said, "When it's necessary, it'll be done. Why worry?"

Baley had the picture of an Earth of unlimited energy. Population could continue to increase. The yeast farms could expand, hydroponic culture intensify. Energy was the only thing indispensable. The raw minerals could be brought in from the uninhabited rocks of the System. If ever water became a bottleneck, more could be brought in from the moons of Jupiter. Hell, the oceans could be frozen and dragged out into Space where they could circle Earth as moonlets of ice. There they would be, always available for use, while the ocean bottoms would represent more land for exploitation, more room to live. Even carbon and oxygen could be maintained and increased on Earth through utilization of the methane atmosphere of Titan and the frozen oxygen of Umbriel.

Earth's population could reach a trillion or two. Why not? There was a time when the current population of eight billion would have been viewed as impossible. There was a time when a population of a single billion would have been unthinkable. There had always been prophets of Malthusian doom in every generation since Medieval times and they had always proven wrong.

But what would Fastolfe say? A world of a trillion? Surely! But they would be dependent on imported air and water and upon an energy supply from complicated storehouses fifty million miles away. How incredibly unstable that would be. Earth would be, and remain, a feather's weight away from complete catastrophe at the slightest failure of any part of the System-wide mechanism.

Baley said, "I think it would be easier to ship off some of the surplus population, myself." It was more an answer to the picture he had himself conjured up than to anything Norris had said.

"Who'd have us?" said Norris with a bitter lightness.

"Any uninhabited planet."

Norris rose, patted Baley on the shoulder. "Lije, you eat your chicken, and recover. You *must* be living on knockout pills." He left, chuckling.

Baley watched him leave with a humorless twist to his mouth. Norris would spread the news and it would be weeks before the humor boys of the office (every office has them) would lay off. But at least it got him off the subject of young Vince, robots, of declassification.

He sighed as he put a fork into the now cold and somewhat stringy chicken.

Baley finished the last of the yeast-nut and it was only then that R. Daneel left his own desk (assigned him that morning) and approached.

Baley eyed him uncomfortably. "Well?"

R. Daneel said, "The Commissioner is not in his office and it is not known when he'll be back. I've told R. Sammy we will use it and that he is to allow no one but the Commissioner to enter."

"What are we going to use it for?"

"Greater privacy. Surely you agree that we must plan our next move. After all, you do not intend to abandon the investigation, do you?"

That was precisely what Baley most longed to do, but obviously, he could not say so. He rose and led the way to Enderby's office.

Once in the office, Baley said, "All right, Daneel. What is it?"

The robot said, "Partner Elijah, since last night, you are not yourself. There is a definite alteration in your mental aura."

A horrible thought sprang full-grown into Baley's mind. He cried, "Are you telepathic?"

It was not a possibility he would have considered at a less disturbed moment.

"No. Of course not," said R. Daneel.

Baley's panic ebbed. He said, "Then what the devil do you mean by talking about my mental aura?"

"It is merely an expression I use to describe a sensation that you do not share with me."

"What sensation?"

"It is difficult to explain, Elijah. You will recall that I was originally designed to study human psychology for our people back in Spacetown."

"Yes, I know. You were adjusted to detective work by the simple installation of a justice-desire circuit." Baley did not try to keep the sarcasm out of his voice.

"Exactly, Elijah. But my original design remains essentially unaltered. I was constructed for the purpose of cerebroanalysis."

"For analyzing brain waves?"

"Why, yes. It can be done by field-measurements without the necessity of direct electrode contact, if the proper receiver exists. My mind is such a receiver. Is that principle not applied on Earth?"

Baley didn't know. He ignored the question and said, cautiously, "If you measure the brain waves, what do you get out of it?"

"Not thoughts, Elijah. I get a glimpse of emotion and most of all, I can analyze temperament, the underlying drives and attitudes of a man. For instance, it was I who was able to ascertain that Commissioner Enderby was incapable of killing a man under the circumstances prevailing at the time of the murder."

"And they eliminate him as a suspect on your say-so."

"Yes. It was safe enough to do so. I am a very delicate machine in that respect."

Again a thought struck Baley. "Wait! Commissioner Enderby didn't know he was being cerebroanalyzed, did he?"

"There was no necessity of hurting his feelings."

"I mean you just stood there and looked at him. No machinery. No electrodes. No needles and graphs."

"Certainly not. I am a self-contained unit."

Baley bit his lower lip in anger and chagrin. It had been the one remaining inconsistency, the one loophole through which a forlorn stab might yet be made in an attempt to pin the crime on Spacetown.

R. Daneel had stated that the Commissioner had been cerebroanalyzed and one hour later the Commissioner himself had, with apparent candor, denied any knowledge of the term. Certainly no man could have undergone the shattering experience of electroencephalographic measurements by electrode and graph under the suspicion of murder without an unmistakable impression of what cerebroanalysis must be.

But now that discrepancy had evaporated. The Commissioner had been cerebroanalyzed and had never known it. R. Daneel told the truth; so had the Commissioner.

"Well," said Baley sharply, "what does cerebroanalysis tell you about me?"

"You are disturbed."

"That's a great discovery, isn't it? Of course, I'm disturbed."

"Specifically, though, your disturbance is due to a clash between motivations within you. On the one hand your devotion to the principles of your profession urges you to look deeply into this conspiracy of Earthmen who lay siege to us last night. Another motivation, equally

strong, forces you in the opposite direction. This much is clearly written in the electric field on your cerebral cells."

"My cerebral cells, *nuts*," said Baley, feverishly. "Look, I'll tell you
why there's no point in investigating your so-called conspiracy. It has
nothing to do with the murder. I thought it might have. I'll admit
that. Yesterday in the kitchen, I thought we were in danger. But what
happened? They followed us out, were quickly lost on the strips, and
that was that. That was not the action of well-organized and desperate
men.

"My own son found out where we were staying easily enough. He
called the Department. He didn't even have to identify himself. Our
precious conspirators could have done the same if they had really
wanted to hurt us."

"Didn't they?"

"Obviously not. If they had wanted riots, they could have started
one at the shoe counter, and yet they backed out tamely enough before one man and a blaster. One *robot*, and a blaster which they must
have known you would be unable to fire once they recognized what
you were. They're Medievalists. They're harmless crackpots. You
wouldn't know that, but I should have. And I would have, if it weren't
for the fact that this whole business has me thinking in—in foolish
melodramatic terms.

"I tell you I know the type of people that become Medievalists.
They're soft, dreamy people who find life too hard for them here and
get lost in an ideal world of the past that never really existed. If you
could cerebroanalyze a movement as you do an individual, you would
find they are no more capable of murder than Julius Enderby himself."

R. Daneel said slowly, "I cannot accept your statements at face
value."

"What do you mean?"

"Your conversion to this view is too sudden. There are certain dis-
crepancies, too. You arranged the appointment with Dr. Gerrigel hours
before the evening meal. You did not know of my food sac then and
could not have suspected me as the murderer. Why *did* you call him,
then?"

"I suspected you even then."

"And last night you spoke as you slept."

Baley's eyes widened. "What did I say?"

"Merely the one word 'Jessie' several times repeated. I believe you
were referring to your wife."

Baley let his tight muscles loosen. He said, shakily, "I had a nightmare. Do you know what it is?"

"I do not know by personal experience, of course. The dictionary
definition has it that it is a bad dream."

"And do you know what a dream is?"

"Again, the dictionary definition only. It is an illusion of reality experienced during the temporary suspension of conscious thought which you call sleep."

"All right. I'll buy that. An illusion. Sometimes the illusion can seem damned real. Well, I dreamed my wife was in danger. It's the sort of dream people often have. I called her name. That happens under such circumstances, too. You can take my word for it."

"I am only too glad to do so. But it brings up a thought. How did Jessie find out I was a robot?"

Baley's forehead went moist again. "We're not going into that again, are we? The rumor——"

"I am sorry to interrupt, partner Elijah, but there is no rumor. If there were, the City would be alive with unrest today. I have checked reports coming into the Department and this is not so. There simply is no rumor. Therefore, how did your wife find out?"

"Jehoshaphat! What are you trying to say? Do you think my wife is one of the members of—of . . ."

"Yes, Elijah."

Baley gripped his hands together tightly. "Well, she isn't, and we won't discuss that point any further."

"This is not like you, Elijah. In the course of duty, you accused me of murder twice."

"And is this your way of getting even?"

"I am not sure I understand what you mean by the phrase. Certainly, I approve your readiness to suspect me. You had your reasons. They were wrong, but they might easily have been right. Equally strong evidence points to your wife."

"As a murderess? Why, damn you, Jessie wouldn't hurt her worst enemy. She couldn't set foot outside the City. She couldn't . . . Why, if you were flesh and blood I'd——"

"I merely say that she is a member of the conspiracy. I say that she should be questioned."

"Not on your life. Not on whatever it is you call your life. Now, listen to me. The Medievalists aren't after our blood. It's not the way they do things. But they are trying to get you out of the City. That much is obvious. And they're trying to do it by a kind of psychological attack. They're trying to make life unpleasant for you and for me, since I'm with you. They could easily have found out Jessie was my wife, and it was an obvious move for them to let the news leak to her. She's like any other human being. She doesn't *like* robots. She wouldn't want me to associate with one, especially if she thought it involved danger, and surely they would imply that. I tell you it worked. She begged all night to have me abandon the case or to get you out of the City somehow."

"Presumably," said R. Daneel, "you have a very strong urge to protect your wife against questioning. It seems obvious to me that you are constructing this line of argument without really believing it."

"What the hell do you think you are?" ground out Baley. "You're not a detective. You're a cerebroanalysis machine like the electroencephalographs we have in this building. You've got arms, legs, a head, and can talk, but you're not one inch more than a machine. Putting a lousy circuit into you doesn't make you a detective, so what do you know? You keep your mouth shut, and let me do the figuring out."

The robot said quietly, "I think it would be better if you lowered your voice, Elijah. Granted that I am not a detective in the sense that you are, I would still like to bring one small item to your attention."

"I'm not interested in listening."

"Please do. If I am wrong, you will tell me so, and it will do no harm. It is only this. Last night you left our room to call Jessie by corridor phone. I suggested that your son go in your place. You told me it was not the custom among Earthmen for a father to send his son into danger. Is it then the custom for a mother to do so?"

"No, of cour——" began Baley, and stopped.

"You see my point," said R. Daneel. "Ordinarily, if Jessie feared for your safety and wished to warn you, she would risk her own life, *not* send her son. The fact that she did send Bentley could only mean that she felt that he would be safe while she herself would not. If the conspiracy consisted of people unknown to Jessie, that would not be the case, or at least she would have no reason to think it to be the case. On the other hand, if she were a member of the conspiracy, she would know, she would *know*, Elijah, that she would be watched for and recognized, whereas Bentley might get through unnoticed."

"Wait now," said Bentley, sick at heart, "that's feather-fine reasoning, but——"

There was no need to wait. The signal on the Commissioner's desk was flickering madly. R. Daneel waited for Baley to answer, but the latter could only stare at it helplessly. The robot closed contact.

"What is it?"

R. Sammy's slurring voice said, "There is a lady here who wishes to see Lije. I told her he was busy, but she will not go away. She says her name is Jessie."

"Let her in," said R. Daneel calmly, and his brown eyes rose unemotionally to meet the panicky glare of Baley's.

14.

**Power of
a Name**

Baley remained standing in a tetany of shock, as Jessie ran to him, seizing his shoulders, huddling close.

His pale lips formed the word, "Bentley?"

She looked at him and shook her head, her brown hair flying with the force of her motion. "He's all right."

"Well, then . . ."

Jessie said through a sudden torrent of sobs, in a low voice that could scarcely be made out, "I can't go on, Lije. I can't. I can't sleep or eat. I've got to tell you."

"Don't say anything," Baley said in anguish. "For God's sake, Jessie, not now."

"I must. I've done a terrible thing. Oh, Lije . . ." She lapsed into incoherence.

Baley said, hopelessly, "We're not alone, Jessie."

She looked up and stared at R. Daneel with no signs of recognition. The tears in which her eyes were swimming might easily be refracting the robot into a featureless blur.

R. Daneel said in a low murmur, "Good afternoon, Jessie."

She gasped. "Is it the—the robot?"

She dashed the back of her hand across her eyes and stepped out of Baley's encircling right arm. She breathed deeply and for a moment, a tremulous smile wavered on her lips. "It *is* you, isn't it?"

"Yes, Jessie."

"You don't mind being called a robot?"

"No, Jessie. It is what I am."

"And I don't mind being called a fool and an idiot and a—a subversive agent, because it's what *I* am."

"Jessie!" groaned Baley.

"It's no use, Lije," she said. "He might as well know if he's your partner. I can't live with it anymore. I've had such a time since yesterday. I don't care if I go to jail. I don't care if they send me down to the lowest levels and make me live on raw yeast and water. I don't care if . . . You won't let them, will you, Lije? Don't let them do anything to me. I'm fuh—frightened."

Baley patted her shoulder and let her cry.

He said to R. Daneel, "She isn't well. We can't keep her here. What time is it?"

R. Daneel said without any visible signs of consulting a timepiece, "Fourteen-forty-five."

"The Commissioner could be back any minute. Look, commandeer a squad car and we can talk about this in the motorway."

Jessie's head jerked upright. "The motorway? Oh, no, Lije."

He said, in as soothing a tone as he could manage, "Now, Jessie, don't be superstitious. You can't go on the expressway the way you are. Be a good girl and calm down or we won't even be able to go through the common room. I'll get you some water."

She wiped her face with a damp handkerchief and said drearily, "Oh, look at my makeup."

"Don't worry about your makeup," said Baley. "Daneel, what about the squad car?"

"It's waiting for us now, partner Elijah."

"Come on, Jessie."

"Wait. Wait just a minute, Lije. I've got to do something to my face."

"It doesn't matter now."

But she twisted away. "Please. I can't go through the common room like this. I won't take a second."

Jessie rummaged through her purse for the necessary equipment. (If there were one thing, Baley had once said solemnly, that had resisted mechanical improvement since Medieval times, it was a woman's purse. Even the substitution of magnetic clotures for metal clasps had not proven successful.) Jessie pulled out a small mirror and the silver-chased cosmetokit that Baley had bought her on the occasion of three birthdays before.

The cosmetokit had several orifices and she used each in turn. All but the last spray were invisible. She used them with that fineness of touch and delicacy of control that seems to be the birthright of women even at times of the greatest stress.

The base went on first in a smooth even layer that removed all shininess and roughness from the skin and left it with the faintly golden glow which long experience had taught Jessie was just the shade most suited to the natural coloring of her hair and eyes. Then the touch of tan along the forehead and chin, a gentle brush of rouge on either cheek, tracing back to the angle of the jaw; and a delicate drift of blue on the upper eyelids and along the earlobes. Finally there was the application of the smooth carmine to the lips. That involved the one visible spray, a faintly pink mist that glistened liquidly in air, but dried and deepened richly on contact with the lips.

"There," said Jessie, with several swift pats at her hair and a look of deep satisfaction. "I suppose that will do."

The process had taken more than the promised second, but less than fifteen seconds. Nevertheless, it had seemed interminable to Baley.

"Come," he said.

She barely had time to return the cosmetokit to the purse before he had pushed her through the door.

The eerie silence of the motorway lay thick on either side.

Baley said, "All right, Jessie."

The impassivity that had covered Jessie's face since they first left the Commissioner's office showed signs of cracking. She looked at her husband and at Daneel with a helpless silence.

Baley said, "Get it over with, Jessie. Please. Have you committed a crime? An actual crime?"

"A crime?" She shook her head uncertainly.

"Now hold on to yourself. No hysterics. Just say yes or no, Jessie. Have you—" he hesitated a trifle, "killed anyone?"

The look on Jessie's face was promptly transmitted to indignation. "Why, Lije Baley!"

"Yes or no, Jessie."

"No, of course not."

The hard knot in Baley's stomach softened perceptibly. "Have you stolen anything? Falsified ration data? Assaulted anyone? Destroyed property? Speak up, Jessie."

"I haven't done anything—anything specific. I didn't mean anything like that." She looked over his shoulder. "Lije, do we have to stay down here?"

"Right here until this is over. Now, start at the beginning. What did you come to tell us?" Over Jessie's bowed head, Baley's eyes met R. Daneel's.

Jessie spoke in a soft voice that gained in strength and articulateness as she went on.

"It's these people, these Medievalists; you know, Lije. They're always around, always talking. Even in the old days when I was an assistant dietitian, it was like that. Remember Elizabeth Thornbowe? She was a Medievalist. She was always talking about how all our troubles came from the City and how things were better before the Cities started.

"I used to ask her how she was so sure that was so, especially after you and I met, Lije (remember the talks we used to have), and then she would quote from those small book-reels that are always floating around. You know, like *Shame of the Cities* that the fellow wrote. I don't remember his name."

Baley said, absently, "Ogrinsky."

"Yes, only most of them were lots worse. Then, when I married you, she was really sarcastic. She said, 'I suppose you're going to be a real City woman now that you've married a policeman.' After that, she didn't talk to me much and then I quit the job and that was that. Lots of things she used to say were just to shock me, I think, or to make herself look mysterious and glamorous. She was an old maid, you know; never got married till the day she died. Lots of those Medievalists don't fit in, one way or another. Remember, you once said, Lije, that people sometimes mistake their own shortcomings for those of society and want to fix the Cities because they don't know how to fix themselves."

Baley remembered, and his words now sounded flip and superficial in his own ears. He said, gently, "Keep to the point, Jessie."

She went on, "Anyway, Lizzy was always talking about how there'd come a day and people had to get together. She said it was all the fault of the Spacers because they wanted to keep Earth weak and decadent. That was one of her favorite words, 'decadent.' She'd look at the menus I'd prepare for the next week and sniff and say, 'Decadent, decadent.' Jane Myers used to imitate her in the cook room and we'd die laughing. She said, Elizabeth did, that someday we were going to break up the Cities and go back to the soil and have an accounting with the Spacers, who were trying to tie us forever to the Cities by forcing robots on us. Only she never called them robots. She used to say 'soulless monster-machines,' if you'll excuse the expression, Daneel."

The robot said, "I am not aware of the significance of the adjective you used, Jessie, but in any case, the expression is excused. Please go on."

Baley stirred restlessly. It was that way with Jessie. No emergency, no crisis could make her tell a story in any way but her own circuitous one.

She said, "Elizabeth always tried to talk as though there were lots of people in it with her. She would way, 'At the last meeting,' and then stop and look at me sort of half proud and half scared as though she wanted me to ask about it so she could look important, and yet scared I might get her in trouble. Of course, I never asked her. I wouldn't give her the satisfaction."

"Anyway, after I married you, Lije, it was all over, until . . . ." She stopped.

"Go on Jessie," said Baley.

"You remember, Lije, that argument we had? About Jezebel, I mean?"

"What about it?" It took a second or two for Baley to remember that it was Jessie's own name, and not a reference to another woman.

He turned to R. Daneel in an automatically defensive explanation. "Jessie's full name is Jezebel. She is not fond of it and doesn't use it."

R. Daneel nodded gravely and Baley thought: Jehoshaphat, why waste worry on *him*?

"It bothered me a lot, Lije," Jessie said. "It really did. I guess it was silly, but I kept thinking and thinking about what you said. I mean

about your saying that Jezebel was only a conservative who fought for
the ways of her ancestors against the strange ways the newcomers had
brought. After all, *I* was Jezebel and I always . . ."

She groped for a word and Baley supplied it. "Identified yourself?"

"Yes." But she shook her head almost immediately and looked away.
"Not really, of course. Not literally. The way I thought she was, you
know. I wasn't like that."

"I know that, Jessie. Don't be foolish."

"But still I thought of her a lot and, somehow, I got to thinking, it's
just the same now as it was then. I mean, we Earth people had our
old ways and here were the Spacers coming in with a lot of new ways
and trying to encourage the new ways we had stumbled into ourselves
and maybe the Medievalists were right. Maybe we *should* go back to
our old, good ways. So I went back and found Elizabeth."

"Yes. Go on."

"She said she didn't know what I was talking about and besides I
was a cop's wife. I said that had nothing to do with it and finally she
said, well, she'd speak to somebody, and then about a month later she
came to me and said it was all right and I joined and I've been at
meetings ever since."

Baley looked at her sadly. "And you never told me?"

Jessie's voice trembled. "I'm sorry, Lije."

"Well, that won't help. Being sorry, I mean. I want to know about
the meetings. In the first place, where were they held?"

A sense of detachment was creeping over him, a numbing of emotions. What he had tried not to believe was so, was openly so, was
unmistakably so. In a sense, it was a relief to have the uncertainty
over.

She said, "Down here."

"Down here? You mean on this spot? What *do* you mean?"

"Here in the motorway. That's why I didn't want to come
down here. It was a wonderful place to meet, though. We'd get together——"

"How many?"

"I'm not sure. About sixty or seventy. It was just a sort of local
branch. There'd be folding chairs and some refreshments and someone would make a speech, mostly about how wonderful life was in the
old days, and how someday we'd do away with the monsters, the robots, that is, and the Spacers, too. The speeches were sort of dull
really, because they were all the same. We just endured them. Mostly,
it was the fun of getting together and feeling important. We would
pledge ourselves to oaths and there'd be secret ways we would greet
each other on the outside."

"Weren't you ever interrupted? No squad cars or fire engines
passed?"

"No. Never."

R. Daneel interrupted. "Is that unusual, Elijah?"

"Maybe not," Baley answered thoughtfully. "There are some side-passages that are practically never used. It's quite a trick, knowing which they are, though. Is that all you did at the meetings, Jessie? Make speeches and play at conspiracy?"

"It's about all. And sing songs, sometimes. And of course, refreshments. Not much. Sandwiches, usually, and juice."

"In that case," he said, almost brutally, "what's bothering you now?"

Jessie winced. "You're angry."

"Please," said Baley, with iron patience, "answer my question. If it were all as harmless as that, why have you been in such panic for the last day and a half?"

"I thought they would hurt you, Lije. For heaven's sake, why do you act as though you don't understand? I've explained it to you."

"No, you haven't. Not yet. You've told me about a harmless little secret kaffee-klatsch you belonged to. Did they ever hold open demonstrations? Did they ever destroy robots? Start riots? Kill people?"

"Never! Lije, I wouldn't do any of those things. I wouldn't stay a member if they tried it."

"Well, then, why do you say you've done a terrible thing? Why do you expect to be sent to jail?"

"Well . . . Well, they used to talk about someday when they'd put pressure on the government. We were supposed to get organized and then afterward there would be huge strikes and work stoppages. We could force the government to ban all robots and make the Spacers go back where they came from. I thought it was just talk and then, this thing started; about you and Daneel, I mean. Then they said, 'Now we'll see action,' and 'We're going to make an example of them and put a stop to the robot invasion right now.' Right there in Personal they said it, not knowing it was you they were talking about. But I knew. Right away."

Her voice broke.

Baley softened. "Come on, Jessie. It was all nothing. It was just talk. You can see for yourself that nothing has happened."

"I was so—so suh—scared. And I thought: I'm part of it. If there were going to be killing and destruction, you might be killed and Bentley and somehow it would be all muh—my fault for taking part in it, and I ought to be sent to jail."

Baley let her sob herself out. He put his arm about her shoulder and stared tight-lipped at R. Daneel, who gazed calmly back.

He said, "Now, I want you to think, Jessie. Who was the head of your group?"

She was quieter now, patting the corners of her eyes with a hand-kerchief. "A man called Joseph Klemin was the leader, but he wasn't really anybody. He wasn't more than five feet four inches tall and I think he was terribly hen-pecked at home. I don't think there's any harm in him. You aren't going to arrest him, are you, Lije? On my say-so?" She looked guiltily troubled.

"I'm not arresting anyone just yet. How did Klemin get his instructions?"

"I don't know."

"Did any strangers come to meetings? You know what I mean: big shots from Central Headquarters?"

"Sometimes people would come to make speeches. That wasn't very often, maybe twice a year or so."

"Can you name them?"

"No. They were always just introduced as 'one of us' or 'a friend from Jackson Heights' or wherever."

"I see. Daneel!"

"Yes, Elijah," said R. Daneel.

"Describe the men you think you've tabbed. We'll see if Jessie can recognize them."

R. Daneel went through the list with clinical exactness. Jessie listened with an expression of dismay as the categories of physical measurements lengthened and shook her head with increasing firmness.

"It's no use. It's no use," she cried. "How can I remember? I can't remember how any of them looked. I can't——"

She stopped, and seemed to consider. Then she said, "Did you say one of them was a yeast farmer?"

"Francis Clousarr," said R. Daneel, "is an employee at New York Yeast."

"Well, you know, once a man was making a speech and I happened to be sitting in the first row and I kept getting a whiff, just a whiff, really, of raw yeast smell. You know what I mean. The only reason that I remember is that I had an upset stomach that day and the smell kept making me sick. I had to stand up and move to the back and of course I couldn't explain what was wrong. It was so embarrassing. Maybe that's the man you're speaking of. After all, when you work with yeast all the time, the odor gets to stick to your clothes." She wrinkled her nose.

"You don't remember what he looked like?" said Baley.

"No," she replied, with decision.

"All right, then. Look, Jessie, I'm going to take you to your mother's. Bentley will stay with you, and none of you will leave the Section. Ben can stay away from school and I'll arrange to have meals sent in and the corridors around the apartment watched by the police."

"What about you?" quavered Jessie.

"I'll be in no danger."

"But how long?"

"I don't know. Maybe just a day or two." The words sounded hollow even to himself.

They were back in the motorway, Baley and R. Daneel, alone now. Baley's expression was dark with thought.

"It would seem to me," he said, "that we are faced with an organization built up on two levels. First, a ground level with no specific program, designed only to supply mass support for an eventual coup. Secondly, a much smaller elite we must find. The comic-opera groups that Jessie spoke of can be ignored."

"All this," said R. Daneel, "follows, perhaps, if we can take Jessie's story at face value."

"I think," Baley said stiffly, "that Jessie's story can be accepted as completely true."

"So it would seem," said R. Daneel. "There is nothing about her cerebro-impulses that would indicate a pathological addiction to lying."

Baley turned an offended look upon the robot. "I should say not. And there will be no necessity to mention her name in our reports. Do you understand that?"

"If you wish it so, partner Elijah," said R. Daneel calmly, "but our report will then be neither complete nor accurate."

Baley said, "Well, maybe so, but no real harm will be done. She has come to us with whatever information she had and to mention her name will only put her in the police records. I do not want that to happen."

"In that case, certainly not, provided we are certain that nothing more remains to be found out."

"Nothing remains as far as she's concerned. My guarantee."

"Could you then explain why the word, Jezebel, the mere sound of a name, should lead her to abandon previous convictions and assume a new set? The motivation seems obscure."

They were traveling slowly through the curving, empty tunnel.

Baley said, "It is hard to explain. Jezebel is a rare name. It belonged once to a woman of very bad reputation. My wife treasured that fact. It gave her a vicarious feeling of wickedness and compensated for a life that was uniformly proper."

"Why should a law-abiding woman wish to feel wicked?"

Baley almost smiled. "Women are women, Daneel. Anyway, I did a very foolish thing. In a moment of irritation, I insisted that the historic Jezebel was not particularly wicked and was, if anything, a good wife. I've regretted that ever since.

"It turned out," he went on, "that I had made Jessie bitterly unhappy. I had spoiled something for her that couldn't be replaced. I

suppose what followed was her way of revenge. I imagine she wished
to punish me by engaging in activity of which she knew I wouldn't
approve. I don't say the wish was a conscious one."

"Can a wish be anything but conscious? Is that not a contradiction
in terms?"

Baley stared at R. Daneel and despaired of attempting to explain
the unconscious mind. He said, instead, "Besides that, the Bible has
a great influence on human thought and emotion."

"What is the Bible?"

For a moment Baley was surprised, and then was surprised at himself for having felt surprised. The Spacers, he knew, lived under a
thoroughly mechanistic personal philosophy, and R. Daneel could
know only what the Spacers knew; no more.

He said, curtly, "It is the sacred book of about half of Earth's population."

"I do not grasp the meaning here of the adjective."

"I mean that it is highly regarded. Various portions of it, when properly interpreted, contain a code of behavior which many men consider
best suited to the ultimate happiness of mankind."

R. Daneel seemed to consider that. "Is this code incorporated into
your laws?"

"I'm afraid not. The code doesn't lend itself to legal enforcement.
It must be obeyed spontaneously by each individual out of a longing
to do so. It is in a sense higher than any law can be."

"Higher than law? Is that not a contradiction in terms?"

Baley smiled wryly. "Shall I quote a portion of the Bible for you?
Would you be curious to hear it?"

"Please do."

Baley let the car slow to a halt and for a few moments sat with his
eyes closed, remembering. He would have liked to use the sonorous
Middle English of the Medieval Bible, but to R. Daneel, Middle English would be gibberish.

He began, speaking almost casually in the words of the Modern
Revision, as though he were telling a story of contemporary life, instead of dredging a tale out of Man's dimmest past:

" 'Jesus went to the mount of Olives, and at dawn returned to the
temple. All the people came to him, and he sat down and preached
to them. And the scribes and Pharisees brought to him a woman caught
in adultery, and when they had placed her before him, they said to
him, "Master, this woman was caught in adultery, in the very act. Now
Moses, in the law, commanded us to stone such offenders. What do
you say?"

" 'They said this, hoping to trap him, that they might have grounds
for accusations against him. But Jesus stooped down, and with his

finger wrote on the ground, as though he had not heard them. But when they continued asking him, he stood up and said to them, "He that is without sin among you let him first cast a stone at her."

" 'And again he stooped down and wrote on the ground. And those that heard this, being convicted by their own conscience, went away one by one, beginning with the oldest down to the last: Jesus was left alone, with the woman standing before him. When Jesus stood up and saw no one but the woman, he said to her, "Woman, where are your accusers? Has no one condemned you?"

" 'She said, "No one, Lord."

" 'And Jesus said to her, "Nor do I condemn you. Go, and sin no more." ' "

R. Daneel listened attentively. He said, "What is adultery?"

"That doesn't matter. It was a crime and at the time, the accepted punishment was stoning; that is, stones were thrown at the guilty one until she was killed."

"And the woman was guilty?"

"She was."

"Then why was she not stoned?"

"None of the accusers felt he could after Jesus's statement. The story is meant to show that there is something even higher than the justice which you have been filled with. There is a human impulse known as mercy; a human act known as forgiveness."

"I am not acquainted with those words, partner Elijah."

"I know," muttered Baley. "I know."

He started the squad car with a jerk and let it tear forward savagely. He was pressed back against the cushions of the seat.

"Where are we going?" asked R. Daneel.

"To Yeast-town," said Baley, "to get the truth out of Francis Clousarr, conspirator."

"You have a method for doing this, Elijah?"

"Not I, exactly. But you have, Daneel. A simple one."

They sped onward.

# 15.

Arrest of a Conspirator

Baley could sense the vague aroma of Yeast-town growing stronger, more pervasive. He did not find it as unpleasant as some did; Jessie, for instance. He even liked it, rather. It had pleasant connotations.

Every time he smelled raw yeast, the alchemy of sense perception threw him more than three decades into the past. He was a ten-year-old again, visiting Uncle Boris, who was a yeast farmer. Uncle Boris always had a little supply of yeast delectables: small cookies, chocolaty things filled with sweet liquid, hard confections in the shape of cats and dogs. Young as he was, he knew that Uncle Boris shouldn't really have had them to give away and he always ate them very quietly, sitting in a corner with his back to the center of the room. He would eat them quickly for fear of being caught.

They tasted all the better for that.

Poor Uncle Boris! He had an accident and died. They never told him exactly how, and he had cried bitterly because he thought Uncle Boris had been arrested for smuggling yeast out of the plant. He expected to be arrested and executed himself. Years later, he poked carefully through police files and found the truth. Uncle Boris had fallen beneath the treads of a transport. It was a disillusioning ending to a romantic myth.

Yet the myth would always arise in his mind, at least momentarily, at the whiff of raw yeast.

Yeast-town was not the official name of any part of New York City. It could be found in no gazetteer and on no official map. What was called Yeast-town in popular speech was, to the Post Office, merely the boroughs of Newark, New Brunswick, and Trenton. It was a broad strip across what was once Medieval New Jersey, dotted with residential areas, particularly in Newark Center and Trenton Center, but given over mostly to the many-layered farms in which a thousand varieties of yeast grew and multiplied.

One fifth of the City's population worked in the yeast farms; another fifth worked in the subsidiary industries. Beginning with the mountains of wood and coarse cellulose that were dragged into the City from the tangled forests of the Alleghenies, through the vats of acid that hydrolyzed it to glucose, the carloads of niter and phosphate rock that were the most important additives, down to the jars of organics supplied by the chemical laboratories—it all came to one thing, yeast and more yeast.

Without yeast, six of Earth's eight billions would starve in a year.

Baley felt cold at the thought. Three days before the possibility existed as deeply as it did now, but three days before it would never have occurred to him.

They whizzed out of the motorway through an exit on the Newark outskirts. The thinly populated avenues, flanked on either side by the featureless blocks that were the farms, offered little to act as a brake on their speed.

"What time is it, Daneel?" asked Baley.

"Sixteen-oh-five," replied R. Daneel.

"Then he'll be at work, if he's on day shift."

Baley parked the squad car in a delivery recess and froze the controls.

"This is New York then, Elijah?" asked the robot.

"Part of it," said Baley.

They entered into a corridor flanked by a double row of offices. A receptionist at a bend in the corridor was instantly smiles. "Whom do you wish to see?"

Baley opened his wallet. "Police. Is there a Francis Clousarr working for New York Yeast?"

The girl looked perturbed. "I can check."

She connected her switchboard through a line plainly marked "Personnel," and her lips moved slightly, though no sound could be heard.

Baley was no stranger to throat phones that translated the small movements of the larynx into words. He said. "Speak up, please. Let me hear you."

Her words became audible, but consisted only of ". . . he says he's a policeman, sir."

A dark, well-dressed man came out a door. He had a thin mustache and his hairline was beginning to retreat. He smiled whitely, and said, "I'm Prescott of Personnel. What's the trouble, Officer?"

Baley stared at him coldly and Prescott's smile grew strained.

Prescott said, "I just don't want to upset the workers. They're touchy about the police."

Baley said, "Tough, isn't it? Is Clousarr in the building now?"

"Yes, Officer."

"Let's have a rod, then. And if he's gone when we get there, I'll be speaking to you again."

The other's smile was quite dead. He muttered, "I'll get you a rod, Officer."

The guide rod was set for Department CG, Section 2. What that meant in factory terminology, Baley didn't know. He didn't have to. The rod was an inconspicuous thing which could be palmed in the hand. Its tip warmed gently when lined up in the direction for which it was set, cooled quickly when turned away. The warmth increased as the final goal was approached.

To an amateur, the guide rod was almost useless, with its quick little differences of heat content, but few City dwellers were amateurs at this particular game. One of the most popular and perennial of the games of childhood was hide-and-seek through the school-level corridors with the use of toy guide rods. ("Hot or Not, Let Hot-Spot Spot. Hot-Spot Guide Rods Are Keen.")

Baley had found his way through hundreds of massive piles by guide rods, and he could follow the shortest course with one of them in his hands as though it had been mapped out for him.

When he stepped into a large and brilliantly lit room after ten minutes, the guide rod's tip was almost hot.

Baley said to the worker nearest the door, "Francis Clousarr here?"

The worker jerked his head. Baley walked in the indicated direction. The odor of yeast was sharply penetrating, despite the laboring air pumps, whose humming made a steady background noise.

A man had risen at the other end of the room, and was taking off an apron. He was of moderate height, his face deeply lined despite his comparative youth, and his hair just beginning to grizzle. He had large, knobby hands, which he wiped slowly on a celltex towel.

"I'm Francis Clousarr," he said.

Baley looked briefly at R. Daneel. The robot nodded.

"Okay," said Baley. "Anywhere here we can talk?"

"Maybe," said Clousarr slowly, "but it's just about the end of my shift. How about tomorrow?"

"Lot of hours between now and tomorrow. Let's make it now." Baley opened his wallet and palmed it at the yeast farmer.

But Clousarr's hands did not waver in their somber wiping motions. He said, coolly, "I don't know the system in the Police Department, but around here you get tight eating hours with no leeway. I eat at 17:00 to 17:45, or I don't eat."

"It's all right," said Baley. "I'll arrange to have your supper brought to you."

"Well, well," said Clousarr, joylessly. "Just like an aristocrat, or a C-class copper. What's next? Private bath?"

"You just answer questions, Clousarr," said Baley, "and save your big jokes for your girl friend. Where can we talk?"

"If you want to talk, how about the balance room? Suit yourself to that. Me, I've got nothing to say."

Baley thumbed Clousarr into the balance room. It was square and antiseptically white, air-conditioned independently of the larger room (and more efficiently), and with its walls lined with delicate electronic balances, glassed off and manipulable by field forces only. Baley had used cheaper models in his college days. One make, which he recognized, could weigh a mere billion atoms.

Clousarr said, "I don't expect anyone will be in here for a while."

Baley grunted, then turned to Daneel and said, "Would you step out and have a meal sent up here? And if you don't mind, wait outside for it."

He watched R. Daneel leave, then said to Clousarr, "You're a chemist?"

"I'm a zymologist, if you don't mind."

"What's the difference?"

Clousarr looked loftly. "A chemist is a soup-pusher, a stink-operator. A zymologist is a man who helps keep a few billion people alive. I'm a yeast-culture specialist."

"All right," said Baley.

But Clousarr went on, "This laboratory keeps New York Yeast going. There isn't one day, not one damned hour, that we haven't got cultures of every strain of yeast in the company growing in our kettles. We check and adjust the food factor requirements. We make sure it's breeding true. We twist the genetics, start the new strains and weed them out, sort out their properties and mold them again.

"When New York started getting strawberries out of season a couple of years back, those weren't strawberries, fella. Those were a special high-sugar yeast culture with true-bred color and just a dash of flavor additive. It was developed right here in this room.

"Twenty years ago *Saccharomyces olei Benedictae* was just a scrub strain with a lousy taste of tallow and good for nothing. It still tastes of tallow, but its fat content has been pushed up from 15 per cent to 87 per cent. If you used the expressway today, just remember that it's greased strictly with *S. O. Benedictae, Strain AG–7*. Developed right here in this room.

"So don't call me a chemist. I'm a zymologist."

Despite himself, Baley retreated before the fierce pride of the other.

He said abruptly, "Where were you last night between the hours of eighteen and twenty?"

Clousarr shrugged. "Walking. I like to take a little walk after dinner."

"You visit friends? Or a subetheric?"

"No. Just walked."

Baley's lips tightened. A visit to the subetherics would have involved a notch in Clousarr's ration plack. A meeting with a friend would have involved naming a man or woman, and a cross check. "No one saw you, then?"

"Maybe someone did. I don't know. Not that I know of, though."

"What about the night before last?"

"Same thing."

"You have no alibi for either night?"

"If I had done anything criminal, Officer, I'd have one. What do I need an alibi for?"

Baley didn't answer. He consulted his little book. "You were up before the magistrate once. Inciting a riot."

"All right. One of the R things pushed past me and I tripped him up. Is that inciting to riot?"

"The courts thought so. You were convicted and fined."

"That ends it, doesn't it? Or do you want to fine me again?"

"Night before last, there was a near riot at a shoe department in the Bronx. You were seen there."

"By whom?"

Baley said, "It was at mealtime for you here. Did you eat the evening meal night before last?"

Clousarr hesitated, then shook his head. "Upset stomach. Yeast gets you that way sometimes. Even an old-timer."

"Last night, there was a near riot in Williamsburg and you were seen *there*."

"By whom?"

"Do you deny you were present on both occasions?"

"You're not giving me anything to deny. Exactly where did these things happen and who says he saw me?"

Baley stared at the zymologist levelly. "I think you know exactly what I'm talking about. I think you're an important man in an unregistered Medievalist organization."

"I can't stop you from thinking, Officer, but thinking isn't evidence. Maybe you know that." Clousarr was grinning.

"Maybe," said Baley, his long face stony, "I can get a little truth out of you right now."

Baley stepped to the door of the balance room and opened it. He said to R. Daneel, who was waiting stolidly outside, "Has Clousarr's evening meal arrived?"

"It is coming now, Elijah."

"Bring it in, will you, Daneel?"

R. Daneel entered a moment later with a metal compartmented tray.

"Put it down in front of Mr. Clousarr, Daneel," said Baley. He sat down on one of the stools lining the balance wall, legs crossed, one shoe swinging rhythmically. He watched Clousarr edge stiffly away as R. Daneel placed the tray on a stool near the zymologist.

"Mr. Clousarr," said Baley. "I want to introduce you to my partner, Daneel Olivaw."

Daneel put out his hand and said, "How do you do, Francis."

Clousarr said nothing. He made no move to grasp Daneel's extended hand. Daneel maintained his position and Clousarr began to redden.

Baley said softly, "You are being rude, Mr. Clousarr. Are you too proud to shake hands with a policeman?"

Clousarr muttered, "If you don't mind, I'm hungry." He unfolded a pocket fork out of a clasp knife he took from his pocket and sat down, eyes bent on his meal.

Baley said, "Daneel, I think our friend is offended by your cold attitude. You are not angry with him, are you?"

"Not at all, Elijah," said R. Daneel.

"Then show that there are no hard feelings. Put your arm about his shoulder."

"I will be glad to," said R. Daneel, and stepped forward.

Clousarr swung backhanded, wildly, knocking R. Daneel's arm to one side. "Damn it, don't touch me."

He jumped up and away, the tray of food tipping and hitting the floor in a messy clatter.

Baley, hard-eyed, nodded curtly to R. Daneel, who thereupon continued a stolid advance toward the retreating zymologist. Baley stepped in front of the door.

Clousarr yelled, "Keep that thing off me."

"That's no way to speak," said Baley with equanimity. "The man's my partner."

"You mean he's a damn robot," shrieked Clousarr.

"Get away from him, Daneel," said Baley promptly.

R. Daneel stepped back and stood quietly against the door just behind Baley. Clousarr, panting harshly, fists clenched, faced Baley.

Baley said, "All right, smart boy. What makes you think Daneel's a robot?"

"Anyone can tell!"

"We'll leave that to a judge. Meanwhile, I think we want you at headquarters, Clousarr. We'd like to have you explain exactly how you knew Daneel was a robot. And lots more, mister, lots more. Daneel, step outside and get through to the Commissioner. He'll be at his home by now. Tell him to come down to the office. Tell him I have a fellow who can't wait to be questioned."

R. Daneel stepped out.

Baley said, "What makes your wheels go round, Clousarr?"

"I want a lawyer."

"You'll get one. Meanwhile, suppose you tell me what makes you Medievalists tick?"

Clousarr looked away in a determined silence.

Baley said, "Jehoshaphat, man, we know all about you *and* your organization. I'm not bluffing. Just tell me for my own curiosity: What do you Medievalists *want*?"

"Back to the soil," said Clousarr in a stifled voice. "That's simple, isn't it?"

"It's simple to say," said Baley. "But it isn't simple to do. How's the soil going to feed eight billions?"

"Did I say back to the soil overnight? Or in a year? Or in a hundred years? Step by step, mister policeman. It doesn't matter how long it takes, but let's get started out of these caves we live in. Let's get out into the fresh air."

"Have *you* ever been out into the fresh air?"

Clousarr squirmed. "All right, so I'm ruined, too. But the children aren't ruined yet. There are babies being born continuously. Get them out, for God's sake. Let them have space and open air and sun. If we've got to, we'll cut our population little by little, too."

"Backward, in other words, to an impossible past." Baley did not really know why he was arguing, except for the strange fever that was burning in his own veins. "Back to the seed, to the egg, to the womb. Why not move forward? Don't cut Earth's population. Use it for export. Go back to the soil, but go back to the soil of other planets. Colonize!"

Clousarr laughed harshly. "And make more Outer Worlds? More Spacers?"

"We won't. The Outer Worlds were settled by Earthmen who came from a planet that did not have Cities, by Earthmen who were individualists and materialists. Those qualities were carried to an unhealthy extreme. We can now colonize out of a society that has built co-operation, if anything, too far. Now environment and tradition can interact to form a new middle way, distinct from either old Earth or the Outer Worlds. Something newer and better."

He was parroting Dr. Fastolfe, he knew, but it was coming out as though he himself had been thinking of it for years.

Clousarr said, "Nuts! Colonize desert worlds with a world of our own at our fingertips? What fools would try?"

"Many. And they wouldn't be fools. There'd be robots to help."

"No," said Clousarr, fiercely. "Never! No robots!"

"Why not, for the love of Heaven? I don't like them, either, but I'm not going to knife myself for the sake of a prejudice. What are we afraid of in robots? If you want my guess, it's a sense of inferiority. We, all of us, feel inferior to the Spacers and hate it. We've got to feel superior somehow, somewhere, to make up for it, and it kills us that we can't at least feel superior to robots. They seem to be better than us—only they're *not*. That's the damned irony of it."

Baley felt his blood heating as he spoke. "Look at this Daneel I've been with for over two days. He's taller than I am, stronger, handsomer. He looks like a Spacer, in fact. He's got a better memory and knows more facts. He doesn't have to sleep or eat. He's not troubled by sickness or panic or love or guilt.

"But he's a machine. I can do anything I want to him, the way I can to that microbalance right there. If I slam the microbalance, it won't hit me back. Neither will Daneel. I can order him to take a blaster to himself and he'll do it.

"We can't ever build a robot that will be even as good as a human being in anything that counts, let alone better. We can't create a robot with a sense of beauty or a sense of ethics or a sense of religion. There's no way we can raise a positronic brain one inch above the level of perfect materialism.

"We can't, damn it, we can't. Not as long as we don't understand what makes our own brains tick. Not as long as things exist that science can't measure. What *is* beauty, or goodness, or art, or love, or God? We're forever teetering on the brink of the unknowable, and trying to understand what can't be understood. It's what makes us men.

"A robot's brain must be finite or it can't be built. It must be calculated to the final decimal place so that it has an end. Jehoshaphat, what are you afraid of? A robot can look like Daneel, he can look like a god, and be no more human than a lump of wood is. Can't you see that?"

Clousarr had tried to interrupt several times and failed against Baley's furious torrent. Now, when Baley paused in sheer emotional exhaustion, he said weakly, "Copper turned philosopher. What do you know?"

R. Daneel re-entered.

Baley looked at him and frowned, partly with the anger that had not yet left him, partly with new annoyance.

He said, "What kept you?"

R. Daneel said, "I had trouble in reaching Commissioner Enderby, Elijah. It turned out he was still at his office."

Baley looked at his watch. "*Now?* What for?"

"There is a certain confusion at the moment. A corpse has been discovered in the Department."

"*What?* For God's sake, who?"

"The errand boy, R. Sammy."

Baley gagged. He stared at the robot and said in an outraged voice, "I thought you said a corpse."

R. Daneel amended smoothly, "A robot with a completely deactivated brain, if you prefer."

Clousarr laughed suddenly and Baley turned on him, saying huskily, "Nothing out of you! Understand?" Deliberately, he unlimbered his blaster. Clousarr was very silent.

Baley said, "Well, what of it? R. Sammy blew a fuse. So what?"

"Commissioner Enderby was evasive, Elijah, but while he did not say so outright, my impression is that the Commissioner believes R. Sammy to have been deliberately deactivated."

Then, as Baley absorbed that silently, R. Daneel added gravely. "Or, if you prefer the phrase—murdered."

16. Questions Concerning a Motive

Baley replaced his blaster, but kept his hand unobtrusively upon its butt.

He said, "Walk ahead of us, Clousarr, to Seventeenth Street Exit B."

Clousarr said, "I haven't eaten."

"Tough," said Baley, impatiently. "There's your meal on the floor where you dumped it."

"I have a right to eat."

"You'll eat in detention, or you'll miss a meal. You won't starve. Get going."

All three were silent as they threaded the maze of New York Yeast, Clousarr moving stonily in advance, Baley right behind him, and R. Daneel in the rear.

It was after Baley and R. Daneel had checked out at the receptionist's desk, after Clousarr had drawn a leave of absence and requested that a man be sent in to clean up the balance room, after they were out in the open just to one side of the parked squad car, that Clousarr said, "Just a minute."

He hung back, turned toward R. Daneel, and, before Baley could make a move to stop him, stepped forward and swung his open hand full against the robot's cheek.

"What the devil," cried Baley, snatching violently at Clousarr.

Clousarr did not resist the plain-clothes man's grasp. "It's all right. I'll go. I just wanted to see for myself." He was grinning.

R. Daneel, having faded with the slap, but not having escaped it entirely, gazed quietly at Clousarr. There was no reddening of his cheek, no mark of any blow.

He said, "That was a dangerous action, Francis. Had I not moved

backward, you might easily have damaged your hand. As it is, I regret
that I must have caused you pain."

Clousarr laughed.

Baley said, "Get in, Clousarr. You, too, Daneel. Right in the back
seat with him. And make sure he doesn't move. I don't care if it means
breaking his arm. That's an order."

"What about the First Law?" mocked Clousarr.

"I think Daneel is strong enough and fast enough to stop you without hurting you, but it might do you good to have an arm or two
broken at that."

Baley got behind the wheel and the squad car gathered speed. The
empty wind ruffled his hair and Clousarr's, but R. Daneel's remained
smoothly in place.

R. Daneel said quietly to Clousarr, "Do you fear robots for the sake
of your job, Mr. Clousarr?"

Baley could not turn to see Clousarr's expression, but he was certain
it would be a hard and rigid mirror of detestation, that he would be
sitting stiffly apart, as far as he might, from R. Daneel.

Clousarr's voice said, "And my kids' jobs. And everyone's kids."

"Surely adjustments are possible," said the robot. "If your children,
for instance, were to accept training for emigration——"

Clousarr broke in. "You, too? The policeman talked about emigration. He's got good robot training. Maybe he *is* a robot."

Baley growled, "That's enough, you!"

R. Daneel said, evenly, "A training school for emigrants would involve security, guaranteed classification, an assured career. If you are
concerned over your children, that is something to consider."

"I wouldn't take anything from a robot, or a Spacer, or any of your
trained hyenas in the Government."

That was all. The silence of the motorway engulfed them and there
was only the soft whirr of the squad-car motor and the hiss of its
wheels on the pavement.

Back at the Department, Baley signed a detention certificate for Clousarr and left him in appropriate hands. Following that, he and R. Daneel took the motorspiral up the levels to Headquarters.

R. Daneel showed no surprise that they had not taken the elevators,
nor did Baley expect him to. He was becoming used to the robot's
queer mixture of ability and submissiveness and tended to leave him
out of his calculations. The elevator was the logical method of leaping
the vertical gap between Detention and Headquarters. The long moving stairway that was the motorspiral was useful only for short climbs
or drops of two or three levels at most. People of all sorts and varieties
of administrative occupation stepped on and then off in less than a

minute. Only Baley and R. Daneel remained on continuously, moving
upward in a slow and stolid measure.

Baley felt that he needed the time. It was only minutes at best, but
up in Headquarters he would be thrown violently into another phase
of the problem and he wanted a rest. He wanted time to think and
orient himself. Slowly as it moved, the motorspiral went too quickly
to satisfy him.

R. Daneel said, "It seems, then, we will not be questioning Clousarr
just yet."

"He'll keep," said Baley, irritably. "Let's find out what the R. Sammy
thing is all about." He added in a mutter, far more to himself than to
R. Daneel, "It can't be independent; there must be a connection."

R. Daneel said, "It is a pity. Clousarr's cerebric qualities——"

"What about them?"

"They have changed in a strange way. What was it that took place
between the two of you in the balance room while I was not present?"

Baley said, absently, "The only thing I did was to preach at him. I
passed along the gospel according to St. Fastolfe."

"I do not understand you, Elijah."

Baley sighed and said, "Look, I tried to explain that Earth might as
well make use of robots and get its population surplus onto other
planets. I tried to knock some of the Medievalist hogwash out of his
head. God knows why. I've never thought of myself as the missionary
type. Anyway, that's all that happened."

"I see. Well, that makes some sense. Perhaps that can be fitted in.
Tell me, Elijah, what did you tell him about robots?"

"You really want to know? I told him robots were simply machines.
That was the gospel according to St. Gerrigel. There are any number
of gospels, I think."

"Did you by any chance tell him that one could strike a robot without fear of a return blow, much as one could strike any other mechanical object?"

"Except for a punching bag, I suppose. Yes. But what made you
guess that?" Baley looked curiously at the robot.

"It fits the cerebric changes," said R. Daneel, "and it explains his
blow to my face just after we left the factory. He must have been
thinking of what you said, so he simultaneously tested your statement,
worked off his aggressive feelings, and had the pleasure of seeing me
placed in what seemed to him a position of inferiority. In order to be
so motivated and allowing for the delta variations in his quintic . . ."

He paused a long moment and said, "Yes, it is quite interesting, and
now I believe I can form a self-consistent whole of the data."

Headquarters level was approaching. Baley said, "What time is it?"

He thought, pettishly: Nuts, I could look at my watch and take less
time that way.

But he knew why he asked him, nevertheless. The motive was not so different from Clousarr's in punching R. Daneel. To give the robot a trivial order that he must fulfill emphasized his roboticity and, contrariwise, Baley's humanity.

Baley thought. We're all brothers. Under the skin, over it, everywhere. Jehoshaphat!

R. Daneel said, "Twenty-ten."

They stepped off the motorspiral and for a few seconds Baley had the usual queer sensation that went with the necessary adjustment to non-motion after long minutes of steady movement.

He said, "And I haven't eaten. Damn this job, anyway."

Baley saw and heard Commissioner Enderby through the open door of his office. The common room was empty, as though it had been wiped clean, and Enderby's voice rang through it with unusual hollowness. His round face looked bare and weak without its glasses, which he had in his hand, while he mopped his smooth forehead with a flimsy paper napkin.

His eyes caught Baley just as the latter reached the door and his voice rose into a petulant tenor.

"Good God, Baley, where the devil were you?"

Baley shrugged off the remark and said, "What's doing? Where's the night shift?" and then caught sight of the second person in the office with the Commissioner.

He said, blankly, "Dr. Gerrigel!"

The gray-haired roboticist returned the involuntary greeting by nodding briefly. "I'm glad to see you again, Mr. Baley."

The Commissioner readjusted his glasses and stared at Baley through them. "The entire staff is being questioned downstairs. Signing statements. I was going mad trying to find you. It looked queer, your being away."

"*My* being away!" cried Baley, strenuously.

"Anybody's being away. Someone in the Department did it and there's going to be hell to pay for that. What an unholy mess! What an unholy, *rotten* mess!"

He raised his hands as though in expostulation to heaven and as he did so, his eyes fell on R. Daneel.

Baley thought sardonically: First time you've looked Daneel in the face. Take a good look, Julius!

The Commissioner said in a subdued voice, "*He'll* have to sign a statement. Even *I've* had to do it. I!"

Baley said, "Look, Commissioner, what makes you so sure that R. Sammy didn't blow a gasket all by himself? What makes it deliberate destruction?"

The Commissioner sat down heavily. "Ask him," he said, and pointed to Dr. Gerrigel.

Dr. Gerrigel cleared his throat. "I scarcely know how to go about this, Mr. Baley. I take it from your expression that you are surprised to see me."

"Moderately," admitted Baley.

"Well, I was in no real hurry to return to Washington and my visits to New York are few enough to make me wish to linger. And what's more important, I had a growing feeling that it would be criminal for me to leave the City without having made at least one more effort to be allowed to analyze your fascinating robot, whom, by the way," (he looked very eager) "I see you have with you."

Baley stirred restlessly. "That's quite impossible."

The roboticist looked disappointed. "Now, yes. Perhaps later?"

Baley's long face remained woodenly unresponsive.

Dr. Gerrigel went on. "I called you, but you weren't in and no one knew where you could be located. I asked the Commissioner and he asked me to come to headquarters and wait for you."

The Commissioner interposed quickly. "I thought it might be important. I knew you wanted to see the man."

Baley nodded. "Thanks."

Dr. Gerrigel said, "Unfortunately my guide rod was somewhat off, or perhaps in my overanxiety I misjudged its temperature. In either case I took a wrong turning and found myself in a small room——"

The Commissioner interrupted again. "One of the photographic supply rooms, Lije."

"Yes," said Dr. Gerrigel. "And it was the prone figure of what was obviously a robot. It was quite clear to me after brief examination that he was irreversibly deactivated. Dead, you might say. Nor was it very difficult to determine the cause of the deactivation."

"What was it?" asked Baley.

"In the robot's partly clenched right fist," said Dr. Gerrigel, "was a shiny ovoid about two inches long and half an inch wide with a mica window at one end. The fist was in contact with his skull as though the robot's last act had been to touch his head. The thing he was holding was an alpha-sprayer. You know what they are, I suppose?"

Baley nodded. He needed neither dictionary nor handbook to be told what an alpha-sprayer was. He had handled several in his lab courses in physics: a lead-alloy casing with a narrow pit dug into it longitudinally, at the bottom of which was a fragment of a plutonium salt. The pit was capped with a sliver of mica, which was transparent to alpha particles. In that one direction, hard radiation sprayed out.

An alpha-sprayer had many uses, but killing robots was not one of them, not a legal one, at least.

Baley said, "He held it to his head mica first, I take it."

Dr. Gerrigel said, "Yes, and his positronic brain paths were immediately randomized. Instant death, so to speak."

Baley turned to the pale Commissioner. "No mistake? It really *was* an alpha-sprayer?"

The Commissioner nodded, his plump lips thrust out. "Absolutely. The counters could spot it ten feet away. Photographic film in the storeroom was fogged. Cut and dried."

He seemed to brood about it for a moment or two, then said abruptly, "Dr. Gerrigel, I'm afraid you'll have to stay in the City a day or two until we can get your evidence down on wire-film. I'll have you escorted to a room. You don't mind being under guard, I hope?"

Dr. Gerrigel said nervously, "Do you think it's necessary?"

"It's safer."

Dr. Gerrigel, seeming quite abstracted, shook hands all around, even with R. Daneel, and left.

The Commissioner heaved a sigh. "It's one of us. Lije. That's what bothers me. No outsider would come into the Department just to knock off a robot. Plenty of them outside where it's safer. And it had to be somebody who could pick up an alpha-sprayer. They're hard to get hold of."

R. Daneel spoke, his cool, even voice cutting through the agitated words of the Commissioner. He said, "But what is the motive for this murder?"

The Commissioner glanced at R. Daneel with obvious distaste, then looked away. "We're human, too. I suppose policemen can't get to like robots any more than anybody else can. He's gone now and maybe it's a relief to somebody. He used to annoy you considerably, Lije, remember?"

"That is scarcely murder motive," said R. Daneel.

"No," agreed Baley, with decision.

"It isn't murder," said the Commissioner. "It's property damage. Let's keep our legal terms straight. It's just that it was done inside the Department. Anywhere else it would be nothing. Nothing. Now it could be a first-class scandal. Lije!"

"Yes?"

"When did you last see R. Sammy?"

Baley said, "R. Daneel spoke to R. Sammy after lunch. I should judge it was about 13:30. He arranged to have us use your office, Commissioner."

"My office? What for?"

"I wanted to talk over the case with R. Daneel in moderate privacy. You weren't in, so your office was an obvious place."

"I see." The Commissioner looked dubious, but let the matter ride. "You didn't see him yourself?"

"No, but I heard his voice perhaps an hour afterward."

"Are you sure it was he?"

"Perfectly."

"That would be about 14:30?"

"Or a little sooner."

The Commissioner bit his pudgy lower lip thoughtfully. "Well, that settles one thing."

"It does?"

"Yes. The boy, Vincent Barrett, was here today. Did you know that?"

"Yes. But, Commissioner, he wouldn't do anything like this."

The Commissioner lifted his eyes to Baley's face. "Why not? R. Sammy took his job away. I can understand how he feels. There would be a tremendous sense of justice. He would want a certain revenge. Wouldn't you? But the fact is that he left the building at 14:00 and you heard R. Sammy alive at 14:30. Of course, he might have given the alpha-sprayer to R. Sammy before he left with instructions not to use it for an hour, but then where could he have gotten an alpha-sprayer? It doesn't bear thinking of. Let's get back to R. Sammy. When you spoke to him at 14:30, what did he say?"

Baley hesitated a perceptible moment, then said carefully, "I don't remember. We left shortly afterward."

"Where did you go?"

"Yeast-town, eventually. I want to talk about that, by the way."

"Later. Later." The Commissioner rubbed his chin. "Jessie was in today, I noticed. I mean, we were checking on all visitors today and I just happened to see her name."

"She was here," said Baley, coldly.

"What for?"

"Personal family matters."

"She'll have to be questioned as a pure formality."

"I understand police routine, Commissioner. Incidentally, what about the alpha-sprayer itself? Has it been traced?"

"Oh, yes. It came from one of the power plants."

"How do they account for having lost it?"

"They don't. They have no idea. But look, Lije, except for routine statements, this has nothing to do with you. You stick to your case. It's just that . . . Well, you stick to the Spacetown investigation."

Baley said, "May I give my routine statements later, Commissioner? The fact is, I haven't eaten yet."

Commissioner Enderby's glassed eyes turned full on Baley. "By all means get something to eat. But stay inside the Department, will you? Your partner's right, though, Lije"—he seemed to avoid addressing R. Daneel or using his name—"it's the motive we need. The motive."

Baley felt suddenly frozen.

Something outside himself, something completely alien, took up the events of this day and the day before and the day before and juggled them. Once again pieces began to dovetail; a pattern began to form.

He said, "Which power plant did the alpha-sprayer come from, Commissioner?"

"The Williamsburg plant. Why?"

"Nothing. Nothing."

The last word Baley heard the Commissioner mutter as he strode out of the office, with R. Daneel immediately behind him, was, "Motive. Motive."

Baley ate a sparse meal in the small and infrequently used Department lunchroom. He devoured the stuffed tomato on lettuce without being entirely aware of its nature and for a second or so after he had gulped down the last mouthful his fork still slithered aimlessly over the slick cardboard of his plate, searching automatically for something that was no longer there.

He became aware of that and put down his fork with a muffled, "Jehoshaphat!"

He said, "Daneel!"

R. Daneel had been sitting at another table, as though he wished to leave the obviously preoccupied Baley in peace, or as though he required privacy himself. Baley was past caring which.

Daneel stood up, moved to Baley's table, and sat down again. "Yes, partner Elijah?"

Baley did not look at him. "Daneel, I'll need your cooperation."

"In what way?"

"They will question Jessie and myself. That is certain. Let me answer the questions in my own way. Do you understand?"

"I understand what you say, of course. Nevertheless, if I am asked a direct question, how is it possible for me to say anything but what is so?"

"*If* you are asked a direct question, that's another matter. I ask only that you don't volunteer information. You can do that, can't you?"

"I believe so, Elijah, provided it does not appear that I am hurting a human being by remaining silent."

Baley said, grimly, "You will be hurting *me* if you don't. I assure you of that."

"I do not quite understand your point of view, partner Elijah. Surely the matter of R. Sammy cannot concern you."

"No? It all centers about motive, doesn't it? You've questioned the motive. The Commissioner questioned it. I do, for that matter. Why should anyone want to kill R. Sammy? Mind you, it's not just a question of who would want to smash up robots in general. Any Earthman, practically, would want to do that. The question is, who would want to single out R. Sammy. Vincent Barrett might, but the Commissioner said he couldn't get hold of an alpha-sprayer, and he's right. We have to look somewhere else, and it so happens that one other person has a motive. It glares out. It yells. It stinks to top level."

"Who is the person, Elijah?"

And Baley said, softly, "I am, Daneel."

R. Daneel's expressionless face did not change under the impact of the statement. He merely shook his head.

Baley said, "You don't agree. My wife came to the office today. They know that already. The Commissioner is even curious. If I weren't a personal friend, he wouldn't have stopped his questioning so soon. Now they'll find out why. That's certain. She was part of a conspiracy; a foolish and harmless one, but a conspiracy just the same. And a policeman can't afford to have his wife mixed up with anything like that. It would be to my obvious interest to see that the matter was hushed up.

"Well, who knew about it? You and I, of course, and Jessie—*and R. Sammy*. He saw her in a state of panic. When he told her that we had left orders not to be disturbed, she must have lost control. You saw the way she was when she first came in."

R. Daneel said, "It is unlikely that she said anything incriminating to him."

"That may be so. But I'm reconstructing the case the way they will. They'll say she did. There's my motive. I killed him to keep him quiet."

"They will not think so."

"They *will* think so. The murder was arranged deliberately in order to throw suspicion on me. Why use an alpha-sprayer? It's a rather risky way. It's hard to get and it can be traced. I think that those were the very reasons it *was* used. The murderer even ordered R. Sammy to go into the photographic supply room and kill himself there. It seems obvious to me that the reason for that was to have the method of murder unmistakable. Even if everyone was so infantile as not to recognize the alpha-sprayer immediately, someone would be bound to notice fogged photographic film in fairly short order."

"How does all that relate to you, Elijah?"

Baley grinned tightly, his long face completely devoid of humor. "Very neatly. The alpha-sprayer was taken from the Williamsburg power plant. You and I passed through the Williamsburg power plant yesterday. We were seen, and the fact will come out. That gives me opportunity to get the weapon as well as the motive for the crime. And it may turn out that we were the last ones to see or hear R. Sammy alive, except for the real murderer, of course."

"I was with you in the power plant and I can testify that you did not have the opportunity to steal an alpha-sprayer."

"Thanks," said Baley sadly, "but you're a robot and your testimony will be invalid."

"The Commissioner is your friend. He will listen."

"The Commissioner has a job to keep, and he already is a bit uneasy about me. There's only one chance of saving myself from this very nasty situation."

"Yes?"

"I ask myself, *why* am I being framed? Obviously to get rid of me. But why? Again obviously, because I am dangerous to someone. I am doing my best to be dangerous to whoever killed Dr. Sarton in Spacetown. That might mean the Medievalists, of course, or at least, the inner group among them. It would be this inner group that would know I had passed through the power plant; at least one of them might have followed me along the strips that far, even though you thought we had lost them.

"So the chances are that if I find the murderer of Dr. Sarton, I find the man or men who are trying to get me out of the way. If I think it through, if I crack the case, if I can only crack it, I'll be safe. And Jessie. I couldn't stand to have her . . . But I don't have much time." His fist clenched and unclenched spasmodically. "I don't have much time."

Baley looked at R. Daneel's chiseled face with a sudden burning hope. Whatever the creature was, he was strong and faithful, animated by no selfishness. What more could you ask of any friend? Baley needed a friend and he was in no mood to cavil at the fact that a gear replaced a blood vessel in this particular one.

But R. Daneel was shaking his head.

The robot said, "I am sorry, Elijah"—there was no trace of sorrow on his face, of course—"but I anticipated none of this. Perhaps my action was to your harm. I am sorry if the general good requires that."

"What general good?" stammered Baley.

"I have been in communication with Dr. Fastolfe."

"Jehoshaphat! When?"

"While you were eating."

Baley's lips tightened.

"Well?" he managed to say. "What happened?"

"You will have to clear yourself of suspicion of the murder of R. Sammy through some means other than the investigation of the murder of my designer, Dr. Sarton. Our people at Spacetown, as a result of my information, have decided to bring that investigation to an end, as of today, and to begin plans for leaving Spacetown and Earth."

17.

Conclusion of a Project

Baley looked at his watch with something approaching detachment. It was 21:45. In two and a quarter hours it would be midnight. He had been awake since before six and had been under tension now for two and a half days. A vague sense of unreality pervaded everything.

He kept his voice painfully steady as he reached for his pipe and for the little bag that held his precious crumbs of tobacco. He said, "What's it all about, Daneel?"

R. Daneel said, "Do you not understand? Is it not obvious?"

Baley said, patiently, "I do not understand. It is not obvious."

"We are here," said the robot, "and by we, I mean our people at Spacetown, to break the shell surrounding Earth and force its people into new expansion and colonization."

"I know that. Please don't labor the point."

"I must, since it is the essential one. If we were anxious to exact punishment for the murder of Dr. Sarton, it was not that in doing so we expected to bring Dr. Sarton back to life, you understand; it was only that failure to do so would strengthen the position of our home planet politicians who are against the very idea of Spacetown."

"But now," said Baley, with sudden violence, "you say you're getting ready to go home of your own accord. Why? In heaven's name, why? The answer to the Sarton case is close. It *must* be close or they wouldn't be trying so hard to blast me out of the investigation. I have a feeling I have all the facts I need to work out the answer. It must be in here somewhere." He knuckled his temple wildly. "A sentence might bring it out. A word."

He clenched his eyes fiercely shut, as though the quivering opaque jelly of the last sixty hours were indeed on the point of clarifying and becoming transparent. But it did not. It did not.

Baley drew a shuddering breath and felt ashamed. He was making a weak spectacle of himself before a cold and unimpressed machine that could only stare at him silently.

He said harshly, "Well, never mind that. Why are the Spacers breaking off?"

The robot said, "Our project is concluded. We are satisfied that Earth will colonize."

"You've switched to optimism then?" The plain-clothes man drew in his first calming puff of tobacco smoke and felt his grip upon his own emotions grow firmer.

"I have. For a long time now, we of Spacetown have tried to change

149

Earth by changing its economy. We have tried to introduce our own C/Fe culture. Your planetary and various City governments co-operated with us because it was expedient to do so. Still, in twenty-five years, we have failed. The harder we tried, the stronger the opposing party of the Medievalists grew."

"I know all this," said Baley. He thought: No use. He's got to tell this in his own way, like a field recording. He yelled silently at R. Daneel: *Machine!*

R. Daneel went on, "It was Dr. Sarton who first theorized that we must reverse our tactics. We must first find a segment of Earth's population that desired what we desired or could be persuaded to do so. By encouraging and helping them, we could make the movement a native one rather than a foreign one. The difficulty was in finding the native element best suited for our purposes. You, yourself, Elijah, were an interesting experiment."

"I? *I?* What do you mean?" demanded Baley.

"We were glad your Commissioner recommended you. From your psychic profile we judged you to be a useful specimen. Cerebroanalysis, a process I conducted upon you as soon as I met you, confirmed my judgment. You are a practical man, Elijah. You do not moon romantically over Earth's past, despite your healthy interest in it. Nor do you stubbornly embrace the City culture of Earth's present day. We felt that people such as yourself were the ones that could lead Earthmen to the stars once more. It was one reason Dr. Fastolfe was anxious to see you yesterday morning.

"To be sure, your practical nature was embarrassingly intense. You refused to understand that the fanatical service of an ideal, even a mistaken ideal, could make a man do things quite beyond his ordinary capacity, as, for instance, crossing open country at night to destroy someone he considered an archenemy of his cause. We were not overly surprised, therefore, that you were stubborn enough and daring enough to attempt to prove the murder a fraud. In a way, it proved you were the man we wanted for our experiment."

"For God's sake, what experiment?" Baley brought his fist down on the table.

"The experiment of persuading you that colonization was the answer to Earth's problems."

"Well, I was persuaded. I'll grant you that."

"Yes, under the influence of the appropriate drug."

Baley's teeth loosened their grip on his pipestem. He caught the pipe as it fell. Once again, he was seeing that scene in the Spacetown dome. Himself swinging back to awareness after the shock of learning that R. Daneel was a robot after all; R. Daneel's smooth fingers pinching up the flesh of his arm; a hypo-sliver standing out darkly under his skin and then fading away.

He said, chokingly, "What was in the hypo-sliver?"

"Nothing that need alarm you, Elijah. It was a mild drug intended only to make your mind more receptive."

"And so I believed whatever was told me. Is that it?"

"Not quite. You would not believe anything that was foreign to the basic pattern of your thought. In fact, the results of the experiment were disappointing. Dr. Fastolfe had hoped you would become fanatical and single-minded on the subject. Instead you became rather distantly approving, no more. Your practical nature stood in the way of anything further. It made us realize that our only hope was the romantics after all, and the romantics, unfortunately, were all Medievalists, actual or potential."

Baley felt incongruously proud of himself, glad of his stubbornness, and happy that he had disappointed them. Let them experiment with someone else.

He grinned savagely. "And so now you've given up and are going home?"

"Why, this is not it. I said a few moments ago that we were satisfied Earth would colonize. It was you that gave us the answer."

"I gave it to you? How?"

"You spoke to Francis Clousarr of the advantages of colonization. You spoke rather fervently, I judge. At least our experiment on you had that result. And Clousarr's cerebroanalytic properties changed. Very subtly, to be sure, but they changed."

"You mean I convinced him that I was right? I don't believe that."

"No, conviction does not come that easily. But the cerebroanalytic changes demonstrated conclusively that the Medievalist mind is open to that sort of conviction. I experimented further myself. When leaving Yeast-town, guessing what might have happened between you two from his cerebric changes, I made the proposition of a school of emigrants as a way of insuring his children's future. He rejected that, but again his aura changed, and it seemed to me quite obvious that it was the proper method of attack."

R. Daneel paused, then spoke on.

"The thing called Medievalism shows a craving for pioneering. To be sure, the direction in which that craving turns itself is toward Earth itself, which is near and which has the precedent of a great past. But the vision of worlds beyond is a similar something and the romantic can turn to it easily, just as Clousarr felt the attraction as a result of one lecture from you.

"So you see, we of Spacetown had already succeeded without knowing it. We ourselves, rather than anything we tried to introduce, were the unsettling factor. We crystallized the romantic impulses on Earth into Medievalism and induced an organization in them. After all, it is the Medievalist who wishes to break the cake of custom, not the City officials who have most to gain from preserving the *status quo*. If we leave Spacetown now, if we do not irritate the Medievalist by our continued presence until he has committed himself to Earth, and only Earth, past redemption, if we leave behind a few obscure individuals or robots such as myself who, together with sympathetic Earthmen such as yourself, can establish the training schools for emigrants that I spoke of, the Medievalist will eventually turn away from Earth. He will need robots and will either get them from us or build his own. He will develop a C/Fe culture to suit himself."

It was a long speech for R. Daneel. He must have realized that himself, for, after another pause, he said, "I tell you all this to explain why it is necessary to do something that may hurt you."

Baley thought bitterly: A robot must not hurt a human being, unless he can think of a way to prove it is for the human being's ultimate good after all.

Baley said, "Just a minute. Let me introduce a practical note. You'll go back to your worlds and say that an Earthman killed a Spacer and is unpunished. The Outer Worlds will demand an indemnity from Earth, and I warn you, Earth is no longer in a mood to endure such treatment. There will be trouble."

"I am not sure that will not happen, Elijah. The elements on our planets that would be most interested in pressing for an indemnity would be also most interested in forcing an end to Spacetown. We can easily offer the latter as an inducement to abandon the former. It is what we plan to do, anyway. Earth will be left in peace."

And Baley broke out, his voice hoarse with sudden despair, "And where does that leave me? The Commissioner will drop the Sarton investigation at once if Spacetown is willing, but the R. Sammy thing will have to continue, since it points to corruption inside the Department. He'll be in any minute with a ream of evidence against me. I know that. It's been arranged. I'll be declassified, Daneel. There's Jessie to consider. She'll be smeared as a criminal. There's Bentley——"

R. Daneel said, "You must not think, Elijah, that I do not understand the position in which you find yourself. In the service of humanity's good, the minor wrongs must be tolerated. Dr. Sarton has a surviving wife, two children, parents, a sister, many friends. All must grieve at his death and be saddened at the thought that his murderer has not been found and punished."

"Then why not stay and find him?"

"It is no longer necessary."

Baley said, bitterly, "Why not admit that the entire investigation was an excuse to study us under field conditions? You never gave a damn who killed Dr. Sarton."

"We would have liked to know," said R. Daneel, coolly, "but we were never under any delusions as to which was more important, an individual or humanity. To continue the investigation now would involve interfering with a situation which we now find satisfactory. We could not foretell what damage we might do."

"You mean the murderer might turn out to be a prominent Medievalist and right now the Spacers don't want to do anything to antagonize their new friends."

"It is not as I would say it, but there is truth in your words."

"Where's your justice circuit, Daneel? Is this justice?"

"There are degrees of justice, Elijah. When the lesser is incompatible with the greater, the lesser must give way."

It was as though Baley's mind were circling the impregnable logic of R. Daneel's positronic brain, searching for a loophole, a weakness.

He said, "Have you no personal curiosity, Daneel? You've called yourself a detective. Do you know what that implies? Do you understand that an investigation is more than a job of work? It is a challenge. Your mind is pitted against that of the criminal. It is a clash of intellect. Can you abandon the battle and admit defeat?"

"If no worthy end is served by a continuation, certainly."

"Would you feel no loss? No wonder? Would there be no little speck of dissatisfaction? Frustrated curiosity?"

Baley's hopes, not strong in the first place, weakened as he spoke. The word "curiosity," second time repeated, brought back his own remarks to Francis Clousarr four hours before. He had known well enough then the qualities that marked off a man from a machine. Curiosity *had* to be one of them. A six-week-old kitten was curious, but how could there be a curious machine, be it ever so humanoid?

R. Daneel echoed those thoughts by saying, "What do you mean by curiosity?"

Baley put the best face on it. "Curiosity is the name we give to a desire to extend one's knowledge."

"Such a desire exists within me, when the extension of knowledge is necessary for the performance of an assigned task."

"Yes," said Baley, sarcastically, "as when you ask questions about Bentley's contact lenses in order to learn more of Earth's peculiar customs."

"Precisely," said R. Daneel, with no sign of any awareness of sarcasm. "Aimless extension of knowledge, however, which is what I think you really mean by the term of curiosity, is merely inefficiency. I am designed to avoid inefficiency."

It was in that way that the "sentence" he had been waiting for came to Elijah Baley, and the opaque jelly shuddered and settled and changed into luminous transparency.

While R. Daneel spoke, Baley's mouth opened and stayed so.

It could not all have burst full-grown into his mind. Things did not work so. Somewhere, deep inside his unconscious, he had built a case, built it carefully and in detail, but had been brought up short by a single inconsistency. One inconsistency that could be neither jumped over, burrowed under, nor shunted aside. While that inconsistency existed, the case remained buried below his thoughts, beyond the reach of his conscious probing.

But the sentence had come; the inconsistency had vanished; the case was his.

The glare of mental light appeared to have stimulated Baley mightily. At least he suddenly knew what R. Daneel's weakness must be, the weakness of any thinking machine. He thought feverishly, hopefully: The thing *must* be literal-minded.

He said, "Then Project Spacetown is concluded as of today and with it the Sarton investigation. Is that it?"

"That is the decision of our people at Spacetown," agreed R. Daneel, calmly.

"But today is not yet over." Baley looked at his watch. It was 22:30. "There is an hour and a half until midnight."

R. Daneel said nothing. He seemed to consider.

Baley spoke rapidly. "Until midnight, the project continues, then. You are my partner and the investigation continues." He was becoming almost telegraphic in his haste. "Let us go on as before. Let me work. It will do your people no harm. It will do them great good. My word upon it. If, in your judgment, I am doing harm, stop me. It is only an hour and a half I ask."

R. Daneel said, "What you say is correct. Today is not over. I had not thought of that, partner Elijah."

Baley was "partner Elijah" again.

He grinned, and said, "Didn't Dr. Fastolfe mention a film of the scene of the murder when I was in Spacetown?"

"He did," said R. Daneel.

Baley said, "Can you get a copy of the film?"

"Yes, partner Elijah."

"I mean now! Instantly!"

"In ten minutes, if I can use the Department transmitter."

The process took less time than that. Baley stared at the small aluminum block he held in his trembling hands. Within it the subtle forces transmitted from Spacetown had strongly fixed a certain atomic pattern.

And at that moment, Commissioner Julius Enderby stood in the doorway. He saw Baley and a certain anxiety passed from his round face, leaving behind it a look of growing thunder.

He said, uncertainly, "Look here, Lije, you're taking a devil of a time, eating."

"I was bone-tired, Commissioner. Sorry if I've delayed you."

"I wouldn't mind, but . . . You'd better come to my office."

Baley's eyes flicked toward R. Daneel, but met no answering look. Together they moved out of the lunchroom.

Julius Enderby tramped the floor before his desk, up and down, up and down. Baley watched him, himself far from composed. Occasionally, he glanced at his watch.

22:45.

The Commissioner moved his glasses up onto his forehead and rubbed his eyes with thumb and forefinger. He left red splotches in the flesh around them, then restored the glasses to their place, blinking at Baley from behind them.

"Lije," he said suddenly, "when were you last in the Williamsburg power plant?"

Baley said, "Yesterday, after I left the office. I should judge at about eighteen or shortly thereafter."

The Commissioner shook his head. "Why didn't you say so?"

"I was going to. I haven't given an official statement yet."

"What were you doing there?"

"Just passing through on my way to our temporary sleeping quarters."

The Commissioner stopped short, standing before Baley, and said, "That's no good, Lije. No one just passes through a power plant to get somewhere else."

Baley shrugged. There was no point in going through the story of the pursuing Medievalists, of the dash along the strips. Not now.

He said, "If you're trying to hint that I had an opportunity to get the alpha-sprayer that knocked out R. Sammy, I'll remind you that Daneel was with me and will testify that I went right through the plant without stopping and that I had no alpha-sprayer on me when I left."

Slowly, the Commissioner sat down. He did not look in R. Daneel's direction or offer to speak to him. He put his pudgy white hands on the desk before him and regarded them with a look of acute misery on his face.

He said, "Lije, I don't know what to say or what to think. And it's no use having your—your partner as alibi. He can't give evidence."

"I still deny that I took an alpha-sprayer."

The Commissioner's fingers intertwined and writhed. He said, "Lije, why did Jessie come to see you here this afternoon?"

"You asked me that before, Commissioner. Same answer. Family matters."

"I've got information from Francis Clousarr, Lije."

"What kind of information?"

"He claims that a Jezebel Baley is a member of a Medievalist society dedicated to the overthrow of the government by force."

"Are you sure he has the right person? There are many Baleys."

"There aren't many Jezebel Baleys."

"He used her name, did he?"

"He said Jezebel. I heard him, Lije. I'm not giving you a second-hand report."

"All right. Jessie was a member of a harmless lunatic-fringe organization. She never did anything but attend meetings and feel devilish about it."

"It won't look that way to a board of review, Lije."

"You mean I'm going to be suspended and held on suspicion of destroying government property in the form of R. Sammy?"

"I hope not, Lije, but it looks awfully bad. Everyone knows you didn't like R. Sammy. Your wife was seen talking to him this afternoon. She was in tears and some of her words were heard. They were harmless in themselves, but two and two can be added up, Lije. You might feel it was dangerous to leave him in a position to talk. *And* you had an opportunity to obtain the weapon."

Baley interrupted. "If I were wiping out all evidences against Jessie, would I bring in Francis Clousarr? He seems to know a lot more about her than R. Sammy could have. Another thing. I passed through the power plant eighteen hours before R. Sammy spoke to Jessie. Did I know that long in advance that I would have to destroy him and pick up an alpha-sprayer out of clairvoyance."

The Commissioner said, "Those are good points. I'll do my best. I'm sorry about this, Lije."

"Yes? Do you really believe I didn't do it, Commissioner?"

Enderby said slowly, "I don't know what to think, Lije. I'll be frank with you."

"Then I'll tell you what to think. Commissioner, this is all a careful and elaborate frame."

The Commissioner stiffened. "Now, wait, Lije. Don't strike out blindly. You won't get any sympathy with that line of defense. It's been used by too many bad eggs."

"I'm not after sympathy. I'm just telling the truth. I'm being taken out of circulation to prevent me from learning the facts about the Sarton murder. Unfortunately for my framing pal, it's too late for that."

"*What!*"

Baley looked at his watch. It was 23:00.

He said, "I know who is framing me, and I know how Dr. Sarton was killed and by whom, and I have one hour to tell you about it, catch the man, and end the investigation."

 **End of an Investigation**

Commissioner Enderby's eyes narrowed and he glared at Baley. "What are you going to do? You tried something like this in Fastolfe's dome yesterday morning. Not again. Please."

Baley nodded. "I know. I was wrong the first time."

He thought, fiercely: Also the second time. But not now, not *this* time, not . . .

The thought faded out, spluttering like a micropile under a positronic damper.

He said, "Judge for yourself, Commissioner. Grant that the evidence against me has been planted. Go that far with me and see where it takes you. Ask yourself who could have planted that evidence. Obviously only someone who'd known I was in the Williamsburg plant yesterday evening."

"All right. Who would that be?"

Baley said, "I was followed out of the kitchen by a Medievalist group. I lost them, or I thought I did, but obviously at least one of them saw me pass through the plant. My only purpose in doing so, you understand, was to help me lose them."

The Commissioner considered. "Clousarr? Was he with them?"

Baley nodded.

Enderby said, "All right, we'll question him. If he's got anything in him, we'll have it out of him. What more can I do, Lije?"

"Wait, now. Don't quit on me. Do you see my point?"

"Well, let's see if I do?" The Commissioner clasped his hands. "Clousarr saw you go into the Williamsburg power plant, or else someone in his group did and passed the information along to him. He decided to utilize that fact to get you into trouble and off the investigation. Is that what you're saying?"

"It's close to it."

"Good." The Commissioner seemed to warm to the task. "He knew your wife was a member of his organization, naturally, and so he knew you wouldn't face a really close probe into your private life. He thought you would resign rather than fight circumstantial evidence. By the way, Lije, what about a resignation? I mean, if things looked really bad. We could keep things quiet——"

"Not in a million years, Commissioner."

Enderby shrugged. "Well, where was I? Oh, yes, so he got an alpha-sprayer, presumably through a confederate in the plant, and had another confederate arrange the destruction of R. Sammy." His fingers drummed lightly on the desk. "No good, Lije."

"Why not?"

"Too farfetched. Too many confederates. And he has a cast-iron alibi for the night and morning of the Spacetown murder, by the way. We checked that almost right away, though I was the only one who knew the reason for checking that particular time."

Baley said, "I never said it was Clousarr, Commissioner. *You* did. It could be anyone in the Medievalist organization. Clousarr is just the owner of a face that Daneel happened to recognize. I don't even think he's particularly important in the organization. Though there is one queer thing about him."

"What?" asked Enderby, suspiciously.

"He did know Jessie was a member. Does he know every member in the organization, do you suppose?"

"I don't know. He knew about Jessie, anyway. Maybe she was important because she was the wife of a policeman. Maybe he remembered her for that reason."

"You say he came right out and said that Jezebel Baley was a member. Just like that? Jezebel Baley?"

Enderby nodded. "I keep telling you I heard him."

"That's the funny thing, Commissioner. Jessie hasn't used her full first name since before Bentley was born. Not once. I know that for certain. She joined the Medievalists after she dropped her full name. I know that for sure, too. How would Clousarr come to know her as Jezebel, then?"

The Commissioner flushed and said, hastily, "Oh, well, if it comes to that, he probably said Jessie. I just filled it in automatically and gave her full name. In fact, I'm sure of that. He said Jessie."

"Until now you were quite sure he said Jezebel. I asked several times."

The Commissioner's voice rose. "You're not saying I'm a liar, are you?"

"I'm just wondering if Clousarr, perhaps, said nothing at all. I'm wondering if you made that up. You've known Jessie for twenty years, and *you* knew her name was Jezebel."

"You're off your head, man."

"Am I? Where were you after lunch today? You were out of your office for two hours at least."

"Are you questioning *me*?"

"I'll answer for you, too. You were in the Williamsburg power plant."

The Commissioner rose from his seat. His forehead glistened and there were dry, white flecks at the corners of his lips. "What the hell are you trying to say?"

"Weren't you?"

"Baley, you're suspended. Hand me your credentials."

"Not yet. Hear me out."

"I don't intend to. You're guilty. You're guilty as the devil, and what gets me is your cheap attempt to make me, *me*, look as though I were conspiring against you." He lost his voice momentarily in a squeak of indignation. He managed to gasp out, "In fact, you're under arrest."

"No," said Baley, tightly. "Not yet. Commissioner, I've got a blaster on you. It's pointed straight and it's cocked. Don't fool with me, please, because I'm desperate and I *will* have my say. Afterward, you can do what you please."

With widening eyes, Julius Enderby stared at the wicked muzzle in Baley's hands.

He stammered, "Twenty years for this, Baley, in the deepest prison level in the City."

R. Daneel moved suddenly. His hand clamped down on Baley's wrist. He said, quietly, "I cannot permit this, partner Elijah. You must do no harm to the Commissioner."

For the first time since R. Daneel had entered the City, the Commissioner spoke directly to him. "Hold him, you. First Law!"

Baley said quickly, "I have no intention of hurting him, Daneel, if you will keep him from arresting me. You said you would help me clear this up. I have forty-five minutes."

R. Daneel, without releasing Baley's wrist, said, "Commissioner, I believe Elijah should be allowed to speak. I am in communication with Dr. Fastolfe at this moment——"

"How? How?" demanded the Commissioner, wildly.

"I possess a self-contained subetheric unit," said R. Daneel. The Commissioner stared.

"I am in communication with Dr. Fastolfe," the robot went on inexorably, "and it would make a bad impression, Commissioner, if you were to refuse to listen to Elijah. Damaging inferences might be drawn."

The Commissioner fell back in his chair, quite speechless.

Baley said, "I say you were in the Williamsburg power plant today, Commissioner, and you got the alpha-sprayer and gave it to R. Sammy. You deliberately chose the Williamsburg power plant in order to incriminate me. You even seized Dr. Gerrigel's reappearance to invite him down to the Department and give him a deliberately maladjusted guide rod to lead him to the photographic supply room and allow him to find R. Sammy's remains. You counted on him to make a correct diagnosis."

Baley put away his blaster. "If you want to have me arrested now, go ahead, but Spacetown won't take that for an answer."

"Motive," spluttered Enderby breathlessly. His glasses were fogged and he removed them, looking once again curiously vague and helpless in their absence. "What motive could I have for this?"

"You got me into trouble, didn't you? It will put a spoke in the Sarton investigation, won't it? And all that aside, R. Sammy knew too much."

"About *what*, in Heaven's name?"

"About the way in which a Spacer was murdered five and a half days ago. You see, Commissioner, *you* murdered Dr. Sarton of Space-town."

It was R. Daneel who spoke. Enderby could only clutch feverishly at his hair and shake his head.

The robot said, "Partner Elijah, I am afraid that this theory is quite untenable. As you know, it is impossible for Commissioner Enderby to have murdered Dr. Sarton."

"Listen, then. Listen to me. Enderby begged *me* to take the case, not any of the men who overranked me. He did that for several reasons. In the first place, we were college friends and he thought he could count on its never occurring to me that an old buddy and respected superior could be a criminal. He counted on my well-known loyalty, you see. Secondly, he knew Jessie was a member of an underground organization and expected to be able to maneuver me out of the investigation or blackmail me into silence if I got too close to the truth. And he wasn't really worried about that. At the very beginning he did his best to arouse my distrust of you, Daneel, and make certain that the two of us worked at cross-purposes. He knew about my father's declassification. He could guess how I would react. You see, it is an advantage for the murderer to be in charge of the murder investigation."

The Commissioner found his voice. He said, weakly, "How could I know about Jessie?" He turned to the robot. "You! If you're transmitting this to Spacetown, tell them it's a lie! It's all a lie!"

Baley broke in, raising his voice for a moment and then lowering it into a queer sort of tense calm. "Certainly you would know about Jessie. You're a Medievalist, and part of the organization. Your old-fashioned spectacles! Your windows! It's obvious your temperament is turned that way. But there's better evidence than that.

"How did Jessie find out Daneel was a robot? It puzzled me at the time. Of course we know now that she found out through her Medievalist organization, but that just shoves the problem one step backward. How did *they* know? You, Commissioner, dismissed it with a theory that Daneel was recognized as a robot during the incident at the shoe counter. I didn't quite believe that. I couldn't. I took him for human when I first saw him, and there's nothing wrong with my eyes.

"Yesterday, I asked Dr. Gerrigel to come in from Washington. Later

I decided I needed him for several reasons, but, at the time I first called him, my only purpose was to see if he would recognize Daneel for what he was with no prompting on my part.

"Commissioner, he didn't! I introduced him to Daneel, he shook hands with him, we all talked together, and it was only after the subject got around to humanoid robots that he suddenly caught on. Now, that was Dr. Gerrigel, Earth's greatest expert on robots. Do you mean to say a few Medievalist rioters could do better than he under conditions of confusion and tension, and be so certain about it that they would throw their entire organization into activity based on the feeling that Daneel was a robot?

"It's obvious now that the Medievalists must have known Daneel to be a robot to begin with. The incident at the shoe counter was deliberately designed to show Daneel and, through him, Spacetown, the extent of antirobot feeling in the City. It was meant to confuse the issue, to turn suspicion away from individuals and toward the population as a whole.

"Now, if they knew the truth about Daneel to begin with, who told them? I didn't. I once thought it was Daneel himself, but that's out. The only other Earthman who knew about it was you, Commissioner."

Enderby said, with surprising energy, "There could be spies in the Department, too. The Medievalists could have us riddled with them. Your wife was one, and if you don't find it impossible that I should be one, why not others in the Department?"

The corners of Baley's lips pulled back a savage trifle. "Let's not bring up mysterious spies until we see where the straightforward solution leads us. I say you're the obvious informer and the real one.

"It's interesting now that I look back on it, Commissioner, to see how your spirits rose and fell accordingly as I seemed to be far from a solution or possibly close to it. You were nervous to begin with. When I wanted to visit Spacetown yesterday morning and wouldn't tell you the reason, you were practically in a state of collapse. Did you think I had you pinned, Commissioner? That it was a trap to get you into their hands? You hated them, you told me. You were virtually in tears. For a time, I thought that to be caused by the memory of humiliations in Spacetown when you yourself were a suspect, but then Daneel told me that your sensibilities had been carefully regarded. You had never known you were a suspect. Your panic was due to fear, not humiliation.

"Then when I came out with my completely wrong solution, while you listened over trimensional circuit, and you saw how far, how immensely far, from the truth I was, you were confident again. You even argued with me, defended the Spacers. After that, you were quite master of yourself for a while, quite confident. It surprised me at the time that you so easily forgave my false accusations against the Spacers when earlier you had so lectured me on their sensitivity. You enjoyed my mistake.

"Then I put in my call for Dr. Gerrigel and you wanted to know why and I wouldn't tell you. That plunged you into the abyss again because you feared——"

R. Daneel suddenly raised his hand. "Partner Elijah!"

Baley looked at his watch. 23:42! He said, "What is it?"

R. Daneel said, "He might have been disturbed at thinking you would find out his Medievalist connections, if we grant their existence. There is nothing, though, to connect him with the murder. He cannot have had anything to do with that."

Baley said, "You're quite wrong, Daneel. He didn't know what I wanted Dr. Gerrigel for, but it was quite safe to assume that it was in connection with information about robots. This frightened the Commissioner, because a robot had an intimate connection with this greater crime. Isn't that so, Commissioner?"

Enderby shook his head. "When this is over——" he began, but choked into inarticulacy.

"How was the murder committed?" demanded Baley with a suppressed fury. "C/Fe, damn it! C/Fe! I use your own term, Daneel. You're so full of the benefits of a C/Fe culture, yet you don't see where an Earthman might have used it for at least a temporary advantage. Let me sketch it in for you.

"There is no difficulty in the notion of a robot crossing open country. Even at night. Even alone. The Commissioner put a blaster into R. Sammy's hand, told him where to go and when. He himself entered Spacetown through the Personal and was relieved of his own blaster. He received the other from R. Sammy's hands, killed Dr. Sarton, returned the blaster to R. Sammy, who took it back across the fields to New York City. And today he destroyed R. Sammy, whose knowledge had become dangerous.

"That explains everything. The presence of the Commissioner, the absence of a weapon. And it makes it unnecessary to suppose any human New Yorker had crawled a mile under the open sky at night."

But at the end of Baley's recitation, R. Daneel said, "I am sorry, partner Elijah, though happy for the Commissioner, that your story explains nothing. I have told you that the cerebroanalytic properties of the Commissioner are such that it is impossible for him to have committed deliberate murder. I don't know what English word would be applied to the psychological fact: cowardice, conscience, or compassion. I know the dictionary meanings of all these, but I cannot judge. At any rate, the Commissioner did not murder."

"Thank you," muttered Enderby. His voice gained strength and confidence. "I don't know what your motives are, Baley, or why you should try to ruin me this way, but I'll get to the bottom——"

"Wait," said Baley. "I'm not through. I've got this."

He slammed the aluminum cube on Enderby's desk, and tried to feel the confidence he hoped he was radiating. For half an hour now, he had been hiding from himself one little fact: that he did *not* know what the picture showed. He was gambling, but it was all that was left to do.

Enderby shrank away from the small object. "What is it?"

"It isn't a bomb," said Baley, sardonically. "Just an ordinary micro-projector."

"Well? What will that prove?"

"Suppose we see." His fingernail probed at one of the slits in the cube, and a corner of the Commissioner's office blanked out, then lit up in an alien scene in three dimensions.

It reached from floor to ceiling and extended out past the walls of the room. It was awash with a gray light of a sort the City's utilities never provided.

Baley thought, with a pang of mingled distaste and perverse attraction: It must be the dawn they talk about.

The picture scene was of Dr. Sarton's dome. Dr. Sarton's dead body, a horrible, broken remnant, filled its center.

Enderby's eyes bulged as he stared.

Baley said, "I know the Commissioner isn't a killer. I don't need you to tell me that, Daneel. If I could have gotten around that one fact earlier, I would have had the solution earlier. Actually, I didn't see a way out of it until an hour ago when I carelessly said to you that you had once been curious about Bentley's contact lenses.—That was it, Commissioner. It occurred to me then that your nearsightedness and your glasses were the key. They don't have nearsightedness on the Outer Worlds, I suppose, or they might have reached the true solution of the murder almost at once. Commissioner, when did you break your glasses?"

The Commissioner said, "What do you mean?"

Baley said, "When I first saw you about this case, you told me you had broken your glasses in Spacetown. I assumed that you broke them in your agitation on hearing the news of the murder, but *you* never said so, and I had no reason for making that assumption. Actually, if you were entering Spacetown with crime in your mind, you were already sufficiently agitated to drop and break your *glasses* before the murder. Isn't that so, and didn't that, in fact, happen?"

R. Daneel said, "I do not see the point, partner Elijah."

Baley thought: I'm partner Elijah for ten minutes more. Fast! Talk fast! And think fast!

He was manipulating Sarton's dome image as he spoke. Clumsily, he expanded it, his fingernails unsure in the tension that was overwhelming him. Slowly, in jerks, the corpse widened, broadened, heightened, came closer. Baley could almost smell the stench of its scorched flesh. Its head, shoulders, and one upper arm lolled crazily, connected to hips and legs by a blackened remnant of spine from which charred rib stumps jutted.

Baley cast a side glance at the Commissioner. Enderby had closed his eyes. He looked sick. Baley felt sick, too, but he *had* to look. Slowly he circled the trimensional image by means of the transmitter controls, rotating it, bringing the ground about the corpse to view in successive quadrants. His fingernail slipped and the imaged floor tilted suddenly and expanded 'til floor and corpse alike were a hazy mess, beyond the resolving power of the transmitter. He brought the expansion down, let the corpse slide away.

He was still talking. He had to. He couldn't stop till he found what he was looking for. And if he didn't, all his talk might be useless. Worse than useless. His heart was throbbing, and so was his head.

He said, "The Commissioner can't commit deliberate murder. True! *Deliberate*. But any man can kill by accident. The Commissioner didn't enter Spacetown to kill Dr. Sarton. He came in to kill you, Daneel, *you!* Is there anything in his cerebroanalysis that says he is incapable of wrecking a machine? *That's* not murder, merely sabotage.

"He is a Medievalist, an earnest one. He worked with Dr. Sarton and knew the purpose for which you were designed, Daneel. He feared that purpose might be achieved, that Earthmen would eventually be weaned away from Earth. So he decided to destroy you, Daneel. You were the only one of your type manufactured as yet and he had good reason to think that by demonstrating the extent and determination of Medievalism on Earth, he would discourage the Spacers. He knew how strong popular opinion was on the Outer Worlds to end the Spacetown project altogether. Dr. Sarton must have discussed that with him. This, he thought, would be the last nudge in the proper direction.

"I don't say even the thought of killing you, Daneel, was a pleasant one. He would have had R. Sammy do it, I imagine, if you didn't look so human that a primitive robot such as Sammy could not have told the difference, or understood it. First Law would stop him. Or the Commissioner would have had another human do it if he, himself, were not the only one who had ready access to Spacetown at all times.

"Let me reconstruct what the Commissioner's plan might have been. I'm guessing, I admit, but I think I'm close. He made the appointment with Dr. Sarton, but deliberately came early, at dawn, in fact. Dr. Sarton would be sleeping, I imagine, but you, Daneel, would be awake. I assume, by the way, you were living with Dr. Sarton, Daneel."

The robot nodded. "You are quite right, partner Elijah."

Baley said, "Then let me go on. You would come to the come door, Daneel, receive a blaster charge in the chest or head, and be done with. The Commissioner would leave quickly, through the deserted streets of Spacetown's dawn, and back to where R. Sammy waited. He would give him back the blaster, then slowly walk again to Dr. Sarton's dome. If necessary, he would 'discover' the body himself, though he would prefer to have someone else do that. If questioned concerning his early arrival, he could say, I suppose, that he had come to tell Dr. Sarton of rumors of a Medievalist attack on Spacetown, urge him to take secret precautions to avoid open trouble between Spacers and Earthmen. The dead robot would lend point to his words.

"If they asked about the long interval between your entering Spacetown, Commissioner, and your arrival at Dr. Sarton's dome, you could say—let's see—that you saw someone lurking through the streets and headed for open country. You pursued for a while. That would also encourage them along a false path. As for R. Sammy, no one would notice him. A robot among the truck farms outside the City is just another robot.

"How close am I, Commissioner?"

Enderby writhed, "I didn't——"

"No," said Baley, "you didn't kill Daneel. He's here, and in all the time he's been in the City, you haven't been able to look him in the face or address him by name. Look at him now, Commissioner."

Enderby couldn't. He covered his face with shaking hands.

Baley's shaking hands almost dropped his transmitter. He had found it.

The image was now centered upon the main door to Dr. Sarton's dome. The door was open; it had been slid into its wall receptacle along its shining metal runner grooves. Down within them. There! There!

The sparkle was unmistakable.

"I'll tell you what happened," said Baley. "You were at the dome when you dropped your glasses. You must have been nervous and I've seen you when you're nervous. You take them off; you wipe them. You did that then. But your hands were shaking and you dropped them; maybe you stepped on them. Anyway, they were broken, and just then; the door opened and a figure that looked like Daneel faced you.

"You blasted him, scrabbled up the remains of your glasses, and ran. *They* found the body, not you, and when they came to find you, you discovered that it was not Daneel, but the early-rising Dr. Sarton, that you had killed. Dr. Sarton had designed Daneel in his own image, to his great misfortune, and without your glasses in that moment of tension, you could not tell them apart.

"And if you want the tangible proof, it's there!" The image of Sarton's dome quivered and Baley put the transmitter carefully upon the desk, his hand tightly upon it.

Commissioner Enderby's face was distorted with terror and Baley's with tension. R. Daneel seemed indifferent.

Baley's finger was pointing. "That glitter in the grooves of the door. What was it, Daneel?"

"Two small slivers of glass," said the robot, coolly. "It meant nothing to us."

"It will now. They're portions of concave lenses. Measure their optical properties and compare them with those of the glasses Enderby is wearing now. *Don't smash them, Commissioner!*"

He lunged at the Commissioner and wrenched the spectacles from the other's hands. He held them out to R. Daneel, panting, "That's proof enough, I think, that he was at the dome earlier than he was thought to be."

R. Daneel said, "I am quite convinced. I can see now that I was thrown completely off the scent by the Commissioner's cerebroanalysis. I congratulate you, partner Elijah."

Baley's watch said 24:00. A new day was beginning.

Slowly, the Commissioner's head went down on his arms. His words were muffled wails. "It was a mistake. A mistake. I never meant to kill him." Without warning, he slipped from the chair and lay crumpled on the floor.

R. Daneel sprang to him, saying, "You have hurt him, Elijah. That is too bad."

"He isn't dead, is he?"

"No. But unconscious."

"He'll come to. It was too much for him, I suppose. I had to do it, Daneel, I had to. I had no evidence that would stand up in court, only inferences. I had to badger him and badger him and let it out little by little, hoping he would break down. He did, Daneel. You heard him confess, didn't you?"

"Yes."

"Now, then, I promised this would be to the benefit of Spacetown's project, so——Wait, he's coming to."

The Commissioner groaned. His eyes fluttered and opened. He stared speechlessly at the two.

Baley said, "Commissioner, do you hear me?"

The Commissioner nodded listlessly.

"All right. Now, the Spacers have more on their minds than your prosecution. If you co-operate with them——"

"What? What?" There was a dawning flicker of hope in the Commissioner's eyes.

"You must be a big wheel in New York's Medievalist organization, maybe even in the planetary setup. Maneuver them in the direction of the colonization of space. You can see the propaganda line, can't you? We can go back to the soil all right—but on other planets."

"I don't understand," mumbled the Commissioner.

"It's what the Spacers are after. And God help me, it's what I'm after now, too, since a small conversation I had with Dr. Fastolfe. It's what they want more than anything. They risk death continually by coming to Earth and staying here for that purpose. If Dr. Sarton's murder will make it possible for you to swing Medievalism into line for the resumption of Galactic colonization, they'll probably consider it a worthwhile sacrifice. Do you understand now?"

R. Daneel said, "Elijah is quite correct. Help us, Commissioner, and we will forget the past. I am speaking for Dr. Fastolfe and our people generally in this. Of course, if you should agree to help and later betray us, we would always have the fact of your guilt to hold over your head. I hope you understand that, too. It pains me to have to mention that."

"I won't be prosecuted?" asked the Commissioner.

"Not if you help us."

Tears filled his eyes. "I'll do it. It was an accident. Explain that. An accident. I did what I thought right."

Baley said, "If you help us, you *will* be doing right. The colonization of space is the only possible salvation of Earth. You'll realize that if you think about it without prejudice. If you find you cannot, have a short talk with Dr. Fastolfe. And now, you can begin helping by quashing the R. Sammy business. Call it an accident or something. End it!"

Baley got to his feet. "And remember, I'm not the only one who knows the truth, Commissioner. Getting rid of me will ruin you. All Spacetown knows. You see that, don't you?"

R. Daneel said, "It is unnecessary to say more, Elijah. He is sincere and he will help. So much is obvious from his cerebroanalysis."

"All right. Then I'll go home. I want to see Jessie and Bentley and take up a natural existence again. And I want to sleep.—Daneel, will you stay on Earth after the Spacers go?"

R. Daneel said, "I have not been informed. Why do you ask?"

Baley bit his lip, then said, "I didn't think I would ever say anything like this to anyone like you, Daneel, but I trust you. I even—admire you. I'm too old ever to leave Earth myself, but when schools for emigrants are finally established, there's Bentley. If someday, perhaps, Bentley and you, together . . ."

"Perhaps." R. Daneel's face was emotionless.

The robot turned to Julius Enderby, who was watching them with a flaccid face into which a certain vitality was only now beginning to return.

The robot said, "I have been trying, friend Julius, to understand some remarks Elijah made to me earlier. Perhaps I am beginning to, for it suddenly seems to me that the destruction of what should not be, that is, the destruction of what you people call evil, is less just and desirable than the conversion of this evil into what you call good."

He hesitated, then, almost as though he were surprised at his own words, he said, "Go, and sin no more!"

Baley, suddenly smiling, took R. Daneel's elbow, and they walked out the door, arm in arm.

The
Naked
Sun

To Noreen and Nick Falasca, for inviting me,
To Tony Boucher, for introducing me, and
To One Hundred Unusual Hours

Contents

**A Question
Is Asked**

Stubbornly Elijah Baley fought panic.

For two weeks it had been building up. Longer than that, even. It had been building up ever since they had called him to Washington and there calmly told him he was being reassigned.

The call to Washington had been disturbing enough in itself. It came without details, a mere summons; and that made it worse. It included travel slips directing round trip by plane and that made it still worse.

Partly it was the sense of urgency introduced by any order for plane travel. Partly it was the thought of the plane; simply that. Still, that was just the beginning of uneasiness and, as yet, easy to suppress.

After all, Lije Baley had been in a plane four times before. Once he had even crossed the continent. So, while plane travel is never pleasant, it would, at least, not be a complete step into the unknown.

And then, the trip from New York to Washington would take only an hour. The take-off would be from New York Runway Number 2, which, like all official Runways, was decently enclosed, with a lock opening to the unprotected atmosphere only after air speed had been achieved. The arrival would be at Washington Runway Number 5, which was similarly protected.

Furthermore, as Baley well knew, there would be no windows on the plane. There would be good lighting, decent food, all necessary conveniences. The radio-controlled flight would be smooth; there would scarcely be any sensation of motion once the plane was airborne.

He explained all this to himself, and to Jessie, his wife, who had never been air-borne and who approached such matters with terror.

She said, "But I don't *like* you to take a plane, Lije. It isn't natural. Why can't you take the Expressways?"

"Because that would take ten hours"—Baley's long face was set in dour lines—"and because I'm a member of the City Police Force and have to follow the orders of my superiors. At least, I do if I want to keep my C-6 rating."

There was no arguing with that.

Baley took the plane and kept his eyes firmly on the news-strip that unreeled smoothly and continuously from the eye-level dispenser. The City was proud of that service: news, features, humorous articles, educational bits, occasional fiction. Someday the strips would be converted to film, it was said, since enclosing the eyes with a viewer would be an even more efficient way of distracting the passenger from his surroundings.

Baley kept his eyes on the unreeling strip, not only for the sake of distraction, but also because etiquette required it. There were five other passengers on the plane (he could not help noticing that much) and each one of them had his private right to whatever degree of fear and anxiety his nature and upbringing made him feel.

Baley would certainly resent the intrusion of anyone else on his own uneasiness. He wanted no strange eyes on the whiteness of his knuckles where his hands gripped the armrest, or the dampish stain they would leave when he took them away.

He told himself: I'm enclosed. This plane is just a little City.

But he didn't fool himself. There was an inch of steel at his left; he could feel it with his elbow. Past that, nothing——

Well, air! But that was nothing, really.

A thousand miles of it in one direction. A thousand in another. One mile of it, maybe two, straight down.

He almost wished he could see straight down, glimpse the top of the buried Cities he was passing over; New York, Philadelphia, Baltimore, Washington. He imagined the rolling, low-slung cluster-complexes of domes he had never seen but knew to be there. And under them, for a mile underground and dozens of miles in every direction, would be the Cities.

The endless, hiving corridors of the Cities, he thought, alive with people; apartments, community kitchens, factories, Expressways; all comfortable and warm with the evidence of man.

And he himself was isolated in the cold and featureless air in a small bullet of metal, moving through emptiness.

His hands trembled, and he forced his eyes to focus on the strip of paper and read a bit.

It was a short story dealing with Galactic exploration and it was quite obvious that the hero was an Earthman.

Baley muttered in exasperation, then held his breath momentarily in dismay at his boorishness in making a sound.

It was completely ridiculous, though. It was pandering to childishness, this pretense that Earthmen could invade space. Galactic exploration! The Galaxy was closed to Earthmen. It was pre-empted by the Spacers, whose ancestors had been Earthmen centuries before. Those ancestors had reached the Outer Worlds first, found themselves comfortable, and their descendants had lowered the bars to immigration. They had penned in Earth and their Earthman cousins. And Earth's City civilization completed the task, imprisoning Earthmen within the Cities by a wall of fear of open spaces that barred them from the robot-run farming and mining areas of their own planet; from even that.

Baley thought bitterly: Jehoshaphat! If we don't like it, let's do something about it. Let's not just waste time with fairy tales.

But there was nothing to do about it, and he knew it.

Then the plane landed. He and his fellow-passengers emerged and scattered away from one another, never looking.

Baley glanced at his watch and decided there was time for freshening before taking the Expressway to the Justice Department. He was glad there was. The sound and clamor of life, the huge vaulted chamber of the airport with City corridors leading off on numerous levels, everything else he saw and heard, gave him the feeling of being safely and warmly enclosed in the bowels and womb of the City. It washed away anxiety and only a shower was necessary to complete the job.

He needed a transient's permit to make use of one of the community bathrooms, but presentation of his travel orders eliminated any difficulties. There was only the routine stamping, with private-stall privileges (the date carefully marked to prevent abuse) and a slim strip of directions for getting to the assigned spot.

Baley was thankful for the feel of the strips beneath his feet. It was with something amounting to luxury that he felt himself accelerate as he moved from strip to moving strip inward toward the speeding Expressway. He swung himself aboard lightly, taking the seat to which his rating entitled him.

It wasn't a rush hour; seats were available. The bathroom, when he reached it, was not unduly crowded either. The stall assigned to him was in decent order with a launderette that worked well.

With his water ration consumed to good purpose and his clothing freshened he felt ready to tackle the Justice Department. Ironically enough, he even felt cheerful.

Undersecretary Albert Minnim was a small, compact man, ruddy of skin, and graying, with the angles of his body smoothed down and softened. He exuded an air of cleanliness and smelled faintly of tonic. It all spoke of the good things of life that came with the liberal rations obtained by those high in Administration.

Baley felt sallow and rawboned in comparison. He was conscious of his own large hands, deep-set eyes, a general sense of cragginess.

Minnim said cordially, "Sit down, Baley. Do you smoke?"

"Only a pipe, sir," said Baley.

He drew it out as he spoke, and Minnim thrust back a cigar he had half drawn.

Baley was instantly regretful. A cigar was better than nothing and he would have appreciated the gift. Even with the increased tobacco ration that went along with his recent promotion from C-5 to C-6 he wasn't exactly swimming in pipe fixings.

"Please light up, if you care to," said Minnim, and waited with a

kind of paternal patience while Baley measured out a careful quantity
of tobacco and affixed the pipe baffle.

Baley said, his eyes on his pipe, "I have not been told the reason
for my being called to Washington, sir."

"I know that," said Minnim. He smiled. "I can fix that right now.
You are being reassigned temporarily."

"Outside New York City?"

"Quite a distance."

Baley raised his eyebrows and looked thoughtful. "How temporarily,
sir?"

"I'm not sure."

Baley was aware of the advantages and disadvantages of reassignment. As a transient in a City of which he was not a resident, he would
probably live on a scale better than his official rating entitled him to.
On the other hand, it would be very unlikely that Jessie and their son,
Bentley, would be allowed to travel with him. They would be taken
care of, to be sure, there in New York, but Baley was a domesticated
creature and he did not enjoy the thought of separation.

Then, too, a reassignment meant a specific job of work, which was
good, and a responsibility greater than that ordinarily expected of the
individual detective, which could be uncomfortable. Baley had, not
too many months earlier, survived the responsibility of the investigation of the murder of a Spacer just outside New York. He was not
overjoyed at the prospect of another such detail, or anything approaching it.

He said, "Would you tell me where I'm going? The nature of the
reassignment? What it's all about?"

He was trying to weigh the Undersecretary's "Quite a distance" and
make little bets with himself as to his new base of operations. The
"Quite a distance" had sounded emphatic and Baley thought: Cal-
cutta? Sydney?

Then he noticed that Minnim was taking out a cigar after all and
was lighting it carefully.

Baley thought: Jehoshaphat! He's having trouble telling me. He
doesn't want to say.

Minnim withdrew his cigar from between his lips. He watched the
smoke and said, "The Department of Justice is assigning you to temporary duty on Solaria."

For a moment Baley's mind groped for an illusive identification:
Solaria, Asia; Solaria, Australia . . . ?

Then he rose from his seat and said tightly, "You mean, one of the
Outer Worlds?"

Minnim didn't meet Baley's eyes. "That is right."

Baley said, "But that's impossible. They wouldn't allow an Earthman on an Outer World."

"Circumstances do alter cases, Plainclothesman Baley. There has been a murder on Solaria."

Baley's lips quirked into a sort of reflex smile. "That's a little out of our jurisdiction, isn't it?"

"They've requested help."

"From us? Earth?" Baley was torn between confusion and disbelief. For an Outer World to take any attitude other than contempt toward the despised mother planet or, at best, a patronizing social benevolence was unthinkable. To come for help?

"From Earth?" he repeated.

"Unusual," admitted Minnim, "but there it is. They want a Terrestrial detective assigned to the case. It's been handled through diplomatic channels on the highest levels."

Baley sat down again. "Why me? I'm not a young man. I'm forty-three. I've got a wife and child. I couldn't leave Earth."

"That's not our choice, Plainclothesman. You were specifically asked for."

"I?"

"Plainclothesman Elijah Baley, C-6, of the New York City Police Force. They knew what they wanted. Surely you see why."

Baley said stubbornly, "I'm not qualified."

"They think you are. The way you handled the Spacer murder has apparently reached them."

"They must have got it all mixed up. It must have seemed better than it was."

Minnim shrugged. "In any case, they've asked for you and we have agreed to send you. You are reassigned. The papers have all been taken care of and you must go. During your absence, your wife and child will be taken care of at a C-7 level since that will be your temporary rating during your discharge of this assignment." He paused significantly. "Satisfactory completion of the assignment may make the rating permanent."

It was happening too quickly for Baley. None of this could be so. He *couldn't* leave Earth. Didn't they see that?

He heard himself ask in a level voice that sounded unnatural in his own ears, "What kind of a murder? What are the circumstances? Why can't they handle it themselves?"

Minnim rearranged small objects on his desk with carefully kept fingers. He shook his head. "I don't know anything about the murder. I don't know the circumstances."

"Then who does, sir? You don't expect me to go there cold, do you?" And again a despairing inner voice: But I *can't* leave Earth.

"Nobody knows anything about it. Nobody on Earth. The Solarians didn't tell us. That will be your job; to find out what is so important about the murder that they must have an Earthman to solve it. Or, rather, that will be *part* of your job."

Baley was desperate enough to say, "What if I refuse?" He knew the answer, of course. He knew exactly what declassification would mean to himself and, more than that, to his family.

Minnim said nothing about declassification. He said softly, "You can't refuse, Plainclothesman. You have a job to do."

"For Solaria? The hell with them."

"For *us*, Baley. For us." Minnim paused. Then he went on, "You know the position of Earth with respect to the Spacers. I don't have to go into that."

Baley knew the situation and so did every man on Earth. The fifty Outer Worlds, with a far smaller population, in combination, than that of Earth alone, nevertheless maintained a military potential perhaps a hundred times greater. With their underpopulated worlds resting on a positronic robot economy, their energy production per human was thousands of times that of Earth. And it was the amount of energy a single human could produce that dictated military potential, standard of living, happiness, and all besides.

Minnim said, "One of the factors that conspires to keep us in that position is ignorance. Just that. Ignorance. The Spacers know all about us. They send missions enough to Earth, heaven knows. We know nothing about them except what they tell us. No man on Earth has ever as much as set foot on an Outer World. *You* will, though."

Baley began, "I can't . . . ."

But Minnim repeated, "You *will*. Your position will be unique. You will be on Solaria on their invitation, doing a job to which they will assign you. When you return, you will have information useful to Earth."

Baley watched the Undersecretary through somber eyes. "You mean I'm to spy for Earth."

"No question of spying. You need do nothing they don't ask you to do. Just keep your eyes and mind open. Observe! There will be specialists on Earth when you return to analyze and interpret your observations."

Baley said, "I take it there's a crisis, sir."

"Why do you say that?"

"Sending an Earthman to an Outer World is risky. The Spacers hate us. With the best will in the world and even though I'm there on invitation, I could cause an interstellar incident. The Terrestrial Government could easily avoid sending me if they chose. They could say I was ill. The Spacers are pathologically afraid of disease. They wouldn't want me for any reason if they thought I were ill."

"Do you suggest," said Minnim, "we try that trick?"

"No. If the government had no other motive for sending me, they would think of that or something better without my help. So it follows that it is the question of spying that is the real essential. And if that is so, there must be more to it than just a see-what-you-can-see to justify the risk."

Baley half expected an explosion and would have half welcomed one as a relief of pressure, but Minnim only smiled frostily and said, "You can see past the nonessentials, it seems. But then, I expected no less."

The Undersecretary leaned across his desk toward Baley. "Here is certain information which you will discuss with no one, not even with other government officials. Our sociologists have been coming to certain conclusions concerning the present Galactic situation. Fifty Outer Worlds, underpopulated, roboticized, powerful, with people that are healthy and long-lived. We ourselves, crowded, technologically underdeveloped, short-lived, under their domination. It is unstable."

"Everything is in the long run."

"This is unstable in the short run. A hundred years is the most we're allowed. The situation will last our time, to be sure, but we have children. Eventually we will become too great a danger to the Outer Worlds to be allowed to survive. There are eight billions on Earth who hate the Spacers."

Baley said, "The Spacers exclude us from the Galaxy, handle our trade to their own profit, dictate to our government, and treat us with contempt. What do they expect? Gratitude?"

"True, and yet the pattern is fixed. Revolt, suppression, revolt, suppression—and within a century Earth will be virtually wiped out as a populated world. So the sociologists say."

Baley stirred uneasily. One didn't question sociologists and their computers. "But what do you expect me to accomplish if all this is so?"

"Bring us information. The big flaw in sociological forecast is our lack of data concerning the Spacers. We've had to make assumptions on the basis of the few Spacers they sent out here. We've had to rely on what they choose to tell us of themselves, so it follows we know their strengths and only their strengths. Damn it, they have their robots and their low numbers and their long lives. But do they have weaknesses? Is there some factor or factors which, if we but knew, would alter the sociologic inevitability of destruction; something that could guide our actions and better the chance of Earth's survival."

"Hadn't you better send a sociologist, sir?"

Minnim shook his head. "If we could send whom we pleased, we would have sent someone out ten years ago, when these conclusions were first being arrived at. This is our first excuse to send someone and they ask for a detective and that suits us. A detective is a sociologist, too; a rule-of-thumb, practicing sociologist, or he wouldn't be a good detective. Your record proves you a good one."

"Thank you, sir," said Baley mechanically. "And if I get into trouble?"

Minnim shrugged. "That's the risk of a policeman's job." He dismissed the point with a wave of his hand and added, "In any case, you must go. Your time of departure is set. The ship that will take you is waiting."

Baley stiffened. "Waiting? When do I leave?"

"In two days."

"I've got to get back to New York then. My wife——"

"We will see your wife. She can't know the nature of your job, you know. She will be told not to expect to hear from you."

"But this is inhuman. I must see her. I may never see her again."

Minnim said, "What I say now may sound even more inhuman, but isn't it true there is never a day you set about your duties on which you cannot tell yourself she may never see you again? Plainclothesman Baley, we must all do our duty."

Baley's pipe had been out for fifteen minutes. He had never noticed it.

No one had more to tell him. No one knew anything about the murder. Official after official simply hurried him on to the moment when he stood at the base of a spaceship, all unbelieving still.

It was like a gigantic cannon aimed at the heavens, and Baley shivered spasmodically in the raw, open air. The night closed in (for which Baley was thankful) like dark black walls melting into a black ceiling overhead. It was cloudy, and though he had been to Planetaria, a bright star, stabbing through a rift in the cloud, startled him when it caught his eyes.

A little spark, far, far away. He stared curiously, almost unafraid of it. It looked quite close, quite insignificant, and yet around things like that circled planets of which the inhabitants were lords of the Galaxy. The sun was a thing like that, he thought, except much closer, shining now on the other side of the Earth.

He thought of the Earth suddenly as a ball of stone with a film of moisture and gas, exposed to emptiness on every side, with its Cities barely dug into the outer rim, clinging precariously between rock and air. His skin crawled!

The ship was a Spacer vessel, of course. Interstellar trade was entirely in Spacer hands. He was alone now, just outside the rim of the City. He had been bathed and scraped and sterilized until he was considered safe, by Spacer standards, to board the ship. Even so, they

sent only a robot out to meet him, bearing as he did a hundred varieties of disease germs from the sweltering City to which he himself
was resistant but to which the eugenically hothoused Spacers were
not.

The robot bulked dimly in the night, its eyes a dull red glow.

"Plainclothesman Elijah Baley?"

"That's right," said Baley crisply, the hair on the nape of his neck
stirring a bit. He was enough of an Earthman to get angry goose flesh
at the sight of a robot doing a man's job. There had been R. Daneel
Olivaw, who had partnered with him in the Spacer murder affair, but
that had been different. Daneel had been——

"You will follow me, please," said the robot, and a white light flooded
a path toward the ship.

Baley followed. Up the ladder and into the ship he went, along
corridors, and into a room.

The robot said, "This will be your room, Plainclothesman Baley. It
is requested that you remain in it for the duration of the trip."

Baley thought: Sure, seal me off. Keep me safe. Insulated.

The corridors along which he had traveled had been empty. Robots
were probably disinfecting them now. The robot facing him would
probably step through a germicidal bath when it left.

The robot said, "There is a water supply and plumbing. Food
will be supplied. You will have viewing matter. The ports are controlled from this panel. They are closed now but if you wish to view
space——"

Baley said with some agitation, "That's all right, boy. Leave the
ports closed."

He used the "boy" address that Earthmen always used for robots,
but the robot showed no adverse response. It couldn't, of course. Its
responses were limited and controlled by the Laws of Robotics.

The robot bent its large metal body in the travesty of a respectful
bow and left.

Baley was alone in his room and could take stock. It was better than
the plane, at least. He could see the plane from end to end. He could
see its limits. The spaceship was large. It had corridors, levels, rooms.
It was a small City in itself. Baley could almost breathe freely.

Then lights flashed and a robot's metallic voice sounded over the
communo and gave him specific instructions for guarding himself
against take-off acceleration.

There was the push backward against webbing and a yielding hydraulic system, a distant rumble of force-jets heated to fury by the
proton micro-pile. There was the hiss of tearing atmosphere, growing
thinner and high-pitched and fading into nothingness after an hour.

They were in space.

·   ·   ·

It was as though all sensation had numbed, as though nothing were real. He told himself that each second found him thousands of miles farther from the Cities, from Jessie, but it didn't register.

On the second day (the third?—there was no way of telling time except by the intervals of eating and sleeping) there was a queer momentary sensation of being turned inside out. It lasted an instant and Baley knew it was a Jump, that oddly incomprehensible, almost mystical, momentary transition through hyperspace that transferred a ship and all it contained from one point in space to another, light-years away. Another lapse of time and another Jump, still another lapse, still another Jump.

Baley told himself now that he was light-years away, tens of light-years, hundreds, thousands.

He didn't know how many. No one on Earth as much as knew Solaria's location in space. He would bet on that. They were ignorant, every one of them.

He felt terribly alone.

There was the feel of deceleration and the robot entered. Its somber, ruddy eyes took in the details of Baley's harness. Efficiently it tightened a wing nut; quickly it surveyed the details of the hydraulic system.

It said, "We will be landing in three hours. You will remain, if you please, in this room. A man will come to escort you out and to take you to your place of residence."

"Wait," said Baley tensely. Strapped in as he was, he felt helpless. "When we land, what time of day will it be?"

The robot said at once, "By Galactic Standard Time, it will be——"

"Local time, boy. Local time! Jehoshaphat!"

The robot continued smoothly, "The day on Solaria is twenty-eight point thirty-five Standard hours in length. The Solarian hour is divided into ten decads, each of which is divided into a hundred centads. We are scheduled to arrive at an airport at which the day will be at the twentieth centad of the fifth decad."

Baley hated that robot. He hated it for its obtuseness in not understanding; for the way it was making him ask the question directly and exposing his own weakness.

He had to. He said flatly, "Will it be daytime?"

And after all that the robot answered, "Yes, sir," and left.

It would be day! He would have to step out onto the unprotected surface of a planet in daytime.

He was not quite sure how it would be. He had seen glimpses of planetary surfaces from certain points within the City; he had even been out upon it for moments. Always, though, he had been surrounded by walls or within reach of one. There was always safety at hand.

Where would there be safety now? Not even the false walls of darkness.

And because he would not display weakness before the Spacers— he'd be damned if he would—he stiffened his body against the webbing that held him safe against the forces of deceleration, closed his eyes, and stubbornly fought panic.

2. A Friend Is Encountered

Baley was losing his fight. Reason alone was not enough.

Baley told himself over and over: Men live in the open all their lives. The Spacers do so now. Our ancestors on Earth did it in the past. There is no real harm in wall-lessness. It is only my mind that tells me differently, and it is wrong.

But all that did not help. Something above and beyond reason cried out for walls and would have none of space.

As time passed, he thought he would not succeed. He would be cowering at the end, trembling and pitiful. The Spacer they would send for him (with filters in his nose to keep out germs, and gloves on his hands to prevent contact) would not even honestly despise him. The Spacer would feel only disgust.

Baley held on grimly.

When the ship stopped and the deceleration harness automatically uncoupled, while the hydraulic system retracted into the wall, Baley remained in his seat. He was afraid, and determined not to show it.

He looked away at the first quiet sound of the door of his room opening. There was the eye-corner flash of a tall, bronze-haired figure entering; a Spacer, one of those proud descendants of Earth who had disowned their heritage.

The Spacer spoke. "Partner Elijah!"

Baley's head turned toward the speaker with a jerk. His eyes rounded and he rose almost without volition.

He stared at the face; at the broad, high cheekbones, the absolute calm of the facial lines, the symmetry of the body, most of all at that level look out of nerveless blue eyes.

"D-daneel."

The Spacer said, "It is pleasant that you remember me, Partner Elijah."

"Remember you!" Baley felt relief wash over him. This being was a bit of Earth, a friend, a comfort, a savior. He had an almost unbearable desire to rush to the Spacer and embrace him, to hug him wildly, and laugh and pound his back and do all the foolish things old friends did when meeting once again after a separation.

But he didn't. He couldn't. He could only step forward, and hold out his hand and say, "I'm not likely to forget you, Daneel."

"That is pleasant," said Daneel, nodding gravely. "As you are well aware, it is quite impossible for me, while in working order, to forget you. It is well that I see you again."

Daneel took Baley's hand and pressed it with firm coolness, his fingers closing to a comfortable but not painful pressure and then releasing it.

Baley hoped earnestly that the creature's unreadable eyes could not penetrate Baley's mind and see that wild moment, just past and not yet entirely subsided, when all of Baley had concentrated into a feeling of an intense friendship that was almost love.

After all, one could not love as a friend this Daneel Olivaw, who was not a man at all, but only a robot.

The robot that looked so like a man said, "I have asked that a robot-driven ground-transport vessel be connected to this ship by air-tube——"

Baley frowned. "An air-tube?"

"Yes. It is a common technique, frequently used in space, in order that personnel and matériel be transferred from one vessel to another without the necessity of special equipment against vacuum. It would seem then that you are not acquainted with the technique."

"No," said Baley, "but I get the picture."

"It is, of course, rather complicated to arrange such a device between spaceship and ground vehicle, but I have requested that it be done. Fortunately, the mission on which you and I are engaged is one of high priority. Difficulties are smoothed out quickly."

"Are you assigned to the murder case too?"

"Have you not been informed of that? I regret not having told you at once." There was, of course, no sign of regret on the robot's perfect face. "It was Dr. Han Fastolfe, whom you met on Earth during our previous partnership and whom I hope you remember, who first suggested you as an appropriate investigator in this case. He made it a condition that I be assigned to work with you once more."

Baley managed a smile. Dr. Fastolfe was a native of Aurora and Aurora was the strongest of the Outer Worlds. Apparently the advice of an Auroran bore weight.

Baley said, "A team that works shouldn't be broken up, eh?" (The first exhilaration of Daneel's appearance was fading and the compression about Baley's chest was returning.)

"I do not know if that precise thought was in his mind, Partner Elijah. From the nature of his orders to me, I should think that he was interested in having assigned to work with you one who would have experience with your world and would know of your consequent peculiarities."

"Peculiarities!" Baley frowned and felt offended. It was not a term he liked in connection with himself.

"So that I could arrange the air-tube, for example. I am well aware of your aversion to open spaces as a result of your upbringing in the Cities of Earth."

Perhaps it was the effect of being called "peculiar," the feeling that he had to counterattack or lose caste to a machine, that drove Baley to change the subject sharply. Perhaps it was just that life-long training prevented him from leaving any logical contradiction undisturbed.

He said, "There was a robot in charge of my welfare on board this ship; a robot" (a touch of malice intruded itself here) "that looks like a robot. Do you know it?"

"I spoke to it before coming on board."

"What's its designation? How do I make contact with it?"

"It is RX-2475. It is customary on Solaria to use only serial numbers for robots." Daneel's calm eyes swept the control panel near the door. "This contact will signal it."

Baley looked at the control panel himself and, since the contact to which Daneel pointed was labeled RX, its identification seemed quite unmysterious.

Baley put his finger over it and in less than a minute, the robot, the one that looked like a robot, entered.

Baley said, "You are RX-2475."

"Yes, sir."

"You told me earlier that someone would arrive to escort me off the ship. Did you mean him?" Baley pointed at Daneel.

The eyes of the two robots met. RX-2475 said, "His papers identify him as the one who was to meet you."

"Were you told in advance anything about him other than his papers? Was he described to you?"

"No, sir. I was given his name, however."

"Who gave you the information?"

"The captain of the ship, sir."

"Who is a Solarian?"

"Yes, sir."

Baley licked his lips. The next question would be decisive.

He said, "What were you told would be the name of the one you were expecting?"

RX-2475 said, "Daneel Olivaw, sir."

"Good boy! You may leave now."

There was the robotic bow and then the sharp about-face. RX-2475 left.

Baley turned to his partner and said thoughtfully, "You are not telling me all the truth, Daneel."

"In what way, Partner Elijah?" asked Daneel.

"While I was talking to you earlier, I recalled an odd point. RX-2475, when it told me I would have an escort said a *man* would come for me. I remember that quite well."

Daneel listened quietly and said nothing.

Baley went on. "I thought the robot might have made a mistake. I thought also that perhaps a man had indeed been assigned to meet me and had later been replaced by you, RX-2475 not being informed of the change. But you heard me check that. Your papers were described to it and it was given your name. But it was not quite given your name at that, was it, Daneel?"

"Indeed, it was not given my entire name," agreed Daneel.

"Your name is not Daneel Olivaw, but R. Daneel Olivaw, isn't it? Or, in full, Robot Daneel Olivaw."

"You are quite correct, Partner Elijah."

"From which it all follows that RX-2475 was never informed that you are a robot. It was allowed to think of you as a man. With your manlike appearance, such a masquerade is possible."

"I have no quarrel with your reasoning."

"Then let's proceed." Baley was feeling the germs of a kind of savage delight. He was on the track of something. It couldn't be anything much, but this was the kind of tracking he could do well. It was something he could do well enough to be called half across space to do. He said, "Now why should anyone want to deceive a miserable robot? It doesn't matter to it whether you are man or robot. It follows orders in either case. A reasonable conclusion then is that the Solarian captain who informed the robot and the Solarian officials who informed the Captain did not themselves know you were a robot. As I say, that is one reasonable conclusion, but perhaps not the only one. Is this one true?"

"I believe it is."

"All right, then. Good guess. Now why? Dr. Han Fastolfe, in recommending you as my partner allows the Solarians to think you are a human. Isn't that a dangerous thing? The Solarians, if they find out, may be quite angry. Why was it done?"

The humanoid robot said, "It was explained to me thus, Partner Elijah. Your association with a human of the Outer Worlds would raise your status in the eyes of the Solarians. Your association with a robot would lower it. Since I was familiar with your ways and could work with you easily, it was thought reasonable to allow the Solarians to accept me as a man without actually deceiving them by a positive statement to that effect."

Baley did not believe it. It seemed like the kind of careful consideration for an Earthman's feelings that did not come naturally to a Spacer, not even to as enlightened a one as Fastolfe.

He considered an alternative and said, "Are the Solarians well known among the Outer Worlds for the production of robots?"

"I am glad," said Daneel, "that you have been briefed concerning the inner economy of Solaria."

"Not a word," said Baley. "I can guess the spelling of the word Solaria and there my knowledge stops."

"Then I do not see, Partner Elijah, what it was that impelled you to ask that question, but it is a most pertinent one. You have hit the mark. My mind-store of information includes the fact that, of the fifty Outer Worlds, Solaria is by far the best known for the variety and excellence of robot models it turns out. It exports specialized models to all the other Outer Worlds."

Baley nodded in grim satisfaction. Naturally Daneel did not follow an intuitive mental leap that used human weakness as a starting point. Nor did Baley feel impelled to explain the reasoning. If Solaria turned out to be a world expert in robotics, Dr. Han Fastolfe and his associates might have purely personal and very human motives for demonstrating their own prize robot. It would have nothing at all to do with an Earthman's safety or feelings.

They would be asserting their own superiority by allowing the expert Solarians to be fooled into accepting a robot of Auroran handiwork as a fellow-man.

Baley felt much better. Strange that all the thought, all the intellectual powers he could muster, could not succeed in lifting him out of panic; and yet a sop to his own vainglory succeeded at once.

The recognition of the vainglory of the Spacers helped too.

He thought: Jehoshaphat, we're all human; even the Spacers.

Aloud he said, almost flippantly, "How long do we have to wait for the ground-car? I'm ready."

The air-tube gave signs of not being well adapted to its present use. Man and humanoid stepped out of the spaceship erect, moving along flexible mesh that bent and swayed under their weight. (In space, Baley imagined hazily, men transferring weightlessly from ship to ship might easily skim along the length of the tube, impelled by an initial Jump.)

Toward the other end the tube narrowed clumsily, its meshing bunching as though some giant hand had constricted it. Daneel, carrying the flashlight, got down on all fours and so did Baley. They traveled the last twenty feet in that fashion, moving at last into what was obviously a ground-car.

Daneel closed the door through which they had entered, sliding it shut carefully. There was a heavy, clicking noise that might have been the detachment of the air-tube.

Baley looked about curiously. There was nothing too exotic about the ground-car. There were two seats in tandem, each of which could hold three. There were doors at each end of each seat. The glossy sections that might ordinarily have been windows were black and opaque, as a result, undoubtedly, of appropriate polarization. Baley was acquainted with that.

The interior of the car was lit by two round spots of yellow illumination in the ceiling and, in short, the only thing Baley felt to be strange was the transmitter set into the partition immediately before the front seat and, of course, the added fact that there were no visible controls.

Baley said, "I suppose the driver is on the other side of this partition."

Daneel said, "Exactly so, Partner Elijah. And we can give our orders in this fashion." He leaned forward slightly and flicked a toggle switch that set a spot of red light to flickering. He said quietly, "You may start now. We are ready."

There was a muted whir that faded almost at once, a very slight, very transitory pressing against the back of the seat, and then nothing.

Baley said in surprise, "Are we moving?"

Daneel said, "We are. The car does not move on wheels but glides along a diamagnetic force-field. Except for acceleration and deceleration, you will feel nothing."

"What about curves?"

"The car will bank automatically to compensate. Its level is maintained when traveling up- or downhill."

"The controls must be complicated," said Baley dryly.

"Quite automatic. The driver of the vehicle is a robot."

"Umm." Baley had about all he wanted on the ground-car. He said, "How long will this take?"

"About an hour. Air travel would have been speedier, but I was concerned to keep you enclosed and the aircraft models available on Solaria do not lend themselves to complete enclosure as does a ground-car such as that in which we are now riding."

Baley felt annoyed at the other's "concern." He felt like a baby in the charge of its nurse. He felt almost as annoyed, oddly enough, at Daneel's sentences. It seemed to him that such needlessly formal sentence structure might easily betray the robotic nature of the creature.

For a moment Baley stared curiously at R. Daneel Olivaw. The robot, looking straight ahead, was motionless and unself-conscious under the other's gaze.

Daneel's skin texture was perfect, the individual hair on head and body had been lovingly and intricately manufactured and placed. The muscle movement under the skin was most realistic. No pains, however extravagant, had been spared. Yet Baley knew, from personal knowledge, that limbs and chest could be split open along invisible seams so that repairs might be made. He knew there was metal and silicone under that realistic skin. He knew a positronic brain, most advanced but only positronic, nestled in the hollow of the skull. He knew that Daneel's "thoughts" were only short-lived positronic currents flowing along paths rigidly designed and foreordained by the manufacturer.

But what were the signs that would give that away to the expert eye that had no foreknowledge? The trifling unnaturalness of Daneel's manner of speech? The unemotional gravity that rested so steadily upon him? The very perfection of his humanity?

But he was wasting time. Baley said, "Let's get on with it, Daneel. I suppose that before arriving here, you were briefed on matters Solarian?"

"I was, Partner Elijah."

"Good. That's more than they did for me. How large is the world?"

"Its diameter is 9500 miles. It is the outermost of three planets and the only inhabited one. In climate and atmosphere it resembles Earth; its percentage of fertile land is higher; its useful mineral content lower, but of course less exploited. The world is self-supporting and can, with the aid of its robot exports, maintain a high standard of living."

Baley said, "What's the population?"

"Twenty thousand people, Partner Elijah."

Baley accepted that for a moment, then he said mildly, "You mean twenty million, don't you?" His scant knowledge of the Outer Worlds was enough to tell him that, although the worlds were underpopulated by Earthly standards, the individual populations *were* in the millions.

"Twenty thousand people, Partner Elijah," said the robot again.

"You mean the planet has just been settled?"

"Not at all. It has been independent for nearly two centuries, and it was settled for a century or more before that. The population is deliberately maintained at twenty thousand, that being considered optimum by the Solarians themselves."

"How much of the planet do they occupy?"

"All the fertile portions."

"Which is, in square miles?"

"Thirty million square miles, including marginal areas."

"For twenty thousand people?"

"There are also some two hundred million working positronic robots, Partner Elijah."

"Jehoshaphat! That's—that's ten thousand robots per human."

"It is by far the highest such ratio among the Outer Worlds, Partner Elijah. The next highest, on Aurora, is only fifty to one."

"What can they use so many robots for? What do they want with all that food?"

"Food is a relatively minor item. The mines are more important, and power production more important still."

Baley thought of all those robots and felt a trifle dizzy. Two hundred million robots! So many among so few humans. The robots must litter the landscape. An observer from without might think Solaria a world of robots altogether and fail to notice the thin human leaven.

He felt a sudden need to see. He remembered the conversation with Minnim and the sociologic prediction of Earth's danger. It seemed far off, a bit unreal, but he remembered. His personal dangers and difficulties since leaving Earth dimmed the memory of Minnim's voice stating enormities with cool and precise enunciation, but never blotted it out altogether.

Baley had lived too long with duty to allow even the overwhelming fact of open space to stop him in its performance. Data collected from a Spacer's words, or from those of a Spacer robot for that matter, was the sort of thing that was already available to Earth's sociologists. What was needed was direct observation and it was his job, however unpleasant, to collect it.

He inspected the upper portion of the ground-car. "Is this thing a convertible, Daneel?"

"I beg your pardon, Partner Elijah, but I do not follow your meaning."

"Can the car's top be pushed back? Can it be made open to the—the sky?" (He had almost said "dome" out of habit.)

"Yes, it can."

"Then have that done, Daneel. I would like to take a look."

The robot responded gravely, "I am sorry, but I cannot allow that."

Baley felt astonished. He said, "Look, R. Daneel" (he stressed the R.). "Let's rephrase that. I order you to lower the top."

The creature was a robot, manlike or not. It *had* to follow orders.

But Daneel did not move. He said, "I must explain that it is my first concern to spare you harm. It has been clear to me on the basis both of my instructions and of my own personal experience that you would suffer harm at finding yourself in large, empty spaces. I cannot, therefore, allow you to expose yourself to that."

Baley could feel his face darkening with an influx of blood and at the same time could feel the complete uselessness of anger. The creature *was* a robot, and Baley knew the First Law of Robotics well.

It went: *A robot may not injure a human being, or, through inaction, allow a human being to come to harm.*

Everything else in a robot's positronic brain—that of any robot on any world in the Galaxy—had to bow to that prime consideration. Of course a robot had to follow orders, but with one major, all-important qualification. Following orders was only the Second Law of Robotics.

It went: *A robot must obey the orders given it by human beings except where such orders would conflict with the First Law.*

Baley forced himself to speak quietly and reasonably. "I think I can endure it for a short time, Daneel."

"That is not my feeling, partner Elijah."

"Let me be the judge, Daneel."

"If that is an order, Partner Elijah, I cannot follow it."

Baley let himself lounge back against the softly upholstered seat. The robot would, of course, be quite beyond the reach of force. Daneel's strength, if exerted fully, would be a hundred times that of flesh and blood. He would be perfectly capable of restraining Baley without ever hurting him.

Baley was armed. He could point a blaster at Daneel, but, except for perhaps a momentary sensation of mastery, that action would only succeed in greater frustration. A threat of destruction was useless against a robot. Self-preservation was only the Third Law.

It went: *A robot must protect its own existence, as long as such protection does not conflict with the First or Second Laws.*

It would not trouble Daneel to be destroyed if the alternative were breaking the First Law. And Baley did not wish to destroy Daneel. Definitely not.

Yet he did want to see out the car. It was becoming an obsession with him. He couldn't allow this nurse-infant relationship to build up.

For a moment he thought of pointing the blaster at his own temple. Open the car top or I'll kill myself. Oppose one application of the First Law by a greater and more immediate one.

Baley knew he couldn't do it. Too undignified. He disliked the picture conjured up by the thought.

He said wearily, "Would you ask the driver how close in miles we are to destination?"

"Certainly, Partner Elijah."

Daneel bent forward and pushed the toggle switch. But as he did so, Baley leaned forward too, crying out, "Driver! Lower the top of the car!"

And it was the human hand that moved quickly to the toggle switch and closed it again. The human hand held its place firmly thereafter.

Panting a bit, Baley stared at Daneel.

For a second Daneel was motionless, as though his positronic paths were momentarily out of stability in their effort to adjust to the new situation. But that passed quickly and then the robot's hand was moving.

Baley had anticipated that. Daneel would remove the human hand from the switch (gently, not hurting it), reactivate the transmitter, and countermand the order.

Baley said, "You won't get my hand away without hurting me. I warn you. You will probably have to break my fingers."

That was not so. Baley knew that. But Daneel's movements stopped. Harm against harm. The positronic brain had to weigh probabilities and translate them into opposing potentials. It meant just a bit more hesitation.

Baley said, "It's too late."

His race was won. The top was sliding back and pouring into the car, now open, was the harsh white light of Solaria's sun.

Baley wanted to shut his eyes in initial terror, but fought the sensation. He faced the enormous wash of blue and green, incredible quantities of it. He could feel the undisciplined rush of air against his face, but could make out no details of anything. A moving something flashed past. It might have been a robot or an animal or an unliving something caught in a puff of air. He couldn't tell. The car went past it too quickly.

Blue, green, air, noise, motion—and over it all, beating down, furiously, relentlessly, frighteningly, was the white light that came from a ball in the sky.

For one fleeting split moment he bent his head back and stared directly at Solaria's sun. He stared at it, unprotected by the diffusing glass of the Cities' uppermost-Level sunporches. He stared at the naked sun.

And at the very moment he felt Daneel's hands clamping down upon his shoulders. His mind crowded with thought during that unreal, whirling moment. He had to see! He had to see all he could. And Daneel must be there with him to keep him from seeing.

But surely a robot would not dare use violence on a man. That thought was dominant. Daneel could not prevent him forcibly, and yet Baley felt the robot's hands forcing him down.

Baley lifted his arms to force those fleshless hands away and lost all sensation.

⊃3o   A Victim Is Named

Baley was back in the safety of enclosure. Daneel's face wavered before his eyes, and it was splotched with dark spots that turned to red when he blinked.

Baley said, "What happened?"

"I regret," said Daneel, "that you have suffered harm despite my presence. The direct rays of the sun are damaging to the human eye, but I believe that the damage from the short exposure you suffered will not be permanent. When you looked up, I was forced to pull you down and you lost consciousness."

Baley grimaced. That left the question open as to whether he had fainted out of overexcitement (or fright?) or had been knocked unconscious. He felt his jaw and head and found no pain. He forbore asking the question direct. In a way he didn't want to know.

He said, "It wasn't so bad."

"From your reactions, Partner Elijah, I should judge you had found it unpleasant."

"Not at all," said Baley stubbornly. The splotches before his eyes were fading and they weren't tearing so. "I'm only sorry I saw so little. We were moving too fast. Did we pass a robot?"

"We passed a number of them. We are traveling across the Kinbald estate, which is given over to fruit orchards."

"I'll have to try again," said Baley.

"You must not, in my presence," said Daneel. "Meanwhile, I have done as you requested."

"As I requested?"

"You will remember, Partner Elijah, that before you ordered the driver to lower the top of the car, you had ordered me to ask the driver how close in miles we were to destination. We are ten miles away now and shall be there in some six minutes."

Baley felt the impulse to ask Daneel if he were angry at having been outwitted if only to see that perfect face become imperfect, but he repressed it. Of course Daneel would simply answer no, without rancor or annoyance. He would sit there as calm and as grave as ever, unperturbed and imperturbable.

Baley said quietly, "Just the same, Daneel, I'll have to get used to it, you know."

The robot regarded his human partner. "To what is it that you refer?"

193

"Jehoshaphat! To the—the outdoors. It's all this planet is made of."

"There will be no necessity for facing the outdoors," said Daneel. Then, as though that disposed of the subject, he said, "We are slowing down, Partner Elijah. I believe we have arrived. It will be necessary to wait now for the connection of another air-tube leading to the dwelling that will serve as our base of operations."

"An air-tube is unnecessary, Daneel. If I am to be working outdoors, there is no point in delaying the indoctrination."

"There will be no reason for you to work outdoors, Partner Elijah."

The robot started to say more, but Baley waved him quiet with a peremptory motion of the hand.

At the moment he was not in the mood for Daneel's careful consolations, for soothings, for assurances that all would be well and that he would be taken care of.

What he really wanted was an inner knowledge that he could take care of himself and fulfill his assignment. The sight and feel of the open had been hard to take. It might be that when the time came he would lack the hardihood to dare face it again, at the cost of his self-respect and, conceivably, of Earth's safety. All over a small matter of emptiness.

His face grew grim even at the glancing touch of that thought. He would face air, sun, and empty space yet!

Elijah Baley felt like an inhabitant of one of the smaller Cities, say, Helsinki, visiting New York and counting the Levels in awe. He had thought of a "dwelling" as something like an apartment unit, but this was nothing like it at all. He passed from room to room endlessly. Panoramic windows were shrouded closely, allowing no hint of disturbing day to enter. Lights came to life noiselessly from hidden sources as they stepped into a room and died again as quietly when they left.

"So many rooms," said Baley with wonder. "So many. It's like a very tiny City, Daneel."

"It would seem so, Partner Elijah," said Daneel with equanimity.

It seemed strange to the Earthman. Why was it necessary to crowd so many Spacers together with him in close quarters? He said, "How many will be living here with me?"

Daneel said, "There will be myself, of course, and a number of robots."

Baley thought: He ought to have said, a number of *other* robots.

Again he found it obvious that Daneel had the intention of playing the man thoroughly even for no other audience than Baley, who knew the truth so well.

And then that thought popped into nothing under the force of a second, more urgent one. He cried, "*Robots*? How many *humans*?"

"None, Partner Elijah."

They had just stepped into a room, crowded from floor to ceiling with book films. Three fixed viewers with large twenty-four-inch viewing panels set vertically were in three corners of the room. The fourth contained an animation screen.

Baley looked about in annoyance. He said, "Did they kick everyone out just to leave me rattling around alone in this mausoleum?"

"It is meant only for you. A dwelling such as this for one person is customary on Solaria."

"Everyone lives like this?"

"Everyone."

"What do they need all the rooms for?"

"It is customary to devote a single room to a single purpose. This is the library. There is also a music room, a gymnasium, a kitchen, a bakery, a dining room, a machine shop, various robot-repair and testing rooms, two bedrooms——"

"Stop! How do you know all this?"

"It is part of the information pattern," said Daneel smoothly, "made available to me before I left Aurora."

"Jehoshaphat! Who takes care of all of this?" He swung his arm in a wide arc.

"There are a number of household robots. They have been assigned to you and will see to it that you are comfortable."

"But I don't need all this," said Baley. He had the urge to sit down and refuse to budge. He wanted to see no more rooms.

"We can remain in one room if you so desire, Partner Elijah. That was visualized as a possibility from the start. Nevertheless, Solarian customers being what they are, it was considered wiser to allow this house to be built——"

"*Built*!" Baley stared. "You mean this was built for me? All this? Specially?"

"A thoroughly roboticized economy——"

"Yes, I see what you're going to say. What will they do with the house when all this is over?"

"I believe they will tear it down."

Baley's lips clamped together. Of course! Tear it down! Build a tremendous structure for the special use of one Earthman and then tear down everything he touched. Sterilize the soil the house stood on! Fumigate the air he breathed! The Spacers might seem strong, but they, too, had their foolish fears.

Daneel seemed to read his thoughts, or to interpret his expression at any rate. He said, "It may appear to you, Partner Elijah, that it is to escape contagion that they will destroy the house. If such are your thoughts, I suggest that you refrain from making yourself uncomfortable over the matter. The fear of disease on the part of Spacers is by no means so extreme. It is just that the effort involved in building the house is, to them, very little. Nor does the waste involved in tearing it down once more seem great to them.

"And by law, Partner Elijah, this place cannot be allowed to remain standing. It is on the estate of Hannis Gruer and there can only be one legal dwelling place on any estate, that of the owner. This house was built by special dispensation, for a specific purpose. It is meant to house us for a specific length of time, till our mission is completed."

"And who is Hannis Gruer?" asked Baley.

"The head of Solarian security. We are to see him on arrival."

"Are we? Jehoshaphat, Daneel, when do I begin to learn anything at all about anything? I'm working in a vacuum and I don't like it. I might as well go back to Earth. I might as well——"

He felt himself working up into resentment and cut himself short. Daneel never wavered. He merely waited his chance to speak. He said, "I regret the fact that you are annoyed. My general knowledge of Solaria does seem to be greater than yours. My knowledge of the murder case itself is as limited as your own. It is Agent Gruer who will tell us what we must know. The Solarian Government has arranged this."

"Well, then, let's go to this Gruer. How long a trip will it be?" Baley winced at the thought of more travel and the familiar constriction in his chest was making itself felt again.

Daneel said, "No travel is necessary, Partner Elijah. Agent Gruer will be waiting for us in the conversation room."

"A room for conversation, too?" Baley murmured wryly. Then, in a louder voice, "Waiting for us now?"

"I believe so."

"Then let's get to him, Daneel!"

Hannis Gruer was bald, and that without qualification. There was not even a fringe of hair at the sides of his skull. It was completely naked.

Baley swallowed and tried, out of politeness, to keep his eyes off that skull, but couldn't. On Earth there was the continuous acceptance of Spacers at the Spacers' own evaluation. The Spacers were the unquestioned lords of the Galaxy; they were tall, bronze of skin and hair, handsome, large, cool, aristocratic.

In short, they were all R. Daneel Olivaw was, but with the fact of humanity in addition.

And the Spacers who were sent to Earth often did look like that; perhaps were deliberately chosen for that reason.

But here was a Spacer who might have been an Earthman for all his appearance. He was bald. And his nose was misshapen, too. Not much, to be sure, but on a Spacer even a slight asymmetry was noteworthy.

Baley said, "Good afternoon, sir, I am sorry if we kept you waiting."

No harm in politeness. He would have to work with these people.

He had the momentary urge to step across the expanse of room (how ridiculously large) and offer his hand in greeting. It was an urge easy to fight off. A Spacer certainly would not welcome such a greeting: a hand covered with Earthly germs?

Gruer sat gravely, as far away from Baley as he could get, his hands resting within long sleeves, and probably there were filters in his nostrils, although Baley couldn't see them.

It even seemed to him that Gruer cast a disapproving look at Daneel as though to say: You're a queer Spacer, standing that close to an Earthman.

That would mean Gruer simply did not know the truth. Then Baley noticed suddenly that Daneel was standing at some distance, at that; farther than he usually did.

Of course! Too close, and Gruer might find the proximity unbelievable. Daneel was intent on being accepted as human.

Gruer spoke in a pleasant, friendly voice, but his eyes tended to remain furtively on Daneel; looking away, then drifting back. He said, "I haven't been waiting long. Welcome to Solaria, gentlemen. Are you comfortable?"

"Yes, sir. Quite," said Baley. He wondered if etiquette would require that Daneel as the "Spacer" should speak for the two, but rejected that possibility resentfully. Jehoshaphat! It was he, himself, who had been requested for the investigation and Daneel had been added afterward. Under the circumstances Baley felt he would not play the secondary to a genuine Spacer; it was out of the question when a robot was involved, even such a robot as Daneel.

But Daneel made no attempt to take precedence over Baley, nor did Gruer seem surprised or displeased at that. Instead, he turned his attention at once to Baley to the exclusion of Daneel.

Gruer said, "You have been told nothing, Plainclothesman Baley, about the crime for which your services have been solicited. I imagine you are quite curious about that." He shook his arms so that the sleeves fell backward and clasped his hands loosely in his lap. "Won't you gentlemen sit down?"

They did so and Baley said, "We *are* curious." He noted that Gruer's hands were not protected by gloves.

Gruer went on. "That was on purpose, Plainclothesman. We wanted you to arrive here prepared to tackle the notions. You will have available to you shortly a full report of the details of the crime and of the investigations we have been able to conduct. I am afraid, Plainclothes-man, that you will find our investigations ridiculously incomplete from the standpoint of your own experience. We have no police force on Solaria."

"None at all?" asked Baley.

Gruer smiled and shrugged. "No crime, you see. Our population is tiny and widely scattered. There is no occasion for crime; therefore no occasion for police."

"I see. But for all that, you *do* have crime now."

"True, but the first crime of violence in two centuries of history."

"Unfortunate, then, that you must begin with murder."

"Unfortunate, yes. More unfortunately still, the victim was a man we could scarcely afford to lose. A most inappropriate victim. And the circumstances of the murder were particularly brutal."

Baley said, "I suppose the murderer is completely unknown." (Why else would the crime be worth the importation of an Earthly detective?)

Gruer looked particularly uneasy. He glanced sideways at Daneel, who sat motionless, an absorptive, quiet mechanism. Baley knew that Daneel would, at any time in the future, be able to reproduce any conversation he heard, of whatever length. He was a recording machine that walked and talked like a man.

Did Gruer know that? His look at Daneel had certainly something of the furtive about it.

Gruer said, "No, I cannot say the murderer is completely unknown. In fact, there is only one person that can possibly have done the deed."

"Are you sure you don't mean only one person who is *likely* to have done the deed?" Baley distrusted overstatement and had no liking for the armchair deducer who discovered certainty rather than probability in the workings of logic.

But Gruer shook his bald head. "No. Only one possible person. Anyone else is impossible. Completely impossible."

"Completely?"

"I assure you."

"Then you have no problem."

"On the contrary. We do have a problem. That one person couldn't have done it either."

Baley said calmly, "Then no one did it."

"Yet the deed was done. Rikaine Delmarre is dead."

That's something, thought Baley. Jehoshaphat, I've got *something*. I've got the victim's name.

He brought out his notebook and solemnly made note of it, partly out of a wry desire to indicate that he had scraped up, at last, a nubbin of fact, and partly to avoid making it too obvious that he sat by the side of a recording machine who needed no notes.

He said, "How is the victim's name spelled?"

Gruer spelled it.

"His profession, sir?"

"Fetologist."

Baley spelled that as it sounded and let it go. He said, "Now who would be able to give me a personal account of the circumstances surrounding the murder? As firsthand as possible."

Gruer's smile was grim and his eyes shifted to Daneel again, and then away. "His wife, Plainclothesman."

"His wife . . . ?"

"Yes. Her name is Gladia." Gruer pronounced it in three syllables, accenting the second.

"Any children?" Baley's eyes were fixed on his notebook. When no answer came, he looked up. "Any children?"

But Gruer's mouth had pursed up as though he had tasted something sour. He looked sick. Finally he said, "I would scarcely know."

Baley said, "What?"

Gruer added hastily, "In any case, I think you had better postpone actual operations till tomorrow. I know you've had a hard trip, Mr. Baley, and that you are tired and probably hungry."

Baley, about to deny it, realized suddenly that the thought of food had an uncommon attraction for him at the moment. He said, "Will you join us at our meal?" He didn't think Gruer would, being a Spacer. (Yet he had been brought to the point of saying "Mr. Baley" rather than "Plainclothesman Baley," which was something.)

As expected, Gruer said, "A business engagement makes that impossible. I will have to leave. I am sorry."

Baley rose. The polite thing would be to accompany Gruer to the door. In the first place, however, he wasn't at all anxious to approach the door and the unprotected open. And in the second he wasn't sure where the door was.

He remained standing in uncertainty.

Gruer smiled and nodded. He said, "I will see you again. Your robots will know the combination if you wish to talk to me."

And he was gone.

Baley exclaimed sharply.

Gruer and the chair he was sitting on were simply not there. The wall behind Gruer, the floor under his feet changed with explosive suddenness.

Daneel said calmly, "He was not there in the flesh at any time. It was a trimensional image. It seemed to me you would know. You have such things on Earth."

"Not like this," muttered Baley.

A trimensional image on Earth was encased in a cubic force-field that glittered against the background. The image itself had a tiny flicker. On Earth there was no mistaking image for reality. Here . . .

No wonder Gruer had worn no gloves. He needed no nose filters, for that matter.

Daneel said, "Would you care to eat now, Partner Elijah?"

Dinner was an unexpected ordeal. Robots appeared. One set the table, one brought in the food.

"How many are there in the house, Daneel?" Baley asked.

"About fifty, Partner Elijah."

"Will they stay here while we eat?" (One had backed into a corner, his glossy, glowing-eyed face turned toward Baley.)

"It is the usual practice," said Daneel, "for one to do so in case its service is called upon. If you do not wish that, you have only to order it to leave."

Baley shrugged. "Let it stay!"

Under normal conditions Baley might have found the food delicious. Now he ate mechanically. He noted abstractedly that Daneel ate also, with a kind of unimpassioned efficiency. Later on, of course, he would empty the fluorocarbon sac within him into which the "eaten" food was now being stored. Meanwhile, Daneel maintained his masquerade.

"Is it night outside?" asked Baley.

"It is," replied Daneel.

Baley stared somberly at the bed. It was too large. The whole bedroom was too large. There were no blankets to burrow under, only sheets. They would make a poor enclosure.

Everything was difficult! He had already gone through the unnerving experience of showering in a stall that actually adjoined the bedroom. It was the height of luxury in a way, yet, on the other hand, it seemed an unsanitary arrangement.

He said abruptly, "How is the light put out?" The headboard of the bed gleamed with soft light. Perhaps that was to facilitate book viewing before sleeping, but Baley was in no mood for that.

"It will be taken care of once you're in bed, if you compose yourself for sleep."

"The robots watch, do they?"

"It is their job."

"Jehoshaphat! What do these Solarians do for *themselves*?" Baley muttered. "I wonder now why a robot didn't scrub my back in the shower."

With no trace of humor Daneel said, "One would have, had you required it. As for the Solarians, they do what they choose. No robot performs his duty if ordered not to, except, of course, where the performance is necessary to the well-being of the human."

"Well, good night, Daneel."

"I will be in another bedroom, Partner Elijah. If, at any time during the night, you need anything——"

"I know. The robots will come."

"There is a contact patch on the side table. You have only to touch it. I will come too."

Sleep eluded Baley. He kept picturing the house he was in, balanced precariously at the outer skin of the world, with emptiness waiting just outside like a monster.

On Earth his apartment—his snug, comfortable, crowded apartment—sat nestled beneath many others. There were dozens of levels and thousands of people between himself and the rim of the Earth.

Even on Earth, he tried to tell himself, there were people on the topmost Level. They would be immediately adjacent to the outside. Sure! But that's what made those apartments low-rent.

Then he thought of Jessie, a thousand light-years away.

He wanted terribly to get out of bed right now, dress, and walk to her. His thoughts grew mistier. If there were only a tunnel, a nice, safe tunnel burrowing its way through safe, solid rock and metal from Solaria to Earth, he would walk and walk and walk. . . .

He would walk back to Earth, back to Jessie, back to comfort and security. . . .

Security.

Baley's eyes opened. His arms grew rigid and he rose up on his elbow, scarcely aware that he was doing so.

Security! This man, Hannis Gruer, was head of Solarian security. So Daneel had said. What did "security" mean? If it meant the same as it meant on Earth, and surely it must, this man Gruer was responsible for the protection of Solaria against invasion from without and subversion from within.

Why was he interested in a murder case? Was it because there were no police on Solaria and the Department of Security would come the closest to knowing what to do about a murder?

Gruer had seemed at ease with Baley, yet there had been those furtive glances, again and again, in the direction of Daneel.

Did Gruer suspect the motives of Daneel? Baley, himself, had been ordered to keep his eyes open and Daneel might very likely have received similar instructions.

It would be natural for Gruer to suspect that espionage was possible.

His job made it necessary for him to suspect that in any case where it was conceivable. And he would not fear Baley overmuch, an Earthman, representative of the least formidable world in the Galaxy.

But Daneel was a native of Aurora, the oldest and largest and strongest of the Outer Worlds. That would be different.

Gruer, as Baley now remembered, had not addressed one word to Daneel.

For that matter, why should Daneel pretend so thoroughly to be a man? The earlier explanation that Baley had posed for himself, that it was a vainglorious game on the part of Daneel's Auroran designers, seemed trivial. It seemed obvious now that the masquerade was something more serious.

A man could be expected to receive diplomatic immunity; a certain courtesy and gentleness of treatment. A robot could not. But then why did not Aurora send a real man in the first place. Why gamble so desperately on a fake? The answer suggested itself instantly to Baley. A real man of Aurora, a real Spacer, would not care to associate too closely or for too long a time with an Earthman.

But if all this were true, why should Solaria find a single murder so important that it must allow an Earthman and an Auroran to come to their planet?

Baley felt trapped.

He was trapped on Solaria by the necessities of his assignment. He was trapped by Earth's danger, trapped in an environment he could scarcely endure, trapped by a responsibility he could not shirk. And, to add to all this, he was trapped somehow in the midst of a Spacer conflict the nature of which he did not understand.

 A Woman Is Viewed

He slept at last. He did not remember when he actually made the transition to sleep. There was just a period when his thoughts grew more erratic and then the headboard of his bed was shining and the ceiling was alight with a cool, daytime glow. He looked at his watch.

Hours had passed. The robots who ran the house had decided it was time for him to wake up and had acted accordingly.

He wondered if Daneel were awake and at once realized the illogic of the thought. Daneel could not sleep. Baley wondered if he had counterfeited sleep as part of the role he was playing. Had he undressed and put on nightclothes?

As though on cue Daneel entered. "Good morning, Partner Elijah."

The robot was completely dressed and his face was in perfect repose. He said, "Did you sleep well?"

"Yes," said Baley dryly, "did you?"

He got out of bed and tramped into the bathroom for a shave and for the remainder of the morning ritual. He shouted, "If a robot comes in to shave me, send him out again. They get on my nerves. Even if I don't see them, they get on my nerves."

He stared at his own face as he shaved, marveling a bit that it looked so like the mirrored face he saw on Earth. If only the image were another Earthman with whom he could consult instead of the light-mimicry of himself. If he could go over what he had already learned, small as it was . . .

"Too small! Get more," he muttered to the mirror.

He came out, mopping his face, and pulled trousers over fresh shorts. (Robots supplied everything, damn them.)

He said, "Would you answer a few questions, Daneel?"

"As you know, Partner Elijah, I answer all questions to the best of my knowledge."

Or to the letter of your instructions, thought Baley. He said, "Why are there only twenty thousand people on Solaria?"

"That is a mere fact," said Daneel. "A datum. A figure that is the result of a counting process."

"Yes, but you're evading the matter. The planet can support millions; why, then, only twenty thousand? You said the Solarians consider twenty thousand optimum. Why?"

"It is their way of life."

"You mean they practice birth control?"

"Yes."

"And leave the planet empty?" Baley wasn't sure why he was pounding away at this one point, but the planet's population was one of the few hard facts he had learned about it and there was little else he could ask about.

Daneel said, "The planet is not empty. It is parceled out into estates, each of which is supervised by a Solarian."

"You mean each lives on his estate. Twenty thousand estates, each with a Solarian."

"Fewer estates than those, Partner Elijah. Wives share the estate."

"No Cities?" Baley felt cold.

"None at all, Partner Elijah. They live completely apart and never see one another except under the most extraordinary circumstances."

"Hermits?"

"In a way, yes. In a way, no."

"What does that mean?"

"Agent Gruer visited you yesterday by trimensional image. Solarians visit one another freely that way and in no other way."

Baley stared at Daneel. He said, "Does that include us? Are we expected to live that way?"

"It is the custom of the world."

"Then how do I investigate this case? If I want to see some-one——"

"From this house, Partner Elijah, you can obtain a trimensional view of anyone on the planet. There will be no problem. In fact, it will save you the annoyance of leaving this house. It was why I said when we arrived that there would be no occasion for you to feel it necessary to grow accustomed to facing the outdoors. And that is well. Any other arrangement would be most distasteful to you."

"I'll judge what's distasteful to me," said Baley. "First thing today, Daneel, I get in touch with the Gladia woman, the wife of the murdered man. If the trimensional business is unsatisfactory, I will go out to her place, personally. It's a matter for my decision."

"We shall see what is best and most feasible, Partner Elijah," said Daneel noncommittally. "I shall arrange for breakfast." He turned to leave.

Baley stared at the broad robotic back and was almost amused. Daneel Olivaw acted the master. If his instructions had been to keep Baley from learning any more than was absolutely necessary, a trump card had been left in Baley's hand.

The other was only R. Daneel Olivaw, after all. All that was necessary was to tell Gruer, or any Solarian, that Daneel was a robot and not a man.

And yet, on the other hand, Daneel's pseudo humanity could be of great use, too. A trump card need not be played at once. Sometimes it was more useful in the hand.

Wait and see, he thought, and followed Daneel out to breakfast.

Baley said, "Now how does one go about establishing trimensional contact?"

"It is done for us, Partner Elijah," said Daneel, and his finger sought out one of the contact patches that summoned robots.

A robot entered at once.

Where do they come from, Baley wondered. As one wandered aimlessly about the uninhabited maze that constituted the mansion, not one robot was ever visible. Did they scramble out of the way as humans approached? Did they send messages to one another and clear the path?

Yet whenever a call went out, one appeared without delay.

Baley stared at the robotic newcomer. It was sleek, but not glossy.

Its surface had a muted, grayish finish, with a checkerboard pattern on the right shoulder as the only bit of color. Squares in white and yellow (silver and gold, really, from the metallic luster) were placed in what seemed an aimless pattern.

Daneel said, "Take us to the conversation room."

The robot bowed and turned, but said nothing.

Baley said, "Wait, boy. What's your name?"

The robot faced Baley. It spoke in clear tones and without hesitation. "I have no name, master. My serial number"—and a metal finger lifted and rested on the shoulder patch—"is ACX-2745."

Daneel and Baley followed into a large room, which Baley recognized as having held Gruer and his chair the day before.

Another robot was waiting for them with the eternal, patient nonboredom of the machine. The first bowed and left.

Baley compared shoulder patches of the two as the first bowed and started out. The pattern of silver and gold was different. The checkerboard was made up of a six-by-six square. The number of possible arrangements would be 2^{36} then, or seventy billion. More than enough.

Baley said, "Apparently, there is one robot for everything. One to show us here. One to run the viewer."

Daneel said, "There is much robotic specialization in Solaria, Partner Elijah."

"With so many of them, I can understand why." Baley looked at the second robot. Except for the shoulder patch, and, presumably, for the invisible positronic patterns within its spongy platinum-iridium brain, it was the duplicate of the first. He said, "And your serial number?"

"ACC-1129, master."

"I'll just call you boy. Now I want to speak to a Mrs. Gladia Delmarre, wife of the late Rikaine Delmarre——Daneel, is there an address, some way of pin-pointing her location?"

Daneel said gently, "I do not believe any further information is necessary. If I may question the robot——"

"Let me do that," Baley said. "All right, boy, do you know how the lady is to be reached?"

"Yes, master. I have knowledge of the connection pattern of all masters." This was said without pride. It was a mere fact, as though it were saying: I am made of metal, master.

Daneel interposed, "That is not surprising, Partner Elijah. There are less than ten thousand connections that need be fed into the memory circuits and that is a small number."

Baley nodded. "Is there more than one Gladia Delmarre, by any chance? There might be that chance of confusion."

"Master?" After the question the robot remained blankly silent.

"I believe," said Daneel, "that this robot does not understand your question. It is my belief that duplicate names do not occur on Solaria. Names are registered at birth and no name may be adopted unless it is unoccupied at the time."

"All right," said Baley, "we learn something every minute. Now see here, boy, you tell me how to work whatever it is I am supposed to work; give me the connection pattern, or whatever you call it, and then step out."

There was a perceptible pause before the robot answered. It said, "Do you wish to make contact yourself, sir?"

"That's right."

Daneel touched Baley's sleeve gently. "One moment, Partner Elijah."

"Now what is it?"

"It is my belief that the robot could make the necessary contact with greater ease. It is his specialization."

Baley said grimly, "I'm sure he can do it better than I can. Doing it myself, I may make a mess of it." He stared levelly at the impassive Daneel. "Just the same, I prefer to make contact myself. Do I give the orders or don't I?"

Daneel said, "You give the orders, Partner Elijah, and your orders, where First Law permits, will be obeyed. However, with your permission, I would like to give you what pertinent information I have concerning the Solarian robots. Far more than on any other world, the robots on Solaria are specialized. Although Solarian robots are physically capable of many things, they are heavily equipped mentally for one particular type of job. To perform functions outside their specialty requires the high potentials produced by direct application of one of the Three Laws. Again, for them *not* to perform the duty for which they *are* equipped also requires the direct application of the Three Laws."

"Well, then, a direct order from me brings the Second Law into play, doesn't it?"

"True. Yet the potential set up by it is 'unpleasant' to the robot. Ordinarily, the matter would not come up, since almost never does a Solarian interfere with the day-to-day workings of a robot. For one thing, he would not care to do a robot's work; for another, he would feel no need to."

"Are you trying to tell me, Daneel, that it hurts the robot to have me do its work?"

"As you know, Partner Elijah, pain in the human sense is not applicable to robotic reactions."

Baley shrugged. "Then?"

"Nevertheless," went on Daneel, "the experience which the robot undergoes is as upsetting to it as pain is to a human, as nearly as I can judge."

"And yet," said Baley, "I'm not a Solarian. I'm an Earthman. I don't like robots doing what I want to do."

"Consider, too," said Daneel, "that to cause distress to a robot might be considered on the part of our hosts to be an act of impoliteness since in a society such as this there must be a number of more or less rigid beliefs concerning how it is proper to treat a robot and how it is not. To offend our hosts would scarcely make our task easier."

"All right," said Baley. "Let the robot do its job."

He settled back. The incident had not been without its uses. It was an educational example of how remorseless a robotic society could be. Once brought into existence, robots were not so easily removed, and a human who wished to dispense with them even temporarily found he could not.

His eyes half closed, he watched the robot approach the wall. Let the sociologists on Earth consider what had just occurred and draw their conclusions. He was beginning to have certain notions of his own.

Half a wall slid aside and the control panel that was revealed would have done justice to a City Section power station.

Baley longed for his pipe. He had been briefed that smoking on non-smoking Solaria would be a terrible breach of decorum, so he had not even been allowed to take his fixings. He sighed. There were moments when the feel of pipestem between teeth and a warm bowl in his hand would have been infinitely comforting.

The robot was working quickly, adjusting variable resistances a trifle here and there and intensifying field-forces in proper pattern by quick finger pressures.

Daneel said, "It is necessary first to signal the individual one desires to view. A robot will, of course, receive the message. If the individual being signaled is available and wishes to receive the view, full contact is established."

"Are all those controls necessary?" asked Baley. "The robot's hardly touching most of the panel."

"My information on the matter is not complete, Partner Elijah. There is, however, the necessity of arranging, upon occasion, for multiple viewings and for mobile viewings. The latter, particularly, call for complicated and continuing adjustments."

The robot said, "Masters, contact is made and approved. When you are ready, it will be completed."

"Ready," growled Baley, and as though the word were a signal, the far half of the room was alive with light.

•   •   •

Daneel said at once, "I neglected to have the robot specify that all visible openings to the outside be draped. I regret that and we must arrange——"

"Never mind," said Baley, wincing. "I'll manage. Don't interfere."

It was a bathroom he was staring at, or he judged it to be so from its fixtures. One end of it was, he guessed, a kind of beautician's establishment and his imagination pictured a robot (or robots?) working with unerring swiftness on the details of a woman's coiffure and on the externals that made up the picture she presented to the world.

Some gadgets and fittings he simply gave up on. There was no way of judging their purpose in the absence of experience. The walls were inlaid with an intricate pattern that all but fooled the eye into believing some natural object was being represented before fading away into an abstraction. The result was soothing and almost hypnotic in the way it monopolized attention.

What might have been the shower stall, a large one, was shielded off by nothing that seemed material, but rather by a trick of lighting that set up a wall of flickering opacity. No human was in sight.

Baley's glance fell to the floor. Where did his room end and the other begin? It was easy to tell. There was a line where the quality of the light changed and that must be it.

He stepped toward the line and after a moment's hesitation pushed his hand beyond it.

He felt nothing, any more than he would have had he shoved the hand into one of Earth's crude trimensionals. There, at least, he would have seen his own hand still; faintly, perhaps, and overlaid by the image, but he would have seen it. Here it was lost completely. To his vision, his arm ended sharply at the wrist.

What if he stepped across the line altogether? Probably his own vision would become inoperative. He would be in a world of complete blackness. The thought of such efficient enclosure was almost pleasant.

A voice interrupted him. He looked up and stepped backward with an almost clumsy haste.

Gladia Delmarre was speaking. At least Baley assumed it was she. The upper portion of the flickering light across the shower stall had faded and a head was clearly visible.

It smiled at Baley. "I said hello, and I'm sorry to keep you waiting. I'll be dry soon."

Hers was a triangular face, rather broad at the cheekbones (which grew prominent when she smiled) and narrowing with a gentle curve past full lips to a small chin. Her head was not high above the ground. Baley judged her to be about five feet two in height. (That was not typical. At least not to Baley's way of thinking. Spacer women were supposed to lean toward the tall and stately.) Nor was her hair the Spacer bronze. It was light brown, tinging toward yellow, and worn moderately long. At the moment it was fluffed out in what Baley imagined must be a stream of warm air. The whole picture was quite pleasing.

Baley said in confusion, "If you want us to break contact and wait till you're through——"

"Oh no. I'm almost done, and we can talk meanwhile. Hannis Gruer told me you would be viewing. You're from Earth, I understand." Her eyes rested full on him, seemed to drink him in.

Baley nodded and sat down. "My companion is from Aurora."

She smiled and kept her glance fixed on Baley as though *he* remained the curiosity nevertheless, and of course, Baley thought, so he was.

She lifted her arms above her head, running her fingers through the hair and spreading it out as though to hasten drying. Her arms were slim and graceful. Very attractive, Baley thought.

Then he thought uneasily: Jessie wouldn't like this.

Daneel's voice broke in. "Would it be possible, Mrs. Delmarre, to have the window we see polarized or draped. My partner is disturbed by the sight of daylight. On Earth, as you may have heard——"

The young woman (Baley judged her to be twenty-five but had the doleful thought that the apparent ages of Spacers could be most deceptive) put her hands to her cheeks and said, "Oh my, yes. I know all about that. How ridiculously silly of me. Forgive me, please, but it won't take a moment. I'll have a robot in here——"

She stepped out of the drying cabinet, her hand extended toward the contact-patch, still talking. "I'm always thinking I ought to have more than one contact-patch in this room. A house is just no good if it doesn't have a patch within reach no matter where you stand—say not more than five feet away. It just——Why, what's the matter?"

She stared in shock at Baley, who, having jumped out of his chair and upset it behind him, had reddened to his hairline and hastily turned away.

Daneel said calmly, "It would be better, Mrs. Delmarre, if, after you have made contact with the robot, you would return to the stall or, failing that, proceed to put on some articles of clothing."

Gladia looked down at her nudity in surprise and said, "Well, of course."

5. A Crime Is Discussed

"It was only viewing, you see," said Gladia contritely. She was wrapped in something that left her arms and shoulders free. One leg showed to mid-thigh, but Baley, entirely recovered and feeling an utter fool, ignored it stoically.

He said, "It was the surprise, Mrs. Delmarre——"

"Oh, please. You can call me Gladia, unless—unless that's against your customs."

"Gladia, then. It's all right. I just want to assure you there was nothing repulsive about it, you understand. Just the surprise." Bad enough for him to have acted the fool, he thought, without having the poor girl think he found her unpleasant. As a matter of fact, it had been rather—rather . . .

Well, he didn't have the phrase, but he knew quite certainly that there was no way he would ever be able to talk of this to Jessie.

"I know I offended you," Gladia said, "but I didn't mean to. I just wasn't thinking. Of course I realize one must be careful about the customs of other planets, but the customs are so queer sometimes; at least, not queer," she hastened to add, "I don't mean queer. I mean strange, you know, and it's so easy to forget. As I forgot about keeping the windows darkened."

"Quite all right," muttered Baley. She was in another room now with all the windows draped and the light had the subtly different and more comfortable texture of artificiality.

"But about the other thing," she went on earnestly, "it's just *viewing*, you see. After all, you didn't mind talking to me when I was in the drier and I wasn't wearing anything then, either."

"Well," said Baley, wishing she would run down as far as that subject was concerned, "hearing you is one thing, and seeing you is another."

"But that's exactly it. Seeing isn't involved." She reddened a trifle and looked down. "I hope you don't think I'd ever do anything like that, I mean, just step out of the drier, if anyone were *seeing* me. It was just *viewing*."

"Same thing, isn't it?" said Baley.

"Not at all the same thing. You're viewing me right now. You can't touch me, can you, or smell me, or anything like that. You could if you were seeing me. Right now, I'm two hundred miles away from you at *least*. So how can it be the same thing?"

Baley grew interested. "But I see you with my eyes."

"No, you don't see me. You see my image. You're viewing me."

"And that makes a difference?"

"All the difference there is."

"I see." In a way he did. The distinction was not one he could make easily, but it had a kind of logic to it.

She said, bending her head a little to one side, "Do you *really* see?"

"Yes."

"Does that mean you wouldn't mind if I took off my wrapper?" She was smiling.

He thought: She's teasing and I ought to take her up on it.

But aloud he said, "No, it would take my mind off my job. We'll discuss it another time."

"Do you mind my being in the wrapper, rather than something more formal? Seriously."

"I don't mind."

"May I call you by your first name?"

"If you have the occasion."

"What is your first name?"

"Elijah."

"All right." She snuggled into a chair that looked hard and almost ceramic in texture, but it slowly gave as she sat until it embraced her gently.

Baley said, "To business, now."

She said, "To business."

Baley found it all extraordinarily difficult. There was no way even to make a beginning. On Earth he would ask name, rating, City and Sector of dwelling, a million different routine questions. He might even know the answers to begin with, yet it would be a device to ease into the serious phase. It would serve to introduce him to the person, make his judgment of the tactics to pursue something other than a mere guess.

But here? How could he be certain of anything? The very verb "to see" meant different things to himself and to the woman. How many other words would be different? How often would they be at cross-purposes without his being aware of it?

He said, "How long were you married, Gladia?"

"Ten years, Elijah."

"How old are you?"

"Thirty-three."

Baley felt obscurely pleased. She might easily have been a hundred thirty-three.

He said, "Were you happily married?"

Gladia looked uneasy. "How do you mean that?"

"Well——" For a moment Baley was at a loss. How do you define a happy marriage. For that matter, what would a Solarian consider a happy marriage? He said, "Well, you saw one another often?"

"What? I should hope not. We're not animals, you know."

Baley winced. "You did live in the same mansion? I thought——"

"Of course, we did. We were married. But I had my quarters and he had his. He had a very important career which took much of his time and I have my own work. We viewed each other whenever necessary."

"He *saw* you, didn't he?"

"It's not a thing one talks about but he *did* see me."

"Do you have any children?"

Gladia jumped to her feet in obvious agitation. "That's too much. Of all the indecent——"

"Now wait. *Wait!*" Baley brought his fist down on the arm of his chair. "Don't be difficult. This is a murder investigation. Do you understand? Murder. And it was your husband who was murdered. Do you want to see the murderer found and punished or don't you?"

"Then *ask* about the murder, not about—about——"

"I have to ask all sorts of things. For one thing I want to know whether you're sorry your husband is dead." He added with calculated brutality, "You don't seem to be."

She stared at him haughtily. "I'm sorry when anyone dies, especially when he's young and useful."

"Doesn't the fact that he was your husband make it just a little more than that?"

"He was assigned to me and, well, we *did* see each other when scheduled and—and"—she hurried the next words—"and, if you must know, we don't have children because none have been assigned us yet. I don't see what all that has to do with being sorry over someone being dead."

Maybe it had nothing to do with it, Baley thought. It depended on the social facts of life and with those he was not acquainted.

He changed the subject. "I'm told you have personal knowledge of the circumstances of the murder."

For a moment she seemed to grow taut. "I—discovered the body. Is that the way I should say it?"

"Then you didn't witness the actual murder?"

"Oh no," she said faintly.

"Well, suppose you tell me what happened. Take your time and use your own words." He sat back and composed himself to listen.

She began, "It was on three-two of the fifth——"

"When was that in Standard Time?" asked Baley quickly.

"I'm not sure. I really don't know. You can check, I suppose."

Her voice seemed shaky and her eyes had grown large. They were a little too gray to be called blue, he noted.

She said, "He came to my quarters. It was our assigned day for seeing and I knew he'd come."

"He always came on an assigned day?"

"Oh yes. He was a very conscientious man, a good Solarian. He never skipped an assigned day and always came at the same time. Of course, he didn't stay long. We have not been assigned to ch——"

She couldn't finish the word, but Baley nodded.

"Anyway," she said, "he always came at the same time, you know, so that everything would be comfortable. We spoke a few minutes; seeing *is* an ordeal, but he spoke quite normally to me. It was his way. Then he left to attend to some project he was involved with; I'm not sure what. He had a special laboratory in my quarters to which he could retire on seeing days. He had a much bigger one in his quarters, of course."

Baley wondered what he did in those laboratories. Fetology, perhaps, whatever that was.

He said, "Did he seem unnatural in any way? Worried?"

"No. No. He was never worried." She came to the edge of a small laugh and buried it at the last moment. "He always had perfect control, like your friend there." For a brief moment her small hand reached out and indicated Daneel, who did not stir.

"I see. Well, go on."

Gladia didn't. Instead she whispered, "Do you mind if I have myself a drink?"

"Please do."

Gladia's hand slipped along the arm of her chair momentarily. In less than a minute, a robot moved in silently and a warm drink (Baley could see the steam) was in her hand. She sipped slowly, then set the drink down.

She said, "That's better. May I ask a personal question?"

Baley said, "You may always ask."

"Well, I've read a lot about Earth. I've always been interested, you know. It's such a *queer* world." She gasped and added immediately, "I didn't mean that."

Baley frowned a little. "Any world is queer to people who don't live on it."

"I mean it's different. You know. Anyway, I want to ask a rude question. At least, I hope it doesn't seem rude to an Earthman. I wouldn't ask it of a Solarian, of course. Not for anything."

"Ask what, Gladia?"

"About you and your friend—Mr. Olivaw, is it?"

"Yes."

"You two aren't viewing, are you?"

"How do you mean?"

"I mean each other. You're seeing. You're there, both of you."

Baley said, "We're physically together. Yes."

"You could touch him, if you wanted to."

"That's right."

She looked from one to the other and said, "Oh."

It may have meant anything. Disgust? Revulsion?

Baley toyed with the idea of standing up, walking to Daneel and placing his hand flat on Daneel's face. It might be interesting to watch her reaction.

He said, "You were about to go on with the events of that day when your husband came to see you." He was morally certain that her digression, however interesting it might have been intrinsically to her, was primarily motivated by a desire to avoid just that.

She returned to her drink for a moment. Then: "There isn't much to tell. I saw he would be engaged, and I knew he would be, anyway, because he was always at some sort of constructive work, so I went back to my own work. Then, perhaps fifteen minutes later, I heard a shout."

There was a pause and Baley prodded her. "What kind of a shout?"

She said, "Rikaine's. My husband's. Just a shout. No words. A kind of fright. No! Surprise, shock. Something like that. I'd never heard him shout before."

She lifted her hands to her ears as though to shut out even the memory of the sound and her wrapper slipped slowly down to her waist. She took no notice and Baley stared firmly at his notebook.

He said, "What did you do?"

"I ran. I ran. I didn't know where he was——"

"I thought you said he had gone to the laboratory he maintained in your quarters."

"He did, E-Elijah, but I didn't know where that was. Not for sure, anyway. I never went there. It was his. I had a general idea of its direction. I knew it was somewhere in the west, but I was so upset, I didn't even think to summon any robot. One of them would have guided me easily, but of course none came without being summoned. When I did get there—I found it somehow—he was dead."

She stopped suddenly and, to Baley's acute discomfort, she bent her head and wept. She made no attempt to obscure her face. Her eyes simply closed and tears slowly trickled down her cheeks. It was quite soundless. Her shoulders barely trembled.

Then her eyes opened and looked at him through swimming tears. "I never saw a dead man before. He was all bloody and his head was— just—all——I managed to get a robot and he called the others and

I suppose they took care of me and Rikaine. I don't remember. I don't——"

Baley said, "What do you mean, they took care of Rikaine?"

"They took him away and cleaned up." There was a small wedge of indignation in her voice, the lady of the house careful of its condition. "Things were a mess."

"And what happened to the body?"

She shook her head. "I don't know. Burned, I suppose. Like any dead body."

"You didn't call the police?"

She looked at him blankly and Baley thought: No police.

He said. "You told somebody, I suppose. People found out about the matter."

She said, "The robots called a doctor. And I had to call Rikaine's place of work. The robots there had to know he wouldn't be back."

"The doctor was for you, I suppose."

She nodded. For the first time, she seemed to notice her wrapper draped about her hips. She pulled it up into position, murmuring forlornly, "I'm sorry, I'm sorry."

Baley felt uncomfortable, watching her as she sat there helpless, shivering, her face contorted with the absolute terror that had come over her with the memory.

She had never seen a dead body before. She had never seen blood and a crushed skull. And if the husband-wife relationship on Solaria was something thin and shallow, it was still a dead human being with whom she had been confronted.

Baley scarcely knew what to say or do next. He had the impulse to apologize, and yet, as a policeman, he was doing only his duty.

But there were no police on this world. Would she understand that this was his duty?

Slowly, and as gently as he could, he said, "Gladia, did you hear anything at all? Anything besides your husband's shout."

She looked up, her face as pretty as ever, despite its obvious distress—perhaps because of it. She said, "Nothing."

"No running footsteps? No other voice?"

She shook her head. "I didn't hear anything."

"When you found your husband, he was completely alone? You two were the only ones present?"

"Yes."

"No signs of anyone else having been there?"

"None that I could see. I don't see how anyone could have been there, anyway."

"Why do you say that?"

For a moment she looked shocked. Then she said dispiritedly,

"You're from Earth. I keep forgetting. Well, it's just that nobody could have been there. My husband never saw anybody except me; not since he was a boy. He certainly wasn't the sort to see anybody. Not Rikaine. He was very strict; very custom-abiding."

"It might not have been his choice. What if someone had just come to see him without an invitation, without your husband knowing anything about it? He couldn't have helped seeing the intruder regardless of how custom-abiding he was."

She said, "Maybe, but he would have called robots at once and had the man taken away. He would have! Besides, no one would try to see my husband without being invited to. I couldn't conceive of such a thing. And Rikaine certainly would never invite anyone to see him. It's ridiculous to think so."

Baley said softly, "Your husband was killed by being struck on the head, wasn't he? You'll admit that."

"I suppose so. He was—all——"

"I'm not asking for the details at the moment. Was there any sign of some mechanical contrivance in the room that would have enabled someone to crush his skull by remote control."

"Of course not. At least, I didn't see any."

"If anything like that had been there, I imagine you would have seen it. It follows then that a hand held something capable of crushing a man's skull and that hand swung it. Some person had to be within four feet of your husband to do that. So someone did see him."

"No one would," she said earnestly. "A Solarian just wouldn't see anyone."

"A Solarian who would commit murder wouldn't stick at a bit of seeing, would he?"

(To himself that statement sounded dubious. On Earth he had known the case of a perfectly conscienceless murderer who had been caught only because he could not bring himself to violate the custom of absolute silence in the community bathroom.)

Gladia shook her head. "You don't understand about seeing. Earthmen just see anybody they want to all the time, so you don't understand it. . . ."

Curiosity seemed to be struggling within her. Her eyes lightened a bit. "Seeing does seem perfectly normal to you, doesn't it?"

"I've always taken it for granted," said Baley.

"It doesn't trouble you?"

"Why should it?"

"Well, the films don't say, and I've always wanted to know——Is it all right if I ask a question?"

"Go ahead," said Baley stolidly.

"Do you have a wife assigned to you?"

"I'm married. I don't know about the assignment part."

"And I know you see your wife any time you want to and she sees you and neither of you thinks anything of it."

Baley nodded.

"Well, when you see her, suppose you just want to——" She lifted her hands elbow-high, pausing as though searching for the proper phrase. She tried again, "Can you just—any time . . ." She let it dangle.

Baley didn't try to help.

She said, "Well, never mind. I don't know why I should bother you with that sort of thing now anyway. Are you through with me?" She looked as though she might cry again.

Baley said, "One more try, Gladia. Forget that no one would see your husband. Suppose someone *did*. Who might it have been?"

"It's just useless to guess. It couldn't be anyone."

"It has to be someone. Agent Gruer says there is reason to suspect some one person. So you see there must be someone."

A small, joyless smile flickered over the girl's face. "I know who he thinks did it."

"All right. Who?"

She put a small hand on her breast. "I."

A Theory Is Refuted

"I should have said, Partner Elijah," said Daneel, speaking suddenly, "that that is an obvious conclusion."

Baley cast a surprised look at his robot partner. "Why obvious?" he asked.

"The lady herself," said Daneel, "states that she was the only person who did or who would see her husband. The social situation on Solaria is such that even she cannot plausibly present anything else as the truth. Certainly Agent Gruer would find it reasonable, even obligatory, to believe that a Solarian husband would be seen only by his wife. Since only one person could be in seeing range, only one person could be the murderer. Or murderess, rather. Agent Gruer, you will remember, said that only one person could have done it. Anyone else he considered impossible. Well?"

"He also said," said Baley, "that that one person couldn't have done it, either."

"By which he probably meant that there was no weapon found at the scene of the crime. Presumably Mrs. Delmarre could explain that anomaly."

He gestured with cool robotic politeness toward where Gladia sat, still in viewing focus, her eyes cast down, her small mouth compressed.

Jehoshaphat, thought Baley, we're forgetting the lady.

Perhaps it was annoyance that had caused him to forget. It was Daneel who annoyed him, he thought, with his unemotional approach to problems. Or perhaps it was himself, with his emotional approach. He did not stop to analyze the matter.

He said, "That will be all for now, Gladia. However one goes about it, break contact. Good-by."

She said softly, "Sometimes one says, 'Done viewing,' but I like 'Good-by' better. You seem disturbed, Elijah. I'm sorry, because I'm used to having people think I did it, so you don't need to feel disturbed."

Daneel said, "*Did* you do it, Gladia?"

"No," she said angrily.

"Good-by, then."

With the anger not yet washed out of her face she was gone. For a moment, though, Baley could still feel the impact of those quite extraordinary gray eyes.

She might say she was used to having people think her a murderess, but that was very obviously a lie. Her anger spoke more truly than her words. Baley wondered of how many other lies she was capable.

And now Baley found himself alone with Daneel. He said, "All right, Daneel, I'm not altogether a fool."

"I have never thought you were, Partner Elijah."

"Then tell me what made you say there was no murder weapon found at the site of the crime? There was nothing in the evidence so far, nothing in anything I've heard that would lead us to that conclusion."

"You are correct. I have additional information not yet available to you."

"I was sure of that. What kind?"

"I felt that it would perhaps be more fruitful for you to conduct your investigation, at least in the initial stages, according to your own ideas, without being prejudiced by the conclusions of other people who, self-admittedly, have reached no satisfactory conclusions. It was because I, myself, felt my logical processes might be influenced by those conclusions that I contributed nothing to the discussion."

Logical processes! Unbidden, there leaped into Baley's mind the fragment of a conversation he had once had with a roboticist. A robot, the man had said, is logical but not reasonable.

He said, "You entered the discussion at the end."

"So I did, Partner Elijah, but only because by that time I had independent evidence bearing out Agent Gruer's suspicions."

"What kind of independent evidence?"

"That which could be deduced from Mrs. Delmarre's own behavior."

"Let's be specific, Daneel."

"Consider that if the lady were guilty and were attempting to prove herself innocent, it would be useful to her to have the detective in the case believe her innocent."

"Well?"

"If she could warp his judgment by playing upon a weakness of his, she might do so, might she not?"

"Strictly hypothetical."

"Not at all," was the calm reply. "You will have noticed, I think, that she concentrated her attention entirely on you."

"I was doing the talking," said Baley.

"Her attention was on you from the start; even before she could guess that you would be doing the talking. In fact, one might have thought she would, logically, have expected that I, as an Auroran, would take the lead in the investigation. Yet she concentrated on you."

"And what do you deduce from this?"

"That it was upon you, Partner Elijah, that she pinned her hopes. You were the Earthman."

"What of that?"

"She had studied Earth. She implied that more than once. She knew what I was talking about when I asked her to blank out the outer daylight at the very start of the interview. She did not act surprised or uncomprehending, as she would most certainly have done had she not had actual knowledge of conditions on Earth."

"Well?"

"Since she has studied Earth, it is quite reasonable to suppose that she discovered one weakness Earthmen possess. She must know of the nudity tabu, and of how such a display must impress an Earthman."

"She—she explained about the viewing——"

"So she did. Yet did it seem entirely convincing to you? Twice she allowed herself to be seen in what you would consider a state of improper clothing——"

"Your conclusion," said Baley, "is that she was trying to seduce me. Is that it?"

"Seduce you away from your professional impersonality. So it would seem to me. And though I cannot share human reactions to stimuli, I would judge, from what has been imprinted on my instruction circuits, that the lady meets any reasonable standard of physical attractiveness. From your behavior, moreover, it seems to me that you were aware of that and that you approved her appearance. I would even judge that Mrs. Delmarre acted rightly in thinking her mode of behavior would predispose you in her favor."

"Look," said Baley uncomfortably, "regardless of what effect she might have had on me, I am still an officer of the law in full possession of my sense of professional ethics. Get that straight. Now let's see the report."

Baley read through the report in silence. He finished, turned back, and read it through a second time.

"That brings in a new item," he said. "The robot."

Daneel Olivaw nodded.

Baley said thoughtfully, "She didn't mention it."

Daneel said, "You asked the wrong question. You asked if he was alone when she found the body. You asked if anyone else had been present at the death scene. A robot isn't 'anybody else.' "

Baley nodded. If he himself were a suspect and were asked who else had been at the scene of the crime, he would scarcely have replied: "No one but this table."

He said, "I suppose I should have asked if any robots were present?" (Damn it, what questions does one ask anyway on a strange world?) He said, "How legal is robotic evidence, Daneel?"

"What do you mean?"

"Can a robot bear witness on Solaria? Can it give evidence?"

"Why should you doubt it?"

"A robot isn't human, Daneel. On Earth, it cannot be a legal witness."

"And yet a footprint can, Partner Elijah, although that is much less a human than a robot is. The position of your planet in this respect is illogical. On Solaria, robotic evidence, when competent, is admissible."

Baley did not argue the point. He rested his chin on the knuckles of one hand and went over this matter of the robot in his mind.

In the extremity of terror Gladia Delmarre, standing over her husband's body, had summoned robots. By the time they came she was unconscious.

The robots reported having found her there together with the dead body. And something else was present as well; a robot. That robot had not been summoned; it was already there. It was not one of the regular staff. No other robot had seen it before or knew its function or assignment.

Nor could anything be discovered from the robot in question. It was not in working order. When found, its motions were disorganized and so, apparently, was the functioning of its positronic brain. It could give none of the proper responses, either verbal or mechanical, and after exhaustive investigation by a robotics expert it was declared a total loss.

Its only activity that had any trace of organization was its constant repetition of "You're going to kill me—you're going to kill me—you're going to kill me . . . ."

No weapon that could possibly have been used to crush the dead man's skull was located.

Baley said suddenly, "I'm going to eat, Daneel, and then we see Agent Gruer again—or view him, anyway."

Hannis Gruer was still eating when contact was established. He ate slowly, choosing each mouthful carefully from a variety of dishes, peering at each anxiously as though searching for some hidden combination he would find most satisfactory.

Baley thought: He may be a couple of centuries old. Eating may be getting dull for him.

Gruer said, "I greet you, gentlemen. You received our report, I believe." His bald head glistened, as he leaned across the table to reach a tidbit.

"Yes. We have spent an interesting session with Mrs. Delmarre also," said Baley.

"Good, good," said Gruer. "And to what conclusion, if any, did you come?"

Baley said, "That she is innocent, sir."

Gruer looked up sharply. "Really?"

Baley nodded.

Gruer said, "And yet she was the only one who could see him, the only one who could possibly be within reach. . . ."

Baley said, "That's been made clear to me, and no matter how firm social customs are on Solaria, the point is not conclusive. May I explain?"

Gruer had returned to his dinner. "Of course."

"Murder rests on three legs," said Baley, "each equally important. They are motive, means, and opportunity. For a good case against any suspect, each of the three must be satisfied. Now I grant you that Mrs. Delmarre had the opportunity. As for the motive, I've heard of none."

Gruer shrugged. "We know of none." For a moment his eyes drifted to the silent Daneel.

"All right. The suspect has no known motive, but perhaps she's a pathological killer. We can let the matter ride for a while, and continue. She is in his laboratory with him and there's some reason why she wants to kill him. She waves some club or other heavy object threateningly. It takes him a while to realize that his wife really intends to hurt him. He shouts in dismay, 'You're going to kill me,' and so she does. He turns to run as the blow descends and it crushes the back of his head. Did a doctor examine the body, by the way?"

"Yes and no. The robots called a doctor to attend Mrs. Delmarre and, as a matter of course, he looked at the dead body, too."

"That wasn't mentioned in the report."

"It was scarcely pertinent. The man was dead. In fact, by the time the doctor could view the body, it had been stripped, washed, and prepared for cremation in the usual manner."

"In other words, the robots had destroyed evidence," said Baley, annoyed. Then: "Did you say he *viewed* the body? He didn't *see* it?"

"Great Space," said Gruer, "what a morbid notion. He viewed it, of course, from all necessary angles and a close focus, I'm sure. Doctors can't avoid seeing patients under some conditions, but I can't conceive of any reason why they should have to see corpses. Medicine is a dirty job, but even doctors draw the line somewhere."

"Well, the point is this. Did the doctor report anything about the nature of the wound that killed Dr. Delmarre?"

"I see what you're driving at. You think that perhaps the wound was too severe to have been caused by a woman."

"A woman is weaker than a man, sir. And Mrs. Delmarre is a small woman."

"But quite athletic, Plainclothesman. Given a weapon of the proper type, gravity and leverage would do most of the work. Even not allowing for that, a woman in frenzy can do surprising things."

Baley shrugged. "You speak of a weapon. Where is it?"

Gruer shifted position. He held out his hand toward an empty glass and a robot entered the viewing field and filled it with a colorless fluid that might have been water.

Gruer held the filled glass momentarily, then put it down as though he had changed his mind about drinking. He said, "As is stated in the report, we have not been able to locate it."

"I know the report says that. I want to make absolutely certain of a few things. The weapon was searched for?"

"Thoroughly."

"By yourself?"

"By robots, but under my own viewing supervision at all times. We could locate nothing that might have been the weapon."

"That weakens the case against Mrs. Delmarre, doesn't it?"

"It does," said Gruer calmly. "It is one of several things about the case we don't understand. It is one reason why we have not acted against Mrs. Delmarre. It is one reason why I told you that the guilty

party could not have committed the crime, either. Perhaps I should
say that she apparently could not have committed the crime."

"Apparently?"

"She must have disposed of the weapon some way. So far, we have
lacked the ingenuity to find it."

Baley said dourly, "Have you considered all possibilities?"

"I think so."

"I wonder. Let's see. A weapon has been used to crush a man's skull
and it is not found at the scene of the crime. The only alternative is
that it has been carried away. It could not have been carried away
by Rikaine Delmarre. He was dead. Could it have been carried away
by Gladia Delmarre?"

"It must have been," said Gruer.

"How? When the robots arrived, she was on the floor unconscious.
Or she may have been feigning unconsciousness, but anyway she was
there. How long a time between the murder and the arrival of the first
robot?"

"That depends upon the exact time of the murder, which we don't
know," said Gruer uneasily.

"I read the report, sir. One robot reported hearing a disturbance
and a cry it identified as Dr. Delmarre's. It was apparently the closest
to the scene. The summoning signal flashed five minutes afterward. It
would take the robot less than a minute to appear on the scene."
(Baley remembered his own experiences with the rapid-fire appearance of robots when summoned.) "In five minutes, even ten, how far
could Mrs. Delmarre have carried a weapon and returned in time to
assume unconsciousness?"

"She might have destroyed it in a disposer unit."

"The disposer unit was investigated, according to the report, and
the residual gamma-ray activity was quite low. Nothing sizable had
been destroyed in it for twenty-four hours."

"I know that," said Gruer. "I simply present it as an example of
what might have been done."

"True," said Baley, "but there may be a very simple explanation. I
suppose the robots belonging to the Delmarre household have been
checked and all were accounted for."

"Oh yes."

"And all in reasonable working order?"

"Yes."

"Could any of those have carried away the weapon, perhaps without
being aware of what it was?"

"Not one of them had removed anything from the scene of the
crime. Or touched anything, for that matter."

"That's not so. They certainly removed the body and prepared it
for cremation."

"Well, yes, of course, but that scarcely counts. You would expect them to do that."

"Jehoshaphat!" muttered Baley. He had to struggle to keep calm.

He said, "Now suppose someone else had been on the scene."

"Impossible," said Gruer. "How could someone invade Dr. Delmarre's personal presence?"

"Suppose!" cried Baley. "Now there was never any thought in the robots' minds that an intruder might have been present. I don't suppose any of them made an immediate search of the grounds about the house. It wasn't mentioned in the report."

"There was no search till we looked for the weapon, but that was a considerable time afterward."

"Nor any search for signs of a ground-car or an air vehicle on the grounds?"

"No."

"Then if someone had nerved himself to invade Dr. Delmarre's personal presence, as you put it, he could have killed him and then walked away leisurely. No one would have stopped him or even seen him. Afterward, he could rely on everyone being sure no one could have been there."

"And no one could," said Gruer positively.

Baley said, "One more thing. Just one more. There was a robot involved. A robot was at the scene."

Daneel interposed for the first time. "The robot was not at the scene. Had it been there, the crime would not have been committed."

Baley turned his head sharply. And Gruer, who had lifted his glass a second time as though about to drink, put it down again to stare at Daneel.

"Is that not so?" asked Daneel.

"Quite so," said Gruer. "A robot would have stopped one person from harming another. First Law."

"All right," said Baley. "Granted. But it must have been close. It was on the scene when the other robots arrived. Say it was in the next room. The murderer is advancing on Delmarre and Delmarre cries out, 'You're going to kill me.' The robots of the household did not hear those words; at most they heard a cry, so, unsummoned, they did not come. But this particular robot heard the words and First Law made it come unsummoned. It was too late. Probably, it actually saw the murder committed."

"It must have seen the last stages of the murder," agreed Gruer. "That is what disordered it. Witnessing harm to a human without having prevented it is a violation of the First Law and, depending upon circumstances, more or less damage to the positronic brain is induced. In this case, it was a great deal of damage."

Gruer stared at his fingertips as he turned the glass of liquid to and fro.

Baley said, "Then the robot was a witness. Was it questioned?"

"What use? He was disordered. It could only say 'You're going to kill me.' I agree with your reconstruction that far. They were probably Delmarre's last words burned into the robot's consciousness when everything else was destroyed."

"But I'm told Solaria specializes in robots. Was there no way in which the robot could be repaired? No way in which its circuits could be patched?"

"None," said Gruer sharply.

"And where is the robot, now?"

"Scrapped," said Gruer.

Baley raised his eyebrows. "This is a rather peculiar case. No motive, no means, no witnesses, no evidence. Where there was some evidence to begin with, it was destroyed. You have only one suspect and everyone seems convinced of her guilt; at least, everyone is certain no one else can be guilty. That's your opinion, too, obviously. The question then is: Why was I sent for?"

Gruer frowned. "You seem upset, Mr. Baley." He turned abruptly to Daneel. "Mr. Olivaw."

"Yes, Agent Gruer."

"Won't you please go through the dwelling and make sure all windows are closed and blanked out? Plainclothesman Baley may be feeling the effects of open space."

The statement astonished Baley. It was his impulse to deny Gruer's assumption and order Daneel to keep his place when, on the brink, he caught something of panic in Gruer's voice, something of glittering appeal in his eyes.

He sat back and let Daneel leave the room.

It was as though a mask had dropped from Gruer's face, leaving it naked and afraid. Gruer said, "That was easier than I had thought. I'd planned so many ways of getting you alone. I never thought the Auroran would leave at a simple request, and yet I could think of nothing else to do."

Baley said, "Well, I'm alone now."

Gruer said, "I couldn't speak freely in his presence. He's an Auroran and he is here because he was forced on us as the price of having you." The Solarian leaned forward. "There's something more to this than murder. I am not concerned only with the matter of who did it. There are parties on Solaria, secret organizations. . . ."

Baley stared. "Surely, I can't help you there."

"Of course you can. Now understand this: Dr. Delmarre was a Traditionalist. He believed in the old ways, the good ways. But there are

new forces among us, forces for change, and Delmarre has been silenced."

"By Mrs. Delmarre?"

"Hers must have been the hand. That doesn't matter. There is an
organization behind her and that is the important matter."

"Are you sure? Do you have evidence?"

"Vague evidence, only. I can't help that. Rikaine Delmarre was on
the track of something. He assured me *his* evidence was good, and I
believe him. I knew him well enough to know him as neither fool nor
child. Unfortunately, he told me very little. Naturally, he wanted to
complete his investigation before laying the matter completely open
to the authorities. He must have gotten close to completion, too, or
they wouldn't have dared the risk of having him openly slaughtered
by violence. One thing Delmarre told me, though. The whole human
race is in danger."

Baley felt himself shaken. For a moment it was as though he were
listening to Minnim again, but on an even larger scale. Was *everyone*
going to turn to him with cosmic dangers?

"Why do you think I can help?" he asked.

"Because you're an Earthman," said Gruer. "Do you understand?
We on Solaria have no experience with these things. In a way, we
don't understand people. There are too few of us here."

He looked uneasy. "I don't like to say this, Mr. Baley. My colleagues
laugh at me and some grow angry, but it is a definite feeling I have.
It seems to me that you Earthmen *must* understand people far better
than we do, just by living among such crowds of them. And a detective
more than anyone. Isn't that so?"

Baley half nodded and held his tongue.

Gruer said, "In a way, this murder was fortunate. I have not dared
speak to the others about Delmarre's investigation, since I wasn't sure
who might be involved in the conspiracy, and Delmarre himself was
not ready to give any details till his investigation was complete. And
even if Delmarre had completed his work, how would we deal with
the matter afterward? How does one deal with hostile human beings?
I don't know. From the beginning, I felt we needed an Earthman.
When I heard of your work in connection with the murder in Spacetown on Earth, I knew we needed you. I got in touch with Aurora,
with whose men you have worked most closely, and through them
approached the Earth government. Yet my own colleagues could not
be persuaded into agreeing to this. Then came the murder and that
was enough of a shock to give me the agreement I needed. At the
moment, they would have agreed to anything."

Gruer hesitated, then added, "It's not easy to ask an Earthman to
help, but I must do so. Remember, whatever it is, the human race is
in danger. Earth, too."

Earth was doubly in danger, then. There was no mistaking the desperate sincerity in Gruer's voice.

But then, if the murder were so fortunate a pretext for allowing Gruer to do what he so desperately wanted to do all the time, was it entirely fortune? It opened new avenues of thought that were not reflected in Baley's face, eyes, or voice.

Baley said, "I have been sent here, sir, to help. I will do so to the best of my ability."

Gruer finally lifted his long-delayed drink and looked over the rim of the glass at Baley. "Good," he said. "Not a word to the Auroran, please. Whatever this is about, Aurora may be involved. Certainly they took an unusually intense interest in the case. For instance, they insisted on including Mr. Olivaw as your partner. Aurora is powerful; we had to agree. They say they include Mr. Olivaw only because he worked with you before, but it may well be that they wish a reliable man of their own on the scene, eh?"

He sipped slowly, his eyes on Baley.

Baley passed the knuckles of one hand against his long cheek, rubbing it thoughtfully. "Now if that——"

He didn't finish, but leaped from his chair and almost hurled himself toward the other, before remembering it was only an image he was facing.

For Gruer, staring wildly at his drink, clutched his throat, whispered hoarsely, "Burning . . . burning . . ."

The glass fell from his hand, its contents spilling. And Gruer dropped with it, his face distorted with pain.

7. A Doctor Is Prodded

Daneel stood in the doorway. "What happened, Partner Eli——"

But no explanation was needed. Daneel's voice changed to a loud ringing shout. "Robots of Hannis Gruer! Your master is hurt! Robots!"

At once a metal figure strode into the dining room and after it, in a minute or two, a dozen more entered. Three carried Gruer gently away. The others busily engaged in straightening the disarray and picking up the tableware strewn on the floor.

Daneel called out suddenly, "You there, robots, never mind the crockery. Organize a search. Search the house for any human being.

Alert any robots on the grounds outside. Have them go over every acre of the estate. If you find a master, hold him. Do not hurt him" (unnecessary advice) "but do not let him leave, either. If you find no master present, let me know. I will remain at this viewer combination."

Then, as robots scattered, Elijah muttered to Daneel, "That's a beginning. It was poison, of course."

"Yes. That much is obvious, Partner Elijah." Daneel sat down queerly, as though there were a weakness in his knees. Baley had never seen him give way so, not for an instant, to any action that resembled anything so human as a weakness in the knees.

Daneel said, "It is not well with my mechanism to see a human being come to harm."

"There was nothing you could do."

"That I understand and yet it is as though there were certain cloggings in my thought paths. In human terms what I feel might be the equivalent to shock."

"If that's so, get over it." Baley felt neither patience nor sympathy for a queasy robot. "We've got to consider the little matter of responsibility. There is no poison without a poisoner."

"It might have been food-poisoning."

"Accidental food-poisoning? On a world this neatly run? Never. Besides, the poison was in a liquid and the symptoms were sudden and complete. It was a poisoned dose and a large one. Look, Daneel, I'll go into the next room to think this out a bit. You get Mrs. Delmarre. Make sure she's at home and check the distance between her estate and Gruer's."

"Is it that you think she——"

Baley held up a hand. "Just find out, will you?"

He strode out of the room, seeking solitude. Surely there could not be two independent attempts at murder so close together in time on a world like Solaria. And if a connection existed, the easiest assumption to make was that Gruer's story of a conspiracy was true.

Baley felt a familiar excitement growing within him. He had come to this world with Earth's predicament in his mind, and his own. The murder itself had been a faraway thing, but now the chase was really on. The muscles in his jaw knotted.

After all, the murderer or murderers (or murderess) had struck in his presence and he was stung by that. Was he held in so little account? It was professional pride that was hurt and Baley knew it and welcomed the fact. At least it gave him a firm reason to see this thing through as a murder case, simply, even without reference to Earth's dangers.

Daneel had located him now and was striding toward him. "I have done as you asked me to, Partner Elijah. I have viewed Mrs. Delmarre.

She is at home, which is somewhat over a thousand miles from the estate of Agent Gruer."

Baley said, "I'll see her myself later. View her, I mean." He stared thoughtfully at Daneel. "Do you think she has any connection with this crime?"

"Apparently not a direct connection, Partner Elijah."

"Does that imply there might be an indirect connection?"

"She might have persuaded someone else to do it."

"Someone else?" Baley asked quickly. "Who?"

"That, Partner Elijah, I cannot say."

"If someone were acting for her, that someone would have to be at the scene of the crime."

"Yes," said Daneel, "someone must have been there to place the poison in the liquid."

"Isn't it possible that the poisoned liquid might have been prepared earlier in the day? Perhaps much earlier?"

Daneel said quietly, "I had thought of that, Partner Elijah, which is why I used the word 'apparently' when I stated that Mrs. Delmarre had no direct connection with the crime. It is within the realm of possibility for her to have been on the scene earlier in the day. It would be well to check her movements."

"We will do that. We will check whether she was physically present at any time."

Baley's lips twitched. He had guessed that in some ways robotic logic must fall short and he was convinced of it now. As the roboticist had said: Logical but not reasonable.

He said, "Let's get back into the viewing room and get Gruer's estate back in view."

The room sparkled with freshness and order. There was no sign at all that less than an hour before a man had collapsed in agony.

Three robots stood, backs against the wall, in the usual robotic attitude of respectful submission.

Baley said, "What news concerning your master?"

The middle robot said, "The doctor is attending him, master."

"Viewing or seeing?"

"Viewing, master."

"What does the doctor say? Will your master live?"

"It is not yet certain, master."

Baley said, "Has the house been searched?"

"Thoroughly, master."

"Was there any sign of another master beside your own?"

"No, master."

"Were there any signs of such presence in the near past?"

"Not at all, master."

"Are the grounds being searched?"

"Yes, master."

"Any results so far?"

"No, master."

Baley nodded and said, "I wish to speak to the robot that served at the table this night."

"It is being held for inspection, master. Its reactions are erratic."

"Can it speak?"

"Yes, master."

"Then get it here without delay."

There *was* delay and Baley began again. "I said——"

Daneel interrupted smoothly. "There is interradio communication among these Solarian types. The robot you desire is being summoned. If it is slow in coming, it is part of the disturbance that has overtaken it as the result of what has occurred."

Baley nodded. He might have guessed at interradio. In a world so thoroughly given over to robots some sort of intimate communication among them would be necessary if the system were not to break down. It explained how a dozen robots could follow when one robot had been summoned, but only when needed and not otherwise.

A robot entered. It limped, one leg dragging. Baley wondered why and then shrugged. Even among the primitive robots on Earth reactions to injury of the positronic paths were never obvious to the layman. A disrupted circuit might strike a leg's functioning, as here, and the fact would be most significant to a roboticist and completely meaningless to anyone else.

Baley said cautiously, "Do you remember a colorless liquid on your master's table, some of which you poured into a goblet for him?"

The robot said, "Yeth, mathter."

A defect in oral articulation, too!

Baley said, "What was the nature of the liquid?"

"It wath water, mathter."

"Just water? Nothing else?"

"Jutht water, mathter."

"Where did you get it?"

"From the rethervoir tap, mathter."

"Had it been standing in the kitchen before you brought it in?"

"The mathter preferred it not too cold, mathter. It wath a thtanding order that it be poured an hour before mealth."

How convenient, thought Baley, for anyone who knew that fact.

He said, "Have one of the robots connect me with the doctor viewing your master as soon as he is available. And while that is being done, I want another one to explain how the reservoir tap works. I want to know about the water supply here."

•   •   •

The doctor was available with little delay. He was the oldest Spacer Baley had ever seen, which meant, Baley thought, that he might be over three hundred years old. The veins stood out on his hands and his close-cropped hair was pure white. He had a habit of tapping his ridged front teeth with a fingernail, making a little clicking noise that Baley found annoying. His name was Altim Thool.

The doctor said, "Fortunately, he threw up a good deal of the dose. Still, he may not survive. It is a tragic event." He sighed heavily.

"What was the poison, Doctor?" asked Baley.

"I'm afraid I don't know." (Click-click-click.)

Baley said, "What? Then how are you treating him?"

"Direct stimulation of the neuromuscular system to prevent paralysis, but except for that I am letting nature take its course." His face, with its faintly yellow skin, like well-worn leather of superior quality, wore a pleading expression. "We have very little experience with this sort of thing. I don't recall another case in over two centuries of practice."

Baley stared at the other with contempt. "You know there are such things as poisons, don't you?"

"Oh, yes." (Click-click.) "Common knowledge."

"You have book-film references where you can gain some knowledge."

"It would take days. There are numerous mineral poisons. We make use of insecticides in our society, and it is not impossible to obtain bacterial toxins. Even with descriptions in the films it would take a long time to gather the equipment and develop the techniques to test for them."

"If no one on Solaria knows," said Baley grimly, "I'd suggest you get in touch with one of the other worlds and find out. Meanwhile, you had better test the reservoir tap in Gruer's mansion for poison. Get there in person, if you have to, and do it."

Baley was prodding a venerable Spacer roughly, ordering him about like a robot, and was quite unconscious of the incongruity of it. Nor did the Spacer make any protest.

Dr. Thool said doubtfully, "How could the reservoir tap be poisoned? I'm sure it couldn't be."

"Probably not," agreed Baley, "but test it anyway to make sure."

The reservoir tap was a dim possibility indeed. The robot's explanation had shown it to be a typical piece of Solarian self-care. Water might enter it from whatever source and be tailored to suit. Microorganisms were removed and non-living organic matter eliminated. The proper amount of aeration was introduced, as were various ions in just those trace amounts best suited to the body's needs. It was very unlikely that any poison could survive one or another of the control devices.

Still, if the safety of the reservoir were directly established, then the time element would be clear. There would be the matter of the hour before the meal, when the pitcher of water (exposed to *air*, thought Baley sourly) was allowed to warm slowly, thanks to Gruer's idiosyncrasy.

But Dr. Thool, frowning, was saying, "But how would I test the reservoir tap?"

"Jehoshaphat! Take an animal with you. Inject some of the water you take out of the tap into its veins, or have it drink some. Use your head, man. And do the same for what's left in the pitcher, and if that's poisoned, as it must be, run some of the tests the reference films describe. Find some simple one. Do *something*."

"Wait, wait. What pitcher?"

"The pitcher in which the water was standing. The pitcher from which the robot poured the poisoned drink."

"Well, dear me—I presume it has been cleaned up. The household retinue would surely not leave it standing about."

Baley groaned. Of course not. It was *impossible* to retain evidence with eager robots forever destroying it in the name of household duty. He should have *ordered* it preserved, but of course, this society was not his own and he never reacted properly to it.

Jehoshaphat!

Word eventually came through that the Gruer estate was clear; no sign of any unauthorized human present anywhere.

Daneel said, "That rather intensifies the puzzle, Partner Elijah, since it seems to leave no one in the role of poisoner."

Baley, absorbed in thought, scarcely heard. He said, "What? . . . Not at all. Not at all. It clarifies the matter." He did not explain, knowing quite well that Daneel would be incapable of understanding or believing what Baley was certain was the truth.

Nor did Daneel ask for an explanation. Such an invasion of a human's thoughts would have been most unrobotic.

Baley prowled back and forth restlessly, dreading the approach of the sleep period, when his fears of the open would rise and his longing for Earth increase. He felt an almost feverish desire to keep things happening.

He said to Daneel, "I might as well see Mrs. Delmarre again. Have the robot make contact."

They walked to the viewing room and Baley watched a robot work with deft metal fingers. He watched through a haze of obscuring thought that vanished in startled astonishment when a table, elaborately spread for dinner, suddenly filled half the room.

Gladia's voice said, "Hello." A moment later she stepped into view and sat down. "Don't look surprised, Elijah. It's just dinnertime. And I'm very carefully dressed. See?"

She was. The dominant color of her dress was a light blue and it shimmered down the length of her limbs to wrists and ankles. A yellow ruff clung about her neck and shoulders, a little lighter than her hair, which was now held in disciplined waves.

Baley said, "I did not mean to interrupt your meal."

"I haven't begun yet. Why don't you join me?"

He eyed her suspiciously. "Join you?"

She laughed. "You Earthmen are so funny. I don't mean join me in personal presence. How could you do that? I mean, go to your own dining room and then you and the other one can dine with me."

"But if I leave——"

"Your viewing technician can maintain contact."

Daneel nodded gravely at that, and with some uncertainty Baley turned and walked toward the door. Gladia, together with her table, its setting, and its ornaments moved with him.

Gladia smiled encouragingly. "See? Your viewing technician is keeping us in contact."

Baley and Daneel traveled up a moving ramp that Baley did not recall having traversed before. Apparently there were numerous possible routes between any two rooms in this impossible mansion and he knew only few of them. Daneel, of course, knew them all.

And, moving through walls, sometimes a bit below floor level, sometimes a bit above, there was always Gladia and her dinner table.

Baley stopped and muttered, "This takes getting used to."

Gladia said at once, "Does it make you dizzy?"

"A little."

"Then I tell you what. Why don't you have your technician freeze me right here. Then when you're in your dining room and all set, he can join us up."

Daneel said, "I will order that done, Partner Elijah."

Their own dinner table was set when they arrived, the plates steaming with a dark brown soup in which diced meat was bobbing, and in the center a large roast fowl was ready for the carving. Daneel spoke briefly to the serving robot and, with smooth efficiency, the two places that had been set were drawn to the same end of the table.

As though that were a signal, the opposite wall seemed to move outward, the table seemed to lengthen and Gladia was seated at the opposite end. Room joined to room and table to table so nearly that but for the varying pattern in wall and floor covering and the differing designs in tableware it would have been easy to believe they were all dining together in actual fact.

"There," said Gladia with satisfaction. "Isn't this comfortable?"

"Quite," said Baley. He tasted his soup gingerly, found it delicious, and helped himself more generously. "You know about Agent Gruer?"

Trouble shadowed her face at once and she put her spoon down. "Isn't it terrible? Poor Hannis."

"You use his first name. Do you know him?"

"I know almost all the important people on Solaria. Most Solarians do know one another. Naturally."

Naturally, indeed, thought Baley. How many of them were there, after all?

Baley said, "Then perhaps you know Dr. Altim Thool. He's taking care of Gruer."

Gladia laughed gently. Her serving robot sliced meat for her and added small, browned potatoes and slivers of carrots. "Of course I know him. He treated me."

"Treated you when?"

"Right after the—trouble. About my husband, I mean."

Baley said in astonishment, "Is he the only doctor on the planet?"

"Oh no." For a moment her lips moved as though she were counting to herself. "There are at least ten. And there's one youngster I know of who's studying medicine. But Dr. Thool is one of the best. He has the most experience. Poor Dr. Thool."

"Why poor?"

"Well, you know what I mean. It's such a nasty job, being a doctor. Sometimes you just have to see people when you're a doctor and even touch them. But Dr. Thool seems so resigned to it and he'll always do some seeing when he feels he must. He's always treated me since I was a child and was always so friendly and kind and I honestly feel I almost wouldn't mind if he did have to see me. For instance, he saw me this last time."

"After your husband's death, you mean?"

"Yes. You can imagine how he felt when he saw my husband's dead body and me lying there."

"I was told he viewed the body," said Baley.

"The body, yes. But after he made sure I was alive and in no real danger, he ordered the robots to put a pillow under my head and give me an injection of something or other, and then get out. He came over by jet. Really! By jet. It took less than half an hour and he took care of me and made sure all was well. I was so woozy when I came to that I was sure I was only viewing him, you know, and it wasn't till he touched me that I knew we were seeing, and I screamed. Poor Dr. Thool. He was awfully embarrassed, but I knew he meant well."

Baley nodded. "I suppose there's not much use for doctors on Solaria?"

"I should hope *not.*"

"I know there are no germ diseases to speak of. What about metabolic disorders? Atherosclerosis? Diabetes? Things like that?"

"It happens and it's pretty awful when it does. Doctors can make life more livable for such people in a physical way, but that's the least of it."

"Oh?"

"Of course. It means the gene analysis was imperfect. You don't suppose we allow defects like diabetes to develop on purpose. Anyone who develops such things has to undergo very detailed re-analysis. The mate assignment has to be retracted, which is terribly embarrassing for the mate. And it means no—no"—her voice sank to a whisper—"children."

Baley said in a normal voice, "No children?"

Gladia flushed. "It's a terrible thing to say. Such a word! Ch-children!"

"It comes easy after a while," said Baley dryly.

"Yes, but if I get into the habit, I'll say it in front of another Solarian someday and I'll just sink into the ground. . . . Anyway, if the two of them have had children (see, I've said it again) already, the children have to be found and examined—that was one of Rikaine's jobs, by the way—and well, it's just a mess."

So much for Thool, thought Baley. The doctor's incompetence was a natural consequence of the society, and held nothing sinister. Nothing *necessarily* sinister. Cross him off, he thought, but lightly.

He watched Gladia as she ate. She was neat and precisely delicate in her movements and her appetite seemed normal. (His own fowl was delightful. In one respect, anyway—food—he could easily be spoiled by these Outer Worlds.)

He said, "What is your opinion of the poisoning, Gladia?"

She looked up. "I'm trying not to think of it. There are so many horrors lately. Maybe it wasn't poisoning."

"It was."

"But there wasn't anyone around?"

"How do you know?"

"There couldn't have been. He has no wife, these days, since he's all through with his quota of ch—you know what. So there was no one to put the poison in anything, so how could he be poisoned?"

"But he was poisoned. That's a fact and must be accepted."

Her eyes clouded over. "Do you suppose," she said, "he did it himself?"

"I doubt it. Why should he? And so publicly?"

"Then it couldn't be done, Elijah. It just couldn't."

Baley said, "On the contrary, Gladia. It could be done very easily. And I'm sure I know exactly how."

A Spacer Is Defied

Gladia seemed to be holding her breath for a moment. It came out through puckered lips in what was almost a whistle. She said, "I'm sure *I* don't see how. Do you know *who* did it?"

Baley nodded. "The same one who killed your husband."

"Are you sure?"

"Aren't you? Your husband's murder was the first in the history of Solaria. A month later there is another murder. Could that be a coincidence? Two separate murders striking within a month of each other on a crime-free world? Consider, too, that the second victim was investigating the first crime and therefore represented a violent danger to the original murderer."

"Well!" Gladia applied herself to her dessert and said between mouthfuls, "If you put it that way, I'm innocent."

"How so, Gladia?"

"Why, Elijah. I've never been near the Gruer estate, never in my whole life. So I certainly couldn't have poisoned Agent Gruer. And if I haven't—why, neither did I kill my husband."

Then, as Baley maintained a stern silence, her spirit seemed to fade and the corners of her small mouth drooped. "Don't you think so, Elijah?"

"I can't be sure," said Baley. "I've told you I know the method used to poison Gruer. It's an ingenious one and anyone on Solaria could have used it, whether they were ever on the Gruer estate or not."

Gladia clenched her hands into fists. "Are you saying I did it?"

"I'm not saying that."

"You're implying it." Her lips were thin with fury and her high cheekbones were splotchy. "Is that all your interest in viewing me? To ask me sly questions? To trap me?"

"Now wait——"

"You seemed so sympathetic. So understanding. You—you Earthman!"

Her contralto had become a tortured rasp with the last word.

Daneel's perfect face leaned toward Gladia and he said, "If you will pardon me, Mrs. Delmarre, you are holding a knife rather tightly and may cut yourself. Please be careful."

Gladia stared wildly at the short, blunt, and undoubtedly quite harmless knife she held in her hand. With a spasmodic movement she raised it high.

Baley said, "You couldn't reach me, Gladia."

She gasped, "Who'd want to reach you? Ugh!" She shuddered in exaggerated disgust and called out, "Break contact at once!"

The last must have been to a robot out of the line of sight, and Gladia and her end of the room were gone and the original wall sprang back.

Daneel said, "Am I correct in believing you now consider this woman guilty?"

"No," said Baley flatly. "Whoever did this needed a great deal more of certain characteristics than this poor girl has."

"She has a temper."

"What of that? Most people do. Remember, too, that she has been under a considerable strain for a considerable time. If I had been under a similar strain and someone had turned on me as she imagined I had turned on her, I might have done a great deal more than wave a foolish little knife."

Daneel said, "I have not been able to deduce the technique of poisoning at a distance, as you say you have."

Baley found it pleasant to be able to say, "I know you haven't. You lack the capacity to decipher this particular puzzle."

He said it with finality and Daneel accepted the statement as calmly and as gravely as ever.

Baley said, "I have two jobs for you, Daneel."

"And what are they, Partner Elijah?"

"First, get in touch with this Dr. Thool and find out Mrs. Delmarre's condition at the time of the murder of her husband. How long she required treatment and so on."

"Do you want to determine something in particular?"

"No. I'm just trying to accumulate data. It isn't easy on this world. Secondly, find out who will be taking Gruer's place as head of security and arrange a viewing session for me first thing in the morning. As for me," he said without pleasure in his mind, and with none in his voice, "I'm going to bed and eventually, I hope, I'll sleep." Then, almost petulantly, "Do you suppose I could get a decent book-film in this place?"

Daneel said, "I would suggest that you summon the robot in charge of the library."

.   .   .

Baley felt only irritation at having to deal with the robot. He would much rather have browsed at will.

"No," he said, "not a classic; just an ordinary piece of fiction dealing with everyday life on contemporary Solaria. About half a dozen of them."

The robot submitted (it would have to) but even as it manipulated the proper controls that plucked the requisite book-films out of their niches and transferred them first to an exit slot and then to Baley's hand, it rattled on in respectful tones about all the other categories in the library.

The master might like an adventure romance of the days of exploration, it suggested, or an excellent view of chemistry, perhaps, with animated atom models, or a fantasy, or a Galactography. The list was endless.

Baley waited grimly for his half dozen, said, "These will do," reached with his own hands (his *own* hands) for a scanner and walked away.

When the robot followed and said, "Will you require help with the adjustment, master?" Baley turned and snapped, "No. Stay where you are."

The robot bowed and stayed.

Lying in bed, with the headboard aglow, Baley almost regretted his decision. The scanner was like no model he had ever used and he began with no idea at all as to the method for threading the film. But he worked at it obstinately, and, eventually, by taking it apart and working it out bit by bit, he managed something.

At least he could view the film and, if the focus left a bit to be desired, it was small payment for a moment's independence from the robots.

In the next hour and a half he had skipped and switched through four of the six films and was disappointed.

He had had a theory. There was no better way, he thought, to get an insight into Solarian ways of life and thought than to read their novels. He needed that insight if he were to conduct the investigation sensibly.

But now he had to abandon his theories. He had viewed the novels and had succeeded only in learning of the people with ridiculous problems who behaved foolishly and reacted mysteriously. Why should a woman abandon her job on discovering her child had entered the same profession and refuse to explain her reasons until unbearable and ridiculous complications had resulted? Why should a doctor and an artist be humiliated at being assigned to one another and what was so noble about the doctor's insistence on entering robotic research?

He threaded the fifth novel into the scanner and adjusted it to his eyes. He was bone-weary.

So weary, in fact, that he never afterward recalled anything of the fifth novel (which he believed to be a suspense story) except for the opening in which a new estate owner entered his mansion and looked through the past account films presented him by a respectful robot.

Presumably he fell asleep then with the scanner on his head and all lights blazing. Presumably a robot, entering respectfully, had gently removed the scanner and put out the lights.

In any case, he slept and dreamed of Jessie. All was as it had been. He had never left Earth. They were ready to travel to the community kitchen and then to see a subetheric show with friends. They would travel over the Expressways and see people and neither of them had a care in the world. He was happy.

And Jessie was beautiful. She had lost weight somehow. Why should she be so slim? And so beautiful?

And one other thing was wrong. Somehow the sun shone down on them. He looked up and there was only the vaulted base of the upper Levels visible, yet the sun shone down, blazing brightly on everything, and no one was afraid.

Baley woke up, disturbed. He let the robots serve breakfast and did not speak to Daneel. He said nothing, asked nothing, downed excellent coffee without tasting it.

Why had he dreamed of the visible-invisible sun? He could understand dreaming of Earth and of Jessie, but what had the sun to do with it? And why should the thought of it bother him, anyway?

"Partner Elijah," said Daneel gently.

"What?"

"Corwin Attlebish will be in viewing contact with you in half an hour. I have arranged that."

"Who the hell is Corwin Whatchamacullum?" asked Baley sharply, and refilled his coffee cup.

"He was Agent Gruer's chief aide, Partner Elijah, and is now Acting Head of Security."

"Then get him now."

"The appointment, as I explained, is for half an hour from now."

"I don't care when it's for. Get him now. That's an order."

"I will make the attempt, Partner Elijah. He may not, however, agree to receive the call."

"Let's take the chance, and get on with it, Daneel."

The Acting Head of Security accepted the call and, for the first time on Solaria, Baley saw a Spacer who looked the usual Earthly conception of one. Attlebish was tall, lean, and bronze. His eyes were a light brown, his chin large and hard.

He looked faintly like Daneel. But whereas Daneel was idealized, almost godlike, Corwin Attlebish had lines of humanity in his face.

Attlebish was shaving. The small abrasive pencil gave out its spray of fine particles that swept over cheek and chin, biting off the hair neatly and then disintegrating into impalpable dust.

Baley recognized the instrument through hearsay but had never seen one used before.

"You the Earthman?" asked Attlebish slurringly through barely cracked lips, as the abrasive dust passed under his nose.

Baley said, "I'm Elijah Baley, Plainclothesman C-7. I'm from Earth."

"You're early." Attlebish snapped his shaver shut and tossed it somewhere outside Baley's range of vision. "What's on your mind, Earthman?"

Baley would not have enjoyed the other's tone of voice at the best of times. He burned now. He said, "How is Agent Gruer?"

Attlebish said, "He's still alive. He may stay alive."

Baley nodded. "Your poisoners here on Solaria don't know dosages. Lack of experience. They gave Gruer too much and he threw it up. Half the dose would have killed him."

"Poisoners? There is no evidence for poison."

Baley stared. "Jehoshaphat! What else do you think it is?"

"A number of things. Much can go wrong with a person." He rubbed his face, looking for roughness with his fingertips. "You would scarcely know the metabolic problems that arise past the age of two fifty."

"If that's the case, have you obtained competent medical advice?"

"Dr. Thool's report——"

That did it. The anger that had been boiling inside Baley since waking burst through. He cried at the top of his voice, "I don't care about Dr. Thool. I said competent medical advice. Your doctors don't know anything, any more than your detectives do, if you had any. You had to get a detective from Earth. Get a doctor as well."

The Solarian looked at him coolly. "Are you telling me what to do?"

"Yes, and without charge. Be my guest. Gruer *was* poisoned. I witnessed the process. He drank, retched, and yelled that his throat was burning. What do you call it when you consider that he was investigating——" Baley came to a sudden halt.

"Investigating what?" Attlebish was unmoved.

Baley was uncomfortably aware of Daneel at his usual position some ten feet away. Gruer had not wanted Daneel, an Auroran, to know of the investigation. He said lamely, "There were political implications."

Attlebish crossed his arms and looked distant, bored, and faintly hostile. "We have no politics on Solaria in the sense we hear of it on other worlds. Hannis Gruer has been a good citizen, but he is imaginative. It was he who, having heard some story about you, urged that we import you. He even agreed to accept an Auroran companion for you as a condition. I did not think it necessary. There is no mystery. Rikaine Delmarre was killed by his wife and we shall find out how and why. Even if we do not, she will be genetically analyzed and the proper measures taken. As for Gruer, your fantasy concerning poisoning is of no importance."

Baley said incredulously, "You seem to imply that I'm not needed here."

"I believe not. If you wish to return to Earth, you may do so. I may even say we urge you to."

Baley was amazed at his own reaction. He cried, "No, sir. I don't budge."

"We hired you, Plainclothesman. We can discharge you. You will return to your home planet."

"No! You listen to me. I'd advise you to. You're a bigtime Spacer and I'm an Earthman, but with all respect, with deepest and most humble apologies, you're scared."

"Withdraw that statement!" Attlebish drew himself to his six-foot-plus, and stared down at the Earthman haughtily.

"You're scared as hell. You think you'll be next if you pursue this thing. You're giving in so they'll let you alone; so they'll leave you and your miserable life." Baley had no notion who the "they" might be or if there were any "they" at all. He was striking out blindly at an arrogant Spacer and enjoying the thud his phrases made as they hit against the other's self-control.

"You will leave," said Attlebish, pointing his finger in cold anger, "within the hour. There'll be no diplomatic considerations about this, I assure you."

"Save your threats, Spacer. Earth is nothing to you, I admit, but I'm not the only one here. May I introduce my partner, Daneel Olivaw. He's from Aurora. He doesn't talk much. He's not here to talk. I handle that department. But he listens awfully well. He doesn't miss a word.

"Let me put it straight, Attlebish"—Baley used the unadorned name with some relish—"whatever monkeyshines are going on here on Solaria, Aurora and forty-odd other Outer Worlds are interested. If you kick us off, the next deputation to visit Solaria will consist of warships. I'm from Earth and I know how the system works. Hurt feelings mean warships by return trip."

Attlebish transferred his regard to Daneel and seemed to be considering. His voice was gentler. "There is nothing going on here that need concern anyone outside the planet."

"Gruer thought otherwise and my partner heard him." This was no time to cavil at a lie.

Daneel turned to look at Baley, at the Earthman's last statement, but Baley paid no attention. He drove on: "I intend to pursue this investigation. Ordinarily, there's nothing I wouldn't do to get back to Earth. Even just dreaming about it gets me so restless I can't sit. If I owned this robot-infested palace I'm living in now, I'd give it with the robots thrown in and you and all your lousy world to boot for a ticket home.

"But I won't be ordered off by you. Not while there's a case to which I've been assigned that's still open. Try getting rid of me against my will and you'll be looking down the throats of space-based artillery.

"What's more, from now on, this murder investigation is going to be run *my* way. I'm in charge. I see the people I want to see. I *see* them. I don't view them. I'm used to seeing and that's the way it's going to be. I'll want the official approval of your office for all of that."

"This is impossible, unbearable——"

"Daneel, you tell him."

The humanoid's voice said dispassionately, "As my partner has informed you, Agent Attlebish, we have been sent here to conduct a murder investigation. It is essential that we do so. We, of course, do not wish to disturb any of your customs and perhaps actual seeing will be unnecessary, although it would be helpful if you were to give approval for such seeing as becomes necessary as Plainclothesman Baley has requested. As to leaving the planet against our will, we feel that would be inadvisable, although we regret any feeling on your part or on the part of any Solarian that our remaining would be unpleasant."

Baley listened to the stilted sentence structure with a dour stretching of his lips that was not a smile. To one who knew Daneel as a robot, it was all an attempt to do a job without giving offense to any human, not to Baley and not to Attlebish. To one who thought Daneel was an Auroran, a native of the oldest and most powerful militarily of the Outer Worlds, it sounded like a series of subtly courteous threats.

Attlebish put the tips of his fingers to his forehead. "I'll think about it."

"Not too long," said Baley, "because I have some visiting to do within the hour, and not by a viewer. Done viewing!"

He signaled the robot to break contact, then he stared with surprise and pleasure at the place where Attlebish had been. None of this had been planned. It had all been impulse born of his dream and of Attlebish's unnecessary arrogance. But now that it had happened, he was glad. It was what he had wanted, really—to take control.

He thought: Anyway, that was telling the dirty Spacer!

He wished the entire population of Earth could have been here to watch. The man *looked* such a Spacer, and that made it all the better, of course. All the better.

Only, why this feeling of vehemence in the matter of seeing? Baley scarcely understood that. He knew what he planned to do, and seeing (not viewing) was part of it. All right. Yet there had been the tight lift to his spirit when he spoke of seeing, as though he were ready to break down the walls of this mansion even though it served no purpose.

Why?

There was something impelling besides the case, something that had nothing to do even with the question of Earth's safety. But what?

Oddly, he remembered his dream again; the sun shining down through all the opaque layers of the gigantic underground Cities of Earth.

Daneel said with thoughtfulness (as far as his voice could carry a recognizable emotion), "I wonder, Partner Elijah, if this is entirely safe."

"Bluffing this character? It worked. And it wasn't really a bluff. I think it *is* important to Aurora to find out what's going on on Solaria, and that Aurora knows it. Thank you, by the way, for not catching me out in a misstatement."

"It was the natural decision. To have borne you out did Agent Attlebish a certain rather subtle harm. To have given you the lie would have done you a greater and more direct harm."

"Potentials countered and the higher one won out, eh, Daneel?"

"So it was, Partner Elijah. I understand that this process, in a less definable way, goes on within the human mind. I repeat, however, that this new proposal of yours is not safe."

"Which new proposal is this?"

"I do not approve your notion of seeing people. By that I mean seeing as opposed to viewing."

"I understand you. I'm not asking for your approval."

"I have my instructions, Partner Elijah. What it was that Agent Hannis Gruer told you during my absence last night I cannot know. That he did say something is obvious from the change in your attitude toward this problem. However, in the light of my instructions, I can guess. He must have warned you of the possibility of danger to other planets arising from the situation on Solaria."

Slowly Baley reached for his pipe. He did that occasionally and always there was the feeling of irritation when he found nothing and remembered he could not smoke. He said, "There are only twenty thousand Solarians. What danger can they represent?"

"My masters on Aurora have for some time been uneasy about Solaria. I have not been told all the information at their disposal——"

"And what little you have been told you have been told not to repeat to me. Is that it?" demanded Baley.

Daneel said, "There is a great deal to find out before this matter can be discussed freely."

"Well, what are the Solarians doing? New weapons? Paid subversion? A campaign of individual assassination? What can twenty thousand people do against hundreds of millions of Spacers?"

Daneel remained silent.

Baley said, "I intend to find out, you know."

"But not the way you have now proposed, Partner Elijah. I have been instructed most carefully to guard your safety."

"You would have to anyway. First Law!"

"Over and above that, as well. In conflict between your safety and that of another I must guard yours."

"Of course. I understand that. If anything happens to me, there is no further way in which you can remain on Solaria without complications that Aurora is not yet ready to face. As long as I'm alive, I'm here at Solaria's original request and so we can throw our weight around, if necessary, and make them keep us. If I'm dead, the whole situation is changed. Your orders are, then, to keep Baley alive. Am I right, Daneel?"

Daneel said, "I cannot presume to interpret the reasoning behind my orders."

Baley said, "All right, don't worry. The open space won't kill me, if I do find it necessary to see anyone. I'll survive. I may even get used to it."

"It is not the matter of open space alone, Partner Elijah," said Daneel. "It is this matter of seeing Solarians. I do not approve of it."

"You mean the Spacers won't like it. Too bad if they don't. Let them wear nose filters and gloves. Let them spray the air. And if it offends their nice morals to see me in the flesh, let them wince and blush. But I intend to see them. I consider it necessary to do so and I *will* do so."

"But I cannot allow you to."

"*You* can't allow *me*?"

"Surely you see why, Partner Elijah."

"I do not."

"Consider, then, that Agent Gruer, the key Solarian figure in the investigation of this murder, has been poisoned. Does it not follow that if I permit you to proceed in your plan for exposing yourself indiscriminately in actual person, the next victim will necessarily be you yourself. How then can I possibly permit you to leave the safety of this mansion?"

"How will you stop me, Daneel?"

"By force, if necessary, Partner Elijah," said Daneel calmly. "Even if I must hurt you. If I do not do so, you will surely die."

A Robot Is Stymied

Baley said, "So the higher potential wins out again, Daneel. You will hurt me to keep me alive."

"I do not believe hurting you will be necessary, Partner Elijah. You know that I am superior to you in strength and you will not attempt a useless resistance. If it should become necessary, however, I will be compelled to hurt you."

"I could blast you down where you stand," said Baley. "Right now! There is nothing in *my* potentials to prevent me."

"I had thought you might take this attitude at some time in our present relationship, Partner Elijah. Most particularly, the thought occurred to me during our trip to this mansion, when you grew momentarily violent in the ground-car. The destruction of myself is unimportant in comparison with your safety, but such destruction would cause you distress eventually and disturb the plans of my masters. It was one of my first cares, therefore, during your first sleeping period, to deprive your blaster of its charge."

Baley's lips tightened. He was left without a charged blaster! His hand dropped instantly to his holster. He drew his weapon and stared at the charge reading. It hugged zero.

For a moment he balanced the lump of useless metal as though to hurl it directly into Daneel's face. What good? The robot would dodge efficiently.

Baley put the blaster back. It could be recharged in good time.

Slowly, thoughtfully, he said, "I'm not fooled by you, Daneel."

"In what way, Partner Elijah?"

"You are too much the master. I am too completely stopped by you. Are you a robot?"

"You have doubted me before," said Daneel.

"On Earth last year I doubted whether R. Daneel Olivaw was truly a robot. It turned out he was. I believe he still is. My question, however is this: Are you R. Daneel Olivaw?"

"I am."

"Yes? Daneel was designed to imitate a Spacer closely. Why could not a Spacer be made up to imitate Daneel closely?"

"For what reason?"

"To carry on an investigation here with greater initiative and capacity than ever a robot could. And yet by assuming Daneel's role, you could keep me safely under control by giving me a false consciousness of mastery. After all, you are working through me and I must be kept pliable."

"All this is not so, Partner Elijah."

"Then why do all the Solarians we meet assume you to be human? They are robotic experts. Are they so easily fooled? It occurs to me that I cannot be one right against many wrong. It is far more likely that I am one wrong against many right."

"Not at all, Partner Elijah."

"Prove it," said Baley, moving slowly toward an end table and lifting a scrap-disposal unit. "You can do that easily enough, if you *are* a robot. Show the metal beneath your skin."

Daneel said, "I assure you——"

"Show the metal," said Baley crisply. "That is an order! Or don't you feel compelled to obey orders?"

Daneel unbuttoned his shirt. The smooth, bronze skin of his chest was sparsely covered with light hair. Daneel's fingers exerted a firm pressure just under the right nipple, and flesh and skin split bloodlessly the length of the chest, with the gleam of metal showing beneath.

And as that happened, Baley's fingers, resting on the end table, moved half an inch to the right and stabbed at a contact patch. Almost at once a robot entered.

"Don't move, Daneel," cried Baley. "That's an order! Freeze!"

Daneel stood motionless, as though life, or the robotic imitation thereof, had departed from him.

Baley shouted to the robot, "Can you get two more of the staff in here without yourself leaving? If so, do it."

The robot said, "Yes, master."

Two more robots entered, answering a radioed call. The three lined up abreast.

"Boys!" said Baley. "Do you see this creature whom you thought a master?"

Six ruddy eyes had turned solemnly on Daneel. They said in unison, "We see him, master."

Baley said, "Do you also see that this so-called master is actually a robot like yourself since it is metal within. It is only designed to look like a man."

"Yes, master."

"You are not required to obey any order it gives you. Do you understand that?"

"Yes, master."

"I, on the other hand," said Baley, "am a true man."

For a moment the robots hesitated. Baley wondered if, having had it shown to them that a thing might seem a man yet be a robot, they would accept *anything* in human appearance as a man, anything at all.

But then one robot said, "You are a man, master," and Baley drew breath again.

He said, "Very well, Daneel. You may relax."

Daneel moved into a more natural position and said calmly, "Your expressed doubt as to my identity, then, was merely a feint designed to exhibit my nature to these others, I take it."

"So it was," said Baley, and looked away. He thought: The thing is a machine, not a man. You can't doublecross a machine.

And yet he couldn't entirely repress a feeling of shame. Even as Daneel stood there, chest open, there seemed something so human about him, something capable of being betrayed.

Baley said, "Close your chest, Daneel, and listen to me. Physically, you are no match for three robots. You see that, don't you?"

"That is clear, Partner Elijah."

"Good! . . . Now you boys," and he turned to the other robots again. "You are to tell no one, human or master, that this creature is a robot. Never at any time, without further instructions from myself and myself alone."

"I thank you," interposed Daneel softly.

"However," Baley went on, "this manlike robot is not to be allowed to interfere with my actions in any way. If it attempts any such interference, you will restrain it by force, taking care not to damage it unless absolutely necessary. Do not allow it to establish contact with humans other than myself, or with robots other than yourselves, either by seeing or by viewing. And do not leave it at any time. Keep it in this room and remain here yourselves. Is all this clear?"

"Yes, master," they chorused.

Baley turned to Daneel again. "There is nothing you can do now, so don't try to stop me."

Daneel's arms hung loosely at his sides. He said, "I may not, through inaction, allow you to come to harm, Partner Elijah. Yet under the circumstances, nothing but inaction is possible. The logic is unassailable. I shall do nothing. I trust you will remain safe and in good health."

There it was, thought Baley. Logic was logic and robots had nothing else. Logic told Daneel he was completely stymied. Reason might have told him that all factors are rarely predictable, that the opposition might make a mistake.

None of that. A robot is logical only, not reasonable.

Again Baley felt a twinge of shame and could not forbear an attempt at consolation. He said, "Look, Daneel, even if I were walking into danger, *which I'm not*" (he added that hurriedly, with a quick glance at the other robots), "it would only be my job. It is what I'm paid to do. It is as much my job to prevent harm to mankind as a whole as yours is to prevent harm to man as an individual. Do you see?"

"I do not, Partner Elijah."

"Then that is because you're not made to see. Take my word for it that if you were a man, you would see."

Daneel bowed his head in acquiescence and remained standing, motionless, while Baley walked slowly toward the door of the room. The three robots parted to make room for him and kept their photo-electric eyes fixed firmly on Daneel.

Baley was walking to a kind of freedom and his heart beat rapidly in anticipation of the fact, then skipped a beat.

Another robot was approaching the door from the other side.

Had something gone wrong?

"What is it, boy?" he snapped.

"A message has been forwarded to you, master, from the office of Acting Head of Security Attlebish."

Baley took the personal capsule handed to him and it opened at once. A finely inscribed strip of paper unrolled. (He wasn't startled. Solaria would have his fingerprints on file and the capsule would be adjusted to open at the touch of his particular convolutions.)

He read the message and his long face mirrored satisfaction. It was his official permission to arrange "seeing" interviews, subject to the wishes of the interviewees, who were nevertheless urged to give "Agents Baley and Olivaw" every possible co-operation.

Attlebish had capitulated, even to the extent of putting the Earthman's name first. It was an excellent omen with which to begin, finally, an investigation conducted as it should be conducted.

Baley was in an air-borne vessel again, as he had been on that trip from New York to Washington. This time, however, there was a difference. The vessel was not closed in. The windows were left transparent.

It was a clear bright day and from where Baley sat the windows were so many patches of blue. Unrelieved, featureless. He tried not to huddle. He buried his head in his knees only when he could absolutely no longer help it.

The ordeal was of his own choosing. His state of triumph, his unusual sense of freedom at having beaten down first Attlebish and then Daneel, his feeling of having asserted the dignity of Earth against the Spacers, almost demanded it.

He had begun by stepping across open ground to the waiting plane with a kind of lighthearted dizziness that was almost enjoyable, and he had ordered the windows left unblanked in a kind of manic self-confidence.

I have to get used to it, he thought, and stared at the blue until his heart beat rapidly and the lump in his throat swelled beyond endurance.

He had to close his eyes and bury his head under the protective cover of his arms at shortening intervals. Slowly his confidence trickled away and even the touch of the holster of his freshly recharged blaster could not reverse the flow.

He tried to keep his mind on his plan of attack. First, learn the ways of the planet. Sketch in the background against which everything must be placed or fail to make sense.

See a sociologist!

He had asked a robot for the name of the Solarian most eminent as a sociologist. And there was that comfort about robots; they asked no questions.

The robot gave the name and vital statistics, and paused to remark that the sociologist would most probably be at lunch and would, therefore, possibly ask to delay contact.

"Lunch!" said Baley sharply. "Don't be ridiculous. It's not noon by two hours."

The robot said, "I am using local time, master."

Baley stared, then understood. On Earth, with its buried Cities, day and night, waking and sleeping, were man-made periods, adjusted to suit the needs of the community and the planet. On a planet such as this one, exposed nakedly to the sun, day and night were not a matter of choice at all, but were imposed on man willy-nilly.

Baley tried to picture a world as a sphere being lit and unlit as it turned. He found it hard to do and felt scornful of the so-superior Spacers who let such an essential thing as time be dictated to them by the vagaries of planetary movements.

He said, "Contact him anyway."

Robots were there to meet the plane when it landed and Baley, stepping out into the open again, found himself trembling badly.

He muttered to the nearest of the robots, "Let me hold your arm, boy."

The sociologist waited for him down the length of a hall, smiling tightly. "Good afternoon, Mr. Baley."

Baley nodded breathlessly. "Good evening, sir. Would you blank out the windows?"

The sociologist said, "They are blanked out already. I know something of the ways of Earth. Will you follow me?"

Baley managed it without robotic help, following at a considerable distance, across and through a maze of hallways. When he finally sat down in a large and elaborate room, he was glad of the opportunity to rest.

The walls of the room were set with curved, shallow alcoves. Statuary in pink and gold occupied each niche; abstract figures that pleased the eye without yielding instant meaning. A large, boxlike affair with white and dangling cylindrical objects and numerous pedals suggested a musical instrument.

Baley looked at the sociologist standing before him. The Spacer looked precisely as he had when Baley had viewed him earlier that day. He was tall and thin and his hair was pure white. His face was strikingly wedge-shaped, his nose prominent, his eyes deep-set and alive.

His name was Anselmo Quemot.

They stared at one another until Baley felt he could trust his voice to be reasonably normal. And then his first remark had nothing to do with the investigation. In fact it was nothing he had planned.

He said, "May I have a drink?"

"A drink?" The sociologist's voice was a trifle too high-pitched to be entirely pleasant. He said, "You wish water?"

"I'd prefer something alcoholic."

The sociologist's look grew sharply uneasy, as though the obligations of hospitality were something with which he was unacquainted.

And that, thought Baley, was literally so. In a world where viewing was the thing, there would be no sharing of food and drink.

A robot brought him a small cup of smooth enamel. The drink was a light pink in color. Baley sniffed at it cautiously and tasted it even more cautiously. The small sip of liquid evaporated warmly in his mouth and sent a pleasant message along the length of his esophagus. His next sip was more substantial.

Quemot said, "If you wish more——"

"No, thank you, not now. It is good of you, sir, to agree to see me."

Quemot tried a smile and failed rather markedly. "It has been a long time since I've done anything like this. Yes."

He almost squirmed as he spoke.

Baley said, "I imagine you find this rather hard."

"Quite." Quemot turned away sharply and retreated to a chair at the opposite end of the room. He angled the chair so that it faced more away from Baley than toward him and sat down. He clasped his gloved hands and his nostrils seemed to quiver.

Baley finished his drink and felt warmth in his limbs and even the return of something of his confidence.

He said, "Exactly how *does* it feel to have me here, Dr. Quemot?"

The sociologist muttered, "That is an uncommonly personal question."

"I know it is. But I think I explained when I viewed you earlier that I was engaged in a murder investigation and that I would have to ask a great many questions, some of which were bound to be personal."

"I'll help if I can," said Quemot. "I hope the questions will be decent ones." He kept looking away as he spoke. His eyes, when they struck Baley's face, did not linger, but slipped away.

Baley said, "I don't ask about your feelings out of curiosity only. This is essential to the investigation."

"I don't see how."

"I've got to know as much as I can about this world. I must understand how Solarians feel about ordinary matters. Do you see that?"

Quemot did not look at Baley at all now. He said slowly, "Ten years ago, my wife died. Seeing her was never very easy, but, of course, it is something one learns to bear in time and she was not the intrusive sort. I have been assigned no new wife since I am past the age of— of"—he looked at Baley as though requesting him to supply the phrase, and when Baley did not do so, he continued in a lower voice—"siring. Without even a wife, I have grown quite unused to this phenomenon of seeing."

"But how does it feel?" insisted Baley. "Are you in panic?" He thought of himself on the plane.

"No. Not in panic." Quemot angled his head to catch a glimpse of Baley and almost instantly withdrew. "But I will be frank, Mr. Baley. I imagine I can smell you."

Baley automatically leaned back in his chair, painfully self-conscious. "Smell me?"

"Quite imaginary, of course," said Quemot. "I cannot say whether you do have an odor or how strong it is, but even if you had a strong one, my nose filters would keep it from me. Yet, imagination . . ." He shrugged.

"I understand."

"It's worse. You'll forgive me, Mr. Baley, but in the actual presence of a human, I feel strongly as though something slimy were about to touch me. I keep shrinking away. It is most unpleasant."

Baley rubbed his ear thoughtfully and fought to keep down annoyance. After all, it was the other's neurotic reaction to a simple state of affairs.

He said, "If all this is so, I'm surprised you agreed to see me so readily. Surely you anticipated this unpleasantness."

"I did. But you know, I was curious. You're an Earthman."

Baley thought sardonically that that should have been another argument against seeing, but he said only, "What does that matter?"

A kind of jerky enthusiasm entered Quemot's voice. "It's not something I can explain easily. Not even to myself, really. But I've worked on sociology for ten years now. Really worked. I've developed propositions that are quite new and startling, and yet basically true. It is one of these propositions that makes me most extraordinarily interested in Earth and Earthmen. You see, if you were to consider Solaria's society and way of life carefully, it will become obvious to you that the said society and way of life is modeled directly and closely on that of Earth itself."

 **A Culture Is Traced**

Baley could not prevent himself from crying out, "What!"

Quemot looked over his shoulder as the moments of silence passed and said finally, "Not Earth's present culture. No."

Baley said, "Oh."

"But in the past, yes, Earth's ancient history. As an Earthman, you know it, of course."

"I've viewed books," said Baley cautiously.

"Ah. Then you understand."

Baley, who did not, said, "Let me explain exactly what I want, Dr. Quemot. I want you to tell me what you can about why Solaria is so different from the other Outer Worlds, why there are so many robots, why you behave as you do. I'm sorry if I seem to be changing the subject."

Baley most definitely wanted to change the subject. Any discussion of a likeness or unlikeness between Solaria's culture and Earth's would prove too absorbing by half. He might spend the day there and come away none the wiser as far as useful information was concerned.

Quemot smiled. "You want to compare Solaria and the Outer Worlds and not Solaria and Earth."

"I know Earth, sir."

"As you wish." The Solarian coughed slightly. "Do you mind if I turn my chair completely away from you. It would be more—more comfortable."

"As you wish, Dr. Quemot," said Baley stiffly.

"Good." A robot turned the chair at Quemot's low-voiced order, and as the sociologist sat there, hidden from Baley's eyes by the substantial chair back, his voice took on added life and even deepened and strengthened in tone.

Quemot said, "Solaria was first settled about three hundred years ago. The original settlers were Nexonians. Are you acquainted with Nexon?"

"I'm afraid not."

"It is close to Solaria, only about two parsecs away. In fact, Solaria and Nexon represented the closest pair of inhabited worlds in the Galaxy. Solaria, even when uninhabited by man, was life-bearing and eminently suited for human occupation. It represented an obvious attraction to the well-to-do of Nexon, who found it difficult to maintain a proper standard of living as their own planet filled up."

Baley interrupted. "Filled up? I thought Spacers practiced population control."

"Solaria does, but the Outer Worlds in general control it rather laxly. Nexon was completing its second million of population at the time I speak of. There was sufficient crowding to make it necessary to regulate the number of robots that might be owned by a particular family. So those Nexonians who could established summer homes on Solaria, which was fertile, temperate, and without dangerous fauna.

"The settlers on Solaria could still reach Nexon without too much trouble and while on Solaria they could live as they pleased. They could use as many robots as they could afford or felt a need for. Estates could be as large as desired since, with an empty planet, room was no problem, and with unlimited robots, exploitation was no problem.

"Robots grew to be so many that they were outfitted with radio contact and that was the beginning of our famous industries. We began to develop new varieties, new attachments, new capabilities. Culture dictates invention; a phrase I believe I have invented." Quemot chuckled.

A robot, responding to some stimulus Baley could not see beyond the barrier of the chair, brought Quemot a drink similar to that Baley had had earlier. None was brought to Baley, and he decided not to ask for one.

Quemot went on, "The advantages of life on Solaria were obvious to all who watched. Solaria became fashionable. More Nexonians established homes, and Solaria became what I like to call a 'villa planet.' And of the settlers, more and more took to remaining on the planet all year round and carrying on their business on Nexon through proxies. Robot factories were established on Solaria. Farms and mines began to be exploited to the point where exports were possible.

"In short, Mr. Baley, it became obvious that Solaria, in the space of a century or less, would be as crowded as Nexon had been. It seemed ridiculous and wasteful to find such a new world and then lose it through lack of foresight.

"To spare you a great deal of complicated politics, I need say only that Solaria managed to establish its independence and make it stick without war. Our usefulness to other Outer Worlds as a source of specialty robots gained us friends and helped us, of course.

"Once independent, our first care was to make sure that population did not grow beyond reasonable limits. We regulate immigration and births and take care of all needs by increasing and diversifying the robots we use."

Baley said, "Why is it the Solarians object to seeing one another?" He felt annoyed at the manner in which Quemot chose to expound sociology.

Quemot peeped round the corner of his chair and retreated almost at once. "It follows inevitably. We have huge estates. An estate ten thousand square miles in area is not uncommon, although the largest ones contain considerable unproductive areas. My own estate is nine hundred fifty square miles in area but every bit of it is good land.

"In any case, it is the size of an estate, more than anything else, that determines a man's position in society. And one property of a large estate is this: You can wander about in it almost aimlessly with little or no danger of entering a neighbor's territory and thus encountering your neighbor. You see?"

Baley shrugged. "I suppose I do."

"In short, a Solarian takes pride in not meeting his neighbor. At the same time, his estate is so well run by robots and so self-sufficient that there is no reason for him to have to meet his neighbor. The desire not to do so led to the development of ever more perfect viewing equipment, and as the viewing equipment grew better there was less and less need ever to see one's neighbor. It was a reinforcing cycle, a kind of feed-back. Do you see?"

Baley said, "Look here, Dr. Quemot. You don't have to make all this so simple for me. I'm not a sociologist but I've had the usual elementary courses in college. It's only an Earth college, of course," Baley added with a reluctant modesty designed to ward off the same comment, in more insulting terms, from the other, "but I can follow mathematics."

"Mathematics?" said Quemot, his voice squeaking the last syllable.

"Well, not the stuff they use in robotics, which I *wouldn't* follow, but sociological relationships I can handle. For instance, I'm familiar with the Teramin Relationship."

"The what, sir?"

"Maybe you have a different name for it. The differential of inconveniences suffered with privileges granted: dee eye sub jay taken to the nth——"

"What are you talking about?" It was the sharp and peremptory tone of a Spacer that Baley heard and he was silenced in bewilderment.

Surely the relationship between inconveniences suffered and privileges granted was part of the very essentials of learning how to handle people without an explosion. A private stall in the community bathroom for one person, given for cause, would keep x persons waiting patiently for the same lightning to strike them, the value of x varying in known ways with known variations in environment and human temperament, as quantitatively described in the Teramin Relationship.

But then again, in a world where all was privilege and nothing inconvenience, the Teramin Relationship might reduce to triviality. Perhaps he had chosen the wrong example.

He tried again. "Look, sir, it's one thing to get a qualitative fill-in on the growth of this prejudice against seeing, but it isn't helpful for my purposes. I want to know the exact analysis of the prejudice so I can counteract it effectively. I want to persuade people to see me, as you are doing now."

"Mr. Baley," said Quemot, "you can't treat human emotions as though they were built about a positronic brain."

"I'm not saying you can. Robotics is a deductive science and sociology an inductive one. But mathematics can be made to apply in either case."

There was silence for a moment. Then Quemot spoke in a voice that trembled. "You have admitted you are not a sociologist."

"I know. But I was told you *were* one. The best on the planet."

"I am the only one. You might almost say I have invented the science."

"Oh?" Baley hesitated over the next question. It sounded impertinent even to himself. "Have you viewed books on the subject?"

"I've looked at some Auroran books."

"Have you looked at books from Earth?"

"Earth?" Quemot laughed uneasily. "It wouldn't have occurred to me to read any of Earth's scientific productions. No offense intended."

"Well, I'm sorry. I had thought I would be able to get specific data that would make it possible for me to interview others face to face without having to——"

Quemot made a queer, grating inarticulate sound and the large chair in which he sat scraped backward, then went over with a crash.

A muffled "My apologies" was caught by Baley.

Baley had a momentary glimpse of Quemot running with an ungainly stride, then he was out of the room and gone.

Baley's eyebrows lifted. What the devil had he said this time? Jehoshaphat! What wrong button had he pushed?

Tentatively he rose from his seat, and stopped halfway as a robot entered.

"Master," said the robot, "I have been directed to inform you that the master will view you in a few moments."

"*View* me, boy?"

"Yes, master. In the meanwhile, you may desire further refreshment."

Another beaker of pink liquid was at Baley's elbow and this time a dish of some confectionary, warm and fragrant, was added.

Baley took his seat again, sampled the liquor cautiously and put it down. The confectionary was hard to the touch and warm, but the crust broke easily in the mouth and the inner portion was at once considerably warmer and softer. He could not identify the components of the taste and wondered if it might not be a product of the native spices or condiments of Solaria.

Then he thought of the restricted, yeast-derived dietary of Earth and wondered if there might be a market for yeast strains designed to imitate the tastes of Outer World products.

But his thoughts broke off sharply as sociologist Quemot appeared out of nowhere and faced him. *Faced* him this time! He sat in a smaller chair in a room in which the walls and floor clashed sharply with those surrounding Baley. And he was smiling now, so that fine wrinkles in his face deepened and, paradoxically, gave him a more youthful appearance by accentuating the life in his eyes.

He said, "A thousand pardons, Mr. Baley. I thought I was enduring personal presence so well, but that was a delusion. I was quite on edge and your phrase pushed me over it, in a manner of speaking."

"What phrase was that, sir?"

"You said something about interviewing people face to——" He shook his head, his tongue dabbing quickly at his lips. "I would rather not say it. I think you know what I mean. The phrase conjured up the most striking picture of the two of us breathing—breathing one another's breath." The Solarian shuddered. "Don't you find that repulsive?"

"I don't know that I've ever thought of it so."

"It seems so filthy a habit. And as you said it and the picture rose in my mind, I realized that after all we *were* in the same room and even though I was not facing you, puffs of air that had been in your lungs must be reaching me and entering mine. With my sensitive frame of mind——"

Baley said, "Molecules all over Solaria's atmosphere have been in thousands of lungs. Jehoshaphat! They've been in the lungs of animals and the gills of fish."

"That *is* true," said Quemot with a rueful rub of his cheek, "and I'd just as soon not think of that, either. However there was a sense of immediacy to the situation with yourself actually there and with both of us inhaling and exhaling. It's amazing the relief I feel in viewing."

"I'm still in the same house, Dr. Quemot."

"That's precisely what is so amazing about the relief. You are in the same house and yet just the use of the trimensionals make all the difference. At least I know what seeing a stranger feels like now. I won't try it again."

"That sounds as though you were experimenting with seeing."

"In a way," said the Spacer, "I suppose I was. It was a minor motivation. And the results were interesting, even if they were disturbing as well. It was a good test and I may record it."

"Record what?" asked Baley, puzzled.

"My feelings!" Quemot returned puzzled stare for puzzled stare.

Baley sighed. Cross-purposes. Always cross-purposes. "I only asked because somehow I assumed you would have instruments of some sort to measure emotional responses. An electroencephalograph, perhaps." He looked about fruitlessly. "Though I suppose you could have a pocket version of the same that works without direct electrical connection. We don't have anything like that on Earth."

"I trust," said the Solarian stiffly, "that I am able to estimate the nature of my own feelings without an instrument. They were pronounced enough."

"Yes, of course, but for quantitative analysis . . ." began Baley.

Quemot said querulously, "I don't know what you're driving at. Besides, I'm trying to tell you something else, my own theory, in fact, something I have viewed in no books, something I am quite proud of——"

Baley said, "Exactly what is that, sir?"

"Why, the manner in which Solaria's culture is based on one existing in Earth's past."

Baley sighed. If he didn't allow the other to get it off his chest, there might be very little co-operation thereafter. He said, "And that is?"

"Sparta!" said Quemot, lifting his head so that for a moment his white hair glistened in the light and seemed almost a halo. "I'm sure you've heard of Sparta!"

Baley felt relieved. He had been mightily interested in Earth's ancient past in his younger days (it was an attractive study to many Earthmen—an Earth supreme because it was an Earth alone; Earthmen the masters because there were no Spacers), but Earth's past was a large one. Quemot might well have referred to some phase with which Baley was unacquainted and that would have been embarrassing.

As it was, he could say cautiously, "Yes, I've viewed films on the subject."

"Good. Good. Now Sparta in its heyday consisted of a relatively small number of Spartiates, the only full citizens, plus a somewhat larger number of second-class individuals, the Perioeci, and a really large number of outright slaves, the Helots. The Helots outnumbered the Spartiates a matter of twenty to one, and the Helots were men with human feelings and human failings.

"In order to make certain that a Helot rebellion could never be successful despite their overwhelming numbers, the Spartans became military specialists. Each lived the life of a military machine, and the society achieved its purpose. There was never a successful Helot revolt.

"Now we human beings on Solaria are equivalent, in a way, to the Spartiates. We have our Helots, but our Helots aren't men but machines. They cannot revolt and need not be feared even though they outnumber us a thousand times as badly as the Spartans' human Helots outnumbered them. So we have the advantage of Spartiate exclusiveness without any need to sacrifice ourselves to rigid mastery. We can, instead, model ourselves on the artistic and cultural way of life of the Athenians, who were contemporaries of the Spartans and who——"

Baley said, "I viewed films on the Athenians, too."

Quemot grew warmer as he spoke. "Civilizations have always been pyramidal in structure. As one climbs toward the apex of the social edifice, there is increased leisure and increasing opportunity to pursue happiness. As one climbs, one finds also fewer and fewer people to enjoy this more and more. Invariably, there is a preponderance of the dispossessed. And remember this, no matter how well off the bottom layers of the pyramid might be on an absolute scale, they are always dispossessed in comparison with the apex. For instance, even the most poorly off humans on Aurora are better off than Earth's aristocrats, but they are dispossessed with respect to Aurora's aristocrats, and it is with the masters of their own world that they compare themselves.

"So there is always social friction in ordinary human societies. The action of social revolution and the reaction of guarding against such revolution or combating it once it has begun are the causes of a great deal of the human misery with which history is permeated.

"Now here on Solaria, for the first time, the apex of the pyramid stands alone. In the place of the dispossessed are the robots. We have the first new society, the first really new one, the first great social invention since the farmers of Sumeria and Egypt invented cities."

He sat back now, smiling.

Baley nodded. "Have you published this?"

"I may," said Quemot with an affectation of carelessness, "someday. I haven't yet. This is my third contribution."

"Were the other two as broad as this?"

"They weren't in sociology. I have been a sculptor in my time. The work you see about you"—he indicated the statuary—"is my own. And I have been a composer, too. But I am getting older and Rikaine Delmarre always argued strongly in favor of the applied arts rather than the fine arts and I decided to go into sociology."

Baley said, "That sounds as though Delmarre was a good friend of yours."

"We knew one another. At my time in life, one knows all adult

Solarians. But there is no reason not to agree that Rikaine Delmarre and I were well acquainted."

"What sort of a man was Delmarre?" (Strangely enough, the name of the man brought up the picture of Gladia in Baley's mind and he was plagued with a sudden, sharp recall of her as he had last seen her, furious, her face distorted with anger at him.)

Quemot looked a bit thoughtful. "He was a worthy man; devoted to Solaria and to its way of life."

"An idealist, in other words."

"Yes. Definitely. You could see that in the fact that he volunteered for his job as—as fetal engineer. It was an applied art, you see, and I told you his feelings about that."

"Was volunteering unusual?"

"Wouldn't *you* say——But I forget you're an Earthman. Yes, it is unusual. It's one of those jobs that must be done, yet finds no voluntary takers. Ordinarily, someone must be assigned to it for a period of so many years and it isn't pleasant to be the one chosen. Delmarre volunteered, and for life. He felt the position was too important to be left to reluctant draftees, and he persuaded me into that opinion, too. Yet I certainly would never have volunteered. I couldn't possibly make the personal sacrifice. And it was more of a sacrifice for him, since he was almost a fanatic in personal hygiene."

"I'm still not certain I understand the nature of his job."

Quemot's old cheeks flushed gently. "Hadn't you better discuss that with his assistant?"

Baley said, "I would certainly have done so by now, sir, if anyone had seen fit to tell me before this moment that he had an assistant."

"I'm sorry about that," said Quemot, "but the existence of the assistant is another measure of his social responsibility. No previous occupant of the post provided for one. Delmarre, however, felt it necessary to find a suitable youngster and conduct the necessary training himself so as to leave a professional heir behind when the time came for him to retire or, well, to die." The old Solarian sighed heavily. "Yet I outlived him and he was so much younger. I used to play chess with him. Many times."

"How did you manage that?"

Quemot's eyebrows lifted. "The usual way."

"You saw one another?"

Quemot looked horrified. "What an idea! Even if I could stomach it, Delmarre would never allow it for an instant. Being fetal engineer didn't blunt his sensibilities. He was a finicky man."

"Then how——"

"With two boards as any two people would play chess." The Solarian shrugged in a sudden gesture of tolerance. "Well, you're an Earthman. My moves registered on his board, and his on mine. It's a simple matter."

Baley said, "Do you know Mrs. Delmarre?"

"We've viewed one another. She's a field colorist, you know, and I've viewed some of her showings. Fine work in a way but more interesting as curiosities than as creations. Still, they're amusing and show a perceptive mind."

"Is she capable of killing her husband, would you say?"

"I haven't given it a thought. Women are surprising creatures. But then, there's scarcely room for argument, is there? Only Mrs. Delmarre could have been close enough to Rikaine to kill him. Rikaine would never, under any circumstances, have allowed anyone else seeing privileges for any reason. Extremely finicky. Perhaps finicky is the wrong word. It was just that he lacked any tract of abnormality; anything of the perverse. He was a good Solarian."

"Would you call your granting me seeing privileges perverse?" asked Baley.

Quemot said, "Yes, I think I would. I should say there was a bit of scatophilia involved."

"Could Delmarre have been killed for political reasons?"

"What?"

"I've heard him called a Traditionalist."

"Oh, we all are."

"You mean there is no group of Solarians who are *not* Traditionalists?"

"I dare say there are some," said Quemot slowly, "who think it is dangerous to be too Traditionalist. They are overconscious of our small population, of the way the other worlds outnumber us. They think we are defenseless against possible aggression from the other Outer Worlds. They're quite foolish to think so and there aren't many of them. I don't think they're a force."

"Why do you say they are foolish? Is there anything about Solaria that would affect the balance of power in spite of the great disadvantage of numbers? Some new type of weapon?"

"A weapon, certainly. But not a new one. The people I speak of are more blind than foolish not to realize that such a weapon is in operation continuously and cannot be resisted."

Baley's eyes narrowed. "Are you serious?"

"Certainly."

"Do you know the nature of the weapon?"

"All of us must. *You* do, if you stop to think of it. I see it a trifle easier than most, perhaps, since I am a sociologist. To be sure, it isn't used as a weapon ordinarily is used. It doesn't kill or hurt, but it is irresistible even so. All the more irresistible because no one notices it."

Baley said with annoyance, "And just what is this nonlethal weapon?"

Quemot said, "The positronic robot."

A Farm Is Inspected

For a moment Baley went cold. The positronic robot was the symbol of Spacer superiority over Earthmen. That was weapon enough.

He kept his voice steady. "It's an economic weapon. Solaria is important to the Outer Worlds as a source of advanced models and so it will not be harmed by them."

"That's an obvious point," said Quemot indifferently. "That helped us establish our independence. What I have in mind is something else, something more subtle and more cosmic." Quemot's eyes were fixed on his fingers' ends and his mind was obviously fixed on abstractions.

Baley said, "Is this another of your sociological theories?"

Quemot's poorly suppressed look of pride all but forced a short smile out of the Earthman.

The sociologist said, "It is indeed mine. Original, as far as I know, and yet obvious if population data on the Outer Worlds is carefully studied. To begin with, ever since the positronic robot was invented, it has been used more and more intensively everywhere."

"Not on Earth," said Baley.

"Now, now, Plainclothesman. I don't know much of your Earth, but I know enough to know that robots are entering your economy. You people live in large Cities and leave most of your planetary surface unoccupied. Who runs your farms and mines, then?"

"Robots," admitted Baley. "But if it comes to that, Doctor, Earthmen invented the positronic robot in the first place."

"They did? Are you sure?"

"You can check. It's true."

"Interesting. Yet robots made the least headway there." The sociologist said thoughtfully, "Perhaps that is because of Earth's large population. It would take that much longer. Yes . . . . Still, you have robots even in your Cities."

"Yes," said Baley.

"More now than, say, fifty years ago."

Baley nodded impatiently. "Yes."

"Then it fits. The difference is only one of time. Robots tend to displace human labor. The robot economy moves in only one direction. More robots and fewer humans. I've studied population data *very* carefully and I've plotted it and made a few extrapolations." He paused in sudden surprise. "Why, that's rather an application of mathematics to sociology, isn't it?"

"It is," said Baley.

"There may be something to it, at that. I will have to give the matter thought. In any case, these are the conclusions I have come to, and I am convinced there is no doubt as to their correctness. The robot-human ratio in any economy that has accepted robot labor tends continuously to increase despite any laws that are passed to prevent it. The increase is slowed, but never stopped. At first the human population increases, but the robot population increases much more quickly. Then, after a certain critical point is reached . . ."

Quemot stopped again, then said, "Now let's see. I wonder if the critical point could be determined exactly; if you could really put a figure to it. There's your mathematics again."

Baley stirred restlessly. "What happens after the critical point is reached, Dr. Quemot?"

"Eh? Oh, the human population begins actually to decline. A planet approaches a true social stability. Aurora will have to. Even your Earth will have to. Earth may take a few more centuries, but it is inevitable."

"What do you mean by social stability?"

"The situation here. In Solaria. A world in which the humans are the leisure class only. So there is no reason to fear the other Outer Worlds. We need only wait a century perhaps and they shall all be Solarias. I suppose that will be the end of human history, in a way; at least, its fulfillment. Finally, finally, all men will have all they can need and want. You know, there is a phrase I once picked up; I don't know where it comes from; something about the pursuit of happiness."

Baley said thoughtfully, "All men are 'endowed by their Creator with certain unalienable rights . . . among these are life, liberty, and the pursuit of happiness.' "

"You've hit it. Where's that from?"

"Some old document," said Baley.

"Do you see how that is changed here on Solaria and eventually in all the Galaxy? The pursuit will be over. The rights mankind will be heir to will be life, liberty, and happiness. Just that. Happiness."

Baley said dryly, "Maybe so, but a man has been killed on your Solaria and another may yet die."

He felt regret almost the moment he spoke, for the expression on Quemot's face was as though he had been struck with an open palm. The old man's head bowed. He said without looking up, "I have answered your questions as well as I could. Is there anything else you wish?"

"I have enough. Thank you, sir. I am sorry to have intruded on your grief at your friend's death."

Quemot looked up slowly. "It will be hard to find another chess partner. He kept our appointments most punctually and he played an extraordinarily even game. He was a good Solarian."

"I understand," said Baley softly. "May I have your permission to use your viewer to make contact with the next person I must see?"

"Of course," said Quemot. "My robots are yours. And now I will leave you. Done viewing."

A robot was at Baley's side within thirty seconds of Quemot's disappearance and Baley wondered once again how these creatures were managed. He had seen Quemot's fingers move toward a contact as he had left and that was all.

Perhaps the signal was quite a generalized one, saying only, "Do your duty!" Perhaps robots listened to all that went on and were always aware of what a human might desire at any given moment, and if the particular robot was not designed for a particular job in either mind or body, the radio web that united all robots went into action and the correct robot was spurred into action.

For a moment Baley had the vision of Solaria as a robotic net with holes that were small and continually growing smaller, with every human being caught neatly in place. He thought of Quemot's picture of worlds turning into Solarias; of nets forming and tightening even on Earth, until——

His thoughts were disrupted as the robot who had entered spoke with the quiet and even respect of the machine.

"I am ready to help you, master."

Baley said, "Do you know how to reach the place where Rikaine Delmarre once worked?"

"Yes, master."

Baley shrugged. He would never teach himself to avoid asking useless questions. The robots knew. Period. It occurred to him that, to handle robots with true efficiency, one must needs be expert, a sort of roboticist. How well did the average Solarian do, he wondered? Probably only so-so.

He said, "Get Delmarre's place and contact his assistant. If the assistant is not there, locate him wherever he is."

"Yes, master."

As the robot turned to go, Baley called after it, "Wait! What time is it at the Delmarre workplace?"

"About 0630, master."

"In the morning?"

"Yes, master."

Again Baley felt annoyance at a world that made itself victim of the coming and going of a sun. It was what came of living on bare planetary surface.

He thought fugitively of Earth, then tore his mind away. While he kept firmly to the matter in hand, he managed well. Slipping into homesickness would ruin him.

He said, "Call the assistant, anyway, boy, and tell him it's government business—and have one of the other boys bring something to eat. A sandwich and a glass of milk will do."

He chewed thoughtfully at the sandwich, which contained a kind of smoked meat, and with half his mind thought that Daneel Olivaw would certainly consider every article of food suspect after what had happened to Gruer. And Daneel might be right, too.

He finished the sandwich without ill effects, however (immediate ill effects, at any rate), and sipped at the milk. He had not learned from Quemot what he had come to learn, but he had learned something. As he sorted it out in his mind, it seemed he had learned a good deal.

Little about the murder, to be sure, but more about the larger matter.

The robot returned. "The assistant will accept contact, master."

"Good. Was there any trouble with it?"

"The assistant was asleep, master."

"Awake now, though?"

"Yes, master."

The assistant was facing him suddenly, sitting up in bed and wearing an expression of sullen resentment.

Baley reared back as though a force-barrier had been raised before him without warning. Once again a piece of vital information had been withheld from him. Once again he had not asked the right questions.

No one had thought to tell him that Rikaine Delmarre's assistant was a woman.

Her hair was a trifle darker than ordinary Spacer bronze and there was a quantity of it, at the moment in disorder. Her face was oval, her nose a trifle bulbous, and her chin large. She scratched slowly at her side just above the waist and Baley hoped the sheet would remain in position. He remembered Gladia's free attitude toward what was permitted while viewing.

Baley felt a sardonic amusement at his own disillusion at the moment. Earthmen assumed, somehow, that all Spacer women were beautiful, and certainly Gladia had reinforced that assumption. This one, though, was plain even by Earthly standards.

It therefore surprised Baley that he found her contralto attractive when she said, "See here, do you know what time it is?"

"I do," said Baley, "but since I will be seeing you, I felt I should warn you."

"*Seeing* me? Skies above——" Her eyes grew wide and she put a hand to her chin. (She wore a ring on one finger, the first item of personal adornment Baley had yet seen on Solaria.) "Wait, you're not my new assistant, are you?"

"No. Nothing like that. I'm here to investigate the death of Rikaine Delmarre."

"Oh? Well, investigate, then."

"What is your name?"

"Klorissa Cantoro."

"And how long have you been working with Dr. Delmarre?"

"Three years."

"I assume you're now at the place of business." (Baley felt uncomfortable at the noncommittal phrase, but he did not know what to call a place where a fetal engineer worked.)

"If you mean, am I at the farm?" said Klorissa discontentedly, "I certainly am. I haven't left it since the old man was done in, and I won't leave it, looks like, till an assistant is assigned me. Can you arrange that, by the way?"

"I'm sorry, ma'am. I have no influence with anyone here."

"Thought I'd ask."

Klorissa pulled off the sheet and climbed out of bed without any self-consciousness. She was wearing a one-piece sleeping suit and her hand went to the notch of the seam, where it ended at the neck.

Baley said hurriedly, "Just one moment. If you'll agree to see me, that will end my business with you for now and you may dress in privacy."

"In privacy?" She put out her lower lip and stared at Baley curiously. "You're finicky, aren't you? Like the boss."

"Will you see me? I would like to look over the farm."

"I don't get this business about seeing, but if you want to view the farm I'll tour you. If you'll give me a chance to wash and take care of a few things and wake up a little, I'll enjoy the break in routine."

"I don't want to view anything. I want to *see*."

The woman cocked her head to one side and her keen look had something of professional interest in it. "Are you a pervert or something? When was the last time you underwent a gene analysis?"

"Jehoshaphat!" muttered Baley. "Look, I'm Elijah Baley. I'm from Earth."

"From Earth?" She cried vehemently. "Skies above! Whatever are you doing here? Or is this some kind of complicated joke?"

"I'm not joking. I was called in to investigate Delmarre's death. I'm a plainclothesman, a detective."

"You mean that kind of investigation. But I thought everyone knew his wife did it."

"No, ma'am, there's some question about it in my mind. May I have your permission to see the farm and you. As an Earthman you understand, I'm not accustomed to viewing. It makes me uncomfortable. I have permission from the Head of Security to see people who might help me. I will show you the document, if you wish."

"Let's see it."

Baley held the official strip up before her imaged eyes.

She shook her head. "Seeing! It's filthy. Still, skies above, what's a little more filth in this filthy job? Look here, though, don't you come close to me. You stay a good distance away. We can shout or send messages by robot, if we have to. You understand?"

"I understand."

Her sleeping suit split open at the seam just as contact broke off and the last word he heard from her was a muttered: "Earthman!"

"That's close enough," said Klorissa.

Baley, who was some twenty-five feet from the woman, said, "It's all right this distance, but I'd like to get indoors quickly."

It had not been so bad this time, somehow. He had scarcely minded the plane trip, but there was no point in overdoing it. He kept himself from yanking at his collar to allow himself to breathe more freely.

Klorissa said sharply, "What's wrong with you? You look kind of beat."

Baley said, "I'm not used to the outdoors."

"That's right! Earthman! You've got to be cooped up or something. Skies above!" Her tongue passed over her lips as though it tasted something unappetizing. "Well, come in, then, but let me move out of the way first. All right. Get in."

Her hair was in two thick braids that wound about her head in a complicated geometrical pattern. Baley wondered how long it took to arrange like that and then remembered that, in all probability, the unerring mechanical fingers of a robot did the job.

The hair set off her oval face and gave it a kind of symmetry that made it pleasant if not pretty. She did not wear any facial make-up, nor, for that matter, were her clothes meant to do more than cover her serviceably. For the most part they were a subdued dark blue except for her gloves, which covered her to mid-arm and were a badly clashing lilac in color. Apparently they were not part of her ordinary costume. Baley noted the thickening of one finger of the gloves owing to the presence of the ring underneath.

They remained at opposite ends of the room, facing one another.

Baley said, "You don't like this, do you, ma'am?"

Klorissa shrugged. "Why should I like it? I'm not an animal. But I can stand it. You get pretty hardened, when you deal with—with"— she paused, and then her chin went up as though she had made up her mind to say what she had to say without mincing—"with children." She pronounced the word with careful precision.

"You sound as though you don't like the job you have."

"It's an important job. It must be done. Still, I don't like it."

"Did Rikaine Delmarre like it?"

"I suppose he didn't, but he never showed it. He was a good Solarian."

"And he was finicky."

Klorissa looked surprised.

Baley said, "You yourself said so. When we were viewing and I said you might dress in private, you said I was finicky like the boss."

"Oh. Well, he *was* finicky. Even viewing he never took any liberties. Always proper."

"Was that unusual?"

"It shouldn't be. Ideally, you're supposed to be proper, but no one ever is. Not when viewing. There's no personal presence involved so why take any pains? You know? I don't take pains when viewing, except with the boss. You had to be formal with him."

"Did you admire Dr. Delmarre?"

"He was a good Solarian."

Baley said, "You've called this place a farm and you've mentioned children. Do you bring up children here?"

"From the age of a month. Every fetus on Solaria comes here."

"Fetus?"

"Yes." She frowned. "We get them a month after conception. Does this embarrass you?"

"No," Baley said shortly. "Can you show me around?"

"I can. But keep your distance."

Baley's long face took on a stony grimness as he looked down the length of the long room from above. There was glass between the room and themselves. On the other side, he was sure, was perfectly controlled heat, perfectly controlled humidity, perfectly controlled asepsis. Those tanks, row on row, each contained its little creature floating in a watery fluid of precise composition, infused with a nutrient mixture of ideal proportions. Life and growth went on.

Little things, some smaller than half his fist, curled on themselves, with bulging skulls and tiny budding limbs and vanishing tails.

Klorissa, from her position twenty feet away, said, "How do you like it, Plainclothesman?"

Baley said, "How many do you have?"

"As of this morning, one hundred and fifty-two. We receive fifteen to twenty each month and we graduate as many to independence."

"Is this the only such institution on the planet?"

"That's right. It's enough to keep the population steady, counting on a life expectancy of three hundred years and a population of twenty thousand. This building is quite new. Dr. Delmarre supervised its construction and made many changes in our procedures. Our fetal death rate now is virtually zero."

Robots threaded their way among the tanks. At each tank they stopped and checked controls in a tireless, meticulous way, looking at the tiny embryos within.

"Who operates on the mother?" asked Baley. "I mean, to get the little things."

"Doctors," answered Klorissa.

"Dr. Delmarre?"

"Of course not. *Medical* doctors. You don't think Dr. Delmarre would ever stoop to——Well, never mind."

"Why can't robots be used?"

"Robots in surgery? First Law makes that very difficult, Plainclothes-man. A robot might perform an appendectomy to save a human life, if he knew how, but I doubt that he'd be usable after that without major repairs. Cutting human flesh would be quite a traumatic experience for a positronic brain. Human doctors can manage to get hardened to it. Even to the personal presence required."

Baley said, "I notice that robots tend the fetuses, though. Do you and Dr. Delmarre ever interfere?"

"We have to, sometimes, when things go wrong. If a fetus has developmental trouble, for instance. Robots can't be trusted to judge the situation accurately when human life is involved."

Baley nodded. "Too much risk of a misjudgment and a life lost, I suppose."

"Not at all. Too much risk of overvaluing a life and saving one improperly." The woman looked stern. "As fetal engineers, Baley, we see to it that healthy children are born, *healthy* ones. Even the best gene analysis of parents can't assure that all gene permutations and combinations will be favorable, to say nothing of the possibility of mutations. That's our big concern, the unexpected mutation. We've got the rate of those down to less than one in a thousand, but that means that, on the average, once a decade, we have trouble."

She motioned him along the balcony and he followed her.

She said, "I'll show you the infants' nurseries and the youngsters' dormitories. They're much more a problem than the fetuses are. With them, we can rely on robot labor only to a limited extent."

"Why is that?"

"You would know, Baley, if you ever tried to teach a robot the importance of discipline. First Law makes them almost impervious to that fact. And don't think youngsters don't learn that about as soon as they can talk. I've seen a three-year-old holding a dozen robots motionless by yelling, 'You'll hurt me. I'm hurt.' It takes an extremely advanced robot to understand that a child might be deliberately lying."

"Could Delmarre handle the children?"

"Usually."

"How did he do that? Did he get out among them and shake sense into them?"

"Dr. Delmarre? Touch them? Skies above! Of course not! But he could *talk* to them. And he could give a robot specific orders. I've seen him viewing a child for fifteen minutes, and keeping a robot in spanking position all that time, getting it to spank—spank—spank. A few like that and the child would risk fooling with the boss no more. And the boss was skillful enough about it so that usually the robot didn't need more than a routine readjustment afterward."

"How about you? Do you get out among the children?"

"I'm afraid I have to sometimes. I'm not like the boss. Maybe someday I'll be able to handle the long-distance stuff, but right now if I tried, I'd just ruin robots. There's an art to handling robots really well, you know. When I think of it, though. Getting out among the children. Little animals!"

She looked back at him suddenly. "I suppose you wouldn't mind seeing them."

"It wouldn't bother me."

She shrugged and stared at him with amusement. "Earthman!" She walked on again. "What's this all about, anyway? You'll have to end up with Gladia Delmarre as murderess. You'll *have* to."

"I'm not quite sure of that," said Baley.

"How could you be anything else but sure? Who else could it possibly be?"

"There are possibilities, ma'am."

"Who, for instance?"

"Well, you, for instance!"

And Klorissa's reaction to that quite surprised Baley.

A Target Is Missed

She laughed.

The laughter grew and fed on itself till she was gasping for breath and her plump face had reddened almost to purple. She leaned against the wall and gasped for breath.

"No, don't come—closer," she begged. "I'm all right."

Baley said gravely, "Is the possibility that humorous?"

She tried to answer and laughed again. Then, in a whisper, she said, "Oh, you *are* an Earthman? How could it ever be me?"

"You knew him well," said Baley. "You knew his habits. You could have planned it."

"And you think I would *see* him? That I would get close enough to bash him over the head with something? You just don't know anything at all about it, Baley."

Baley felt himself redden. "Why couldn't you get close enough to him, ma'am. You've had practice—uh—mingling."

"With the *children*."

"One thing leads to another. You seem to be able to stand my presence."

"At twenty feet," she said contemptuously.

"I've just visited a man who nearly collapsed because he had to endure my presence for a while."

Klorissa sobered and said, "A difference in degree."

"I suggest that a difference in degree is all that is necessary. The habit of seeing children makes it possible to endure seeing Delmarre just long enough."

"I would like to point out, Mr. Baley," said Klorissa, no longer appearing the least amused, "that it doesn't matter a speck what I can endure. Dr. Delmarre was the finicky one. He was almost as bad as Leebig himself. Almost. Even if I could endure seeing him, he would never endure seeing me. Mrs. Delmarre is the only one he could possibly have allowed within seeing distance."

Baley said, "Who's this Leebig you mentioned?"

Klorissa shrugged. "One of these odd-genius types, if you know what I mean. He'd done work with the boss on robots."

Baley checked that off mentally and returned to the matter at hand. He said, "It could also be said you had a motive."

"What motive?"

"His death put you in charge of this establishment, gave you position."

"You call that a motive? Skies above, who could *want* this position? Who on Solaria? This is a motive for keeping him alive. It's a motive for hovering over him and protecting him. You'll have to do better than that, Earthman."

Baley scratched his neck uncertainly with one finger. He saw the justice of that.

Klorissa said, "Did you notice my ring, Mr. Baley?"

For a moment it seemed she was about to strip the glove from her right hand, but she refrained.

"I noticed it," said Baley.

"You don't know its significance, I suppose?"

"I don't." (He would never have done with ignorance, he thought bitterly.)

"Do you mind a small lecture, then?"

"If it will help me make sense of this damned world," blurted out Baley, "by all means."

"Skies above!" Klorissa smiled. "I suppose we seem to you as Earth would seem to us. Imagine. Say, here's an empty chamber. Come in here and we'll sit down—no, the room's not big enough. Tell you what, though. You take a seat in there and I'll stand out here."

She stepped farther down the corridor, giving him space to enter the room, then returned, taking up her stand against the opposite wall at a point which she could see him.

Baley took his seat with only the slightest quiver of chivalry countering it. He thought rebelliously: Why not? Let the Spacer woman stand.

Klorissa folded her muscular arms across her chest and said, "Gene analysis is the key to our society. We don't analyze for genes directly, of course. Each gene, however, governs one enzyme, and we can analyze for enzymes. Know the enzymes, know the body chemistry. Know the body chemistry, know the human being. You see all that?"

"I understand the theory," said Baley. "I don't know how it's applied."

"That part's done here. Blood samples are taken while the infant is still in the late fetal stage. That gives us our rough first approximation. Ideally, we should catch all mutations at that point and judge whether birth can be risked. In actual fact, we still don't quite know enough to eliminate all possibility of mistake. Someday, maybe. Anyway, we continue testing after birth; biopsies as well as body fluids. In any case, long before adulthood, we know exactly what our little boys and girls are made of."

(Sugar and spice ... A nonsense phrase went unbidden through Baley's mind.)

"We wear coded rings to indicate our gene constitution," said Klorissa. "It's an old custom, a bit of the primitive left behind from the days when Solarians had not yet been weeded eugenically. Nowadays, we're all healthy."

Baley said, "But you still wear yours. Why?"

"Because I'm exceptional," she said with an unembarrassed, unblunted pride. "Dr. Delmarre spent a long time searching for an assistant. He *needed* someone exceptional. Brains, ingenuity, industry, stability. Most of all, stability. Someone who could learn to mingle with children and not break down."

"He couldn't, could he? Was that a measure of his instability?"

Klorissa said, "In a way, it was, but at least it was a desirable type of instability under most circumstances. You wash your hands, don't you?"

Baley's eyes dropped to his hands. They were as clean as need be. "Yes," he said.

"All right. I suppose it's a measure of instability to feel such revulsion at dirty hands as to be unable to clean an oily mechanism by hand even in an emergency. Still, in the *ordinary* course of living, the revulsion keeps you clean, which is good."

"I see. Go ahead."

"There's nothing more. My genic health is the third-highest ever recorded on Solaria, so I wear my ring. It's a record I enjoy carrying with me."

"I congratulate you."

"You needn't sneer. It may not be my doing. It may be the blind permutation of parental genes, but it's a proud thing to own, anyway. And no one would believe me capable of so seriously psychotic an act as murder. Not with my gene make-up. So don't waste accusations on me."

Baley shrugged and said nothing. The woman seemed to confuse gene make-up and evidence and presumably the rest of Solaria would do the same.

Klorissa said, "Do you want to see the youngsters now?"

"Thank you. Yes."

The corridors seemed to go on forever. The building was obviously a tremendous one. Nothing like the huge banks of apartments in the Cities of Earth, of course, but for a single building clinging to the outside skin of a planet it must be a mountainous structure.

There were hundreds of cribs, with pink babies squalling, or sleeping, or feeding. Then there were playrooms for the crawlers.

"They're not too bad even at this age," said Klorissa grudgingly, "though they take up a tremendous sum of robots. It's practically a robot per baby till walking age."

"Why is that?"

"They sicken if they don't get individual attention."

Baley nodded. "Yes, I suppose the requirement for affection is something that can't be done away with."

Klorissa frowned and said brusquely, "Babies require attention."

Baley said, "I am a little surprised that robots can fulfill the need for affection."

She whirled toward him, the distance between them not sufficing to hide her displeasure. "See here, Baley, if you're trying to shock me by using unpleasant terms, you won't succeed. Skies above, don't be childish."

"Shock you?"

"I can use the word too. Affection! Do you want a short word, a good four-letter word. I can say that, too. Love! Love! Now if it's out of your system, behave yourself."

Baley did not trouble to dispute the matter of obscenity He said, "Can robots really give the necessary attention, then?"

"Obviously, or this farm would not be the success it is. They fool with the child. They nuzzle it and snuggle it. The child doesn't care that it's only a robot. But then, things grow more difficult between three and ten."

"Oh?"

"During that interval, the children insist on playing with one another. Quite indiscriminately."

"I take it you let them."

"We have to, but we never forget our obligation to teach them the requirements of adulthood. Each has a separate room that can be closed off. Even from the first, they must sleep alone. We insist on that. And then we have an isolation time every day and that increases with the years. By the time a child reaches ten, he is able to restrict himself to viewing for a week at a time. Of course, the viewing arrangements are elaborate. They can view outdoors, under mobile conditions, and can keep it up all day."

Baley said, "I'm surprised you can counter an instinct so thoroughly. You do counter it; I see that. Still, it surprises me."

"What instinct?" demanded Klorissa.

"The instinct of gregariousness. There is one. You say yourself that as children they insist on playing with each other."

Klorissa shrugged. "Do you call that instinct? But then, what if it is? Skies above, a child has an instinctive fear of falling, but adults can be trained to work in high places even where there is constant danger of falling. Haven't you ever seen gymnastic exhibitions on high wires? There are some worlds where people live in tall buildings. And children have instinctive fear of loud noises, too, but are you afraid of them?"

"Not within reason," said Baley.

"I'm willing to bet that Earth people couldn't sleep if things were really quiet. Skies above, there isn't an instinct around that can't give way to a good, persistent education. Not in human beings, where instincts are weak anyway. In fact, if you go about it right, education gets easier with each generation. It's a matter of evolution."

Baley said, "How is that?"

"Don't you see? Each individual repeats his own evolutionary history as he develops. Those fetuses back there have gills and a tail for a time. Can't skip those steps. The youngster has to go through the social-animal stage in the same way. But just as a fetus can get through in one month a stage that evolution took a hundred million years to

get through, so our children can hurry through the social-animal stage.
Dr. Delmarre was of the opinion that with the generations, we'd get
through that stage faster and faster."

"Is that so?"

"In three thousand years, he estimated, at the present rate of progress, we'd have children who'd take to viewing at once. The boss had
other notions, too. He was interested in improving robots to the point
of making them capable of disciplining children without becoming
mentally unstable. Why not? Discipline today for a better life tomorrow is a true expression of First Law if robots could only be made to
see it."

"Have such robots been developed yet?"

Klorissa shook her head. "I'm afraid not. Dr. Delmarre and Leebig
had been working hard on some experimental models."

"Did Dr. Delmarre have some of the models sent out to his estate?
Was he a good enough roboticist to conduct tests himself?"

"Oh yes. He tested robots frequently."

"Do you know that he had a robot with him when he was murdered?"

"I've been told so."

"Do you know what kind of a model it was?"

"You'll have to ask Leebig. As I told you, he's the roboticist who
worked with Dr. Delmarre."

"You know nothing about it?"

"Not a thing."

"If you think of anything, let me know."

"I will. And don't think new robot models are all that Dr. Delmarre
was interested in. Dr. Delmarre used to say the time would come
when unfertilized ova would be stored in banks at liquid-air tempera-
tures and utilized for artificial insemination. In that way, eugenic principles could be truly applied and we could get rid of the last vestige
of any need for seeing. I'm not sure that I quite go along with him so
far, but he was a man of advanced notions; a very good Solarian."

She added quickly, "Do you want to go outside? The five-through-
eight group are encouraged to take part in outdoor play and you could
see them in action."

Baley said cautiously, "I'll try that. I may have to come back inside
on rather short notice."

"Oh yes, I forgot. Maybe you'd rather not go out at all?"

"No." Baley forced a smile. "I'm trying to grow accustomed to the
outdoors."

The wind was hard to bear. It made breathing difficult. It wasn't cold,
in a direct physical sense, but the feel of it, the feel of his clothes
moving against his body, gave Baley a kind of chill.

His teeth chattered when he tried to talk and he had to force his words out in little bits. It hurt his eyes to look so far at a horizon so hazy green and blue and there was only limited relief when he looked at the pathway immediately before his toes. Above all, he avoided looking up at the empty blue, empty, that is, but for the piled-up white of occasional clouds and the glare of the naked sun.

And yet he could fight off the urge to run, to return to enclosure.

He passed a tree, following Klorissa by some ten paces, and he reached out a cautious hand to touch it. It was rough and hard to the touch. Frondy leaves moved and rustled overhead, but he did not raise his eyes to look at them. A living tree!

Klorissa called out. "How do you feel?"

"All right."

"You can see a group of youngsters from here," she said. "They're involved in some kind of game. The robots organize the games and see to it that the little animals don't kick each other's eyes out. With personal presence you can do just that, you know."

Baley raised his eyes slowly, running his glance along the cement of the pathway out to the grass and down the slope, farther and farther out—very carefully—ready to snap back to his toes if he grew frightened—feeling with his eyes . . .

There were the small figures of boys and girls racing madly about, uncaring that they raced at the very outer rim of a world with nothing but air and space above them. The glitter of an occasional robot moved nimbly among them. The noise of the children was a far-off incoherent squeaking in the air.

"They love it," said Klorissa. "Pushing and pulling and squabbling and falling down and getting up and just generally contacting. Skies above! How do children ever manage to grow up?"

"What are those older children doing?" asked Baley. He pointed to a group of isolated youngsters standing to one side.

"They're viewing. They're not in a state of personal presence. By viewing, they can walk together, talk together, race together, play together. Anything except physical contact."

"Where do children go when they leave here?"

"To estates of their own. The number of deaths is, on the average, equal to the number of graduations."

"To their parents' estates?"

"Skies above, no! It would be an amazing coincidence, wouldn't it, to have a parent die just as a child is of age. No, the children take any one that falls vacant. I don't know that any of them would be particularly happy, anyway, living in a mansion that once belonged to their parents, supposing, of course, they knew who their parents were."

"Don't they?"

She raised her eyebrows. "Why should they?"

"Don't parents visit their children here?"

"What a mind you have. Why should they want to?"

Baley said, "Do you mind if I clear up a point for myself? Is it bad manners to ask a person if they have had children?"

"It's an intimate question, wouldn't you say?"

"In a way."

"I'm hardened. Children are my business. Other people aren't."

Baley said, "Have you any children?"

Klorissa's Adam's apple made a soft but clearly visible motion in her throat as she swallowed. "I deserve that, I suppose. And you deserve an answer. I haven't."

"Are you married?"

"Yes, and I have an estate of my own and I would be there but for the emergency here. I'm just not confident of being able to control all the robots if I'm not here in person."

She turned away unhappily, and then pointed. "Now there's one of them gone tumbling and of course he's crying."

A robot was running with great space-devouring strides.

Klorissa said, "He'll be picked up and cuddled and if there's any real damage, I'll be called in." She added nervously, "I hope I don't have to be."

Baley took a deep breath. He noted three trees forming a small triangle fifty feet to the left. He walked in that direction, the grass soft and loathsome under his shoes, disgusting in its softness (like walking through corrupting flesh, and he nearly retched at the thought).

He was among them, his back against one trunk. It was almost like being surrounded by imperfect walls. The sun was only a wavering series of flitters through the leaves, so disconnected as almost to be robbed of horror.

Klorissa faced him from the path, then slowly shortened the distance by half.

"Mind if I stay here awhile?" asked Baley.

"Go ahead," said Klorissa.

Baley said, "Once the youngsters graduate out of the farm, how do you get them to court one another?"

"Court?"

"Get to know one another," said Baley, vaguely wondering how the thought could be expressed safely, "so they can marry."

"That's not their problem," said Klorissa. "They're matched by gene analysis, usually when they are quite young. That's the sensible way, isn't it?"

"Are they always willing?"

"To be married? They never are! It's a very traumatic process. At first they have to grow accustomed to one another, and a little bit of seeing each day, once the initial queasiness is gone, can do wonders."

"What if they don't like their partner?"

"What? If the gene analysis indicates a partnership what difference does it——"

"I understand," said Baley hastily. He thought of Earth and sighed.

Klorissa said, "Is there anything else you would like to know?"

Baley wondered if there were anything to be gained from a longer stay. He would not be sorry to be done with Klorissa and fetal engineering so that he might pass on to the next stage.

He had opened his mouth to say as much, when Klorissa called out at some object far off, "You, child, you there! What are you doing?" Then, over her shoulder: "Earthman! Baley! Watch out! Watch *out!*"

Baley scarcely heard her. He responded to the note of urgency in her voice. The nervous effort that held his emotions taut snapped wide and he flamed into panic. All the terror of the open air and the endless vault of heaven broke in upon him.

Baley gibbered. He heard himself mouth meaningless sounds and felt himself fall to his knees and slowly roll over to his side as though he were watching the process from a distance.

Also from a distance he heard the sighing hum piercing the air above him and ending with a sharp thwack.

Baley closed his eyes and his fingers clutched a thin tree root that skimmed the surface of the ground and his nails burrowed into dirt.

He opened his eyes (it must only have been moments after). Klorissa was scolding sharply at a youngster who remained at a distance. A robot, silent, stood closer to Klorissa. Baley had only time to notice the youngster held a stringed object in his hand before his eyes sheered away.

Breathing heavily, Baley struggled to his feet. He stared at the shaft of glistening metal that remained in the trunk of the tree against which he had been standing. He pulled at it and it came out readily. It had not penetrated far. He looked at the point but did not touch it. It was blunted, but it would have sufficed to tear his skin had he not dropped when he did.

It took him two tries to get his legs moving. He took a step toward Klorissa and called. "You. Youngster."

Klorissa turned, her face flushed. She said, "It was an accident. Are you hurt?"

"No! What is this thing?"

"It's an arrow. It is fired by a bow, which makes a taut string do the work."

"Like this," called the youngster impudently, and he shot another arrow into the air, then burst out laughing. He had light hair and a lithe body.

Klorissa said, "You will be disciplined, now leave!"

"Wait, wait," cried Baley. He rubbed his knee where a rock had caught and bruised him as he had fallen. "I have some questions. What is your name?"

"Bik," he said carelessly.

"Did you shoot that arrow at me, Bik?"

"That's right," said the boy.

"Do you realize you would have hit me if I hadn't been warned in time to duck?"

Bik shrugged. "I was aiming to hit."

Klorissa spoke hurriedly. "You must let me explain. Archery is an encouraged sport. It is competitive without requiring contact. We have contests among the boys using viewing only. Now I'm afraid some of the boys will aim at robots. It amuses them and it doesn't hurt the robots. I'm the only adult human on the estate and when the boy saw you, he must have assumed you were a robot."

Baley listened. His mind was clearing, and the natural dourness of his long face intensified. He said, "Bik, did you think I was a robot?"

"No," said the youngster. "You're an Earthman."

"All right. Go now."

Bik turned and raced off whistling. Baley turned to the robot. "You! How did the youngster know I was an Earthman, or weren't you with him when he shot?"

"I was with him, master. I told him you were an Earthman."

"Did you tell him what an Earthman was?"

"Yes, master."

"What is an Earthman?"

"An inferior sort of human that ought not to be allowed on Solaria because he breeds disease, master."

"And who told you that, boy?"

The robot maintained silence.

Baley said, "Do you know who told you?"

"I do not, master. It is in my memory store."

"So you told the boy I was a disease-breeding inferior and he immediately shot at me. Why didn't you stop him?"

"I would have, master. I would not have allowed harm to come to a human, even an Earthman. He moved too quickly and I was not fast enough."

"Perhaps you thought I was just an Earthman, not completely a human, and hesitated a bit."

"No, master."

It was said with quiet calm, but Baley's lips quirked grimly. The robot might deny it in all faith, but Baley felt that was exactly the factor involved.

Baley said, "What were you doing with the boy?"

"I was carrying his arrows, master."

"May I see them?"

He held out his hand. The robot approached and delivered a dozen of them. Baley put the original arrow, the one that had hit the tree, carefully at his feet, and looked the others over one by one. He handed them back and lifted the original arrow again.

He said, "Why did you give this particular arrow to the boy?"

"No reason, master. He had asked for an arrow some time earlier and this was the one my hand touched first. He looked about for a target, then noticed you and asked who the strange human was. I explained——"

"I know what you explained. This arrow you handed him is the only one with gray vanes at the rear. The others have black vanes."

The robot simply stared.

Baley said, "Did you guide the youngster here?"

"We walked randomly, master."

The Earthman looked through the gap between two trees through which the arrow had hurled itself toward its mark.

He said, "Would it happen, by any chance, that this youngster, Bik, was the best archer you have here?"

The robot bent his head. "He is the best, master."

Klorissa gaped. "How did you ever come to guess that?"

"It follows," said Baley dryly. "Now please observe this gray-vaned arrow and the others. The gray-vaned arrow is the only one that seems oily at the point. I'll risk melodrama, ma'am, by saying that your warning saved my life. This arrow that missed me is poisoned."

 **A Roboticist Is Confronted**

Klorissa said, "Impossible! Skies above, absolutely impossible!"

"Above or below or any way you wish it. Is there an animal on the farm that's expendable? Get it and scratch it with the arrow and see what happens."

"But why should anyone want to——"

Baley said harshly, "I know why. The question is, who?"

"No one."

Baley felt the dizziness returning and he grew savage. He threw the arrow at her and she eyed the spot where it fell.

"Pick it up," Baley cried, "and if you don't want to test it, destroy it. Leave it there and you'll have an accident if the children get at it."

She picked it up hurriedly, holding it between forefinger and thumb.

Baley ran for the nearest entrance to the building and Klorissa was still holding the arrow, gingerly, when she followed him back indoors.

Baley felt a certain measure of equanimity return with the comfort of enclosure. He said, "Who poisoned the arrow?"

"I can't imagine."

"I suppose it isn't likely the boy did it himself. Would you have any way of telling who his parents were?"

"We could check the records," said Klorissa gloomily.

"Then you do keep records of relationships?"

"We have to for gene analysis."

"Would the youngster know who his parents were?"

"Never," said Klorissa energetically.

"Would he have any way of finding out?"

"He would have to break into the records room. Impossible."

"Suppose an adult visited the estate and wanted to know who his child was——"

Klorissa flushed. "Very unlikely."

"But suppose. Would he be told if he were to ask?"

"I don't know. It isn't exactly illegal for him to know. It certainly isn't customary."

"Would *you* tell him?"

"I'd try not to. I know Dr. Delmarre wouldn't have. He believed knowledge of relationship was for gene analysis only. Before him things may have been looser. . . . Why do you ask all this, anyway?"

"I don't see how the youngster could have a motive on his own account. I thought that through his parents he might have."

"This is all horrible." In her disturbed state of mind Klorissa approached more closely than at any previous time. She even stretched out an arm in his direction. "How can it all be happening? The boss killed; you nearly killed. We have no motives for violence on Solaria. We all have all we can want, so there is no personal ambition. We have no knowledge of relationship, so there is no family ambition. We are all in good genetic health."

Her face cleared all at once. "Wait. This arrow can't be poisoned. I shouldn't let you convince me it is."

"Why have you suddenly decided that?"

"The robot with Bik. He would never have allowed poison. It's inconceivable that he could have done anything that might bring harm to a human being. The First Law of Robotics makes sure of that."

Baley said, "Does it? What is the First Law, I wonder?"

Klorissa stared blankly. "What do you mean?"

"Nothing. You have the arrow tested and you will find it poisoned."

Baley himself was scarcely interested in the matter. He knew it for poison beyond any internal questionings. He said, "Do you still believe Mrs. Delmarre to have been guilty of her husband's death?"

"She was the only one present."

"I see. And you are the only other human adult present on this estate at a time when I have just been shot at with a poisoned arrow."

She cried energetically, "I had nothing to do with it."

"Perhaps not. And perhaps Mrs. Delmarre is innocent as well. May I use your viewing apparatus?"

"Yes, of course."

Baley knew exactly whom he intended to view and it was not Gladia. It came as a surprise to himself then to hear his voice say, "Get Gladia Delmarre."

The robot obeyed without comment, and Baley watched the manipulations with astonishment, wondering why he had given the order.

Was it that the girl had just been the subject of discussion, or was it that he had been a little disturbed over the manner of the end of their last viewing, or was it simply the sight of the husky, almost overpoweringly practical figure of Klorissa that finally enforced the necessity of a glimpse of Gladia as a kind of counterirritant?

He thought defensively: Jehoshaphat! Sometimes a man has to play things by ear.

She was there before him all at once, sitting in a large, upright chair that made her appear smaller and more defenseless than ever. Her hair was drawn back and bound into a loose coil. She wore pendant earrings bearing gems that looked like diamonds. Her dress was a simple affair that clung tightly at the waist.

She said in a low voice, "I'm glad you viewed, Elijah. I've been trying to reach you."

"Good morning, Gladia." (Afternoon? Evening? He didn't know Gladia's time and he couldn't tell from the manner in which she was dressed what time it might be.) "Why have you been trying to reach me?"

"To tell you I was sorry I had lost my temper last time we viewed. Mr. Olivaw didn't know where you were to be reached."

Baley had a momentary vision of Daneel still bound fast by the overseeing robots and almost smiled. He said, "That's all right. In a few hours, I'll be seeing you."

"Of course, if——Seeing me?"

"Personal presence," said Baley gravely.

Her eyes grew wide and her fingers dug into the smooth plastic of the chair arms. "Is there any reason for that?"

"It is necessary."

"I don't think——"

"Would you allow it?"

She looked away. "Is it absolutely necessary?"

"It is. First, though, there is something else I must see. Your husband was interested in robots. You told me that, and I have heard it from other sources, but he wasn't a roboticist, was he?"

"That wasn't his training, Elijah." She still avoided his eyes.

"But he worked with a roboticist, didn't he?"

"Jothan Leebig," she said at once. "He's a good friend of mine."

"He is?" said Baley energetically.

Gladia looked startled. "Shouldn't I have said that?"

"Why not, if it's the truth?"

"I'm always afraid that I'll say things that will make me seem as though——You don't know what it's like when everyone is sure you've done something."

"Take it easy. How is it that Leebig is a friend of yours?"

"Oh, I don't know. He's in the next estate, for one thing. Viewing energy is just about nil, so we can just view all the time in free motion with hardly any trouble. We go on walks together all the time; or we did, anyway."

"I didn't know you could go on walks together with anyone."

Gladia flushed. "I said *viewing*. Oh well, I keep forgetting you're an Earthman. Viewing in free motion means we focus on ourselves and we can go anywhere we want to without losing contact. I walk on my estate and he walks on his and we're together." She held her chin high. "It can be pleasant."

Then, suddenly, she giggled. "Poor Jothan."

"Why do you say that?"

"I was thinking of you thinking we walked together without viewing. He'd die if he thought anyone could think that."

"Why?"

"He's terrible that way. He told me that when he was five years old he stopped seeing people. Insisted on viewing only. Some children are like that. Rikaine"——she paused in confusion, then went on——"Rikaine, my husband, once told me, when I talked about Jothan, that more and more children would be like that too. He said it was a kind of social evolution that favored survival of pro-viewing. Do you think that's so?"

"I'm no authority," said Baley.

"Jothan won't even get married. Rikaine was angry with him, told him he was anti-social and that he had genes that were necessary in the common pool, but Jothan just refused to consider it."

"Has he a right to refuse?"

"No-o," said Gladia hesitantly, "but he's a very brilliant roboticist, you know, and roboticists are valuable on Solaria. I suppose they stretched a point. Except I think Rikaine was going to stop working with Jothan. He told me once Jothan was a bad Solarian."

"Did he tell Jothan that?"

"I don't know. He was working with Jothan to the end."

"But he thought Jothan was a bad Solarian for refusing to marry?"

"Rikaine once said that marriage was the hardest thing in life, but that it had to be endured."

"What did you think?"

"About what, Elijah?"

"About marriage. Did you think it was the hardest thing in life?"

Her expression grew slowly blank as though she were painstakingly washing emotion out of it. She said, "I never thought about it."

Baley said, "You said you go on walks with Jothan Leebig all the time, then corrected yourself and put that in the past. You don't go on walks with him any more, then?"

Gladia shook her head. Expression was back in her face. Sadness. "No. We don't seem to. I viewed him once or twice. He always seemed busy and I didn't like to——You know."

"Was this since the death of your husband?"

"No, even some time before. Several months before."

"Do you suppose Dr. Delmarre ordered him not to pay further attention to you?"

Gladia looked startled. "Why should he? Jothan isn't a robot and neither am I. How can we take orders and why should Rikaine give them?"

Baley did not bother to try to explain. He could have done so only in Earth terms and that would make things no clearer to her. And if it did manage to clarify, the result could only be disgusting to her.

Baley said, "Only a question. I'll view you again, Gladia, when I'm done with Leebig. What time do you have, by the way?" He was sorry at once for asking the question. Robots would answer in Terrestrial equivalents, but Gladia might answer in Solarian units and Baley was weary of displaying ignorance.

But Gladia answered in purely qualitative terms. "Mid-afternoon," she said.

"Then that's it for Leebig's estate also?"

"Oh yes."

"Good. I'll view you again as soon as I can and we'll make arrangements for seeing."

Again she grew hesitant. "Is it absolutely necessary?"

"It is."

She said in a low voice, "Very well."

* * *

There was some delay in contacting Leebig and Baley utilized it in consuming another sandwich, one that was brought to him in its original packaging. But he had grown more cautious. He inspected the seal carefully before breaking it, then looked over the contents painstakingly.

He accepted a plastic container of milk, not quite unfrozen, bit an opening with his own teeth, and drank from it directly. He thought gloomily that there were such things as odorless, tasteless, slow-acting poisons that could be introduced delicately by means of hypodermic needles or high-pressure needle jets, then put the thought aside as being childish.

So far murders and attempted murders had been committed in the most direct possible fashion. There was nothing delicate or subtle about a blow on the head, enough poison in a glass to kill a dozen men, or a poisoned arrow shot openly at the victim.

And then he thought, scarcely less gloomily, that as long as he hopped between time zones in this fashion, he was scarcely likely to have regular meals. Or, if this continued, regular sleep.

The robot approached him. "Dr. Leebig directs you to call sometime tomorrow. He is engaged in important work."

Baley bounced to his feet and roared, "You tell that guy——"

He stopped. There was no use in yelling at a robot. That is, you could yell if you wished, but it would achieve results no sooner than a whisper.

He said in a conversational tone, "You tell Dr. Leebig, or his robot if that is as far as you've reached, that I am investigating the murder of a professional associate of his and a good Solarian. You tell him that I cannot wait on his work. You tell him that if I am not viewing him in five minutes, I will be in a plane and at his estate *seeing* him in less than an hour. You use that word, seeing, so there's no mistake."

He returned to his sandwich.

The five minutes were not quite gone, when Leebig, or at least a Solarian whom Baley presumed to be Leebig, was glaring at him.

Baley glared back. Leebig was a lean man, who held himself rigidly erect. His dark, prominent eyes had a look of intense abstraction about them, compounded now with anger. One of his eyelids dropped slightly.

He said, "Are you the Earthman?"

"Elijah Baley," said Baley, "Plainclothesman C-7, in charge of the investigation into the murder of Dr. Rikaine Delmarre. What is your name?"

"I am Dr. Jothan Leebig. Why do you presume to annoy me at my work?"

"It's easy," said Baley quietly. "It's my business."

"Then take your business elsewhere."

"I have a few questions to ask first, Doctor. I believe you were a close associate of Dr. Delmarre. Right?"

One of Leebig's hands clenched suddenly into a fist and he strode hastily toward a mantelpiece on which tiny clockwork contraptions went through complicated periodic motions that caught hypnotically at the eye.

The viewer kept focused on Leebig so that his figure did not depart from central projection as he walked. Rather the room behind him seemed to move backward in little rises and dips as he strode.

Leebig said, "If you are the foreigner whom Gruer threatened to bring in——"

"I am."

"Then you are here against my advice. Done viewing."

"Not yet. Don't break contact." Baley raised his voice sharply and a finger as well. He pointed it directly at the roboticist, who shrank visibly away from it, full lips spreading into an expression of disgust.

Baley said, "I wasn't bluffing about seeing you, you know."

"No Earthman vulgarity, please."

"A straightforward statement is what it is intended to be. I will see you, if I can't make you listen any other way. I will grab you by the collar and make you listen."

Leebig stared back. "You are a filthy animal."

"Have it your way, but I will do as I say."

"If you try to invade my estate, I will——I will——"

Baley lifted his eyebrows. "Kill me? Do you often make such threats?"

"I made no threat."

"Then talk now. In the time you have wasted, a good deal might have been accomplished. You were a close associate of Dr. Delmarre. Right?"

The roboticist's head lowered. His shoulders moved slightly to a slow, regular breathing. When he looked up, he was in command of himself. He even managed a brief, sapless smile.

"I was."

"Delmarre was interested in new types of robots, I understand."

"He was."

"What kind?"

"Are you a roboticist?"

"No. Explain it for the layman."

"I doubt that I can."

"Try! For instance, I think he wanted robots capable of disciplining children. What would that involve?"

Leebig raised his eyebrows briefly and said, "To put it very simply, skipping all the subtle details, it means a strengthening of the C-integral governing the Sikorovich tandem route response at the W-65 level."

"Double-talk," said Baley.

"The truth."

"It's double-talk to me. How else can you put it?"

"It means a certain weakening of the First Law."

"Why so? A child is disciplined for its own future good. Isn't that the theory?"

"Ah, the future good!" Leebig's eyes glowed with passion and he seemed to grow less conscious of his listener and correspondingly more talkative. "A simple concept, you think. How many human beings are willing to accept a trifling inconvenience for the sake of a large future good? How long does it take to train a child that what tastes good now means a stomach-ache later, and what tastes bad now will correct the stomach-ache later? Yet you want a robot to be able to understand?

"Pain inflicted by a robot on a child sets up a powerful disruptive potential in the positronic brain. To counteract that by an anti-potential triggered through a realization of future good requires enough paths and bypaths to increase the mass of the positronic brain by 50 per cent, unless other circuits are sacrificed."

Baley said, "Then you haven't succeeded in building such a robot."

"No, nor am I likely to succeed. Nor anyone."

"Was Dr. Delmarre testing an experimental model of such a robot at the time of his death?"

"Not of *such* a robot. We were interested in other more practical things also."

Baley said quietly, "Dr. Leebig, I am going to have to learn a bit more about robotics and I am going to ask you to teach me."

Leebig shook his head violently, and his drooping eyelid dipped further in a ghastly travesty of a wink. "It should be obvious that a course in robotics takes more than a moment. I lack the time."

"Nevertheless, you must teach me. The smell of robots is the one thing that pervades everything on Solaria. If it is time we require, then more than ever I must see you. I am an Earthman and I cannot work or think comfortably while viewing."

It would not have seemed possible to Baley for Leebig to stiffen his stiff carriage further, but he did. He said, "Your phobias as an Earthman don't concern me. Seeing is impossible."

"I think you will change your mind when I tell you what I chiefly want to consult you about."

"It will make no difference. Nothing can."

"No? Then listen to this. It is my belief that throughout the history of the positronic robot, the First Law of Robotics has been deliberately misquoted."

Leebig moved spasmodically. "Misquoted? Fool! Madman! Why?"

"To hide the fact," said Baley with complete composure, "that robots can commit murder."

14.

A Motive Is
Revealed

Leebig's mouth widened slowly. Baley took it for a snarl at first and then, with considerable surprise, decided that it was the most unsuccessful attempt at a smile that he had ever seen.

Leebig said, "Don't say that. Don't ever say that."

"Why not?"

"Because anything, however small, that encourages distrust of robots is harmful. Distrusting robots is a human *disease!*"

It was as though he were lecturing a small child. It was as though he were saying something gently that he wanted to yell. It was as though he were trying to persuade when what he really wanted was to enforce on penalty of death.

Leebig said, "Do you know the history of robotics?"

"A little."

"On Earth, you should. Yes. Do you know robotics started with a Frankenstein complex against them? They were suspect. Men distrusted and feared robots. Robotics was almost an undercover science as a result. The Three Laws were first built into robots in an effort to overcome distrust and even so Earth would never allow a robotic society to develop. One of the reasons the first pioneers left Earth to colonize the rest of the Galaxy was so that they might establish societies in which robots would be allowed to free men of poverty and toil. Even *then*, there remained a latent suspicion not far below, ready to pop up at any excuse."

"Have you yourself had to counter distrust of robots?" asked Baley.

"Many times," said Leebig grimly.

"Is that why you and other roboticists are willing to distort the facts just a little in order to avoid suspicion as much as possible?"

"There is no distortion!"

"For instance, aren't the Three Laws misquoted?"

"*No!*"

"I can demonstrate that they are, and unless you convince me otherwise, I will demonstrate it to the whole Galaxy, if I can."

"You're mad. Whatever argument you may think you have is fallacious, I assure you."

"Shall we discuss it?"

"If it does not take too long."

"Face to face? Seeing?"

Leebig's thin face twisted. "*No!*"

"Good-by, Dr. Leebig. Others will listen to me."

"Wait. Great Galaxy, man, wait!"

"Seeing?"

The roboticist's hands wandered upward, hovered about his chin. Slowly a thumb crept into his mouth and remained there. He stared, blankly, at Baley.

Baley thought: Is he regressing to the pre-five-year-old stage so that it will be legitimate for him to see me?

"Seeing?" he said.

But Leebig shook his head slowly. "I can't. I can't," he moaned, the words all but stifled by the blocking thumb. "Do whatever you want."

Baley stared at the other and watched him turn away and face the wall. He watched the Solarian's straight back bend and the Solarian's face hide in shaking hands.

Baley said, "Very well, then, I'll agree to view."

Leebig said, back still turned, "Excuse me a moment. I'll be back."

Baley tended to his own needs during the interval and stared at his fresh-washed face in the bathroom mirror. Was he getting the feel of Solaria and Solarians? He wasn't sure.

He sighed and pushed a contact and a robot appeared. He didn't turn to look at it. He said, "Is there another viewer at the farm, besides the one I'm using?"

"There are three other outlets, master."

"Then tell Klorissa Cantoro——tell your mistress that I will be using this one till further notice and that I am not to be disturbed."

"Yes, master."

Baley returned to his position where the viewer remained focused on the empty patch of room in which Leebig had stood. It was still empty and he settled himself to wait.

It wasn't long. Leebig entered and the room once more jiggled as the man walked. Evidently focus shifted from room center to man center without delay. Baley remembered the complexity of viewing controls and began to feel a kind of appreciation of what was involved.

Leebig was quite master of himself now, apparently. His hair was slicked back and his costume had been changed. His clothes fit loosely and were of a material that glistened and caught highlights. He sat down in a slim chair that folded out of the wall.

He said soberly, "Now what is this notion of yours concerning First Law?"

"Will we be overheard?"

"No, I've taken care."

Baley nodded. He said, "Let me quote the First Law."

"I scarcely need that."

"I know, but let me quote it, anyway: A robot may not harm a human being or, through inaction, allow a human being to come to harm."

"Well?"

"Now when I first landed on Solaria, I was driven to the estate assigned for my use in a ground-car. The ground-car was a specially enclosed job designed to protect me from exposure to open space. As an Earthman——"

"I know about that," said Leebig impatiently. "What has this to do with the matter?"

"The robots who drove the car did *not* know about it. I asked that the car be opened and was at once obeyed. Second Law. They had to follow orders. I was uncomfortable, of course, and nearly collapsed before the car was enclosed again. Didn't the robots harm me?"

"At your order," snapped Leebig.

"I'll quote the Second Law: A robot must obey the orders given it by human beings except where such orders would conflict with the First Law. So you see, my order should have been ignored."

"This is nonsense. The robot lacked knowledge——"

Baley leaned forward in his chair. "Ah! We have it. Now let's recite the First Law as it should be stated: A robot may do nothing that, *to its knowledge*, will harm a human being; nor, through inaction, *knowingly* allow a human being to come to harm."

"This is all understood."

"I think not by ordinary men. Otherwise, ordinary men would realize robots could commit murder."

Leebig was white. "Mad! Lunacy!"

Baley stared at his finger ends. "A robot may perform an innocent task, I suppose; one that has no damaging effect on a human being?"

"If ordered to do so," said Leebig.

"Yes, of course. If ordered to do so. And a second robot may perform an innocent task, also, I suppose; one that also can have no damaging effect on a human being? If ordered to do so?"

"Yes."

"And what if the two innocent tasks, each completely innocent, completely, amount to murder when added together?"

"What?" Leebig's face puckered into a scowl.

"I want your expert opinion on the matter," said Baley. "I'll set you a hypothetical case. Suppose a man says to a robot, 'Place a small quantity of this liquid into a glass of milk that you will find in such and such a place. The liquid is harmless. I wish only to know its effect on milk. Once I know the effect, the mixture will be poured out. After you have performed this action, forget you have done so.'"

Leebig, still scowling, said nothing.

Baley said, "If I had told the robot to add a mysterious liquid to milk and then offer it to a man, First Law would force it to ask, 'What is the nature of the liquid? Will it harm a man?' And if it were assured the liquid was harmless, First Law might still make the robot hesitate and refuse to offer the milk. Instead, however, it is told the milk will be poured out. First Law is not involved. Won't the robot do as it is told?"

Leebig glared.

Baley said, "Now a second robot has poured out the milk in the first place and is unaware that the milk has been tampered with. In all innocence, it offers the milk to a man and the man dies."

Leebig cried out, "*No!*"

"Why not? Both actions are innocent in themselves. Only together are they murder. Do you deny that that sort of thing can happen?"

"The murderer would be the man who gave the order," cried Leebig.

"If you want to be philosophical, yes. The robots would have been the immediate murderers, though, the instruments of murder."

"No man would give such orders."

"A man would. A man has. It was exactly in this way that the murder attempt on Dr. Gruer must have been carried through. You've heard about that, I suppose."

"On Solaria," muttered Leebig, "one hears about everything."

"Then you know Gruer was poisoned at his dinner table before the eyes of myself and my partner, Mr. Olivaw of Aurora. Can you suggest any other way in which the poison might have reached him? There was no other human on the estate. As a Solarian, you must appreciate that point."

"I'm not a detective. I have no theories."

"I've presented you with one. I want to know if it is a possible one. I want to know if two robots might not perform two separate actions, each one innocent in itself, the two together resulting in murder. You're the expert, Dr. Leebig. *Is it possible?*"

And Leebig, haunted and harried, said, "Yes," in a voice so low that Baley scarcely heard him.

Baley said, "Very well, then. So much for the First Law."

Leebig stared at Baley and his drooping eyelid winked once or twice in a slow tic. His hands, which had been clasped, drew apart, though the fingers maintained their clawed shape as though each hand still entwined a phantom hand of air. Palms turned downward and rested on knees and only then did the fingers relax.

Baley watched it all in abstraction.

Leebig said, "Theoretically, yes. Theoretically! But don't dismiss the First Law that easily, Earthman. Robots would have to be ordered very cleverly in order to circumvent the First Law."

"Granted," said Baley. "I am only an Earthman. I know next to nothing about robots and my phrasing of the orders was only by way of example. A Solarian would be much more subtle and do much better. I'm sure of that."

Leebig might not have been listening. He said loudly, "If a robot can be manipulated into doing harm to a man, it means only that we must extend the powers of the positronic brain. One *might* say we ought to make the human better. That is impossible, so we will make the robot more foolproof.

"We advance continuously. Our robots are more varied, more specialized, more capable, and more unharming than those of a century ago. A century hence, we will have still greater advances. Why have a robot manipulate controls when a positronic brain can be built into the controls itself? That's specialization, but we can generalize, also. Why not a robot with replaceable and interchangeable limbs. Eh? Why not? If we——"

Baley interrupted. "Are you the only roboticist on Solaria?"

"Don't be a fool."

"I only wondered. Dr. Delmarre was the only——uh——fetal engineer, except for an assistant."

"Solaria has over twenty roboticists."

"Are you the best?"

"I am," Leebig said without self-consciousness.

"Delmarre worked with you."

"He did."

Baley said, "I understand that he was planning to break the partnership toward the end."

"No sign of it. What gave you the idea?"

"I understand he disapproved of your bachelorhood."

"He may have. He was a thorough Solarian. However, it did not affect our business relationships."

"To change the subject. In addition to developing new model robots, do you also manufacture and repair existing types?"

Leebig said, "Manufacture and repair are largely robot-conducted. There is a large factory and maintenance shop on my estate."

"Do robots require much in the way of repair, by the way?"

"Very little."

"Does that mean that robot repair is an undeveloped science?"

"Not at all." Leebig said that stiffly.

"What about the robot that was at the scene of Dr. Delmarre's murder?"

Leebig looked away, and his eyebrows drew together as though a painful thought were being barred entrance to his mind. "It was a complete loss."

"Really complete? Could it answer any questions at all?"

"None at all. It was absolutely useless. Its positronic brain was completely short-circuited. Not one pathway was left intact. Consider! It had witnessed a murder it had been unable to halt——"

"Why was it unable to halt the murder, by the way?"

"Who can tell? Dr. Delmarre was experimenting with that robot. I do not know in what mental condition he had left it. He might have ordered it, for instance, to suspend all operations while he checked one particular circuit element. If someone whom neither Dr. Delmarre nor the robot suspected of harm were suddenly to launch a homicidal attack, there might be a perceptible interval before the robot could use First Law potential to overcome Dr. Delmarre's freezing order. The length of the interval would depend on the nature of the attack and the nature of Dr. Delmarre's freezing order. I could invent a dozen other ways of explaining why the robot was unable to prevent the murder. Being unable to do so was a First Law violation, however, and that was sufficient to blast every positronic pathway in the robot's mind."

"But if the robot was physically unable to prevent the murder, was it responsible? Does the First Law ask impossibilities?"

Leebig shrugged. "The First Law, despite your attempts to make little of it, protects humanity with every atom of possible force. It allows no excuses. If the First Law is broken, the robot is ruined."

"That is a universal rule, sir?"

"As universal as robots."

Baley said, "Then I've learned something."

"Then learn something else. Your theory of murder by a series of robotic actions, each innocent in itself, will not help you in the case of Dr. Delmarre's death."

"Why not?"

"The death was not by poisoning, but by bludgeoning. Something had to hold the bludgeon, and that had to be a human arm. No robot could swing a club and smash a skull."

"Suppose," said Baley, "a robot were to push an innocent button which dropped a booby-trap weight on Delmarre's head."

Leebig smiled sourly. "Earthman, I've viewed the scene of the crime. I've heard all the news. The murder was a big thing on Solaria, you know. So I know there was no sign of any machinery at the scene of the crime, or of any fallen weight."

Baley said, "Or of any blunt instrument, either."

Leebig said scornfully, "You're a detective. Find it."

"Granting that a robot was not responsible for Dr. Delmarre's death, who was, then?"

"Everyone knows who was," shouted Leebig. "His wife! Gladia!"

Baley thought: At least there's a unanimity of opinion.

Aloud he said, "And who was the mastermind behind the robots who poisoned Gruer?"

"I suppose . . ." Leebig trailed off.

"You don't think there are two murderers, do you? If Gladia was responsible for one crime, she must be responsible for the second attempt, also."

"Yes. You must be right." His voice gained assurance. "No doubt of it."

"No doubt?"

"Nobody else could get close enough to Dr. Delmarre to kill him. He allowed personal presence no more than I did, except that he made an exception in favor of his wife, and I make no exceptions. The wiser I." The roboticist laughed harshly.

"I believe you knew her," said Baley abruptly.

"Whom?"

"Her. We are discussing only one 'her.' Gladia!"

"Who told you I knew her any more than I know anyone else?" demanded Leebig. He put his hand to his throat. His fingers moved slightly and opened the neckseam of his garment for an inch downward, leaving more freedom to breathe.

"Gladia herself did. You two went for walks."

"So? We were neighbors. It is a common thing to do. She seemed a pleasant person."

"You approved of her, then?"

Leebig shrugged. "Talking to her was relaxing."

"What did you talk about?"

"Robotics." There was a flavor of surprise about the word as though there were wonder that the question could be asked.

"And she talked robotics too?"

"She knew nothing about robotics. Ignorant! But she listened. She has some sort of field-force rigmarole she plays with; field coloring, she calls it. I have no patience with that, but I listened."

"All this without personal presence?"

Leebig looked revolted and did not answer.

Baley tried again. "Were you attracted to her?"

"What?"

"Did you find her attractive? Physically?"

Even Leebig's bad eyelid lifted and his lips quivered. "Filthy animal," he muttered.

"Let me put it this way, then. When did you cease finding Gladia pleasant? You used that word yourself, if you remember."

"What do you mean?"

"You said you found her pleasant. Now you believe she murdered her husband. That isn't the mark of a pleasant person."

"I was mistaken about her."

"But you decided you were mistaken before she killed her husband, if she did so. You stopped walking with her some time before the murder. Why?"

Leebig said, "Is that important?"

"Everything is important till proven otherwise."

"Look, if you want information from me as a roboticist, ask it. I won't answer personal questions."

Baley said, "You were closely associated with both the murdered man and the chief suspect. Don't you see that personal questions are unavoidable? Why did you stop walking with Gladia?"

Leebig snapped, "There came a time when I ran out of things to say; when I was too busy; when I found no reason to continue the walks."

"When you no longer found her pleasant, in other words."

"All right. Put it so."

"Why was she no longer pleasant?"

Leebig shouted, "I have no reason."

Baley ignored the other's excitement. "You are still someone who has known Gladia well. What could her motive be?"

"Her motive?"

"No one suggested any motive for the murder. Surely Gladia wouldn't commit murder without a motive."

"Great Galaxy!" Leebig leaned his head back as though to laugh, but didn't. "No one told you? Well, perhaps no one knew. I knew, though. She told me. She told me frequently."

"Told you what, Dr. Leebig?"

"Why, that she quarreled with her husband. Quarreled bitterly and frequently. She hated him, Earthman. Didn't anyone tell you that? Didn't *she* tell you?"

15. A Portrait Is Colored

Baley took it between the eyes and tried not to show it.

Presumably, living as they did, Solarians considered one another's private lives to be sacrosanct. Questions concerning marriage and children were in bad taste. He supposed then that chronic quarreling

would exist between husband and wife and be a matter into which
curiosity was equally forbidden.

But even when murder had been committed? Would no one commit
the social crime of asking the suspect if she quarreled with her husband? Or of mentioning the matter if they happened to know of it?

Well, Leebig had.

Baley said, "What did the quarrel concern?"

"You had better ask her, I think."

He better had, thought Baley. He rose stiffly, "Thank you, Dr. Leebig, for your co-operation. I may need your help again later. I hope
you will keep yourself available."

"Done viewing," said Leebig, and he and the segment of his room
vanished abruptly.

For the first time Baley found himself not minding a plane flight
through open space. Not minding it at all. It was almost as though he
were in his own element.

He wasn't even thinking of Earth or of Jessie. He had been away
from Earth only a matter of weeks, yet it might as well have been
years. He had been on Solaria only the better part of three days and
yet it seemed forever.

How fast could a man adapt to nightmare?

Or was it Gladia? He would be seeing her soon, not viewing her.
Was that what gave him confidence and this odd feeling of mixed
apprehension and anticipation?

Would she endure it? he wondered. Or would she slip away after a
few moments of seeing, begging off as Quemot had done?

She stood at the other end of a long room when he entered. She
might almost have been an impressionistic representation of herself,
she was reduced so to essentials.

Her lips were faintly red, her eyebrows lightly penciled, her earlobes
faintly blue, and, except for that, her face was untouched. She looked
pale, a little frightened, and very young.

Her brown-blond hair was drawn back, and her gray-blue eyes were
somehow shy. Her dress was a blue so dark as to be almost black, with
a thin white edging curling down each side. Not an inch of skin showed
anywhere but in her face. Even her neck was covered by a kind of
unobtrusive ruching.

Baley stopped where he was. "Is this close enough, Gladia?"

She was breathing with shallow quickness. She said, "I had forgotten what to expect really. It's just like viewing, isn't it? I mean, if you
don't think of it as seeing."

Baley said, "It's all quite normal to me."

"Yes, on Earth." She closed her eyes. "Sometimes I try to imagine
it. Just crowds of people everywhere. You walk down a road and there

are others walking with you and still others walking in the other direction. Dozens——"

"Hundreds," said Baley. "Did you ever view scenes on Earth in a book-film? Or view a novel with an Earth setting?"

"We don't have many of those, but I've viewed novels set on the other Outer Worlds where seeing goes on all the time. It's different in a novel. It just seems like a multiview."

"Do people ever kiss in novels?"

She flushed painfully. "I don't read that kind."

"Never?"

"Well—there are always a few dirty films around, you know, and sometimes, just out of curiosity——It's sickening, really."

"Is it?"

She said with sudden animation, "But Earth is so different. So many people. When you walk, Elijah, I suppose you even t-touch people. I mean, by accident."

Baley half smiled. "You even knock them down by accident." He thought of the crowds on the Expressways, tugging and shoving, bounding up and down the strips, and for a moment, inevitably, he felt the pang of homesickness.

Gladia said, "You don't have to stay way out there."

"Would it be all right if I came closer?"

"I think so. I'll tell you when I'd rather you wouldn't any more."

Stepwise Baley drew closer, while Gladia watched him, wide-eyed.

She said suddenly, "Would you like to see some of my field colorings?"

Baley was six feet away. He stopped and looked at her. She seemed small and fragile. He tried to visualize her, something in her hand (what?), swinging furiously at the skull of her husband. He tried to picture her, mad with rage, homicidal with hate and anger.

He had to admit it could be done. Even a hundred and five pounds of woman could crush a skull if she had the proper weapon and were wild enough. And Baley had known murderesses (on Earth, of course) who, in repose, were bunny rabbits.

He said, "What are field colorings, Gladia?"

"An art form," she said.

Baley remembered Leebig's reference to Gladia's art. He nodded. "I'd like to see some."

"Follow me, then."

Baley maintained a careful six-foot distance between them. At that, it was less than a third the distance Klorissa had demanded.

They entered a room that burst with light. It glowed in every corner and every color.

Gladia looked pleased, proprietary. She looked up at Baley, eyes anticipating.

Baley's response must have been what she expected, though he said nothing. He turned slowly, trying to make out what he saw, for it was light only, no material object at all.

The gobbets of light sat on embracing pedestals. They were living geometry, lines and curves of color, entwined into a coalescing whole yet maintaining distinct identities. No two specimens were even remotely alike.

Baley groped for appropriate words and said, "Is it supposed to mean anything?"

Gladia laughed in her pleasant contralto. "It means whatever you like it to mean. They're just light-forms that might make you feel angry or happy or curious or whatever I felt when I constructed one. I could make one for you, a kind of portrait. It might not be very good, though, because I would just be improvising quickly."

"Would you? I would be very interested."

"All right," she said, and half-ran to a light-figure in one corner, passing within inches of him as she did so. She did not seem to notice.

She touched something on the pedestal of the light-figure and the glory above died without a flicker.

Baley gasped and said, "Don't do that."

"It's all right. I was tired of it, anyway. I'll just fade the others temporarily so they don't distract me." She opened a panel along one featureless wall and moved a rheostat. The colors faded to something scarcely visible.

Baley said, "Don't you have a robot to do this? Closing contact?"

"Shush, now," she said impatiently. "I don't keep robots in here. This is me." She looked at him, frowning. "I don't know you well enough. That's the trouble."

She wasn't looking at the pedestal, but her fingers rested lightly on its smooth upper surface. All ten fingers were curved, tense, waiting.

One finger moved, described a half curve over smoothness. A bar of deep yellow light grew and slanted obliquely across the air above. The finger inched backward a fraction and the light grew slightly less deep in shade.

She looked at it momentarily. "I suppose that's it. A kind of strength without weight."

"Jehoshaphat," said Baley.

"Are you offended?" Her fingers lifted and the yellow slant of light remained solitary and stationary.

"No, not at all. But what is it? How do you do it?"

"That's hard to explain," said Gladia, looking at the pedestal thoughtfully, "considering I don't really understand it myself. It's a kind of optical illusion, I've been told. We set up force-fields at different energy levels. They're extrusions of hyperspace, really, and don't have the properties of ordinary space at all. Depending on the energy level, the human eye sees light of different shades. The shapes and colors are controlled by the warmth of my fingers against the appropriate spots on the pedestal. There are all sorts of controls inside each pedestal."

"You mean if I were to put my finger there——" Baley advanced and Gladia made way for him. He put a hesitant forefinger down upon the pedestal and felt a soft throbbing.

"Go ahead. Move your finger, Elijah," said Gladia.

Baley did so and a dirty-gray jag of light lifted upward, skewing the yellow light. Baley withdrew his finger sharply and Gladia laughed and then was instantly contrite.

"I shouldn't laugh," she said. "It's really very hard to do, even for people who've tried a long time." Her own hand moved lightly and too quickly for Baley to follow and the monstrosity he had set up disappeared, leaving the yellow light in isolation again.

"How did you learn to do this?" asked Baley.

"I just kept on trying. It's a new art form, you know, and only one or two really know how——"

"And you're the best," said Baley somberly. "On Solaria everyone is either the only or the best or both."

"You needn't laugh. I've had some of my pedestals on display. I've given shows." Her chin lifted. There was no mistaking her pride.

She continued, "Let me go on with your portrait." Her fingers moved again.

There were few curves in the light-form that grew under her ministrations. It was all sharp angles. And the dominant color was blue.

"That's Earth, somehow," said Gladia, biting her lower lip. "I always think of Earth as blue. All those people and seeing, seeing, seeing. Viewing is more rose. How does it seem to you?"

"Jehoshaphat, I can't picture things as colors."

"Can't you?" she asked abstractedly. "Now you say 'Jehoshaphat' sometimes and that's just a little blob of violet. A little sharp blob because it usually comes out ping, like that." And the little blob was there, glowing just off-center.

"And then," she said, "I can finish it like this." And a flat, lusterless hollow cube of slate gray sprang up to enclose everything. The light within shone through it, but dimmer, imprisoned, somehow.

Baley felt a sadness at it, as though it were something enclosing him, keeping him from something he wanted. He said, "What's that last?"

Gladia said, "Why, the walls about you. That's what's most in you, the way you can't go outside, the way you have to be inside. You *are* inside there. Don't you see?"

Baley saw and somehow he disapproved. He said, "Those walls aren't permanent. I've been out today."

"You have? Did you mind?"

He could not resist a counterdig. "The way you mind seeing me. You don't like it but you can stand it."

She looked at him thoughtfully. "Do you want to come out now? With me? For a walk?"

It was Baley's impulse to say: Jehoshaphat, no.

She said, "I've never walked with anyone, seeing. It's still daytime, and it's pleasant weather."

Baley looked at his abstractionist portrait and said, "If I go, will you take away the gray?"

She smiled and said, "I'll see how you behave."

The structure of light remained as they left the room. It stayed behind, holding Baley's imprisoned soul fast in the gray of the Cities.

Baley shivered slightly. Air moved against him and there was a chill to it.

Gladia said, "Are you cold?"

"It wasn't like this before," muttered Baley.

"It's late in the day now, but it isn't really cold. Would you like a coat? One of the robots could bring one in a minute."

"No. It's all right." They stepped forward along a narrow paved path. He said, "Is this where you used to walk with Dr. Leebig?"

"Oh no. We walked way out among the fields, where you can only see an occasional robot working and you can hear the animal sounds. You and I will stay near the house though, just in case."

"In case what?"

"Well, in case you want to go in."

"Or in case you get weary of seeing?"

"It doesn't bother me," she said recklessly.

There was the vague rustle of leaves above and an all-pervading yellowness and greenness. There were sharp, thin cries in the air about, plus a strident humming, and shadows, too.

He was especially aware of the shadows. One of them stuck out before him, in shape like a man, that moved as he did in horrible mimicry. Baley had heard of shadows, of course, and he knew what they were, but in the pervasive indirect lighting of the Cities he had never been specifically aware of one.

Behind him, he knew, was the Solarian sun. He took care not to look at it, but he knew it was there.

Space was large, space was lonely, yet he found it drawing him. His mind pictured himself striding the surface of a world with thousands of miles and light-years of room all about him.

Why should he find attraction in this thought of loneliness? He didn't want loneliness. He wanted Earth and the warmth and companionship of the man-crammed Cities.

The picture failed him. He tried to conjure up New York in his mind, all the noise and fullness of it, and found he could remain conscious only of the quiet, air-moving chill of the surface of Solaria.

Without quite willing it Baley moved closer to Gladia until he was two feet away, then grew aware of her startled face.

"I beg your pardon," he said at once, and drew off.

She gasped, "It's all right. Won't you walk this way? We have some flower beds you might like."

The direction she indicated lay away from the sun. Baley followed silently.

Gladia said, "Later in the year, it will be wonderful. In the warm weather I can run down to the lake and swim, or just run across the fields, run as fast as I can until I'm just glad to fall down and lie still."

She looked down at herself. "But this is no costume for it. With all this on, I've *got* to walk. Sedately, you know."

"How would you prefer to dress?" asked Baley.

"Halter and shorts at the *most*," she cried, lifting her arms as though feeling the freedom of that in her imagination. "Sometimes less. Sometimes just sandals so you can feel the air with every inch——Oh, I'm sorry, I've offended you."

Baley said, "No. It's all right. Was that your costume when you went walking with Dr. Leebig?"

"It varied. It depended on the weather. Sometimes I wore very little, but it was viewing, you know. You *do* understand, I hope."

"I understand. What about Dr. Leebig, though? Did he dress lightly too?"

"Jothan dress lightly?" Gladia smiled flashingly. "Oh no. He's very solemn, always." She twisted her face into a thin look of gravity and half winked, catching the very essence of Leebig and forcing a short grunt of appreciation out of Baley.

"This is the way he talks," she said. " 'My dear Gladia, in considering the effect of a first-order potential on positron flow——' "

"Is that what he talked to you about? Robotics?"

"Mostly. Oh, he takes it so seriously, you know. He was always trying to teach me about it. He never gave up."

"Did you learn anything?"

"Not one thing. Nothing. It's just all a complete mix-up to me. He'd get angry with me sometimes, but when he'd scold, I'd dive into the water, if we were anywhere near the lake, and splash him."

"*Splash* him? I thought you were viewing."

She laughed. "You're *such* an Earthman. I'd splash where he was standing in his own room or on his own estate. The water couldn't touch him, but he would duck just the same. Look at that."

Baley looked. They had circled a wooded patch and now came upon a clearing, centered about an ornamental pond. Small bricked walks penetrated the clearing and broke it up. Flowers grew in profusion and order. Baley knew them for flowers from book-films he had viewed.

In a way the flowers were like the light-patterns that Gladia constructed and Baley imagined that she constructed them in the spirit of flowers. He touched one cautiously, then looked about. Reds and yellows predominated.

In turning to look about Baley caught a glimpse of the sun.

He said uneasily, "The sun is low in the sky."

"It's late afternoon," called Gladia back to him. She had run toward the pond and was sitting on a stone bench at its edge. "Come here," she shouted, waving. "You can stand if you don't like to sit on stone."

Baley advanced slowly. "Does it get this low every day?" and at once he was sorry he asked. If the planet rotated, the sun must be low in the sky both mornings and afternoons. Only at midday could it be high.

Telling himself this couldn't change a lifetime of pictured thought. He knew there was such a thing as night and had even experienced it, with a planet's whole thickness interposing safely between a man and the sun. He knew there were clouds and a protective grayness hiding the worst of outdoors. And still, when he thought of planetary surfaces, it was always a picture of a blaze of light with a sun high in the sky.

He looked over his shoulder, just quickly enough to get a flash of sun, and wondered how far the house was if he should decide to return.

Gladia was pointing to the other end of the stone bench.

Baley said, "That's pretty close to you, isn't it?"

She spread out her little hands, palms up. "I'm getting used to it. Really."

He sat down, facing toward her to avoid the sun.

She leaned over backward toward the water and pulled a small cup-shaped flower, yellow without and white-streaked within, not at all flamboyant. She said, "This is a native plant. Most of the flowers here are from Earth originally."

Water dripped from its severed stem as she extended it gingerly toward Baley.

Baley reached for it as gingerly. "You killed it," he said.

"It's only a flower. There are thousands more." Suddenly, before his fingers more than touched the yellow cup, she snatched it away, her eyes kindling. "Or are you trying to imply I could kill a human being because I pulled a flower?"

Baley said in soft conciliation, "I wasn't implying anything. May I see it?"

Baley didn't really want to touch it. It had grown in wet soil and there was still the effluvium of mud about it. How could these people, who were so careful in contact with Earthmen and even with one another, be so careless in their contact with ordinary dirt?

But he held the stalk between thumb and forefinger and looked at it. The cup was formed of several thin pieces of papery tissue, curving up from a common center. Within it was a white convex swelling, damp with liquid and fringed with dark hairs that trembled lightly in the wind.

She said, "Can you smell it?"

At once Baley was aware of the odor that emanated from it. He leaned toward it and said, "It smells like a woman's perfume."

Gladia clapped her hands in delight. "How like an Earthman. What you really mean is that a woman's perfume smells like *that*."

Baley nodded ruefully. He was growing weary of the outdoors. The shadows were growing longer and the land was becoming somber. Yet he was determined not to give in. He wanted those gray walls of light that dimmed his portrait removed. It was quixotic, but there it was.

Gladia took the flower from Baley, who let it go without reluctance. Slowly she pulled its petals apart. She said, "I suppose every woman smells different."

"It depends on the perfume," said Baley indifferently.

"Imagine being close enough to tell. I don't wear perfume because no one is close enough. Except now. But I suppose you smell perfume often, all the time. On Earth, your wife is always with you, isn't she?" She was concentrating very hard on the flower, frowning as she plucked it carefully to pieces.

"She's not always with me," said Baley. "Not every minute."

"But most of the time. And whenever you want to——"

Baley said suddenly, "Why did Dr. Leebig try so hard to teach you robotics, do you suppose?"

The dismembered flower consisted of a stalk and the inner swelling. Gladia twirled it between her fingers, then tossed it away, so that it floated for a moment on the surface of the pond. "I think he wanted me to be his assistant," she said.

"Did he tell you so, Gladia?"

"Toward the end, Elijah. I think he grew impatient. Anyway, he asked me if I didn't think it would be exciting to work in robotics. Naturally, I told him I could think of nothing duller. He was quite angry."

"And he never walked with you again after that."

She said, "You know, I think that may have been it. I suppose his feelings were hurt. Really, though, what could I do?"

"It was before that, though, that you told him about your quarrels with Dr. Delmarre."

Her hands became fists and held so in a tight spasm. Her body held stiffly to its position, head bent and a little to one side. Her voice was unnaturally high. "What quarrels?"

"Your quarrels with your husband. I understand you hated him."

Her face was distorted and blotched as she glared at him. "Who told you that? Jothan?"

"Dr. Leebig mentioned it. I think it's true."

She was shaken. "You're still trying to prove I killed him. I keep thinking you're my friend and you're only——only a detective."

She raised her fists and Baley waited.

He said, "You know you can't touch me."

Her hands dropped and she began crying without a sound. She turned her head away.

Baley bent his own head and closed his eyes, shutting out the disturbing long shadows. He said, "Dr. Delmarre was not a very affectionate man, was he?"

She said in a strangled way, "He was a very busy man."

Baley said, "You *are* affectionate, on the other hand. You find a man interesting. Do you understand?"

"I c-can't help it. I know it's disgusting, but I can't help it. It's even disgusting t-to talk about it."

"You did talk about it to Dr. Leebig, though?"

"I *had* to do something and Jothan was handy and he didn't seem to mind and it made me feel better."

"Was this the reason you quarreled with your husband? Was it that he was cold and unaffectionate and you resented it?"

"Sometimes I hated him." She shrugged her shoulders helplessly. "He was just a good Solarian and we weren't scheduled for ch—for ch——" She broke down.

Baley waited. His own stomach was cold and open air pressed down heavily upon him. When Gladia's sobs grew quieter, he asked, as gently as he could, "Did you kill him, Gladia?"

"No-no." Then, suddenly, as though all resistance had corroded within her: "I haven't told you everything."

"Well, then, please do so now."

"We were quarreling that time, the time he died. The old quarrel. I screamed at him but he never shouted back. He hardly ever even said anything and that just made it worse. I was so angry, so angry. I don't remember after that."

"Jehoshaphat!" Baley swayed slightly and his eyes sought the neutral stone of the bench. "What do you mean you don't remember?"

"I mean he was dead and I was screaming and the robots came——"

"Did you kill him?"

"I don't remember it, Elijah, and I would remember it if I did, wouldn't I? Only I don't remember anything else, either, and I've been so frightened, so frightened. Help me, please, Elijah."

"Don't worry, Gladia. I'll help you." Baley's reeling mind fastened on the murder weapon. What happened to it? It must have been removed. If so, only the murderer could have done it. Since Gladia was found immediately after the murder on the scene, she could not have done it. The murderer would have to be someone else. No matter how it looked to everyone in Solaria, it had to be someone else.

Baley thought sickly: I've got to get back to the house.

He said, "Gladia——"

Somehow he was staring at the sun. It was nearly at the horizon. He had to turn his head to look at it and his eyes locked with a morbid fascination. He had never seen it so. Fat, red, and dim somehow, so that one could look at it without blinding, and see the bleeding clouds above it in thin lines, with one crossing it in a bar of black.

Baley mumbled, "The sun is so red."

He heard Gladia's choked voice say drearily, "It's always red at sunset, red and dying."

Baley had a vision. The sun was moving down to the horizon because the planet's surface was moving away from it, a thousand miles an hour, spinning under that naked sun, spinning with nothing to guard the microbes called men that scurried over its spinning surface, spinning madly forever, spinning—spinning . . .

It was his head that was spinning and the stone bench that was slanting beneath him and the sky heaving, blue, dark blue, and the sun was gone, and the tops of the trees and the ground rushing up and Gladia screaming thinly and another sound . . .

 # A Solution Is Offered

Baley was aware first of enclosure, the absence of the open, and then of a face bending over him.

He stared for a moment without recognition. Then: *"Daneel!"*

The robot's face showed no sign of relief or of any other recognizable emotion at being addressed. He said, "It is well that you have recovered consciousness, Partner Elijah. I do not believe you have suffered physical injury."

"I'm all right," said Baley testily, struggling to his elbows. "Jehoshaphat, am I in bed? What for?"

"You have been exposed to the open a number of times today. The effects upon you have been cumulative and you need rest."

"I need a few answers first." Baley looked about and tried to deny to himself that his head was spinning just a little. He did not recognize the room. The curtains were drawn. Lights were comfortably artificial. He was feeling much better. "For instance, where am I?"

"In a room of Mrs. Delmarre's mansion."

"Next, let's get something straight. What are you doing here? How did you get away from the robots I set over you?"

Daneel said, "It had seemed to me that you would be displeased at this development and yet in the interests of your safety and of my orders, I felt that I had no choice but——"

"What did you do? Jehoshaphat!"

"It seems Mrs. Delmarre attempted to view you some hours ago."

"Yes." Baley remembered Gladia saying as much earlier in the day. "I know that."

"Your order to the robots that held me prisoner was, in your words: 'Do not allow him' (meaning myself) 'to establish contact with other humans or other robots, either by seeing or by viewing.' However, Partner Elijah, you said nothing about forbidding other humans or robots to contact me. You see the distinction?"

Baley groaned.

Daneel said, "No need for distress, Partner Elijah. The flaw in your orders was instrumental in saving your life, since it brought me to the scene. You see, when Mrs. Delmarre viewed me, being allowed to do so by my robot guardians, she asked after you and I answered, quite truthfully, that I did not know of your whereabouts, but that I could attempt to find out. She seemed anxious that I do so. I said I thought it possible you might have left the house temporarily and that I would check that matter and would she, in the meanwhile, order the robots in the room with me, to search the mansion for your presence."

"Wasn't she surprised that you didn't deliver the orders to the robots yourself?"

"I gave her the impression, I believe, that as an Auroran I was not as accustomed to robots as she was; that she might deliver the orders with greater authority and effect a more speedy consummation. Solarians, it is quite clear, are vain of their skill with robots and contemptuous of the ability of natives of other planets to handle them. Is that not your opinion as well, Partner Elijah?"

"And she ordered them away, then?"

"With difficulty. They protested previous orders but, of course, could not state the nature thereof since you had ordered them to tell no one of my own true identity. She overrode them, although the final orders had to be shrilled out in fury."

"And then you left."

"I did, Partner Elijah."

A pity, thought Baley, that Gladia did not consider that episode important enough to relay to him when he viewed her. He said, "It took you long enough to find me, Daneel."

"The robots on Solaria have a network of information through sub-etheric contact. A skilled Solarian could obtain information readily, but, mediated as it is through millions of individual machines, one such as myself, without experience in the matter, must take time to unearth a single datum. It was better than an hour before the information as to your whereabouts reached me. I lost further time by visiting Dr. Delmarre's place of business after you had departed."

"What were you doing there?"

"Pursuing researches of my own. I regret that this had to be done in your absence, but the exigencies of the investigation left me no choice."

Baley said, "Did you view Klorissa Cantoro, or see her?"

"I viewed her, but from another part of her building, not from our own estate. There were records at the farm I had to see. Ordinarily viewing would have been sufficient, but it might have been inconvenient to remain on our own estate since three robots knew my real name and might easily have imprisoned me once more."

Baley felt almost well. He swung his legs out of bed and found himself in a kind of nightgown. He stared at it with distaste. "Get me my clothes."

Daneel did so.

As Baley dressed, he said, "Where's Mrs. Delmarre?"

"Under house arrest, Partner Elijah."

"What? By whose order?"

"By my order. She is confined to her bedroom under robotic guard and her right to give orders other than to meet personal needs has been neutralized."

"By yourself?"

"The robots on this estate are not aware of my identity."

Baley finished dressing. "I know the case against Gladia," he said. "She had the opportunity; more of it, in fact, than we thought at first. She did not rush to the scene at the sound of her husband's cry, as she first said. She was there all along."

"Does she claim to have witnessed the murder and seen the murderer?"

"No. She remembers nothing of the crucial moments. That happens sometimes. It turns out, also, that she has a motive."

"What was it, Partner Elijah?"

"One that I had suspected as a possibility from the first. I said to myself, if this were Earth, and Dr. Delmarre were as he was described to be and Gladia Delmarre as she seemed to be, I would say that she was in love with him, or had been, and that he was in love only with himself. The difficulty was to tell whether Solarians felt love or reacted to love in any Earthly sense. My judgment as to their emotions and reactions wasn't to be trusted. It was why I had to see a few. Not view them, but see them."

"I do not follow you, Partner Elijah."

"I don't know if I can explain it to you. These people have their gene possibilities carefully plotted before birth and the actual gene distribution tested after birth."

"I know that."

"But genes aren't everything. Environment counts too, and environment can bend into actual psychosis where genes indicate only a potentiality for a particular psychosis. Did you notice Gladia's interest in Earth?"

"I remarked upon it, Partner Elijah, and considered it an assumed interest designed to influence your opinions."

"Suppose it were a real interest, even a fascination. Suppose there were something about Earth's crowds that excited her. Suppose she were attracted against her will by something she had been taught to consider filthy. There was possibly abnormality. I had to test it by seeing Solarians and noticing how *she* reacted to it. It was why I had to get away from you, Daneel, at any cost. It was why I had to abandon viewing as a method for carrying on the investigation."

"You did not explain this, Partner Elijah."

"Would the explanation have helped against what you conceived your duty under First Law to be?"

Daneel was silent.

Baley said, "The experiment worked. I saw or tried to see several people. An old sociologist tried to see me and had to give up midway. A roboticist refused to see me at all even under terrific force. The bare possibility sent him into an almost infantile frenzy. He sucked his finger and wept. Dr. Delmarre's assistant was used to personal presence in the way of her profession and so she tolerated me, but at twenty feet only. Gladia, on the other hand——"

"Yes, Partner Elijah?"

"Gladia consented to see me without more than a slight hesitation. She tolerated my presence easily and actually showed signs of decreasing strain as time went on. It all fits into a pattern of psychosis. She didn't mind seeing me; she was interested in Earth; she might have felt an abnormal interest in her husband. All of it could be explained by a strong and, for this world, psychotic interest in the personal presence of members of the opposite sex. Dr. Delmarre, himself, was not the type to encourage such a feeling or co-operate with it. It must have been very frustrating for her."

Daneel nodded. "Frustrating enough for murder in a moment of passion."

"In spite of everything, I don't think so, Daneel."

"Are you perhaps influenced by extraneous motives of your own, Partner Elijah? Mrs. Delmarre is an attractive woman and you are an Earthman in whom a preference for the personal presence of an attractive woman is not psychotic."

"I have better reasons," said Baley uneasily. (Daneel's cool glance was too penetrating and soul-dissecting by half. Jehoshaphat! The thing was only a machine.) He said, "If she were the murderess of her husband, she would also have to be the attempted murderess of Gruer." He had almost the impulse to explain the way murder could be manipulated through robots, but held back. He was not sure how Daneel would react to a theory that made unwitting murderers of robots.

Daneel said, "And the attempted murderess of yourself as well."

Baley frowned. He had had no intention of telling Daneel of the poisoned arrow that had missed; no intention of strengthening the other's already too strong protective complex vis-à-vis himself.

He said angrily, "What did Klorissa tell you?" He ought to have warned her to keep quiet, but then, how was he to know that Daneel would be about, asking questions?

Daneel said calmly, "Mrs. Cantoro had nothing to do with the matter. I witnessed the murder attempt myself."

Baley was thoroughly confused. "You were nowhere about."

Daneel said, "I caught you myself and brought you here an hour ago."

"What are you talking about?"

"Do you not remember, Partner Elijah? It was almost a perfect murder. Did not Mrs. Delmarre suggest that you go into the open? I was not a witness to that, but I feel certain she did."

"She did suggest it. Yes."

"She may even have enticed you to leave the house."

Baley thought of the "portrait" of himself, of the enclosing gray walls. Could it have been clever psychology? Could a Solarian have that much intuitive understanding of the psychology of an Earthman?

"No," he said.

Daneel said, "Was it she who suggested you go down to the ornamental pond and sit on the bench?"

"Well, yes."

"Does it occur to you that she might have been watching you, noticing your gathering dizziness?"

"She asked once or twice if I wanted to go back."

"She might not have meant it seriously. She might have been watching you turn sicker on that bench. She might even have pushed you, or perhaps a push wasn't necessary. At the moment I reached you and caught you in my arms, you were in the process of falling backward off the stone bench and into three feet of water, in which you would surely have drowned."

For the first time Baley recalled those last fugitive sensations. "Jehoshaphat!"

"Moreover," said Daneel with calm relentlessness, "Mrs. Delmarre sat beside you, watching you fall, without a move to stop you. Nor would she have attempted to pull you out of the water. She would have let you drown. She might have called a robot, but the robot would surely have arrived too late. And afterward, she would explain merely that, of course, it was impossible for her to touch you even to save your life."

True enough, thought Baley. No one would question her inability to touch a human being. The surprise, if any, would come at her ability to be as close to one as she was.

Daneel said, "You see, then, Partner Elijah, that her guilt can scarcely be in question. You stated that she would have to be the attempted murderess of Agent Gruer as though this were an argument against her guilt. You see now that she must have been. Her only motive to murder you was the same as her motive for trying to murder Gruer; the necessity of getting rid of an embarrassingly persistent investigator of the first murder."

Baley said, "The whole sequence might have been an innocent one. She might never have realized how the outdoors would affect me."

"She studied Earth. She knew the peculiarities of Earthmen."

"I assured her I had been outdoors and that I was growing used to it."

"She may have known better."

Baley pounded fist against palm. "You're making her too clever. It doesn't fit and I don't believe it. In any case, no murder accusation can stick unless and until the absence of the murder weapon can be accounted for."

Daneel looked steadily at the Earthman. "I can do that, too. Partner Elijah."

Baley looked at his robot partner with a stunned expression. "How?"

"Your reasoning, you will remember, Partner Elijah, was this. Were Mrs. Delmarre the murderess, then the weapon, whatever it was, must have remained at the scene of the murder. The robots, appearing almost at once, saw no sign of such a weapon, hence it must have been removed from the scene, hence the murderer must have removed it, hence the murderer could not be Mrs. Delmarre. Is all that correct?"

"Correct."

"Yet," continued the robot, "there is one place where the robots did not look for the weapon."

"Where?"

"Under Mrs. Delmarre. She was lying in a faint, brought on by the excitement and passion of the moment, whether murderess or not, and the weapon, whatever it was, lay under her and out of sight."

Baley said, "Then the weapon would have been discovered as soon as she was moved."

"Exactly," said Daneel, "but she was not moved by the robots. She herself told us yesterday at dinner that Dr. Thool ordered the robots to put a pillow under her head and leave her. She was first moved by Dr. Altim Thool, himself, when he arrived to examine her."

"So?"

"It follows, therefore, Partner Elijah, that a new possibility arises. Mrs. Delmarre was the murderess, the weapon was at the scene of the crime, but Dr. Thool carried it off and disposed of it to protect Mrs. Delmarre."

Baley felt contemptuous. He had almost been seduced into expecting something reasonable. He said, "Completely motiveless. Why should Dr. Thool do such a thing?"

"For a very good reason. You remember Mrs. Delmarre's remarks concerning him: 'He always treated me since I was a child and was always so friendly and kind.' I wondered if he might have some motive for being particularly concerned about her. It was for that reason that I visited the baby farm and inspected the records. What I had merely guessed at as a possibility turned out to be the truth."

"What?"

"Dr. Altim Thool was the father of Gladia Delmarre, and what is more, he knew of the relationship."

Baley had not thought of disbelieving the robot. He felt only a deep chagrin that it had been Robot Daneel Olivaw and not himself that had carried through the necessary piece of logical analysis. Even so, it was not complete.

He said, "Have you spoken to Dr. Thool?"

"Yes. I have placed him under house arrest, also."

"What does he say?"

"He admits that he is the father of Mrs. Delmarre. I confronted him with the records of the fact and the records of his inquiries into her health when she was a youngster. As a doctor, he was allowed more

leeway in this respect than another Solarian might have been allowed."

"Why should he have inquired into her health?"

"I have considered that, too, Partner Elijah. He was an old man
when he was given special permission to have an additional child and,
what is more, he succeeded in producing one. He considers this a
tribute, to his genes and to his physical fitness. He is prouder of the
result, perhaps, than is quite customary on this world. Moreover, his
position as physician, a profession little regarded on Solaria because it
involves personal presence, made it the more important to him to
nurture this sense of pride. For that reason, he maintained unobtrusive contact with his offspring."

"Does Gladia know anything of it?"

"As far as Dr. Thool is aware, Partner Elijah, she does not."

Baley said, "Does Thool admit removing the weapon?"

"No. That he does not."

"Then you've got nothing, Daneel.

"Nothing?"

"Unless you can find the weapon and prove he took it, or at the
very least induce him to confess, you have no evidence. A chain of
deduction is pretty, but it isn't evidence."

"The man would scarcely confess without considerable questioning
of a type I myself could not carry through. His daughter is dear to
him."

"Not at all," said Baley. "His feeling for his daughter is not at all
what you and I are accustomed to. Solaria is different!"

He strode the length of the room and back, letting himself cool. He
said, "Daneel, you have worked out a perfect exercise in logic, but
none of it is reasonable, just the same." (Logical but not reasonable.
Wasn't that the definition of a robot?)

He went on, "Dr. Thool is an old man and past his best years,
regardless of whether he was capable of siring a daughter thirty years
or so ago. Even spacers get senile. Picture him then examining his
daughter in a faint and his son-in-law dead by violence. Can you imagine the unusual nature of the situation for him? Can you suppose he
could have remained master of himself? So much the master of himself, in fact, as to carry out a series of amazing actions?

"Look! First, he would have had to notice a weapon under his
daughter, one that must have been so well covered by her body that
the robots never noticed it. Secondly, from whatever small scrap of
object he noted, he must have deduced the presence of the weapon
and seen at once that if he could but sneak off with that weapon,
unseen, a murder accusation against his daughter would be hard to
substantiate. That's pretty subtle thinking for an old man in a panic.

Then, thirdly, he would have had to carry the plan through, also tough for an old man in a panic. And now lastly, he would have to dare to compound the felony further by sticking to his lie. It all may be the result of logical thinking, but none of it is reasonable."

Daneel said, "Do you have an alternate solution to the crime, Partner Elijah?"

Baley had sat down during the course of his last speech and now he tried to rise again, but a combination of weariness and the depth of the chair defeated him. He held out his hand petulantly. "Give me a hand, will you, Daneel?"

Daneel stared at his own hand. "I beg your pardon, Partner Elijah?"

Baley silently swore at the other's literal mind and said, "Help me out of the chair."

Daneel's strong arm lifted him out of the chair effortlessly.

Baley said, "Thanks. No, I haven't an alternate solution. At least, I have, but the whole thing hinges on the location of the weapon."

He walked impatiently to the heavy curtains that lined most of one wall and lifted a corner without quite realizing what he was doing. He stared at the black patch of glass until he became aware of the fact that he was looking out into the early night, and then dropped the curtain just as Daneel, approaching quietly, took it out of his fingers.

In the split fraction of a moment in which Baley watched the robot's hand take the curtain away from him with the loving caution of a mother protecting her child from the fire, a revolution took place within him.

He snatched the curtain back, yanking it out of Daneel's grasp. Throwing his full weight against it, he tore it away from the window, leaving shreds behind.

"Partner Elijah!" said Daneel softly. "Surely you know now what the open will do to you."

"I know," said Baley, "what it will do *for* me."

He stared out the window. There was nothing to see, only blackness, but that blackness was open air. It was unbroken, unobstructed space, even if unlit, and he was facing it.

And for the first time he faced it freely. It was no longer bravado, or perverse curiosity, or the pathway to a solution of a murder. He faced it because he knew he wanted to and because he needed to. That made all the difference.

Walls were crutches! Darkness and crowds were crutches! He must have thought them so, unconsciously, and hated them even when he most thought he loved and needed them. Why else had he so resented Gladia's gray enclosure of his portrait?

He felt himself filling with a sense of victory, and, as though victory were contagious, a new thought came, bursting like an inner shout.

Baley turned dizzily to Daneel. "I know," he whispered. "Jehosha-phat! I know!"

"Know what, Partner Elijah?"

"I know what happened to the weapon; I know who is responsible. All at once, everything falls into place."

17. A Meeting Is Held

Daneel would allow no immediate action.

"Tomorrow!" he had said with respectful firmness. "That is my sug-gestion, Partner Elijah. It is late and you are in need of rest."

Baley had to admit the truth of it, and besides there was the need for preparation; a considerable quantity of it. He had the solution of the murder, he felt sure of that, but it rested on deduction, as much as had Daneel's theory, and it was worth as little as evidence. Solarians would have to help him.

And if he were to face them, one Earthman against half a dozen Spacers, he would have to be in full control. That meant rest and preparation.

Yet he would not sleep. He was certain he would not sleep. Not all the softness of the special bed set up for him by smoothly functioning robots nor all the soft perfume and softer music in the special room of Gladia's mansion would help. He was sure of it.

Daneel sat unobtrusively in one darkened corner.

Baley said, "Are you still afraid of Gladia?"

The robot said, "I do not think it wise to allow you to sleep alone and unprotected."

"Well, have your way. Are you clear as to what I want you to do, Daneel?"

"I am, Partner Elijah."

"You have no reservations under the First Law, I hope."

"I have some with respect to the conference you wish arranged. Will you be armed and careful of your own safety?"

"I assure you, I will."

Daneel delivered himself of a sigh that was somehow so human that for a moment Baley found himself trying to penetrate the darkness that he might study the machine-perfect face of the other.

Daneel said, "I have not always found human behavior logical."

"We need Three Laws of our own," said Baley, "but I'm glad we don't have them."

He stared at the ceiling. A great deal depended on Daneel and yet he could tell him very little of the whole truth. Robots were too involved. The planet, Aurora, had its reasons for sending a robot as representative of their interests, but it was a mistake. Robots had their limitations.

Still, if all went right, this could all be over in twelve hours. He could be heading back to Earth in twenty-four, bearing hope. A strange kind of hope. A kind he could scarcely believe himself, yet it was Earth's way out. It must be Earth's way out.

Earth! New York! Jessie and Ben! The comfort and familiarity and dearness of home!

He dwelled on it, half asleep, and the thought of Earth failed to conjure the comfort he expected. There was an estrangement between himself and the Cities.

And at some unknown point in time it all faded and he slept.

Baley, having slept and then wakened, showered and dressed. Physically he was quite prepared. Yet he was unsure. It was not that his reasoning seemed any less cogent to himself in the pallor of morning. It was rather the necessity of facing Solarians.

Could he be sure of their reactions after all? Or would he still be working blind?

Gladia was the first to appear. It was simple for her, of course. She was on an intramural circuit, since she was in the mansion herself. She was pale and expressionless, in a white gown that draped her into a cold statue.

She stared helplessly at Baley. Baley smiled back gently and she seemed to take comfort from that.

One by one, they appeared now. Attlebish, the Acting Head of Security, appeared next after Gladia, lean and haughty, his large chin set in disapproval. Then Leebig, the roboticist, impatient and angry, his weak eyelid fluttering periodically. Quemot, the sociologist, a little tired, but smiling at Baley out of deep-set eyes in a condescending way, as though to say: We have seen one another, we have been intimate.

Klorissa Cantoro, when she appeared, seemed uneasy in the presence of the others. She glanced at Gladia for a moment with an audible sniff, then stared at the floor. Dr. Thool, the physician, appeared last. He looked haggard, almost sick.

They were all there, all but Gruer, who was slowly recovering and for whom attendance was physically impossible. (Well, thought Baley, we'll do without him.) All were dressed formally; all sat in rooms that were well curtained into enclosure.

Daneel had arranged matters well. Baley hoped fervently that what remained for Daneel to do would work as well.

Baley looked from one Spacer to the other. His heart thudded. Each figure viewed him out of a different room and the clash of lighting, furniture, and wall decoration was dizzying.

Baley said, "I want to discuss the matter of the killing of Dr. Rikaine Delmarre under the heading of motive, opportunity, and means, in that order——"

Attlebish interrupted. "Will this be a long speech?"

Baley said sharply, "It may be. I have been called here to investigate a murder and such a job is my specialty and my profession. I know best how to go about it." (Take nothing from them now, he thought, or this whole thing won't work. Dominate! Dominate!)

He went on, making his words as sharp and incisive as he could. "Motive first. In a way, motive is the most unsatisfactory of the three items. Opportunity and means are objective. They can be investigated factually. Motive is subjective. It may be something that can be observed by others; revenge for a known humiliation, for instance. But it may also be completely unobservable; an irrational, homicidal hate on the part of a well-disciplined person who never lets it show.

"Now almost all of you have told me at one time or another that you believe Gladia Delmarre to have committed the crime. Certainly, no one has suggested an alternate suspect. Has Gladia a motive? Dr. Leebig suggested one. He said that Gladia quarreled frequently with her husband and Gladia later admitted this to me. The rage that can arise out of a quarrel can, conceivably, move a person to murder. Very well.

"The question remains, though, whether she is the only one with a motive. I wonder. Dr. Leebig, himself——"

The roboticist almost jumped. His hand extended rigidly in the direction of Baley. "Watch what you say, Earthman."

"I am only theorizing," said Baley coldly. "You, Dr. Leebig, were working with Dr. Delmarre on new robot models. You are the best man in Solaria as far as robotics is concerned. You say so and I believe it."

Leebig smiled with open condescension.

Baley went on, "But I have heard that Dr. Delmarre was about to break off relations with you for matters concerning yourself of which he disapproved."

"False! False!"

"Perhaps. But what if it were true? Wouldn't you have a motive to get rid of him before he humiliated you publicly by breaking with you? I have a feeling you could not easily bear such humiliation."

Baley went on rapidly to give Leebig no chance to retort. "And you, Mrs. Cantoro. Dr. Delmarre's death leaves you in charge of fetal engineering, a responsible position."

"Skies above, we talked about that before," cried Klorissa in anguish.

"I know we did, but it's a point that must be considered, anyway. As for Dr. Quemot, he played chess with Dr. Delmarre regularly. Perhaps he grew annoyed at losing too many games."

The sociologist interposed quietly. "Losing a chess game is insufficient motive surely, Plainclothesman."

"It depends on how seriously you take your chess. Motives can seem all the world to the murderer and completely insignificant to everyone else. Well, it doesn't matter. My point is that motive alone is insufficient. Anyone can have a motive, particularly for the murder of a man such as Dr. Delmarre."

"What do you mean by that remark," demanded Quemot in indignation.

"Why, only that Dr. Delmarre was a 'good Solarian.' You all described him as such. He rigidly fulfilled all the requirements of Solarian custom. He was an ideal man, almost an abstraction. Who could feel love, or even liking, for such a man? A man without weaknesses serves only to make everyone else conscious of his own imperfections. A primitive poet named Tennyson once wrote: 'He is all fault who has no fault at all.' "

"No one would kill a man for being too good," said Klorissa, frowning.

"You little know," said Baley, and went on without amplification. "Dr. Delmarre was aware of a conspiracy on Solaria, or thought he was; a conspiracy that was preparing an assault on the rest of the Galaxy for purposes of conquest. He was interested in preventing that. For that reason, those concerned in the conspiracy might find it necessary to do away with him. Anyone here could be a member of the conspiracy, including, to be sure, Mrs. Delmarre, but including even the Acting Head of Security, Corwin Attlebish."

"I?" said Attlebish, unmoved.

"You certainly attempted to end the investigation as soon as Gruer's mishap put you in charge."

Baley took a few slow sips at his drink (straight from its original container, untouched by human hands other than his own, or robotic hands, either) and gathered his strength. So far, this was a waiting game, and he was thankful the Solarians were sitting still for it. They hadn't the Earthman's experience of dealing with people at close quarters. They weren't in-fighters.

He said, "Opportunity next. It is the general opinion that only Mrs.

Delmarre had opportunity since only she could approach her husband in actual personal presence.

"Are we sure of that? Suppose someone other than Mrs. Delmarre had made up his or her mind to kill Dr. Delmarre? Would not such a desperate resolution make the discomfort of personal presence secondary? If any of you were set on murder, wouldn't you bear personal presence just long enough to do the job? Couldn't you sneak into the Delmarre mansion——"

Attlebish interposed frigidly. "You are ignorant of the matter, Earthman. Whether we would or would not doesn't matter. The fact is that Dr. Delmarre himself would not allow seeing, I assure you. If anyone came into his personal presence, regardless of how valued and longstanding a friendship there was between them, Dr. Delmarre would order him away and, if necessary, call robots to help with the ejection."

"True," said Baley, "*if* Dr. Delmarre were aware that personal presence was involved."

"What do you mean by that?" demanded Dr. Thool in surprise, his voice quavering.

"When you treated Mrs. Delmarre at the scene of the murder," replied Baley, looking full at his questioner, "she assumed you were viewing her, until you actually touched her. So she told me and so I believe. I am, myself, accustomed only to seeing. When I arrived at Solaria and met Security Head Gruer, I assumed I was seeing him. When at the end of our interview, Gruer disappeared, I was taken completely by surprise.

"Now assume the reverse. Suppose that for all a man's adult life, he had been viewing only; never seeing anyone, except on rare occasions his wife. Now suppose someone other than his wife walked up to him in personal presence. Would he not automatically assume that it was a matter of viewing, particularly if a robot had been instructed to advise Delmarre that viewing contact was being set up?"

"Not for a minute," said Quemot. "The sameness of background would give it away."

"Maybe, but how many of you are aware of background now? There would be a minute or so, at least, before Dr. Delmarre would grow aware that something was wrong and in that time, his friend, whoever he was, could walk up to him, raise a club, and bring it down."

"Impossible," said Quemot stubbornly.

"I think not," said Baley. "I think opportunity must be canceled out as absolute proof that Mrs. Delmarre is the murderess. She had opportunity, but so might others."

Baley waited again. He felt perspiration on his forehead, but wiping it away would have made him look weak. He must maintain absolute charge of the proceedings. The person at whom he was aiming must be placed in self-convinced inferiority. It was hard for an Earthman to do that to a Spacer.

Baley looked from face to face and decided that matters were at least progressing satisfactorily. Even Attlebish looked quite humanly concerned.

"And so we come," he said, "to means, and that is the most puzzling factor of all. The weapon with which the murder was committed was never found."

"We know that," said Attlebish. "If it were not for that point, we would have considered the case against Mrs. Delmarre conclusive. We would never had required an investigation."

"Perhaps," said Baley. "Let's analyze the matter of means, then. There are two possibilities. Either Mrs. Delmarre committed the murder, or someone else did. If Mrs. Delmarre committed the murder, the weapon would have had to remain at the scene of the crime, unless it were removed later. It has been suggested by my partner, Mr. Olivaw of Aurora, who is not present at the moment, that Dr. Thool had the opportunity to remove the weapon. I ask Dr. Thool now, in the presence of all of us, if he did this, if he removed a weapon while examining the unconscious Mrs. Delmarre?"

Dr. Thool was shaking. "No, no. I swear it. I'll abide any questioning. I swear I removed nothing."

Baley said, "Is there anyone who wishes to suggest at this point that Dr. Thool is lying?"

There was a silence, during which Leebig looked at an object outside of Baley's field of vision and muttered something about the time.

Baley said, "The second possibility is that someone else committed the crime and carried the weapon off with him. But if that were so, one must ask why. Carrying the weapon away is an advertisement of the fact that Mrs. Delmarre was not the murderess. If an outsider were the murderer, he would have to be a complete imbecile not to leave the weapon with the corpse to convict Mrs. Delmarre. Either way, then, *the weapon must be there!* Yet it was not seen."

Attlebish said, "Do you take us for fools or for blind men?"

"I take you for Solarians," said Baley calmly, "and therefore incapable of recognizing the particular weapon that was left at the scene of the crime as a weapon."

"I don't understand a word," muttered Klorissa in distress.

Even Gladia, who had scarcely moved a muscle during the course of the meeting, was staring at Baley in surprise.

Baley said, "Dead husband and unconscious wife were not the only individuals on the scene. There was also a disorganized robot."

"Well?" said Leebig angrily.

"Isn't it obvious, then, that, in having eliminated the impossible, what remains, however improbable, is the truth. The robot at the scene of the crime was the murder weapon, a murder weapon none of you could recognize by force of your training."

They all talked at once; all but Gladia, who simply stared.

Baley raised his arms. "Hold it. Quiet! Let me explain!" And once again he told the story of the attempt on Gruer's life and the method by which it could have been accomplished. This time he added the attempt on his own life at the baby farm.

Leebig said impatiently, "I suppose that was managed by having one robot poison an arrow without knowing it was using poison, and having a second robot hand the poisoned arrow to the boy after telling him that you were an Earthman, without its knowing that the arrow was poisoned."

"Something like that. Both robots would be completely instructed."

"Very farfetched," said Leebig.

Quemot was pale and looked as though he might be sick at any moment. "No Solarian could possibly use robots to harm a human."

"Maybe so," said Baley with a shrug, "but the point is that robots can be so manipulated. Ask Dr. Leebig. He is the roboticist."

Leebig said, "It does not apply to the murder of Dr. Delmarre. I told you that yesterday. How can anyone arrange to have a robot smash a man's skull?"

"Shall I explain how?"

"Do so if you can."

Baley said, "It was a new-model robot that Dr. Delmarre was testing. The significance of that wasn't plain to me until last evening, when I had occasion to say to a robot, in asking for his help in rising out of a chair, 'Give me a hand!' The robot looked at his own hand in confusion as though he thought he was expected to detach it and give it to me. I had to repeat my order less idiomatically. But it reminded me of something Dr. Leebig had told me earlier that day. There was experimentation among robots with replaceable limbs.

"Suppose this robot that Dr. Delmarre had been testing was one such, capable of using any of a number of interchangeable limbs of various shapes for different kinds of specialized tasks. Suppose the murderer knew this and suddenly said to the robot, 'Give me your arm.' The robot would detach its arm and give it to him. The detached arm would make a splendid weapon. With Dr. Delmarre dead, it could be snapped back into place."

Stunned horror gave way to a babble of objection as Baley talked. His last sentence had to be shouted, and, even so, was all but drowned out.

Attlebish, face flushed, raised himself from his chair and stepped forward. "Even if what you say is so, then Mrs. Delmarre is the murderess. She was there, she quarreled with him, she would be watching her husband working with the robot, and would know of the replaceable-limb situation—which I don't believe, by the way. No matter what you do, Earthman, everything points to her."

Gladia began to weep softly.

Baley did not look at her. He said, "On the contrary, it is easy to show that, whoever committed the murder, Mrs. Delmarre did not."

Jothan Leebig suddenly folded his arms and allowed an expression of contempt to settle on his face.

Baley caught that and said, "You'll help me do so, Dr. Leebig. As a roboticist, you know that maneuvering robots into action such as indirect murder takes enormous skill. I had occasion yesterday to try to put an individual under house arrest. I gave three robots detailed instructions intended to keep this individual safe. It was a simple thing, but I am a clumsy man with robots. There were loopholes in my instructions and my prisoner escaped."

"Who was the prisoner?" demanded Attlebish.

"Beside the point," said Baley impatiently. "What *is* the point is the fact that amateurs can't handle robots well. And some Solarians may be pretty amateurish as Solarians go. For instance, what does Gladia Delmarre know about robotics? . . . Well, Dr. Leebig?"

"What?" The roboticist stared.

"You tried to teach Mr. Delmarre robotics. What kind of a pupil was she? Did she learn anything?"

Leebig looked about uneasily. "She didn't . . ." and stalled.

"She was completely hopeless, wasn't she? Or would you prefer not to answer?"

Leebig said stiffly, "She might have pretended ignorance."

"Are you prepared to say, as a roboticist, that you think Mrs. Delmarre is sufficiently skilled to drive robots to indirect murder?"

"How can I answer that?"

"Let me put it another way. Whoever tried to have me killed at the baby farm must have had to locate me by using interrobot communications. After all, I told no human where I was going and only the robots who conveyed me from point to point knew of my whereabouts. My partner, Daneel Olivaw, managed to trace me later in the day, but only with considerable difficulty. The murderer, on the other hand, must have done it easily, since, in addition to locating me, he had to arrange for arrow poisoning and arrow shooting, all before I left the farm and moved on. Would Mrs. Delmarre have the skill to do that?"

Corwin Attlebish leaned forward. "Who do you suggest would have the necessary skill, Earthman?"

Baley said, "Dr. Jothan Leebig is self-admittedly the best robot man on the planet."

"Is that an accusation?" cried Leebig.

"Yes!" shouted Baley.

The fury in Leebig's eyes faded slowly. It was replaced not by calm, exactly, but by a kind of clamped-down tension. He said, "I studied the Delmarre robot after the murder. It had no detachable limbs. At least, they were detachable only in the usual sense of requiring special tools and expert handling. So the robot wasn't the weapon used in killing Delmarre and you have no argument."

Baley said, "Who else can vouch for the truth of your statement?"

"My word is not to be questioned."

"It is here. I'm accusing you, and your unsupported word concerning the robot is valueless. If someone else will bear you out, that would be different. Incidentally, you disposed of that robot quickly. Why?"

"There was no reason to keep it. It was completely disorganized. It was useless."

"Why?"

Leebig shook his finger at Baley and said violently, "You asked me that once before, Earthman, and I told you why. It had witnessed a murder which it had been powerless to stop."

"And you told me that that always brought about complete collapse; that that was a universal rule. Yet when Gruer was poisoned, the robot that had presented him with the poisoned drink was harmed only to the extent of a limp and a lisp. It had actually itself been the agent of what looked like murder at that moment, and not merely a witness, and yet it retained enough sanity to be questioned.

"This robot, the robot in the Delmarre case, must therefore have been still more intimately concerned with murder than the Gruer robot. This Delmarre robot must have had its own arm used as the murder weapon."

"All nonsense," gasped out Leebig. "You know nothing about robotics."

Baley said, "That's as may be. But I will suggest that Security Head Attlebish impound the records of your robot factory and maintenance shop. Perhaps we can find out whether you have built robots with detachable limbs and, if so, whether any were sent to Dr. Delmarre, and, if so, when."

"No one will tamper with my records," cried Leebig.

"Why? If you have nothing to hide, why?"

"But why on Solaria would I want to kill Delmarre? Tell me that. What's my motive?"

"I can think of two," said Baley. "You were friendly with Mrs. Delmarre. Overly friendly. Solarians are human, after a fashion. You never consorted with women, but that didn't keep you immune from, shall we say, animal urges. You saw Mrs. Delmarre—I beg your pardon, you viewed her—when she was dressed rather informally and——"

"No," cried Leebig in agony.

And Gladia whispered energetically, "No."

"Perhaps you didn't recognize the nature of your feelings yourself," said Baley, "or if you had a dim notion of it, you despised yourself for your weakness, and hated Mrs. Delmarre for inspiring it. And yet you might have hated Delmarre, too, for having her. You did ask Mrs. Delmarre to be your assistant. You compromised with your libido that far. She refused and your hatred was the keener for that. By killing Dr. Delmarre in such a way as to throw suspicion on Mrs. Delmarre, you could be avenged on both at once."

"Who would believe that cheap, melodramatic filth?" demanded Leebig in a hoarse whisper. "Another Earthman, another animal, maybe. No Solarian."

"I don't depend on that motive," said Baley. "I think it was there, unconsciously, but you had a plainer motive, too. Dr. Rikaine Delmarre was in the way of your plans, and had to be removed."

"What plans?" demanded Leebig.

"Your plans aiming at the conquest of the Galaxy, Dr. Leebig," said Baley.

18. A Question Is Answered

"The Earthman is mad," cried Leebig, turning to the others. "Isn't that obvious?"

Some stared at Leebig wordlessly, some at Baley.

Baley gave them no chance to come to decisions. He said, "You know better, Dr. Leebig. Dr. Delmarre was going to break off with you. Mrs. Delmarre thought it was because you wouldn't marry. I don't think so. Dr. Delmarre himself was planning a future in which ectogenesis would be possible and marriage unnecessary. But Dr. Delmarre was working with you; he would know, and guess, more about your work than anyone else. He would know if you were attempting dangerous experiments and he would try to stop you. He hinted about such matters to Agent Gruer, but gave no details, because he was not yet certain of the details. Obviously, you discovered his suspicions and killed him."

"Mad!" said Leebig again. "I will have nothing more to do with this."

But Attlebish interrupted. "Hear him out, Leebig!"

Baley bit his lip to keep from a premature display of satisfaction at the obvious lack of sympathy in the Security Head's voice. He said, "In the same discussion with me in which you mentioned robots with detachable limbs, Dr. Leebig, you mentioned spaceships with built-in positronic brains. You were definitely talking too much then. Was it that you thought I was only an Earthman and incapable of understanding the implications of robotics? Or was it that you had just been threatened with personal presence, had the threat lifted, and were a little delirious with relief? In any case, Dr. Quemot had already told me that the secret weapon of Solaria against the Outer Worlds was the positronic robot."

Quemot, thus unexpectedly referred to, started violently, and cried, "I meant——"

"You meant it sociologically, I know. But it gives rise to thoughts. Consider a spaceship with a built-in positronic brain as compared to a manned spaceship. A manned spaceship could not use robots in active warfare. A robot could not destroy humans on enemy spaceships or on enemy worlds. It would not grasp the distinction between friendly humans and enemy humans.

"Of course, a robot could be told that the opposing spaceship had no humans aboard. It could be told that it was an uninhabited planet that was being bombarded. That would be difficult to manage. A robot could see that its own ship carried humans; it would know its own world held humans. It would assume that the same was true of enemy ships and worlds. It would take a real expert in robotics, such as you, Dr. Leebig, to handle them properly in that case, and there are very few such experts.

"But a spaceship that was equipped with its own positronic brain would cheerfully attack any ship it was directed to attack, it seems to me. It would naturally assume all other ships were unmanned. A positronic-brained ship could easily be made incapable of receiving messages from enemy ships that might undeceive it. With its weapons and defenses under the immediate control of a positronic brain, it would be more maneuverable than any manned ship. With no room necessary for crewmen, for supplies, for water or air purifiers, it could carry more armor, more weapons and be more invulnerable than any ordinary ship. One ship with a positronic brain could defeat fleets of ordinary ships. Am I wrong?"

The last question was shot at Dr. Leebig, who had risen from his seat and was standing, rigid, almost cataleptic with—what? Anger? Horror?

There was no answer. No answer could have been heard. Something tore loose and the others were yelling madly. Klorissa had the face of a Fury and even Gladia was on her feet, her small fist beating the air threateningly.

And all had turned on Leebig.

Baley relaxed and closed his eyes. He tried for just a few moments to unknot his muscles, unfreeze his tendons.

It had worked. He had pressed the right button at last. Quemot had made an analogy between the Solarian robots and the Spartan Helots. He said the robots could not revolt so that the Solarians could relax.

But what if some humans threatened to teach the robots how to harm humans; to make them, in other words, capable of revolting?

Would that not be the ultimate crime? On a world such as Solaria would not every last inhabitant turn fiercely against anyone even suspected of making a robot capable of harming a human; on Solaria, where robots outnumbered humans by twenty thousand to one?

Attlebish cried, "You are under arrest. You are absolutely forbidden to touch your books or records until the government has a chance to inspect them——" He went on, almost incoherent, scarcely heard in the pandemonium.

A robot approached Baley. "A message, master, from the master Olivaw."

Baley took the message gravely, turned, and cried, "One moment."

His voice had an almost magical effect. All turned to look at him solemnly and in no face (outside Leebig's frozen glare) was there any sign of anything but the most painful attention to the Earthman.

Baley said, "It is foolish to expect Dr. Leebig to leave his records untouched while waiting for some official to reach them. So even before this interview began, my partner, Daneel Olivaw, left for Dr. Leebig's estate. I have just heard from him. He is on the grounds now and will be with Dr. Leebig in a moment in order that he may be put under restraint."

"*Restraint!*" howled Leebig in an almost animal terror. His eyes widened into staring holes in his head. "Someone coming here? Personal presence? No! No!" The second "No" was a shriek.

"You will not be harmed," said Baley coldly, "if you co-operate."

"But I don't see him. I can't see him." The roboticist fell to his knees without seeming aware of the motion. He put his hands together in a desperate clasped gesture of appeal. "What do you want? Do you want a confession? Delmarre's robot had detachable limbs. Yes. Yes. Yes. I arranged Gruer's poisoning. I arranged the arrow meant for you. I even planned the spaceships as you said. I haven't succeeded, but, yes, I planned it. Only keep the man away. Don't let him come. Keep him away!"

He was babbling.

Baley nodded. Another right button. The threat of personal presence would do more to induce confession than any physical torture.

But then, at some noise or movement outside the field of sound or vision of any of the others, Leebig's head twisted and his mouth opened. He lifted a pair of hands, holding something off.

"Away," he begged. "Go away. Don't come. Please don't come. Please——"

He scrambled away on hands and knees, then his hand went suddenly to a pocket in his jacket. It came out with something and moved rapidly to his mouth. Swaying twice, he fell prone.

Baley wanted to cry: You fool, it isn't a human that's approaching you; only one of the robots you love.

Daneel Olivaw darted into the field of vision and for a moment stared down at the crumpled figure.

Baley held his breath. If Daneel should realize it was his own pseudo humanity that had killed Leebig, the effect on his First Law-enslaved brain might be drastic.

But Daneel only knelt and his delicate fingers touched Leebig here and there. Then he lifted Leebig's head as though it were infinitely precious to him, cradling it, caressing it.

His beautifully chiseled face stared out at the others and he whispered, "A human is dead!"

Baley was expecting her; she had asked for a last interview; but his eyes widened when she appeared.

He said, "I'm seeing you."

"Yes," said Gladia, "how can you tell?"

"You're wearing gloves."

"Oh." She looked at her hands in confusion. Then, softly, "Do you mind?"

"No, of course not. But why have you decided to see, rather than view?"

"Well"—she smiled weakly—"I've got to get used to it, don't I, Elijah? I mean, if I'm going to Aurora."

"Then it's all arranged?"

"Mr. Olivaw seems to have influence. It's all arranged. I'll never come back."

"Good. You'll be happier, Gladia. I know you will."

"I'm a little afraid."

"I know. It will mean seeing all the time and you won't have all the comforts you had on Solaria. But you'll get used to it and, what's more, you'll forget all the terror you've been through."

"I don't want to forget everything," said Gladia softly.

"You will." Baley looked at the slim girl who stood before him and said, not without a momentary pang, "And you will be married someday, too. Really married, I mean."

"Somehow," she said mournfully, "that doesn't seem so attractive to me—right now."

"You'll change your mind."

And they stood there, looking at each other for a wordless moment. Gladia said, "I've never thanked you."

Baley said, "It was only my job."

"You'll be going back to Earth now, won't you?"

"Yes."

"I'll never see you again."

"Probably not. But don't feel badly about that. In forty years at most, I'll be dead and you won't look a bit different from the way you do now."

Her face twisted. "Don't say that."

"It's true."

She said rapidly, as though forced to change the subject, "It's all true about Jothan Leebig, you know."

"I know. Other roboticists went over his records and found experiments toward unmanned intelligent spaceships. They also found other robots with replaceable limbs."

Gladia shuddered. "Why did he do such a horrible thing, do you suppose?"

"He was afraid of people. He killed himself to avoid personal presence and he was ready to kill other worlds to make sure that Solaria and its personal-presence taboo would never be touched."

"How could he feel so," she murmured, "when personal presence can be so very——"

Again a silent moment while they faced each other at ten paces.

Then Gladia cried suddenly, "Oh, Elijah, you'll think it abandoned of me."

"Think what abandoned?"

"May I touch you? I'll never see you again, Elijah."

"If you want to."

Step by step, she came closer, her eyes glowing, yet looking apprehensive, too. She stopped three feet away, then slowly, as though in a trance, she began to remove the glove on her right hand.

Baley started a restraining gesture. "Don't be foolish, Gladia."

"I'm not afraid," said Gladia.

Her hand was bare. It trembled as she extended it.

And so did Baley's as he took her hand in his. They remained so for one moment, her hand a shy thing, frightened as it rested in his. He opened his hand and hers escaped, darted suddenly and without warning toward his face until her fingertips rested feather-light upon his cheek for the barest moment.

She said, "Thank you, Elijah. Good-by."

He said, "Good-by, Gladia," and watched her leave.

Even the thought that a ship was waiting to take him back to Earth did not wipe out the sense of loss he felt at that moment.

Undersecretary Albert Minnim's look was intended to be one of prim welcome. "I am glad to see you back on Earth. Your report, of course, arrived before you did and is being studied. You did a good job. The matter will look well in your record."

"Thank you," said Baley. There was no room for further elation in him. Being back on Earth; being safe in the Caves; being in hearing of Jessie's voice (he had spoken to her already) had left him strangely empty.

"However," said Minnim, "your report concerned only the murder investigation. There was another matter we were interested in. May I have a report on that, verbally?"

Baley hesitated and his hand moved automatically toward the inner pocket where the warm comfort of his pipe could once more be found.

Minnim said at once, "You may smoke, Baley."

Baley made of the lighting process a rather drawn-out ritual. He said, "I am not a sociologist."

"Aren't you?" Minnim smiled briefly. "It seems to me we discussed that once. A successful detective must be a good rule-of-thumb sociologist even if he never heard of Hackett's Equation. I think, from your discomfort at the moment, that you have notions concerning the Outer Worlds but aren't sure how it will sound to me?"

"If you put it that way, sir . . . When you ordered me to Solaria, you asked a question; you asked what the weaknesses of the Outer Worlds were. Their strengths were their robots, their low population, their long lives, but what were their weaknesses?"

"Well?"

"I believe I know the weaknesses of the Solarians, sir."

"You can answer my question? Good. Go ahead."

"Their weaknesses, sir, are their robots, their low population, their long lives."

Minnim stared at Baley without any change of expression. His hands worked in jerky finger-drawn designs along the papers on his desk.

He said, "Why do you say that?"

Baley had spent hours organizing his thoughts on the way back from Solaria; had confronted officialdom, in imagination, with balanced, well-reasoned arguments. Now he felt at a loss.

He said, "I'm not sure I can put them clearly."

"No matter. Let me hear. This is first approximation only."

Baley said, "The Solarians have given up something mankind has had for a million years; something worth more than atomic power, cities, agriculture, tools, fire, everything; because it's something that made everything else possible."

"I don't want to guess, Baley. What is it?"

"The tribe, sir. Co-operation between individuals. Solaria has given it up entirely. It is a world of isolated individuals and the planet's only sociologist is delighted that this is so. That sociologist, by the way, never heard of sociomathematics, because he is inventing his own science. There is no one to teach him, no one to help him, no one to think of something he himself might miss. The only science that really flourishes on Solaria is robotics and there are only a handful of men involved in that, and when it came to an analysis of the interaction of robots and men, they had to call in an Earthman to help.

"Solarian art, sir, is abstract. We have abstract art on Earth as *one* form of art; but on Solaria it is the *only* form. The human touch is gone. The looked-for future is one of ectogenesis and complete isolation from birth."

Minnim said, "It all sounds horrible. But is it harmful?"

"I think so. Without the interplay of human against human, the chief interest in life is gone; most of the intellectual values are gone; most of the reason for living is gone. Viewing is no substitute for seeing. The Solarians, themselves, are conscious that viewing is a long-distance sense.

"And if isolation isn't enough to induce stagnation, there is the matter of their long lives. On Earth, we have a continuous influx of young people who are willing to change because they haven't had time to grow hard-set in their ways. I suppose there's some optimum. A life long enough for real accomplishment and short enough to make way for youth at a rate that's not too slow. On Solaria, the rate *is* too slow."

Minnim still drew patterns with his finger. "Interesting! Interesting!" He looked up, and it was as though a mask had fallen away. There was glee in his eyes. "Plainclothesman, you're a man of penetration."

"Thank you," said Baley stiffly.

"Do you know why I encouraged you to describe your views to me?" He was almost like a little boy, hugging his pleasure. He went on without waiting for an answer. "Your report has already undergone preliminary analysis by our sociologists and I was wondering if you had any idea yourself as to the excellent news for Earth you had brought with you. I see you have."

"But wait," said Baley. "There's more to this."

"There is, indeed," agreed Minnim jubilantly. "Solaria cannot possibly correct its stagnation. It has passed a critical point and their dependence on robots has gone too far. Individual robots can't discipline an individual child, even though discipline may do the child eventual good. The robot can't see past the immediate pain. And robots collectively cannot discipline a planet by allowing its institutions to collapse when the institutions have grown harmful. They can't see past the immediate chaos. So the only end for the Outer Worlds is perpetual stagnation and Earth will be freed of their domination. This new data changes everything. Physical revolt will not even be necessary. Freedom will come of itself."

"Wait," said Baley again, more loudly. "It's only Solaria we're discussing, not any other Outer World."

"It's the same thing. Your Solaria sociologist—Kimot——"

"Quemot, sir."

"Quemot, then. He said, did he not, that the other Outer Worlds were moving in the direction of Solaria?"

"He did, but he knew nothing about the other Outer Worlds firsthand, and he was no sociologist. Not really. I thought I made that clear."

"Our own men will check."

"They'll lack data too. We know nothing about the really big Outer Worlds. Aurora, for instance; Daneel's world. To me, it doesn't seem reasonable to expect them to be anything like Solaria. In fact, there's only one world in the Galaxy which resembles Solaria——"

Minnim was dismissing the subject with a small, happy wave of his neat hand. "Our men will check. I'm sure they will agree with Quemot."

Baley's stare grew somber. If Earth's sociologists were anxious enough for happy news, they would find themselves agreeing with Quemot, at that. Anything could be found in figures if the search were long enough and hard enough and if the proper pieces of information were ignored or overlooked.

He hesitated. Was it best now to speak while he had the ear of a man high in the government or——

He hesitated a trifle too long. Minnim was speaking again, shuffling a few papers and growing more matter-of-fact. "A few minor matters, Plainclothesman, concerning the Delmarre case itself and then you will be free to go. Did you intend to have Leebig commit suicide?"

"I intended to force a confession, sir. I had not anticipated suicide at the approach, ironically, of someone who was only a robot and who would not really be violating the taboo against personal presence. But, frankly, I don't regret his death. He was a dangerous man. It will be a long time before there will be another man who will combine his sickness and his brilliance."

"I agree with that," said Minnim dryly, "and consider his death fortunate, but didn't you consider your danger if the Solarians had stopped to realize that Leebig couldn't possibly have murdered Delmarre?"

Baley took his pipe out of his mouth and said nothing.

"Come, Plainclothesman," said Minnim. "You know he didn't. The murder required personal presence and Leebig would die rather than allow that. He *did* die rather than allow it."

Baley said, "You're right, sir. I counted on the Solarians being too horrified at his misuse of robots to stop to think of that."

"Then who did kill Delmarre?"

Baley said slowly, "If you mean who struck the actual blow, it was the person everyone knew had done so. Gladia Delmarre, the man's wife."

"And you let her go?"

Baley said, "Morally, the responsibility wasn't hers. Leebig knew Gladia quarreled bitterly with her husband, and often. He must have known how furious she could grow in moments of anger. Leebig wanted the death of the husband under circumstances that would incriminate the wife. So he supplied Delmarre with a robot and, I imagine, instructed it with all the skill he possessed to hand Gladia one of its detachable limbs at the moment of her full fury. With a weapon on her hand at the crucial moment, she acted in a temporary black-out before either Delmarre or the robot could stop her. Gladia was as much Leebig's unwitting instrument as the robot itself."

Minnim said, "The robot's arm must have been smeared with blood and matted hair."

"It probably was," said Baley. "But it was Leebig who took the murder robot in charge. He could easily have instructed any other robots who might have noticed the fact to forget it. Dr. Thool might have noticed it, but he inspected only the dead man and the unconscious woman. Leebig's mistake was to think that guilt would rest so obviously on Gladia that the matter of the absence of an obvious weapon at the scene wouldn't save her. Nor could he anticipate that an Earthman would be called in to help with the investigation."

"So with Leebig dead, you arranged to have Gladia leave Solaria. Was that to save her in case any Solarians began thinking about the case?"

Baley shrugged. "She had suffered enough. She had been victimized by everyone; by her husband, by Leebig, by the world of Solaria."

Minnim said, "Weren't you bending the law to suit a personal whim?"

Baley's craggy face grew hard. "It was not a whim. I was not bound by Solarian law. Earth's interests were paramount, and for the sake of those interests, I had to see that Leebig, the dangerous one, was dealt with. As for Mrs. Delmarre." He faced Minnim now, and felt himself taking a crucial step. He *had* to say this. "As for Mrs. Delmarre, I made her the basis of an experiment."

"What experiment?"

"I wanted to know if she would consent to face a world where personal presence was permitted and expected. I was curious to know if she had the courage to face disruption of habits so deeply settled in her. I was afraid she might refuse to go; that she might insist on remaining on Solaria, which was purgatory to her, rather than bring herself to abandon her distorted Solarian way of life. But she chose change and I was glad she did, because to me it seemed symbolic. It seemed to open the gates of salvation for *us*."

"For *us*?" said Minnim with energy. "What the devil do you mean?"

"Not for you and me, particularly, sir," said Baley gravely, "but for all mankind. You're wrong about the other Outer Worlds. They have few robots; they permit personal presence; and they have been investigating Solaria. R. Daneel Olivaw was there with me, you know, and he'll bring back a report. There is a danger they may become Solarias someday, but they will probably recognize that danger and work to keep themselves in a reasonable balance and in that way remain the leaders of mankind."

"That is your opinion," said Minnim testily.

"And there's more to it. There *is* one world like Solaria and that's Earth."

"Plainclothesman Baley!"

"It's so, sir. We're Solarian inside out. They retreated into isolation from one another. We retreated into isolation from the Galaxy. They are at the dead end of their inviolable estate. We are at the dead end of underground Cities. They're leaders without followers, only robots who can't talk back. We're followers without leaders, only enclosing Cities to keep us safe." Baley's fists clenched.

Minnim disapproved. "Plainclothesman, you have been through an ordeal. You need a rest and you will have one. A month's vacation, full pay, and a promotion at the end of it."

"Thank you, but that's not all I want. I want you to listen. There's only one direction out of our dead end and that's outward, toward Space. There are a million worlds out there and the Spacers own only fifty. They are few and long-lived. We are many and short-lived. We are better suited than they for exploration and colonization. We have population pressure to push us and a rapid turn-over of generation to keep us supplied with the young and reckless. It was our ancestors who colonized the Outer Worlds in the first place."

"Yes, I see—but I'm afraid our time is up."

Baley could feel the other's anxiety to be rid of him and he remained stolidly in place. He said, "When the original colonization established worlds superior to our own in technology, we escaped by building wombs beneath the ground for ourselves. The Spacers made us feel inferior and we hid from them. That's no answer. To avoid the destructive rhythm of rebellion and suppression, we must *compete* with them, follow them, if we must, lead them, if we can. To do that, we must face the open; we must teach ourselves to face the open. If it is too late to teach ourselves, then we must teach our children. It's vital!"

"You need a rest, Plainclothesman."

Baley said violently, "Listen to me, sir. If the Spacers are strong and we remain as we are, then Earth will be destroyed within a century. That has been computed, as you yourself told me. If the Spacers are really weak and are growing weaker, then we may escape, but who says the Spacers are weak? The Solarians, yes, but that's all we know."

"But——"

"I'm not through. One thing we *can* change, whether the Spacers are weak or strong. We can change the way we are. Let us face the open and we'll never need rebellion. We can spread out into our own crowd of worlds and become Spacers ourselves. If we stay here on Earth, cooped up, then useless and fatal rebellion can't be stopped. It will be all the worse if the people build any false hopes because of supposed spacer weakness. Go ahead, ask the sociologists. Put my argument to them. And if they're still in doubt, find a way to send me to Aurora. Let me bring back a report on the *real* Spacers, and you'll see what Earth must do."

Minnim nodded. "Yes, yes. Good day, now, Plainclothesman Baley."

Baley left with a feeling of exaltation. He had not expected an open victory over Minnim. Victories over ingrained patterns of thought are not won in a day or a year. But he had seen the look of pensive uncertainty that had crossed Minnim's face and had blotted out, at least for a while, the earlier uncritical joy.

He felt he could see into the future. Minnim would ask the sociologists and one or two of them would be uncertain. They would wonder. They would consult Baley.

Give it one year, thought Baley, one year, and I'll be on my way to Aurora. One generation, and we'll be out in space once more.

Baley stepped onto the northbound Expressway. Soon he would see Jessie. Would *she* understand? And his son, Bentley, now seventeen. When Ben had a seventeen-year-old of his own, would he be standing on some empty world, building a spacious life?

It was a frightening thought. Baley still feared the open. But he no longer feared the fear! It was not something to run from, that fear, but something to fight.

Baley felt as though a touch of madness had come over him. From the very first the open had had its weird attraction over him; from the

time in the ground-car when he had tricked Daneel in order to have
the top lowered so that he might stand up in the open air.

He had failed to understand then. Daneel thought he was being
perverse. Baley himself thought he was facing the open out of professional necessity, to solve a crime. Only on that last evening on Solaria,
with the curtain tearing away from the window, did he realize his need
to face the open for the open's own sake; for its attraction and its
promise of freedom.

There must be millions on Earth who would feel that same urge, if
the open were only brought to their attention, if they could be made
to take the first step.

He looked about.

The Expressway was speeding on. All about him was artificial light
and huge banks of apartments gliding backward and flashing signs and
store windows and factories and lights and noise and crowds and more
noise and people and people and people . . .

It was all he had loved, all he had hated and feared to leave, all he
had thought he longed for on Solaria.

And it was all strange to him.

He couldn't make himself fit back in.

He had gone out to solve a murder and something had happened
to him.

He had told Minnim the Cities were wombs, and so they were. And
what was the first thing a man must do before he can be a man? He
must be born. He must leave the womb. And once left, it could not
be re-entered.

Baley had left the City and could not re-enter. The City was no
longer his; the Caves of Steel were alien. This *had* to be. And it would
be so for others and Earth would be born again and reach outward.

His heart beat madly and the noise of life about him sank to an
unheard murmur.

He remembered his dream on Solaria and he understood it at last.
He lifted his head and he could see through all the steel and concrete
and humanity above him. He could see the beacon set in space to lure
men outward. He could see it shining down. The naked sun!

The Robots of Dawn

Dedicated to Marvin Minsky and
Joseph F. Engelberger, who epitomize
(respectively) the theory and practice
of robotics.

Contents

Baley

I

Elijah Baley found himself in the shade of the tree and muttered to himself, "I knew it. I'm sweating."

He paused, straightened up, wiped the perspiration from his brow with the back of his hand, then looked dourly at the moisture that covered it.

"I *hate* sweating," he said to no one, throwing it out as a cosmic law. And once again he felt annoyance with the Universe for making something both essential and unpleasant.

One *never* perspired (unless one wished to, of course) in the City, where temperature and humidity were absolutely controlled and where it was never absolutely necessary for the body to perform in ways that made heat production greater than heat removal.

Now *that* was civilized.

He looked out into the field, where a straggle of men and women were, more or less, in his charge. They were mostly youngsters in their late teens, but included some middle-aged people like himself. They were hoeing inexpertly and doing a variety of other things that robots were designed to do—and could do much more efficiently had they not been ordered to stand aside and wait while the human beings stubbornly practiced.

There were clouds in the sky and the sun, at the moment, was going behind one of them. He looked up uncertainly. On the one hand, it meant the direct heat of the sun (and the sweating) would be cut down. On the other hand, was there a chance of rain?

That was the trouble with the Outside. One teetered forever between unpleasant alternatives.

It always amazed Baley that a relatively small cloud could cover the sun completely, darkening Earth from horizon to horizon yet leaving most of the sky blue.

He stood beneath the leafy canopy of the tree (a kind of primitive wall and ceiling, with the solidity of the bark comforting to the touch) and looked again at the group, studying it. Once a week they were out there, whatever the weather.

They were gaining recruits, too. They were definitely more in number than the stout-hearted few who had started out. The City government, if not an actual partner in the endeavor, was benign enough to raise no obstacles.

To the horizon on Baley's right—eastward, as one could tell by the position of the late-afternoon sun—he could see the blunt, many-fingered domes of the City, enclosing all that made life worthwhile. He saw, as well, a small moving speck that was too far off to be made out clearly.

From its manner of motion and from indications too subtle to describe, Baley was quite sure it was a robot, but that did not surprise him. The Earth's surface, outside the Cities, was the domain of robots, not of human beings—except for those few, like himself, who were dreaming of the stars.

Automatically, his eyes turned back toward the hoeing stardreamers and went from one to the other. He could identify and name each one. All working, all learning how to endure the Outside, and—

He frowned and muttered in a low voice, "Where's Bentley?"

And another voice, sounding behind with a somewhat breathless exuberance, said, "Here I am, Dad."

Baley whirled. "Don't *do* that, Ben."

"Do what?"

"Sneak up on me like that. It's hard enough trying to keep my equilibrium in the Outside without my having to worry about surprises, too."

"I wasn't trying to surprise you. It's tough to make much noise walking on the grass. One can't help that. —But don't you think you ought to go in, Dad? You've been out two hours now and I think you've had enough."

"Why? Because I'm forty-five and you're a punk kid of nineteen? You think you have to take care of your decrepit father, do you?"

Ben said, "Yes, I guess that's it. And a bit of good detective work on your part, too. You cut right through to the nub."

Ben smiled broadly. His face was round, his eyes sparkling. There was a lot of Jessie in him, Baley thought, a lot of his mother. There was little trace of the length and solemnity of Baley's own face.

And yet Ben had his father's way of thinking. He could at times furrow into a grave solemnity that made it quite clear that he was of perfectly legitimate origin.

"I'm doing very well," said Baley.

"You are, Dad. You're the best of us, considering—"

"Considering what?"

"Your age, of course. And I'm not forgetting that you're the one who started this. Still, I saw you take cover under the tree and I thought—well, maybe the old man has had enough."

"I'll 'old man' you," said Baley. The robot he had noted in the direction of the City was now close enough to be made out clearly, but Baley dismissed it as unimportant. He said, "It makes sense to get under a tree once in a while when the sun's too bright. We've got to learn to use the advantages of the Outside, as well as learning to bear its disadvantages. —And there's the sun coming out from behind that cloud."

"Yes, it will do that. —Well, then, don't you want to go in?"

"I can stick it out. Once a week, I have an afternoon off and I spend it here. That's my privilege. It goes with my C-7 rating."

"It's not a question of privilege, Dad. It's a question of getting over-tired."

"I feel fine, I tell you."

"Sure. And when you get home, you'll go straight to bed and lie in the dark."

"Natural antidote to overbrightness."

"And Mom worries."

"Well, let her worry. It will do her good. Besides, what's the harm in being out here? The worst part is I *sweat*, but I just have to get used to it. I can't run away from it. When I started, I couldn't even walk this far from the City without having to turn back—and you were the only one with me. Now look at how many we've got and how far I can come without trouble. I can do plenty of work, too. I can last another hour. Easy. —I tell you, Ben, it would do your mother good to come out here herself."

"Who? Mom? Surely you jest."

"Some jest. When the time comes to take off, I won't be able to go along—because she won't."

"And you'll be glad of it. Don't kid yourself, Dad. It won't be for quite a while—and if you're not too old now, you'll be too old then. It's going to be a game for young people."

"You know," said Baley, half-balling his fist, "you are such a wise guy with your 'young people.' Have you ever been off Earth? Have any of those people in the field been off Earth? *I* have. Two years ago. That was before I had any of this acclimatization—and I sur-vived."

"I know, Dad, but that was briefly, and in the line of duty, and you were taken care of in a going society. It's not the same."

"It *was* the same," said Baley stubbornly, knowing in his heart that it wasn't. "And it won't take us so long to be able to leave. If I could get permission to go to Aurora, we could get this act off the ground."

"Forget it. It's not going to happen that easily."

"We've got to try. The government won't let us go without Aurora giving us the go-ahead. It's the largest and strongest of the Spacer worlds and what it says—"

"Goes! I know. We've all talked this over a million times. But you don't have to go there to get permission. There are such things as hyper-relays. You can talk to them from here. I've said that any num-ber of times before."

"It's not the same. We'll need face-to-face contact—and I've said *that* any number of times before."

"In any case," said Ben, "we're not ready yet."

"We're not ready because Earth won't give us the ships. The Spacers will, together with the necessary technical help."

"Such faith! Why should the Spacers do it? When did they start feeling kindly toward us short-lived Earthpeople?"

"If I could talk to them—"

Ben laughed. "Come on, Dad. You just want to go to Aurora to see that woman again."

Baley frowned and his eyebrows beetled over his deep-set eyes. "Woman? Jehoshaphat, Ben, what are you talking about?"

"Now, Dad, just between us—and not a word to Mom—what *did* happen with that woman on Solaria? I'm old enough. You can tell me."

"*What* woman on Solaria?"

"How can you look at me and deny any knowledge of the woman everyone on Earth saw in the hyperwave dramatization? Gladia Delmarre. *That* woman!"

"*Nothing* happened. That hyperwave thing was nonsense. I've told you that a thousand times. She didn't look that way. *I* didn't look that way. It was all made up and you know it was produced over my protests, just because the government thought it would put Earth in a good light with the Spacers. —And you make sure you don't imply anything different to your mother."

"Wouldn't dream of it. Still, this Gladia went to Aurora and you keep wanting to go there, too."

"Are you trying to tell me that you honestly think the reason I want to go to Aurora—Oh, *Jehoshaphat!*"

His son's eyebrows raised. "What's the matter?"

"The robot. That's R. Geronimo."

"Who?"

"One of our Department messenger robots. And it's out here! I'm off-time and I *deliberately* left my receiver at home because I didn't want them to get at me. That's my C-7 privilege and yet they send for me by robot."

"How do you know it's coming to you, Dad?"

"By very clever deduction. One: there's no one else here who has any connection with the Police Department; and two: that miserable thing is heading right toward me. From that I deduce that it wants me. I should get on the other side of the tree and stay there."

"It's not a wall, Dad. The robot can walk around the tree."

And the robot called out, "Master Baley, I have a message for you. You are wanted at Headquarters."

The robot stopped, waited, then said again, "Master Baley, I have a message for you. You are wanted at Headquarters."

"I hear and understand," Baley said tonelessly. He had to say that or the robot would have continued to repeat.

Baley frowned slightly as he studied the robot. It was a new model, a little more humaniform than the older models were. It had been uncrated and activated only a month before and with some degree of fanfare. The government was always trying for something—anything—that might produce more acceptance of robots.

It had a grayish surface with a dull finish and a somewhat resilient touch (perhaps like soft leather). The facial expression, while largely changeless, was not quite as idiotic as that of most robots. It was, though, in actual fact, quite as idiotic, mentally, as all the rest.

For a moment, Baley thought of R. Daneel Olivaw, the Spacer robot who had been on two assignments with him, one on Earth and one on Solaria, and whom he had last encountered when Daneel had consulted him in the mirror-image case. Daneel was a robot who was so human that Baley could treat him as a friend and could still miss him, even now. If all robots were like that—

Baley said, "This is my day off, boy. There is no necessity for me to go to Headquarters."

R. Geronimo paused. There was a trifling vibration in his hands. Baley noticed that and was quite aware that it meant a certain amount of conflict in the robot's positronic pathways. They had to obey human beings, but it was quite common for two human beings to want two different types of obedience.

The robot made a choice. It said, "It is your day off, master. —You are wanted at Headquarters."

Ben said uneasily, "If they want you, Dad—"

Baley shrugged. "Don't be fooled, Ben. If they really wanted me badly, they'd have sent an enclosed car and probably used a human volunteer, instead of ordering a robot to do the walking—and irritate me with one of its messages."

Ben shook his head. "I don't think so, Dad. They wouldn't know where you were or how long it would take to find you. I don't think they would want to send a human being on an uncertain search."

"Yes? Well, let's see how strong the order is. —R. Geronimo, go back to Headquarters and tell them I'll be at work at 0900." Then sharply, "Go back! That's an order!"

The robot hesitated perceptibly, then turned, moved away, turned again, made an attempt to come back toward Baley, and finally remained in one spot, its whole body vibrating.

Baley recognized it for what it was and muttered to Ben, "I may have to go. Jehoshaphat!"

What was troubling the robot was what the roboticists called an equipotential of contradiction on the second level. Obedience was the Second Law and R. Geronimo was now suffering from two roughly equal and contradictory orders. Robot-block was what the general population called it or, more frequently, roblock for short.

Slowly, the robot turned. Its original order was the stronger, but not by much, so that its voice was slurred. "Master, I was told you might say that. If so I was to say—" It paused, then added hoarsely, "I was to say—if you are alone."

Baley nodded curtly to his son and Ben didn't wait. He knew when his father was Dad and when he was a policeman. Ben retreated hastily.

For a moment, Baley played irritably with the notion of strengthening his own order and making the roblock more nearly complete, but that would surely cause the kind of damage that would require positronic analysis and reprogramming. The expense of that would be taken out of his salary and it might easily amount to a year's pay.

He said, "I withdraw my order. What were you told to say?"

R. Geronimo's voice at once cleared. "I was told to say that you are wanted in connection with Aurora."

Baley turned toward Ben and called out, "Give them another half hour and then say I want them back in. I've got to leave now."

And as he walked off with long strides, he said petulantly to the robot, "Why couldn't they tell you to say that at once? And why can't they program you to use a car so I wouldn't have to walk?"

He knew very well why that wasn't done. Any accident involving a robot-driven car would set off another antirobot riot.

He did not slacken his pace. There were two kilometers to walk before they even got to the City wall and, thereafter, they would have to reach Headquarters through heavy traffic.

Aurora? What kind of crisis was brewing now?

2

It took half an hour for Baley to reach the entranceway into the City and he stiffened himself for what he suspected ahead. Perhaps— *perhaps*—it wouldn't happen this time.

He reached the dividing plane between Outside and City, the wall that marked off chaos from civilization. He placed his hand over the signal patch and an opening appeared. As usual, he didn't wait for the opening to be completed, but slipped in as soon as it was wide enough. R. Geronimo followed.

The police sentry on duty looked startled, as he always did when someone came in from Outside. Each time there was the same look of disbelief, the same coming to attention, the same sudden hand upon the blaster, the same frown of uncertainty.

Baley presented his identity card with a scowl and the sentry saluted. The door closed behind him—and it happened.

Baley was inside the City. The walls closed around him and the City became the Universe. He was again immersed in the endless, eternal hum and odor of people and machinery that would soon fade below the threshold of consciousness; in the soft, indirect artificial light that was nothing at all like the partial and varying glare of the Outside, with its green and brown and blue and white and its interruptions of red and yellow. Here there was no erratic wind, no heat, no cold, no threat of rain; here there was instead the quiet permanence of unfelt air currents that kept everything fresh. Here was a designed combination of temperature and humidity so perfectly adjusted to humans it remained unsensed.

Baley felt his breath drawn in tremulously and he gladdened in the realization that he was home and safe with the known and *knowable*.

That was what always happened. Again he had accepted the City as the womb and moved back into it with glad relief. He knew that such a womb was something from which humanity must emerge and be born. Why did he always sink back this way?

And would that always be? Would it really be that, though he might lead countless numbers out of the City and off the Earth and out to the stars, he would not, in the end, be able to go himself? Would he always feel at home only in the City?

He clenched his teeth—but there was no use thinking about it.

He said to the robot, "Were you brought to this point by car, boy?"

"Yes, master."

"Where is it now?"

"I do not know, master."

Baley turned to the sentry. "Officer, this robot was brought to this spot two hours ago. What has happened to the car that brought him?"

"Sir, I went on duty less than an hour ago."

Actually, it was foolish to ask. Those in the car did not know how long it would take the robot to find him, so they would not wait. Baley had a brief impulse to call in, but they would tell him to take the Expressway; it would be quicker.

The only reason he hesitated was the presence of R. Geronimo. He didn't want its company on the Expressway and yet he could not expect the robot to make its way back to Headquarters through hostile crowds.

Not that he had a choice. Undoubtedly, the Commissioner was not eager to make this easy for him. He would be annoyed at not having had him on call, free time or not.

Baley said, "This way, boy."

The City covered over five thousand square kilometers and contained over four hundred kilometers of Expressway, plus hundreds of kilometers of Feederway, to serve its well over twenty million people. The intricate net of movement existed on eight levels and there were hundreds of interchanges of varying degrees of complexity.

As a plainclothesman, Baley was expected to know them all—and he did. Put him down blindfolded in any corner of the City, whip off the blindfold, and he could make his way flawlessly to any other designated portion.

There was no question then but that he knew how to get to Headquarters. There were eight reasonable routes he could follow, however, and for a moment he hesitated over which might be least crowded at this time.

Only for a moment. Then he decided and said, "Come with me, boy." The robot followed docilely at his heels.

They swung onto a passing Feeder and Baley seized one of the vertical poles: white, warm, and textured to give a good grip. Baley did not want to sit down; they would not be on for long. The robot had waited for Baley's quick gesture before placing its hand upon the same pole. It might as well have remained standing without a grip—it would not have been difficult to maintain balance—but Baley wanted to take no chance of being separated. He was responsible for the robot and did not wish to risk being asked to replace the financial loss to the City should anything happen to R. Geronimo.

The Feeder had a few other people on board and the eyes of each turned curiously—and inevitably—to the robot. One by one, Baley caught those glances. Baley had the look of one used to authority and the eyes he caught turned uneasily away.

Baley gestured again as he swung off the Feeder. It had reached the strips now and was moving at the same speed as the nearest strip, so that there was no necessity for it to slow down. Baley stepped onto that nearest strip and felt the whipping of air once they were no longer protected by plastic enclosure.

He leaned into the wind with the ease of long practice, lifting one arm to break the force at eye level. He ran the strips downward to the intersection with the Expressway and then began the run upward to the speed-strip that bordered the Expressway.

He heard the teenage cry of "Robot!" (he had been a teenager himself once) and knew exactly what would happen. A group of them—two or three or half a dozen—would swarm up or down the strips and somehow the robot would be tripped and would go clanging down.

Then, if it ever came before a magistrate, any teenager taken into custody would claim the robot had collided with him and was a menace on the strips—and would undoubtedly be let go.

The robot could neither defend itself in the first instance, nor testify in the second.

Baley moved rapidly and was between the first of the teenagers and the robot. He sidestepped onto a faster strip, brought his arm higher, as though to adjust to the increase in wind speed, and somehow the young man was nudged off course and onto a slower strip for which he was not prepared. He called out wildly, "Hey!" as he went sprawling. The others stopped, assessed the situation quickly, and veered away.

Baley said, "Onto the Expressway, boy."

The robot hesitated briefly. Robots were not allowed, unaccompanied, on the Expressway. Baley's order had been a firm one, however, and it moved aboard. Baley followed, which relieved the pressure on the robot.

Baley moved brusquely through the crowd of standees, forcing R. Geronimo ahead of him, making his way up to the less crowded upper level. He held on to a pole and kept one foot firmly on the robot's, again glaring down all eye contact.

Fifteen and a half kilometers brought him to the close-point for the Police Headquarters and he was off. R. Geronimo came off with him. It hadn't been touched, not a scuff. Baley delivered it at the door and accepted a receipt. He carefully checked the date, the time, and the robot's serial number, then placed the receipt in his wallet. Before the day was over, he would check and make certain that the transaction had been computer-registered.

Now he was going to see the Commissioner—and he knew the Commissioner. Any failing on Baley's part would be suitable cause for demotion. He was a harsh man, the Commissioner. He considered Baley's past triumphs a personal offense.

3

The Commissioner was Wilson Roth. He had held the post for two and a half years, since Julius Enderby had resigned once the furor roused by the murder of a Spacer had subsided and the resignation could be safely offered.

Baley had never quite reconciled himself to the change. Julius, with all his shortcomings, had been a friend as well as a superior; Roth was merely a superior. He was not even Citybred. Not *this* City. He had been brought in from outside.

Roth was neither unusually tall nor unusually fat. His head

was large, though, and seemed to be set on a neck that slanted slightly forward from his torso. It made him appear heavy: heavy-bodied and heavy-headed. He even had heavy lids half-obscuring his eyes.

Anyone would think him sleepy, but he never missed anything. Baley had found that out very soon after Roth had taken over the office. He was under no illusion that Roth liked him. He was under less illusion that he liked Roth.

Roth did not sound petulant—he never did—but his words did not exude pleasure, either. "Baley, why is it so hard to find you?" he said.

Baley said in a carefully respectful voice, "It is my afternoon off, Commissioner."

"Yes, your C-7 privilege. You've heard of a Waver, haven't you? Something that receives official messages? You are subject to recall, even on your off-time."

"I know that very well, Commissioner, but there are no longer any regulations concerning the wearing of a Waver. We can be reached without one."

"Inside the City, yes, but you were Outside—or am I mistaken?"

"You are not mistaken, Commissioner. I was Outside. The regulations do not state that, in such a case, I am to wear a Waver."

"You hide behind the letter of the statute, do you?"

"Yes, Commissioner," said Baley calmly.

The Commissioner rose, a powerful and vaguely threatening man, and sat on the desk. The window to the Outside, which Enderby had installed, had long been closed off and painted over. In the closed-in room (warmer and more comfortable for that), the Commissioner seemed the larger.

He said, without raising his voice, "You rely, Baley, on Earth's gratitude, I think."

"I rely on doing my job, Commissioner, as best I can and in accord with the regulations."

"And on Earth's gratitude when you bend the spirit of those regulations."

Baley said nothing to that.

The Commissioner said, "You are considered as having done well in the Sarton murder case three years ago."

"Thank you, Commissioner," said Baley. "The dismantling of Spacetown was a consequence, I believe."

"It was—and that was something applauded by all Earth. You are also considered as having done well on Solaria two years ago and, before you remind me, the result was a revision in the terms of the trade treaties with the Spacer worlds, to the considerable advantage of Earth."

"I believe that is on record, sir."

"And you are very much the hero as a result."

"I make no such claim."

"You have received two promotions, one in the aftermath of each affair. There has even been a hyperwave drama based on the events on Solaria."

"Which was produced without my permission and against my will, Commissioner."

"Which nevertheless made you a kind of hero."

Baley shrugged.

The Commissioner, having waited for a spoken comment for a few seconds, went on. "But you have done nothing of importance in nearly two years."

"It is natural for Earth to ask what I have done for it lately."

"Exactly. It probably does ask. It knows that you are a leader in this new fad of venturing Outside, in fiddling with the soil, and in pretending to be a robot."

"It is permitted."

"Not all that is permitted is admired. It is possible that more people think of you as peculiar than as heroic."

"That is, perhaps, in accord with my own opinion of myself," said Baley.

"The public has a notoriously short memory. The heroic is vanishing rapidly behind the peculiar in your case, so that if you make a mistake you will be in serious trouble. The reputation you rely on—"

"With respect, Commissioner, I do not rely on it."

"The reputation the Police Department *feels* you rely on will not save you and I will not be able to save you."

The shadow of a smile seemed to pass for one moment over Baley's dour features. "I would not want you, Commissioner, to risk your position in a wild attempt to save me."

The Commissioner shrugged and produced a smile precisely as shadowy and fleeting. "You need not worry about that."

"Then why are you telling me all this, Commissioner?"

"To warn you. I am not trying to destroy you, you understand, so I am warning you *once*. You are going to be involved in a very delicate matter, in which you may easily make a mistake, and I am warning you that you must not make one." Here his face relaxed into an unmistakable smile.

Baley did not respond to the smile. He said, "Can you tell me what the very delicate matter is?"

"I do not know."

"Does it involve Aurora?"

"R. Geronimo was instructed to tell you that it did, if it had to, but I know nothing about it."

"Then how can you tell, Commissioner, that it is a very delicate matter?"

"Come, Baley, you are an investigator of mysteries. What brings a member of the Terrestrial Department of Justice to the City, when you might easily have been asked to go to Washington, as you did two years ago in connection with the Solaria incident? And what makes the person from Justice frown and seem ill-tempered and grow impatient at the fact that you were not reached instantly? Your decision to make yourself unavailable was a mistake, one that was in no way my responsibility. It is perhaps not fatal in itself, but you are off on the wrong foot, I believe."

"You are delaying me further, however," said Baley, frowning.

"Not really. The official from Justice is having some light refreshment—you know the perks that the Terries allow themselves. We will be joined when that is done. The news of your arrival has been transmitted, so just continue to wait, as I am doing."

Baley waited. He had known, at the time, that the hyperwave drama, forced upon him against his will, however it might have helped Earth's position, had ruined him in the Department. It had cast him in three-dimensional relief against the two-dimensional flatness of the organization and had made him a marked man.

He had risen to higher rank and greater privileges, but that, too, had increased Department hostility against him. And the higher he rose, the more easily he would shatter in case of a fall.

If he made a mistake—

4

The official from Justice entered, looked about casually, walked to the other side of Roth's desk, and took the seat. As highest-classified individual, the official behaved properly. Roth calmly took a secondary seat.

Baley remained standing, laboring to keep his face unsurprised.

Roth might have warned him, but he had not. He had clearly chosen his words deliberately, in order to give no sign.

The official was a woman.

There was no reason for this not to be. Any official might be a woman. The Secretary-General might be a woman. There were women on the police force, even a woman with the rank of captain.

It was just that, without warning, one didn't expect it in any given case. There were times in history when women entered administrative posts in considerable numbers. Baley knew that; he knew history well. But this wasn't one of those times.

She was quite tall and sat stiffly upright in the chair. Her uniform was not very different from that of a man, nor was her hair styling or facial adornment. What gave her sex away immediately were her breasts, the prominence of which she made no attempt to hide.

She was fortyish, her facial features regular and cleanly chiseled. She had middle-aged attractively, with, as yet, no visible gray in her dark hair.

She said, "You are Plainclothesman Elijah Baley, Classification C-7." It was a statement, not a question.

"Yes, ma'am," Baley answered, nevertheless.

"I am Undersecretary Lavinia Demachek. You don't look very much as you did in that hyperwave drama concerning you."

Baley had been told that often. "They couldn't very well portray me as I am and collect much of an audience, ma'am," said Baley dryly.

"I'm not sure of that. You look stronger than the baby-faced actor they used."

Baley hesitated a second or so and decided to take the chance—or perhaps felt he couldn't resist taking it. Solemnly, he said, "You have a cultivated taste, ma'am."

She laughed and Baley let out his breath very gently. She said, "I like to think I have. —Now what do you mean by keeping me waiting?"

"I was not informed you would come, ma'am, and it was off-time for me."

"Which you spent Outside, I understand."

"Yes, ma'am."

"You are one of those cranks, as I would say were my taste not a cultivated one. Let me ask, instead, if you are one of those enthusiasts."

"Yes, ma'am."

"You expect to emigrate some day and found new worlds in the wilderness of the Galaxy?"

"Perhaps not I, ma'am. I may prove to be too old, but—"

"How old are you?"

"Forty-five, ma'am."

"Well, you look it. I am forty-five also, as it happens."

"You do not look it, ma'am."

"Older or younger?" She broke into laughter again, then said, "But let's not play games. Do you imply I am too old to be a pioneer?"

"No one can be a pioneer in our society, without training Outside. The training works best with the young. My son, I hope, will someday stand on another world."

"Indeed? You know, of course, that the Galaxy belongs to the Spacer worlds."

"There are only fifty of them, ma'am. There are millions of worlds in the Galaxy that are habitable—or can be made habitable—and that probably do not possess indigenous intelligent life."

"Yes, but not one ship can leave Earth without Spacer permission."

"That might be granted, ma'am."

"I do not share your optimism, Mr. Baley."

"I have spoken to Spacers who—"

"I know you have," said Demachek. "My superior is Albert Minnim, who, two years ago, sent you to Solaria." She permitted herself a small curve of the lips. "An actor portrayed him in a bit role on that hyperwave drama, one that resembled him closely, as I recall. He was not pleased, as I also recall."

Baley changed the subject. "I asked Undersecretary Minnim—"

"He has been promoted, you know."

Baley thoroughly understood the importance of grades in classification. "His new title, ma'am?"

"Vice-Secretary."

"Thank you. I asked Vice-Secretary Minnim to request permission for me to visit Aurora to deal with this subject."

"When?"

"Not very long after my return from Solaria. I have renewed the request twice since."

"But have not received a favorable reply?"

"No, ma'am."

"Are you surprised?"

"I am disappointed, ma'am."

"No point in that." She leaned back a trifle in the chair. "Our relationship with the Spacer worlds is very touchy. You may feel that your two feats of detection have eased the situation—and so they have. That awful hyperwave drama has also helped. The total easing, however, has been this much"—she placed her thumb and forefinger close together—"out of this much," and she spread her hands far apart.

"Under those circumstances," she went on, "we could scarcely take the risk of sending you to Aurora, the leading Spacer world, and having you perhaps do something that could create interstellar tension."

Baley's eyes met hers. "I have been on Solaria and have done no harm. On the contrary—"

"Yes, I know, but you were there at Spacer request, which is parsecs distant from being there at our request. You cannot fail to see that."

Baley was silent.

She made a soft snorting sound of nonsurprise and said, "The situation has grown worse since your requests were placed with—and very correctly ignored by—the Vice-Secretary. It has grown particularly worse in the last month."

"Is that the reason for this conference, ma'am?"

"Do you grow impatient, sir?" She addressed him sardonically in the to-a-superior intonation. "Do you direct me to come to the point?"

"No, ma'am."

"Certainly you do. And why not? I grow tedious. Let me approach the point by asking if you know Dr. Han Fastolfe."

Baley said carefully, "I met him once, nearly three years ago, in what was then Spacetown."

"You liked him, I believe."

"He was friendly—for a Spacer."

She made another soft snorting sound. "I imagine so. Are you aware that he has been an important political power on Aurora over the last two years?"

"I had heard he was in the government from a—a partner I once had."

"From R. Daneel Olivaw, your Spacer robot friend?"

"My ex-partner, ma'am."

"On the occasion when you solved a small problem concerning two mathematicians on board a Spacer ship?"

Baley nodded. "Yes, ma'am."

"We keep informed, you see. Dr. Han Fastolfe has been, more or less, the guiding light of the Auroran government for two years, an important figure in their World Legislature, and he is even spoken of as a possible future Chairman. —The Chairman, you understand, is the closest thing to a chief executive that the Aurorans have."

Baley said, "Yes, ma'am," and wondered when she would get to the very delicate matter of which the Commissioner had spoken.

Demachek seemed in no hurry. She said, "Fastolfe is a—moderate. That's what he calls himself. He feels Aurora—and the Spacer worlds generally—have gone too far in their direction, as you, perhaps, feel that we on Earth have gone too far in ours. He wishes to step backward to less robotry, to a more rapid turnover of generations, and to alliance and friendship with Earth. Naturally, we support him—but very quietly. If we were too demonstrative in our affection, that might well be the kiss of death for him."

Baley said, "I believe he would support Earth's exploration and settlement of other worlds."

"I believe so, too. I am of the opinion he said as much to you."

"Yes, ma'am, when we met."

Demachek steepled her hands and put the tips of her fingers to her chin. "Do you think he represents public opinion on the Spacer worlds?"

"I don't know, ma'am."

"I'm afraid he does not. Those who are with him are lukewarm. Those who are against him are an ardent legion. It is only his political skills and his personal warmth that have kept him as close to the seats of power as he is. His greatest weakness, of course, is his sympathy for Earth. That is constantly used against him and it influences many who would share his views in every other respect. If you were sent to Aurora, any mistake you made would help strengthen anti-Earth feeling and would therefore weaken him, possibly fatally. Earth simply cannot take that risk."

Baley muttered, "I see."

"Fastolfe is willing to take the risk. It was he who arranged to have you sent to Solaria at a time when his political power was barely beginning and when he was very vulnerable. But then, he has only his personal power to lose, whereas we must be concerned with the welfare of over eight billion Earthpeople. That is what makes the present political situation almost unbearably delicate."

She paused and, finally, Baley was forced to ask the question. "What is the situation that you are referring to, ma'am?"

"It seems," said Demachek, "that Fastolfe has become implicated in a serious and unprecedented scandal. If he is clumsy, the chances are that he will undergo political destruction in a matter of weeks. If he is superhumanly clever, perhaps he will hold out for some months. A little sooner, a little later, he could be destroyed as a political force on Aurora—and *that* would be a real disaster for Earth, you see."

"May I ask what he is accused of? Corruption? Treason?"

"Nothing that small. His personal integrity is, in any case, unquestioned even by his enemies."

"A crime of passion, then? Murder?"

"Not *quite* murder."

"I don't understand, ma'am."

"There are human beings on Aurora, Mr. Baley. And there are robots, too, most of them something like ours, not very much more advanced in most cases. However, there are a few humaniform robots, robots so humaniform that they can be taken for human."

Baley nodded. "I know that very well."

"I suppose that destroying a humaniform robot is not exactly murder in the strict sense of the word."

Baley leaned forward, eyes widening. He shouted, "Jehoshaphat, woman! Stop playing games. Are you telling me that Dr. Fastolfe has killed R. Daneel?"

Roth leaped to his feet and seemed about to advance on Baley, but Undersecretary Demachek waved him back. She seemed unruffled.

She said, "Under the circumstances, I excuse your disrespect, Baley. No, R. Daneel has *not* been killed. He is not the only humaniform robot on Aurora. Another such robot, *not* R. Daneel, has been killed, if you wish to use the term loosely. To be more precise, its mind has been totally destroyed; it was placed into permanent and irreversible roblock."

Baley said, "And they say that Dr. Fastolfe did it?"

"His enemies are saying so. The extremists, who wish only Spacers to spread through the Galaxy and who wish Earthpeople to vanish from the Universe, are saying so. If these extremists can maneuver another election within the next few weeks, they will surely gain total control of the government, with incalculable results."

"Why is this roblock so important politically? I don't understand."

"I am not myself certain," said Demachek. "I do not pretend to understand Auroran politics. I gather that the humaniforms were in some way involved with the extremist plans and that the destruction has infuriated them." She wrinkled her nose. "I find their politics very confusing and I will only mislead you if I try to interpret it."

Baley labored to control himself under the Undersecretary's level stare. He said in a low voice, "Why am I here?"

"Because of Fastolfe. Once before you went out into space in order to solve a murder and succeeded. Fastolfe wants you to try again. You are to go to Aurora and discover who was responsible for the roblock. He feels that to be his only chance of turning back the extremists."

"I am not a roboticist. I know nothing about Aurora—"

"You knew nothing about Solaria, either, yet you managed. The point is, Baley, we are as eager to find out what really happened as Fastolfe is. We don't want him destroyed. If he is, Earth will be subject to a kind of hostility from these Spacer extremists that will probably be greater than anything we have yet experienced. We don't want that to happen."

"I can't take on this responsibility, ma'am. The task is—"

"Next to impossible. We know that, but we have no choice. Fastolfe insists—and behind him, for the moment, stands the Auroran government. If you refuse to go or if we refuse to let you go, we will have to face the Auroran fury. If you do go and are successful, we'll be saved and you will be suitably rewarded."

"And if I go—and fail?"

"We will do our best to see to it that the blame will be yours and not Earth's."

"The skins of officialdom will be saved, in other words."

Demachek said, "A kinder way of putting it is that you will be thrown to the wolves in the hope that Earth will not suffer too badly. One man is not a bad price to pay for our planet."

"It seems to me that, since I am sure to fail, I might as well not go."

"You know better than that," said Demachek softly. "Aurora has asked for you and you cannot refuse. —And why should you want to refuse? You've been trying to go to Aurora for two years and you've been bitter over your failure to get our permission."

"I've wanted to go in peace to arrange for help in the settlement of other worlds, not to—"

"You might still try to get their help for your dream of settling other worlds, Baley. After all, suppose you *do* succeed. It's possible, after all. In that case, Fastolfe will be much beholden to you and he may do far more for you than he ever would have otherwise. And we ourselves will be sufficiently grateful to you to help. Isn't that worth a risk, even a large one? However small your chances of success are if you go, those chances are zero if you do not go. Think of that, Baley, but please—not too long."

Baley's lips tightened and, finally, realizing there was no alternative, he said, "How much time do I have to—"

And Demachek said calmly, "Come. Haven't I been explaining that we have no choice—and no time, either? You leave," she looked at the timeband on her wrist, "in just under six hours."

5

The spaceport was at the eastern outskirts of the City in an all-but-deserted Sector that was, strictly speaking, Outside. This was palliated by the fact that the ticket offices and the waiting rooms were actually in the City and that the approach to the ship itself was by vehicle through a covered path. By tradition, all takeoffs were at night, so that a pall of darkness further deadened the effect of Outside.

The spaceport was not very busy, considering the populous character of Earth. Earthmen very rarely left the planet and the traffic consisted entirely of commercial activity organized by robots and Spacers.

Elijah Baley, waiting for the ship to be ready for boarding, felt already cut off from Earth.

Bentley sat with him and there was a glum silence between the two. Finally, Ben said, "I didn't think Mom would want to come."

Baley nodded. "I didn't think so, either. I remember how she was when I went to Solaria. This is no different."

"Did you manage to calm her down?"

"I did what I could, Ben. She thinks I'm bound to be in a space crash or that the Spacers will kill me once I'm on Aurora."

"You got back from Solaria."

"That just makes her the less eager to risk me a second time. She assumes the luck will run out. However, she'll manage. —You rally round, Ben. Spend some time with her and, whatever you do, don't talk about heading out to settle a new planet. That's what really bothers her, you know. She feels you'll be leaving her one of these years. She knows she won't be able to go and so she'll never see you again."

"She may not," said Ben. "That's the way it might work out."

"You can face that easily, maybe, but she can't, so just don't discuss it while I'm gone. All right?"

"All right. —I think she's a little upset about Gladia."

Baley looked up sharply. "Have you been—"

"I haven't said a word. But she saw that hyperwave thing, too, you know, and she knows Gladia's on Aurora."

"What of it? It's a big planet. Do you think Gladia Delmarre will be waiting at the spaceport for me? —Jehoshaphat, Ben, doesn't your mother *know* that hyperwave axle grease was nine-tenths fiction?"

Ben changed the subject with a tangible effort. "It seems funny— you sitting here with no luggage of any kind."

"I'm sitting here with too much. I've got the clothes I'm wearing, don't I? They'll get rid of those as soon as I'm on board. Off they go— to be chemically treated, then dumped into space. After that, they'll give me a totally new wardrobe, after I have been personally fumigated and cleaned and polished, inside and out. I've been through that once before."

Again silence and then Ben said, "You know, Dad—" and stopped suddenly. He tried again. "You know Dad—" and did no better.

Baley looked at him steadily. "What are you trying to say, Ben?"

"Dad, I feel like an awful jackass saying this, but I think I'd better. You're not the hero type. Even I never thought you were. You're a nice guy and the best father there could be, but not the hero type."

Baley grunted.

"Still," said Ben, "when you stop to think of it, it was you who got Spacetown off the map; it was you who got Aurora on our side; it was you who started this whole project of settling other worlds. Dad, you've done more for Earth than everyone in the government put together. So why aren't you appreciated more?"

Baley said, "Because I'm not the hero type and because this stupid hyperwave drama was foisted on me. It has made an enemy of every man in the Department, it's unsettled your mother, and it's given me a reputation I can't live up to." The light flashed on his wrist-caller and he stood up. "I've got to go now, Ben."

"I know. But what I want to say, Dad, is that I appreciate you. And this time when you come back, you'll get that from everybody and not just from me."

Baley felt himself melting. He nodded rapidly, put a hand on his son's shoulder, and muttered, "Thanks. Take care of yourself—and your mother—while I'm gone."

He walked away, not looking back. He had told Ben that he was going to Aurora to discuss the settlement project. If that were so, he *might* come back in triumph. As it was—

He thought: I'll come back in disgrace—if I come back at all.

2. 　Daneel

6

It was Baley's third time on a spaceship and the passage of two years had in no way dimmed his memory of the first two times. He knew exactly what to expect.

There would be the isolation—the fact that no one would see him or have anything to do with him, with the exception (perhaps) of a robot. There would be the constant medical treatment—the fumigation and sterilization. (No other way of putting it.) There would be the attempt to make him fit to approach the disease-conscious Spacers who thought of Earthpeople as walking bags of multifarious infections.

There would be differences, too, however. He would not, this time, be quite so afraid of the process. Surely the feeling of loss at being out of the womb would be less dreadful.

He would be prepared for the wider surroundings. This time, he told himself boldly (but with a small knot in his stomach, for all that), he might even be able to insist on being given a view of space.

Would it look different from photographs of the night sky as seen from Outside? he wondered.

He remembered his first view of a planetarium dome (safely within the City, of course). It had given him no sensation of being Outside, no discomfort at all.

Then there were the two times—no, three—that he had been in the open at night and saw the real stars in the real dome of the sky. That had been far less impressive than the planetarium dome had been, but there had been a cool wind each time and a feeling of distance, which made it more frightening than the dome—but less frightening than daytime, for the darkness was a comforting wall about him.

Would, then, the sight of the stars through a spaceship viewing window seem more like a planetarium or more like Earth's night sky? Or would it be a different sensation altogether?

He concentrated on that, as though to wash out the thought of leaving Jessie, Ben, and the City.

With nothing less than bravado, he refused the car and insisted on walking the short distance from the gate to the ship in the company of the robot who had come for him. It was just a roofed-over arcade, after all.

The passage was slightly curved and he looked back while he could still see Ben at the other end. He lifted his hand casually, as though he were taking the Expressway to Trenton, and Ben waved both arms wildly, holding up the first two fingers of each hand outspread in the ancient symbol of victory.

Victory? A useless gesture, Baley was certain.

He switched to another thought that might serve to fill and occupy him. What would it be like to board a spaceship by day, with the sun shining brightly on its metal and with himself and the others who were boarding all exposed to the Outside.

How would it feel to be entirely aware of a tiny cylindrical world, one that would detach itself from the infinitely larger world to which it was temporarily attached and that would then lose itself in an Out-side infinitely larger than any Outside on Earth, until after an endless stretch of Nothingness it would find another—

He held himself grimly to a steady walk, letting no change in expression show—or so he thought, at least. The robot at his side, however, brought him to a halt.

"Are you ill, sir?" (Not "master," merely "sir." It was an Auroran robot.)

"I'm all right, boy," said Baley hoarsely. "Move on."

He kept his eyes turned to the ground and did not lift them again till the ship itself was towering above him.

An Auroran ship!

He was sure of that. Outlined by a warm spotlight, it soared taller, more gracefully, and yet more powerfully than the Solarian ships had.

Baley moved inside and the comparison remained in favor of Aurora. His room was larger than the ones two years before had been: more luxurious, more comfortable.

He knew exactly what was coming and removed all his clothes without hesitation. (Perhaps they would be disintegrated by plasma torch. Certainly, he would not get them back on returning to Earth—if he returned. He hadn't the first time.)

He would receive no other clothes till he had been thoroughly bathed, examined, dosed, and injected. He almost welcomed the humiliating procedures imposed on him. After all, it served to keep his mind off what was taking place. He was scarcely aware of the initial acceleration and scarcely had time to think of the moment during which he left earth and entered space.

When he was finally dressed again, he surveyed the results unhappily in a mirror. The material, whatever it was, was smooth and reflective and shifted color with any change in angle. The trouser legs hugged his ankles and were, in turn, covered by the tops of shoes that molded themselves softly to his feet. The sleeves of his blouse hugged his wrists and his hands were covered by thin, transparent gloves. The top of the blouse covered his neck and an attached hood could, if desired, cover his head. He was being so covered, not for his own comfort, he knew, but to reduce his danger to the Spacers.

He thought, as he looked at the outfit, that he should feel uncomfortably enclosed, uncomfortably hot, uncomfortably damp. But he did not. He wasn't, to his enormous relief, even sweating.

He made the reasonable deduction. He said to the robot that had walked him to the ship and was still with him, "Boy, are these clothes temperature-controlled?"

The robot said, "Indeed they are, sir. It is all-weather clothing and is considered very desirable. It is also exceedingly expensive. Few on Aurora are in a position to wear it."

"That so? Jehoshaphat!"

He stared at the robot. It seemed a fairly primitive model, not very much different from Earth models, in fact. Still, there was a certain subtlety of expression that Earth models lacked. It could change expression in a limited way, for instance. It had smiled very slightly when it indicated that Baley had been given that which few on Aurora could afford.

The structure of its body resembled metal and yet had the look of something woven, something shifting slightly with movement, something with colors that matched and contrasted pleasingly. In short, unless one looked very closely and steadily, the robot, though definitely nonhumaniform, seemed to be wearing clothing.

Baley said, "What ought I to call you, boy?"

"I am Giskard, sir."

"R. Giskard?"

"If you wish, sir."

"Do you have a library on this ship?"

"Yes, sir."

"Can you get me book-films on Aurora?"

"What kind, sir?"

"Histories—political science—geographies—anything that will let me know about the planet."

"Yes, sir."

"And a viewer."

"Yes, sir."

The robot left through the double door and Baley nodded grimly to himself. On his trip to Solaria, it had never occurred to him to spend the useless time crossing space in learning something useful. He had come along a bit in the last two years.

He tried the door the robot had just passed through. It was locked and utterly without give. He would have been enormously surprised at anything else.

He investigated the room. There was a hyperwave screen. He handled the controls idly, received a blast of music, managed to lower the volume eventually, and listened with disapproval. Tinkly and discordant. The instruments of the orchestra seemed vaguely distorted.

He touched other contacts and finally managed to change the view. What he saw was a space-soccer game that was played, obviously, under conditions of zero-gravity. The ball flew in straight lines and the players (too many of them on each side—with fins on backs, elbows, and knees that must serve to control movement) soared in graceful sweeps. The unusual movements made Baley feel dizzy. He leaned forward and had just found and used the off-switch when he heard the door open behind him.

He turned and, because he thoroughly expected to see R. Giskard, he was aware at first only of someone who was *not* R. Giskard. It took a blink or two to realize that he saw a thoroughly human shape, with a broad, high-cheekboned face and with short, bronze hair lying flatly backward, someone dressed in clothing with a conservative cut and color scheme.

"Jehoshaphat!" said Baley in a nearly strangled voice.

"Partner Elijah," said the other, stepping forward, a small grave smile on his face.

"Daneel!" cried Baley, throwing his arms around the robot and hugging tightly. "Daneel!"

7

Baley continued to hold Daneel, the one unexpected familiar object on the ship, the one strong link to the past. He clung to Daneel in a gush of relief and affection.

And then, little by little, he collected his thoughts and knew that he was hugging not Daneel but R. Daneel—*Robot* Daneel Olivaw. He was hugging a robot and the robot was holding him lightly, allowing himself to be hugged, judging that the action gave pleasure to a human being and enduring that action because the positronic potentials of his brain made it impossible to repel the embrace and so cause disappointment and embarrassment to the human being.

The insurmountable First Law of Robotics states: "A robot may not injure a human being—" and to repel a friendly gesture would do injury.

Slowly, so as to reveal no sign of his own chagrin, Baley released his hold. He even gave each upper arm of the robot a final squeeze, so that there might seem to be no shame to the release.

"Haven't seen you, Daneel," said Baley, "since you brought that ship to Earth with the two mathematicians. Remember?"

"Of a certainty, Partner Elijah. It is a pleasure to see you."

"You feel emotion, do you?" said Baley lightly.

"I cannot say what I feel in any human sense, Partner Elijah. I can say, however, that the sight of you seems to make my thoughts flow more easily, and the gravitational pull on my body seems to assault my senses with lesser insistence, and that there are other changes I can identify. I imagine that what I sense corresponds in a rough way to what it is that you may sense when you feel pleasure."

Baley nodded. "Whatever it is you sense when you see me, old partner, that makes it seem preferable to the state in which you are when you don't see me, suits me well—if you follow my meaning. But how is it you are here?"

"Giskard Reventlov, having reported you—" R. Daneel paused.

"Purified?" asked Baley sardonically.

"Disinfected," said R. Daneel. "I felt it appropriate to enter then."

"Surely you would not fear infection otherwise?"

"Not at all, Partner Elijah, but others on the ship might then be reluctant to have me approach them. The people of Aurora are sensitive to the chance of infection, sometimes to a point beyond a rational estimate of the probabilities."

"I understand, but I wasn't asking why you were here at this moment. I meant why are you here at all?"

"Dr. Fastolfe, of whose establishment I am part, directed me to board the ship that had been sent to pick you up for several reasons. He felt it desirable that you have one immediate item of the known in what he was certain would be a difficult mission for you."

"That was a kindly thought on his part. I thank him."

R. Daneel bowed gravely in acknowledgment. "Dr. Fastolfe also felt that the meeting would give me"—the robot paused—"appropriate sensations."

"Pleasure, you mean, Daneel."

"Since I am permitted to use the term, yes. And as a third reason— and the most important—"

The door opened again at that point and R. Giskard walked in.

Baley's head turned toward it and he felt a surge of displeasure. There was no mistaking R. Giskard as a robot and its presence emphasized, somehow, the robotism of Daneel (R. Daneel, Baley suddenly thought again), even though Daneel was far the superior of the two. Baley didn't *want* the robotism of Daneel emphasized; he didn't want himself humiliated for his inability to regard Daneel as anything but a human being with a somewhat stilted way with the language.

He asked impatiently, "What is it, boy?"

R. Giskard said, "I have brought the book-films you wished to see, sir, and the viewer."

"Well, put them down. Put them down. —And you needn't stay. Daneel will be here with me."

"Yes, sir." The robot's eyes—faintly glowing, Baley noticed, as Daneel's were not—turned briefly to R. Daneel, as though seeking orders from a superior being.

R. Daneel said quietly, "It will be appropriate, friend Giskard, to remain just outside the door."

"I shall, friend Daneel," said R. Giskard.

It left and Baley said with some discontent, "Why does it have to stay just outside the door? Am I a prisoner?"

"In the sense," said R. Daneel, "that it would not be permitted for you to mingle with the ship's company in the course of this voyage, I regret to be forced to say you are indeed a prisoner. Yet that is not the reason for the presence of Giskard. —And I should tell you at this point that it might well be advisable, Partner Elijah, if you did not address Giskard—or any robot—as 'boy.' "

Baley frowned. "Does it resent the expression?"

"Giskard does not resent any action of a human being. It is simply that 'boy' is not a customary term of address for robots on Aurora and it would be inadvisable to create friction with the Aurorans by unintentionally stressing your place of origin through habits of speech that are nonessential."

"How do I address it, then?"

"As you address me, by the use of his accepted identifying name. That is, after all, merely a sound indicating the particular person you are addressing—and why should one sound be preferable to another? It is merely a matter of convention. And it is also the custom on Aurora to refer to a robot as 'he'—or sometimes 'she'—rather than as 'it.' Then, too, it is not the custom on Aurora to use the initial 'R.' except under formal conditions where the entire name of the robot is appropriate—and even then the initial is nowadays left out."

"In that case—Daneel" (Baley repressed the sudden impulse to say "R. Daneel"), "how do you distinguish between robots and human beings?"

"The distinction is usually self-evident, Partner Elijah. There would seem to be no need to emphasize it unnecessarily. At least that is the Auroran view and, since you have asked Giskard for films on Aurora, I assume you wish to familiarize yourself with things Auroran as an aid to the task you have undertaken."

"The task which has been dumped on me, yes. And what if the

distinction between robot and human being is *not* self-evident, Daneel? As in your case?"

"Then why make the distinction, unless the situation is such that it is essential to make it?"

Baley took a deep breath. It was going to be difficult to adjust to this Auroran pretense that robots did not exist. He said, "But then, if Giskard is not here to keep me prisoner, why is it—he—outside the door?"

"Those are according to the instructions of Dr. Fastolfe, Partner Elijah. Giskard is to protect you."

"Protect me? Against what? —Or against whom?"

"Dr. Fastolfe was not precise on that point, Partner Elijah. Still, as human passions are running high over the matter of Jander Panell—"

"Jander Panell?"

"The robot whose usefulness was terminated."

"The robot, in other words, who was killed?"

"Killed, Partner Elijah, is a term that is usually applied to human beings."

"But on Aurora distinctions between robots and human beings are avoided, are they not?"

"So they are! Nevertheless, the possibility of distinction or lack or distinction in the particular case of the ending of functioning has never arisen—to my knowledge. I do not know what the rules are."

Baley pondered the matter. It was a point of no real importance, purely a matter of semantics. Still, he wanted to probe the manner of thinking of the Aurorans. He would get nowhere otherwise.

He said slowly, "A human being who is functioning is alive. If that life is violently ended by the deliberate action of another human being, we call that 'murder' or 'homicide.' 'Murder' is, somehow, the stronger word. To be witness, suddenly, to an attempted violent end to the life of a human being, one would shout 'Murder!' It is not at all likely that one would shout 'Homicide!' It is the more formal word, the less emotional word."

R. Daneel said, "I do not understand the distinction you are making, Partner Elijah. Since 'murder' and 'homicide' are both used to represent the violent ending of the life of a human being, the two words must be interchangeable. Where, then, is the distinction?"

"Of the two words, one screamed out will more effectively chill the blood of a human being than the other will, Daneel."

"Why is that?"

"Connotations and associations; the subtle effect, not of dictionary meaning, but of years of usage; the nature of the sentences and conditions and events in which one has experienced the use of one word as compared with that of the other."

"There is nothing of this in my programming," said Daneel, with a curious sound of helplessness hovering over the apparent lack of emotion with which he said this (the same lack of emotion with which he said everything).

Baley said, "Will you accept my word for it, Daneel?"

Quickly, Daneel said, almost as though he had just been presented with the solution to a puzzle, "Without doubt."

"Now, then, we might say that a robot that is functioning is alive," said Baley. "Many might refuse to broaden the word so far, but we are free to devise definitions to suit ourselves if it is useful. It is easy to treat a functioning robot as alive and it would be unnecessarily complicated to try to invent a new word for the condition to avoid the use of the familiar one. You are alive, for instance, Daneel, aren't you?"

Daneel said, slowly and with emphasis, "I am functioning!"

"Come. If a squirrel is alive, or a bug, or a tree, or a blade of grass, why not you? I would never remember to say—or to think—that I am alive but that you are merely functioning, especially if I am to live for a while on Aurora, where I am to try not to make unnecessary distinctions between a robot and myself. Therefore, I tell you that we are both alive and I ask you to take my word for it."

"I will do so, Partner Elijah."

"And yet can we say that the ending of robotic life by the deliberate violent action of a human being is also 'murder'? We might hesitate. If the crime is the same, the punishment should be the same, but would that be right? If the punishment of the murder of a human being is death, should one actually execute a human being who puts an end to a robot?"

"The punishment of a murderer is psychic-probing, Partner Elijah, followed by the construction of a new personality. It is the personal structure of the mind that has committed the crime, not the life of the body."

"And what is the punishment on Aurora for putting a violent end to the functioning of a robot?"

"I do not know, Partner Elijah. Such an incident has never occurred on Aurora, as far as I know."

"I suspect the punishment would not be psychic-probing," said Baley. "How about 'roboticide'?"

"Roboticide?"

"As the term used to describe the killing of a robot."

Daneel said, "But what about the verb derived from the noun, Partner Elijah? One never says 'to homicide' and it would therefore not be proper to say 'to roboticide.' "

"You're right. You would have to say 'to murder' in each case."

"But murder applies specifically to human beings. One does not murder an animal, for instance."

Baley said, "True. And one does not murder even a human being by accident, only by deliberate intent. The more general term is 'to kill.' That applies to accidental death as well as to deliberate murder—and it applies to animals as well as human beings. Even a tree may be killed by disease, so why may not a robot be killed, eh, Daneel?"

"Human beings and other animals and plants as well, Partner Elijah, are all living things," said Daneel. "A robot is a human artifact, as much as this viewer is. An artifact is 'destroyed,' 'damaged,' 'demolished,' and so on. It is never 'killed.' "

"Nevertheless, Daneel, I shall say 'killed.' Jander Panell was killed."

Daneel said, "Why should a difference in a word make any difference to the thing described?"

" 'That which we call a rose by any other name would smell as sweet.' Is that it, Daneel?"

Daneel paused, then said, "I am not certain what is meant by the smell of a rose, but if a rose on Earth is the common flower that is called a rose on Aurora, and if by its 'smell' you mean a property that can be detected, sensed, or measured by human beings, then surely calling a rose by another sound-combination—and holding all else equal—would not affect the smell or any other of its intrinsic properties."

"True. And yet changes in name do result in changes in perception where human beings are concerned."

"I do not see why, Partner Elijah."

"Because human beings are often illogical, Daneel. It is not an admirable characteristic."

Baley sank deeper into his chair and fiddled with his viewer, allowing his mind, for a few minutes, to retreat into private thought. The discussion with Daneel was useful in itself, for while Baley played with the question of words, he managed to forget that he was in space, to forget that the ship was moving forward until it was far enough from the mass centers of the Solar System to make the Jump through hyperspace; to forget that he would soon be several million kilometers from Earth and, not long after that, several light-years from Earth.

More important, there were positive conclusions to be drawn. It was clear that Daneel's talk about Aurorans making no distinction between robots and human beings was misleading. The Aurorans might virtuously remove the initial "R.," the use of the "boy" as a form of address, and the use of "it" as the customary pronoun, but from Daneel's resistance to the use of the same word for the violent ends of a robot and of a human being (a resistance inherent in his programming which was, in turn, the natural consequence of Auroran assumptions about how Daneel ought to behave) one had to conclude that these were merely superficial changes. In essence, Aurorans were as firm as Earthmen in their belief that robots were machines that were infinitely inferior to human beings.

That meant that his formidable task of finding a useful resolution of the crisis (if that were possible at all) would not be hampered by at least one particular misperception of Auroran society.

Baley wondered if he ought to question Giskard, in order to confirm the conclusions he reached from his conversation with Daneel—and, without much hesitation, decided not to. Giskard's simple and rather unsubtle mind would be of no use. He would "Yes, sir" and "No, sir" to the end. It would be like questioning a recording.

Well, then, Baley decided, he would continue with Daneel, who was at least capable of responding with something approaching subtlety.

He said, "Daneel, let us consider the case of Jander Panell, which I assume, from what you have said so far, is the first case of roboticide in the history of Aurora. The human being responsible—the killer— is, I take it, not known."

"If," said Daneel, "one assumes that a human being was responsible, then his identity is not known. In that, you are right, Partner Elijah."

"What about the motive? Why was Jander Panell killed?"

"That, too, is not known."

"But Jander Panell was a humaniform robot, one like yourself and not one like, for instance, R. Gis—I mean, Giskard."

"That is so. Jander was a humaniform robot like myself."

"Might it not be, then, that no case of roboticide was intended?"

"I do not understand, Partner Elijah."

Baley said, a little impatiently, "Might not the killer have thought this Jander was a human being, that the intention was homicide, not roboticide?"

Slowly, Daneel shook his head. "Humaniform robots are quite like human beings in appearance, Partner Elijah, down to the hairs and pores in our skin. Our voices are thoroughly natural, we can go through the motions of eating, and so on. And yet, in our behavior there are noticeable differences. There may be fewer such differences with time and with refinement of technique, but as yet they are many. You—and other Earthmen not used to humaniform robots—may not easily note these differences, but Aurorans would. No Auroran would mistake Jander—or me—for a human being, not for a moment."

"Might some Spacer, other than an Auroran, make the mistake?"

Daneel hesitated. "I do not think so. I do not speak from personal observation or from direct programmed knowledge, but I do have the programming to know that all Spacer worlds are as intimately acquainted with robots as Aurora is—some, like Solaria, even more so—and I deduce, therefore, that no Spacer would miss the distinction between human and robot."

"Are there humaniform robots on the other Spacer worlds?"

"No, Partner Elijah, they exist only on Aurora so far."

"Then other Spacers would not be intimately acquainted with humaniform robots and might well miss the distinctions and mistake them for human beings."

"I do not think that is likely. Even humaniform robots will behave in a robotic fashion in certain definite ways that any Spacer would recognize."

"And yet surely there are Spacers who are not as intelligent as most, not as experienced, not as mature. There are Spacer children, if nothing else, who could miss the distinction."

"It is quite certain, Partner Elijah, that the—roboticide—was not committed by anyone unintelligent, inexperienced, or young. Completely certain."

"We're making eliminations. Good. If no Spacer would miss the distinction, what about an Earthman? Is it possible that—"

"Partner Elijah, when you arrive in Aurora, you will be the first Earthman to set foot on the planet since the period of original settlement was over. All Aurorans now alive were born on Aurora or, in a relatively few cases, on other Spacer worlds."

"The first Earthman," muttered Baley. "I am honored. Might not an Earthman be present on Aurora without the knowledge of Aurorans?"

"No!" said Daneel with simple certainty.

"Your knowledge, Daneel, might not be absolute."

"No!" came the repetition, in tones precisely similar to the first.

"We conclude, then," said Baley with a shrug, "that the roboticide was intended to be roboticide and nothing else."

"That was the conclusion from the start."

Baley said, "Those Aurorans who concluded this at the start had all the information to begin with. I am getting it now for the first time."

"My remark, Partner Elijah, was not meant in any pejorative manner. I know better than to belittle your abilities."

"Thank you, Daneel. I know there was no intended sneer in your remark. —You said just a while ago that the roboticide was not committed by anyone unintelligent, inexperienced, or young, and that this is completely certain. Let us consider your remark—"

Baley knew that he was taking the long route. He had to. Considering his lack of understanding of Auroran ways and of their manner of thought, he could not afford to make assumptions and skip steps. If he were dealing with an intelligent human being in this way, that person would be likely to grow impatient and blurt out information—and consider Baley an idiot into the bargain. Daneel, however, as a robot, would follow Baley down the winding road with total patience.

That was one type of behavior that gave away Daneel as a robot, however humaniform he might be. An Auroran might be able to judge him a robot from a single answer to a single question. Daneel was right as to the subtle distinctions.

Baley said, "One might eliminate children, perhaps also most women, and many male adults by presuming that the method of roboticide involved great strength—that Jander's head was perhaps crushed by a violent blow or that his chest was smashed inward. This would not, I imagine, be easy for anyone who was not a particularly large and strong human being." From what Demachek had said on Earth, Baley knew that this was not the manner of the roboticide, but how was he to tell that Demachek herself had not been misled?

Daneel said, "It would not be possible at all for any human being."

"Why not?"

"Surely, Partner Elijah, you are aware that the robotic skeleton is metallic in nature and much stronger than human bone. Our movements are more strongly powered, faster, and more delicately controlled. The Third Law of Robotics states: 'A robot must protect its own existence.' An assault by a human being could easily be fended off. The strongest human being could be immobilized. Nor is it likely that a robot can be caught unaware. We are always aware of human beings. We could not fulfill our functions otherwise."

Baley said, "Come now, Daneel. The Third Law states: 'A robot must protect its own existence, as long as such protection does not conflict with the First or Second Law.' The Second law states: 'A robot must obey the orders given it by a human being, except where such orders would conflict with the First Law,' and the First Law states: 'A robot may not injure a human being or, through inaction, allow a human being to come to harm.' A human being could order a robot to smash his own skull. And if a human being attacked a robot, that robot could not fend off the attack without harming the human being, which would violate First Law."

Daneel said, "You are, I suppose, thinking of Earth's robots. On Aurora—or on any of the Spacer worlds—robots are regarded more highly than on Earth, and are, in general, more complex, versatile, and valuable. The Third Law is distinctly stronger in comparison to the Second Law on Spacer worlds than it is on Earth. An order for self-destruction would be questioned and there would have to be a truly legitimate reason for it to be carried through—a clear and present danger. And in fending off an attack, the First Law would not be violated, for Auroran robots are deft enough to immobilize a human being without hurting him."

"Suppose, though, that a human being maintained that, unless a robot destroyed himself, he—the human being—would be destroyed? Would not the robot then destroy himself?"

"An Auroran robot would surely question a mere statement to that effect. There would have to be clear evidence of the possible destruction of a human being."

"Might not a human being be sufficiently subtle to so arrange matters in such a way as to make it seem to a robot that the human being was indeed in great danger? Is it the ingenuity that would be required that makes you eliminate the unintelligent, inexperienced, and young?"

And Daneel said, "No, Partner Elijah, it is not."

"Is there an error in my reasoning?"

"None."

"Then the error may lie in my assumption that he was physically damaged. He was not, in actual fact, physically damaged. Is that right?"

"Yes, Partner Elijah."

(That meant Demachek had had her facts straight, Baley thought.)

"In that case, Daneel, Jander was mentally damaged. Roblock! Total and irreversible!"

"Roblock?"

"Short for robot-block, the permanent shutdown of the functioning of the positronic pathways."

"We do not use the word 'roblock' on Aurora, Partner Elijah."

"What do you say?"

"We say 'mental freeze-out.' "

"Either way, it is the same phenomenon being described."

"It might be wise, Partner Elijah, to use our expression or the Aurorans you speak to may not understand; conversation may be impeded. You stated a short while ago that different words make a difference."

"Very well. I will say 'freeze-out.'—Could such a thing happen spontaneously?"

"Yes, but the chances are infinitesimally small, roboticists say. As a humaniform robot, I can report that I have never myself experienced any effect that could even approach mental freeze-out."

"Then one must assume that a human being deliberately set up a situation in which mental freeze-out would take place."

"That is precisely what Dr. Fastolfe's opposition contends, Partner Elijah."

"And since this would take robotic training, experience, and skill, the unintelligent, the inexperienced, and the young cannot have been responsible."

"That is the natural reasoning, Partner Elijah."

"It might even be possible to list the number of human beings on Aurora with sufficient skills and thus set up a group of suspects that might not be very large in number."

"That has, in actual fact, been done, Partner Elijah."

"And how long is the list?"

"The longest list suggested contains only one name."

It was Baley's turn to pause. His brows drew together in an angry frown and he said, quite explosively, "Only one name?"

Daneel said quietly, "Only one name, Partner Elijah. That is the judgment of Dr. Han Fastolfe, who is Aurora's greatest theoretical roboticist."

"But what is, then, the mystery in all this? Whose is the one name?"

R. Daneel said, "Why, that of Dr. Han Fastolfe, of course. I have just stated that he is Aurora's greatest theoretical roboticist and, in Dr. Fastolfe's professional opinion, he himself is the only one who could possibly have maneuvered Jander Panell into total mental freeze-out without leaving any sign of the process. However, Dr. Fastolfe also states that he did not do it."

"But that no one else could have, either?"

"Indeed, Partner Elijah. There lies the mystery."

"And what if Dr. Fastolfe—" Baley paused. There would be no point in asking Daneel if Dr. Fastolfe was lying or was somehow mistaken, either in his own judgment that no one but he could have done it or in the statement that he himself had not done it. Daneel had been programmed by Fastolfe and there would be no chance that the programming included the ability to doubt the programmer.

Baley said, therefore, with as close an approach to mildness as he could manage, "I will think about this, Daneel, and we will talk again."

"That is well, Partner Elijah. It is, in any case, time for sleep. Since it is possible that, on Aurora, the pressure of events may force an irregular schedule upon you, it would be wise to seize the opportunity for sleep now. I will show you how one produces a bed and how one manages the bedclothes."

"Thank you, Daneel," muttered Baley. He was under no illusion that sleep would come easily. He was being sent to Aurora for the specific purpose of demonstrating that Fastolfe was innocent of roboticide—and success in that was required for Earth's continued security and (much less important but equally dear to Baley's heart) for the continued prospering of Baley's own career—yet, even before

reaching Aurora, he had discovered that Fastolfe had virtually con-
fessed to the crime.

8

Baley did sleep—eventually, after Daneel demonstrated how to
reduce the field intensity that served as a form of pseudo-gravity.
This was not true antigravity and it consumed so much energy that
the process could only be used at restricted times and under unusual
conditions.

Daneel was not programmed to be able to explain the manner in
which this worked and, if he had, Baley was quite certain he would
not have understood it. Fortunately, the controls could be operated
without any understanding of the scientific justification.

Daneel said, "The field intensity cannot be reduced to zero—at least,
not by these controls. Sleeping under zero-gravity is not, in any case,
comfortable, certainly not for those inexperienced in space travel.
What one needs is an intensity low enough to give one a feeling of
freedom from the pressure of one's own weight, but high enough to
maintain an up-down orientation. The level varies with the individual.
Most people would feel most comfortable at the minimum intensity
allowed by the control, but you might find that, on first use, you would
wish a higher intensity, so that you might retain the familiarity of the
weight sensation to a somewhat greater extent. Simply experiment
with different levels and find the one that suits."

Lost in the novelty of the sensation, Baley found his mind drifting
away from the problem of Fastolfe's affirmation/denial, even as his
body drifted away from wakefulness. Perhaps the two were one process.

He dreamed he was back on Earth (of course), moving along an
Expressway but not in one of the seats. Rather, he was floating along
beside the high-speed strip, just over the head of the moving people,
gaining on them slightly. None of the ground-bound people seemed
surprised; none looked up at him. It was a rather pleasant sensation
and he missed it upon waking.

After breakfast the following morning—

Was it morning actually? Could it be morning—or any other time
of day—in space?

Clearly, it couldn't. He thought awhile and decided he would define
morning as the time after waking, and he would define breakfast as
the meal eaten after waking, and abandon specific timekeeping as ob-
jectively unimportant. —For him, at least, if not for the ship.

After breakfast, then, the following morning, he studied the news

sheets offered him only long enough to see that they said nothing
about the roboticide on Aurora and then turned to those book-films
that had been brought to him the previous day ("wake period"?) by
Giskard.

He chose those whose titles sounded historical and, after viewing
through several hastily, he decided that Giskard had brought him books
for adolescents. They were heavily illustrated and simply written. He
wondered if that was Giskard's estimate of Baley's intelligence—or,
perhaps, of his needs. After some thought, Baley decided that Giskard,
in his robotic innocence, had chosen well and that there was no point
in brooding over a possible insult.

He settled down to viewing with greater concentration and noted
at once that Daneel was viewing the book-film with him. Actual curiosity? Or just to keep his eyes occupied?

Daneel did not once ask to have a page repeated. Nor did he stop
to ask a question. Presumably, he merely accepted what he read with
robotic trust and did not permit himself the luxury of either doubt or
curiosity.

Baley did not ask Daneel any questions concerning what he read,
though he did ask for instructions on the operation of the print-out
mechanism of the Auroran viewer, with which he was not familiar.

Occasionally, Baley stopped to make use of the small room that
adjoined his room and could be used for the various private physiological functions, so private that the room was referred to as "the
Personal," with the capital letters always understood, both on Earth
and—as Baley discovered when Daneel referred to it—on Aurora. It
was just large enough for one person—which made it bewildering to
a City-dweller accustomed to huge banks of urinals, excretory seats,
washbasins, and showers.

In viewing the book-films, Baley did not attempt to memorize details. He had no intention of becoming an expert on Auroran society,
nor even of passing a high school test on the subject. Rather, he wished
to get the feel of it.

He noticed, for instance, even through the hagiographic attitude of
historians writing for young people, that the Auroran pioneers—the
founding fathers, the Earthpeople who had first come to Aurora to
settle in the early days of interstellar travel—had been very much
Earthpeople. Their politics, their quarrels, every facet of their behavior had been Earthish; what happened on Aurora was, in ways, similar
to the events that took place when the relatively empty sections of
Earth had been settled a couple of thousand years before.

Of course, the Aurorans had no intelligent life to encounter and to
fight, no thinking organisms to puzzle the invaders from Earth with
questions of treatment, humane or cruel. There was precious little life
of any kind, in fact. So the planet was quickly settled by human be-

ings, by their domesticated plants and animals, and by the parasites and other organisms that were adventitiously brought along. And, of course, the settlers brought robots with them.

The first Aurorans quickly felt the planet to be theirs, since it fell into their laps with no sense of competition, and they had called the planet New Earth to begin with. That was natural, since it was the first extrasolar planet—the first Spacer world—to be settled. It was the first fruit of interstellar travel, the first dawn of an immense new era. They quickly cut the umbilical cord, however, and renamed the planet Aurora after the Roman goddess of the dawn.

It was the World of the Dawn. And so did the settlers from the start self-consciously declare themselves the progenitors of a new kind. All previous history of humanity was a dark Night and only for the Aurorans on this new world was the Day finally approaching.

It was this great fact, this great self-praise, that made itself felt over all the details: all the names, dates, winners, losers. It was the essential.

Other worlds were settled, some from Earth, some from Aurora, but Baley paid no attention to that or to any of the details. He was after the broad brushstrokes and he noted the two massive changes that took place and pushed the Aurorans ever farther away from their Earthly origins. These were first, the increasing integration of robots into every facet of life and second, the extension of the life-span.

As the robots grew more advanced and versatile, the Aurorans grew more dependent on them. But never helplessly so. Not like the world of Solaria, Baley remembered, on which a very few human beings were in the collective womb of very many robots. Aurora was not like that.

And yet they grew more dependent.

Viewing as he did for intuitive feel—for trend and generality—every step in the course of human/robot interaction seemed to depend on dependence. Even the manner in which a consensus of robotic rights was reached—the gradual dropping of what Daneel would call "unnecessary distinctions"—was a sign of the dependence. To Baley, it seemed not that the Aurorans were growing more humane in their attitude out of a liking for the humane, but that they were denying the robotic nature of the objects in order to remove the discomfort of having to recognize the fact that the human beings were dependent upon objects of artificial intelligence.

As for the extended life-span, that was accompanied by a slowing of the pace of history. The peaks and troughs smoothed out. There was a growing continuity and a growing consensus.

There was no question but that the history he was viewing grew less interesting as it went along; it became almost soporific. For those living through it, this had to be good. History was interesting to the extent that it was catastrophic and, while that might make absorbing viewing, it made horrible living. Undoubtedly, personal lives continued to be interesting for the vast majority of Aurorans and, if the collective interaction of lives grew quiet, who would mind?

If the World of the Dawn had a quiet sunlit day, who on that world would clamor for storm?

—Somewhere in the course of his viewing, Baley felt an indescrib-able sensation. If he had been forced to attempt a description, he would have said it was that of a momentary inversion. It was as though he had been turned inside out—and then back as he had been—in the course of a small fraction of a second.

So momentary had it been that he almost missed it, ignoring it as though it had been a tiny hiccup inside himself.

It was only perhaps a minute later, suddenly going over the feeling in retrospect, that he remembered the sensation as something he had experienced twice before: once when traveling to Solaria and once when returning to Earth from that planet.

It was the "Jump," the passage through hyperspace that, in a time-less, spaceless interval, sent the ship across the parsecs and defeated the speed-of-light limit of the Universe. (No mystery in words, since the ship merely left the Universe and traversed something which in-volved no speed limit. Total mystery in concept, however, for there was no way of describing what hyperspace was, unless one made use of mathematical symbols which could, in any case, not be translated into anything comprehensible.)

If one accepted the fact that human beings had learned to manip-ulate hyperspace without understanding the thing they manipulated, then the effect was clear. At one moment, the ship had been within microparsecs of Earth, and at the next moment, it was within micro-parsecs of Aurora.

Ideally, the Jump took zero-time—literally zero—and, if it were car-ried through with perfect smoothness, there would not, could not be any biological sensation at all. Physicists maintained, however, that perfect smoothness required infinite energy so that there was always an "effective time" that was not quite zero, though it could be made as short as desired. It was that which produced that odd and essentially harmless feeling of inversion.

The sudden realization that he was very far from Earth and very close to Aurora filled Baley with a desire to see the Spacer world.

Partly, it was the desire to see somewhere people lived. Partly, it was a natural curiosity to see something that had been filling his thoughts as a result of the book-films he had been viewing.

Giskard entered just then with the middle meal between waking and sleeping (call it "lunch") and said, "We are approaching Aurora, sir, but it will not be possible for you to observe it from the bridge. There would, in any case, be nothing to see. Aurora's sun is merely a bright star and it will be several days before we are near enough to Aurora itself to see any detail." Then he added, as though in afterthought, "It will not be possible for you to observe it from the bridge at that time, either."

Baley felt strangely abashed. Apparently, it was assumed he would want to observe and that want was simply squashed. His presence as a viewer was not desired.

He said, "Very well, Giskard," and the robot left.

Baley looked after him somberly. How many other constraints would be placed on him? Improbable as successful completion of his task was, he wondered in how many different ways Aurorans would conspire to make it impossible.

3. Giskard

9

Baley turned and said to Daneel, "It annoys me, Daneel, that I must remain a prisoner here because the Aurorans on board this ship fear me as a source of infection. This is pure superstition. I have been treated."

Daneel said, "It is not because of Auroran fears that you are being asked to remain in your cabin, Partner Elijah."

"No? What other reason?"

"Perhaps you remember that, when we first met on this ship, you asked me my reasons for being sent to escort you. I said it was to give you something familiar as an anchor and to please me. I was then about to tell you the third reason, when Giskard interrupted us with your viewer and viewing material—and thereafter we launched into a discussion of roboticide."

"And you never told me the third reason. What is it?"

"Why, Partner Elijah, it is merely that I might help protect you."

"Against what?"

"Unusual passions have been stirred by the incident we have agreed to call roboticide. You are being called to Aurora to help demonstrate Dr. Fastolfe's innocence. And the hyperwave drama——"

"Jehoshaphat, Daneel," said Baley in outrage. "Have they seen that thing on Aurora, too?"

"They have seen it throughout the Spacer worlds, Partner Elijah. It was a most popular program and has made it quite plain that you are a most extraordinary investigator."

"So that whoever might be behind the roboticide may well have exaggerated fears of what I might accomplish and might therefore risk a great deal to prevent my arrival—or to kill me."

"Dr. Fastolfe," said Daneel calmly, "is quite convinced that no one is behind the roboticide, since no human being other than himself could have carried it through. It was a purely fortuitous occurrence in Dr. Fastolfe's view. However, there are those who are trying to capitalize on the occurrence and it would be to their interest to keep you from proving that. For that reason, you must be protected."

Baley took a few hasty steps to one wall of the room and then back to the other, as though to speed his thought processes by physical example. Somehow he did not feel any sense of personal danger.

He said, "Daneel, how many humaniform robots are there all together on Aurora?"

"Do you mean now that Jander no longer functions?"

"Yes, now that Jander is dead."

"One, Partner Elijah."

Baley stared at Daneel in shock. Soundlessly, he mouthed the word: One?

Finally, he said, "Let me understand this, Daneel. You are the only humaniform robot on Aurora?"

"Or on any world, Partner Elijah. I thought you were aware of this. I was the prototype and then Jander was constructed. Since then, Dr. Fastolfe has refused to construct any more and no one else has the skill to do it."

"But in that case, since of two humaniform robots, one has been killed, does it not occur to Dr. Fastolfe that the remaining humaniform—you, Daneel—might be in danger."

"He recognizes the possibility. But the chance that the fantastically unlikely occurrence of mental freeze-out would take place a second time is remote. He doesn't take it seriously. He feels, however, that there might be a chance of other misadventure. That, I think, played some small part in his sending me to Earth to get you. It kept me away from Aurora for a week or so."

"And you are now as much a prisoner as I am, aren't you, Daneel?"

"I am a prisoner," said Daneel gravely, "only in the sense, Partner Elijah, that I am expected not to leave this room."

"In what other sense is one a prisoner?"

"In the sense that the person so restricted in his movements resents the restriction. A true imprisonment has the implication of being involuntary. I quite understand the reason for being here and I concur in the necessity."

"*You* do," grumbled Baley. "I do not. I am a prisoner in the full sense. And what keeps us safe here, anyway?"

"For one thing, Partner Elijah, Giskard is on duty outside."

"Is he intelligent enough for the job?"

"He understands his orders entirely. He is rugged and strong and quite realizes the importance of his task."

"You mean he is prepared to be destroyed to protect the two of us?"

"Yes, of course, just as I am prepared to be destroyed to protect you."

Baley felt abashed. He said, "You do not resent the situation in which you may be forced to give up your existence for me?"

"It is my programming, Partner Elijah," said Daneel in a voice that seemed to soften, "yet somehow it seems to me that, even were it not for my programming, saving you makes the loss of my own existence seem quite trivial in comparison."

Baley could not resist this. He held out his hand and closed it on Daneel's with a fierce grip. "Thank you, Partner Daneel, but please do not allow it to happen. I do not wish the loss of your existence. The preservation of my own would be inadequate compensation, it seems to me."

And Baley was amazed to discover that he really meant it. He was faintly horrified to realize that he would be ready to risk his life for a robot. ——No, not for a robot. For Daneel.

10

Giskard entered without signaling. Baley had come to accept that. The robot, as his guard, had to be able to come and go as he pleased. And Giskard was *only* a robot, in Baley's eyes, however much he might be a "he" and however much one did not mention the "R." If Baley were scratching himself, picking his nose, engaged in any messy biological function, it seemed to him that Giskard would be indifferent, nonjudgmental, incapable of reacting in any way, but coldly recording the observation in some inner memory bank.

It made Giskard simply a piece of mobile furniture and Baley felt no embarrassment in his presence. ——Not that Giskard had ever intruded on him at an inconvenient moment, Baley thought idly.

Giskard brought a small cubicle with him. "Sir, I suspect that you still wish to observe Aurora from space."

Baley started. No doubt, Daneel had noted Baley's irritation and had deduced its cause and taken this way of dealing with it. To have Giskard do it and present it as an idea of his simple-minded own was a touch of delicacy on Daneel's part. It would free Baley of the necessity of expressing gratitude. Or so Daneel would think.

Baley had, as a matter of fact, been more irritated at being, to his way of thinking, needlessly kept from the view of Aurora than at being kept imprisoned generally. He had been fretting over the loss of the view during the two days since the Jump. ——So he turned and said to Daneel, "Thank you, my friend."

"It was Giskard's idea," said Daneel.

"Yes, of course," said Baley with a small smile. "I thank him, too. What is this, Giskard?"

"It is an astrosimulator, sir. It works essentially like a trimensional receiver and is connected to the viewroom. If I might add——"

"Yes?"

"You will not find the view particularly exciting, sir. I would not wish you to be unnecessarily disappointed."

"I will try not to expect too much, Giskard. In any case, I will not hold you responsible for any disappointment I might feel."

"Thank you, sir. I must return to my post, but Daneel will be able to help you with the instrument if any problem arises."

He left and Baley turned to Daneel with approval. "Giskard handled that very well, I thought. He may be a simple model, but he's well-designed."

"He, too, is a Fastolfe robot, Partner Elijah. ——This astrosimulator is self-contained and self-adjusted. Since it is already focused on Aurora, it is only necessary to touch the control-edge. That will put it in operation and you need do nothing more. Would you care to set it going yourself?"

Baley shrugged. "No need. You may do it."

"Very well."

Daneel had placed the cubicle upon the table on which Baley had done his book-film viewing.

"This," he said, indicating a small rectangle in his hand, "is the control, Partner Elijah. You need only hold it by the edges in this manner and then exert a small inward pressure to turn the mechanism on—and then another to turn it off."

Daneel pressed the control-edge and Baley shouted in a strangled way.

Baley had expected the cubicle to light up and to display within itself a holographic representation of a star field. That was not what happened. Instead, Baley found himself in space—in space—with bright, unblinking stars in all directions.

It lasted for only a moment and then everything was back as it was: the room and, within it, Baley, Daneel, and the cubicle.

"My regrets, Partner Elijah," said Daneel. "I turned it off as soon as I understood your discomfort. I did not realize you were not prepared for the event."

"Then prepare me. What happened?"

"The astrosimulator works directly on the visual center of the human brain. There is no way of distinguishing the impression it leaves from three-dimensional reality. It is a comparatively recent device and so far it has been used only for astronomical scenes which are, after all, low in detail."

"Did you see it, too, Daneel?"

"Yes, but very poorly and without the realism a human being experiences. I see the dim outline of a scene superimposed upon the still-clear contents of the room, but it has been explained to me that human beings see the scene only. Undoubtedly, when the brains of those such as myself are still more finely tuned and adjusted——"

Baley had recovered his equilibrium. "The point is, Daneel, that I was aware of *nothing* else. I was not aware of myself. I did not see my hands or sense where they were. I felt as though I were a disembodied spirit or—er—as I imagine I would feel if I were dead but were consciously existing in some sort of immaterial afterlife."

"I see now why you would find that rather disturbing."

"Actually I found it *very* disturbing."

"My regrets, Partner Elijah. I shall have Giskard take this away."

"No. I'm prepared now. Let me have that cube. ——Will I be able to turn it off, even though I am not conscious of the existence of my hands?"

"It will cling to your hand, so that you will not drop it, Partner Elijah. I have been told by Dr. Fastolfe, who has experienced this phenomenon, that the pressure is automatically applied when the human being holding it wills an end. It is an automatic phenomenon based on nerve manipulation, as the vision itself is. At least, that is how it works with Aurorans and I imagine——"

"That Earthmen are sufficiently similar to Aurorans, physiologically, for it to work with us as well. ——Very well, give me the control and I will try."

With a slight internal wince, Baley squeezed the control-edge and was in space again. He was expecting it this time and, once he found he could breathe without difficulty and did not feel in any way as though he were immersed in a vacuum, he labored to accept it all as a visual illusion. Breathing rather stertorously (perhaps to convince himself he was actually breathing), he stared about curiously in all directions.

Suddenly aware he was hearing his breath rasp in his nose, he said, "Can you hear me, Daneel?"

He heard his own voice—a little distant, a little artificial—but he heard it.

And then he heard Daneel's, different enough to be distinguishable.

"Yes, I can," said Daneel. "And you should be able to hear me, Partner Elijah. The visual and kinesthetic senses are interfered with for the sake of a greater illusion of reality, but the auditory sense remains untouched. Largely so, at any rate."

"Well, I see only stars—ordinary stars, that is. Aurora has a sun. We are close enough to Aurora, I imagine, to make the star that is its sun considerably brighter than the others."

"Entirely too bright, Partner Elijah. It is blanked out or you might suffer retinal damage."

"Then where is the planet Aurora?"

"Do you see the constellation of Orion?"

"Yes, I do. ——Do you mean we still see the constellations as we see them in Earth's sky, as in the City planetarium?"

"Just about. As stellar distances go, we are not far from Earth and the Solar System of which it is part, so that they have the starview in common. Aurora's sun is known as Tau Ceti on Earth and is only 3.67 parsecs from there. ——Now if you'll imagine a line from Betelgeuse to the middle star of Orion's belt and continue it for an equal length and a bit more, the middling-bright star you see is actually the planet Aurora. It will become increasingly unmistakable over the next few days, as we approach it rapidly."

Baley regarded it gravely. It was just a bright starlike object. There was no luminous arrow, going on and off, pointing to it. There was no carefully lettered inscription arced over it.

He said, "Where's the sun? Earth's star, I mean."

"It's in the constellation Virgo, as seen from Aurora. It is a second-magnitude star. Unfortunately, the astrosimulator we have is not properly computerized and it would not be easy to point it out to you. It would, in any case, just appear to be a star, quite an ordinary one."

"Never mind," said Baley. "I am going to turn off this thing now. If I have trouble—help out."

He didn't have trouble. It flicked off just as he thought of doing so and he sat blinking in the suddenly harsh light of the room.

It was only then, when he had returned to his normal senses, that it occurred to him that for some minutes he had seemed to himself to have been out in space, without a protecting wall of any kind, and yet his Earthly agoraphobia had not been activated. He had been perfectly comfortable, once he had accepted his own non-existence.

The thought puzzled him and distracted him from his book-film viewing for a while.

Periodically, he returned to the astrosimulator and took another look at space as seen from a vantage point just outside the spaceship, with himself nowhere present (apparently). Sometimes it was just for a moment, to reassure himself that he was still not made uneasy by the infinite void. Sometimes he found himself lost in the pattern of the stars and he began lazily counting them or forming geometrical figures, rather luxuriating in the ability to do something which, on Earth, he would never have been able to do because the mounting agoraphobic uneasiness would quickly have overwhelmed everything else.

Eventually, it grew quite obvious that Aurora was brightening. It soon became easy to detect among the other dots of light, then un-mistakable, and finally unavoidable. It began as a tiny sliver of light and, thereafter, it enlarged rapidly and began to show phases.

It was almost precisely a half-circle of light when Baley became aware of the existence of phases.

Baley inquired and Daneel said, "We are approaching from outside the orbital plane, Partner Elijah. Aurora's south pole is more or less in the center of its disk, somewhat into the lighted half. It is spring in the southern hemisphere."

Baley said, "According to the material I have been reading, Aurora's axis is tipped sixteen degrees." He had glanced over the physical description of the planet with insufficient attention in his anxiety to get to the Aurorans, but he remembered that.

"Yes, Partner Elijah. Eventually, we will move into orbit about Aurora and the phases will then change rapidly. Aurora revolves more rapidly than Earth does——"

"It has a 22-hour day. Yes."

"A day of 22.3 traditional hours. The Auroran day is divided into 10 Auroran hours, with each hour divided into 100 Auroran minutes, which are, in turn, divided into 100 Auroran seconds. An Auroran second is thus roughly equal to 0.8 Earth seconds."

"Is that what the books mean when they refer to metric hours, metric minutes, and so on?"

"Yes. It was difficult to persuade the Aurorans, at first, to abandon the time units to which they were accustomed and both systems—the standard and the metric—were in use. Eventually, of course, the metric won out. At present we speak only of hours, minutes, and seconds, but the decimalized versions are invariably meant. The same system has been adopted throughout the Spacer worlds, even though, on the other worlds, it does not tie in with the natural rotation of the planet. Each planet also uses a local system, of course."

"As Earth does."

"Yes, Partner Elijah, but Earth uses *only* the original standard time units. That inconveniences the Spacer worlds where trade is concerned, but they allow Earth to go its way in this."

"Not out of friendliness, I imagine. I suspect they wish to emphasize Earth's difference. ——How does decimalization fit in with the year? After all, Aurora must have a natural period of revolution about its sun that controls the cycle of its seasons. How is that measured?"

Daneel said, "Aurora revolves about its sun in 373.5 Auroran days or in about 0.95 Earth years. That is not considered a vital matter in chronology. Aurora accepts 30 of its days as equaling a month and 10 months as equaling a metric year. The metric year is equal to about 0.8 seasonal years or about three-quarters of an Earth year.

The relationship is different on each world, of course. Ten days is usually referred to as a decimonth. All the Spacer worlds use this system."

"Surely, there must be some convenient way of following the cycle of the seasons?"

"Each world has its seasonal year, too, but it is little regarded. One can, by computer, convert any day—past or present—into its position in the seasonal year if, for any reason, such information is desired. And this is true on any world, where conversion to and from the local days is also as easily possible. And, of course, Partner Elijah, any robot can do the same and can guide human activity where the seasonal year or local time is relevant. The advantage of metricized units is that it supplies humanity with a unified chronometry that involves little more than decimal point shifts."

It bothered Baley that the books he viewed made none of this clear. But then, from his own knowledge of Earth's history, he knew that, at one time, the lunar month had been the key to the calendar and that there had come a time when, for ease of chronometry, the lunar month came to be ignored and was never missed. Yet if he had given books on Earth to some stranger, that stranger would have very likely found no mention of the lunar month or any historical change in calendars. Dates would have been given without explanation.

What else would be given without explanation?

How far could he rely, then, on the knowledge he was gaining? He would have to ask questions constantly, take nothing for granted.

There would be so many opportunities to miss the obvious, so many chances to misunderstand, so many ways of taking the wrong path.

∎∎

Aurora filled his vision now when he used the astrosimulator and it looked like Earth. (Baley had never seen Earth in the same way, but there had been photographs in astronomy texts and he had seen those.)

Well, what Baley saw on Aurora were the same cloud patterns, the same glimpse of desert areas, the same large stretches of day and night, the same pattern of twinkling light in the expanse of the night hemisphere as the photographs showed on Earth's globe.

Baley watched raptly and thought: What if, for some reason, he had been taken into space, told he was being brought to Aurora, and was in reality being returned to Earth for some reason—for some subtle and insane reason. How could he tell the difference before landing?

Was there reason to be suspicious? Daneel had carefully told him that the constellations were the same in the sky of both planets, but wouldn't that be naturally so for planets circling neighboring stars? The gross appearance of both planets from space was identical, but wouldn't that be expected if both were habitable and comfortably suited to human life?

Was there any reason to suppose such a farfetched deception would be played upon him? What purpose would it serve? And yet why shouldn't it be made to appear farfetched and useless? If there were an obvious reason to do such a thing, he would have seen through it at once.

Would Daneel be party to such a conspiracy? Surely not, if he were a human being. But he was only a robot; might there not be a way to order him to behave appropriately?

There was no way of coming to a decision. Baley found himself watching for glimpses of continental outlines that he could recognize as Earthly or as non-Earthly. That would be the telling test—except that it didn't work.

The glimpses that came and went hazily through the clouds were of no use to him. He was not sufficiently knowledgeable about Earth's geography. What he really knew of Earth were its underground Cities, its caves of steel.

The bits of coastline he saw were unfamiliar to him—whether Aurora or Earth, he did not know.

Why this uncertainty, anyway? When he had gone to Solaria, he had never doubted his destination; he had never suspected that they might be bringing him back to Earth.—— Ah, but then he had gone on a clear-cut mission in which there was reasonable chance for success. Now he felt there was no chance at all.

Perhaps it was, then, that he *wanted* to be returned to Earth and was building a false conspiracy in his mind so that he could imagine it possible.

The uncertainty in his mind had come to have a life of its own. He couldn't let go. He found himself watching Aurora with an almost mad intensity, unable to come back to the cabin-reality.

Aurora was moving, turning slowly——

He had watched long enough to see that. While he had been viewing space, everything had seemed motionless, like a painted backdrop, a silent and static pattern of dots of light, with, later on, a small half-circle included. Was it the motionlessness that had enabled him to be nonagoraphobic?

But now he could see Aurora moving and he realized that the ship was spiraling down in the final stage before landing. The clouds were bellying upward——

No, not the clouds; the ship was spiraling downward. The *ship* was moving. *He* was moving. He was suddenly aware of his own existence.

He was hurtling downward through the clouds. He was falling, unguarded, through thin air toward solid ground.

His throat constricted; it was becoming very hard to breathe.

He told himself desperately: You are enclosed. The walls of the ship
are around you.

But he sensed no walls.

He thought: Even without considering the walls, you are still enclosed. You are wrapped in skin.

·But he sensed no skin.

The sensation was worse than simple nakedness—he was an unaccompanied personality, the essence of identity totally uncovered, a
living point, a singularity surrounded by an open and infinite world,
and he was falling.

He wanted to close off the vision, contract his fist upon the control-
edge, but nothing happened. His nerve-endings had so abnormalized
that the automatic contraction at an effort of will did not work. He
had no will. Eyes would not close, fist would not contract. He was
caught and hypnotized by terror, frightened into immobility.

All he sensed before him were clouds, white—not quite white—
off-white—a slight golden-orange cast——

And all turned to gray—and he was drowning. He could not breathe.
He struggled desperately to open his clogged throat, to call to Daneel
for help——

He could make no sound——

12

Baley was breathing as though he had just breasted the tape at the
end of a long race. The room was askew and there was a hard surface
under his left elbow.

He realized he was on the floor.

Giskard was on his knees beside him, his robot's hand (firm but
somewhat cold) closed on Baley's right fist. The door to the cabin,
visible to Baley just beyond Giskard's shoulder, stood ajar.

Baley knew, without asking, what had happened. Giskard had seized
that helpless human hand and clenched it upon the control-edge to
end the astrosimulation. Otherwise——

Daneel was there as well, his face close to Baley's, with a look on it
that might well have been pain.

He said, "You said nothing, Partner Elijah. Had I been more quickly
aware of your discomfort——"

Baley tried to gesture that he understood, that it did not matter. He
was still unable to speak.

The two robots waited until Baley made a feeble movement to get up. Arms were under him at once, lifting him. He was placed in a chair and the control was gently taken away from him by Giskard.

Giskard said, "We will be landing soon. You will have no further need of the astrosimulator, I believe."

Daneel added gravely, "It would be best to remove it, in any case."

Baley said, "Wait!" His voice was a hoarse whisper and he was not sure the word could be made out. He drew a deep breath, cleared his throat feebly, and said again, "Wait!"—and then, "Giskard."

Giskard turned back. "Sir?"

Baley did not speak at once. Now that Giskard knew he was wanted, he would wait a lengthy interval, perhaps indefinitely. Baley tried to gather his scattered wits. Agoraphobia or not, there still remained his uncertainty about their destination. That had existed first and it might well have intensified the agoraphobia.

He had to find out. Giskard would not lie. A robot could not lie— unless very carefully instructed to do so. And why instruct Giskard? It was Daneel who was his companion, who was to be in his company at all times. If there was lying to be done, that would be Daneel's job. Giskard was merely a fetcher and carrier, a guard at the door. Surely there was no need to undergo the task of carefully instructing *him* in the web of lies.

"Giskard!" said Baley, almost normally now.

"Sir?"

"We are about to land, are we?"

"In a little less than two hours, sir."

That was two metric hours, thought Baley. More than two real hours? Less? It didn't matter. It would only confuse. Forget it.

Baley said, as sharply as he could manage, "Tell me right now the name of the planet we are about to land on."

A human being, if he had answered at all, would have done so only after a pause—and then with an air of considerable surprise.

Giskard answered at once, with a flat and uninflected assertion, "It is Aurora, sir."

"How do you know?"

"It is our destination. Then, too, it could not be Earth, for instance, since Aurora's sun, Tau Ceti, is only ninety percent the mass of Earth's sun. Tau Ceti is a little cooler, therefore, and its light has a distinct orange tinge to fresh and unaccustomed Earth eyes. You may have already seen the characteristic color of Aurora's sun in the reflection upon the upper surface of the cloud bank. You will certainly see it in the appearance of the landscape—until your eyes grow accustomed to it."

Baley's eyes left Giskard's impassive face. He *had* noticed the color difference, Baley thought, and had attached no importance to it. A bad error.

"You may go, Giskard.'

"Yes, sir."

Baley turned bitterly to Daneel. "I've made a fool of myself, Daneel."

"I gather you wondered if perhaps we were deceiving you and taking you somewhere that was not Aurora. Did you have a reason for suspecting this, Partner Elijah?"

"None. It may have been the result of the uneasiness that arose from subliminal agoraphobia. Staring at seemingly motionless space, I felt no perceptible illness, but it may have lain just under the surface, creating a gathering uneasiness."

"The fault was ours, Partner Elijah. Knowing of your dislike for open spaces, it was wrong to subject you to astrosimulation or, having done so, to subject you to no closer supervision."

Baley shook his head in annoyance. "Don't say that, Daneel. I have supervision enough. The question in my mind is how closely I am to be supervised on Aurora itself."

Daneel said, "Partner Elijah, it seems to me it will be difficult to allow you free access to Aurora and Aurorans."

"That is just what I must be allowed, nevertheless. If I'm to get to the truth of this case of roboticide, I must be free to seek information directly on the site—and from the people involved."

Baley was, by now, feeling quite himself though a bit weary. Embarrassingly enough, the intense experience he had passed through left him with a keen desire for a pipe of tobacco, something he thought he had done away with altogether better than a year before. He could feel the taste and odor of the tobacco smoke making its way through his throat and nose.

He would, he knew, have to make do with the memory. On Aurora, he would on no account be allowed to smoke. There was no tobacco on any of the Spacer worlds and, if he had had any on him to begin with, it would have been removed and destroyed.

Daneel said, "Partner Elijah, this must be discussed with Dr. Fastolfe once we land. I have no power to make any decisions in this matter."

"I'm aware of that, Daneel, but how do I speak to Fastolfe? Through the equivalent of an astrosimulator? With controls in my hand?"

"Not at all, Partner Elijah. You will speak face-to-face. He plans to meet you at the spaceport."

13

Baley listened for the noises of landing. He did not know what they might be, of course. He did not know the mechanism of the ship, how many men and women it carried, what they would have to do in the process of landing, what in the way of noise would be involved.

Shouts? Rumbles? A dim vibration?

He heard nothing.

Daneel said, "You seem to be under tension, Partner Elijah. I would prefer that you did not wait to tell me of any discomfort you might feel. I must help you at the very moment you are, for any reason, unhappy."

There was a faint stress on the word "must."

Baley thought absently: The First Law drives him. He surely suffered as much in his way as I suffered in mine when I collapsed and he did not foresee it in time. A forbidden imbalance of positronic potentials may have no meaning to me, but it may produce in him the same discomfort and the same reaction as acute pain would to me.

He thought further: How can I tell what exists inside the pseudoskin and pseudoconsciousness of a robot, any more than Daneel can tell what exists inside me.

And then, feeling remorse at having thought of Daneel as a robot, Baley looked into the other's gentle eyes (when did he start thinking of their expression as gentle?) and said, "I would tell you of any discomfort at once. There is none. I am merely trying to hear any noise that might tell me of the progress of the landing procedure, Partner Daneel."

"Thank you, Partner Elijah," said Daneel gravely. He bowed his head slightly and went on, "There should be no discomfort in the landing. You will feel acceleration, but that will be minimal, for this room will yield, to a certain extent, in the direction of the acceleration. The temperature may go up, but not more than two degrees Celsius. As for sonic effects, there may be a low hiss as we pass through the thickening atmosphere. Will any of this disturb you?"

"It shouldn't. What does disturb me is not being free to participate in the landing. I would like to know about such things. I do not want to be imprisoned and to be kept from the experience."

"You have already discovered, Partner Elijah, that the nature of the experience does not suit your temperament."

"And how am I to get over that, Daneel?" he said strenuously. "That is not enough reason to keep me here!"

"Partner Elijah, I have already explained that you are kept here for your own safety."

Baley shook his head in clear disgust. "I have thought of that and I say it's nonsense. My chances of straightening out this mess are so small, with all the restrictions being placed on me and with the difficulty I will have in understanding anything about Aurora, that I don't think anyone in his right mind would bother to take the trouble to try to stop me. And if they did, why bother attacking me personally? Why not sabotage the ship? If we imagine ourselves to be facing no-holds-barred villains, they should find a ship—and the people aboard it—and you and Giskard—and myself, of course—to be a small price to pay."

"This has, in point of fact, been considered, Partner Elijah. The ship has been carefully studied. Any signs of sabotage would be detected."

"Are you sure? One hundred percent certain?"

"Nothing of this sort can be absolutely certain. Giskard and I were comfortable, however, with the thought that the certainty was quite high and that we might proceed with minimal expectation of disaster."

"And if you were wrong?"

Something like a small sign of spasm crossed Daneel's face, as though he were being asked to consider something that interfered with the smooth working of the positronic pathways in his brain. He said, "But we have not been wrong."

"You cannot say that. We are approaching the landing and that is sure to be the danger moment. In fact, at this point there is no need to sabotage the ship. My personal danger is greatest now—right now. I can't hide in this room if I'm to disembark at Aurora. I will have to pass through the ship and be within reach of others. Have you taken precautions to keep the landing safe?" (He was being petty—striking out at Daneel needlessly because he was chafing at his long imprisonment—and at the indignity of his moment of collapse.)

But Daneel said calmly, "We have, Partner Elijah. And, incidentally, we have landed. We are now resting on the surface of Aurora."

For a moment, Baley was bewildered. He looked around wildly, but of course there was nothing to see but an enclosing room. He had felt and heard nothing of what Daneel had described. None of the acceleration, or heat, or wind whistle. ——Or had Daneel deliberately brought up the matter of his personal danger once again, in order to make sure he would not think of other unsettling—but minor—matters.

Baley said, "And yet there's still the matter of getting off the ship. How do I do that without being vulnerable to possible enemies?"

Daneel walked to one wall and touched a spot upon it. The wall promptly split in two, the two halves moving apart. Baley found himself looking into a long cylinder, a tunnel.

Giskard had entered the room at that moment from the other side and said, "Sir, the three of us will move through the exit tube. Others have it under observation from without. At the other end of the tube, Dr. Fastolfe is waiting."

"We have taken every precaution," said Daneel.

Baley muttered, "My apologies, Daneel—Giskard." He moved into the exit tube somberly. Every effort to assure that precautions had been taken also assured him that those precautions were thought necessary.

Baley liked to think he was no coward, but he was on a strange planet, with no way of telling friend from enemy, with no way of taking comfort in anything familiar (except, of course, Daneel). At crucial moments, he thought with a shiver, he would be without enclosure to warm him and to give him relief.

Fastolfe

14

Dr. Han Fastolfe was indeed waiting—and smiling. He was tall and thin, with light brown hair that was not very thick, and there were, of course, his ears. It was the ears that Baley remembered, even after three years. Large ears, standing away from his head, giving him a vaguely humorous appearance, a pleasant homeliness. It was the ears that made Baley smile, rather than Fastolfe's welcome.

Baley wondered briefly if Auroran medical technology did not extend to the minor plastic surgery required to correct the ungainliness of those ears. ——But then, it might well be that Fastolfe liked their appearance as Baley himself (rather to his surprise) did. There is something to be said about a face that makes one smile.

Perhaps Fastolfe valued being liked at first glance. Or was it that he found it useful to be underestimated? Or just different?

Fastolfe said, "Plainclothesman Elijah Baley. I remember you well, even though I persist in thinking of you as possessing the face of the actor who portrayed you."

Baley's face turned grim. "That hyperwave dramatization haunts me, Dr. Fastolfe. If I knew where I could go to escape it——"

"Nowhere," said Fastolfe genially. "At least ordinarily. So if you don't like it, we'll expunge it from our conversations right now. I shall never mention it again. Agreed?"

"Thank you." With calculated suddenness, he thrust out his hand at Fastolfe.

Fastolfe hesitated perceptibly. Then he took Baley's hand, holding it gingerly—and not for long—and said, "I shall assume you are not a walking sack of infection, Mr. Baley."

Then he said ruefully, staring at his hands, "I must admit, though, that my hands have been treated with an inert film that doesn't feel entirely comfortable. I'm a creature of the irrational fears of my society."

Baley shrugged. "So are we all. I do not relish the thought of being Outside—in the open air, that is. For that matter, I do not relish having had to come to Aurora under the circumstances in which I find myself."

"I understand that well, Mr. Baley. I have a closed car for you here and, when we come to my establishment, we will do our best to continue to keep you enclosed."

"Thank you, but in the course of my stay on Aurora, I feel that it will be necessary for me to stay Outside on occasion. I am prepared for that—as best I can be."

"I understand, but we will inflict the Outside on you only when it is necessary. That is not now the case, so please consent to be enclosed."

The car was waiting in the shadow of the tunnel and there would scarcely be a trace of Outside in passing from the latter to the former. Behind him, Baley was aware of both Daneel and Giskard, quite dissimilar in appearance but both identical in grave and waiting attitude—and both endlessly patient.

Fastolfe opened the back door and said, "Please to get in."

Baley entered. Quickly and smoothly, Daneel entered behind him, while Giskard, virtually simultaneously, in what seemed almost like a well-choreographed dance movement, entered on the other side. Baley found himself wedged, but not oppressively so, between them. In fact, he welcomed the thought that, between himself and the Outside, on both sides, was the thickness of a robotic body.

But there was no Outside. Fastolfe climbed into the front seat and, as the door closed behind him, the windows blanked out and a soft, artificial light suffused the interior.

Fastolfe said, "I don't generally drive this way, Mr. Baley, but I don't mind a great deal and you may find it more comfortable. The car is completely computerized, knows where it's going, and can deal with any obstructions or emergencies. We need interfere in no way."

There was the faintest feeling of acceleration and then a vague, barely noticeable sensation of motion.

Fastolfe said, "This is a secure passage, Mr. Baley. I have gone to considerable trouble to make certain that as few people as possible know you will be in this car and certainly you will not be detected within it. The trip by car—which rides on air-jets, by the way, so that it is an airfoil, actually—will not take long, but, if you wish, you can seize the opportunity to rest. You are quite safe now."

"You speak," said Baley, "as though you think I'm in danger. I was protected to the point of imprisonment on the ship—and again now." Baley looked about the small, enclosed interior of the car, within which he was hemmed by the frame of metal and opacified glass, to say nothing of the metallic frame of two robots.

Fastolfe laughed lightly. "I am overreacting, I know, but feeling runs high on Aurora. You arrive here at a time of crisis for us and I would rather be made to look silly by overreacting than to run the terrible risk that underreacting entails."

Baley said, "I believe you understand, Dr. Fastolfe, that my failure here would be a blow to Earth."

"I understand that well. I am as determined as you are to prevent your failure. Believe me."

"I do. Furthermore, my failure here, for whatever reason, will also be my personal and professional ruin on Earth."

Fastolfe turned in his seat to look at Baley with a shocked expression. "Really? That would not be warranted."

Baley shrugged. "I agree, but it will happen. I will be the obvious target for a desperate Earth government."

"This was not in my mind when I asked for you, Mr. Baley. You may be sure I will do what I can. Though, in all honesty"—his eyes fell away—"that will be little enough, if we lose."

"I know that," said Baley dourly. He leaned back against the soft upholstery and closed his eyes. The motion of the car was limited to a gentle lulling sway, but Baley did not sleep. Instead, he thought hard—for what that was worth.

15

Baley did not experience the Outside at the other end of the trip, either. When he emerged from the airfoil, he was in an underground garage and a small elevator brought him up to ground level (as it turned out).

He was ushered into a sunny room and, as he passed through the direct rays of the sun (yes, faintly orange), he shrank away a bit.

Fastolfe noticed. He said, "The windows are not opacifiable, though they can be darkened. I will do that, if you like. In fact, I should have thought of that——"

"No need," said Baley gruffly. "I'll just sit with my back to it. I must acclimate myself."

"If you wish, but let me know if, at any time, you grow too uncomfortable. ——Mr. Baley, it is late morning here on this part of Aurora. I don't know your personal time on the ship. If you have been awake for many hours and would like to sleep, that can be arranged. If you are wakeful but not hungry, you need not eat. However, if you feel you can manage it, you are welcome to have lunch with me in a short while."

"That would fit in well with my personal time, as it happens."

"Excellent. I'll remind you that our day is about seven percent shorter than Earth's. It shouldn't involve you in too much biorhythmic difficulty, but if it does, we will try to adjust ourselves to your needs."

"Thank you."

"Finally—I have no clear idea what your food preferences might be."

"I'll manage to eat whatever is put before me."

"Nevertheless, I won't feel offended if anything seems—not palatable."

"Thank you."

"And you won't mind if Daneel and Giskard join us?"

Baley smiled faintly. "Will they be eating, too?"

There was no answering smile from Fastolfe. He said seriously, "No, but I want them to be with you at all times."

"Still danger? Even here?"

"I trust nothing entirely. Even here."

A robot entered. "Sir, lunch is served."

Fastolfe nodded. "Very good, Faber. We will be at the table in a few moments."

Baley said, "How many robots do you have?"

"Quite a few. We are not at the Solarian level of ten thousand robots to a human being, but I have more than the average number—fifty-seven. The house is a large one and it serves as my office and my workshop as well. Then, too, my wife, when I have one, must have space enough to be insulated from my work in a separate wing and must be served independently."

"Well, with fifty-seven robots, I imagine you can spare two. I feel the less guilty at your having sent Giskard and Daneel to escort me to Aurora."

"It was no casual choice, I assure you, Mr. Baley. Giskard is my majordomo and my right hand. He has been with me all my adult life."

"Yet you sent him on the trip to get me. I am honored," said Baley.

"It is a measure of your importance, Mr. Baley. Giskard is the most reliable of my robots, strong and sturdy."

Baley's eyes flickered toward Daneel and Fastolfe added, "I don't include my friend Daneel in these calculations. He is not my servant, but an achievement of which I have the weakness to be extremely proud. He is the first of his class and, while Dr. Roj Nemennuh Sarton was his designer and model, the man who——"

He paused delicately, but Baley nodded brusquely and said, "I understand."

He did not require the phrase to be completed with a reference to Sarton's murder on Earth.

"While Sarton supervised the actual construction," Fastolfe went on, "it was I whose theoretical calculations made Daneel possible."

Fastolfe smiled at Daneel, who bowed his head in acknowledgment.

Baley said, "There was Jander, too."

"Yes." Fastolfe shook his head and looked downcast. "I should perhaps have kept him with me, as I do Daneel. But he *was* my second humaniform and that makes a difference. It is Daneel who is my first-born, so to speak—a special case."

"And you construct no more humaniform robots now?"

"No more. But come," said Fastolfe, rubbing his hands. "We must have our lunch. ——I do not think, Mr. Baley, that on Earth the population is accustomed to what I might term natural food. We are having shrimp salad, together with bread and cheese, milk, if you wish, or any of an assortment of fruit juices. It's all very simple. Ice cream for dessert."

"All traditional Earth dishes," said Baley, "which exist now in their original form only in Earth's ancient literature."

"None of it is entirely common here on Aurora, but I didn't think it made sense to subject you to our own version of gourmet dining, which involves food items and spices of Auroran varieties. The taste would have to be acquired."

He rose. "Please come with me, Mr. Baley. There will just be the two of us and we will not stand on ceremony or indulge in unnecessary dining ritual."

"Thank you," said Baley. "I accept that as a kindness. I have relieved the tedium of the trip here by a rather intensive viewing of material relating to Aurora and I know that proper politeness requires many aspects to a ceremonial meal that I would dread."

"You need not dread."

Baley said, "Could we break ceremony even to the extent of talking business over the meal, Dr. Fastolfe? I must not lose time unnecessarily."

"I sympathize with that point of view. We will indeed talk business and I imagine I can rely on you to say nothing to anyone concerning that lapse. I would not want to be expelled from polite society." He chuckled, then said, "Though I should not laugh. It is nothing to laugh at. Losing time may be more than an inconvenience alone. It could easily be fatal."

16

The room that Baley left was a spare one: several chairs, a chest of drawers, something that looked like a piano but had brass valves in the place of keys, some abstract designs on the walls that seemed to shimmer with light. The floor was a smooth checkerboard of several shades of brown, perhaps designed to be reminiscent of wood, and although it shone with highlights as though freshly waxed, it did not feel slippery underfoot.

The dining room, though it had the same floor, was like it in no

other way. It was a long rectangular room, overburdened with decoration. It contained six large square tables that were clearly modules
that could be assembled in various fashions. A bar was to be found
along one short wall, with gleaming bottles of various colors standing
before a curved mirror that seemed to lend a nearly infinite extension
to the room it reflected. Along the other short wall were four recesses,
in each of which a robot waited.

Both long walls were mosaics, in which the colors slowly changed.
One was a planetary scene, though Baley could not tell if it were
Aurora, or another planet, or something completely imaginary. At one
end there was a wheat field (or something of that sort) filled with
elaborate farm machinery, all robot-controlled. As one's eye traveled
along the length of the wall, that gave way to scattered human habi-
tations, becoming, at the other end, what Baley felt to be the Auroran
version of a City.

The other long wall was astronomical. A planet, blue-white, lit by a
distant sun, reflected light in such a manner that not the closest examination could free one from the thought that it was slowly rotating.
The stars that surrounded it—some faint, some bright—seemed also
to be changing their patterns, though when the eye concentrated on
some small grouping and remained fixed there, the stars seemed im-
mobile.

Baley found it all confusing and repellent.

Fastolfe said, "Rather a work of art, Mr. Baley. Far too expensive
to be worth it, though, but Fanya would have it. —Fanya is my current
partner."

"Will she be joining us, Dr. Fastolfe?"

"No, Mr. Baley. As I said, just the two of us. For the duration, I
have asked her to remain in her own quarters. I do not want to subject
her to this problem we have. You understand, I hope?"

"Yes, of course."

"Come. Please take your seat."

One of the tables was set with dishes, cups, and elaborate cutlery,
not all of which were familiar to Baley. In the center was a tall, somewhat tapering cylinder that looked as though it might be a gigantic
chess pawn made out of a gray rocky material.

Baley, as he sat down, could not resist reaching toward it and touching it with a finger.

Fastolfe smiled, "It's a spicer. It possesses simple controls that allow
one to use it to deliver a fixed amount of any of a dozen different
condiments on any portion of a dish. To do it properly, one picks it
up and performs rather intricate evolutions that are meaningless in
themselves but that are much valued by fashionable Aurorans as symbols of the grace and delicacy with which meals should be served.
When I was younger, I could, with my thumb and two fingers, do the

triple genuflection and produce salt as the spicer struck my palm. Now
if I tried it, I'd run a good risk of braining my guest. I trust you won't
mind if I do not try."

"I urge you not to try, Dr. Fastolfe."

A robot placed the salad on the table, another brought a tray of fruit
juices, a third brought the bread and cheese, a fourth adjusted the
napkins. All four operated in close coordination, weaving in and out
without collision or any sign of difficulty. Baley watched them in
astonishment.

They ended, without any apparent sign of prearrangements, one at
each side of the table. They stepped back in unison, bowed in unison,
turned in unison, and returned to the recesses along the wall at the
far end of the room. Baley was suddenly aware of Daneel and Giskard
in the room as well. He had not seen them come in. They waited in
two recesses that had somehow appeared along the wall with the wheat
field. Daneel was the closer.

Fastolfe said, "Now that they've gone——" He paused and shook
his head slowly in rueful conclusion. "Except that they haven't. Ordinarily, it is customary for the robots to leave before lunch actually
begins. Robots do not eat, while human beings do. It therefore makes
sense that those who eat do so and that those who do not leave. And
it has ended by becoming one more ritual. It would be quite unthinkable to eat until the robots left. In this case, though——"

"They have not left," said Baley.

"No. I felt that security came before etiquette and I felt that, not
being an Auroran, you would not mind."

Baley waited for Fastolfe to make the first move. Fastolfe lifted a
fork, so did Baley. Fastolfe made use of it, moving slowly and allowing
Baley to see exactly what he was doing.

Baley bit cautiously into a shrimp and found it delightful. He recognized the taste, which was like the shrimp paste produced on Earth
but enormously more subtle and rich. He chewed slowly and, for a
while, despite his anxiety to get on with the investigation while dining,
he found it quite unthinkable to do anything but give his full attention
to the lunch.

It was, in fact, Fastolfe who made the first move. "Shouldn't we
make a beginning on the problem, Mr. Baley?"

Baley felt himself flush slightly. "Yes. By all means. I ask your pardon. Your Auroran food caught me by surprise, so that it was difficult
for me to think of anything else. ——The problem, Dr. Fastolfe, is of
your making, isn't it?"

"Why do you say that?"

"Someone has committed roboticide in a manner that requires great
expertise—as I have been told."

"Roboticide? An amusing term." Fastolfe smiled. "Of course, I understand what you mean by it. ——You have been told correctly; the manner requires *enormous* expertise."

"And only you have the expertise to carry it out—as I have been told."

"You have been told correctly there, too."

"And even you yourself admit—in fact, you insist—that only you could have put Jander into a mental freeze-out."

"I maintain what is, after all, the truth, Mr. Baley. It would do me no good to lie, even if I could bring myself to do so. It is notorious that I am the outstanding theoretical roboticist in all the Fifty Worlds."

"Nevertheless, Dr. Fastolfe, might not the second-best theoretical roboticist in all the worlds—or the third-best, or even the fifteenth-best—nevertheless possess the necessary ability to commit the deed? Does it really require all the ability of the very best?"

Fastolfe said calmly, "In my opinion, it really requires all the ability of the very best. Indeed, again in my opinion, I, myself, could only accomplish the task on one of my good days. Remember that the best brains in robotics—including mine—have specifically labored to design positronic brains that could *not* be driven into mental freeze-out."

"Are you certain of all that? Really certain?"

"Completely."

"And you stated so publicly?"

"Of course. There was a public inquiry, my dear Earthman. I was asked the questions you are now asking and I answered truthfully. It is an Auroran custom to do so."

Baley said, "I do not, at the moment, question that you were convinced you were answering truthfully. But might you not have been swayed by a natural pride in yourself? That might also be typically Auroran, might it not?"

"You mean that my anxiety to be considered the best would make me willingly put myself in a position where everyone would be forced to conclude I had mentally frozen Jander?"

"I picture you, somehow, as content to have your political and social status destroyed, provided your scientific reputation remained intact."

"I see. You have an interesting way of thinking, Mr. Baley. This would not have occurred to me. Given a choice between admitting I was second-best and admitting I was guilty of, to use your phrase, a roboticide, you are of the opinion I would knowingly accept the latter."

"No, Dr. Fastolfe, I do not wish to present the matter quite so simplistically. Might it not be that you deceive yourself into thinking you are the greatest of all roboticists and that you are completely unrivaled, clinging to that at all costs, because you unconsciously—*unconsciously*, Dr. Fastolfe—realize that, in fact, you are being over-taken—or have even already been overtaken—by others."

Fastolfe laughed, but there was an edge of annoyance in it. "Not so, Mr. Baley. Quite wrong."

"Think, Dr. Fastolfe! Are you certain that none of your roboticist colleagues can approach you in brilliance?"

"There are only a few who are capable of dealing at all with humaniform robots. Daneel's construction created virtually a new profession for which there is not even a name—humaniformicists, perhaps. Of the theoretical roboticists on Aurora, not one, except for myself, understands the workings of Daneel's positronic brain. Dr. Sarton did, but he is dead—and he did not understand it as well as I do. The basic theory is *mine*."

"It may have been yours to begin with, but surely you can't expect to maintain exclusive ownership. Has no one learned the theory?"

Fastolfe shook his head firmly. "Not one. I have taught no one and I defy any other living roboticist to have developed the theory on his own."

Baley said, with a touch of irritation, "Might there not be a bright young man, fresh out of the university, who is cleverer than anyone yet realizes, who——"

"*No*, Mr. Baley, no. I would have known such a young man. He would have passed through my laboratories. He would have worked with me. At the moment, no such young man exists. Eventually, one will; perhaps many will. At the moment, *none!*"

"If you died, then, the new science dies with you?"

"I am only a hundred and sixty-five years old. That's metric years, of course, so it is only a hundred and twenty-four of your Earth years, more or less. I am still quite young by Auroran standards and there is no medical reason why my life should be considered even half over. It is not entirely unusual to reach an age of four hundred years— metric years. There is yet plenty of time to teach."

They had finished eating, but neither man made any move to leave the table. Nor did any robot approach to clear it. It was as though they were transfixed into immobility by the intensity of the back and forth flow of talk.

Baley's eyes narrowed. He said, "Dr. Fastolfe, two years ago I was on Solaria. There I was given the clear impression that the Solarians were, on the whole, the most skilled roboticists in all the worlds."

"On the whole, that's probably true."

"And not one of them could have done the deed?"

"Not one, Mr. Baley. Their skill is with robots who are, at best, no more advanced than my poor, reliable Giskard. The Solarians know nothing of the construction of humaniform robots."

"How can you be sure of that?"

"Since you were on Solaria, Mr. Baley, you know very well that Solarians can approach each other with only the greatest of difficulty, that they interact by trimensional viewing—except where sexual contact is absolutely required. Do you think that any of them would dream of designing a robot so human in appearance that it would activate their neuroses? They would so avoid the possibility of approaching him, since he would look so human, that they could make no reasonable use of him."

"Might not a Solarian here or there display a surprising tolerance for the human body? How can you be sure?"

"Even if a Solarian could, which I do not deny, there are no Solarian nationals on Aurora this year."

"None?"

"None! They do not like to be thrown into contact even with Aurorans and, except on the most urgent business, none will come here— or to any other world. Even in the case of urgent business, they will come no closer than orbit and then they deal with us only by electronic communication."

Baley said, "In that case, if you are—literally and actually—the only person in all the worlds who could have done it, *did* you kill Jander?"

Fastolfe said, "I cannot believe that Daneel did not tell you I have denied this deed."

"He did tell me so, but I want to hear it from *you*."

Fastolfe crossed his arms and frowned. He said, through clenched teeth, "Then I'll tell you so. I did *not* do it."

Baley shook his head. "I believe you believe that statement."

"I do. And most sincerely. I am telling the truth. I did *not* kill Jander."

"But if you did not do it, and if no one else can possibly have done it, then—— But wait. I am, perhaps, making an unwarranted assumption. Is Jander really dead or have I been brought here under false pretenses?"

"The robot is really destroyed. It will be quite possible to show him to you, if the Legislature does not bar my access to him before the day is over—which I don't think they will do."

"In that case, if you did not do it, and if no one else could possibly have done it, and if the robot is actually dead—who committed the crime?"

Fastolfe sighed. "I'm sure Daneel told you what I have maintained at the inquiry—but you want to hear it from my own lips."

"That is right, Dr. Fastolfe."

"Well, then, *no one* committed the crime. It was a spontaneous event in the positronic flow along the brain paths that set up the mental freeze-out in Jander."

"Is that likely?"

"No, it is not. It is extremely unlikely—but if I did not do it, then that is the only thing that can have happened."

"Might it not be argued that there is a greater chance that you are lying than that a spontaneous mental freeze-out took place."

"Many *do* so argue. But I happen to know that I did *not* do it and that leaves only the spontaneous event as a possibility."

"And you have had me brought here to demonstrate—to *prove*—that the spontaneous event did, in fact, take place?"

"Yes."

"But how does one go about proving the spontaneous event? Only by proving it, it seems, can I save you, Earth, and myself."

"In order of increasing importance, Mr. Baley?"

Baley looked annoyed. "Well, then, you, me, and Earth."

"I'm afraid," said Fastolfe, "that after considerable thought, I have come to the conclusion that there is no way of obtaining such a proof."

17

Baley stared at Fastolfe in horror. "No way?"

"No way. None." And then, in a sudden fit of apparent abstraction, he seized the spicer and said, "You know, I am curious to see if I can still do the triple genuflection."

He tossed the spicer into the air with a calculated flip of the wrist. It somersaulted and, as it came down, Fastolfe caught the narrow end on the side of his right palm (his thumb tucked down). It went up slightly and swayed and was caught on the side of the left palm. It went up again in reverse and was caught on the side of the right palm and then again on the left palm. After this third genuflection, it was lifted with sufficient force to produce a flip. Fastolfe caught it in his right fist, with his left hand nearby, palm upward. Once the spicer was caught, Fastolfe displayed his left hand and there was a fine sprinkling of salt in it.

Fastolfe said, "It is a childish display to the scientific mind and the effort is totally disproportionate to the end, which is, of course, a pinch of salt, but the good Auroran host is proud of being able to put on a display. There are some experts who can keep the spicer in the air for a minute and a half, moving their hands almost more rapidly than the eye can follow.

"Of course," he added thoughtfully, "Daneel can perform such actions with greater skill and speed than any human. I have tested him in this manner in order to check on the workings of his brain paths, but it would be totally wrong to have him display such talents in public. It would needlessly humiliate human spicists—a popular term for them, you understand, though you won't find it in dictionaries."

Baley grunted.

Fastolfe sighed. "But we must get back to business."

"You brought me through several parsecs of space for that purpose."

"Indeed, I did. ——Let us proceed!"

Baley said, "Was there a reason for that display of yours, Dr. Fastolfe?"

Fastolfe said, "Well, we seem to have come to an impasse. I've brought you here to do something that can't be done. Your face was rather eloquent and, to tell you the truth, I felt no better. It seemed, therefore, that we could use a breathing space. And now—let us proceed."

"On the impossible task?"

"Why should it be impossible for you, Mr. Baley? Your reputation is that of an achiever of the impossible."

"The hyperwave drama? You believe that foolish distortion of what happened on Solaria?"

Fastolfe spread his arms. "I have no other hope."

Baley said, "And I have no choice. I must continue to try; I cannot return to Earth a failure. That has been made clear to me. ——Tell me, Dr. Fastolfe, how could Jander have been killed? What sort of manipulation of his mind would have been required?".

"Mr. Baley, I don't know how I could possibly explain that, even to another roboticist, which you certainly are not, and even if I were prepared to publish my theories, which I certainly am not. However, let me see if I can't explain something. ——You know, of course, that robots were invented on Earth."

"Very little concerning robotics is dealt with on Earth——"

"Earth's strong antirobot bias is well-known on the Spacer worlds."

"But the Earthly origin of robots is obvious to any person on Earth who thinks about it. It is well-known that hyperspatial travel was developed with the aid of robots and, since the Spacer worlds could not have been settled without hyperspatial travel, it follows that robots existed before settlement had taken place and while Earth was still the only inhabited planet. Robots were therefore invented on Earth by Earthpeople."

"Yet Earth feels no pride in that, does it?"

"We do not discuss it," said Baley shortly.

"And Earthpeople know nothing about Susan Calvin?"

"I have come across her name in a few old books. She was one of the early pioneers in robotics."

"Is that all you know of her?"

Baley made a gesture of dismissal. "I suppose I could find out more if I searched the records, but I have had no occasion to do so."

"How strange," said Fastolfe. "She's a demigod to all Spacers, so much so that I imagine that few Spacers who are not actually roboticists think of her as an Earthwoman. It would seem a profanation. They would refuse to believe it if they were told that she died after having lived scarcely more than a hundred metric years. And yet you know her only as an early pioneer."

"Has she got something to do with all this, Dr. Fastolfe?"

"Not directly, but in a way. You must understand that numerous legends cluster about her name. Most of them are undoubtedly untrue, but they cling to her, nonetheless. One of the most famous legends—and one of the least likely to be true—concerns a robot manufactured in those primitive days that, through some accident on the production lines, turned out to have telepathic abilities——"

"What!"

"A legend! I told you it was a legend—and undoubtedly untrue! Mind you, there is some theoretical reason for supposing this might be possible, though no one has ever presented a plausible design that could even begin to incorporate such an ability. That it could have appeared in positronic brains as crude and simple as those in the pre-hyperspatial era is totally unthinkable. That is why we are quite certain that this particular tale is an invention. But let me go on anyway, for it points out a moral."

"By all means, go on."

"The robot, according to the tale, could read minds. And when asked questions, he read the questioner's mind and told the questioner what he wanted to hear. Now the First Law of Robotics states quite clearly that a robot may not injure a human being or, through inaction, allow a person to come to harm, but to robots generally that means physical harm. A robot who can read minds, however, would surely decide that disappointment or anger or any violent emotion would make the human being feeling those emotions unhappy and the robot would interpret the inspiring of such emotions under the heading of 'harm.' If, then, a telepathic robot knew that the truth might disappoint or enrage a questioner or cause that person to feel envy or unhappiness, he would tell a pleasing lie, instead. Do you see that?"

"Yes, of course."

"So the robot lied even to Susan Calvin herself. The lies could not long continue, for different people were told different things that were not only inconsistent among themselves but unsupported by the gathering evidence of reality, you see. Susan Calvin discovered she had been lied to and realized that those lies had led her into a position of considerable embarrassment. What would have disappointed her somewhat to begin with had now, thanks to false hope, disappointed her unbearably. ——You never heard the story?"

"I give you my word."

"Astonishing! Yet it certainly wasn't invented on Aurora, for it is equally current on all the worlds. ——In any case, Calvin took her revenge. She pointed out to the robot that, whether he told the truth or told a lie, he would equally harm the person with whom he dealt. He could not obey the First Law, whatever action he took. The robot, understanding this, was forced to take refuge in total inaction. If you want to put it colorfully, his positronic pathways burned out. His brain was irrecoverably destroyed. The legend goes on to say that Calvin's last word to the destroyed robot was 'Liar!' "

Baley said, "And something like this, I take it, was what happened to Jander Panell. He was faced with a contradiction in terms and his brain burned out?"

"It's what *appears* to have happened, though that is not as easy to bring about as it would have been in Susan Calvin's day. Possibly because of the legend, roboticists have always been careful to make it as difficult as possible for contradictions to arise. As the theory of positronic brains has grown more subtle and as the practice of positronic brain design has grown more intricate, increasingly successful systems have been devised to have all situations that might arise resolve into non-equality, so that some action can always be taken that will be interpreted as obeying the First Law."

"Well, then, you can't burn out a robot's brain. Is that what you're saying? Because if you are, what happened to Jander?"

"It's *not* what I'm saying. The increasingly successful systems I speak of, are never *completely* successful. They cannot be. No matter how subtle and intricate a brain might be, there is always some way of setting up a contradiction. That is a fundamental truth of mathematics. It will remain forever impossible to produce a brain so subtle and intricate as to reduce the chance of contradiction to zero. Never quite to zero. However, the systems have been made so close to zero that to bring about a mental freeze-out by setting up a suitable contradiction would require a deep understanding of the particular positronic brain being dealt with—and *that* would take a clever theoretician."

"Such as yourself, Dr. Fastolfe?"

"Such as myself. In the case of humaniform robots, *only* myself."

"Or no one at all," said Baley, heavily ironic.

"Or no one at all. Precisely," said Fastolfe, ignoring the irony. "The humaniform robots have brains—and, I might add, bodies—constructed in conscious imitation of the human being. The positronic brains are extraordinarily delicate and they take on some of the fragility of the human brain, naturally. Just as a human being may have a stroke, through some chance event within the brain and without the intervention of any external effect, so a humaniform brain might, through chance alone—the occasional aimless drifting of positrons—go into mental freeze."

"Can you prove that, Dr. Fastolfe?"

"I can demonstrate it mathematically, but of those who could follow the mathematics, not all would agree that the reasoning was valid. It involves certain suppositions of my own that do not fit into the accepted modes of thinking in robotics."

"And how likely is spontaneous mental freeze-out?"

"Given a large number of humaniform robots, say a hundred thousand, there is an even chance that one of them might undergo spontaneous mental freeze-out in an average Auroran lifetime. And yet it could happen much sooner, as it did to Jander, although then the odds would be very greatly against it."

"But look here, Dr. Fastolfe, even if you were to prove conclusively that a spontaneous mental freeze-out *could* take place in robots generally, that would not be the same as proving that such a thing happened to Jander in particular at this particular time."

"No," admitted Fastolfe, "you are quite right."

"You, the greatest expert in robotics, cannot prove it in the specific case of Jander."

"Again, you are quite right."

"Then what do you expect me to be able to do, when I know nothing of robotics."

"There is no need to *prove* anything. It would surely be sufficient to present an ingenious suggestion that would make spontaneous mental freeze-out plausible to the general public."

"Such as——"

"I don't know."

Baley said harshly, "Are you sure you don't know, Dr. Fastolfe?"

"What do you mean? I have just said I don't know."

"Let me point out something. I assume that Aurorans, generally, know that I have come to the planet for the purpose of tackling this problem. It would be difficult to manage to get me here secretly, considering that I am an Earthman and this is Aurora."

"Yes, certainly, and I made no attempt to do that. I consulted the Chairman of the Legislature and persuaded him to grant me permission to bring you here. It is how I've managed to win a stay in judgment. You are to be given a chance to solve the mystery before I go on trial. I doubt that they'll give me a very long stay."

"I repeat, then—Aurorans, in general, know I'm here and I imagine they know precisely why I am here—that I am supposed to solve the puzzle of the death of Jander."

"Of course. What other reason could there be?"

"And from the time I boarded the ship that brought me here, you have kept me under close and constant guard because of the danger that your enemies might try to eliminate me—judging me to be some sort of wonderman who just might solve the puzzle in such a way as to place you on the winning side, even though all the odds are against me."

"I fear that as a possibility, yes."

"And suppose someone who does not want to see the puzzle solved and you, Dr. Fastolfe, exonerated should actually succeed in killing me. Might that not swing sentiment in your favor? Might not people reason that your enemies felt you were, in actual fact, innocent or they would not fear the investigation so much that they would want to kill me?"

"Rather complicated reasoning, Mr. Baley. I suppose that, properly exploited, your death might be used to such a purpose, but it's not going to happen. You are being protected and you will not be killed."

"But *why* protect me, Dr. Fastolfe? Why not let them kill me and use my death as a way of winning?"

"Because I would rather you remained alive and succeeded in actually demonstrating my innocence."

Baley said, "But surely you know that I *can't* demonstrate your innocence."

"Perhaps you can. You have every incentive. The welfare of Earth hangs on your doing so and, as you have told me, your own career."

"What good is incentive? If you ordered me to fly by flapping my arms and told me further that if I failed, I would be promptly killed by slow torture and that Earth would be blown up and all its population destroyed, I would have enormous incentive to flap my wings and fly—and yet still be unable to do so."

Fastolfe said uneasily, "I know the chances are small."

"You know they are nonexistent," said Baley violently, "and that only my death can save you."

"Then I will not be saved, for I am seeing to it that my enemies cannot reach you."

"But *you* can reach me."

"What?"

"I have the thought in my head, Dr. Fastolfe, that you yourself might kill me in such a way as to make it appear that your enemies have done the deed. You would then use my death against them—and that that is why you have brought me to Aurora."

For a moment, Fastolfe looked at Baley with a kind of mild surprise and then, in an excess of passion both sudden and extreme, his face reddened and twisted into a snarl. Sweeping up the spicer from the table, he raised it high and brought his arm down to hurl it at Baley.

And Baley, caught utterly by surprise, barely managed to cringe back against his chair.

5. Daneel and Giskard

18

If Fastolfe had acted quickly, Daneel had reacted far more quickly still.

To Baley, who had all but forgotten Daneel's existence, there seemed a vague rush, a confused sound, and then Daneel was standing to one side of Fastolfe, holding the spicer, and saying, "I trust, Dr. Fastolfe, that I did not in any way hurt you."

Baley noted, in a dazed sort of way, that Giskard was not far from Fastolfe on the other side and that every one of the four robots at the far wall had advanced almost to the dining room table.

Panting slightly, Fastolfe, his hair quite disheveled, said, "No, Daneel. You did very well, indeed." He raised his voice. "You all did well, but remember, you must allow nothing to slow you down, even my own involvement."

He laughed softly and took his seat once more, straightening his hair with his hand.

"I'm sorry," he said, "to have startled you so, Mr. Baley, but I felt the demonstration might be more convincing than any words of mine would have been."

Baley, whose moment of cringing had been purely a matter of reflex, loosened his collar and said, with a touch of hoarseness, "I'm afraid I expected words, but I agree the demonstration was convincing. I'm glad that Daneel was close enough to disarm you."

"Any one of them was close enough to disarm me, but Daneel was the closest and got to me first. He got to me quickly enough to be gentle about it. Had he been farther away, he might have had to wrench my arm or even knock me out."

"Would he have gone that far?"

"Mr. Baley," said Fastolfe. "I have given instructions for your protection and I *know* how to give instructions. They would not have hesitated to save you, even if the alternative was harm to me. They would, of course, have labored to inflict minimum harm, as Daneel did. All he harmed was my dignity and the neatness of my hair. And my fingers tingle a bit." Fastolfe flexed them ruefully.

Baley drew a deep breath, trying to recover from that short period of confusion. He said, "Would not Daneel have protected me even without your specific instruction?"

"Undoubtedly. He would have had to. You must not think, however, that robotic response is a simple yes or no, up or down, in or out. It is a mistake the layman often makes. There is the matter of speed of response. My instructions with regard to you were so phrased that the potential built up within the robots of my establishment, including Daneel, is abnormally high, as high as I can reasonably make it, in fact. The response, therefore, to a clear and present danger to you is extraordinarily rapid. I knew it would be and it was for that reason that I could strike out at you as rapidly as I did—knowing I could give you a *most* convincing demonstration of my inability to harm you."

"Yes, but I don't entirely thank you for it."

"Oh, I was entirely confident in my robots, especially Daneel. It did occur to me, though, a little too late, that if I had not instantly released the spicer, he might, quite against his will—or the robotic equivalent of will—have broken my wrist."

Baley said, "It occurs to me that it was a foolish risk for you to have undertaken."

"It occurs to me, as well—after the fact. Now if you had prepared yourself to hurl the spicer at me, Daneel would have at once countered your move, but not with quite the same speed, for he has received no special instructions as to my safety. I can hope he would have been fast enough to save me, but I'm not sure—and I would prefer not to test that matter." Fastolfe smiled genially.

Baley said, "What if some explosive device were dropped on the house from some airborne vehicle?"

"Or if a gamma beam were trained upon us from a neighboring hilltop. ——My robots do not represent infinite protection, but such radical terrorist attempts are unlikely in the extreme here on Aurora. I suggest we do not worry about them."

"I am willing not to worry about them. Indeed, I did not seriously suspect that you were a danger to me, Dr. Fastolfe, but I needed to eliminate the possibility altogether if I were to continue. We can now proceed."

Fastolfe said, "Yes, we can. Despite this additional and very dramatic distraction, we still face the problem of proving that Jander's mental freeze-out was spontaneous chance."

But Baley had been made aware of Daneel's presence and he now turned to him and said uneasily, "Daneel, does it pain you that we discuss this matter?"

Daneel, who had deposited the spicer on one of the farther of the empty tables, said, "Partner Elijah, I would prefer that past-friend Jander were still operational, but since he is not and since he cannot be restored to proper functioning, the best of what is left is that action be taken to prevent similar incidents in the future. Since the discussion now has that end in view, it pleases rather than pains me."

"Well, then, just to settle another matter, Daneel, do *you* believe that Dr. Fastolfe is responsible for the end of your fellow-robot Jander? ——You'll pardon my inquiring, Dr. Fastolfe?"

Fastolfe gestured his approval and Daneel said, "Dr. Fastolfe has stated that he was not responsible, so he, of course, was not."

"You have no doubts on the matter, Daneel?"

"None, Partner Elijah."

Fastolfe seemed a little amused. "You are cross-examining a robot, Mr. Baley."

"I know that, but I cannot quite think of Daneel as a robot and so I have asked."

"His answers would have no standing before any Board of Inquiry. He is compelled to believe me by his positronic potentials."

"I am not a Board of Inquiry, Dr. Fastolfe, and I am clearing out the underbrush. Let me go back to where I was. Either you burned out Jander's brain or it happened by random circumstance. You assure me that I cannot prove random circumstance and that leaves me only with the task of disproving any action by you. In other words, if I can show that it is *impossible* for you to have killed Jander, we are left with random circumstance as the only alternative."

"And how can you do that?"

"It is a matter of means, opportunity, and motive. You had the means of killing Jander—the theoretical ability to so manipulate him that he would end in a mental freeze-out. But did you have the opportunity? He was your robot, in that you designed his brain paths and supervised his construction, but was he in your actual possession at the time of the mental freeze-out?"

"No, as a matter of fact. He was in the possession of another."

"For how long?"

"About eight months—or a little over half of one of your years."

"Ah. It's an interesting point. Were you with him—or near him— at the time of his destruction? Could you have reached him? In short, can we demonstrate the fact that you were so far from him— or so out of touch with him—that it is not reasonable to suppose that you could have done the deed at the time it is supposed to have been done?"

Fastolfe said, "That, I'm afraid, is impossible. There is a rather broad interval of time during which the deed might have been done. There are no robotic changes after destruction equivalent to rigor mortis or decay in a human being. We can only say that, at a certain time, Jander was known to be in operation and, at a certain other time, he was known not to be in operation. Between the two was a stretch of about eight hours. For that period, I have no alibi."

"None? During that time, Dr. Fastolfe, what were you doing?"

"I was here in my establishment."

"Your robots were surely aware, perhaps, that you were here and could bear witness."

"They were certainly aware, but they cannot bear witness in any legal sense and on that day Fanya was off on business of her own."

"Does Fanya share your knowledge of robotics, by the way?"

Fastolfe indulged in a wry smile. "She knows less than you do. ——Besides, none of this matters."

"Why not?"

Fastolfe's patience was clearly beginning to stretch to the cracking point. "My dear Mr. Baley, this was not a matter of close-range physical assault, such as my recent pretended attack on you. What happened to Jander did not require my physical presence. As it happens, although not actually in my establishment, Jander was not far away geographically, but it wouldn't have mattered if he were on the other side of Aurora. I could always reach him electronically and could, by the orders I gave him and the responses I could educe, send him into mental freeze-out. The crucial step would not even necessarily require much in the way of time——"

Baley said at once, "It's a short process, then, one that someone else might move through by chance, while intending something perfectly routine?"

"No!" said Fastolfe. "For Aurora's sake, Earthman, let me talk. I've already told you that's not the case. Inducing mental freeze-out in Jander would be a long and complicated and tortuous process, requiring the greatest understanding and wit, and could be done by no one accidentally, without incredible and long-continued coincidence. There would be far less chance of accidental progress over that enormously complex route than of spontaneous mental freeze-out, if my mathematical reasoning were only accepted.

"However, if I wished to induce mental freeze-out, I could carefully produce changes and reactions, little by little, over a period of weeks, months, even years, until I had brought Jander to the very point of destruction. And at no time in that process would he show any signs of being at the edge of catastrophe, just as you could approach closer and closer to a precipice in the dark and yet feel no loss in firmness of footing whatever, even at the very edge. Once I had brought him to the very brink, however—the lip of the precipice—a single remark from me would send him over. It is that final step that would take but a moment of time. You see?"

Baley tightened his lips. There was no use trying to mask his disappointment. "In short, then, you had the opportunity."

"*Anyone* would have had the opportunity. Anyone on Aurora, provided he or she had the necessary ability."

"And only you have the necessary ability."

"I'm afraid so."

"Which brings us to motive, Dr. Fastolfe."

"Ah."

"And it's there that we might be able to make a good case. These humaniform robots are yours. They are based on your theory and you were involved in their construction at every step of the way, even if Dr. Sarton supervised that construction. They exist because of you and *only* because of you. You have spoken of Daneel as your 'firstborn.' They are your creations, your children, your gift to humanity, your hold on immortality." (Baley felt himself growing eloquent and, for a moment, imagined himself to be addressing a Board of Inquiry.) "Why on Earth—or Aurora, rather—why on Aurora should you undo this work? Why should you destroy a life you have produced by a miracle of mental labor?"

Fastolfe looked wanly amused. "Why, Mr. Baley, you know nothing about it. How can you possibly know that my theory was the result of a miracle of mental labor? It might have been the very dull extension of an equation that anyone might have accomplished but which none had bothered to do before me."

"I think not," said Baley, endeavoring to cool down. "If no one but you can understand the humaniform brain well enough to destroy it, then I think it likely that no one but you can understand it well enough to create it. Can you deny that?"

Fastolfe shook his head. "No, I won't deny that. And yet, Mr. Baley"—his face grew grimmer than it had been since they had met— "your careful analysis is succeeding only in making matters far worse for us. We have already decided that I am the only one with the means and the opportunity. As it happens, I also have a motive—the best motive in the world—and my enemies know it. How on Earth, then, to quote you—or on Aurora, or on anywhere—are we going to prove I didn't do it?"

19

Baley's face crumpled into a furious frown. He stepped hastily away, making for the corner of the room, as though seeking enclosure. Then he turned suddenly and said sharply, "Dr. Fastolfe, it seems to me that you are taking some sort of pleasure in frustrating me."

Fastolfe shrugged. "No pleasure. I'm merely presenting you with the problem as it is. Poor Jander died the robotic death by the pure uncertainty of positronic drift. Since I know I had nothing to do with it, I know that's how it must be. However, no one else can be sure I'm innocent and all the indirect evidence points to me—and this must be faced squarely in deciding what, if anything, we can do."

Baley said, "Well, then, let's investigate your motive. What seems like an overwhelming motive to you may be nothing of the sort."

"I doubt that. I am no fool, Mr. Baley."

"You are also no judge, perhaps, of yourself and your motives. People sometimes are not. You may be dramatizing yourself for some reason."

"I don't think so."

"Then tell me your motive. What is it? Tell me!"

"Not so quickly, Mr. Baley. It's not easy to explain it. ——Could you come outside with me?"

Baley looked quickly toward the window. Outside?

The sun had sunk lower in the sky and the room was the sunnier for it. He hesitated, then said, rather more loudly than was necessary, "Yes, I will!"

"Excellent," said Fastolfe. And then, with an added note of amiability, he added, "But perhaps you would care to visit the Personal first."

Baley thought for a moment. He felt no immediate urgency, but he did not know what might await him Outside, how long he would be expected to stay, what facilities there might or might not be there. Most of all, he did not know Auroran customs in this respect and he could not recall anything in the book-films he had viewed on the ship that served to enlighten him in this respect. It was safest, perhaps, to acquiesce in whatever one's host suggested.

"Thank you," he said, "if it will be convenient for me to do so."

Fastolfe nodded. "Daneel," he said, "show Mr. Baley to the Visitors' Personal."

Daneel said, "Partner Elijah, would you come with me?"

As they stepped together into the next room, Baley said, "I am sorry, Daneel, that you were not part of the conversation between myself and Dr. Fastolfe."

"It would not have been fitting, Partner Elijah. When you asked me a direct question, I answered, but I was not invited to take part fully."

"I would have issued the invitation, Daneel, if I did not feel constrained by my position as guest. I thought it might be wrong to take the initiative in this respect."

"I understand. ——This is the Visitors' Personal, Partner Elijah. The door will open at a touch of your hand anywhere upon it if the room in unoccupied."

Baley did not enter. He paused thoughtfully, then said, "If you had been invited to speak, Daneel, is there anything you would have said?

Any comment you would have cared to make? I would value your opinion, my friend."

Daneel said, with his usual gravity, "The one remark I care to make is that Dr. Fastolfe's statement that he had an excellent motive for placing Jander out of operation was unexpected to me. I do not know what the motive might be. Whatever he states to be his motive, however, you might ask why he would not have the same motive to put me in mental freeze-out. If they can believe he had a motive to put Jander out of operation, why would the same motive not apply to me? I would be curious to know."

Baley looked at the other sharply, seeking automatically for expression in a face not given to lack of control. He said, "Do you feel insecure, Daneel? Do you feel Fastolfe is a danger to you?"

Daneel said, "By the Third Law, I must protect my own existence, but I would not resist Dr. Fastolfe or any human being if it were their considered opinion that it was necessary to end my existence. That is the Second Law. However, I know that I am of great value, both in terms of investment of material, labor, and time, and in terms of scientific importance. It would therefore be necessary to explain to me carefully the reasons for the necessity of ending my existence. Dr. Fastolfe has never said anything to me—*never*, Partner Elijah—that would sound as though such a thing were in his mind. I do not believe it is remotely in his mind to end my existence or that it ever was in his mind to end Jander's existence. Random positronic drift must have ended Jander and may, someday, end me. There is always an element of chance in the Universe."

Baley said, "You say so, Fastolfe says so, and I believe so—but the difficulty is to persuade people generally to accept this view of the matter." He turned gloomily to the door of the Personal and said, "Are you coming in with me, Daneel?"

Daneel's expression contrived to seem amused. "It is flattering, Partner Elijah, to be taken for human to this extent. I have no need, of course."

"Of course. But you can enter anyway."

"It would not be appropriate for me to enter. It is not the custom for robots to enter the Personal. The interior of such a room is purely human. ——Besides, this is a one-person Personal."

"One person!" Momentarily, Baley was shocked. He rallied, however. Other worlds, other customs! And this one he did not recall being described in the book-films. He said, "That's what you meant, then, by saying that the door would open only if it were unoccupied. What if it is occupied, as it will be in a moment?"

"Then it will *not* open at a touch from outside, of course, and your privacy will be protected. Naturally, it will open at a touch from the inside."

"And what if a visitor fell into a faint, had a stroke or a heart seizure while in there and could not touch the door from inside. Wouldn't that mean no one could enter to help him?"

"There are emergency ways of opening the door, Partner Elijah, if that should seem advisable." Then, clearly disturbed, "Are you of the opinion that something of this sort will occur?"

"No, of course not. ——I am merely curious."

"I will be immediately outside the door," said Daneel uneasily. "If I hear a call, Partner Elijah, I will take action."

"I doubt that you'll have to." Baley touched the door, casually and lightly, with the back of his hand and it opened at once. He waited a moment or two to see if it would close. It didn't. He stepped through and the door then closed promptly.

While the door was open, the Personal had seemed like a room that flatly served its purpose. A sink, a stall (presumably equipped with a shower arrangement), a tub, a translucent half-door with a toilet seat beyond in all likelihood. There were several devices that he did not quite recognize. He assumed they were intended for the fulfilment of personal services of one sort or another.

He had little chance to study any of these, for in a moment it was all gone and he was left to wonder if what he had seen had really been there at all or if the devices had seemed to exist because they were what he had expected to see.

As the door closed, the room darkened, for there was no window. When the door was completely closed, the room lit up again, but nothing of what he had seen returned. It was daylight and he was Outside—or so it appeared.

There was open sky above, with clouds drifting across it in a fashion just regular enough to seem clearly unreal. On every side there seemed an outstretching of greenery moving in equally repetitive fashion.

He felt the familiar knotting of his stomach that arose whenever he found himself Outside—but he was *not* Outside. He had walked into a windowless room. It had to be a trick of the lighting.

He stared directly ahead of him and slowly slid his feet forward. He put his hands out before him. Slowly. Staring hard.

His hands touched the smoothness of a wall. He followed the flatness to either side. He touched what he had seen to be a sink in that moment of original vision and, guided by his hands, he could see it now—faintly, faintly against the overpowering sensation of light.

He found the faucet, but no water came from it. He followed its curve backward and found nothing that was the equivalent of the familiar handles that would control the flow of water. He did find an oblong strip whose slight roughness marked it off from the surrounding wall. As his fingers slid along it, he pushed slightly and experimentally against it and at once the greenery, which stretched far beyond the plane along which his fingers told him the wall existed, was parted by a rivulet of water, falling quickly from a height toward his feet with a loud noise of splashing.

He jumped backward in automatic panic, but the water ended before it reached his feet. It didn't stop coming, but it didn't reach the floor. He put his hand out. It was not water, but a light-illusion of water. It did not wet his hand; he felt nothing. But his eyes stubbornly resisted the evidence. They saw water.

He followed the rivulet upward and eventually came to something that *was* water—a thinner stream issuing from the faucet. It was cold.

His fingers found the oblong again and experimented, pushing here and there. The temperature shifted quickly and he found the spot that produced water of suitable tepidity.

He did not find any soap. Somewhat reluctantly, he began to rub his unsoaped hands against each other under what seemed a natural spring that should have been soaking him from head to foot but did not. And as though the mechanism could read his mind or, more likely, was guided by the rubbing together of his hands, he felt the water grow soapy, while the spring he did/didn't see grew bubbles and developed into foam.

Still reluctant, he bent over the sink and rubbed his face with the same soapy water. He felt the bristles of his beard, but knew that there was no way in which he could translate the equipment of this room into a shave without instruction.

He finished and held his hands helplessly under the water. How did he stop the soap? He did not have to ask. Presumably, his hands, no longer rubbing either themselves or his face, controlled that. The water lost its soapy feel and the soap was rinsed from his hands. He splashed the water against his face—without rubbing—and that was rinsed too. Without the help of vision and with the clumsiness of one unused to the process, he managed to soak his shirt badly.

Towels? Paper?

He stepped back, eyes closed, holding his head forward to avoid dripping more water on his clothes. Stepping back was, apparently, the key action, for he felt the warm flow of an air current. He placed his face within it and then his hands.

He opened his eyes and found the spring no longer flowing. He used his hands and found that he could feel no real water.

The knot in his stomach had long since dissolved into irritation. He recognized that Personals varied enormously from world to world, but somehow this nonsense of simulated Outside went too far.

On Earth, a Personal was a huge community chamber restricted to one gender, with private cubicles to which one had a key. On Solaria, one entered a Personal through a narrow corridor appended to one side of a house, as though Solarians hoped that it would not be considered a part of their home. In both worlds, however, though so different in every possible way, the Personals were clearly defined and the function of everything in them could not be mistaken. Why should there be, on Aurora, this elaborate pretense of rusticity that totally masked every part of a Personal?

Why?

At any rate, his annoyance gave him little emotional room in which to feel uneasy over the pretense of Outside. He moved in the direction in which he recalled having seen the translucent half-door.

It was not the correct direction. He found it only by following the wall slowly and after barking various parts of his body against protuberances.

In the end, he found himself urinating into the illusion of a small pond that did not seem to be receiving the stream properly. His knees told him that he was aiming correctly between the sides of what he took to be a urinal and he told himself that if he were using the wrong receptacle or misjudging his aim, the fault was not his.

For a moment, when done, he considered finding the sink again for a final hand rinse and decided against it. He just couldn't face the search and the false waterfall.

Instead, he found, by groping, the door through which he had entered, but he did not know he had found it until his hand touch resulted in its opening. The light died out at once and the normal nonillusory gleam of day surrounded him.

Daneel was waiting for him, along with Fastolfe and Giskard.

Fastolfe said, "You took nearly twenty minutes. We were beginning to fear for you."

Baley felt himself grow warm with rage. "I had problems with your foolish illusions," he said in a tightly controlled fashion.

Fastolfe's mouth pursed and his eyebrows rose in a silent: Oh-h!

He said, "There is a contact just inside the door that controls the illusion. It can make it dimmer and allow you to see reality through it—or it can wipe out the illusion altogether, if you wish."

"I was not told. Are all your Personals like this?"

Fastolfe said, "No. Personals on Aurora commonly possess illusory qualities, but the nature of the illusion varies with the individual. The illusion of natural greenery pleases me and I vary its details from time to time. One grows tired of anything, you know, after a while. There are some people who make use of erotic illusions, but that is not to my taste.

"Of course, when one is familiar with Personals, the illusions offer no trouble. The rooms are quite standard and one knows where everything is. It's no worse than moving about a well-known place in the dark. —But tell me, Mr. Baley, why didn't you find your way out and ask for directions?"

Baley said, "Because I didn't wish to. I admit that I was extremely irritated over the illusions, but I accepted them. After all, it was Daneel who led me to the Personal and he gave me no instructions, nor any warning. He would certainly have instructed me at length, if he had been left to his own devices, for he would surely have foreseen harm to me otherwise. I had to assume, therefore, that you had carefully instructed him not to warn me and, since I didn't really expect you to play a practical joke on me, I had to assume that you had a serious purpose in doing so."

"Oh?"

"After all, you had asked me to come Outside and, when I agreed, you immediately asked me if I wished to visit the Personal. I decided that the purpose of sending me into an illusion of Outside was to see whether I could endure it—or if I would come running out in panic. If I could endure it, I might be trusted with the real thing. Well, I endured it. I'm a little wet, thank you, but that will dry soon enough."

Fastolfe said, "You are a clear-thinking person, Mr. Baley. I apologize for the nature of the test and for the discomfort I caused you. I was merely trying to ward off the possibility of far greater discomfort. Do you still wish to come out with me?"

"I not only wish it, Dr. Fastolfe. I insist on it."

20

They made their way through a corridor, with Daneel and Giskard following close behind.

Fastolfe said chattily, "I hope you won't mind the robots accompanying us. Aurorans never go anywhere without at least one robot in attendance and, in your case in particular, I must insist that Daneel and Giskard be with you at all times."

He opened a door and Baley tried to stand firm against the beat of sunshine and wind, to say nothing of the envelopment of the strange and subtly alien smell of Aurora's land.

Fastolfe stayed to one side and Giskard went out first. The robot looked keenly about for a few moments. One had the impression that all his senses were intently engaged. He looked back and Daneel joined him and did the same.

"Leave them for a moment, Mr. Baley," said Fastolfe, "and they will tell us when they think it safe for us to emerge. Let me take the opportunity of once again apologizing for the scurvy trick I played on you with respect to the Personal. I assure you we would have known if you were in trouble—your various vital signs were being recorded. I am very pleased, though not entirely surprised, that you penetrated my purpose." He smiled and, with almost unnoticeable hesitation, placed his hand upon Baley's left shoulder and gave it a friendly squeeze.

Baley held himself stiffly. "You seem to have forgotten your earlier scurvy trick—your apparent attack on me with the spicer. If you will assure me that we will now deal with each other frankly and honestly, I will consider these matters as having been of reasonable intent."

"Done!"

"Is it safe to leave now?" Baley looked out to where Giskard and Daneel had moved farther and had separated from each other to right and left, still watching and sensing.

"Not quite yet. They will move all around the establishment. —Daneel tells me that you invited him into the Personal with you. Was that seriously meant?"

"Yes. I knew he had no need, but I felt it might be impolite to exclude him. I wasn't sure of Auroran custom in that respect, despite all the reading I did on Auroran matters."

"I suppose that isn't one of those things Aurorans feel necessary to mention and of course one can't expect the books to make any attempt to prepare visiting Earthmen concerning these subjects——"

"Because there are so few visiting Earthmen?"

"Exactly. The point is, of course, that robots never visit Personals. It is the one place where human beings can be free of them. I suppose there is the feeling that one should feel free of them at some periods and in some places."

Baley said, "And yet when Daneel was on Earth on the occasion of Sarton's death three years ago, I tried to keep him out of the Community Personal by saying he had no need. Still, he insisted on entering."

"And rightly so. He was, on that occasion, strictly instructed to give no indication he was not human, for reasons you well remember. Here on Aurora, however——Ah, they are done."

The robots were coming toward the door and Daneel gestured them outward.

Fastolfe held out his arm to bar Baley's way. "If you don't mind, Mr. Baley, I will go out first. Count to one hundred patiently and then join us."

21

Baley, on the count of one hundred, stepped out firmly and walked toward Fastolfe. His face was perhaps too stiff, his jaws too tightly clenched, his back too straight.

He looked about. The scene was not very different from that which had been presented in the Personal. Fastolfe had, perhaps, used his own grounds as a model. Everywhere there was green and in one place there was a stream filtering down a slope. It was, perhaps, artificial, but it was not an illusion. The water was real. He could feel the spray when he passed near it.

There was somehow a tameness to it all. The Outside on Earth seemed wilder and more grandly beautiful, what little Baley had seen of it.

Fastolfe said, with a gentle touch on Baley's upper arm and a motion of his hand, "Come in this direction. Look there!"

A space between two trees revealed an expanse of lawn.

For the first time, there was a sense of distance and on the horizon one could see a dwelling place: low-roofed, broad, and so green in color that it almost melted into the countryside.

"This is a residential area," said Fastolfe. "It might not seem so to you, since you are accustomed to Earth's tremendous hives, but we are in the Auroran city of Eos, which is actually the administrative center of the planet. There are twenty thousand human beings living here, which makes it the largest city, not only on Aurora but on all the Spacer worlds. There are as many people in Eos as on all of Solaria." Fastolfe said it with pride.

"How many robots, Dr. Fastolfe?"

"In this area? Perhaps a hundred thousand. On the planet as a whole, there are fifty robots to each human being on the average, not ten thousand per human as on Solaria. Most of our robots are on our farms, in our mines, in our factories, in space. If anything, we suffer from a shortage of robots, particularly of household robots. Most Aurorans make do with two or three such robots, some with only one. Still, we don't want to move in the direction of Solaria."

"How many human beings have no household robots at all?"

"None at all. That would not be in the public interest. If a human being, for any reason, could not afford a robot, he or she would be granted one which would be maintained, if necessary, at public expense."

"What happens as the population rises? Do you add more robots?"

Fastolfe shook his head. "The population does not rise. Aurora's population is two hundred million and that has remained stable for three centuries. It is the number desired. Surely you have read that in the books you viewed."

"Yes, I have," admitted Baley, "but I found it difficult to believe."

"Let me assure you it's true. It gives each of us ample land, ample space, ample privacy, and an ample share of the world's resources. There are neither too many people as on Earth, nor too few as on

Solaria." He held out his arm for Baley to take, so they might continue walking.

"What you see," Fastolfe said, "is a tame world. It is what I have brought you out to show you, Mr. Baley."

"There is no danger in it?"

"Always *some* danger. We do have storms, rock slides, earthquakes, blizzards, avalanches, a volcano or two—Accidental death can never be entirely done away with. And there are even the passions of angry or envious persons, the follies of the immature, and the madness of the shortsighted. These things are very minor irritants, however, and do not much affect the civilized quiet that rests upon our world."

Fastolfe seemed to ruminate over his words for a moment, then he sighed and said, "I can scarcely want it to be any other way, but I have certain intellectual reservations. We have brought here to Aurora only those plants and animals we felt would be useful, ornamental, or both. We did our best to eliminate anything we would consider weeds, vermin, or even less than standard. We selected strong, healthy, and attractive human beings, according to our own views, of course. We have tried——But you smile, Mr. Baley."

Baley had not. His mouth had merely twitched. "No, no,' he said. "There is nothing to smile about."

"There is, for I know as well as you do that I myself am not attractive by Auroran standards. The trouble is that we cannot altogether control gene combinations and intrauterine influences. Nowadays, of course, with ectogenesis becoming more common—though I hope it shall never be as common as it is on Solaria—I would be eliminated in the late fetal stage."

"In which case, Dr. Fastolfe, the worlds would have lost a great theoretical roboticist."

"Perfectly correct," said Fastolfe, without visible embarrassment, "but the worlds would never have known that, would they? ——In any case, we have labored to set up a very simple but completely workable ecological balance, an equable climate, a fertile soil, and resources as evenly distributed as is possible. The result is a world that produces all of everything that we need and that is, if I may personify, considerate of our wants. ——Shall I tell you the ideal for which we have striven?"

"Please do," said Baley.

"We have labored to produce a planet which, taken as a whole, would obey the Three Laws of Robotics. It does nothing to harm human beings, either by commission or omission. It does what we want it to do, as long as we do not ask it to harm human beings. And it protects itself, except at times and in places where it must serve us or save us even at the price of harm to itself. Nowhere else, neither on Earth nor in the other Spacer worlds, is this so nearly true as here on Aurora."

Baley said sadly, "Earthmen, too, have longed for this, but we have long since grown too numerous and we have too greatly damaged our planet in the days of our ignorance to be able to do very much about it now. ——But what of Aurora's indigenous life-forms? Surely you did not come to a dead planet."

Fastolfe said, "You know we didn't, if you have viewed books on our history. Aurora had vegetation and animal life when we arrived— and a nitrogen-oxygen atmosphere. This was true of all the fifty Spacer worlds. Peculiarly, in every case, the life-forms were sparse and not very varied. Nor were they particularly tenacious in their hold on their own planet. We took over, so to speak, without a struggle—and what is left of the indigenous life is in our aquaria, our zoos, and in a few carefully maintained primeval areas.

"We do not really understand why the life-bearing planets that human beings have encountered have been so feebly life-bearing, why only Earth itself has been overflowing with madly tenacious varieties of life filling every environmental niche, and why only Earth has developed any sign of intelligence whatever."

Baley said, "Maybe it is coincidence, the accident of incomplete exploration. We know so few planets so far."

"I admit," said Fastolfe, "that that is the most likely explanation. Somewhere there may be an ecological balance as complex as that of Earth. Somewhere there may be intelligent life and a technological civilization. Yet Earth's life and intelligence has spread outward for parsecs in every direction. If there is life and intelligence elsewhere, why have they not spread out as well—and why have we not encountered each other?"

"That might happen tomorrow, for all we know."

"It might. And if such an encounter is imminent, all the more reason why we should not be passively waiting. For we are growing passive, Mr. Baley. No new Spacer world has been settled in two and a half centuries. Our worlds are so tame, so delightful, we do not wish to leave them. This world was originally settled, you see, because Earth had grown so unpleasant that the risks and dangers of new and empty worlds seemed preferable by comparison. By the time our fifty Spacer worlds were developed—Solaria last of all— there was no longer any push, any need to move out elsewhere. And Earth itself had retreated to its underground caves of steel. The End. Finis."

"You don't really mean that."

"If we stay as we are? If we remain placid and comfortable and unmoving? Yes, I do mean that. Humanity must expand its range somehow if it is to flourish. One method of expansion is through space, through a constant pioneering reach toward other worlds. If we fail in this, some other civilization that is undergoing such expansion will reach us and we will not be able to stand against its dynamism."

"You expect a space war—like a hyperwave shoot-'em-up."

"No, I doubt that that would be necessary. A civilization that is expanding through space will not need our few worlds and will probably be too intellectually advanced to feel the need to batter its way into hegemony here. If, however, we are surrounded by a more lively, a more vibrant civilization, we will wither away by the mere force of the comparison; we will die of the realization of what we have become and of the potential we have wasted. Of course, we might substitute other expansions—an expansion of scientific understanding or of cultural vigor, for instance. I fear, however, that these expansions are not separable. To fade in one is to fade in all. Certainly, we are fading in all. We live too long. We are too comfortable."

Baley said, "On Earth, we think of Spacers as all-powerful, as totally self-confident. I cannot believe I'm hearing this from one of you."

"You won't from any other Spacer. My views are unfashionable. Others would find them intolerable and I don't often speak of such things to Aurorans. Instead, I simply talk about a new drive for further settlement, without expressing my fears of the catastrophes which will result if we abandon colonization. In that, at least, I have been winning. Aurora has been seriously—even enthusiastically—considering a new era of exploration and settlement."

"You say that," said Baley, "without any noticeable enthusiasm. What's wrong?"

"It's just that we are approaching my motive for the destruction of Jander Panell."

Fastolfe paused, shook his head, and continued, "I wish, Mr. Baley, I could understand human beings better. I have spent six decades in studying the intricacies of the positronic brain and I expect to spend fifteen to twenty more on the problem. In this time, I have barely brushed against the problem of the *human* brain, which is enormously more intricate. Are there Laws of Humanics as there are Laws of Robotics? How many Laws of Humanics might there be and how can they be expressed mathematically? I don't know.

"Perhaps, though, there may come a day when someone will work out the Laws of Humanics and then be able to predict the broad strokes of the future, and *know* what might be in store for humanity, instead of merely guessing as I do, and *know* what to do to make things better, instead of merely speculating. I dream sometimes of founding a mathematical science which I think of as 'psychohistory,' but I know I can't and I fear no one ever will."

He faded to a halt.

Baley waited, then said softly, "And your motive for the destruction of Jander Panell, Dr. Fastolfe?"

Fastolfe did not seem to hear the question. At any rate, he did not respond. He said, instead, "Daneel and Giskard are again signaling that all is clear. Tell me, Mr. Baley, would you consider walking with me farther afield?"

"Where?" asked Baley cautiously.

"Toward a neighboring establishment. In that direction, across the lawn. Would the openness disturb you?"

Baley pressed his lips together and looked in that direction, as though attempting to measure its effect. "I believe I could endure it. I anticipate no trouble."

Giskard, who was close enough to hear, now approached still closer, his eyes showing no glow in the daylight. If his voice was without human emotion, his words marked his concern. "Sir, may I remind you that on the journey here you suffered serious discomfort on the descent to the planet?"

Baley turned to face him. However he might feel toward Daneel, whatever warmth of past association might paper over his attitude toward robots, there was none here. He found the more primitive Giskard distinctly repellent. He labored to fight down the touch of anger he felt and said, "I was incautious aboard ship, boy, because I was overly curious. I faced a vision I had never experienced before and I had no time for adjustment. This is different."

"Sir, do you feel discomfort now? May I be assured of that?"

"Whether I do or not," said Baley firmly (reminding himself that the robot was helplessly in the grip of the First Law and trying to be polite to a lump of metal who, after all, had Baley's welfare as his only care) "doesn't matter. I have my duty to perform and that cannot be done if I am to hide in enclosures."

"Your duty?" Giskard said it as though he had not been programmed to understand the word.

Baley looked quickly in Fastolfe's direction, but Fastolfe stood quietly in his place and made no move to intervene. He seemed to be listening with abstracted interest, as though weighing the reaction of a robot of a given type to a new situation and comparing it with relationships, variables, constants, and differential equations only he understood.

Or so Baley thought. He felt annoyed at being part of an observation of that type and said (perhaps too sharply, he knew), "Do you know what 'duty' means?"

"That which should be done, sir," said Giskard.

"Your duty is to obey the Laws of Robotics. And human beings have their laws, too—as your master, Dr. Fastolfe, was only this moment saying—which must be obeyed. I must do that which I have been assigned to do. It is important."

"But to go into the open when you are not——"

"It must be done, nevertheless. My son may someday go to another planet, one much less comfortable than this one, and expose himself to the Outside for the rest of his life. And if I could, I would go with him."

"But why would you do that?"

"I have told you. I consider it my duty."

"Sir, I cannot disobey the Laws. Can you disobey yours? For I must urge you to——"

"I can choose not to do my duty, but I do not choose to—and that is sometimes the stronger compulsion, Giskard."

There was silence for a moment and then Giskard said, "Would it do you harm if I were to succeed in persuading you not to walk into the open?"

"Insofar as I would then feel I have failed in my duty, it would."

"More harm than any discomfort you might feel in the open?"

"Much more."

"Thank you for explaining this, sir," said Giskard and Baley imagined there was a look of satisfaction on the robot's largely expressionless face. (The human tendency to personify was irrepressible.)

Giskard stepped back and now Dr. Fastolfe spoke. "That was interesting, Mr. Baley. Giskard needed instructions before he could quite understand how to arrange the positronic potential response to the Three Laws or, rather, how those potentials were to arrange themselves in the light of the situation. Now he knows how to behave."

Baley said, "I notice that Daneel asked no questions."

Fastolfe said, "Daneel knows you. He has been with you on Earth and on Solaria. ——But come, shall we walk? Let us move slowly. Look about carefully and, if at any time you should wish to rest, to wait, even to turn back, I will count on you to let me know."

"I will, but what is the purpose of this walk? Since you anticipate possible discomfort on my part, you cannot be suggesting it idly."

"I am not," said Fastolfe. "I think you will want to see the inert body of Jander."

"As a matter of form, yes, but I rather think it will tell me nothing."

"I'm sure of that, but then you might also have the opportunity to question the one who was Jander's quasi-owner at the time of the tragedy. Surely you would like to speak to some human being other than myself concerning the matter."

22

Fastolfe moved slowly forward, plucking a leaf from a shrub that he passed, bending it in two, and nibbling at it.

Baley looked at him curiously, wondering how Spacers could put something untreated, unheated, even unwashed into their mouths, when they feared infection so badly. He remembered that Aurora was free (*entirely* free?) of pathogenic microorganisms, but found the action repulsive anyway. Repulsion did not have to have a rational basis, he thought defensively—and suddenly found himself on the edge of excusing the Spacers their attitude toward Earthmen.

He drew back! That was different! Human beings were involved there!

Giskard moved ahead, forward and toward the right. Daneel lagged behind and toward the left. Aurora's orange sun (Baley scarcely noted the orange tinge now) was mildly warm on his back, lacking the febrile heat that Earth's sun had in summer (but, then, what was the climate and season on this portion of Aurora right now?).

The grass or whatever it was (it looked like grass) was a bit stiffer and springier than he recalled it being on Earth and the ground was hard, as though it had not rained for a while.

They were moving toward the house up ahead, presumably the house of Jander's quasi-owner.

Baley could hear the rustle of some animal in the grass to the right, the sudden chirrup of a bird somewhere in a tree behind him, the small unplaceable clatter of insects all about. These, he told himself, were all animals with ancestors that had once lived on Earth. They had no way of knowing that this patch of ground they inhabited was not all there was—forever and forever back in time. The very trees and grass had arisen from other trees and grass that had once grown on Earth.

Only human beings could live on this world and know that they were not autochthonous but had stemmed from Earthmen—and yet did the Spacers really know it or did they simply put it out of their mind? Would the time come, perhaps, when they would not know it at all? When they would not remember which world they had come from or whether there was a world of origin at all?

"Dr. Fastolfe," he said suddenly, in part to break the chain of thought that he found to be growing oppressive, "you still have not told me your motive for the destruction of Jander."

"True! I have not! ——Now why do you suppose, Mr. Baley, I have labored to work out the theoretical basis for the positronic brains of humaniform robots?"

"I cannot say."

"Well, think. The task is to design a robotic brain as close to the human as possible and that would require, it would seem, a certain reach into the poetic——" He paused and his small smile became an outright grin. "You know it always bothers some of my colleagues when I tell them that, if a conclusion is not poetically balanced, it cannot be scientifically true. They tell me they don't know what that means."

Baley said, "I'm afraid I don't, either."

"But I know what it means. I can't explain it, but I feel the explanation without being able to put it into words, which may be why I have achieved results my colleagues have not. However, I grow grandiose, which is a good sign I should become prosaic. To imitate a human brain, when I know almost nothing about the workings of the human brain, needs an intuitive leap—something that feels to me like poetry. And the same intuitive leap that would give me the humaniform positronic brain should surely give me a new access of knowledge about the human brain itself. That was my belief—that through humaniformity I might take at least a small step toward the psychohistory I told you about."

"I see."

"And if I succeeded in working out a theoretical structure that would imply a humaniform positronic brain, I would need a humaniform body to place it in. The brain does not exist by itself, you understand. It interacts with the body, so that a humaniform brain in a nonhumaniform body would become, to an extent, itself nonhuman."

"Are you sure of that?"

"Quite. You have only to compare Daneel with Giskard."

"Then Daneel was constructed as an experimental device for furthering the understanding of the human brain?"

"You have it. I labored two decades at the task with Sarton. There were numerous failures that had to be discarded. Daneel was the first true success and, of course, I kept him for further study—and out of"—he grinned lopsidedly, as though admitting to something silly—"affection. After all, Daneel can grasp the notion of human duty, while Giskard, with all his virtues, has trouble doing so. You saw."

"And Daneel's stay on Earth with me, three years ago, was his first assigned task?"

"His first of any importance, yes. When Sarton was murdered, we needed something that was a robot and could withstand the infectious diseases of Earth and yet looked enough like a man to get around the antirobotic prejudices of Earth's people."

"An astonishing coincidence that Daneel should be right at hand at that time."

"Oh? Do you believe in coincidences? It is my feeling that any time at which a development as revolutionary as the humaniform robot came into being, some task that would require its use would present itself. Similar tasks had probably been presenting themselves regularly in all the years that Daneel did not exist—and because Daneel did not exist, other solutions and devices had to be used."

"And have your labors been successful, Dr. Fastolfe? Do you now understand the human brain better than you did?"

Fastolfe had been moving more and more slowly and Baley had been matching his progress to the other's. They were now standing still, about halfway between Fastolfe's establishment and the other's. It was the most difficult point for Baley, since it was equally distant from protection in either direction, but he fought down the growing uneasiness, determined not to provoke Giskard. He did not wish by some motion or outcry—or even expression—to activate the inconvenience of Giskard's desire to save him. He did not want to have himself lifted up and carried off to shelter.

Fastolfe showed no sign of understanding Baley's difficulty. He said, "There's no question but that advances in mentology have been carried through. There remain enormous problems and perhaps these will always remain, but there has been progress. Still——"

"Still?"

"Still, Aurora is not satisfied with a purely theoretical study of the human brain. Uses for humaniform robots have been advanced that I do not approve of."

"Such as the use on Earth."

"No, that was a brief experiment that I rather approved of and was even fascinated by. Could Daneel fool Earthpeople? It turned out he could, though, of course, the eyes of Earthmen for robots are not very keen. Daneel cannot fool the eyes of Aurorans, though I dare say future humaniform robots could be improved to the point where they would. There are other tasks that have been proposed, however."

"Such as?"

Fastolfe gazed thoughtfully into the distance. "I told you this world was tame. When I began my movement to encourage a renewed period of exploration and settlement, it was not to the supercomfortable Aurorans—or Spacers generally—that I looked for leadership. I rather thought we ought to encourage Earthmen to take the lead. With their horrid world—excuse me—and short life-span, they have so little to lose, I thought that they would surely welcome the chance, especially if we were to help them technologically. I spoke to you about such a thing when I saw you on Earth three years ago. Do you remember?" He looked sidelong at Baley.

Baley said stolidly, "I remember quite well. In fact, you started a chain of thought in me that has resulted in a small movement on Earth in that very direction."

"Indeed? It would not be easy, I imagine. There is the claustrophilia of you Earthmen, your dislike of leaving your walls."

"We are fighting it, Dr. Fastolfe. Our organization is planning to move out into space. My son is a leader in the movement and I hope the day may come when he leaves Earth at the head of an expedition to settle a new world. If we do indeed receive the technological help you speak of——" Baley let that dangle.

"If we supplied the ships, you mean?"

"And other equipment. Yes, Dr. Fastolfe."

"There are difficulties. Many Aurorans do not want Earthmen to move outward and settle new worlds. They fear the rapid spread of Earthish culture, its beehive Cities, its chaoticism." He stirred uneasily and said, "Why are we standing here, I wonder? Let's move on."

He walked slowly forward and said, "I have argued that that would not be the way it would be. I have pointed out that the settlers from Earth would not be Earthmen in the classical mode. They would not be enclosed in Cities. Coming to a new world, they would be like the Auroran Fathers coming here. They would develop a manageable ecological balance and would be closer to Aurorans than to Earthmen in attitude."

"Would they not then develop all the weaknesses you find in Spacer culture, Dr. Fastolfe?"

"Perhaps not. They would learn from our mistakes. ——But that is academic, for something has developed which makes the argument moot."

"And what is that?"

"Why, the humaniform robot. You see, there are those who see the humaniform robot as the perfect settler. It is they who can build the new worlds."

Baley said, "You've always had robots. Do you mean this idea was never advanced before?"

"Oh, it was, but it was always clearly unworkable. Ordinary nonhumaniform robots, without immediate human supervision, building a world that would suit their own nonhumaniform selves, could not be expected to tame and build a world that would be suitable for the more delicate and flexible minds and bodies of human beings."

"Surely the world they would build would serve as a reasonable first approximation."

"Surely it would, Mr. Baley. It is a sign of Auroran decay, however, that there is an overwhelming feeling among our people that a reasonable first approximation is unreasonably insufficient. ——A group of humaniform robots, on the other hand, as closely resembling human beings in body and mind as possible, would succeed in building a

world which, in suiting themselves, would also inevitably suit Aurorans. Do you follow the reasoning?"

"Completely."

"They would build a world so well, you see, that when they are
done and Aurorans are finally willing to leave, our human beings will
step out of Aurora and into another Aurora. They will never have left
home; they will simply have another newer home, exactly like the
other one, in which to continue their decay. Do you follow that reasoning, too?"

"I see your point, but I take it that Aurorans do not."

"*May* not. I think I can argue the point effectively, if the opposition
does not destroy me politically via this matter of the destruction of
Jander. Do you see the motive attributed to me? I am supposed to
have embarked on a program of the destruction of humaniform robots
rather than allow them to be used to settle other planets. Or so my
enemies say."

It was Baley now who stopped walking. He looked thoughtfully at
Fastolfe and said, "You understand, Dr. Fastolfe, that it is to Earth's
interest that your point of view win out completely."

"And to your own interests as well, Mr. Baley."

"And to mine. But if I put myself to one side for the moment, it
still remains vital to my world that our people be allowed, encouraged, and helped to explore the Galaxy; that we retain as much of
our own ways as we are comfortable with; that we not be condemned to imprisonment on Earth forever, since there we can only
perish."

Fastolfe said, "Some of you, I think, will insist on remaining imprisoned."

"Of course. Perhaps almost all of us will. However, at least some of
us—as many of us as possible—will escape if given permission. ——It
is therefore my duty, not only as a representative of the law of a large
fraction of humanity but as an Earthman, plain and simple, to help
you clear your name, whether you are guilty or innocent. Nevertheless, I can throw myself wholeheartedly into this task only if I know
that, in fact, the accusations against you are unjustified."

"Of course! I understand."

"In the light, then, of what you have told me of the motive attributed to you, assure me once again that you did not do this thing."

Fastolfe said, "Mr. Baley, I understand completely that you have no
choice in this matter. I am quite aware that I can tell you, with im-
punity, that I am guilty and that you would still be compelled by the
nature of your needs and those of your world to work with me to mask
that fact. Indeed, if I were actually guilty, I would feel compelled to
tell you so, so that you could take that fact into consideration and,

knowing the truth, work the more efficiently to rescue me—and your-self. But I cannot do so, because the fact is I am innocent. However much appearances may be against me, I did not destroy Jander. Such a thing never entered my mind."

"Never?"

Fastolfe smiled sadly. "Oh, I may have thought once or twice that Aurora would have been better off if I had never worked out the in-genious notions that led to the development of the humaniform pos-itronic brain—or that it would be better off if such brains proved unstable and readily subject to mental freeze-out. But those were fu-gitive thoughts. Not for a split second did I contemplate bringing about Jander's destruction for this reason."

"Then we must destroy this motive that they attribute to you."

"Good. But how?"

"We could show that it serves no purpose. What good does it do to destroy Jander? More humaniform robots can be built. Thousands. Millions."

"I'm afraid that's not so, Mr. Baley. None can be built. I alone know how to design them, and, as long as robot colonization is a possible destiny, I refuse to build any more. Jander is gone and only Daneel is left."

"The secret will be discovered by others."

Fastolfe's chin went up. "I would like to see the roboticist capable of it. My enemies have established a Robotics Institute with no other purpose than to work out the methods behind the construction of a humaniform robot, but they won't succeed. They certainly haven't succeeded so far and I know they won't succeed."

Baley frowned. "If you are the only man who knows the secret of the humaniform robots, and if your enemies are desperate for it, will they not try to get it out of you?"

"Of course. By threatening my political existence, by perhaps ma-neuvering some punishment that will forbid my working in the field and thus putting an end to my professional existence as well, they hope to have me agree to share the secret with them. They may even have the Legislature direct me to share the secret on the pain of con-fiscation of property, imprisonment—who knows what? However, I have made up my mind to submit to anything—anything—rather than give in. But I don't want to have to, you understand."

"Do they know of your determination to resist?"

"I hope so. I have told them plainly enough. I presume they think I'm bluffing, that I'm not serious. ——But I am."

"But if they believe you, they might take more serious steps."

"What do you mean?"

"Steal your papers. Kidnap you. Torture you."

Fastolfe broke into a loud laugh and Baley flushed. He said, "I hate to sound like a hyperwave drama, but have you considered that?"

Fastolfe said, "Mr. Baley——First, my robots can protect me. It would take full-scale war to capture me or my work. Second, even if somehow they succeeded, not one of the roboticists opposed to me could bear to make it plain that the only way he could obtain the secret of the humaniform positronic brain is to steal it or force it from me. His or her professional reputation would be completely wiped out. Third, such things on Aurora are unheard of. The merest hint of an unprofessional attempt upon me would swing the Legislature—*and* public opinion—in my favor at once."

"Is that so?" muttered Baley, silently damning the fact of having to work in a culture whose details he simply didn't understand.

"Yes. Take my word for it. I wish they would try something of this melodramatic sort. I wish they were so incredibly stupid as to do so. In fact, Mr. Baley, I wish I could persuade you to go to them, worm your way into their confidence, and cajole them into mounting an attack on my establishment or waylaying me on an empty road—or anything of the sort that, I imagine, is common on Earth."

Baley said stiffly, "I don't think that would be my style."

"I don't think so, either, so I have no intention of trying to implement my wish. And believe me, that is too bad, for if we cannot persuade them to try the suicidal method of force, they will continue to do something much better, from their standpoint. They will destroy me by falsehoods."

"What falsehoods?"

"It is not just the destruction of one robot they attribute to me. That is bad enough and just might suffice. They are whispering—it is only a whisper as yet—that the death is merely an experiment of mine and a dangerous, successful one. They whisper that I am working out a system for destroying humaniform brains rapidly and efficiently, so that when my enemies *do* create their own humaniform robots, I, together with members of my party, will be able to destroy them all, thus preventing Aurora from settling new worlds and leaving the Galaxy to my Earthmen confederates."

"Surely there can be no truth in this."

"Of course not. I told you these are lies. And ridiculous lies, too. No such method of destruction is even theoretically possible and the Robotics Institute people are not on the point of creating their own humaniform robots. I cannot conceivably indulge in an orgy of mass destruction even if I wanted to. I *cannot.*"

"Doesn't the whole thing fall by its own weight, then?"

"Unfortunately, it's not likely to do so in time. It may be silly nonsense, but it will probably last long enough to sway public opinion against me to the point of swinging just enough votes in the Legislature to defeat me. Eventually, it will all be recognized as nonsense, but by then it will be too late. And please notice that Earth is being used as a whipping boy in this. The charge that I am laboring on behalf of Earth is a powerful one and many will choose to believe the whole farrago, against their own better sense, because of their dislike of Earth and Earthpeople."

Baley said, "What you're telling me is that active resentment against Earth is being built up."

Fastolfe said, "Exactly, Mr. Baley. The situation grows worse for me—and for Earth—every day and we have very little time.'

"But isn't there an easy way of knocking this thing on its head?" (Baley, in despair, decided it was time to fall back on Daneel's point.) "If you were indeed anxious to test a method for the destruction of a humaniform robot, why seek out one in another establishment, one with which it might be inconvenient to experiment? You had Daneel, himself, in your own establishment. He was at hand and convenient. Would not the experiment have been conducted upon him if there were any truth at all in the rumor?"

"No, no," said Fastolfe. "I couldn't get anyone to believe that. Daneel was my first success, my triumph. I wouldn't destroy him under any circumstances. Naturally, I would turn to Jander. Everyone would see that and I would be a fool to try to persuade them that it would have made more sense for me to sacrifice Daneel."

They were walking again, nearly at their destination. Baley was in deep silence, his face tight-lipped.

Fastolfe said, "How do you feel, Mr. Baley?"

Baley said in a low voice, "If you mean as far as being Outside is concerned, I am not even aware of it. If you mean as far as our dilemma is concerned, I think I am as close to giving up as I can possibly be without putting myself into an ultrasonic brain-dissolving chamber." Then passionately, "Why did you send for me, Dr. Fastolfe? Why have you given me this job? What have I ever done to you to be treated so?"

"Actually," said Fastolfe, "it was not my idea to begin with and I can only plead my desperation."

"Well, whose idea was it?"

"It was the owner of this establishment we have now reached who suggested it originally—and I had no better idea."

"The owner of this establishment? Why would he——"

"She."

"Well, then, why would she suggest anything of the sort?"

"Oh! I haven't explained that she knows you, have I, Mr. Baley? There she is, waiting for us now."

Baley looked up, bewildered.

"Jehoshaphat," he whispered.

23

The young woman who faced them said with a wan smile, "I knew that when I met you again, Elijah, that would be the first word I would hear."

Baley stared at her. She had changed. Her hair was shorter and her face was even more troubled now than it had been two years ago and seemed more than two years older, somehow. She was still unmistakably Gladia, however. There was still the triangular face, with its pronounced cheekbones and small chin. She was still short, still slight of figure, still vaguely childlike.

He had dreamed of her frequently—though not in an overtly erotic fashion—after returning to Earth. His dreams were always stories of not being able to quite reach her. She was always there, a little too far off to speak to easily. She never quite heard when he called her. She never grew nearer when he approached her.

It was not hard to understand why the dreams had been as they were. She was a Solarian-born person and, as such, was rarely supposed to be in the physical presence of other human beings.

Elijah had been forbidden to her because he was human—and beyond that (of course) because he was from Earth. Though the exigencies of the murder case he was investigating forced them to meet, throughout their relationship she was completely covered, when physically together, to prevent actual contact. And yet, at their last meeting, she had, in defiance of good sense, fleetingly touched his cheek with her bare hand. She must have known she could be infected as a result. He cherished the touch the more, for every aspect of her upbringing combined to make it unthinkable.

The dreams had faded in time.

Baley said, rather stupidly, "It was *you* who owned the——"

He paused and Gladia finished the sentence for him. "The robot. And two years ago, it was I who possessed the husband. Whatever I touch is destroyed."

Without really knowing what he was doing, Baley reached up to place his hand on his cheek. Gladia did not seem to notice.

She said, "You came to rescue me that first time. Forgive me, but I had to call on you again. ——Come in, Elijah. Come in, Dr. Fastolfe."

Fastolfe stepped back to allow Baley to walk in first. He followed.

Behind Fastolfe came Daneel and Giskard—and they, with the char-acteristic self-effacement of robots, stepped to unoccupied wall niches on opposite sides and remained silently standing, backs to the wall.

For one moment, it seemed that Gladia would treat them with the indifference with which human beings commonly treated robots. After a glance at Daneel, however, she turned away and said to Fastolfe in a voice that choked a little, "That one. Please. Ask him to leave."

Fastolfe said, with a small motion of surprise, "Daneel?"

"He's too—too Janderlike!"

Fastolfe turned to look at Daneel and a look of clear pain crossed his face momentarily. "Of course, my dear. You must forgive me. I did not think—Daneel, move into another room and remain there while we are here."

Without a word, Daneel left.

Gladia glanced a moment at Giskard, as though to judge whether he, also, was too Janderlike, and turned away with a small shrug.

She said, "Would either of you like refreshment of any kind? I have an excellent coconut drink, fresh and cold."

"No, Gladia," said Fastolfe. "I have merely brought Mr. Baley here as I promised I would. I will not stay long."

"If I may have a glass of water," said Baley, "I won't trouble you for anything more."

Gladia raised one hand. Undoubtedly, she was under observation, for, in a moment, a robot moved in noiselessly, with a glass of water on a tray and a small dish of what looked like crackers with a pinkish blob on each.

Baley could not forbear taking one, even though he was not certain what it might be. It had to be something Earth-descended, for he could not believe that on Aurora, he—or anyone—would be eating any portion of the planet's sparse indigenous biota or anything syn-thetic either. Nevertheless, the descendants of Earthly food species might change with time, either through deliberate cultivation or the action of a strange environment—and Fastolfe, at lunchtime, had said that much of the Auroran diet was an acquired taste.

He was pleasantly surprised. The taste was sharp and spicy, but he found it delightful and took a second almost at once. He said, "Thank you" to the robot (who would not have objected to standing there indefinitely) and took the entire dish, together with the glass of water.

The robot left.

It was late afternoon now and the sunlight came ruddily through the western windows. Baley had the impression that this house was smaller than Fastolfe's, but it would have been more cheerful had not the sad figure of Gladia standing in its midst provoked a dispiriting effect.

That might, of course, be Baley's imagination. Cheer, in any case, seemed to him impossible in any structure purporting to house and protect human beings that yet remained exposed to the Outside beyond each wall. Not one wall, he thought, had the warmth of human life on the other side. In no direction could one look for companionship and community. Through every outer wall, every side, top and bottom, there was inanimate world. Cold! Cold!

And coldness flooded back upon Baley himself as he thought again of the dilemma in which he found himself. (For a moment, the shock of meeting Gladia again had driven it from his mind.)

Gladia said, "Come. Sit down, Elijah. You must excuse me for not quite being myself. I am, for a second time, the center of a planetary sensation—and the first time was more than enough."

"I understand, Gladia. Please do not apologize," said Baley.

"And as for you, dear Doctor, please don't feel you need go."

"Well——" Fastolfe looked at the time strip on the wall. "I will stay for a short while, but then, my dear, there is work that must be done though the skies fall. All the more so, since I must look forward to a near future in which I may be restrained from doing any work at all."

Gladia blinked rapidly, as though holding back tears. "I know, Dr. Fastolfe. You are in deep trouble because of—of what happened here and I don't seem to have time to think of anything but my own—discomfort."

Fastolfe said, "I'll do my best to take care of my own problem, Gladia, and there is no need for you to feel guilt over the matter. ——Perhaps Mr. Baley will be able to help us both."

Baley pressed his lips together at that, then said heavily, "I was not aware, Gladia, that you were in any way involved in this affair."

"Who else would be?" she said with a sigh.

"You are—were—in possession of Jander Panell?"

"Not truly in possession. I had him on loan from Dr. Fastolfe."

"Were you with him when he——" Baley hesitated over some way of putting it.

"Died? Mightn't we say died? ——No, I was not. And before you ask, there was no one else in the house at the time. I was alone. I am usually alone. Almost always. That is my Solarian upbringing, you remember. Of course, that is not obligatory. You two are here and I do not mind—very much."

"And you were definitely alone at the time Jander died? No mistake?"

"I have said so," said Gladia, sounding a little irritated. "No, never mind, Elijah. I know you must have everything repeated and repeated. I *was* alone. Honestly."

"There were robots present, though."

"Yes, of course. When I say 'alone,' I mean there were no other human beings present."

"How many robots do you possess, Gladia? Not counting Jander."

Gladia paused as though she were counting internally. Finally, she said, "Twenty. Five in the house and fifteen on the grounds. Robots move freely between my house and Dr. Fastolfe's, too, so that it isn't always possible to judge, when a robot is quickly seen at either establishment, whether it is one of mine or one of his."

"Ah," said Baley, "and since Dr. Fastolfe has fifty-seven robots in his establishment, that means, if we combine the two, that there are seventy-seven robots available, altogether. Are there any other establishments whose robots may mingle with yours indistinguishably?"

Fastolfe said, "There's no other establishment near enough to make that practical. Nor is the practice of mixing robots really encouraged. Gladia and I are a special case because she is not Auroran and because I have taken rather a—responsibility for her."

"Even so. Seventy-seven robots," said Baley.

"Yes," said Fastolfe, "but why are you making this point?"

Baley said, "Because it means you can have any of seventy-seven moving objects, each vaguely human in form, that you are used to seeing out of the corner of the eye and to which you would pay no particular attention. Isn't it possible, Gladia, that if an actual human being were to penetrate the house, for whatever purpose, you would scarcely be aware of it? It would be one more moving object, vaguely human in form, and you would pay no attention."

Fastolfe chuckled softly and Gladia, unsmiling, shook her head.

"Elijah," she said, "one can tell you are an Earthman. Do you imagine that any human being, even Dr. Fastolfe here, could possibly approach my house without my being informed of the fact by my robots. I might ignore a moving form, assuming it to be a robot, but no robot ever would. I was waiting for you just now when you arrived, but that was because my robots had informed me you were approaching. No, no, when Jander died, there was no other human being in the house."

"Except yourself?"

"Except myself. Just as there was no one in the house except myself when my husband was killed."

Fastolfe interposed gently. "There is a difference, Gladia. Your husband was killed with a blunt instrument. The physical presence of the murderer was necessary and, if you were the only one present, that was serious. In this case, Jander was put out of operation by a subtle spoken program. Physical presence was not necessary. Your presence here alone means nothing, especially since you do not know how to block the mind of a humaniform robot."

They both turned to look at Baley, Fastolfe with a quizzical look on his face, Gladia with a sad one. (It irritated Baley that Fastolfe, whose future was as bleak as Baley's own, nevertheless seemed to face it with humor. What on Earth is there to the situation to cause one to laugh like an idiot? Baley thought morosely.)

"Ignorance," said Baley slowly, "may mean nothing. A person may not know how to get to a certain place and yet may just happen to reach it while walking blindly. One might talk to Jander and, all unknowingly, push the button for mental freeze-out."

Fastolfe said, "And the chances of that?"

"You're the expert, Dr. Fastolfe, and I suppose you will tell me they are very small."

"Incredibly small. A person may not know how to get to a certain place, but if the only route is a series of tight ropes stretched in sharply changing directions, what are the chances of reaching it by walking randomly while blindfolded?"

Gladia's hands fluttered in extreme agitation. She clenched her fists, as though to hold them steady, and brought them down on her knees. "I didn't do it, accident or not. I wasn't with him when it happened. I *wasn't*. I spoke to him in the morning. He was well, perfectly normal. Hours later, when I summoned him, he never came. I went in search of him and he was standing in his accustomed place, seeming quite normal. The trouble was, he didn't respond to me. He didn't respond at all. He has never responded since."

Baley said, "Could something you had said to him, quite in passing, have produced mind-freeze only after you had left him—an hour after, perhaps?"

Fastolfe interposed sharply, "Quite impossible, Mr. Baley. If mind-freeze is to take place, it takes place at once. Please do not badger Gladia in this fashion. She is incapable of producing mind-freeze deliberately and it is unthinkable that she would produce it accidentally."

"Isn't it unthinkable that it would be produced by random positronic drift, as you say it must have?"

"Not quite as unthinkable."

"Both alternatives are extremely unlikely. What is the difference in unthinkability?"

"A great one. I imagine that a mental freeze-out through positronic drift might have a probability of 1 in 10^{12}; that by accidental pattern-building 1 in 10^{100}. That is just an estimate, but a reasonable one. The difference is greater than that between a single electron and the entire Universe—and it is in favor of the positronic drift."

There was silence for a while.

Baley said, "Dr. Fastolfe, you said earlier that you couldn't stay long."

"I have stayed too long already."

"Good. Then would you leave now?"

Fastolfe began to rise, then said, "Why?"

"Because I want to speak to Gladia alone."

"To badger her?"

"I must question her without your interference. Our situation is entirely too serious to worry about politeness."

Gladia said, "I am not afraid of Mr. Baley, dear Doctor." She added wistfully, "My robots will protect me if his impoliteness becomes extreme."

Fastolfe smiled and said, "Very well, Gladia." He rose and held out his hand to her. She took it briefly.

He said, "I would like to have Giskard remain here for general protection—and Daneel will continue to be in the next room, if you don't mind. Could you lend me one of your own robots to escort me back to my establishment?"

"Certainly," said Gladia, raising her arms. "You know Pandion, I believe."

"Of course! A sturdy and reliable escort." He left, with the robot following closely.

Baley waited, watching Gladia, studying her. She sat there, her eyes on her hands, which were folded limply together in her lap.

Baley was certain there was more for her to tell. How he could persuade her to talk, he couldn't say, but of one thing more he was certain. While Fastolfe was there, she would not tell the whole truth.

24

Finally, Gladia looked up, her face like a little girl's. She said in a small voice, "How are you, Elijah? How do you feel?"

"Well enough, Gladia."

She said, "Dr. Fastolfe said he would lead you here across the open and see to it that you would have to wait some time in the worst of it."

"Oh? Why was that? For the fun of it?"

"No, Elijah. I had told him how you reacted to the open. You remember the time you fainted and fell into the pond?"

Elijah shook his head quickly. He could not deny the event or his memory thereof, but neither did he approve of the reference. He said gruffly, "I'm not quite like that anymore. I've improved."

"But Dr. Fastolfe said he would test you. Was it all right?"

"It was sufficiently all right. I didn't faint." He remembered the episode aboard the spaceship during the approach to Aurora and ground his teeth faintly. That was different and there was no call to discuss the matter.

He said, in a deliberate change of subject, "What do I call you here? How do I address you?"

"You've been calling me Gladia."

"It's inappropriate, perhaps. I could say Mrs. Delmarre, but you may have——"

She gasped and interrupted sharply, "I haven't used that name since arriving here. Please don't you use it."

"What do the Aurorans call you, then?"

"They say Gladia Solaria, but that's just an indication that I'm an alien and I don't want that either. I am simply Gladia. One name. It's not an Auroran name and I doubt that there's another one on this planet, so it's sufficient. I'll continue to call you Elijah, if you don't mind."

"I don't mind."

Gladia said, "I would like to serve tea." It was a statement and Baley nodded.

He said, "I didn't know that Spacers drank tea."

"It's not Earth tea. It's a plant extract that is pleasant but is not considered harmful in any way. We call it tea."

She lifted her arm and Baley noted that the sleeve held tightly at the wrist and that joining it were thin, flesh-colored gloves. She was still exposing the minimum of body surface in his presence. She was still minimizing the chance of infection.

Her arm remained in the air for a moment and, after a few more moments, a robot appeared with a tray. He was patently even more primitive than Giskard, but he distributed the teacups, the small sandwiches, and the bite-size bits of pastry smoothly. He poured tea with what amounted to grace.

Baley said curiously, "How do you do that, Gladia?"

"Do what, Elijah?"

"You lift your arm whenever you want something and the robots always know what it is. How did this one know you wanted tea served?"

"It's not difficult. Every time I lift my arm, it distorts a small electromagnetic field that is maintained continuously across the room. Slightly different positions of my hand and fingers produce different distortions and my robots can interpret these distortions as orders. I only use it for simple orders: Come here! Bring tea! and so on."

"I haven't noticed Dr. Fastolfe using the system at his establishment."

"It's not really Auroran. It's our system in Solaria and I'm used to it. ——Besides, I always have tea at this time. Borgraf expects it."

"This is Borgraf?" Baley eyed the robot with some interest, aware that he had only glanced at him before. Familiarity was quickly breeding indifference. Another day and he would not notice robots at all. They would flutter about him unseen and chores would appear to do themselves.

Nevertheless, he did not want to fail to notice them. He wanted them to fail to be there. He said, "Gladia, I want to be alone with you. Not even robots. ——Giskard, join Daneel. You can stand guard from there."

"Yes, sir," said Giskard, brought suddenly to awareness and response by the sound of his name.

Gladia seemed distantly amused. "You Earthpeople are so odd. I know you have robots on Earth, but you don't seem to know how to handle them. You *bark* your orders, as though they're deaf."

She turned to Borgraf and, in a low voice, said, "Borgraf, none of you are to enter the room until summoned. Do not interrupt us for anything short of a clear and present emergency."

Borgraf said, "Yes, ma'am." He stepped back, glanced over the table as though checking whether he had omitted anything, turned, and left the room.

Baley was amused, in his turn. Gladia's voice had been soft, but her tone had been as crisp as though she were a sergeant-major addressing a recruit. But then, why should he be surprised? He had long known that it was easier to see another's follies than one's own.

Gladia said, "We are now alone, Elijah. Even the robots are gone."

Baley said, "You are not afraid to be alone with me?"

Slowly, she shook her head. "Why should I be? A raised arm, a gesture, a startled outcry—and several robots would be here promptly. No one on any Spacer world has any reason to fear any other human being. This is not Earth. Whyever should you ask, anyway?"

"Because there are other fears than physical ones. I would not offer you violence of any kind or mistreat you physically in any way. But are you not afraid of my questioning and what it might uncover about you? Remember that this is not Solaria, either. On Solaria, I sympathized with you and was intent on demonstrating your innocence."

She said in a low voice, "Don't you sympathize with me now?"

"It's not a husband dead this time. You are not suspected of murder. It's only a robot that has been destroyed and, as far as I know, you are suspected of nothing. Instead, it is Dr. Fastolfe who is my problem. It is of the highest importance to me—for reasons I need not go into— that I be able to demonstrate *his* innocence. If the process turns out to be damaging to you, I will not be able to help it. I do not intend to go out of my way to save you pain. It is only fair that I tell you this."

She raised her head and fixed her eyes on his arrogantly. "Why should anything be damaging to me?"

"Perhaps we will now proceed to find out," said Baley coolly, "without Dr. Fastolfe present to interfere." He plucked one of the small sandwiches out of the dish with a small fork (there was no point in using his fingers and perhaps making the entire dish unusable to Gladia), scraped it off onto his own plate, popped it into his mouth, and then sipped at his tea.

She matched him sandwich for sandwich, sip for sip. If he were going to be cool, so was she, apparently.

"Gladia," said Baley, "it is important that I know, exactly, the relationship between you and Dr. Fastolfe. You live near him and the two of you form what is virtually a single robotic household. He is clearly concerned for you. He has made no effort to defend his own innocence, aside from the mere statement that he is innocent, but he defends you strongly the moment I harden my questioning."

Gladia smiled faintly. "What do you suspect, Elijah?"

Baley said, "Don't fence with me. I don't want to suspect. I want to know."

"Has Dr. Fastolfe mentioned Fanya?"

"Yes, he has."

"Have you asked him whether Fanya is his wife or merely his companion? Whether he has children?"

Baley stirred uneasily. He might have asked such questions, of course. In the close quarters of crowded Earth, however, privacy was cherished, precisely because it had all but perished. It was virtually impossible on Earth not to know all the facts about the family arrangements of others, so one never asked and pretended ignorance. It was a universally maintained fraud.

Here on Aurora, of course, the Earth ways would not hold, yet Baley automatically held with them. Stupid!

He said, "I have not yet asked. Tell me."

Gladia said, "Fanya is his wife. He has been married a number of times, consecutively of course, though simultaneous marriage for either or both sexes is not entirely unheard of on Aurora." The bit of mild distaste with which she said that brought an equally mild defense. "It *is* unheard of on Solaria.

"However, Dr. Fastolfe's current marriage will probably soon be dissolved. Both will then be free to make new attachments, though often either or both parties do not wait for dissolution to do that. ——I don't say I understand this casual way of treating the matter, Elijah, but it is how Aurorans build their relationships. Dr. Fastolfe, to my knowledge, is rather straitlaced. He always maintains one marriage or another and seeks nothing outside of it. On Aurora, that is considered old-fashioned and rather silly."

Baley nodded. "I've gathered something of this in my reading. Marriage takes place when there's the intention to have children, I understand."

"In theory, that is so, but I'm told hardly anyone takes that seriously these days. Dr. Fastolfe already has two children and can't have any more, but he still marries and applies for a third. He gets turned down, of course, and knows he will. Some people don't even bother to apply."

"Then why bother marrying?"

"There are social advantages to it. It's rather complicated and, not being an Auroran, I'm not sure I understand it."

"Well, never mind. Tell me about Dr. Fastolfe's children."

"He has two daughters by two different mothers. Neither of the mothers was Fanya, of course. He has no sons. Each daughter was incubated in the mother's womb, as is the fashion on Aurora. Both daughters are adults now and have their own establishments."

"Is he close with his daughters?"

"I don't know. He never talks about them. One is a roboticist and I suppose he *must* keep in touch with her work. I believe the other is running for office on the council of one of the cities or that she is actually in possession of the office. I don't really know."

"Do you know if there are family strains?"

"None that I am aware of, which may not go for much, Elijah. As far as I know, he is on civil terms with all his past wives. None of the dissolutions were carried through in anger. For one thing, Dr. Fastolfe is not that kind of person. I can't imagine him greeting anything in life with anything more extreme than a good-natured sigh of resignation. He'll joke on his deathbed."

That, at least, rang true, Baley thought. He said, "And Dr. Fastolfe's relationship to you. The truth, please. We are not in a position to dodge the truth in order to avoid embarrassment."

She looked up and met his eyes levelly. She said, "There is no embarrassment to avoid. Dr. Han Fastolfe is my friend, my very good friend."

"How good, Gladia?"

"As I said—very good."

"Are you waiting for the dissolution of his marriage so that you may be his next wife?"

"No." She said it very calmly.

"Are you lovers, then?"

"No."

"Have you been?"

"No. ——Are you surprised?"

"I merely need information," said Baley.

"Then let me answer your questions connectedly, Elijah, and don't bark them at me as though you expected to surprise me into telling you something I would otherwise keep secret." She said it without noticeable anger. It was almost as though she were amused.

Baley, flushing slightly, was about to say that this was not at all his intention, but, of course, it was and he would gain nothing by denying it. He said in a soft growl, "Well, then, go ahead."

The remains of the tea littered the table between them. Baley wondered if, under ordinary conditions, she would not have lifted her arm and bent it just so—and if the robot, Borgraf, would not have then entered silently and cleared the table.

Did the fact that the litter remained upset Gladia—and would it make her less self-controlled in her response? If so, it had better remain—but Baley did not really hope for much, for he could see no signs of Gladia being disturbed over the mess or even of her being aware of it.

Gladia's eyes had fallen to her lap again and her face seemed to sink lower and to become a touch harsh, as though she were reaching into a past she would much rather obliterate.

She said, "You caught a glimpse of my life on Solaria. It was not a happy one, but I knew no other. It was not until I experienced a touch of happiness that I suddenly knew exactly to what an extent—and how intensively—my earlier life was not happy. The first hint came through you, Elijah."

"Through me?" Baley was caught by surprise.

"Yes, Elijah. Our last meeting on Solaria—I hope you remember it, Elijah—taught me something. I touched you! I removed my glove, one that was similar to the glove I am wearing now, and I touched your cheek. The contact did not last long. I don't know what it meant to you—no, don't tell me, it's not important—but it meant a great deal to me."

She looked up, meeting his eyes defiantly. "It meant *everything* to me. It changed my life. Remember, Elijah, that until then, after my few years of childhood, I had never touched a man—or any human being, actually—except for my husband. And I touched my husband very rarely. I had *viewed* men on trimensic, of course, and in the process I had become entirely familiar with every physical aspect of males, every part of them. I had nothing to learn, in that respect.

"But I had no reason to think that one man felt much different from another. I knew what my husband's skin felt like, what his hands felt like when he could bring himself to touch me, what—everything. I had no reason to think that anything would be different with any man. There was no pleasure in contact with my husband, but why should there be? Is there particular pleasure in the contact of my fingers with this table, except to the extent that I might appreciate its physical smoothness?

"Contact with my husband was part of an occasional ritual that he went through because it was expected of him and, as a good Solarian, he therefore carried it through by the calendar and clock and for the length of time and in the manner prescribed by good breeding. Except that, in another sense, it wasn't good breeding, for although this periodic contact was for the precise purpose of sexual intercourse, my husband had not applied for a child and was not interested, I believe, in producing one. And I was too much in awe of him to apply for one on my own initiative, as would have been my right.

"As I look back on it, I can see that the sexual experience was perfunctory and mechanical. I never had an orgasm. Not once. That such a thing existed I gathered from some of my reading, but the descriptions merely puzzled me and—since they were to be found only in imported books—Solarian books never dealt with sex—I could not trust them. I thought they were merely exotic metaphors.

"Nor could I experiment—successfully, at least—with autoeroticism. Masturbation is, I think, the common word. At least, I have heard that word used on Aurora. On Solaria, of course, no aspect of sex is ever discussed, nor is any sex-related word used in polite society. —Nor is there any other kind of society on Solaria.

"From something I occasionally read, I had an idea of how one might go about masturbating and, on a number of occasions, I made a halfhearted attempt to do what was described. I could not carry it through. The taboo against touching human flesh made even my own seem forbidden and unpleasant to me. I could brush my hand against my side, cross one leg over another, feel the pressure of thigh against thigh, but these were casual touches, unregarded. To make the process of touch an instrument of deliberate pleasure was different. Every fiber of me knew it shouldn't be done and, because I knew that, the pleasure wouldn't come.

"And it never occurred to me, never once, that there might be pleasure in touching under other circumstances. Why should it occur to me? How could it occur to me?

"Until I touched you that time. Why I did, I don't know. I felt a gush of affection for you because you had saved me from being a murderess. And besides, you were not altogether forbidden. You were not a Solarian. You were not—forgive me—altogether a man. You were a creature of Earth. You were human in appearance, but you were short-lived and infection-prone, something to be dismissed as semihuman at best.

"So because you had saved me and were not really a man, I could touch you. And what's more, you looked at me not with the hostility and repugnance of my husband—or with the carefully schooled indifference of someone viewing me on trimensic. You were right there, palpable, and your eyes were warm and concerned. You actually trembled when my hand approached your cheek. I saw that.

"Why it was, I don't know. The touch was so fugitive and there was no way in which the physical sensation was different from what it would have been if I had touched my husband or any other man—or, perhaps, even any woman. But there was more to it than the physical sensation. You were there, you welcomed it, you showed me every sign of what I accepted as—affection. And when our skins—my hand, your cheek—made contact, it was as though I had touched gentle fire that made its way up my hand and arm instantaneously and set me all in flame.

"I don't know how long it lasted—it couldn't be for more than a moment or two—but for me time stood still. Something happened to me that had never happened to me before and, looking back on it long afterward, when I had learned about it, I realized that I had very nearly experienced an orgasm.

"I tried not to show it——"

(Baley, not daring to look at her, shook his head.)

"Well, then, I didn't show it. I said, 'Thank you, Elijah.' I said it for what you had done for me in connection with my husband's death. But I said it much more for lighting my life and showing me, without even knowing it, what there was in life; for opening a door; for revealing a path; for pointing out a horizon. The physical act was nothing in itself. Just a touch. But it was the beginning of everything."

Her voice had faded out and, for a moment, she said nothing, remembering.

Then one finger lifted. "No. Don't say anything. I'm not done yet.

"I had had imaginings before, very vague uncertain things. A man and I, doing what my husband and I did, but somehow different—I didn't even know different in what way—and feeling something different—something I could not even imagine when imagining with all my might. I might conceivably have gone through my whole life trying to imagine the unimaginable and I might have died as I suppose women on Solaria—and men, too—often do, never knowing, even after three or four centuries. Never knowing. Having children, but never knowing.

"But one touch of your cheek, Elijah, and I knew. Isn't that amazing? You taught me what I might imagine. Not the mechanics of it, not the dull, reluctant approach of bodies, but something that I could never have conceived as having anything to do with it. The look on a face, the sparkle in an eye, the feeling of—gentleness—kindness—something I can't even describe—acceptance—a lowering of the terrible barrier between individuals. Love, I suppose—a convenient word to encompass all of that and more.

"I felt love for you, Elijah, because I thought you could feel love for me. I don't say you loved me, but it seemed to me you could. I never had that and, although in ancient literature they talked of it, I didn't know what they meant any more than when men in those same books talked about 'honor' and killed each other for its sake. I accepted the word, but never made out its meaning. I still haven't. And so it was with 'love' until I touched you.

"After that I could imagine—and I came to Aurora remembering you, and thinking of you, and talking to you endlessly in my mind, and thinking that in Aurora I would meet a million Elijahs."

She stopped, lost in her own thoughts for a moment, then suddenly went on:

"I didn't. Aurora, it turned out, was, in its way, as bad as Solaria. In Solaria, sex was *wrong*. It was hated and we all turned away from it. We could not love for the hatred that sex aroused.

"In Aurora, sex was *boring*. It was accepted calmly, easily—as easily as breathing. If one felt the impulse, one reached out toward anyone who seemed suitable and, if that suitable person was not at the moment engaged in something that could not be put aside, sex followed in any fashion that was convenient. Like breathing. ——But where is the ecstasy in breathing? If one were choking, then perhaps the first shuddering breath that followed upon deprivation might be an overwhelming delight and relief. But if one never choked?

"And if one never unwillingly went without sex? If it were taught to youngsters on an even basis with reading and programming? If children were expected to experiment as a matter of course, and if older children were expected to help out?

"Sex—permitted and free as water—has nothing to do with love on Aurora, just as sex—forbidden and a thing of shame—has nothing to do with love on Solaria. In either case, children are few and must come about only after formal application. ——And then, if permission in granted, there must be an interlude of sex designed for childbearing only, dull and brackish. If, after a reasonable time, impregnation doesn't follow, the spirit rebels and artificial insemination is resorted to.

"In time, as on Solaria, ectogenesis will be the thing, so that fertilization and fetal development will take place in genotaria and sex will be left to itself as a form of social interaction and play that has no more to do with love than space-polo does.

"I could not move into the Auroran attitude, Elijah. I had not been brought up to it. With terror, I had reached out for sex and no one refused—and no one mattered. Each man's eyes were blank when I offered myself and remained blank as they accepted. Another one, they said, what matter? They were willing, but no more than willing.

"And touching them meant nothing. I might have been touching my husband. I learned to go through with it, to follow their lead, to accept their guidance—and it all still meant nothing. I gained not even the urge to do it to myself and by myself. The feeling you had given me never returned and, in time, I gave up.

"In all this, Dr. Fastolfe was my friend. He alone, on all Aurora, knew everything that happened on Solaria. At least, so I think. You know that the full story was not made public and certainly did not appear in that dreadful hyperwave program that I've heard of—I refused to watch it.

"Dr. Fastolfe protected me against the lack of understanding on the part of Aurorans and against their general contempt for Solarians. He protected me also against the despair that filled me after a while.

"No, we were not lovers. I would have offered myself, but by the time it occurred to me that I might do so, I no longer felt that the feeling you had inspired, Elijah, would ever recur. I thought it might have been a trick of memory and I gave up. I did not offer myself. Nor did he offer himself. I do not know why he did not. Perhaps he could see that my despair arose over my failure to find anything useful in sex and did not want to accentuate the despair by repeating the failure. It would be typically kind of him to be careful of me in this way—so we were not lovers. He was merely my friend at a time when I needed that so much more.

"There you are, Elijah. You have the whole answer to the questions you asked. You wanted to know my relationship with Dr. Fastolfe and said you needed information. You have it. Are you satisfied?"

Baley tried not to let his misery show. "I am sorry, Gladia, that life has been so hard for you. You have given me the information I needed. You have given me more information than, perhaps, you think you have."

Gladia frowned. "In what way?"

Baley did not answer directly. He said, "Gladia, I am glad that your memory of me has meant so much to you. It never occurred to me at any time on Solaria, that I was impressing you so and, even if it had, I would not have tried—You know."

"I know, Elijah," she said, softening. "Nor would it have availed you if you had tried. I couldn't have."

"And I know that. ——Nor do I take what you have told me as an invitation now. One touch, one moment of sexual insight, need be no more than that. Very likely, it can never be repeated and that onetime existence ought not to be spoiled by foolish attempts at resurrection. That is a reason why I do not now—offer myself. My failure to do so is not to be interpreted as one more blank ending for you. Besides——"

"Yes."

"You have, as I said earlier, told me perhaps more than you realize you did. You have told me that the story does not end with your despair."

"Why do you say that?"

"In telling me of the feeling that was inspired by the touch upon my cheek, you said something like 'looking back on it long afterward, when I had learned, I realized that I had very nearly experienced an orgasm.' ——But then you went on to explain that sex with Aurorans was never successful and, I presume, you did not then experience orgasm either. Yet you *must* have, Gladia, if you recognized the sensation you experienced that time on Solaria. You could not look back and recognize it for what it was, unless you had learned to love successfully. In other words, you *have* had a lover and you *ncve* experienced love. If I am to believe that Dr. Fastolfe is not your lover and has not been, then it follows that someone else is—or was.'

"And if so? Why is that your concern, Elijah?"

"I don't know if it is or is not, Gladia. Tell me who it is and, if it proves to be not my concern, that will be the end of it."

Gladia was silent.

Baley said, "If you don't tell me, Gladia, I will have to tell you. I told you earlier that I am not in a position to spare your feelings."

Gladia remained silent, the corners of her lips whitening with pressure.

"It must be someone, Gladia, and your sorrow over Jander's loss is extreme. You sent Daneel out because you could not bear to look at him for the reminder of Jander that his face brought. If I am wrong in deciding that it was Jander Panell——" He paused a moment, then said harshly, "If the robot, Jander Panell, was not your lover, say so."

And Gladia whispered, "Jander Panell, the robot, was not my lover." Then, loudly and firmly, she said, "He was my husband!"

25

Baley's lips moved soundlessly, but there was no mistaking the tetrasyllabic exclamation.

"Yes," said Gladia. "Jehoshaphat! You are startled. Why? Do you disapprove?"

Baley said tonelessly, "It is not my place either to approve or disapprove."

"Which means you disapprove."

"Which means I seek only information. How does one distinguish between a lover and a husband on Aurora?"

"If two people live together in the same establishment for a period of time, they may refer to each other as 'wife' or 'husband,' rather than as 'lover.' "

"How long a period of time?"

"That varies from region to region, I understand, according to local option. In the city of Eos, the period of time is three months."

"It is also required that during this period of time one refrain from sexual relations with others?"

Gladia's eyebrows lifted in surprise. "Why?"

"I merely ask."

"Exclusivity is unthinkable on Aurora. Husband or lover, it makes no difference. One engages in sex at pleasure."

"And did you please while you were with Jander?"

"As it happens I did not, but that was my choice."

"Others offered themselves?"

"Occasionally."

"And you refused?"

"I can always refuse at will. That is part of the nonexclusivity."

"But did you refuse?"

"I did."

"And did those whom you refused know why you refused?"

"What do you mean?"

"Did they know that you had a robot husband?"

"I had a *husband.* Don't call him a robot husband. There is no such expression."

"Did they know?"

She paused. "I don't know if they knew."

"Did you tell them?"

"What reason was there to tell them?"

"Don't answer my questions with questions. Did you tell them?"

"I did not."

"How could you avoid that? Don't you think an explanation for your refusal would have been natural?"

"No explanation is ever required. A refusal is simply a refusal and is always accepted. I don't understand you."

Baley stopped to gather his thoughts. Gladia and he were not at cross-purposes; they were running down parallel tracks.

He started again. "Would it have seemed natural on Solaria to have a robot for a husband?"

"On Solaria, it would have been unthinkable and I would never have thought of such a possibility. On Solaria, everything was unthinkable. ——And on Earth, too, Elijah. Would your wife ever have taken a robot for a husband?"

"That's irrelevant, Gladia."

"Perhaps, but your expression was answer enough. We may not be Aurorans, you and I, but we are on Aurora. I have lived here for two years and I accept its mores."

"Do you mean that human-robot sexual connections are common here on Aurora?"

"I don't know. I merely know that they are accepted because everything is accepted where sex is concerned—everything that is voluntary, that gives mutual satisfaction, and that does no physical harm to anyone. What conceivable difference would it make to anyone else how an individual or any combination of individuals found satisfaction? Would anyone worry about which books I viewed, what food I ate, what hour I went to sleep or awoke, whether I was fond of cats or disliked roses? Sex, too, is a matter of indifference—on Aurora."

"On Aurora," echoed Baley. "But you were not born on Aurora and were not brought up in its ways. You told me just a while ago that you couldn't adjust to this very indifference to sex that you now praise. Earlier, you expressed your distaste for multiple marriages and for easy promiscuity. If you did not tell those whom you refused why you refused, it might have been because, in some hidden pocket of your being, you were ashamed of having Jander as a husband. You might have known—or suspected, or even merely supposed—that you were unusual in this—unusual even on Aurora—and you were ashamed."

"No, Elijah, you won't talk me into being ashamed. If having a robot as a husband is unusual even on Aurora, that would be because robots like Jander are unusual. The robots we have on Solaria, or on Earth—or on Aurora, except for Jander and Daneel—are not designed to give any but the most primitive sexual satisfaction. They might be used as masturbation devices, perhaps, as a mechanical vibrator might be, but nothing much more. When the new humaniform robot becomes widespread, so will human-robot sex become widespread."

Baley said, "How did you come to possess Jander in the first place, Gladia? Only two existed—both in Dr. Fastolfe's establishment. Did he simply give one of them—half of the total—to you?"

"Yes."

"Why?"

"Out of kindness, I suppose. I was lonely, disillusioned, wretched, a stranger in a strange land. He gave me Jander for company and I will never be able to thank him enough for it. It only lasted for half a year, but that half-year may be worth all my life beside."

"Did Dr. Fastolfe know that Jander was your husband?"

"He never referred to it, so I don't know."

"Did you refer to it?"

"No."

"Why not?"

"I saw no need. ——And no, it was not because I felt shame."

"How did it happen?"

"That I saw no need?"

"No. That Jander became your husband."

Gladia stiffened. She said in a hostile voice, "Why do I have to explain that?"

Baley said, "Gladia, it's getting late. Don't fight me every step of the way. Are you distressed that Jander is—is gone?"

"Need you ask?"

"Do you want to find out what happened?"

"Again, need you ask?"

"Then help me. I need all the information I can get if I am to begin—even begin—to make progress in working out an apparently insoluble problem. How did Jander become your husband?"

Gladia sat back in her chair and her eyes were suddenly brimming with tears. She pushed at the plate of crumbs that had once been pastry and said in a choked voice:

"Ordinary robots do not wear clothes. I know robots well, having lived on Solaria, and I have a certain amount of artistic talent——"

"I remember your light-forms," said Baley softly.

Gladia nodded in acknowledgment. "I constructed a few designs for new models that would possess, in my opinion, more style and more interest than some of those in use in Aurora. Some of my paintings, based on those designs, are on the walls here. Others I have in other places in this establishment."

Baley's eyes moved to the paintings. He had seen them. They were of robots, unmistakably. They were not naturalistic, but seemed elongated and unnaturally curved. He noted now that the distortions were so designed as to stress, quite cleverly, those portions which, now that he looked at them from a new perspective, suggested clothing. Somehow there was an impression of servants' costumes he had once viewed in a book devoted to Victorian England of medieval times. Did Gladia know of these things or was it a merely chance, if circumstantial, similarity? It was a question of no account, probably, but not something (perhaps) to be forgotten.

When he had first noticed them, he had thought it was Gladia's way of surrounding herself with robots in imitation of life on Solaria. She hated that life, she said, but that was only a product of her thinking mind. Solaria had been the only home she had really known and that is not easily sloughed off—perhaps not at all. And perhaps that remained a factor in her painting, even if her new occupation gave her a more plausible motive.

She was speaking. "I was successful. Some of the robot-manufacturing concerns paid well for my designs and there were numerous cases of existing robots being resurfaced according to my directions. There was a certain satisfaction in all this that, in a small measure, compensated for the emotional emptiness of my life.

"When Jander was given me by Dr. Fastolfe, I had a robot who, of course, wore ordinary clothing. The dear doctor was, indeed, kind enough to give me a number of changes of clothing for Jander.

"None of it was in the least imaginative and it amused me to buy what I considered more appropriate garb. That meant measuring him

quite accurately, since I intended to have my designs made to order—
and *that* meant having him remove his clothing in stages.

"He did so—and it was only when he was completely unclothed that
I quite realized how close to human he was. Nothing was lacking and
those portions which might be expected to be erectile were, indeed,
erectile. Indeed, they were under what, in a human, would be called
conscious control. Jander could tumesce and detumesce on order. He
told me so when I asked him if his penis was functional in that respect.
I was curious and he demonstrated.

"You must understand that, although he looked very much like a
man, I knew he was a robot. I have a certain hesitation about touching men—you understand—and I have no doubt that played a part
in my inability to have satisfactory sex with Aurorans. But this was
not a man and I had been with robots all my life. I could touch
Jander freely.

"It didn't take me long to realize that I enjoyed touching him and
it didn't take Jander long to realize that I enjoyed it. He was a finely
tuned robot who followed the Three Laws carefully. To have failed to
give joy when he could would have been to disappoint. Disappointment could be reckoned as harm and he could not harm a human
being. He took infinite care then to give me joy and, because I saw in
him the desire to give joy, something I never saw in Auroran men, I
was indeed joyful and, eventually, I found out, to the full, I think,
what an orgasm is."

Baley said, "You were, then, completely happy?"

"With Jander? Of course. Completely."

"You never quarreled?"

"With Jander? How could I? His only aim, his only reason for existence, was to please me."

"Might that not disturb you? He only pleased you because he had
to."

"What motive would anyone have to do anything but that, for one
reason or another, he had to?"

"And you never had the urge to try real—to try Aurorans after you
had learned to experience orgasm?"

"It would have been an unsatisfactory substitute. I wanted only Jander. ——And do you understand, now, what I have lost?"

Baley's naturally grave expression lengthened into solemnity. He
said, "I understand, Gladia. If I gave you pain earlier, please forgive
me, for I did not entirely understand then."

But she was weeping and he waited, unable to say anything more,
unable to think of a reasonable way to console her.

Finally, she shook her head and wiped her eyes with the back of her
hand. She whispered, "Is there anything more?"

Baley said apologetically, "A few questions on another subject and then I will be through annoying you." He added cautiously, "For now."

"What is it?" She seemed very tired.

"Do you know that there are people who seem to think that Dr. Fastolfe was responsible for the killing of Jander?"

"Yes."

"Do you know that Dr. Fastolfe himself admits that only he possesses the expertise to kill Jander in the way that he was killed?"

"Yes. The dear doctor told me so himself."

"Well, then, Gladia, do *you* think Dr. Fastolfe killed Jander?"

She looked up at him, suddenly and sharply, and then said angrily, "Of course not. Why should he? Jander was *his* robot to begin with and he was full of care for him. You don't know the dear doctor as I do, Elijah. He is a gentle person who would hurt no one and who would never hurt a robot. To suppose he would kill one is to suppose that a rock would fall upward."

"I have no further questions, Gladia, and the only other business I have here, at the moment, is to see Jander—what remains of Jander—if I have your permission."

She was suspicious again, hostile. "Why? Why?"

"Gladia! Please! I don't expect it to be of any use, but I must see Jander and *know* that seeing him is of no use. I will try to do nothing that will offend your sensibilities."

Gladia stood up. Her gown, so simple as to be nothing more than a closely fitting sheath, was not black (as it would have been on Earth) but of a dull color that showed no sparkle anywhere in it. Baley, no connoisseur of clothing, realized how well it represented mourning.

"Come with me," she whispered.

26

Baley followed Gladia through several rooms, the walls of which glowed dully. On one or two occasions, he caught a hint of movement, which he took to be a robot getting rapidly out of the way, since they had been told not to intrude.

Through a hallway, then, and up a short flight of stairs into a small room in which one part of one wall gleamed to give the effect of a spotlight.

The room held a cot and a chair—and no other furnishings.

"This was his room," said Gladia. Then, as though answering Baley's thought, she went on to say, "It was all he needed. I left him alone as much as I could—all day if I could. I did not want to ever grow tired of him." She shook her head. "I wish now I had stayed with him every second. I didn't know our time would be so short. ——Here he is."

Jander was lying on the cot and Baley looked at him gravely. The robot was covered with a smooth and shiny material. The spotlighted wall cast its glow on Jander's head, which was smooth and almost inhuman in its serenity. The eyes were wide open, but they were opaque and lusterless. He looked enough like Daneel to give ample point to Gladia's discomfort at Daneel's presence. His neck and bare shoulders showed above the sheet.

Baley said, "Has Dr. Fastolfe inspected him?"

"Yes, thoroughly. I came to him in despair and, if you had seen him rush here, the concern he felt, the pain, the—the panic, you would never think he could have been responsible. There was nothing he could do."

"Is he unclothed?"

"Yes. Dr. Fastolfe had to remove the clothing for a thorough examination. There was no point in replacing them."

"Would you permit me to remove the covering, Gladia?"

"Must you?"

"I do not wish to be blamed for having missed some obvious point of examination."

"What can you possibly find that Dr. Fastolfe didn't?"

"Nothing, Gladia, but I must *know* that there is nothing for me to find. Please cooperate."

"Well, then, go ahead, but *please* put the covering back exactly as it is now when you are done."

She turned her back on him and on Jander, put her left arm against the wall, and rested her forehead on it. There was no sound from her—no motion—but Baley knew that she was weeping again.

The body was, perhaps, not quite human. The muscular contours were somehow simplified and a bit schematic, but all the parts were there: nipples, navel, penis, testicles, pubic hair, and so on. Even fine, light hair on the chest.

How many days was it since Jander had been killed? It struck Baley that he didn't know, but it had been sometime before his trip to Aurora had begun. Over a week had passed and there was no sign of decay, either visually or olfactorily. A clear robotic difference.

Baley hesitated and then thrust one arm under Jander's shoulders and another under his hips, working them through to the other side. He did not consider asking for Gladia's help—*that* would be impossible. He heaved and, with some difficulty, turned Jander over without throwing him off the cot.

The cot creaked. Gladia must know what he was doing, but she did not turn around. Though she did not offer to help, she did not protest either.

Baley withdrew his arms. Jander felt warm to the touch. Presumably, the power unit continued to do so simple a thing as to maintain temperature, even with the brain inoperative. The body felt firm and resilient, too. Presumably, it never went through any stage analogous to rigor mortis.

One arm was now dangling off the cot in quite a human fashion. Baley moved it gently and released it. It swung to and fro slightly and came to a halt. He bent one leg at the knee and studied the foot, then the other. The buttocks were perfectly formed and there was even an anus.

Baley could not get rid of the feeling of uneasiness. The notion that he was violating the privacy of a human being would not go away. If it were a human corpse, its coldness and its stiffness would have deprived it of humanity.

He thought uncomfortably: A robot corpse is much more human than a human corpse.

Again he reached under Jander, lifted, and turned him over.

He smoothed out the sheet as best he could, then replaced the cover as it had been and smoothed that. He stepped back and decided it was as it had been at first—or as near to that as he could manage.

"I'm finished, Gladia," he said.

She turned, looked at Jander with wet eyes, and said, "May we go, then?"

"Yes, of course, but Gladia——"

"Well?"

"Will you be keeping him this way? I imagine he won't decay."

"Does it matter if I do?"

"In some ways, yes. You must give yourself a chance to recover. You can't spend three centuries mourning. What is over is over." (His statements sounded hollowly sententious in his own ear. What must they have sounded like in hers?)

She said, "I know you mean it kindly, Elijah. I have been requested to keep Jander till the investigation is done. He will then be torched at my request."

"Torched?"

"Put under a plasma torch and reduced to his elements, as human corpses are. I will have holograms of him—and memories. Will that satisfy you?"

"Of course. I must return to Dr. Fastolfe's house now."

"Yes. Have you learned anything from Jander's body?"

"I did not expect to, Gladia."

She faced him full. "And Elijah, I want you to find who did this and why. I must know."

"But Gladia——"

She shook her head violently, as though keeping out anything she wasn't ready to hear. "I *know* you can do this."

7. Again Fastolfe

27

Baley emerged from Gladia's house into the sunset. He turned toward what he assumed must be the western horizon and found Aurora's sun, a deep scarlet in color, topped by thin strips of ruddy clouds set in an apple-green sky.

"Jehoshaphat," he murmured. Clearly, Aurora's sun, cooler and more orange than Earth's sun, accentuated the difference at setting, when its light passed through a greater thickness of Aurora.

Daneel was behind him; Giskard, as before, well in front.

Daneel's voice was in his ear. "Are you well, Partner Elijah?"

"Quite well," said Baley, pleased with himself. "I'm handling the Outside well, Daneel. I can even admire the sunset. Is it always like this?"

Daneel gazed dispassionately at the setting sun and said, "Yes. But let us move quickly toward Dr. Fastolfe's establishment. At this time of year, the twilight does not last long, Partner Elijah, and I would wish you there while you can still see easily."

"I'm ready. Let's go." Baley wondered if it might not be better to wait for the darkness. It would not be pleasant not to see, but, then, it would give him the illusion of being enclosed—and he was not, in his heart, sure as to how long this euphoria induced by admiring a sunset (a sunset, mind you, Outside) would last. But that was a cowardly uncertainty and he would not own up to it.

Giskard noiselessly drifted backward toward him and said, "Would you prefer to wait, sir? Would the darkness suit you better? We ourselves will not be discommoded."

Baley became aware of other robots, farther off, on every side. Had Gladia marked off her field robots for guard duty or had Fastolfe sent his?

It accentuated the way they were all caring for him and, perversely, he would not admit to weakness. He said, "No, we'll go now," and struck off at a brisk walk toward Fastolfe's establishment, which he could just see through the distant trees.

Let the robots follow or not, as they wished, he thought boldly. He knew that, if he let himself think about it, there would be something within him that would still quail at the thought of himself on the outer skin of a planet with no protection but air between himself and the great void, but he would *not* think of it.

460

It was the exhilaration at being free of the fear that made his jaws tremble and his teeth click. Or it was the cool wind of evening that did it—and that also set the gooseflesh to appearing on his arms.

It was *not* the Outside.

It was *not*.

He said, trying to unclench his teeth, "How well did you know Jander, Daneel?"

Daneel said, "We were together for some time. From the time of friend Jander's construction, till he passed into the establishment of Miss Gladia, we were together steadily."

"Did it bother you, Daneel, that Jander resembled you so closely?"

"No, sir. He and I each knew ourselves apart, Partner Elijah, and Dr. Fastolfe did not mistake us either. We were, therefore, two individuals."

"And could you tell them apart, too, Giskard?" They were closer to him now, perhaps because the other robots had taken over the long-distance duties.

Giskard said, "There was no occasion, as I recall, on which it was important that I do so."

"And if there had been, Giskard?"

"Then I could have done so."

"What was your opinion of Jander, Daneel?"

Daneel said, "My opinion, Partner Elijah? Concerning what aspect of Jander do you wish my opinion?"

"Did he do his work well, for instance?"

"Certainly."

"Was he satisfactory in every way?"

"In every way, to my knowledge."

"How about you, Giskard? What is your opinion?"

Giskard said, "I was never as close to friend Jander as friend Daneel was and it would not be proper for me to state an opinion. I can say that, to my knowledge, Dr. Fastolfe was uniformly pleased with friend Jander. He seemed equally pleased with friend Jander and with friend Daneel. However, I do not think my programming is such as to allow me to offer certainty in such matters."

Baley said, "What about the period after Jander entered the household of Miss Gladia? Did you know him then, Daneel?"

"No, Partner Elijah. Miss Gladia kept him at her establishment. On those occasions when she visited Dr. Fastolfe, he was never with her, as far as I was aware. On occasions when I accompanied Dr. Fastolfe on a visit to Miss Gladia's establishment, I did not see friend Jander."

Baley felt a little surprised at that. He turned to Giskard in order to ask the same question, paused, and then shrugged. He was not really getting anywhere and, as Dr. Fastolfe had indicated earlier, there is not really much use in cross-examining a robot. They would not knowingly say anything that would harm a human being, nor could they be badgered, bribed, or cajoled into it. They would not openly lie, but they would remain stubbornly—if politely—insistent on giving useless answers.

And—perhaps—it no longer mattered.

They were at Fastolfe's doorstep now and Baley felt his breath quickening. The trembling of his arms and lower lip, he was confident, was, indeed, only because of the cool wind.

The sun had gone now, a few stars were visible, the sky was darkening to an odd greenish-purple that made it seem bruised, and he passed through the door into the warmth of the glowing walls.

He was safe.

Fastolfe greeted him. "You are back in good time, Mr. Baley. Was your session with Gladia fruitful?"

Baley said, "Quite fruitful, Dr. Fastolfe. It is even possible that I hold the key to the answer in my hand."

28

Fastolfe merely smiled politely, in a way that signaled neither surprise, elation, nor disbelief. He led the way into what was obviously a dining róom, a smaller and friendlier one than the one in which they had had lunch.

"You and I, my dear Mr. Baley," said Fastolfe pleasantly, "will eat an informal dinner alone. Merely the two of us. We will even have the robots absent if that will please you. Nor shall we talk business unless you desperately want to."

Baley said nothing, but paused to look at the walls in astonishment. They were a wavering, luminous green, with differences in brightness and in tint that were slowly progressive from bottom to top. There was a hint of fronds of deeper green and shadowy flickers this way and that. The walls made the room appear to be a well-lit grotto at the bottom of a shallow arm of the sea. The effect was vertiginous— at least, Baley found it so.

Fastolfe had no trouble interpreting Baley's expression. He said, "It's an acquired taste, Mr. Baley, I admit. —Giskard, subdue the wall illumination. —Thank you."

Baley drew a breath of relief. "And thank you, Dr. Fastolfe. May I visit the Personal, sir?"

"But of course."

Baley hesitated. "Could you—"

Fastolfe chuckled. "You'll find it perfectly normal, Mr. Baley. You will have no complaints."

Baley bent his head. "Thank you very much."

Without the intolerable make-believe, the Personal—he believed it to be the same one he had used earlier in the day—was merely what it was, a much more luxurious and hospitable one than he had ever seen. It was incredibly different from those on Earth, which were rows of identical units stretching indefinitely, each ticked off for use by one—and only one—individual at a time.

It *gleamed* somehow with hygienic cleanliness. Its outermost molecular layer might have been peeled off after every use and a new layer laid on. Obscurely, Baley felt that, if he stayed on Aurora long enough, he would find it difficult to readjust himself to Earth's crowds, which forced hygiene and cleanliness into the background—something to pay a distant obeisance to—a not quite attainable ideal.

Baley, standing there surrounded by conveniences of ivory and gold (not real ivory, no doubt, nor real gold), gleaming and smooth, suddenly found himself shuddering at Earth's casual exchange of bacteria and wincing at its richness in infectivity. Was that not what the Spacers felt? Could he blame them?

He washed his hands thoughtfully, playing with the tiny touches here and there along the control-strip in order to change the temperature. And yet these Aurorans were so unnecessarily garish in their interior decorations, so insistent in pretending they were living in a state of nature when they had tamed nature and broken it. —Or was that only Fastolfe?

After all, Gladia's establishment had been far more austere. —Or was that only because she had been brought up on Solaria?

The dinner that followed was an unalloyed delight. Again, as at lunch, there was the distinct feeling of being closer to nature. The dishes were numerous—each different, each in small portions—and, in a number of cases, it was possible to see that they had once been part of plants and animals. He was beginning to look upon the inconveniences—the occasional small bone, bit of gristle, strand of fiber, which might have repelled him earlier—as a bit of adventure.

The first course was a little fish—a little fish that one ate whole, with whatever internal organs it might have—and that struck him, at first sight, as another foolish way of rubbing one's nose in Nature with a capital "N." But he swallowed the little fish anyway, as Fastolfe did, and the taste converted him at once. He had never experienced anything like it. It was as though taste buds had suddenly been invented and inserted in his tongue.

Tastes changed from dish to dish and some were distinctly odd and not entirely pleasant, but he found it didn't matter. The thrill of a distinct taste, of *different* distinct tastes (at Fastolfe's instruction, he took a sip of faintly flavored water between dishes) was what counted—and not the inner detail.

He tried not to gobble, nor to concentrate his attention entirely on the food, nor to lick his plate. Desperately, he continued to observe and imitate Fastolfe and to ignore the other's kindly but definitely amused glance.

"I trust," said Fastolfe, "you find this to your taste."

"Quite good," Baley managed to choke out.

"Please don't force yourself into useless politeness. Do not eat anything that seems strange or unpalatable to you. I will have additional helpings of anything you do like brought in its place."

"Not necessary, Dr. Fastolfe. It is all rather satisfactory."

"Good."

Despite Fastolfe's offer to eat without robots present, it was a robot who served. (Fastolfe, accustomed to this, probably did not even notice the fact, Baley thought—and he did not bring the matter up.)

As was to be expected, the robot was silent and his motions were flawless. His handsome livery seemed to be out of historical dramas that Baley had seen on hyperwave. It was only at very close view that one could see how much the costume was an illusion of the lighting and how close the robot exterior was to a smooth metal finish—and no more.

Baley said, "Has the waiter's surface been designed by Gladia?"

"Yes," said Fastolfe, obviously pleased. "How complimented she will feel to know that you recognized her touch. She is good, isn't she? Her work is coming into increasing popularity and she fills a useful niche in Auroran society."

Conversation throughout the meal had been pleasant but unimportant. Baley had had no urge to "talk business" and had, in fact, preferred to be largely silent while enjoying the meal and leaving it to his unconscious—or whatever faculty took over in the absence of hard thought—to decide on how to approach the matter that seemed to him now to be the central point of the Jander problem.

Fastolfe took the matter out of his hands, rather, by saying, "And now that you've mentioned Gladia, Mr. Baley, may I ask how it came about that you left for her establishment rather deep in despair and have returned almost buoyant and speaking of perhaps having the key to the whole affair in your hand? Did you learn something new—and unexpected, perhaps—at Gladia's?"

"That I did," said Baley absently—but he was lost in the dessert, which he could not recognize at all, and of which (after some yearning in his eyes had acted to inspire the waiter) a second small helping was placed before him. He felt replete. He had never in his life so enjoyed the act of eating and for the first time found himself resenting the physiological limits that made it impossible to eat forever. He felt rather ashamed of himself that he should feel so.

"And what was it learned that was new and unexpected?" asked

Fastolfe with quiet patience. "Presumably something I didn't know myself?"

"Perhaps. Gladia told me that you had given Jander to her about half a year ago."

Fastolfe nodded. "I knew *that*. So I did."

Baley said sharply, "Why?"

The amiable look on Fastolfe's face faded slowly. Then he said, "Why not?"

Baley said, "I don't know why not, Dr. Fastolfe. I don't care. My question is: Why?"

Fastolfe shook his head slightly and said nothing.

Baley said, "Dr. Fastolfe, I am here in order to straighten out what seems to be a miserable mess. Nothing you have done— *nothing*—has made things simple. Rather, you have taken what seems to be pleasure in showing me how bad a mess it is and in destroying any speculation I may advance as a possible solution. Now, I don't expect others to answer my questions. I have no official standing on this world and have no right to ask questions, let alone force answers.

"You, however, are different. I am here at your request and I am trying to save your career as well as mine and, according to your own account of matters, I am trying to save Aurora as well as Earth. Therefore, I expect you to answer my questions fully and truthfully. Please don't indulge in stalemating tactics, such as asking me why not when I ask why. Now, once again—and for the last time: Why?"

Fastolfe thrust out his lips and looked grim. "My apologies, Mr. Baley. If I hesitated to answer, it is because, looking back on it, it seems there is no very dramatic reason. Gladia Delmarre—no, she doesn't want her surname used—Gladia is a stranger on this planet; she has undergone traumatic experiences on her home world, as you know, and traumatic experiences on this one, as perhaps you don't know—"

"I do know. Please be more direct."

"Well, then, I was sorry for her. She was alone and Jander, I thought, would make her feel less alone."

"Sorry for her? Just that. Are you lovers? Have you been?"

"No, not at all. I did not offer. Nor did she. —Why? Did she tell you we were lovers?"

"No, she did not, but I need independent confirmation, in any case. I'll let you know when there is a contradiction; you needn't concern yourself about that. How is it that with you sympathizing so with her and—from what I gather from Gladia, she feeling so grateful to you— that neither of you offered yourself? I gather that on Aurora offering sex is about on a par with commenting upon the weather."

Fastolfe frowned. "You know nothing about it, Mr. Baley. Don't judge us by the standards of your own world. Sex is not a matter of great importance to us, but we are careful as to how we use it. It may not seem so to you, but none of us offer it lightly. Gladia, unused to our ways and sexually frustrated on Solaria, perhaps did offer it lightly—or desperately might be the better word—and it may not be surprising, therefore, that she did not enjoy the results."

"Didn't you try to improve matters?"

"By offering myself? I am not what she needs and, for that matter, she is not what I need. I was *sorry* for her. I like her. I admire her artistic talent. And I want her to be happy. —After all, Mr. Baley, surely you'll agree that the sympathy of one human being for another need not rest on sexual desire or on anything but decent human feeling. Have you never felt sympathy for anyone? Have you never wanted to help someone for no reason other than the good feeling it gave you to relieve another's misery? What kind of planet do you come from?"

Baley said, "What you say is justified, Dr. Fastolfe. I do not question the fact that you are a decent human being. Still, bear with me. When I first asked you why you had given Jander to Gladia, you did not tell me then what you have told me just now—and with considerable emotion, too, I might add. Your first impulse was to duck, to hesitate, to play for time by asking why not.

"Granted that what you finally told me is so, what is it about the question that embarrassed you at first? What reason—that you did *not* want to admit—came to you before you settled on the reason you *did* want to admit? Forgive me for insisting, but I must know—and not out of personal curiosity, I assure you. If what you tell me is of no use in this sorry business, then you may consider it thrown into a black hole."

Fastolfe said in a low voice, "In all honesty, I am not sure why I parried your question. You surprised me into something that, perhaps, I don't want to face. Let me think, Mr. Baley."

They sat there together quietly. The server cleared the table and left the room. Daneel and Giskard were elsewhere (presumably, they were guarding the house). Baley and Fastolfe were at last alone in a robot-free room.

Finally, Fastolfe said, "I don't know what I ought to tell you, but let me go back some decades. I have two daughters. Perhaps you know that. They are by two different mothers—"

"Would you rather have had sons, Dr. Fastolfe?"

Fastolfe looked genuinely surprised. "No. Not at all. The mother of my second daughter wanted a son, I believe, but I wouldn't give my consent to artificial insemination with selected sperm—not even with my own sperm—but insisted on the natural throw of the genetic dice. Before you ask why, it is because I prefer a certain operation of chance in life and because I think, on the whole, I wanted a chance to have a daughter. I would have accepted a son, you understand, but I didn't want to abandon the chance of a daughter. I approve of daughters, somehow. Well, my second proved a daughter and that may have been one of the reasons that the mother dissolved the marriage soon after the birth. On the other hand, a sizable percentage of marriages are dissolved after a birth in any case, so perhaps I needn't look for special reasons."

"She took the child with her, I take it."

Fastolfe bent a puzzled glance at Baley. "Why should she do that? —But I forget. You're from Earth. No, of course not. The child would have been brought up in a nursery, where she could be properly cared for, of course. Actually, though" —he wrinkled his nose as though in sudden embarrassment over a peculiar memory—"she wasn't put there. I decided to bring her up myself. It was legal to do so but very unusual. I was quite young, of course, not yet having attained the century mark, but already I had made my mark in robotics."

"Did you manage?"

"You mean to bring her up successfully? Oh yes. I grew quite fond of her. I named her Vasilia. It was my mother's name, you see." He chuckled reminiscently. "I get these odd streaks of sentiment—like my affection for my robots. I never met my mother, of course, but her name was on my charts. And she's still alive, as far as I know, so I could see her—but I think there's something queasy about meeting someone in whose womb you once were. —Where was I?"

"You named your daughter Vasilia."

"Yes—and I did bring her up and actually grew fond of her. Very fond of her. I could see where the attraction lay in doing something like that, but, of course, I was an embarrassment to my friends and I had to keep her out of their way when there was contact to be made, either social or professional. I remember once—" He paused.

"Yes?"

"It's something I haven't thought of for decades. She came running out, weeping for some reason, and threw herself into my arms when Dr. Sarton was with me, discussing one of the very earliest design programs for humaniform robots. She was only seven years old, I think and, of course, I hugged her, and kissed her, and ignored the business at hand, which was quite unforgivable of me. Sarton left, coughing and choking—and *most* indignant. It was a full week before I could renew contact with him and resume deliberation. Children shouldn't have that effect on people, I suppose, but there are so few children and they are so rarely encountered."

"And your daughter—Vasilia—was fond of you?"

"Oh yes—at least, until—She was very fond of me. I saw to her schooling and made sure her mind was allowed to expand to the fullest."

"You said she was fond of you until—something. You did not finish the sentence. There came a time, then, when she was no longer fond of you. When was that?"

"She wanted to have her own establishment once she grew old enough. It was only natural."

"And you did not want it?"

"What do you mean I did not want it? Of course, I wanted it. You keep assuming I'm a monster, Mr. Baley."

"Am I to assume, instead, that once she reached the age when she was to have her own establishment, she no longer felt the same affection for you that she naturally had when she was actively your daughter, living in *your* establishment as a dependent?"

"Not quite that simple. In fact, it was rather complicated. You see—" Fastolfe seemed embarrassed. "I refused her when she offered herself to me."

"She offered herself to *you*?" said Baley, horrified.

"That part was only natural," said Fastolfe indifferently. "She knew me best. I had instructed her in sex, encouraged her experimentation, taken her to the Games of Eros, done my best for her. It was something to be expected and I was foolish for not expecting it and letting myself be caught."

"But *incest*?"

Fastolfe said, "Incest? Oh yes, an Earthly term. On Aurora, there's no such thing, Mr. Baley. Very few Aurorans know their immediate family. Naturally, if marriage is in question and children are applied for, there is a genealogical search, but what has that to do with social sex? No no, the unnatural thing is that I refused my own daughter." He reddened—his large ears most of all.

"I should hope so," muttered Baley.

"I had no decent reasons for it, either—at least none that I could explain to Vasilia. It was criminal of me not to foresee the matter and prepare a foundation for a rational rejection of one so young and inexperienced, if that were necessary, that would not wound her and subject her to a fearful humiliation. I am really unbearably ashamed that I took the unusual responsibility of bringing up a child, only to subject her to such an unpalatable experience. It seemed to me that we could continue our relationship as father and daughter— as friend and friend—but she did not give up. Whenever I rejected her, no matter how affectionately I tried to do so, matters grew worse between us."

"Until finally—"

"Finally, she wanted her own establishment. I opposed it at first, not because I didn't want her to have one, but because I wanted to reestablish our loving relationship before she left. Nothing I did helped. It was, perhaps, the most trying time of my life. Eventually, she simply—and rather violently—insisted on leaving and I could hold out no longer. She was a professional roboticist by then—I am grateful that she didn't abandon the profession out of distaste for me—and she was able to found an establishment without any help from me. She did so, in fact, and since then there has been little contact between us."

Baley said, "It might be, Dr. Fastolfe, that, since she did *not* abandon robotics, she does not feel wholly estranged."

"It is what she does best and is most interested in. It has nothing to do with me. I know that, for to begin with, I thought as you did and I made friendly overtures, but they were not received."

"Do you miss her, Dr. Fastolfe?"

"Of course I miss her, Mr. Baley. —That is an example of the mistake of bringing up a child. You give into an irrational impulse—an atavistic desire—and it leads to inspiring the child with the strongest possible feeling of love and then subjecting yourself to the possibility of having to refuse that same child's first offer of herself and scarring her emotionally for life. And, to add to that, you subject yourself to this thoroughly irrational feeling of regret-of-absence. It's something I never felt before and have never felt since. She and I both suffered needlessly and the fault is entirely mine."

Fastolfe fell into a kind of rumination and Baley said gently, "And what has all this to do with Gladia?"

Fastolfe started. "Oh! I had forgotten. Well, it's rather simple. Everything I've said about Gladia is true. I liked her. I sympathized with her. I admired her talent. But, in addition, she resembles Vasilia. I noticed the similarity when I saw the first hyperwave account of her arrival from Solaria. It was quite startling and it made me take an interest." He sighed. "When I realized that she, like Vasilia, had been sex-scarred, it was more than I could endure. I arranged to have her established near me, as you see. I have been her friend and done my best to cushion the difficulties of adapting to a strange world."

"She is a daughter-substitute, then."

"After a fashion, yes, I suppose you could call it that, Mr. Baley. —And you have no idea how glad I am she never took it into her head to offer herself to me. To have rejected her would have been to relive my rejection of Vasilia. To have accepted her out of an inability to repeat the rejection would have embittered my life, for then I would have felt that I was doing for this stranger—this faint reflection of my daughter—what I would not do for my daughter herself. Either way— But, never mind, you can see now why I hesitated to answer you at first. Somehow, thinking about it led my mind back to this tragedy in my life."

"And your other daughter?"

"Lumen?" said Fastolfe indifferently. "I never had any contact with her, though I hear of her from time to time."

"She's running for political office, I understand."

"A local one. On the Globalist ticket."

"What is that?"

"The Globalists? They favor Aurora alone—just our own globe, you see. Aurorans are to take the lead in settling the Galaxy. Others are to be barred, as far as possible, particularly Earthmen. 'Enlightened self-interest' they call it."

"This is not your view, of course."

"Of course not. I am heading the Humanist party, which believes that all human beings have a right to share in the Galaxy. When I refer to 'my enemies,' I mean the Globalists."

"Lumen, then, is one of your enemies."

"Vasilia is one, also. She is, indeed, a member of the Robotics Institute of Aurora—the RIA—that was founded a few years ago and which is run by roboticists who view me as a demon to be defeated at all costs. As far as I know, however, my various ex-wives are apolitical, perhaps even Humanist." He smiled wryly and said, "Well, Mr. Baley, have you asked the questions you wanted to ask?"

Baley's hands aimlessly searched for pockets in his smooth, loose Auroran breeches—something he had been doing periodically since he had begun wearing them on the ship—and found none. He compromised, as he sometimes did, by folding his arms across his chest.

He said, "Actually, Dr. Fastolfe. I'm not at all sure you have yet answered the first question. It seems to me that you never tire of evading that. *Why did you give Jander to Gladia?* Let's get all of it into the open, so that we may be able to see light in what now seems darkness."

29

Fastolfe reddened again. It might have been anger this time, but he continued to speak softly.

He said, "Do not bully me, Mr. Baley. I have given you your answer. I was sorry for Gladia and I thought Jander would be company for her. I have spoken more frankly to you than I would to anyone else, partly because of the position I am in and partly because you are not an Auroran. In return, I demand a reasonable respect."

Baley bit his lower lip. He was not on Earth. He had no official authority behind him and he had more at stake than his professional pride.

He said, "I apologize, Dr. Fastolfe, if I have hurt your feelings. I do not mean to imply you are being untruthful or uncooperative. Nevertheless, I cannot operate without the whole truth. Let me suggest the possible answer I am looking for and you can then tell me if I am correct, or nearly correct, or totally wrong. Can it be that you have given Jander to Gladia, in order that he might serve as a focus for her sexual drive and so that she might not have occasion to offer herself to you? Perhaps that was not your conscious reason, but think about it now. Is it possible that such a feeling contributed to the gift?"

Fastolfe's hand picked up a light and transparent ornament that had been resting on the dining room table. It turned it over and over, over and over. Except for that motion, Fastolfe seemed frozen. Finally, he said, "That might be so, Mr. Baley. Certainly, after I loaned her Jander—it was never an outright gift, incidentally—I was less concerned about her offering herself to me."

"Do you know whether Gladia made use of Jander for sexual purposes?"

"Did you ask Gladia if she made use of him, Mr. Baley?"

"That has nothing to do with my question. Do you know? Did you witness any overt sexual actions between them? Did any of your robots inform you of such? Did she herself tell you?"

"The answer to all those questions, Mr. Baley, is no. If I stop to think about it, there is nothing particularly unusual about the use of robots for sexual purposes by either men or women. Ordinary robots are not particularly adapted to it, but human beings are ingenious in this respect. As for Jander, he is adapted to it because he is as humaniform as we could make him—"

"So that he might take part in sex."

"No, that was never in our minds. It was the abstract problem of building a totally humaniform robot that exercised the late Dr. Sarton and myself."

"But such humaniform robots are ideally designed for sex, are they not?"

"I suppose they are and, now that I allow myself to think of it—and I admit I may have had it hidden in my mind from the start—Gladia might well have used Jander so. If she did, I hope the process gave her pleasure. I would consider my loan to her a good deed, if it had."

"Could it have been more of a good deed than you counted upon?"

"In what way?"

"What would you say if I told you that Gladia and Jander were wife and husband?"

Fastolfe's hand, still holding the ornament, closed convulsively upon it, held it tightly for a moment, then let it drop. "What? That's ridiculous. It is legally impossible. There is no question of children, so there can't conceivably be an application for any. Without the intention of such an application, there can be no marriage."

"This is not a matter of legality, Dr. Fastolfe. Gladia is a Solarian, remember, and doesn't have the Auroran outlook. It is a matter of emotion. Gladia herself told me that she considered Jander to have been her husband. I think she considers herself now his widow and that she has had another sexual trauma—and a very severe one. If, in any way, you knowingly contributed to this event—"

"By all the stars," said Fastolfe with unwonted emotion, "I didn't. Whatever else was in my mind, I never imagined that Gladia could fantasize *marriage* to a robot, however humaniform he might be. No Auroran could have imagined that."

Baley nodded and raised his hand. "I believe you. I don't think you are actor enough to be drowning me in a faked sincerity. But I had to know. It was, after all, just possible that—"

"No, it was not. Possible that I foresaw this situation? That I deliberately created this abominable widowhood, for some reason? Never. It was not conceivable, so I did not conceive it. Mr. Baley, whatever I meant in placing Jander in her establishment, I meant well. I did not mean *this*. Meaning well is a poor defense, I know, but it is all that I have to offer."

"Dr. Fastolfe, let us refer to that no more," said Baley. "What *I* have now to offer is a possible solution to the mystery."

Fastolfe breathed deeply and sat back in his chair. "You hinted as much when you returned from Gladia's." He looked at Baley with a hint of savagery in his eyes. "Could you not have told me this 'key' you have at the start? Need we have gone through all—this?"

"I'm sorry, Dr. Fastolfe. The key makes no sense without all—this."

"Well, then. Get on with it."

"I will. Jander was in a position that you, the greatest robotics theoretician in all the world, did not foresee, by your own admission. He was pleasing Gladia so well that she was deeply in love with him and considered him her husband. What if it turns out that, in pleasing her, he was also displeasing her?"

"I'm not sure as to your meaning."

"Well, see here, Dr. Fastolfe. She was rather secretive about the matter. I gather that on Aurora sexual matters are not something one hides at all costs."

"We don't broadcast it over the hyperwave," said Fastolfe dryly, "but we don't make a greater secret of it than we do of any other strictly personal matter. We generally know who's been whose latest partner and, if one is dealing with friends, we often get an idea of how good, or how enthusiastic, or how much the reverse one or the other partner—or both—might be. It's a matter of small talk on occasion."

"Yes, but you knew nothing of Gladia's connection with Jander."

"I suspected—"

"Not the same thing. She told you nothing. You saw nothing. Nor could any robots report anything. She kept it secret even from you, her best friend on Aurora. Clearly, her robots were given careful instructions never to discuss Jander and Jander himself must have been thoroughly instructed to give nothing away."

"I suppose that's a fair conclusion."

"Why should she do that, Dr. Fastolfe?"

"A Solarian sense of privacy about sex?"

"Isn't that the same as saying she was ashamed of it?"

"She had no cause to be, although the matter of considering Jander a husband would have made her a laughingstock."

"She might have concealed that portion very easily without concealing everything. Suppose, in her Solarian way, she was ashamed."

"Well, then?"

"No one enjoys being ashamed—and she might have blamed Jander for it, in the rather unreasonable way people have of seeking to attribute to others the blame for unpleasantness that is clearly their own fault."

"Yes?"

"There might have been times when Gladia, who has a shortfused temper, might have burst into tears, let us say, and upbraided Jander for being the source of her shame and her misery. It might not have lasted long and she might have shifted quickly to apologies and caresses, but would not Jander have clearly gotten the idea that he was actually the source of her shame and her misery?"

"Perhaps."

"And might this not have meant to Jander that if he continued the relationship, he would make her miserable, and that if he ended the relationship, he would make her miserable. Whatever he did, he would be breaking the First Law and, unable to act in any way without such a violation, he could only find refuge in not acting at all—and so went into mental freeze-out. —Do you remember the story you told me earlier today of the legendary mind-reading robot who was driven into stasis by that robotics pioneer?"

"By Susan Calvin, yes, I see! You model your scenario on that old legend. Very ingenious, Mr. Baley, but it won't work."

"Why not? When you said only you could bring about a mental freeze-out in Jander, you did not have the faintest idea that he was involved so deeply in so unexpected a situation. It runs exactly parallel to the Susan Calvin situation."

"Let's suppose that the story about Susan Calvin and the mind-reading robot is not merely a totally fictitious legend. Let's take it seriously. There would still be no parallel between that story and the Jander situation. In the case of Susan Calvin, we would be dealing with an incredibly primitive robot, one that today would not even achieve the status of a toy. It could deal only qualitatively with such matters: A creates misery; not-A creates misery; therefore mental freeze-out."

Baley said, "And Jander?"

"Any modern robot—any robot of the last century—would weigh such matters quantitatively. Which of the two situations, A or not-A, would create the *most* misery? The robot would come to a rapid decision and opt for minimum misery. The chance that he would judge the two mutually exclusive alternatives to produce precisely equal quantities of misery is small and, even if that should turn out to be the case, the modern robot is supplied with a randomization factor. If A and not-A are precisely equal misery-producers according to his judgment, he chooses one or the other in a completely unpredictable way and then follows that unquestioningly. He does *not* go into mental freeze-out."

"Are you saying it is impossible for Jander to go into mental freeze-out? You have been saying *you* could have produced it."

"In the case of the humaniform positronic brain, there is a way of sidetracking the randomization factor that depends entirely on the way in which that brain is constructed. Even if you know the basic theory, it is a very difficult and long-sustained process to so lead the robot down the garden path, so to speak, by a skillful succession of questions and orders as to finally induce the mental freeze-out. It is unthinkable that it be done by accident and the mere existence of an apparent contradiction as that produced by simultaneous love and shame could not do the trick without the most careful quantitative adjustment under the most unusual conditions. —Which leaves us, as I keep saying, with indeterministic chance as the only possible way in which it happened."

"But your enemies will insist that your own guilt is the more likely. —Could we not, in our turn, insist that Jander was brought to mental freeze-out by the conflict brought on by Gladia's love and shame? Would this not sound plausible? And would it not win public opinion to your side?"

Fastolfe frowned. "Mr. Baley, you are too eager. Think about it seriously. If we were to try to get out of our dilemma in this rather dishonest fashion, what would be the consequence? I say nothing of the shame and misery it would bring to Gladia, who would suffer not only the loss of Jander but the feeling that she herself had brought about that loss if, in fact, she had really felt and had somehow revealed her shame. I would not want to do that, but let us put that to one side, if we can. Consider, instead, that my enemies would say that I had loaned her Jander precisely to bring about what had happened. I would have done it, they would say, in order to develop a method for mental freeze-out in humaniform robots while escaping all apparent responsibility myself. We would be worse off than we are now, for I would not only be accused of being an underhanded intriguer, as I am now, but, in addition, of having behaved monstrously toward an unsuspecting woman whom I had pretended to befriend, something I have so far been spared."

Baley was staggered. He felt his jaw drop and his voice degenerate to a stutter. "Surely they would not—"

"But they would. You yourself were at least half-inclined to think so not very many minutes ago."

"Merely as a remote—"

"My enemies would not find it remote and they would not publicize it as remote."

Baley knew he had reddened. He felt the wave of heat and found he could not look Fastolfe in the face. He cleared his throat and said, "You are right. I jumped for a way out without thinking and I can only ask your pardon. I am deeply ashamed. —There's no way out, I suppose, but the truth—if we can find it."

Fastolfe said, "Don't despair. You have already uncovered events in connection with Jander that I never dreamed of. You may uncover more and, eventually, what seems altogether a mystery to us now may unfold and become plain. What do you plan to do next?"

But Baley could think of nothing through the shame of his fiasco. He said, "I don't really know."

"Well, then, it was unfair of me to ask. You have had a long day and not an easy one. It is not surprising that your brain is a bit sluggish now. Why not rest, view a film, go to sleep? You will be better off in the morning."

Baley nodded and mumbled, "Perhaps you're right."

But, at the moment, he didn't think he'd be any better off in the morning at all.

30

The bedroom was cold, both in temperature and ambience. Baley shivered slightly. So low a temperature within a room gave it the unpleasant feeling of being Outside. The walls were faintly off-white and (unusual for Fastolfe's establishment) were not decorated. The floor seemed to the sight to be of smooth ivory, but to the bare feet it felt carpeted. The bed was white and the smooth blanket was cold to the touch.

He sat down at the edge of the mattress and found it yielded very slightly to the pressure of his weight.

He said to Daneel, who had entered with him, "Daneel, does it disturb you when a human being tells a lie?"

"I am aware that human beings lie on occasion, Partner Elijah. Sometimes, a lie might be useful or even mandatory. My feeling about a lie depends upon the liar, the occasion, and the reason."

"Can you always tell when a human being lies?"

"No, Partner Elijah."

"Does it seem to you that Dr. Fastolfe often lies?"

"It has never seemed to me that Dr. Fastolfe has told a lie."

"Even in connection with Jander's death?"

"As far as I can tell, he tells the truth in every respect."

"Perhaps he has instructed you to say that—were I to ask?"

"He has not, Partner Elijah."

"But perhaps he instructed you to say that, too—"

He paused. Again—of what use was it to cross-examine a robot? And in this particular case, he was inviting infinite regression.

He was suddenly aware that the mattress had been yielding slowly under him until it now half-enfolded his hips. He rose suddenly and said, "Is there any way of warming the room, Daneel?"

"It will feel warmer when you are under the cover with the light out, Partner Elijah."

"Ah." He looked about suspiciously. "Would you put the light out, Daneel, and remain in the room when you have done so?"

The light went out almost at once and Baley realized that his supposition that this room, at least, was undecorated was totally wrong. As soon as it was dark, he felt he was Outside. There was the soft sound of wind in trees and the small, sleepy mutters of distant lifeforms. There was also the illusion of stars overhead, with an occasional drifting cloud that was just barely visible.

"Put the light back on, Daneel!"

The room flooded with light.

"Daneel," said Baley. "I don't want any of that. I want no stars, no clouds, no sounds, no trees, no wind—no scents, either. I want darkness—featureless darkness. Could you arrange that?"

"Certainly, Partner Elijah."

"Then do so. And show me how I may myself put out the light when I am ready to sleep."

"I am here to protect you, Partner Elijah."

Baley said grumpily, "You can do that, I am sure, from just the other side of the door. Giskard, I imagine, will be just outside the windows, if, indeed, there are windows beyond the draperies."

"There are. —If you cross that threshold, Partner Elijah, you will find a Personal reserved for yourself. That section of the wall is not material and you will move easily through it. The light will turn on as you enter and it will go out as you leave—and there are no decorations. You will be able to shower, if you wish, or do anything else that you care to before retiring or after waking."

Baley turned in the indicated direction. He saw no break in the wall, but the floor molding in that spot did show a thickening as though it were a threshold.

"How do I see it in the dark, Daneel?" he asked.

"That section of the wall—which is not a wall—will glow faintly. As for the room light, there is this depression in the headboard of your bed which, if you place your finger within it, will darken the room if light—or lighten it if dark."

"Thank you. You may leave now."

Half an hour later, he was through with the Personal and found himself huddling beneath the blanket, with the light out, enveloped by a warm spirit-hugging darkness.

As Fastolfe had said, it had been a long day. It was almost unbelievable that it had been only that morning that he had arrived on Aurora. He had learned a great deal and yet none of it had done him any good.

He lay in the dark and went over the events of the day in quiet succession, hoping that something might occur to him that had eluded him before—but nothing like that happened.

So much for the quietly thoughtful, keen-eyed, subtle-brained Elijah Baley of the hyperwave drama.

The mattress was again half-enfolding him and it was like a warm enclosure. He moved slightly and it straightened beneath him, then slowly molded itself to fit his new position.

There was no point in trying, with his worn, sleep-seeking mind, to go over the day again, but he could not help trying a second time, following his own footsteps on this, his first day on Aurora—from the spaceport to Fastolfe's establishment, then to Gladia's, then back to Fastolfe.

Gladia—more beautiful than he remembered but hard—something hard about her—or has she just grown a protective shell—poor woman. He thought warmly of her reaction to the touch of her hand against his cheek—if he could have remained with her, he could have taught her—stupid Aurorans—disgustingly casual attitude toward sex— anything goes—which means nothing really goes—not worthwhile— stupid—to Fastolfe, to Gladia, back to Fastolfe—back to Fastolfe.

He moved a little and then abstractedly felt the mattress remold again. Back to Fastolfe. What happened on the way back to Fastolfe? Something said? Something not said? And on the ship before he ever got to Aurora—something that fit in—

Baley was in the never-never world of half-sleep, when the mind is liberated and follows a law of its own. It is like the body flying, soaring through the air and liberated of gravity.

Of its own accord, it was taking the events—little aspects he had not noted—putting them together—one thing adding to another— clicking into place—forming a web—a fabric—

And then, it seemed to him, he heard a sound and he roused himself to a level of wakefulness. He listened, heard nothing, and sank once more into the half-sleep to take up the line of thought—and it eluded him.

It was like a work of art sinking into a morass. He could still see its outlines, the masses of color. They got dimmer, but he still knew it was there. And even as he scrambled desperately for it, it was gone altogether and he remembered nothing of it. Nothing at all.

Had he actually thought of anything or was the memory of having done so itself an illusion born of some drifting nonsense in a mind asleep? And he was, indeed, asleep.

When he woke briefly during the night, he thought to himself: I had an idea. An important idea.

But he remembered nothing, except that something had been there.

He remained awake a while, staring into the darkness. If, in fact, something had been there—it would come back in time.

Or it might not! (Jehoshaphat!)

—And he slept again.

Fastolfe and Vasilia

31

Baley woke with a start and drew in his breath with sharp suspicion. There was a faint and unrecognizable odor in the air that vanished by his second breath.

Daneel stood gravely at the side of the bed. He said, "I trust, Partner Elijah, that you have slept well."

Baley looked around. The drapes were still closed, but it was clearly daylight Outside. Giskard was laying out clothing, totally different, from shoes to jacket, from anything he had worn the day before.

He said, "Quite well, Daneel. Did something awaken me?"

"There was an injection of antisomnin in the room's air circulation, Partner Elijah. It activates the arousal system. We used a smaller than normal amount, since we were uncertain of your reaction. Perhaps we should have used a smaller amount still."

Baley said, "It did seem to be rather like a paddle over the rear. What time is it?"

Daneel said, "It is 0705, by Auroran measure. Physiologically, breakfast will be ready in half an hour." He said it without a trace of humor, though a human being might have found a smile appropriate.

Giskard said, his voice stiffer and a trifle less intoned than Daneel's, "Sir, friend Daneel and I may not enter the Personal. If you will do so and let us know if there is anything you will need, we will supply it at once."

"Yes, of course." Baley raised himself, swung around, and got out of bed.

Giskard began stripping the bed at once. "May I have your pajamas, sir?"

Baley hesitated for a moment only. It was a robot who asked, nothing more. He disrobed and handed the garment to Giskard, who took it with a small, grave nod of acceptance.

Baley looked at himself with distaste. He was suddenly conscious of a middle-aged body that was very likely in less good condition than Fastolfe's, which was nearly three times as old.

Automatically, he looked for his slippers and found there were none. Presumably, he needed none. The floor seemed warm and soft to his feet.

He stepped into the Personal and called out for instructions. From the other side of the illusory section of the wall, Giskard solemnly

479

explained the working of the shaver, of the toothpaste dispenser, explained how to put the flushing device on automatic, how to control
the temperature of the shower.

Everything was on a grander and more elaborate scale than anything
Earth had to offer and there were no partitions on the other side of
which he could hear the movements and involuntary sounds of someone else, something he had to ignore rigidly to maintain the illusion
of privacy.

It was effete, thought Baley somberly as he went through the luxurious ritual, but it was an effeteness that (he already knew) he could
become accustomed to. If he stayed here on Aurora any length of
time, he would find the culture shock of returning to Earth painfully
intense, *particularly* with respect to the Personal. He hoped that the
readjustment would not take long, but he also hoped that any Earthpeople who settled new worlds would not feel impelled to cling to the
concept of Community Personals.

Perhaps, thought Baley, that was how one ought to define "effete":
That to which one can become easily accustomed.

Baley stepped out of the Personal, various functions completed, chin
new-cropped, teeth glistening, body showered and dry. He said, "Giskard, where do I find the deodorant?"

Giskard said, "I do not understand, sir."

Daneel said quickly, "When you activated the lathering control,
Partner Elijah, that introduced a deodorant effect. I ask pardon for
friend Giskard's failure to understand. He lacks my experience on
Earth."

Baley lifted his eyebrows dubiously and began to dress with Giskard's help.

He said, "I see that you and Giskard are still with me every step of
the way. Has there been any sign of any attempt at putting me out of
the way?"

Daneel said, "None thus far, Partner Elijah. Nevertheless, it would
be wise to have friend Giskard and myself with you at all times, if that
can possibly be managed."

"Why is that, Daneel?"

"For two reasons, Partner Elijah. First, we can help you with any
aspect of Auroran culture or folkways with which you are unfamiliar.
Second, friend Giskard, in particular, can record and reproduce every
word of every conversation you may have. This may be of value to
you. You will recall that there were times in your conversations with
both Dr. Fastolfe and with Miss Gladia when friend Giskard and I
were at a distance or in another room—"

"So that conversations were not recorded by Giskard?"

"Actually, they were, Partner Elijah, but with low fidelity—and
there may be portions that will not be as clear as we would want

them to be. It would be better if we stayed as close to you as is convenient."

Baley said, "Daneel, are you of the opinion that I will be more at ease if I think of you as guides and as recording devices, rather than as guards? Why not simply come to the conclusion that, as guards, you two are completely unnecessary. Since there have been no attempts at me so far, why isn't it possible to conclude that there will be no attempts at me in the future?"

"No, Partner Elijah, that would be incautious. Dr. Fastolfe feels that you are viewed with great apprehension by his enemies. They had made attempts to persuade the Chairman not to give Dr. Fastolfe permission to call you in and they will surely continue to attempt to persuade him to have you ordered back to Earth at the earliest possible moment."

"That sort of peaceful opposition requires no guards."

"No, sir, but if the opposition has reason to fear that you may exculpate Dr. Fastolfe, it is possible that they may feel driven to extremes. You are, after all, not an Auroran and the inhibitions against violence on our world would therefore be weakened in your case."

Baley said dourly, "The fact that I've been here a whole day and that nothing has happened should relieve their minds greatly and reduce the threat of violence considerably."

"It would indeed seem so," said Daneel, showing no signs that he recognized the irony in Baley's voice.

"On the other hand," said Baley, "if I seem to make progress, then the danger to me immediately increases."

Daneel paused to consider, then said, "That would seem to be a logical consequence."

"And, therefore, you and Giskard will come with me wherever I go, just in case I manage to do my job a little too well."

Daneel paused again, then said, "Your way of putting it, Partner Elijah, puzzles me, but you seem to be correct."

"In that case," said Baley, "I'm ready for breakfast, though it does take the edge off my appetite to be told that the alternative to failure is attempted assassination."

32

Fastolfe smiled at Baley across the breakfast table. "Did you sleep well, Mr. Baley?"

Baley studied the slice of ham with fascination. It had to be cut with a knife. It was grainy. It had a discrete strip of fat running down one side. It had, in short, not been processed. The result was that it tasted hammier, so to speak.

There were also fried eggs, with the yolk flattened semisphere in the center, rimmed by white, rather like some daisies that Ben had pointed out to him in the field back on Earth. Intellectually, he knew what an egg looked like before it was processed and he knew that it contained both a yolk and a white, but he had never seen them still separate when ready to eat. Even on the ship coming here and even on Solaria, eggs, when served, were scrambled.

He looked up sharply at Fastolfe. "Pardon me?"

Fastolfe said patiently, "Did you sleep well?"

"Yes. Quite well. I would probably still be sleeping if it hadn't been for the antisomnin."

"Ah yes. Not quite the hospitality a guest has the right to expect, but I felt you might want an early start."

"You are entirely right. And I'm not exactly a guest, either."

Fastolfe ate in silence for a moment or two. He sipped at his hot drink, then said, "Has any enlightenment come overnight? Have you awakened, perhaps, with a new perspective, a new thought?"

Baley looked at Fastolfe suspiciously, but the other's face reflected no sarcasm. As Baley lifted his drink to his lips, he said, "I'm afraid not. I am as ineffectual now as I was last night." He sipped and involuntarily made a face.

Fastolfe said, "I'm sorry. You find the drink unpalatable?"

Baley grunted and cautiously tasted it again.

Fastolfe said, "It is simply coffee, you know. Decaffeinated."

Baley frowned. "It doesn't taste like coffee and— Pardon me, Dr. Fastolfe, I don't want to begin to sound paranoid, but Daneel and I have just had a half-joking exchange on the possibility of violence against me—half-joking on my part, of course, not on Daneel's—and it is in my mind that one way they might get at me is—"

His voice trailed away.

Fastolfe's eyebrows moved upward. He reached for Baley's coffee with a murmur of apology and smelled it. He then ladled out a small portion by spoon and tasted it. He said, "Perfectly normal, Mr. Baley. This is not an attempt at poisoning."

Baley said, "I'm sorry to behave so foolishly, since I know this has been prepared by your own robots—but are you certain?"

Fastolfe smiled. "Robots have been tampered with before now. —However, there has been no tampering this time. It is just that coffee, although universally popular on the various worlds, comes in different strains. It is notorious that each human being prefers the coffee of his own world. I'm sorry, Mr. Baley, I have no Earth strain to give you. Would you prefer milk? That is relatively constant from world to world. Fruit juice? Aurora's grape juice is considered superior throughout the worlds, generally. There are some who hint, darkly, that we allow it to ferment somewhat, but that, of course, is not true. Water?"

"I'll try your grape juice." Baley looked at the coffee dubiously. "I suppose I ought to try to get used to this."

"Not at all," said Fastolfe. "Why seek out the unpleasant if that is unnecessary? —And so"—his smile seemed a bit strained as he returned to his earlier remark—"night and sleep have brought no useful reflection to you?"

"I'm sorry," said Baley. Then, frowning at a dim memory, "Although—"

"Yes?"

"I have the impression that just before falling asleep, in the free-association limbo between sleep and waking, it seemed to me that I had something."

"Indeed? What?"

"I don't know. The thought drove me into wakefulness but didn't follow me there. Or else some imagined sound distracted me. I don't remember. I snatched at the thought, but didn't retrieve it. It's gone. I *think* that this sort of thing is not uncommon."

Fastolfe looked thoughtful. "Are you sure of this?"

"Not really. The thought grew so tenuous so rapidly I couldn't even be sure that I had actually had it. And even if I had, it may have seemed to make sense to me only because I was half-asleep. If it were repeated to me now in broad daylight, it might make no sense at all."

"But whatever it was and however fugitive, it would have left a trace, surely."

"I imagine so, Dr. Fastolfe. In which case, it will come to me again. I'm confident of that."

"Ought we to wait?"

"What else can we do?"

"There's such a thing as a Psychic Probe."

Baley sat back in his chair and stared at Fastolfe for a moment. He said, "I've heard of it, but it isn't used in police work on Earth."

"We're not on Earth, Mr. Baley," said Fastolfe softly.

"It can do brain damage. Am I not right?"

"Not likely, in the proper hands."

"Not impossible, even in the proper hands," said Baley. "It's my understanding that it cannot be used on Aurora except under sharply defined conditions. Those it is used on must be guilty of a major crime or must—"

"Yes, Mr. Baley, but that refers to Aurorans. You are not an Auroran."

"You mean because I'm an Earthman I'm to be treated as inhuman?"

Fastolfe smiled and spread his hands. "Come, Mr. Baley. It was just a thought. Last night you were desperate enough to suggest trying to solve our dilemma by placing Gladia in a horrible and tragic position. I was wondering if you were desperate enough to risk your-self?"

Baley rubbed his eyes and, for a minute or so, remained silent. Then, in an altered voice, he said, "I was wrong last night. I admitted it. As for this matter now, there is no assurance that what I thought of, when half-asleep, had any relevance to the problem. It may have been pure fantasy—illogical nonsense. There may have been no thought at all. Nothing. Would you consider it wise, for so small a likelihood of gain, to risk damage to my brain, when it is upon that for which you say you depend for a solution to the problem?"

Fastolfe nodded. "You plead your case eloquently—and I was not really serious."

"Thank you, Dr. Fastolfe."

"But where are we to go from here?"

"For one thing, I wish to speak to Gladia again. There are points concerning which I need clarification."

"You should have taken them up last night."

"So I should, but I had more than I could properly absorb last night and there were points that escaped me. I am an investigator and not an infallible computer."

Fastolfe said, "I was not imputing blame. It's just that I hate to see Gladia unnecessarily disturbed. In view of what you told me last night, I can only assume she must be in a state of deep distress."

"Undoubtedly. But she is also desperately anxious to find out what happened—who, if anyone, killed the one she viewed as her husband. That's understandable, too. I'm sure she'll be willing to help me. —And I wish to speak to another person as well."

"To whom?"

"To your daughter Vasilia."

"To Vasilia? Why? What purpose will that serve?"

"She is a roboticist. I would like to talk to a roboticist other than yourself."

"I do not wish that, Mr. Baley."

They had finished eating. Baley stood up. "Dr. Fastolfe, once again I must remind you that I am here at your request. I have no formal authority to do police work. I have no connection with any Auroran authorities. The only chance I have of getting to the bottom of this miserable mess is to hope that various people will voluntarily cooper-ate with me and answer my questions.

"If you stop me from attempting this, then it is clear that I can get no farther than I am right now, which is nowhere. It will also look extremely bad for you—and therefore for Earth—so I urge you not to stand in my way. If you make it possible for me to interview anyone I wish—or even simply *try* to make it possible by interceding on my behalf—then the people of Aurora will surely consider that to be a sign of self-conscious innocence on your part. If you hamper my investigation, on the other hand, to what conclusion can they come but that you are guilty and fear exposure?"

Fastolfe said, with poorly suppressed annoyance, "I understand that, Mr. Baley. But why Vasilia? There are other roboticists."

"Vasilia is your daughter. She knows you. She might have strong opinions concerning the likelihood of your destroying a robot. Since she is a member of the Robotics Institute and on the side of your political enemies, any favorable evidence she may give would be persuasive."

"And if she testifies against me?"

"We'll face that when it comes. Would you get in touch with her and ask her to receive me?"

Fastolfe said resignedly, "I will oblige you, but you are mistaken if you think I can easily persuade her to see you. She may be too busy— or think she is. She may be away from Aurora. She may simply not wish to be involved. I tried to explain last night that she has reason— thinks she has reason—to be hostile to me. My asking her to see you may indeed impel her to refuse, merely as a sign of her displeasure with me."

"Would you try, Dr. Fastolfe?"

Fastolfe sighed. "I will try while you are at Gladia's. —I presume you wish to see her directly? I might point out that a trimensional viewing would do. The image is high enough in quality so that you will not be able to tell it from personal presence."

"I'm aware of that, Dr. Fastolfe, but Gladia is a Solarian and has unpleasant associations with trimensional viewing. And, in any case, I am of the opinion that there is an intangible additional effectiveness in being within touching distance. The present situation is too delicate and the difficulties too great for me to want to give up that additional effectiveness."

"Well, I'll alert Gladia." He turned away, hesitated, and turned back. "But, Mr. Baley—"

"Yes, Dr. Fastolfe?"

"Last night you told me that the situation was serious enough for you to disregard any convenience it might cause Gladia. There were, you pointed out, greater things at stake."

"That's so, but you can rely on me not to disturb her if I can help it."

"I am not talking about Gladia now. I merely warn you that this essentially proper view of yours should be extended to myself. I don't expect you to worry about my convenience or pride if you should get a chance to talk to Vasilia. I don't look forward to the results, but if you do talk to her, I will have to endure any ensuing embarrassment and you must not seek to spare me. Do you understand?"

"To be perfectly honest, Dr. Fastolfe, it was never my intention to spare you. If I have to weigh your embarrassment or shame against the welfare of your policies and against the welfare of my world, I would not hesitate a moment to shame you."

"Good!—And Mr. Baley, we must extend that attitude also to yourself. *Your* convenience must not be allowed to stand in the way."

"It wasn't allowed to do so when you decided to have me brought here without consulting me."

"I'm referring to something else. If, after a reasonable time—not a long time, but a reasonable time—you make no progress toward a solution, we will have to consider the possibilities of psychic-probing, after all. Our last chance might be to find out what it is your mind knows that you do not know it knows."

"It may know nothing, Dr. Fastolfe."

Fastolfe looked at Baley sadly. "Agreed. But, as you said concerning the possibility of Vasilia testifying against me—we'll face that when it comes."

He turned away again and walked out of the room.

Baley looked after him thoughtfully. It seemed to him now that if he made progress he would face physical reprisals of an unknown— but possibly dangerous—kind. And if he did not make progress, he would face the Psychic Probe, which could scarcely be better.

"Jehoshaphat!" he muttered softly to himself.

33

The walk to Gladia's seemed shorter than it had on the day before. The day was sunlit and pleasant again, but the vista looked not at all the same. The sunlight slanted from the opposite direction, of course, and the coloring seemed slightly different.

It could be that the plant life looked a bit different in the morning than in the evening—or smelled different. Baley had, on occasion, thought that of Earth's plant life as well, he remembered.

Daneel and Giskard accompanied him again, but they traveled more closely to him and seemed less intensely alert.

Baley said idly, "Does the sun shine here all the time?"

"It does not, Partner Elijah," said Daneel. "Were it to do so, that would be disastrous for the plant world and, therefore, for humanity. The prediction is, in fact, for the sky to cloud over in the course of the day."

"What was that?" asked Baley, startled. A small and gray-brown animal was crouched in the grass. Seeing them, it hopped away in leisurely fashion.

"A rabbit, sir," said Giskard.

Baley relaxed. He had seen them in the fields of Earth, too.

Gladia was not waiting for them at the door this time, but she was clearly expecting them. When a robot ushered them in, she did not stand up, but said, with something between crossness and weariness, "Dr. Fastolfe told me you had to see me again. What now?"

She was wearing a robe that clung tightly to her body and was clearly wearing nothing underneath. Her hair was pulled back shapelessly and her face was pallid. She looked more drawn than she had the day before and it was clear that she had had little sleep.

Daneel, remembering what had happened the day before, did not enter the room. Giskard entered, however, glanced keenly about, then retired to a wall niche. One of Gladia's robots stood in another niche.

Baley said, "I'm terribly sorry, Gladia, to have to bother you again."

Gladia said, "I forgot to tell you last night that, after Jander is torched, he will, of course, be recycled for use in the robot factories again. It will be amusing, I suppose, to know that each time I see a newly formed robot, I can take time to realize that many of Jander's atoms form part of him."

Baley said, "We ourselves, when we die, are recycled—and who knows what atoms of whom are in you and me right now or in whom ours will someday be."

"You are very right, Elijah. And you remind me how easy it is to philosophize over the sorrows of others."

"That is right, too, Gladia, but I did not come to philosophize."

"Do what you came to do, then."

"I must ask questions."

"Weren't yesterday's enough? Have you spent the time since then in thinking up new ones?"

"In part, yes, Gladia.—Yesterday, you said that even after you were with Jander—as wife and husband—there were men who offered themselves to you and that you refused. It is that which I must question you about."

"Why?"

Baley ignored the question. "Tell me," he said, "how many men offered themselves to you during the time you were married to Jander?"

"I don't keep records, Elijah. Three or four."

"Were any of them persistent? Did anyone offer himself more than once?"

Gladia, who had been avoiding his eyes, now looked at him full and said, "Have you talked to others about this?"

Baley shook his head. "I have talked on this subject to no one but you. From your question, however, I suspect that there was at least one who was persistent."

"One. Santirix Gremionis." She sighed. "Aurorans have such pe-

culiar names and he *was* peculiar—for an Auroran. I had never met
one as repetitious in the matter as he. He was always polite, always
accepted my refusal with a small smile and a stately bow, and then, as
like as not, he would try again the next week or even the next day.
The mere repetition was a small discourtesy. A decent Auroran would
accept a refusal permanently unless the prospective partner made it
reasonably plain there was a change of mind."

"Tell me again— Did those who offered themselves to you know of
your relationship with Jander?"

"It was not something I mentioned in casual conversation."

"Well, then, consider this Gremionis, specifically. Did *he* know that
Jander was your husband?"

"I never told him so."

"Don't dismiss it like that, Gladia. It's not a matter of his being told.
Unlike the others, he offered himself repeatedly. How often would you
say, by the way? Three times? Four? How many?"

"I did not count," said Gladia wearily. "It might have been a dozen
times or more. If he weren't a likable person otherwise, I would have
had my robots bar the establishment to him."

"Ah, but you didn't. And it takes time to make multiple offerings.
He came to see you. He encountered you. He had time to note Jander's presence and how you behaved to him. Might he not have
guessed at the relationship?"

Gladia shook her head. "I don't think so. Jander never intruded
when I was with any human being."

"Were those your instructions? I presume they must have been."

"They were. And before you suggest I was ashamed of the relationship, it was merely an attempt to avoid bothersome complications. I
have retained some instinct of privacy about sex that Aurorans don't
have."

"Think again. Might he have guessed? Here he is, a man in
love—"

"In love!" The sound she made was almost a snort. "What do Aurorans know of love?"

"A man who considers himself in love. You are not responsive. Might
he not, with the sensitivity and suspicion of a disappointed lover, have
guessed? Consider! Did he ever make any roundabout reference to
Jander? Anything to cause you the slightest suspicion—"

"No! No! It would be unheard of for any Auroran to comment adversely on the sexual preferences or habits of another."

"Not necessarily adversely. A humorous comment, perhaps. *Any* indication that he suspected the relationship."

"No! If young Gremionis had ever breathed a word of that sort, he
would never have seen the inside of my establishment again and
I would have seen to it that he never approached me again. —But he

wouldn't have done anything of the sort. He was the soul of eager politeness to me."

"You say 'young.' How old is this Gremionis?"

"About my age. Thirty-five. Perhaps even a year or two younger."

"A child," said Baley sadly. "Even younger than I am. But at that age— Suppose he guessed at your relationship with Jander and said nothing—nothing at all. Might he not, nevertheless, have been jealous?"

"Jealous?"

It occurred to Baley that the word might have little meaning on Aurora or Solaria. "Angered that you should prefer another to himself."

Gladia said sharply, "I know the meaning of the word 'jealous.' I repeated it only out of surprise that you should think any Auroran was jealous. On Aurora, people are not jealous over sex. Over other things certainly, but not over sex." There was a definite sneer upon her face. "Even if he were jealous, what would it matter? What could he do?"

"Wasn't it possible he might have told Jander that the relationship with a robot would endanger your position on Aurora—"

"That would not have been true!"

"Jander might have believed it if he were told so—believed he was endangering you, harming you. Might not that have been the reason for the mental freeze-out?"

"Jander would never have believed that. He made me happy every day he was my husband and I told him so."

Baley remained calm. She was missing the point, but he would simply have to make it clearer. "I am sure he believed you, but he might also feel impelled to believe someone else who told him the reverse. If he were then caught in an unbearable First Law dilemma—"

Gladia's face contorted and she shrieked. "That's *mad*. You're just telling me the old fairy tale of Susan Calvin and the mindreading robot. No one over the age of ten can possibly believe that."

"Isn't it possible that—"

"No, it isn't. I'm from Solaria and I know enough about robots to know it isn't possible. It would take an incredible expert to tie First Law knots in a robot. Dr. Fastolfe might be able to do it, but certainly not Santirix Gremionis. Gremionis is a stylist. He works on human beings. He cuts hair, designs clothing. I do the same, but at least I work on robots. Gremionis has never touched a robot. He knows nothing about them, except to order one to close the window or something like that. Are you trying to tell me that it was the relationship between Jander and me—me"—she tapped herself harshly on the breastbone with one rigid finger, the swells of her small breasts scarcely showing under her robe—"that caused Jander's death?"

"It was nothing you did knowingly," said Baley, wanting to stop but unable to quit probing. "What if Gremionis had learned from Dr. Fastolfe how to—"

"Gremionis didn't know Dr. Fastolfe and couldn't have understood anything Dr. Fastolfe might have told him, anyhow."

"You can't know for certain what Gremionis might or might not understand and, as for not knowing Dr. Fastolfe—Gremionis must have been frequently in your establishment if he hounded you so and—"

"And Dr. Fastolfe was almost never in my establishment. Last night, when he came with you, it was only the second time he had crossed my threshold. He was afraid that to be too close to me would drive me away. He admitted that once. He lost his daughter that way, he thought—something foolish like that. —You see, Elijah, when you live several centuries, you have plenty of time to lose *thousands* of things. Be th-thankful for short life, Elijah." She was weeping uncontrollably.

Baley looked and felt helpless. "I'm sorry, Gladia. I have no more questions. Shall I call a robot? Will you need help?"

She shook her head and waved her hand at him. "Just go away—go away," she said in a strangled voice. "Go away."

Baley hesitated and then strode out of the room, taking one last, uncertain look at her as he walked out the door. Giskard followed in his footsteps and Daneel joined him as he left the house. He scarcely noticed. It occurred to him, abstractedly, that he was coming to accept their presence as he would have that of his shadow or of his clothing, that he was reaching a point where he would feel bare without them.

He walked rapidly back toward the Fastolfe establishment, his mind churning. His desire to see Vasilia had at first been a matter of desperation, a lack of any other object of curiosity, but now things had changed. There was just a chance that he had stumbled on something vital.

34

Fastolfe's homely face was set in grim lines when Baley returned. "Any progress?" he asked.

"I eliminated part of a possibility. —Perhaps."

"*Part* of a possibility? How do you eliminate the other part? Better yet, how do you *establish* a possibility?"

Baley said, "By finding it impossible to eliminate a possibility, a beginning is made at establishing one."

"And if you find it impossible to eliminate the other part of the possibility you mysteriously mentioned?"

Baley shrugged. "Before we waste our time considering that, I must see your daughter."

Fastolfe looked dejected. "Well, Mr. Baley, I did as you asked me to do and tried to contact her. It was necessary to awaken her."

"You mean she is in part of the planet where it is night? I hadn't thought of that." Baley felt chagrined. "I'm afraid I'm fool enough to imagine I'm on Earth still. In underground Cities, day and night lose their meaning and time tends to be uniform."

"It's not that bad. Eos is the robotics center of Aurora and you'll find few roboticists who live out of it. She was simply sleeping and being awakened did not improve her temper, apparently. She would not speak to me."

"Call again," said Baley urgently.

"I spoke to her secretarial robot and there was an uncomfortable relaying of messages. She made it quite plain she will not speak to me in any fashion. She was a little more flexible with you. The robot announced that she would give you five minutes on her private viewing channel, if you call" —Fastolfe consulted the time-strip on the wall—"in half an hour. She will not see you in person under any conditions."

"The conditions are insufficient and so is the time. I must see her in person for as long as is needed. Did you explain the importance of this, Dr. Fastolfe?"

"I tried. She is not concerned."

"You are her father. Surely—"

"She is less inclined to bend her decision for my sake than for a randomly chosen stranger. I knew this, so I made use of Giskard."

"Giskard?"

"Oh yes. Giskard is a great favorite of hers. When she was studying robotics at the university, she took the liberty of adjusting some minor aspects of his programming—and nothing makes for a closer relationship with a robot than that—except for Gladia's method, of course. It was almost as though Giskard were Andrew Martin—"

"Who is Andrew Martin?"

"Was, not is," said Fastolfe. "You have never heard of him?"

"Never!"

"How odd! These ancient legends of ours all have Earth as their setting, yet on Earth they are not known. —Andrew Martin was a robot who, gradually, step by step, was supposed to have become humaniform. To be sure, there have been humaniform robots before Daneel, but they were all simple toys, little more than automatons. Nevertheless, amazing stories are told of the abilities of Andrew Martin—a sure sign of the legendary nature of the tale. There was a woman who was part of the legends who is usually known as Little Miss. The relationship is too complicated to describe now, but I suppose that every little girl on Aurora had daydreamed of being Little Miss and of

having Andrew Martin as a robot. Vasilia did—and Giskard was her
Andrew Martin."

"Well, then?"

"I asked her robot to tell her that you would be accompanied by
Giskard. She hasn't seen him in years and I thought that might lure
her into agreeing to see you."

"But it didn't, I presume."

"It didn't."

"Then we must think of something else. There must be some way
of inducing her to see me."

Fastolfe said, "Perhaps you will think of one. In a few minutes, you
will view her on trimensic and you will have five minutes to convince
her that she ought to see you personally."

"Five minutes! What can I do in five minutes?"

"I don't know. It is better, after all, than nothing."

35

Fifteen minutes later, Baley stood before the trimensional viewing
screen, ready to meet Vasilia Fastolfe.

Dr. Fastolfe had left, saying, with a wry smile, that his presence
would certainly make his daughter less amenable to persuasion. Nor
was Daneel present. Only Giskard remained behind to keep Baley
company.

Giskard said, "Dr. Vasilia's trimensic channel is open for reception.
Are you ready, sir?"

"As ready as I can be," said Baley grimly. He had refused to sit,
feeling he might be more imposing if he were standing. (How imposing
could an Earthman be?)

The screen grew bright as the rest of the room dimmed and a woman
appeared—in rather uncertain focus, at first. She was standing facing
him, her right hand resting on a laboratory bench laden with sets of
diagrams. (No doubt *she* planned to be imposing, too.)

As the focus sharpened, the edges of the screen seemed to melt
away and the image of Vasilia (if it were she) deepened and became
three-dimensional. She was standing in the room with every sign of
solid reality, except that the decor of the room she was in did not
match the room Baley was in and the break was a sharp one.

She was wearing a dark brown skirt that divided into loose trouser
legs that were semitransparent, so that her legs, from midthigh down,
were shadowily visible. Her blouse was tight and sleeveless, so that her
arms were bare to the shoulder. Her neckline was low and her hair,
quite blond, was in tight curls.

She had none of her father's plainness and certainly not his large

ears. Baley could only assume she had had a beautiful mother and was
fortunate in the allotment of genes.

She was short and Baley could see a remarkable resemblance to
Gladia in her facial features, although her expression was far colder
and seemed to bear the mark of a dominating personality.

She said sharply, "Are you the Earthman come to solve my father's
problems?"

"Yes, Dr. Fastolfe," said Baley in an equally clipped manner.

"You may call me Dr. Vasilia. I do not wish the confusion of being
mistaken for my father."

"Dr. Vasilia, I must have a chance to deal with you, face-to-face, for
a reasonably extended period."

"No doubt you feel that. You are, of course, an Earthman and a
certain source of infection."

"I have been medically treated and I am quite safe to be with. Your
father has been constantly with me for over a day."

"My father pretends to be an idealist and must do foolish things at
times to support the pretense. I will not imitate him."

"I take it you do not wish him harm. You will bring him harm if
you refuse to see me."

"You are wasting time. I will not see you, except in this manner,
and half the period I have allotted is gone. If you wish, we can stop
this now if you find it unsatisfactory."

"Giskard is here, Dr. Vasilia, and would like to urge you to see me."

Giskard stepped into the field of vision. "Good morning, Little
Miss," he said in a low voice.

For a moment, Vasilia looked embarrassed and, when she spoke, it
was in a somewhat softer tone. "I am glad to view you, Giskard, and
will see you any time you wish, but I will not see this Earthman, even
at your urging."

"In that case," said Baley, throwing in all his reserves desperately,
"I must take the case of Santirix Gremionis to the public without the
benefit of having consulted you."

Vasilia's eyes widened and her hand on the table lifted upward and
clenched into a fist. "What is this about Gremionis?"

"Only that he is a handsome young man and he knows you well.
Am I to deal with these matters without hearing what you have to
say?"

"I will tell you right now that—"

"No," said Baley loudly. "You will tell me nothing unless I see you
face-to-face."

Her mouth twitched. "I will see you, then, but I will not remain
with you one moment more than I choose. I warn you. —And bring
Giskard."

The trimensional connection broke off with a snap and Baley felt himself turn dizzy at the sudden change in background that resulted. He made his way to a chair and sat down.

Giskard's hand was on his elbow, making certain that he reached the chair safely. "Can I help you in any way, sir?" he asked.

"I'm all right," said Baley. "I just need to catch my breath."

Dr. Fastolfe was standing before him. "My apologies, again, for failure in my duties as a host. I listened on an extension that was equipped to receive and not transmit. I wanted to see my daughter, even if she didn't see me."

"I understand," said Baley, panting slightly. "If manners dictate that what you did requires an apology, then I forgive you."

"But what is this about Santirix Gremionis? The name is unfamiliar to me."

Baley looked up at Fastolfe and said, "Dr. Fastolfe, I heard his name from Gladia this morning. I know very little about him, but I took the chance of saying what I did to your daughter anyway. The odds were heavily against me, but the results were what I wanted them to be, nevertheless. As you see, I can make useful deductions, even when I have very little information, so you had better leave me in peace to continue to do so. Please, in the future, cooperate to the full and make no further mention of a Psychic Probe."

Fastolfe was silent and Baley felt a grim satisfaction at having imposed his will first on the daughter, then on the father.

How long he could continue to do so he did not know.

Vasilia

36

Baley paused at the door of the airfoil and said firmly, "Giskard, I do *not* wish the windows opacified. I do *not* wish to sit in the back. I want to sit in the front seat and observe the Outside. Since I will be sitting between you and Daneel, I should be safe enough, unless the car itself is destroyed. And, in that case, we will all be destroyed and it won't matter whether I am in front or in back."

Giskard responded to the force of the statement by retreating into greater respectfulness. "Sir, if you should feel ill—"

"Then you will stop the car and I will climb into the back seat and you can opacify the rear windows. Or you needn't even stop. I can climb over the front seat while you are moving. The point is, Giskard, that it is important for me to become as acquainted with Aurora as is possible and it is important for me, in any case, to become accustomed to the Outside. I am stating this as an order, Giskard."

Daneel said softly, "Partner Elijah is quite correct in his request, friend Giskard. He will be reasonably safe."

Giskard, perhaps reluctantly (Baley could not interpret the expression on his not-quite-human face), gave in and took his place at the controls. Baley followed and looked out of the clear glass of the windshield without quite the assurance he had presented in his voice. However, the pressure of a robot on either side was comforting.

The car rose on its jets of compressed air and swayed a bit as though it were finding its footing. Baley felt a queasy sensation in the pit of his stomach and tried not to regret his brave performance of moments before. There was no use trying to tell himself that Daneel and Giskard showed no signs of fear and should be imitated. They were robots and could not feel fear.

And then the car moved forward suddenly and Baley felt himself pushed hard against the seat. Within a minute he was moving at as fast a speed as he had ever experienced on the Expressways of the City. A wide, grassy road stretched out ahead.

The speed seemed the greater for the fact that there were none of the friendly lights and structures of the City on either side but rather wide gulfs of greenery and irregular formations.

Baley fought to keep his breath steady and to talk as naturally as he might of neutral things.

He said, "We don't seem to be passing any farmland, Daneel. This seems to be unused land."

Daneel said, "This is city territory, Partner Elijah. It is privately owned parkland and estates."

"City?" Baley could not accept the word. He knew what a City was.

"Eos is the largest and most important city on Aurora. The first to be established. The Auroran World Legislature sits here. The Chairman of the Legislature has his estate here and we will be passing it."

Not only a city but the largest. Baley looked about to either side. "I was under the impression that the Fastolfe and Gladia establishments were on the outskirts of Eos. I should think we would have passed the city limits by now."

"Not at all, Partner Elijah. We're passing through its center. The limits are seven kilometers away and our destination is nearly forty kilometers beyond that."

"The center of the city? I see no structures."

"They are not meant to be seen from the road, but there's one you can make out between the trees. That is the establishment of Fuad Labord, a well-known writer."

"Do you know all the establishments by sight?"

"They are in my memory banks," said Daneel solemnly.

"There's no traffic on the road. Why is that?"

"Long distances are covered by air-cars or magnetic subcars. Trimensional connections—"

"They call it viewing on Solaria," said Baley.

"And here, too, in informal conversation, but TVC more formally. That takes care of much communication. Finally, Aurorans are fond of walking and it is not unusual to walk several kilometers for social visiting or even for business meetings where time is not of the essence."

"And we have to get somewhere that's too far to walk, too close for air-cars, and trimensional viewing is not wanted—so we use a ground-car."

"An airfoil, more specifically, Partner Elijah, but that qualifies as a ground-car, I suppose."

"How long will it take to reach Vasilia's establishment?"

"Not long, Partner Elijah. She is at the Robotics Institute, as perhaps you know."

There were some moments of silence and then Baley said, "It looks cloudy near the horizon there."

Giskard negotiated a curve at high speed, the airfoil tipping through an angle of some thirty degrees. Baley choked back a moan and clung to Daneel, who flung his left arm around Baley's shoulders and held

him in a strong viselike grip, one hand on each shoulder. Slowly, Baley
let out his breath as the airfoil righted itself.

Daneel said, "Yes, those clouds will bring precipitation later in the
day, as predicted."

Baley frowned. He had been caught in the rain once—*once*—
during his experimental work in the field Outside on Earth. It was
like standing under a cold shower with his clothes on. There had
been sheer panic for a moment when he realized that there was no
way in which he could reach for any controls that would turn it off.
The water would come down forever! —Then everyone was running
and he ran with them, making for the dryness and controllability of
the City.

But this was Aurora and he had no idea what one did when it began
to rain and there was no City to escape into. Run into the nearest
establishment? Would refugees automatically be welcome?

Then there was another brief turn and Giskard said, "Sir, we are in
the parking lot of the Robotics Institute. We can now enter and visit
the establishment that Dr. Vasilia maintains on the Institute grounds."

Baley nodded. The trip had taken something between fifteen and
twenty minutes (as nearly as he could judge, Earth time) and he was
glad it was over. He said, rather breathlessly, "I want to know something about Dr. Fastolfe's daughter before I meet her. You did not
know her, did you, Daneel?"

Daneel said, "At the time I came into existence, Dr. Fastolfe and
his daughter had been separated for a considerable time. I have never
met her."

"But as for you, Giskard, you and she knew each other well. Is that
not so?"

"It is so, sir," said Giskard impassively.

"And were fond of each other?"

"I believe, sir," said Giskard, "that it gave Dr. Fastolfe's daughter
pleasure to be with me."

"Did it give you pleasure to be with her?"

Giskard seemed to pick his words. "It gives me a sensation that I
think is what human beings mean by 'pleasure' to be with any human
being."

"But more so with Vasilia, I think. Am I right?"

"Her pleasure at being with me, sir," said Giskard, "did seem to
stimulate those positronic potentials that produce actions in me that
are equivalent to those that pleasure produces in human beings. Or
so I was once told by Dr. Fastolfe."

Baley said suddenly, "Why did Vasilia leave her father?"

Giskard said nothing.

Baley said, with the sudden peremptoriness of an Earthman addressing a robot, "I asked you a question, boy."

Giskard turned his head and stared at Baley, who, for a moment, thought the glow in the robot's eyes might be brightening into a blaze of resentment at the demeaning word.

However, Giskard spoke mildly and there was no readable expression in his eyes when he said, "I would like to answer, sir, but in all matters concerning that separation, Miss Vasilia ordered me at that time to say nothing."

"But I'm ordering you to answer me and I can order you very firmly indeed—if I wish to."

Giskard said, "I am sorry. Miss Vasilia, even at that time, was skilled in robotics and the orders she gave me were sufficiently powerful to remain, despite anything you are likely to say, sir."

Baley said, "She must have been skilled in robotics, since Dr. Fastolfe told me she reprogrammed you on occasion."

"It was not dangerous to do so, sir. Dr. Fastolfe himself could always correct any errors."

"Did he have to?"

"He did not, sir."

"What was the nature of the reprogramming?"

"Minor matters, sir."

"Perhaps, but humor me. Just what was it she did?"

Giskard hesitated and Baley knew what that meant at once. The robot said, "I fear that any questions concerning the reprogramming cannot be answered by me."

"You were forbidden?"

"No, sir, but the reprogramming automatically wipes out what went before. If I am changed in any particular, it would seem to me that I have always been as changed and I would have no memory of what I was before I was changed."

"Then how do you know the reprogramming was minor?"

"Since Dr. Fastolfe never saw any need of correcting what Miss Vasilia did—or so he once told me—I can only suppose the changes were minor. You might ask Miss Vasilia, sir."

"I will," said Baley.

"I fear, however, that she will not answer, sir."

Baley's heart sank. So far he had questioned only Dr. Fastolfe, Gladia, and the two robots, all of whom had overriding reasons to cooperate. Now, for the first time, he would be facing an unfriendly subject.

37

Baley stepped out of the airfoil, which was resting on a grassy plot, and felt a certain pleasure in feeling solidity beneath his feet.

He looked around in surprise, for the structures were rather thickly spread, and to his right was a particularly large one, built plainly, rather like a huge right-angled block of metal and glass.

"Is that the Robotics Institute?" he asked.

Daneel said, "This entire complex is the Institute, Partner Elijah. You are seeing only a portion and it is more thickly built up than is common on Aurora because it is a self-contained political entity. It contains home establishments, laboratories, libraries, communal gymnasia, and so on. The large structure is the administrative center."

"This is so un-Auroran, with all these buildings in view—at least judging from what I saw of Eos—that I should think there would be considerable disapproval."

"I believe there was, Partner Elijah, but the head of the Institute is friendly with the Chairman, who has much influence, and there was a special dispensation, I understand, because of research necessities." Daneel looked about thoughtfully. "It is indeed more compact than I had supposed."

"Than you had *supposed*? Have you never been here before, Daneel?"

"No, Partner Elijah."

"How about you, Giskard?"

"No, sir," said Giskard.

Baley said, "You found your way here without trouble—and you seem to know the place."

"We have been suitably informed, Partner Elijah," said Daneel, "since it was necessary that we come with you."

Baley nodded thoughtfully, then said, "Why didn't Dr. Fastolfe come with us?" and decided, once again, that it made no sense to try to catch a robot off-guard. Ask a question rapidly—or unexpectedly—and they simply waited until the question was absorbed and then answered. They were never caught off-guard.

Daneel said, "As Dr. Fastolfe said, he is not a member of the Institute and feels it would be improper to visit uninvited."

"But why is he not a member?"

"The reason for that I have never been told, Partner Elijah."

Baley's eyes turned to Giskard, who said at once, "Nor I, sir."

Did not know? Were told not to know? —Baley shrugged. It did not matter which. Human beings could lie and robots be instructed

Of course, human beings could be browbeaten or maneuvered out of a lie—if the questioner were skillful enough or brutal enough—and robots could be maneuvered out of instruction—if the questioner were skillful enough or unscrupulous enough—but the skills were different and Baley had none at all with respect to robots.

He said, "Where would we be likely to find Dr. Vasilia Fastolfe?"

Daneel said, "This is her establishment immediately before us."

"You have been instructed, then, as to its location?"

"That has been imprinted in our memory banks, Partner Elijah."

"Well, then, lead the way."

The orange sun was well up in the sky now and it was clearly nearing midday. As they approached Vasilia's establishment, they stepped into the shadow of the factory and Baley twitched a little as he felt the temperature drop immediately.

His lips tightened at the thought of occupying and settling worlds without Cities, where the temperature was uncontrolled and subject to unpredictable, idiotic changes. —And, he noted uneasily, the line of clouds at the horizon had advanced somewhat. It could also rain whenever it wished, with water cascading down.

Earth! He longed for the Cities.

Giskard had walked into the establishment first and Daneel held out his arm to prevent Baley from following.

Of course! Giskard was reconnoitering.

So was Daneel, for that matter. His eyes traversed the landscape with an intentness no human being could have duplicated. Baley was certain that those robotic eyes missed nothing. (He wondered why robots were not equipped with four eyes equally distributed about the perimeter of the head—or an optic strip totally circumnavigating it. Daneel could not be expected to, of course, since he had to be human in appearance, but why not Giskard? Or did that introduce complications of vision that the positronic pathways could not handle? For a moment, Baley had a faint vision of the complexities that burdened the life of a roboticist.)

Giskard reappeared in the doorway and nodded. Daneel's arm exerted a respectful pressure and Baley moved forward. The door stood ajar.

There was no lock on Vasilia's establishment, but there had also been none (Baley suddenly remembered) on those of Gladia and of Dr. Fastolfe. A sparse population and separation helped insure privacy and, no doubt, the custom of noninterference helped, too. And, come to think of it, the ubiquitous robot guards were more efficient than any lock could be.

The pressure of Daneel's hand on Baley's upper arm brought the latter to a halt. Giskard, ahead of them, was speaking in a low voice to two robots, who were themselves rather Giskard-like.

A sudden coldness struck the pit of Baley's stomach. What if some rapid maneuver substituted another robot for Giskard? Would he be able to recognize the substitution? Tell two such robots apart? Would he be left with a robot without special instructions to guard him, one who might innocently lead him into danger and then react with insufficient quickness when protection was necessary?

Controlling his voice, he said calmly to Daneel, "Remarkable the similarity in those robots, Daneel. Can you tell them apart?"

"Certainly, Partner Elijah. Their clothing designs are different and their code numbers are different, as well."

"They don't look different to me."

"You are not accustomed to notice that sort of detail."

Baley stared again. "What code numbers?"

"They are easily visible, Partner Elijah, when you know where to look and when your eyes are sensitive farther into the infrared than human eyes are."

"Well, then, I would be in trouble if I had to do the identifying, wouldn't I?"

"Not at all, Partner Elijah. You had but to ask a robot for its full name and serial number. It would tell you."

"Even if instructed to give me a false one?"

"Why should any robot be so instructed?"

Baley decided not to explain.

Giskard was, in any case, returning. He said to Baley, "Sir, you will be received. Come this way, please."

The two robots of the establishment led. Behind them came Baley and Daneel, the latter retaining his grip protectively.

Following in the rear was Giskard.

The two robots stopped before a double door which opened, apparently automatically, in both directions. The room within was suffused with a dim, grayish light—daylight diffusing through thick drapery.

Baley could make out, not very clearly, a small human figure in the room, half-seated on a tall stool, with one elbow resting on a table that ran the length of the wall.

Baley and Daneel entered, Giskard coming up behind them. The door closed, leaving the room dimmer than ever.

A female voice said sharply, "Come no closer! Stay where you are!"

And the room burst into full daylight.

38

Baley blinked and looked upward. The ceiling was glassed and, through it, the sun could be seen. The sun seemed oddly dim, however, and could be looked at, even though that did not seem to affect the quality of the light within. Presumably, the glass (or whatever the transparent substance was) diffused the light without absorbing it.

He looked down at the woman, who still maintained her pose at the stool, and said, "Dr. Vasilia Fastolfe?"

"Dr. Vasilia Aliena, if you want a full name. I do not borrow the names of others. You may call me Dr. Vasilia. It is the name by which I am commonly known at the Institute." Her voice, which had been rather harsh, softened. "And how are you, my old friend Giskard?"

Giskard said, in tones oddly removed from his usual one, "I greet you—" He paused and then said, "I greet you, Little Miss."

Vasilia smiled. "And this, I suppose, is the humaniform robot of whom I have heard—Daneel Olivaw?"

"Yes, Dr. Vasilia," said Daneel briskly.

"And finally, we have—the Earthman."

"Elijah Baley, Doctor," said Baley stiffly.

"Yes, I'm aware that Earthmen have names and that Elijah Baley is yours," she said coolly. "You don't look one blasted thing like the actor who played you in the hyperwave show."

"I am aware of that, Doctor."

"The one who played Daneel was rather a good likeness, however, but I suppose we are not here to discuss the show."

"We are not."

"I gather we are here, Earthman, to talk about whatever it is you want to say about Santirix Gremionis and get it over with. Right?"

"Not entirely," said Baley. "That is not the primary reason for my coming, though I imagine we will get to it."

"Indeed? Are you under the impression that we are here to engage in a long and complicated discussion on whatever topic you choose to deal with?"

"I think, Dr. Vasilia, you would be well-advised to allow me to manage this interview as I wish."

"Is that a threat?"

"No."

"Well, I have never met an Earthman and it might be interesting to see how closely you resemble the actor who played your role—that is, in ways other than appearance. Are you really the masterful person you seemed to be in the show?"

"The show," said Baley with clear distaste, "was overdramatic and exaggerated my personality in every direction. I would rather you accept me as I am and judge me entirely from how I appear to you right now."

Vasilia laughed. "At least you don't seem overawed by me. That's a point in your favor. Or do you think this Gremionis thing you've got in mind puts you in a position to order me about?"

"I am not here to do anything but uncover the truth in the matter of the dead humaniform robot, Jander Panell."

"Dead? Was he ever alive, then?"

"I use one syllable in preference to phrases such as 'rendered in-operative.' Does saying 'dead' confuse you?"

Vasilia said, "You fence well. —Debrett, bring the Earthman a chair. He will grow weary standing if this is to be a long conversation. Then get into your niche. And you may choose one, too, Daneel. —Giskard, come stand by me."

Baley sat down. "Thank you, Debrett. —Dr. Vasilia, I have no authority to question you; I have no legal means of forcing you to answer my questions. However, the death of Jander Panell has put your father in a position of some—"

"It has put *whom* in a position?"

"Your father."

"Earthman, I sometimes refer to a certain individual as my father, but no one else does. Please use a proper name."

"Dr. Han Fastolfe. He is your father, isn't he? As a matter of record?"

Vasilia said, "You are using a biological term. I share genes with him in a manner characteristic of what *on Earth* would be considered a father-daughter relationship. This is a matter of indifference on Aurora, except in medical and genetic matters. I can conceive of my suffering from certain metabolic states in which it would be appropriate to consider the physiology and biochemistry of those with whom I share genes—parents, siblings, children, and so on. Otherwise these relationships are not generally referred to in polite Auroran society. —I explain this to you because you are an Earthman."

"If I have offended against custom," said Baley, "it is through ignorance and I apologize. May I refer to the gentleman under discussion by name?"

"Certainly."

"In that case, the death of Jander Panell has put Dr. Han Fastolfe into a position of some difficulty and I would assume that you would be concerned enough to desire to help him."

"You assume that, do you? Why?"

"He is your— He brought you up. He cared for you. You had a profound affection for each other. He still feels a profound affection for you."

"Did he tell you that?"

"It was obvious from the details of our conversations—even from the fact that he has taken an interest in the Solarian woman, Gladia Delmarre, because of her resemblance to you."

"Did he tell you *that*?"

"He did, but even if he hadn't, the resemblance is obvious."

"Nevertheless, Earthman, I owe Dr. Fastolfe nothing. Your assumptions can be dismissed."

Baley cleared his throat. "Aside from any personal feelings you might or might not have, there is the matter of the future of the Galaxy. Dr. Fastolfe wishes new worlds to be explored and settled by human beings. If the political repercussions of Jander's death lead to the exploration and settlement of the new worlds by robots, Dr. Fastolfe believes that this will be catastrophic for Aurora and humanity. Surely you would not be a party to such a catastrophe."

Vasilia said indifferently, watching him closely, "Surely not, if I agreed with Dr. Fastolfe. I do not. I see no harm in having humaniform robots doing the work. I am here at the Institute, in fact, to make that possible. I am a Globalist. Since Dr. Fastolfe is a Humanist, he is my political enemy."

Her answers were clipped and direct, no longer than they had to be. Each time there followed a definite silence, as though she were waiting, with interest, for the next question. Baley had the impression that she was curious about him, amused by him, making wagers with herself as to what the next question might be, determined to give him just the minimum information necessary to force another question.

He said, "Have you long been a member of this Institute?"

"Since its formation."

"Are there many members?"

"I should judge about a third of Aurora's roboticists are members, though only about half of these actually live and work on the Institute grounds."

"Do other members of the Institute share your views on the robotic exploration of other worlds? Do they oppose Dr. Fastolfe's views one and all?"

"I suspect that most of them are Globalists, but I don't know that we have taken a vote on the matter or even discussed it formally. You had better ask them all individually."

"Is Dr. Fastolfe a member of the Institute?"

"No."

Baley waited a bit, but she said nothing beyond the negative. He said, "Isn't that surprising? I should think he, of all people, would be a member."

"As it happens, we don't want him. What is perhaps less important, he doesn't want us."

"Isn't that even more surprising?"

"I don't think so." —And then, as though goaded into saying something more by an irritation within herself, she said, "He lives in the city of Eos. I suppose you know the significance of the name, Earthman?"

Baley nodded and said, "Eos is the ancient Greek goddess of the dawn, as Aurora is the ancient Roman goddess of the dawn."

"Exactly. Dr. Han Fastolfe lives in the City of the Dawn on the World of the Dawn, but he is not himself a believer in the Dawn. He does not understand the necessary method of expansion through the Galaxy, of converting the Spacer Dawn into broad Galactic Day. The robotic exploration of the Galaxy is the only practical way to carry the task through and he won't accept it—or us."

Baley said slowly, "Why is it the only practical method? Aurora and the other Spacer worlds were not explored and settled by robots but by human beings."

"Correction. By Earthpeople. It was a wasteful and inefficient procedure and there are now no Earthpeople that we will allow to serve as further settlers. We have become Spacers, long-lived and healthy, and we have robots who are infinitely more versatile and flexible than those available to the human beings who originally settled our worlds. Times and matters are wholly different—and *today* only robotic exploration is feasible."

"Let us suppose you are right and Dr. Fastolfe is wrong. Even so, he has a logical view. Why won't he and the Institute accept each other? Simply because they disagree on this point?"

"No, this disagreement is comparatively minor. There is a more fundamental conflict."

Again Baley paused and again she added nothing to her remark. He did not feel it safe to display irritation, so he said quietly, almost tentatively, "What is the more fundamental conflict?"

The amusement in Vasilia's voice came nearer the surface. It softened the lines of her face somewhat and, for a moment, she looked more like Gladia. "You couldn't guess, unless it were explained to you, I think."

"Precisely why I am asking, Dr. Vasilia."

"Well, then, Earthman, I have been told that Earthpeople are short-lived. I have not been misled in that, have I?"

Baley shrugged. "Some of us live to be a hundred years old, Earth time." He thought a bit. "Perhaps a hundred and thirty or so metric years."

"And how old are you?"

"Forty-five standard, sixty metric."

"I am sixty-six metric. I expect to live three metric centuries more at least—if I am careful."

Baley spread his hands wide. "I congratulate you."

"There are disadvantages."

"I was told this morning that, in three or four centuries, many, many losses have a chance to accumulate."

"I'm afraid so," said Vasilia. "And many, many gains have a chance to accumulate, as well. On the whole, it balances."

"What, then, are the disadvantages?"

"You are not a scientist, of course."

"I am a plainclothesman—a policeman, if you like."

"But perhaps you know scientists on your world."

"I have met some," said Baley cautiously.

"You know how they work? We are told that on Earth they coöperate out of necessity. They have, at most, half a century of active labor in the course of their short lives. Less than seven metric decades. Not much can be done in that time."

"Some of our scientists had accomplished quite a deal in considerably less time."

"Because they have taken advantage of the findings others have made before them and profit from the use they can make of contemporary findings by others. Isn't that so?"

"Of course. We have a scientific community to which all contribute, across the expanse of space and of time."

"Exactly. It won't work otherwise. Each scientist, aware of the unlikelihood of accomplishing much entirely by himself, is forced into the community, cannot help becoming part of the clearinghouse. Progress thus becomes enormously greater than it would be if this did not exist."

"Is not this the case on Aurora and the other Spacer worlds, too?" asked Baley.

"In theory it is; in practice not so much. The pressures in a long-lived society are less. Scientists here have three or three and a half centuries to devote to a problem, so that the thought arises that significant progress may be made in that time by a solitary worker. It becomes possible to feel a kind of intellectual greed—to *want* to accomplish something on your own, to assume a property right to a particular facet of progress, to be willing to see the general advance slowed—rather than give up what you conceive to be yours alone. And the general advance *is* slowed on Spacer worlds as a result, to the point where it is difficult to outpace the work done on Earth, despite our enormous advantages."

"I assume you wouldn't say this if I were not to take it that Dr. Han Fastolfe behaves in this manner."

"He certainly does. It is his theoretical analysis of the positronic brain that has made the humaniform robot possible. He has used it to construct—with the help of the late Dr. Sarton—your robot friend Daneel, but he has not published the important details of his theory, nor does he make it available to anyone else. In this way, he—and he alone—holds a stranglehold on the production of humaniform robots."

Baley furrowed his brow. "And the Robotics Institute is dedicated to cooperation among scientists?"

"Exactly. This Institute is made up of over a hundred topnotch roboticists of different ages, advancements, and skills and we hope to

establish branches on other worlds and make it an interstellar association. All of us are dedicated to communicating our separate discoveries or speculations to the common fund—doing voluntarily for the
general good what you Earthpeople do perforce because you live such
short lives.

"This, however, Dr. Han Fastolfe will not do. I'm sure you think
of Dr. Han Fastolfe as a nobly idealistic Auroran patriot, but he will
not put his intellectual property—as he thinks of it—into the common fund and therefore he does not want us. And because he assumes a personal property right upon scientific discoveries, we do
not want him. —You no longer find the mutual distaste a mystery, I
take it."

Baley nodded his head, then said, "You think this will work—this
voluntary giving up of personal glory?"

"It must," said Vasilia grimly.

"And has the Institute, through community endeavor, duplicated
Dr. Fastolfe's individual work and rediscovered the theory of the humaniform positronic brain?"

"We will, in time. It is inevitable."

"And you are making no attempt to shorten the time it will take by
persuading Dr. Fastolfe to yield the secret?"

"I think we are on the way to persuading him."

"Through the working of the Jander scandal?"

"I don't think you really have to ask that question. —Well, have I
told you what you wanted to know, Earthman?"

Baley said, "You have told me some things I didn't know."

"Then it is time for you to tell me about Gremionis. Why have you
brought up the name of this barber in connection with me?"

"Barber?"

"He considers himself a hair stylist, among other things, but he is a
barber, plain and simple. Tell me about him—or let us consider this
interview at an end."

Baley felt weary. It seemed clear to him that Vasilia had enjoyed
the fencing. She had given him enough to whet his appetite and now
he would be forced to buy additional material with information of his
own. —But he had none. Or at least he had only guesses. And if any
of them were wrong, vitally wrong, he was through.

He therefore fenced on his own. "You understand, Dr. Vasilia, that
you can't get away with pretending that it is farcical to suppose there
is a connection between Gremionis and yourself."

"Why not, when it *is* farcical?"

"Oh no. If it were farcical, you would have laughed in my face and
shut off trimensional contact. The mere fact that you were willing to
abandon your earliest stand and receive me—the mere fact that you
have been talking to me at length and telling me a great many things—

is a clear admission that you feel that I just possibly might have my knife at your jugular."

Vasilia's jaw muscles tightened and she said, in a low and angry voice, "See here, little Earthman, my position is vulnerable and you probably know it. I *am* the daughter of Dr. Fastolfe and there are some here at the Institute who are foolish enough—or knavish enough—to mistrust me therefor. I don't know what kind of story you may have heard—or made up—but that it's more or less farcical is certain. Nevertheless, no matter how farcical, it might be used effectively against me. So I am willing to trade for it. I have told you some things and I might tell you more, but only if you now tell me what you have in your hand and convince me you are telling me the truth. So tell me now.

"If you try to play games with me, I will be in no worse position than at present if I kick you out—and I will at least get pleasure out of that. And I will use what leverage *I* have with the Chairman to get him to cancel his decision to let you come here and have you sent right back to Earth. There is considerable pressure on him now to do this and you won't want the addition of mine.

"So talk! Now!"

39

Baley's impulse was to lead up to the crucial point, feeling his way to see if he were right. That, he felt, would not work. She would see what he was doing—she was no fool—and would stop him. He was on the track of something, he knew, and he didn't want to spoil it. What she said about her vulnerable position as the result of her relationship to her father might well be true, but she still would not have been frightened into seeing him if she hadn't suspected that some notion he had was not *completely* farcical.

He had to come out with something, then, with something important that would establish, at once, some sort of domination over her. Therefore—the gamble.

He said, "Santirix Gremionis offered himself to you." And, before Vasilia could react, he raised the ante by saying, with an added touch of harshness, "And not once but many times."

Vasilia clasped her hands over one knee, then pulled herself up and seated herself on the stool, as though to make herself more comfortable. She looked at Giskard, who stood motionless and expressionless at her side.

Then she looked at Baley and said, "Well, the idiot offers himself to everyone he sees, regardless of age and sex. I would be unusual if he paid me no attention."

Baley made the gesture of brushing that to one side. (She had not laughed. She had not brought the interview to an end. She had not even put on a display of fury. She was waiting to see what he would build out of the statement, so he did have *something* by the tail.)

He said, "That is exaggeration, Dr. Vasilia. No one, however undiscriminating, would fail to make choices and, in the case of this Gremionis, you were selected and, despite your refusal to accept him, he continued to offer himself, quite out of keeping with Auroran custom."

Vasilia said, "I am glad you realize I refused him. There are some who feel that, as a matter of courtesy, any offer—or almost any offer—should be accepted, but that is not my opinion. I see no reason why I have to subject myself to some uninteresting event that will merely waste my time. Do you find something objectionable in that, Earthman?"

"I have no opinion to offer—either favorable or unfavorable—in connection with Auroran custom." (She was still waiting, listening to him. What was she waiting for? Would it be for what he wanted to say but yet wasn't sure he dared to?)

She said, with an effort at lightness, "Do you have anything at all to offer—or are we through?"

"Not through," said Baley, who was now forced to take another gamble. "You recognized this non-Auroran perseverance in Gremionis and it occurred to you that you could make use of it."

"Really? How mad! What possible use could I make of it?"

"Since he was clearly attracted to you very strongly, it would not be difficult to arrange to have him attracted by another who resembled you very closely. You urged him to do so, perhaps promising to accept him if the other did not."

"Who is this poor woman who resembles me closely?"

"You do not know? Come now, that is naïve, Dr. Vasilia. I am talking of the Solarian woman, Gladia, whom I already have said has come under the protection of Dr. Fastolfe precisely because she does resemble you. You expressed no surprise when I referred to this at the beginning of our talk. It is too late to pretend ignorance now."

Vasilia looked at him sharply. "And from his interest in her, you deduced that he must first have been interested in me? It was this wild guess with which you approached me?"

"Not entirely a wild guess. There are other substantiating factors. Do you deny all this?"

She brushed thoughtfully at the long desk beside her and Baley wondered what details were carried by the long sheets of paper on it. He could make out, from a distance, complexities of patterns that he knew would be totally meaningless to him, no matter how carefully and thoroughly he studied them.

Vasilia said, "I grow weary. You have told me that Gremionis was interested first in me, and then in my look-alike, the Solarian. And now you want me to deny it. Why should I take the trouble to deny it? Of what importance is it? Even if it were true, how could this damage me in any way? You are saying that I was annoyed by attentions I didn't want and that I ingeniously deflected them. Well?"

Baley said, "It is not so much what you did, as why. You knew that Gremionis was the type of person who would be persistent. He had offered himself to you over and over and he would offer himself to Gladia over and over."

"If she would refuse him."

"She was a Solarian, having trouble with sex, and was refusing everyone, something I dare say you knew, since I imagine that, for all your estrangement from your fa—from Dr. Fastolfe, you have enough feeling to keep an eye on your replacement."

"Well, then, good for her. If she refused Gremionis, she showed good taste."

"You knew there was no 'if' about it. You knew she would."

"Still—what of it?"

"Repeated offers to her would mean that Gremionis would be in Gladia's establishment frequently, that he would cling to her."

"One last time. Well?"

"And in Gladia's establishment was a very unusual object, one of the two humaniform robots in existence, Jander Panell."

Vasilia hesitated. Then, "What are you driving at?"

"I think it struck you that if, somehow, the humaniform robot were killed under circumstances that would implicate Dr. Fastolfe, that could be used as a weapon to force the secret of the humaniform positronic brain out of him. Gremionis, annoyed over Gladia's persistent refusal to accept him and given the opportunity by his constant presence at Gladia's establishment, could be induced to seek a fearful revenge by killing the robot."

Vasilia blinked rapidly. "That poor barber might have twenty such motives and twenty such opportunities and it wouldn't matter. He wouldn't know how to order a robot to shake hands with any efficiency. How would he manage to come within a light-year of imposing mental freeze-out on a robot?"

"Which now," said Baley softly, "finally brings us to the point, a point I think you have been anticipating, for you have somehow restrained yourself from throwing me out because you had to make sure whether I had this point in mind or not. What I'm saying is that Gremionis did the job, with the help of this Robotics Institute, *working through you.*"

 **Again Vasilia**

40

It was as though a hyperwave drama had come to a halt in a holographic still.

None of the robots moved, of course, but neither did Baley and neither did Dr. Vasilia Aliena. Long seconds—abnormally long ones—passed, before Vasilia let out her breath and, very slowly, rose to her feet.

Her face had tightened itself into a humorless smile and her voice was low. "You are saying, Earthman, that I am an accessory in the destruction of the humaniform robot?"

Baley said, "Something of the sort had occurred to me, Doctor."

"Thank you for the thought. The interview is over and you will leave." She pointed to the door.

Baley said, "I'm afraid I do not wish to."

"I don't consult your wishes, Earthman."

"You must, for how can you make me leave against my wishes?"

"I have robots who, at my request, will put you out politely but firmly and without hurting anything but your self-esteem—if you have any."

"You have but one robot here. I have two that will not allow that to happen."

"I have twenty on instant call."

Baley said, "Dr. Vasilia, please understand! You were surprised at seeing Daneel. I suspect that, even though you work at the Robotics Institute, where humaniform robots are the first order of business, you have never actually seen a completed and functioning one. Your robots, therefore, haven't seen one, either. Now look at Daneel. He looks human. He looks more human than any robot who has ever existed, except for the dead Jander. To your robots, Daneel will surely look human. He will know how to present an order in such a way that they will obey him in preference, perhaps, to you."

Vasilia said, "I can, if necessary, summon twenty human beings from within the Institute who will put you out, perhaps *with* a little damage, and your robots, even Daneel, will not be able to interfere effectively."

"How do you intend to call them, since my robots are not going to allow you to move? They have extraordinarily quick reflexes."

Vasilia showed her teeth in something that could not be called a smile. "I cannot speak for Daneel, but I've known Giskard for most of my life. I don't think he will do *anything* to keep me from summoning help and I imagine he will keep Daneel from interfering, too."

Baley tried to keep his voice from trembling as he skated on ever-thinner ice—and knew it. He said, "Before you do anything, perhaps you might ask Giskard what he will do if you and I give conflicting orders."

"Giskard?" said Vasilia with supreme confidence.

Giskard's eyes turned full on Vasilia and he said, with an odd timbre to his voice, "Little Miss, I am compelled to protect Mr. Baley. He takes precedence."

"Indeed? By whose order? By this Earthman's? This stranger's?"

Giskard said, "By Dr. Han Fastolfe's order."

Vasilia's eyes flashed and she slowly sat down on the stool again. Her hands, resting in her lap, trembled and she said through lips that scarcely moved, "He's even taken *you* away."

"If that is not enough, Dr. Vasilia," said Daneel, speaking suddenly, of his own accord, "I, too, would place Partner Elijah's welfare above yours."

Vasilia looked at Daneel with bitter curiosity. "Partner Elijah? Is that what you call him?"

"Yes, Dr. Vasilia. My choice in this matter—the Earthman over you—arises not only out of Dr. Fastolfe's instructions, but because the Earthman and I are partners in this investigation and because—" Daneel paused as though puzzled by what he was about to say, and then said it anyway, "—we are friends."

Vasilia said, "Friends? An Earthman and a humaniform robot? Well, there is a match. Neither quite human."

Baley said, sharply, "Nevertheless bound by friendship. Do not, for your own sake, test the force of our—" Now it was he who paused and, as though to his own surprise, completed the sentence impossibly, "—love."

Vasilia turned to Baley. "What do you want?"

"Information. I have been called to Aurora—this World of the Dawn—to straighten out an event that does not seem to have an easy explanation, one in which Dr. Fastolfe stands falsely accused, with the possibility, therefore, of terrible consequences for your world and mine. Daneel and Giskard understand this situation well and know that nothing but the First Law at its fullest and most immediate can take precedence over my efforts to solve the mystery. Since they have heard what I have said and know that you might possibly be an accessory to the deed, they understand that they must not allow this interview to

end. Therefore, I say again, don't risk the actions they may be forced
to take if you refuse to answer my questions. I have accused you of
being an accessory in the murder of Jander Panell. Do you deny that
accusation or not? You *must* answer."

Vasilia said bitterly, "I will answer. Never fear! Murder? A robot is
put out of commission and that's *murder*? Well, I *do* deny it, murder
or whatever! I deny it with all possible force. I have not given Gremionis information on robotics for the purpose of allowing him to put
an end to Jander. I don't know enough to do so and I suspect that no
one at the Institute knows enough."

Baley said, "I can't say whether you know enough to have helped
commit the crime or whether anyone at the Institute knows enough.
We can, however, discuss motive. First, you might have a feeling of
tenderness for this Gremionis. However much you might reject his
offers—however contemptible you might find him as a possible
lover—would it be so strange that you would feel flattered by his
persistence, sufficiently so to be willing to help him if he turned to
you prayerfully and without any sexual demands with which to annoy you?"

"You mean he may have come to me and said, 'Vasilia, dear, I want
to put a robot out of commission. Please tell me how to do it and I
will be terribly grateful to you.' And I would say, 'Why, certainly, dear,
I would just love to help you commit a crime.' —Preposterous! No
one except an Earthman, who knows nothing of Auroran ways, could
believe anything like this could happen. It would take a particularly
stupid Earthman, too."

"Perhaps, but all possibilities must be considered. For instance, as
a second possibility, might you yourself not be jealous over the fact
that Gremionis has switched his affections, so that you might help
him not out of abstract tenderness but out of a very concrete desire
to win him back?"

"Jealous? That is an Earthly emotion. If I do not wish Gremionis
for myself, how can I possibly care whether he offers himself to another woman and she accepts or, for that matter, if another woman
offers herself to him and he accepts?"

"I have been told before that sexual jealousy is unknown on Aurora and I am willing to admit that is true in theory, but such theories
rarely hold up in practice. There are surely some exceptions. What's
more, jealousy is all too often an irrational emotion and not to be
dismissed by mere logic. Still, let us leave that for the moment.
As a third possibility, you might be jealous of Gladia and wish to
do her harm, even if you don't care the least bit for Gremionis yourself."

"Jealous of Gladia? I have never even seen her, except once on the hyperwave when she arrived in Aurora. The fact that people have commented on her resemblance to me, every once in a long while, hasn't bothered me."

"Does it perhaps bother you that she is Dr. Fastolfe's ward, his favorite, almost the daughter that you were once? She has replaced you."

"She is *welcome* to that. I could not care less."

"Even if they were lovers?"

Vasilia stared at Baley with growing fury and beads of perspiration appeared at her hairline.

She said, "There is no need to discuss this. You have asked me to deny the allegation that I was accessory to what you call murder and I have denied it. I have said I lacked the ability and I lacked the motive. You are welcome to present your case to all Aurora. Present your foolish attempts at supplying me with a motive. Maintain, if you wish, that I have the ability to do so. You will get nowhere. Absolutely nowhere."

And even while she trembled with anger, it seemed to Baley that there was conviction in her voice.

She did not fear the accusation.

She had agreed to see him, so he *was* on the track of something that she feared—perhaps feared desperately.

But she did not fear *this*.

Where, then, had he gone wrong?

41

Baley said (troubled, casting about for some way out), "Suppose I accept your statement, Dr. Vasilia. Suppose I agree that my suspicion that you might have been an accessory in this—roboticide—was wrong. Even that would not mean that it is impossible for you to help me."

"Why should I help you?"

Baley said, "Out of human decency. Dr. Han Fastolfe assures us he did not do it, that he is not a robot-killer, that he did not put this particular robot, Jander, out of operation. You've known Dr. Fastolfe better than anyone ever has, one would suppose. You spent years in an intimate relationship with him as a beloved child and growing daughter. You saw him at times and under conditions that no one else saw him. Whatever your present feelings toward him might be, the past is not changed by them. Knowing him as you do, you must be able to bear witness that his character is such that he could not harm a robot, certainly not a robot that is one of his supreme achievements. Would you be willing to bear such witness openly? To all the worlds? It would help a great deal."

Vasilia's face seemed to harden. "Understand me," she said, pronouncing the words distinctly. "I will not be involved."

"You *must* be involved."

"Why?"

"Do you owe nothing to your father? He *is* your father. Whether the word means anything to you or not, there is a biological connection. And besides that—father or not—he took care of you, nurtured and brought you up, for years. You owe him something for that."

Vasilia trembled. It was a visible shaking and her teeth were chattering. She tried to speak, failed, took a deep breath, another, then tried again. She said, "Giskard, do you hear all that is going on?"

Giskard bowed his head. "Yes, Little Miss."

"And you, the humaniform—Daneel?"

"Yes, Dr. Vasilia."

"You hear all this, too?"

"Yes, Dr. Vasilia."

"You both understand the Earthman insists that I bear evidence on Dr. Fastolfe's character?"

Both nodded.

"Then I will speak—against my will and in anger. It is because I have felt that I did owe this *father* of mine some minimum consideration as my gene-bearer and, after a fashion, my upbringer, that I have *not* borne witness. But now I will. Earthman, listen to me. Dr. Han Fastolfe, some of whose genes I share, did not take care of me— *me*— *me*—as a separate, distinct human being. I was to him nothing more than an experiment, an observational phenomenon."

Baley shook his head. "That is not what I was asking."

She drove furiously over him. "You insisted that I speak and I *will* speak—and it will answer you. —One thing interests Dr. Han Fastolfe. One thing. One thing only. That is the functioning of the human brain. He wishes to reduce it to equations, to a wiring diagram, to a solved maze, and thus found a mathematical science of human behavior which will allow him to predict the human future. He calls the science 'psychohistory.' I can't believe that you have talked to him for as little as an hour without his mentioning it. It is the monomania that drives him."

Vasilia searched Baley's face and cried out in a fierce joy, "I can tell! He *has* talked to you about it. Then he must have told you that he is interested in robots only insofar as they can bring him to the human brain. He is interested in humaniform robots only insofar as they can bring him still closer to the human brain. —Yes, he's told you that, too.

"The basic theory that made humaniform robots possible arose, I am quite certain, out of his attempt to understand the human brain and he hugs that theory to himself and will allow no one else to see it because he wants to solve the problem of the human brain totally by himself in the two centuries or so he has left. Everything is subordinate to that. And that most certainly included me."

Baley, trying to breast his way against the flood of fury, said in a low voice, "In what way did it include you, Dr. Vasilia?"

"When I was born, I should have been placed with others of my kind, with professionals who knew how to care for infants. I should not have been kept by myself in the charge of an amateur—father or not, scientist or not. Dr. Fastolfe should not have been allowed to subject a child to such an environment and would not—if he had been anyone else but Han Fastolfe. He used all his prestige to bring it about, called in every debt he had, persuaded every key person he could, until he had control of me."

"He loved you," muttered Baley.

"Loved me? Any other infant would have done as well, but no other infant was available. What he wanted was a growing child in his presence, a developing brain. He wanted to make a careful study of the method of its development, the fashion of its growth. He wanted a human brain in simple form, growing complex, so that he could study it in detail. For that purpose, he subjected me to an abnormal environment and to subtle experimentation, with no consideration for me as a human being at all."

"I can't believe that. Even if he were interested in you as an experimental object, he could still care for you as a human being."

"No. You speak as an Earthman. Perhaps on Earth there is some sort of regard for biological connections. Here there is not. I was an experimental object to him. Period."

"Even if that were so to start with, Dr. Fastolfe couldn't help but learn to love you—a helpless object entrusted to his care. Even if there were no biological connection at all, even if you were an animal, let us say, he would have learned to love you."

"Oh, would he now?" she said bitterly. "You don't know the force of indifference in a man like Dr. Fastolfe. If it would have advanced his knowledge to snuff out my life, he would have done so without hesitation."

"That is ridiculous, Dr. Vasilia. His treatment of you was so kind and considerate that it evoked love from you. I know that. You—you offered yourself to him."

"He told you that, did he? Yes, he would. Not for a moment, even today, would he stop to question whether such a revelation might not embarrass me. —Yes, I offered myself to him and why not? He was the only human being I really knew. He was superficially gentle to me and I didn't understand his true purposes. He was a natural target for me. Then, too, he saw to it that I was introduced to sexual stimulation under controlled conditions—the controls *he* set up. It was inevitable that eventually I would turn to him. I had to, for there was no one else—and he refused."

"And you hated him for that?"

"*No.* Not at first. Not for years. Even though my sexual development was stunted and distorted, with effects I feel to this day, I did not blame him. I did not know enough. I found excuses for him. He was busy. He had others. He needed older women. You would be astonished at the ingenuity with which I uncovered reasons for his refusal. It was only years later that I became aware that something was wrong and I managed to bring it out openly, face-to-face. 'Why did you refuse me?' I asked. 'Obliging me might have put me on the right track, solved everything.' "

She paused, swallowing, and for a moment covered her eyes. Baley waited, frozen with embarrassment. The robots were expressionless (incapable, for all Baley knew, of experiencing any balance or imbalance of the positronic pathways that would produce a sensation in any way analogous to human embarrassment).

She said, calmer, "He avoided the question for as long as he could, but I faced him with it over and over. 'Why did you refuse me?' 'Why did you refuse me?' He had no hesitation in engaging in sex. I knew of several occasions—I remember wondering if he simply preferred men. Where children are not involved, personal preference in such things is not of any importance and some men can find women distasteful or, for that matter, vice versa. It was not so with this man you call my father, however. He enjoyed women—sometimes young women—as young as I was when I first offered myself. 'Why did you refuse me?' He finally answered me—and you are welcome to guess what that answer was."

She paused and waited sardonically.

Baley stirred uneasily and said in a mumble, "He didn't want to make love to his daughter?"

"Oh, don't be a fool. What difference does that make? Considering that hardly any man on Aurora knows who his daughter is, any man making love to any woman a few decades younger might be—But never mind, it's self-evident. What he answered—and oh, how I remember the words—was 'You great fool! If I involved myself with you in that manner, how could I maintain my objectivity—and of what use would my continuing study of you be?"

"By that time, you see, I knew of his interest in the human brain. I was even following in his footsteps and becoming a roboticist in my own right. I worked with Giskard in this direction and experimented with his programming. I did it very well, too, didn't I, Giskard?"

Giskard said, "So you did, Little Miss."

"But I could see that this man whom you call my father did not view me as a human being. He was willing to see me distorted for life, rather than risk his objectivity. His observations meant more to him than my normality. From that time on, I knew what I was and what he was—and I left him."

The silence hung heavy in the air.

Baley's head was throbbing slightly. He wanted to ask: could you not take into account the self-centeredness of a great scientist? The importance of a great problem? Could you make no allowances for something spoken perhaps in irritation at being forced to discuss what one did not want to discuss? Was not Vasilia's own anger just now much the same thing? Did not Vasilia's concentration on her own "normality" (whatever she meant by that) to the exclusion of perhaps the two most important problems facing humanity—the nature of the human brain and the settling of the Galaxy—represent an equal self-centeredness with much less excuse?

But he could ask none of those things. He did not know how to put it so that it would make real sense to this woman, nor was he sure he would understand her if she answered.

What was he doing on this world? He could not understand their ways, no matter how they explained. Nor could they understand his.

He said wearily, "I am sorry, Dr. Vasilia. I understand that you are angry, but if you would dismiss your anger for a moment and consider, instead, the matter of Dr. Fastolfe and the murdered robot, could you not see that we are dealing with two different things? Dr. Fastolfe might have wanted to observe you in a detached and objective way, even at the cost of your unhappiness, and yet be light-years removed from the desire to destroy an advanced humaniform robot."

Vasilia reddened. She shouted, "Don't you understand what I'm telling you, Earthman? Do you think I have told you what I have just told you because I think you—or anyone—would be interested in the sad story of my life? For that matter, do you think I enjoy revealing myself in this manner?

"I'm telling you this only to show you that Dr. Han Fastolfe—my biological father, as you never tire of pointing out—*did* destroy Jander. Of course he did. I have refrained from saying so because no one—until you—was idiot enough to ask me and because of some foolish remnant of consideration I have for that man. But now that you have asked me, I say so and, by Aurora, I will continue to say so—to anyone and everyone. Publicly, if necessary.

"Dr. Han Fastolfe *did* destroy Jander Panell. I am certain of it. Does that satisfy you?"

42

Baley stared at the distraught woman in horror.

He stuttered and began again. "I don't understand at all, Dr. Vasilia. Please quiet down and consider. Why should Dr. Fastolfe destroy the robot? What has that to do with his treatment of you? Do you imagine it is some kind of retaliation against you?"

Vasilia was breathing rapidly (Baley noted absently and without conscious intention that, although Vasilia was as small-boned as Gladia was, her breasts were larger) and she seemed to wrench at her voice to keep it under control.

She said, "I told you, Earthman, did I not, that Han Fastolfe was interested in observing the human brain? He did not hesitate to put it under stress in order to observe the results. And he preferred brains that were out of the ordinary—that of an infant, for instance—so that he might watch their development. Any brain but a commonplace one."

"But what has that to do—"

"Ask yourself, then, why he gained this interest in the foreign woman."

"In Gladia? I asked *him* and he told me. She reminded him of you and the resemblance is indeed distinct."

"And when you told me this earlier, I was amused and asked if you believed him? I ask again. Do you believe him?"

"Why shouldn't I believe him?"

"Because it's not true. The resemblance may have attracted his attention, but the real key to his interest is that the foreign woman is—foreign. She had been brought up in Solaria, under assumptions and social axioms not like those on Aurora. He could therefore study a brain that was differently molded from ours and could gain an interesting perspective. Don't you understand that? —For that matter, why is he interested in *you*, Earthman? Is he silly enough to imagine that you can solve an Auroran problem when you know nothing about Aurora?"

Daneel suddenly intervened again and Baley started at the sound of the other's voice. Daneel said, "Dr. Vasilia, Partner Elijah solved a problem on Solaria, though he knew nothing of Solaria."

"Yes," said Vasilia sourly, "so all the worlds noted on that hyperwave program. And lightning may strike, too, but I don't think that Han Fastolfe is confident it will strike twice in the same place in rapid succession. No, Earthman, he was attracted to you, in the first place, because you are an Earthman. You possess another alien brain he can study and manipulate."

"Surely you cannot believe, Dr. Vasilia, that he would risk matters of vital importance to Aurora and call in someone he knew to be useless, merely to study an unusual brain."

"Of course he would. Isn't that the whole point of what I am telling you? There is no crisis that could face Aurora that he would believe, for a single moment, to be as important as solving the problem of the brain. I can tell you exactly what he would say if you were to ask him. Aurora might rise or fall, flourish or decay, and that would all be of little concern compared to the problem of the brain, for if human beings really understood the brain, all that might have been lost in the course of a millennium of neglect or wrong decisions would be regained in a decade of cleverly directed human development guided by his dream of 'psychohistory.' He would use the same argument to justify anything—lies, cruelty, *anything*—by merely saying that it is all intended to serve the purpose of advancing the knowledge of the brain."

"I can't imagine that Dr. Fastolfe would be cruel. He is the gentlest of men."

"Is he? How long have you been with him?"

Baley said, "A few hours on Earth three years ago. A day, now, here on Aurora."

"A whole day. A *whole* day. I was with him for thirty years almost constantly and I have followed his career from a distance with some attention ever since. And you have been with him a whole day, Earthman? Well, on that one day, has he done nothing that frightened or humiliated you?"

Baley kept silent. He thought of the sudden attack with the spicer from which Daneel had rescued him; of the Personal that presented him with such difficulty, thanks to its masked nature; the extended walk Outside designed to test his ability to adapt to the open.

Vasilia said, "I see he did. Your face, Earthman, is not quite the mask of disguise you may think it is. Did he threaten you with a Psychic Probe?"

Baley said, "It was mentioned."

"One day—and it was already mentioned. I assume it made you feel uneasy?"

"It did."

"And that there was no reason to mention it?"

"Oh, but there was," said Baley quickly. "I had said that, for a moment, I had a thought which I then lost and it was certainly legitimate to suggest that a Psychic Probe might help me relocate that thought."

Vasilia said, "No, it wasn't. The Psychic Probe cannot be used with sufficient delicacy of touch for that—and, if it were attempted, the chances would be considerable that there would be permanent brain damage."

"Surely not if it were wielded by an expert—by Dr. Fastolfe, for instance."

"By *him*? He doesn't know one end of the Probe from the other. He is a theoretician, not a technician."

"By someone else, then. He did not, in actual fact, specify himself."

"No, Earthman. By *no one*. Think! Think! If the Psychic Probe could be used on human beings safely by *anyone*, and if Han Fastolfe were so concerned about the problem of the inactivation of the robot, then why didn't he suggest the Psychic Probe be used on himself?"

"On himself?"

"Don't tell me this hasn't occurred to you? Any thinking person would come to the conclusion that Fastolfe is guilty. The only point in favor of his innocence is that he himself insists he is innocent. Well, then, why does he not offer to prove his innocence by being psychically probed and showing that no trace of guilt can be dredged up from the recesses of his brain? Has he suggested such a thing, Earthman?"

"No, he hasn't. At least, not to me."

"Because he knows very well that it is deadly dangerous. Yet he does not hesitate to suggest it in your case, merely to observe how your brain works under pressure, how you react to fright. Or perhaps it occurs to him that, however dangerous the Probe is to you, it may come up with some interesting data for *him*, as far as the details of your Earth-molded brain are concerned. Tell me, then, isn't that cruel?"

Baley brushed it aside with a tight gesture of his right arm. "How does this apply to the actual case—to the roboticide?"

"The Solarian woman, Gladia, caught my onetime father's eye. She had an interesting brain—for his purposes. He therefore gave her the robot, Jander, to see what would happen if a woman not raised on Aurora were faced with a robot that seemed human in every particular. He knew that an Auroran woman would very likely make use of the robot for sex immediately and have no trouble doing so. I myself would have some trouble, I admit, because I was not brought up normally, but no ordinary Auroran would. The Solarian woman, on the other hand, would have a great deal of trouble because she was brought up on an extremely robotic world and had unusually rigid mental attitudes toward robots. The difference, you see, might be very instructive to my father, who tried, out of these variations, to build his theory of brain functioning. Han Fastolfe waited half a year for the Solarian woman to get to the point where she could perhaps begin making the first experimental approaches—"

Baley interrupted. "Your father knew nothing at all about the relationship between Gladia and Jander."

"Who told you that, Earthman? My father? Gladia? If the former, he was naturally lying; if the latter, she simply didn't know, very likely. You may be sure Fastolfe knew what was going on; he had to, for it must have been part of his study of how a human brain was bent under Solarian conditions.

"And then he thought—and I am as sure of this as I would be if I could read his thoughts—what would happen now, at the point where the woman is just beginning to rely on Jander, if, suddenly, without reason, she lost him. He knew what an Auroran woman would do. She would feel some disappointment and then seek out some substitute, but what would a Solarian woman do? So he arranged to put Jander out of commission—"

"Destroy an immensely valuable robot just to satisfy a trivial curiosity?"

"Monstrous, isn't it? But that's what Han Fastolfe would do. So go back to him, Earthman, and tell him that his little game is over. If the planet, generally, doesn't believe him to be guilty now, they most certainly will after I have had my say."

43

For a long moment, Baley sat there stunned, while Vasilia looked at him with a kind of grim delight, her face looking harsh and totally unlike that of Gladia.

There seemed nothing to do—

Baley got to his feet, feeling old—much older than his forty-five standard years (a child's age to these Aurorans). So far everything he had done had led to nothing. To worse than nothing, for at every one of his moves, the ropes seemed to tighten about Fastolfe.

He looked upward at the transparent ceiling. The sun was quite high, but perhaps it had passed its zenith, as it was dimmer than ever. Lines of thin clouds obscured it intermittently.

Vasilia seemed to become aware of this from his upward glance.

Her arm moved on the section of the long bench near which she was sitting and the transparency of the ceiling vanished. At the same time, a brilliant light suffused the room, bearing the same faint orange tinge that the sun itself had.

She said, "I think the interview is over. I shall have no reason to see you again, Earthman—or you me. Perhaps you had better leave Aurora. You have done"—she smiled humorlessly and said the next words almost savagely—"my father enough damage, though scarcely as much as he deserves."

Baley took a step toward the door and his two robots closed in on him. Giskard said in a low voice, "Are you well, sir?"

Baley shrugged. What was there to answer to that?

Vasilia called out, "Giskard! When Dr. Fastolfe finds he has no further use for you, come join my staff?"

Giskard looked at her calmly. "If Dr. Fastolfe permits, I will do so, Little Miss."

Her smile grew warm. "Please do so, Giskard. I've never stopped missing you."

"I often think of you, Little Miss."

Baley turned at the door. "Dr. Vasilia, would you have a Personal I might use?"

Vasilia's eyes widened. "Of course not, Earthman. There are Community Personals here and there at the Institute. Your robots should be able to guide you."

He stared at her and shook his head. It was not surprising that she wanted no Earthman infecting her rooms and yet it angered him just the same.

He said out of anger, rather than out of any rational judgment, "Dr. Vasilia, I would not, were I you, speak of the guilt of Dr. Fastolfe."

"What is there to stop me?"

"The danger of the general uncovering of your dealings with Gremionis. The danger to you."

"Don't be ridiculous. You have admitted there was no conspiracy between myself and Gremionis."

"Not really. I agreed there seemed reason to conclude there was no direct conspiracy between you and Gremionis to destroy Jander. There remains the possibility of an indirect conspiracy."

"You are mad. What is an indirect conspiracy?"

"I am not ready to discuss that in front of Dr. Fastolfe's robots—unless you insist. And why should you? You know very well what I mean." There was no reason why Baley should think she would accept this bluff. It might simply worsen the situation still further.

But it didn't! Vasilia seemed to shrink within herself, frowning.

Baley thought: There *is* then an indirect conspiracy, whatever it might be, and this might hold her till she sees through my bluff.

Baley said, his spirits rising a little, "I repeat, say nothing about Dr. Fastolfe."

But, of course, he didn't know how much time he had bought—perhaps very little.

44

They were sitting in the airfoil again—all three in the front, with Baley once more in the middle and feeling the pressure on either side. Baley was grateful to them for the care they unfailingly gave him, even though they were only machines, helpless to disobey instructions.

And then he thought: Why dismiss them with a word—"machines"? They're *good* machines in a Universe of sometimes-evil people. I have no right to favor the machines vs. people sub-categorization over the good vs. evil one. And Daneel, at least, I cannot think of as a machine.

Giskard said, "I must ask again, sir. Do you feel well?"

Baley nodded. "Quite well, Giskard. I am glad to be out here with you two."

The sky was, for the most part, white—off-white, actually. There was a gentle wind and it had felt distinctly cool until they got into the car.

Daneel said, "Partner Elijah, I was listening carefully to the conversation between yourself and Dr. Vasilia. I do not wish to comment unfavorably on what Dr. Vasilia has said, but I must tell you that, in my observation, Dr. Fastolfe is a kind and courteous human being. He has never, to my knowledge, been deliberately cruel, nor has he, as nearly as I can judge, sacrificed a human being's essential welfare to the needs of his curiosity."

Baley looked at Daneel's face, which gave the impression, somehow, of intent sincerity. He said, "Could you say anything against Dr. Fastolfe, even if he were, in fact, cruel and thoughtless?"

"I could remain silent."

"But would you?"

"If, by telling a lie, I were to harm a truthful Dr. Vasilia by casting unjustified doubt on her truthfulness, and if, by remaining silent, I would harm Dr. Fastolfe by lending further color to the true accusations against him, and if the two harms were, to my mind, roughly equal in intensity, then it would be necessary for me to remain silent. Harm through an active deed outweighs, in general, harm through passivity—all things being reasonably equal."

Baley said, "Then, even though the First Law states: 'A robot may not injure a human being or, *through inaction*, allow a human being to come to harm,' the two halves of the law are not equal? A fault of commission, you say, is greater than one of omission?"

"The words of the law are merely an approximate description of the constant variations in positronomotive force along the robotic brain paths, Partner Elijah. I do not know enough to describe the matter mathematically, but I know what my tendencies are."

"And they are always to choose not doing over doing, if the harm is roughly equal in both directions?"

"In general. And always to choose truth over nontruth, if the harm is roughly equal in both directions. In general, that is."

"And, in this case, since you speak to refute Dr. Vasilia and thus do her harm, you can only do so because the First Law is mitigated sufficiently by the fact that you are telling the truth?"

"That is so, Partner Elijah."

"Yet the fact is, you would say what you have said, even though it were a lie—provided Dr. Fastolfe had instructed you, with sufficient intensity, to tell that lie when necessary and to refuse to admit that you had been so instructed."

There was a pause and then Daneel said, "That is so, Partner Elijah."

"It is a complicated mess, Daneel—but you still believe that Dr. Fastolfe did not murder Jander Panell?"

"My experience with him is that he is truthful, Partner Elijah, and that he would not do harm to friend Jander."

"And yet Dr. Fastolfe has himself described a powerful motive for his having committed the deed, while Dr. Vasilia has described a completely different motive, one that is just as powerful and is even more disgraceful than the first." Baley brooded a bit. "If the public were made aware of either motive, belief in Dr. Fastolfe's guilt would be universal."

Baley turned suddenly to Giskard. "How about you, Giskard? You have known Dr. Fastolfe longer than Daneel has. Do you agree that Dr. Fastolfe could not have committed the deed and could not have destroyed Jander, on the basis of your understanding of Dr. Fastolfe's character?"

"I do, sir."

Baley regarded the robot uncertainly. He was less advanced than Daneel. How far could he be trusted as a corroborating witness? Might he not be impelled to follow Daneel in whatever direction Daneel chose to take?

He said, "You knew Dr. Vasilia, too, did you not?"

"I knew her very well," said Giskard.

"And liked her, I gather?"

"She was in my charge for many years and the task did not in any way trouble me."

"Even though she fiddled with your programming?"

"She was very skillful."

"Would she lie about her father—about Dr. Fastolfe, that is?"

Giskard hesitated. "No, sir. She would not."

"Then you are saying that what she says is the truth."

"Not quite, sir. What I am saying is that she herself believes she is telling the truth."

"But why should she believe such evil things about her father to be true if, in actual fact, he is as kind a person as Daneel has just told me he was?"

Giskard said slowly, "She has been embittered by various events in her youth, events for which she considers Dr. Fastolfe to have been responsible and for which he may indeed have been unwittingly responsible—to an extent. It seems to me it was not his intention that the events in question should have the consequences they did. However, human beings are not governed by the straightforward laws of robotics. It is therefore difficult to judge the complexities of their motivations under most conditions."

"True enough," muttered Baley.

Giskard said, "Do you think the task of demonstrating Dr. Fastolfe's innocence to be hopeless?"

Baley's eyebrows moved toward each other in a frown. "It may be. As it happens, I see no way out—and if Dr. Vasilia talks, as she has threatened to do——"

"But you ordered her not to talk. You explained that it would be dangerous to herself if she did."

Baley shook his head. "I was bluffing. I didn't know what else to say."

"Do you intend to give up, then?"

And Baley said forcefully, "No! If it were merely Fastolfe, I might. After all, what physical harm would come to him? Roboticide is not even a crime, apparently, merely a civil offense. At worst, he will lose political influence and, perhaps, find himself unable to continue with his scientific labors for a time. I would be sorry to see that happen, but if there's nothing more I can do, then there's nothing more I can do.

"And if it were just myself, I might give up, too. Failure would damage my reputation, but who can build a brick house without bricks? I would go back to Earth a bit tarnished, I would lead a miserable and unclassified life, but that is the chance that faces every Earthman and woman. Better men than I have had to face that as unjustly.

"However, it is a matter of Earth. If I fail, then along with the grievous loss to Dr. Fastolfe and to myself, there would be an end for any hope Earthpeople might have to move out of Earth and into the Galaxy generally. For that reason, I must not fail and I must keep on somehow, as long as I am not physically thrust off this world."

Having ended in what was almost a whisper, he suddenly looked up and said in a peevish tone, "Why are we sitting here parked, Giskard? Are you running the motor for your own amusement?"

"With respect, sir," said Giskard, "you have not told me where to take you."

"True!—I beg your pardon, Giskard. First, take me to the nearest of the Community Personals that Dr. Vasilia made mention of. You two may be immune to such things, but I have a bladder that needs emptying. After that, find someplace nearby where I can get something to eat. I have a stomach that needs filling. And after that——"

"Yes, Partner Elijah?" asked Daneel.

"To tell you the truth, Daneel, I don't know. However, after I tend to these purely physical needs, I will think of something."

And how Baley wished he could believe that.

45

The airfoil did not skim the ground for long. It came to a halt, swaying a bit, and Baley felt the usual odd tightening of his stomach. That small unsteadiness told him he was in a vehicle and it drove away the temporary feeling of being safe within walls and between robots. Through the glass ahead and on either side (and backward, if he craned his neck) was the whiteness of sky and the greenness of foliage, all amounting to Outside—that is, to nothing. He swallowed uneasily.

They had stopped at a small structure.

Baley said, "Is this the Community Personal?"

Daneel said, "It is the nearest of a number on the Institute grounds, Partner Elijah."

"You found it quickly. Are these structures also included in the map that has been pumped into your memory?"

"That is the case, Partner Elijah."

"Is this one in use now?"

"It may be, Partner Elijah, but three or four may use it simultaneously."

"Is there room for me?"

"Very likely, Partner Elijah."

"Well, then, let me out. I'll go there and see——"

The robots did not move. Giskard said, "Sir, we may not enter with you."

"Yes, I am aware of that, Giskard."

"We will not be able to guard you properly, sir."

Baley frowned. The lesser robot would naturally have the more rigid mind and Baley suddenly recognized the danger that he would simply not be allowed out of their sight and, therefore, not allowed to enter the Personal. He put a note of urgency into his voice and turned his

attention to Daneel, who might be expected to more nearly understand human needs. "I can't help that, Giskard.—Daneel, I have no
choice in the matter. Let me out of the car."

Giskard looked at Baley without moving and, for one horrid moment, Baley thought the robot would suggest that he unburden himself in the nearby field—in the open, like an animal.

The moment passed. Daneel said, "I think we must allow Partner
Elijah to have his way in this respect."

Whereupon Giskard said to Baley, "If you can wait for a short while,
sir, I will approach the structure first."

Baley grimaced. Giskard walked slowly toward the building and then,
deliberately, circumnavigated it. Baley might have predicted the fact
that, once Giskard disappeared, his own sense of urgency would increase.

He tried to distract his own nerve endings by staring around at the
prospect. After some study, he became aware of thin wires in the air,
here and there—fine, dark hairs against the white sky. He did not see
them, to begin with. What he saw first was an oval object sliding along
beneath the clouds. He became aware of it as a vehicle and realized
that it was not floating but was suspended from a long horizontal wire.
He followed that long wire with his eyes, forward and back, noting
others of the sort. He then saw another vehicle farther off—and yet
another still farther off. The farthest of the three was a featureless
speck whose nature he understood only because he had seen the nearer
ones.

Undoubtedly, these were cable-cars for internal transportation from
one part of the Robotics Institute to another.

How spread out it all was, thought Baley. How needlessly the Institute consumed space.

And yet, in doing so, it did not consume the surface. The structures
were sufficiently widely spaced so that the greenery seemed untouched and the plant and animal life continued (Baley imagined) as
they might in emptiness.

Solaria, Baley remembered, had been empty. No doubt all the Spacer
worlds were empty, since Aurora, the most populous, was so empty,
even here in the most built-up region of the planet. For that matter,
even Earth—outside the Cities—was empty.

But there *were* the Cities and Baley felt a sharp pang of homesickness, which he had to push to one side.

Daneel said, "Ah, friend Giskard has completed his examination."

Giskard was back and Baley said tartly, "Well? Will you be so kind
as to grant me permission——" He stopped. Why expend sarcasm on
the impenetrable hide of a robot?

Giskard said, "It seems quite certain that the Personal is unoccupied."

"Good! Then get out of my way." Baley flung open the door of the airfoil and stepped out onto the gravel of a narrow path. He strode rapidly, with Daneel following.

When he reached the door of the structure, Daneel wordlessly indicated the contact that would open it. Daneel did not venture to touch the contact himself. Presumably, thought Baley, to have done so without specific instructions would have indicated an intention to enter—and even the intention was not permitted.

Baley pushed the contact and entered, leaving the two robots behind.

It was not until he was inside that it occurred to him that Giskard could not possibly have entered the Personal to see that it was unoccupied, that the robot must have been judging the matter from external appearance—a dubious proceeding at best.

And Baley realized, with some discomfort, that, for the first time, he was isolated and separated from all protectors—and that the protectors on the other side of the door couldn't easily enter if he were suddenly in trouble. What, then, if he were. at this moment, not alone? What if some enemy had been alerted by Vasilia, who knew he would be in search of a Personal, and what if that enemy was in hiding right now in the structure?

Baley grew suddenly and uncomfortably aware that (as would not have been the case on Earth) he was totally unarmed.

46

To be sure, the structure was not large. There were small urinals, side by side, half a dozen of them; small washbasins, side by side, again half a dozen. No showers, no clothes-fresheners, no shaving devices.

There were half a dozen stalls, separated by partitions and with small doors to each. Might there not be someone waiting inside one of them——

The doors did not come down to the ground. Moving softly, he bent and glanced under each door, looking for any sign of legs. He then approached each door, testing it, swinging it open tensely, ready to slam it shut at the least sign of anything untoward, and then to dash to the door that led to the Outside.

All the stalls were empty.

He looked around to make sure there were no other hiding places. He could find none.

He went to the door to the Outside and found no indication of a way of locking it. It occurred to him that there would naturally be no way of locking it. The Personal was clearly for the use of several men at the same time. Others would have to be able to enter at need.

Yet he could not very well leave and try another, for the danger would exist at any—and besides, he could delay no longer.

For a moment, he found himself unable to decide which of the series of urinals he should use. He could approach and use any of them. So could anyone else.

He forced the choice of one upon himself and, aware of openness all around, was afflicted at once with bashful bladder. He felt the urgency, but had to wait impatiently for the feeling of apprehension at the possible entrance of others to dissipate itself.

He no longer feared the entrance of enemies, just the entrance of anyone.

And then he thought: The robots will at least delay anyone approaching.

With that, he managed to relax——

He was quite done, greatly relieved, and about to turn to a washbasin, when he heard a moderately high-pitched, rather tense voice. "Are you Elijah Baley?"

Baley froze. After all his apprehension and all his precautions, he had been unaware of someone entering. In the end, he had been entirely wrapped up in the simple act of emptying his bladder, something that should not have taken up even the tiniest fraction of his conscious mind. (Was he getting old?)

To be sure, there seemed no threat of any kind in the voice he heard. It seemed empty of menace. It may have been that Baley simply felt certain—and had the sure confidence within him—that Daneel, at least, if not Giskard, would not have allowed a threat to enter.

What bothered Baley was merely the entrance. In his whole life, he had never been approached—let alone addressed—by a man in a Personal. On Earth that was the most strenuous taboo and on Solaria (and, until now, on Aurora) he had used only one-person Personals.

The voice came again. Impatient. "Come! You *must* be Elijah Baley."

Slowly, Baley turned. It was a man of moderate height, delicately dressed in well-fitted clothing in various shades of blue. He was light-skinned, light-haired, and had a small mustache that was a shade darker than the hair on his head. Baley found himself staring with fascination at the small strip of hair on the upper lip. It was the first time he had seen a Spacer with a mustache.

Baley said (and was filled with shame at speaking in a Personal), "I am Elijah Baley." His voice, even in his own ears, seemed a scratchy and unconvincing whisper.

The Spacer seemed to find it unconvincing, certainly. He said, narrowing his eyes and staring, "The robots outside said Elijah Baley was in here, but you don't look at all the way you looked on hyperwave. Not at all."

That foolish dramatization! thought Baley fiercely. No one would meet him to the end of time without having been preliminarily poisoned by that impossible representation. No one would accept him as a human being at the start, as a fallible human being—and when they discovered the fallibility, they would, in disappointment, consider him a fool.

He turned resentfully to the washbasin and splashed water, then shook his hands vaguely in the air, while wondering where the hot-air jet might be found. The Spacer touched a contact and seemed to pluck a thin bit of absorbent fluff out of midair.

"Thank you," said Baley, taking it. "That was not me in the hyperwave show. It was an actor."

"I know that, but they might have picked one that looked more like you, mightn't they?" It seemed to be a source of grievance to him. "I want to speak to you."

"How did you get past my robots?"

That was another source of grievance, apparently. "I nearly didn't," said the Spacer. "They tried to stop me and I only had one robot with me. I had to pretend I had to get in here on an emergency basis and they *searched* me. They absolutely laid *hands* on me to see if I was carrying anything dangerous. I'd have you up on charges—if you weren't an Earthman. You can't give robots the kind of orders that embarrass a human being."

"I'm sorry," said Baley stiffly, "but I am not the one who gave them their orders. What can I do for you?"

"I want to speak to you."

"You *are* speaking to me. ——Who are you?"

The other seemed to hesitate, then said, "Gremionis."

"Santirix Gremionis?"

"That's right."

"Why do you want to speak to me?"

For a moment, Gremionis stared at Baley, apparently with embarrassment. Then he mumbled, "Well, as long as I'm here—if you don't mind—I might as well——" and he stepped toward the line of urinals.

Baley realized, with the last refinement of horrified queasiness, what it was Gremionis intended to do. He turned hastily and said, "I'll wait for you outside."

"No no, don't go," said Gremionis desperately, in what was almost a squeak. "This won't take a second. Please!"

It was only that Baley now wanted, just as desperately, to talk to Gremionis and did not want to do anything that might offend the other and make him unwilling to talk; otherwise he would not have been willing to accede to the request.

He kept his back turned and squinted his eyes nearly shut in a sort of horrified reflex. It was only when Gremionis came up around him, his hands kneading a fluffy towel of his own, that Baley could relax again, after a fashion.

"Why do you want to speak to me?" he said again.

"Gladia—the woman from Solaria——" Gremionis looked dubious and stopped.

"I know Gladia," said Baley coldly.

"Gladia viewed me—trimensionally, you know—and told me you had asked about me. And she asked me if I had, in any way, mistreated a robot she owned—a human-looking robot like one of those outside——"

"Well, did you, Mr. Gremionis?"

"No! I didn't even know she owned a robot like that, until—Did you tell her I did?"

"I was only asking questions, Mr. Gremionis."

Gremionis had made a fist of his right hand and was grinding it nervously into his left. He said intensely, "I don't want to be falsely accused of anything—and especially where such a false accusation would affect my relationship with Gladia."

Baley said, "How did you find me?"

Gremionis said, "She asked me about that robot and said you had asked about me. I had heard you had been called to Aurora by Dr. Fastolfe to solve this—puzzle—about the robot. It was on the hyperwave news. And——" The words ground out as though they were emerging from him with the utmost difficulty.

"Go on," said Baley.

"I had to talk to you and explain that I had had nothing to do with that robot. Nothing! Gladia didn't know where you were, but I thought Dr. Fastolfe would know."

"So you called him?"

"Oh no, I—I don't think I'd have the nerve to—He's such an important scientist. But Gladia called him for me. She's—that kind of person. He told her you had gone to see his daughter, Dr. Vasilia Aliena. That was good because I know her."

"Yes, I know you do," said Baley.

Gremionis looked uneasy. "How did you—Did you ask her about me, too?" His uneasiness seemed to be degenerating to misery. "I finally called Dr. Vasilia and she said you had just left and I'd probably find you at some Community Personal—and this one is the closest to her establishment. I was sure there would be no reason for you to delay in order to find a farther one. I mean why should you?"

"You reason quite correctly, but how is it you got here so quickly?"

"I work at the Robotics Institute and my establishment is on the Institute grounds. My scooter brought me here in minutes."

"Did you come here alone?"

"Yes! With only one robot. The scooter is a two-seater, you see."

"And your robot is waiting outside?"

"Yes."

"Tell me again why you want to see me."

"I've got to make sure you don't think I've had anything to do with that robot. I never even *heard* of him till this whole thing exploded in the news. So can I talk to you *now?*"

"Yes, but not here," said Baley firmly. "Let's get out."

How strange it was, thought Baley, that he was so pleased to get out from behind walls and into the Outside. There was something more totally alien to this Personal than anything else he had encountered on either Aurora or Solaria. Even more disconcerting than the fact of planet-wide indiscriminate use had been the horror of being openly and casually addressed—of behavior that drew no distinction between this place and its purpose and any other place and purpose.

The book-films he had viewed had said nothing of this. Clearly, as Fastolfe had pointed out, they were not written for Earthpeople but for Aurorans and, to a lesser extent, for possible tourists from the other forty-nine Spacer worlds. Earthpeople, after all, almost never went to the Spacer worlds, least of all to Aurora. They were not welcome there. Why, then, should they be addressed?

And why should the book-films expand on what everyone knew? Should they make a fuss over the fact that Aurora was spherical in shape, or that water was wet, or that one man might address another freely in a Personal?

Yet did that not make a mockery of the very name of the structure? Yet Baley found himself unable to avoid thinking of the Women's Personals on Earth where, as Jessie had frequently told him, women chattered incessantly and felt no discomfort about it. Why women, but not men? Baley had never thought seriously about it before, but had accepted it merely as custom—as unbreakable custom—but if women, why not men?

It didn't matter. The thought only affected his intellect and not whatever it was about his mind that made him feel overwhelming and ineradicable distaste for the whole idea. He repeated, "Let's get out."

Gremionis protested, "But your robots are out there."

"So they are. What of it?"

"But this is something I want to talk about privately, man to m-man." He stumbled over the phrase.

"I suppose you mean Spacer to Earthman."

"If you like."

"My robots are necessary. They are my partners in my investigation."

"But this has nothing to do with the investigation. That's what I'm trying to tell you."

"I'll be the judge of that," said Baley firmly, walking out of the Personal.

Gremionis hesitated and then followed.

47

Daneel and Giskard were waiting—impassive, expressionless, patient. On Daneel's face, Baley thought he could make out a trace of concern, but, on the other hand, he might merely be reading that emotion into those inhumanly human features. Giskard, the less human-looking, showed nothing, of course, even to the most willing personifier.

A third robot waited as well—presumably that of Gremionis. He was simpler in appearance even than Giskard and had an air of shabbiness about him. It was clear that Gremionis was not very well-to-do.

Daneel said, with what Baley automatically assumed to be the warmth of relief, "I am pleased that you are well, Partner Elijah."

"Entirely well. I am curious, however, about something. If you had heard me call out in alarm from within, would you have come in?"

"At once, sir," said Giskard.

"Even though you are programmed not to enter Personals?"

"The need to protect a human being—you, in particular—would be paramount, sir."

"That is so, Partner Elijah," said Daneel.

"I'm glad to hear that," said Baley. "This person is Santirix Gremionis. Mr. Gremionis, this is Daneel and this is Giskard."

Each robot bent his head solemnly. Gremionis merely glanced at them and lifted one hand in indifferent acknowledgment. He made no effort to introduce his own robot.

Baley looked around. The light was distinctly dimmer, the wind was brisker, the air was cooler, the sun was completely hidden by clouds. There was a gloom to the surroundings that did not seem to affect Baley, who continued to be delighted at having escaped from the Personal. It lifted his spirits amazingly that he was actually experiencing the feeling of being pleased at being Outside. It was a special case, he knew, but it was a beginning and he could not help but consider it a triumph.

Baley was about to turn to Gremionis to resume the conversation, when his eye caught movement. Walking across the lawn came a woman with an accompanying robot. She was coming toward them but seemed totally oblivious to them. She was clearly making for the Personal.

Baley put out his arm in the direction of the woman, as though to stop her, even though she was still thirty meters away, and muttered, "Doesn't she know that's a Men's Personal?"

"What?" said Gremionis.

The woman continued to approach, while Baley watched in total puzzlement. Finally, the woman's robot stepped to one side to wait and the woman entered the structure.

Baley said helplessly, "But she can't go in there."

Gremionis said, "Why not? It's communal."

"But it's for men."

"It's for people," said Gremionis. He seemed utterly confused.

"Either sex? Surely you can't mean that."

"Any human being. Of course I mean it! How would you want it to be? I don't understand."

Baley turned away. It had not been many minutes before that he had thought that open conversation in a Personal was the acme in bad taste, of Things Not Done.

If he had tried to think of something worse yet, he would have completely failed to dredge up the possibility of encountering a woman in a Personal. Convention on Earth required him to ignore the presence of others in the large Community Personals on that world, but not all the conventions ever invented would have prevented him from knowing whether a person passing him was a man or a woman.

What if, while he had been in the Personal, a woman had entered—casually, indifferently—as this one had just done? Or, worse still, what if he had entered a Personal and found a woman already there?

He could not estimate his reaction. He had never weighed the possibility, let alone met with such a situation, but he found the thought totally intolerable.

And the book-films had told him nothing about that, either.

He had viewed those films in order that he might not approach the investigation in total ignorance of the Auroran way of life—and they had left him in total ignorance of all that was important.

Then how could he handle this triply knotted puzzle of Jander's death, when at every step he found himself lost in ignorance?

A moment before he had felt triumph at a small conquest over the terrors of Outside, but now he was faced with the feeling of being ignorant of everything, ignorant even of the nature of his ignorance.

It was now, while fighting not to picture the woman passing through the airspace lately occupied by himself, that he came near to utter despair.

48

Again Giskard said (and in a way that made it possible to read concern into his words—if not into the tone), "Are you unwell, sir? Do you need help?"

Baley muttered, "No no. I'm all right. —But let's move away. We're in the path of people wishing to use that structure."

He walked rapidly toward the airfoil that was resting in the open stretch beyond the gravel path. On the other side was a small two-wheeled vehicle, with two seats, one behind the other. Baley assumed it to be Gremionis' scooter.

His feeling of depression and misery, Baley realized, was accentuated by the fact that he felt hungry. It was clearly past lunchtime and he had not eaten.

He turned to Gremionis. "Let's talk—but if you don't mind, let's do it over lunch. That is, if you haven't already eaten—and if you don't mind eating with me."

"Where are you going to eat?"

"I don't know. Where does one eat at the Institute?"

Gremionis said, "Not at the Community Diner. We can't talk there."

"Is there an alternative?"

"Come to my establishment," said Gremionis at once. "It isn't one of the fancier ones here. I'm not one of your high executives. Still, I have a few serviceable robots and we can set a decent table. —I tell you what. I'll get on my scooter with Brundij—my robot, you know—and you follow me. You'll have to go slowly, but I'm only a little over a kilometer away. It will just take two or three minutes."

He moved away at an eager half-run. Baley watched him and thought there seemed to be a kind of gangly youthfulness about him. There was no easy way of actually judging his age, of course; Spacers didn't show age and Gremionis might easily be fifty. But he *acted* young, almost what an Earthman would consider teenage young. Baley wasn't sure exactly what there was about him that gave that impression.

Baley turned suddenly to Daneel. "Do you know Gremionis, Daneel?"

"I have never met him before, Partner Elijah."

"You, Giskard?"

"I have met him once, sir, but only in passing."

"Do you know anything about him, Giskard?"

"Nothing that is not apparent on the surface, sir."

"His age? His personality?"

"No, sir."

Gremionis shouted, "Ready?" His scooter was humming rather roughly. It was clear that it was not air-jet assisted. The wheels would not leave the ground. Brundij sat behind Gremionis.

Giskard, Daneel, and Baley moved quickly into their airfoil once again.

Gremionis moved outward in a loose circle. Gremionis' hair flew backward in the wind and Baley had a sudden sensation of how the wind must feel when one traveled in an open vehicle such as a scooter. He was thankful he was totally enclosed in an airfoil—which suddenly seemed to him a much more civilized way of traveling.

The scooter straightened out and darted off with a muted roar, Gremionis waving one hand in a follow-me gesture. The robot behind him maintained his balance with almost negligent ease and did not hold on to Gremionis' waist, as Baley was certain a human being would have needed to.

The airfoil followed. Although the scooter's smooth forward progression seemed high-speed, that was apparently the illusion of its small size. The airfoil had some difficulty maintaining a speed low enough to avoid running it down.

"Just the same," said Baley thoughtfully, "one thing puzzles me."

"What is that, Partner Elijah?" asked Daneel.

"Vasilia referred to this Gremionis disparagingly as a 'barber.' Apparently, he deals with hair, clothes, and other matters of personal human adornment. How is it, then, that he has an establishment on the grounds of the Robotics Institute?"

12. Again Gremionis

49

It took only a few minutes before Baley found himself in the fourth Auroran establishment he had seen since his arrival on the planet a day and a half before: Fastolfe's, Gladia's, Vasilia's, and now Gremionis'.

Gremionis' establishment appeared smaller and drabber than the others, even though it showed, to Baley's unpracticed eye in Auroran matters, signs of recent construction. The distinctive mark of the Auroran establishment—the robotic niches—were, however, present. On entering, Giskard and Daneel moved quickly into two that were empty and faced the room, unmoving and silent. Gremionis' robot, Brundij, moved into a third niche almost as quickly.

There was no sign of any difficulty in making their choices or of any tendency for any one niche to be the target of two robots, however briefly. Baley wondered how the robots avoided conflict and decided there must be signal communication among them of a kind that was subliminal to human beings. It was something (provided he remembered to do so) concerning which he might consult Daneel.

Gremionis was studying the niches also, Baley noticed.

Gremionis' hand had gone to his upper lip and, for a moment, his forefinger stroked the small mustache. He said, a bit uncertainly, "Your robot, the human-looking one, doesn't seem right in the niche. That's Daneel Olivaw, isn't it? Dr. Fastolfe's robot?"

"Yes," said Baley. "He was in the hyperwave drama, too. Or at least an actor was—one who better fit the part."

"Yes, I remember."

Baley noted that Gremionis—like Vasilia and even like Gladia and Fastolfe—kept a certain distance. There seemed to be a repulsion field—unseen, unfelt, unsensed in any way—around Baley that kept these Spacers from approaching too closely, that sent them into a gentle curve of avoidance when they passed him.

Baley wondered if Gremionis was aware of this or if it was entirely automatic. And what did they do with the chairs he sat in while in their establishments, the dishes he ate from, the towels he used? Would ordinary washing suffice? Were there special sterilizing procedures? Would they discard and replace everything? Would the establishments be fumigated once he left the planet—or every night? What about the Community Personal he used? Would they tear it down and rebuild it? What about the woman who had ignorantly entered it after he had left? Or could she possibly have been the fumigator?

He realized he was getting silly.

To outer space with it. What the Aurorans did and how they dealt with their problems was their affair and he would bother his head no more with them. Jehoshaphat! He had his own problems and, right now, the particular splinter of it was Gremionis—and he would tackle that after lunch.

Lunch was rather simple, largely vegetarian, but for the first time he had a little trouble. Each separate item was too sharply defined in taste. The carrots tasted rather strongly of carrots and the peas of peas, so to speak.

A little too much so, perhaps.

He ate rather reluctantly and tried not to show a slightly rising gorge.

And, as he did so, he became aware that he grew used to it—as though his taste buds saturated and could handle the excess more easily. It dawned on Baley, in a rather sad way, that if his exposure to Auroran food was to continue for any length of time, he would return to Earth missing that distinctiveness of flavor and resenting the flowing together of Earth tastes.

Even the crispness of various items—which had startled him at first, as each closing of his teeth seemed to create a noise that surely (he thought) must interfere with conversation—had already grown to seem exciting evidence that he was, in fact, eating. There would be a silence about an Earth meal that would leave him missing something.

He began to eat with attention, to study the tastes. Perhaps, when Earthpeople established themselves on other worlds, this Spacer-fashion food would be the mark of the new diet, especially if there were no robots to prepare and serve the meals.

And then he thought uncomfortably, not when but *if* Earthpeople established themselves on other worlds—and the ifness of it all depended on him, on Plainclothesman Elijah Baley. The burden of it weighed him down.

The meal was over. A pair of robots brought in the heated, moistened napkins with which one could clean one's hands. Except that they weren't ordinary napkins, for when Baley put his down on the plate, it seemed to move slightly, thin out, and grow cobwebby. Then, quite suddenly, it leaped up insubstantially and was carried into an outlet in the ceiling. Baley jumped slightly and his eyes moved upward, following the disappearing item open-mouthed.

Gremionis said, "That's something new I just picked up. Disposable, you see, but I don't know if I like it yet. Some people say it will clog the disposal vent after a while and others worry about pollution because they say some of it will surely get in your lungs. The manufacturer says not, but—"

Baley realized suddenly that he had said not a word during the meal and that this was the first time either of them had spoken since the short exchange on Daneel before the meal had been served. —And there was no use in small talk about napkins.

Baley said, rather gruffly, "Are you a barber, Mr. Gremionis?"

Gremionis flushed, his light skin reddening to the hairline. He said in a choked voice, "Who told you that?"

Baley said, "If that is an impolite way of referring to your profession, I apologize. It is a common way of speaking on Earth and is no insult there."

Gremionis said, "I am a hair designer and a clothing designer. It is a recognized branch of art. I am, in fact, a personnel artist." His finger went to his mustache again.

Baley said gravely, "I notice your mustache. Is it common to grow them on Aurora?"

"No, it is not. I hope it will become so. You take your masculine face— A great many of them can be strengthened and improved by the artful design of facial hair. Everything is in the design—that's part of my profession. You can go too far, of course. On the world of Pallas, facial hair is common, but it is the practice there to indulge in parti-colored dying. Each individual hair is separately dyed to produce some sort of mixture. —Now, that's foolish. It doesn't last, the colors change with time, and it looks terrible. But even so, it's better than facial baldness in some ways. Nothing is less attractive than a facial desert. —That's my own phrase. I use it in my personal talks with potential clients and it's very effective. Females can get by with no facial hair because they make up for it in other ways. On the world of Smitheus—"

There was a hypnotic quality to his quiet, rapid words and his earnest expression, the way in which his eyes widened and remained fixed on Baley with an intense sincerity. Baley had to shake loose with an almost physical force.

He said, "Are you a roboticist, Mr. Gremionis?"

Gremionis looked startled and a little confused at being interrupted in midflow. "A roboticist?"

"Yes. A roboticist."

"No, not at all. I use robots as everyone does, but I don't know what's inside them. —Don't care really."

"But you live here on the grounds of the Robotics Institute. How is that?"

"Why shouldn't I?" Gremionis' voice was measurably more hostile.

"If you're not a roboticist—"

Gremionis grimaced. "That's stupid! The Institute, when it was designed some years ago, was intended to be a self-contained community. We have our own transport vehicle repair shops, our own personal robot maintenance shops, our own physicians, our own structuralists. Our personnel live here and, if they have use for a personnel artist, that's Santirix Gremionis and I live here, too. —Is there something wrong with my profession that I should not?"

"I haven't said that."

Gremionis turned away with a residual petulance that Baley's hasty disclaimer had not allayed. He pressed a button, then, after studying a varicolored rectangular strip, did something that was remarkably like drumming his fingers briefly.

A sphere dropped gently from the ceiling and remained suspended a meter or so above their heads. It opened as though it were an orange that was unsegmenting and a play of colors began within it, together with a soft wash of sound. The two melted together so skillfully that Baley, watching with astonishment, discovered that, after a short while, it was hard to distinguish one from the other.

The windows opacified and the segments grew brighter.

"Too bright?" asked Gremionis.

"No," said Baley, after some hesitation.

"It's meant for background and I've picked a soothing combination that will make it easier for us to talk in a civilized way, you know." Then he said briskly, "Shall we get to the point?"

Baley withdrew his attention from the—whatever it was (Gremionis had not given it a name)—with some difficulty and said, "If you please. I would like to."

"Have you been accusing me of having anything to do with the immobilization of that robot Jander?"

"I've been inquiring into the circumstances of the robot's ending."

"But you've mentioned me in connection with that ending. —In fact, just a little while ago, you asked me if I were a roboticist. I know what you had in mind. You were trying to get me to admit I knew something about robotics, so that you could build up a case against me as the—as the—*ender* of the robot."

"You might say the killer."

"The killer? You can't kill a robot. —In any case, I didn't end it, or kill it, or anything you want to call it. I told you, I'm not a roboticist. I know *nothing* about robotics. How can you even *think* that—"

"I must investigate all connections, Mr. Gremionis. Jander belonged to Gladia—the Solarian woman—and you were friendly with her. That's a connection."

"There could be any number of people friendly with her. That's no connection."

"Are you willing to state that you never saw Jander in all the times you may have been in Gladia's establishment?"

"Never! Not once!"

"You never knew she had a humaniform robot?"

"No!"

"She never mentioned him."

"She had robots all over the place. All ordinary robots She said nothing about having anything else."

Baley shrugged. "Very well. I have no reason—so far—to suppose that that is not the truth."

"Then say so to Gladia. That is why I wanted to see you. To ask you to do that. To insist."

"Has Gladia any reason to think otherwise?"

"Of course. You poisoned her mind. You questioned her about me in that connection and she assumed—she was made uncertain— The fact is, she called this morning and asked me if I had anything to do with it. I told you that."

"And you denied it?"

"Of course I denied it and very strenuously, too, because I didn't have anything to do with it. But it's not convincing if I do the denying. I want you to do it. I want you to tell her that, in your opinion, I had nothing to do with the whole business. You just said I didn't and you can't, without any evidence at all, destroy my reputation. I can report you."

"To whom?"

"To the Committee on Personal Defense. To the Legislature. The head of this Institute is a close personal friend of the Chairman himself and I've already sent a full report to him on this matter. I'm not waiting, you understand. I'm taking action."

Gremionis shook his head with an attitude that might have been intended for fierceness but that did not entirely carry conviction, considering the mildness of his face. "Look," he said, "this isn't Earth. We are protected here. Your planet, with its overpopulation, makes your people exist in so many beehives, so many anthills. You push against each other, suffocate each other—and it doesn't matter. One life or a million lives—it doesn't matter."

Baley, fighting to keep contempt from showing in his voice, said, "You've been reading historical novels."

"Of course I have—and they describe it as it is. You can't have billions of people on a single world without its being so. —On Aurora, we are each a valuable life. We are protected physically, each of us, by our robots, so that there is never an assault, let alone murder, on Aurora."

"Except for Jander."

"That's not murder; it's only a robot. And we are protected from the kinds of harm more subtle than assault by our Legislature. The Committee on Personal Defense takes a dim view—a very dim view—

of any action that unfairly damages the reputation or the social status of any individual citizen. An Auroran, acting as you did, would be in trouble enough. As for an Earthman—well—"

Baley said, "I am carrying on an investigation at the invitation, I presume, of the Legislature. I don't suppose Dr. Fastolfe could have brought me here without Legislative permission."

"Maybe so, but that wouldn't give you the right to overstep the limits of fair investigation."

"Are you going to put this up to the Legislature, then?"

"I'm going to have the Institute head—"

"What is his name, by the way?"

"Kelden Amadiro. I'm going to ask him to put it up to the Legislature—and he's *in* the Legislature, you know—he's one of the leaders of the Globalist party. So I think you had better make it plain to Gladia that I am completely innocent."

"I would like to, Mr. Gremionis, because I suspect that you *are* innocent, but how can I change suspicion to certainty, unless you will allow me to ask you some questions?"

Gremionis hesitated. Then, with an air of defiance, he leaned back in his chair and placed his hands behind his neck, the picture of a man utterly failing to appear at ease. He said, "Ask away. I have nothing to hide. And after you're done, you'll have to call Gladia, right on that trimensional transmitter behind you and say your piece—or you will be in more trouble than you can imagine."

"I understand. But first— How long have you known Dr. Vasilia Fastolfe, Mr. Gremionis? Or Dr. Vasilia Aliena, if you know her by that name?"

Gremionis hesitated, then said in a tense voice, "Why do you ask that? What does that have to do with it?"

Baley sighed and his dour face seemed to sadden further. "I remind you, Mr. Gremionis, that you have nothing to hide and that you want to convince me of your innocence, so that I can convince Gladia of the same. Just tell me how long you have known her. If you have not known her, just say so—but before you do, it is only fair to tell you that Dr. Vasilia has stated that you knew her well—well enough, at least, to offer yourself to her."

Gremionis looked chagrined. He said in a shaky voice, "I don't know why people have to make a big thing out of it. An offer is a perfectly natural social interaction that concerns no one else. —Of course, you're an Earthman, so *you'd* make a fuss about it."

"I understand she didn't accept your offer."

Gremionis brought his hands down upon his lap, fists clenched. "Accepting or rejecting is entirely up to her. There've been people who've offered themselves to me and whom *I've* rejected. It's no large matter."

"Well, then. How long have you known her?"

"For some years. About fifteen."

"Did you know her when she was still living with Dr. Fastolfe?"

"I was just a boy then," he said, flushing.

"How did you get to know her?"

"When I finished my training as a personnel artist, I was called in to design a wardrobe for her. It gave her pleasure and after that she used my services—in that respect—exclusively."

"Was it on her recommendation, then, that you received your present position as—might we say—official personnel artist for the members of the Robotics Institute?"

"She recognized my qualifications. I was tested, along with others, and won the position on my merits."

"But she did recommend you?"

Briefly and with annoyance, Gremionis said, "Yes."

"And you felt the only decent return you could make was to offer yourself to her."

Gremionis grimaced and drew his tongue across his lips, as though tasting something unpleasant. "That—is—disgusting! I suppose an Earthman would think in such a way. My offer meant only that it pleased me to do so."

"Because she is attractive and has a warm personality?"

Gremionis hesitated. "Well, I wouldn't say she has a warm personality," he said cautiously, "but certainly she's attractive."

"I've been told that you offer yourself to everybody—without distinction."

"That is a lie."

"What is a lie? That you offer yourself to everybody or that I have been told so?"

"That I offer myself to everybody. Who said that?"

"I don't know that it would serve any purpose to answer that question. Would you expect me to quote you as a source of embarrassing information? Would you speak freely to me if you thought I would?"

"Well, whoever said it is a liar."

"Perhaps it was merely dramatic exaggeration. Had you offered yourself to others before you offered yourself to Dr. Vasilia?"

Gremionis looked away. "Once or twice. Never seriously."

"But Dr. Vasilia was someone you were serious about?"

"Well—"

"It is my understanding you offered yourself to her repeatedly, which is quite against Auroran custom."

"Oh, Auroran custom—" Gremionis began furiously. Then he pressed his lips together firmly and his forehead furrowed. "See here, Mr. Baley, can I speak to you confidentially?"

"Yes. All my questions are intended to satisfy myself that you had nothing to do with Jander's death. Once I am satisfied of that, you may be sure I'll keep your remarks in confidence."

"Very well, then. It's nothing wrong—it's nothing I'm ashamed of, you understand. It's just that I have a strong sense of privacy and I have a right to that if I wish, don't I?"

"Absolutely," said Baley consolingly.

"You see, I feel that social sex is best when there is a profound love and affection between partners."

"I imagine that's very true."

"And then there's no need for others, wouldn't you say?"

"It sounds—plausible."

"I've always dreamed of finding the perfect partner and never seeking anyone else. They call it monogamy. It doesn't exist on Aurora, but on some worlds it does—and they have it on Earth don't they, Mr. Baley?"

"In theory, Mr. Gremionis."

"It's what I want. I've looked for it for years. When I experimented with sex sometimes, I could tell something was missing. Then I met Dr. Vasilia and she told me—well, people get confidential with their personnel artists because it's *very* personal work—and this is the *really* confidential part—"

"Well, go on."

Gremionis licked his lips. "If what I say now gets out, I'm ruined. She'll do her best to see to it that I get no further commissions. Are you *sure* this has something to do with the case?"

"I assure you with as much force as I can, Mr. Gremionis, that this can be totally important."

"Well, then"—Gremionis did not look quite convinced—"the fact is, that I gathered from what Dr. Vasilia told me, in bits and pieces, that she is"—his voice dropped to a whisper—"a virgin."

"I see," said Baley quietly (remembering Vasilia's certainty that her father's refusal had distorted her life and getting a firmer understanding of her hatred of her father).

"That excited me. It seemed to me I could have her all to myself and I would be the only one that she would ever have. I can't explain how much that meant to me. It made her look gloriously beautiful in my eyes and I just wanted her so much."

"So you offered yourself to her?"

"Yes."

"Repeatedly. You weren't discouraged by her refusals?"

"It just reinforced her virginity, so to speak, and made me more eager. It was more exciting that it wasn't easy. I can't explain and I don't expect you to understand."

"Actually, Mr. Gremionis, I do understand. —But there came a time when you stopped offering yourself to Dr. Vasilia?"

"Well, yes."

"And began offering yourself to Gladia?"

"Well, yes."

"Repeatedly?"

"Well, yes."

"Why? Why the change?"

Gremionis said, "Dr. Vasilia finally made it clear that there was no chance and then Gladia came along and she looked like Dr. Vasilia and—and—that was it."

Baley said, "But Gladia is no virgin. She was married on Solaria and she experimented rather widely on Aurora, I am told."

"I knew about that, but she—stopped. You see, she's a Solarian by birth, not an Auroran, and she didn't quite understand Auroran customs. But she stopped because she doesn't like what she calls 'promiscuity.' "

"Did she tell you that?"

"Yes. Monogamy is the custom on Solaria. She wasn't happily married, but it is still the custom she's used to, so she never enjoyed the Auroran way when she tried it—and monogamy is what I want, too. Do you see?"

"I see. But how did you meet her in the first place?"

"I just met her. She was on the hyperwave when she arrived in Aurora, a romantic refugee from Solaria. And she played a part in that hyperwave drama—"

"Yes yes, but there was something else, wasn't there?"

"I don't know what else you want."

"Well, let me guess. Didn't there come a point when Dr. Vasilia said she was rejecting you forever—and didn't she suggest an alternative to you?"

Gremionis, in sudden fury, shouted, "Did Dr. Vasilia tell you *that?*"

"Not in so many words, but I think I know what happened, even so. Did she not tell you that it might be advantageous if you looked up a new arrival on the planet, a young lady from Solaria who was a ward or protégée of Dr. Fastolfe—who you know is Dr. Vasilia's father? Did Dr. Vasilia perhaps not tell you that people thought this young lady, Gladia, rather resembled herself, but that she was younger and had a warmer personality? Did Dr. Vasilia not, in short, encourage you to transfer your attentions from herself to Gladia?"

Gremionis was visibly suffering. His eyes flicked to those of Baley and away again. It was the first time that Baley saw in the eyes of any Spacer a look of fright—or was it awe? (Baley shook his head slightly. He must not take too much satisfaction at having overawed a Spacer. It could damage his objectivity.)

He said, "Well? Am I right or wrong?"

And Gremionis said in a low voice, "That hyperwave show was no exaggeration, then. —Do you read minds?"

50

Baley said calmly, "I just ask questions. —And you haven't answered directly. Am I right or wrong?"

Gremionis said, "It didn't quite happen like that. Not just like that. She did talk about Gladia, but—" He bit at his lower lip and then said, "Well, it amounted to what you said. It was just about the way you described it."

"And you were not disappointed? You found that Gladia did resemble Dr. Vasilia?"

"In a way, she did." Gremionis' eyes brightened. "But not really. Stand them side by side and you'll see the difference. Gladia has much greater delicacy and grace. A greater spirit of—of fun."

"Have you offered yourself to Vasilia since you met Gladia?"

"Are you mad? Of course not."

"But you have offered yourself to Gladia?"

"Yes."

"And she rejected you?"

"Well, yes, but you have to understand that she has to be sure, as I would have to be. Think what a mistake I would have made if I had moved Dr. Vasilia to accept me. Gladia doesn't want to make that mistake and I don't blame her."

"But *you* don't think it would be a mistake for her to accept you, so you have offered yourself again—and again—and again."

Gremionis stared vacantly at Baley for a moment and then seemed to shudder. He thrust out his lower lip, as though he were a rebellious child. "You say it in an insulting way—"

"I'm sorry. I don't mean it to be insulting. Please answer the question."

"Well, I have."

"How many times have you offered yourself?"

"I haven't counted. Four times. Well, five. Or maybe more."

"And she has always rejected you."

"Yes. Or I wouldn't have to offer again, would I?"

"Did she reject you angrily?"

"Oh no. That's not Gladia. Very kindly."

"Has it made you offer yourself to anyone else?"

"What?"

"Well, Gladia has rejected you. One way of responding would be to offer yourself to someone else. Why not? If Gladia doesn't want you—"

"*No.* I don't want anyone else."

"Why is that, do you suppose?"

And, strenuously, Gremionis said, "How should I know why that is? I want Gladia. It's a—it's a kind of madness, except that I think it's the best kind of insanity. I'd be mad *not* to have that kind of madness. —I don't expect you to understand."

"Have you tried to explain this to Gladia? She might understand."

"Never. I'd distress her. I'd embarrass her. You don't talk about such things. I should see a mentologist."

"Have you?"

"No."

"Why not?"

Gremionis frowned. "You have a way of asking the rudest questions, Earthman."

"Perhaps because I'm an Earthman. I know no better. But I'm also an investigator and I must know these things. Why have you not seen a mentologist?"

Surprisingly, Gremionis laughed. "I told you. The cure would be greater madness than the disease. I would rather be with Gladia and be rejected than be with anyone else and be accepted. —Imagine having your mind out of whack and wanting it to *stay* out of whack. Any mentologist would put me in for major treatment."

Baley thought awhile, then said, "Do you know whether Dr. Vasilia is a mentologist in any way?"

"She's a roboticist. They say that's the closest thing to it. If you know how a robot works, you've got a hint as to how a human brain works. Or so they say."

"Does it occur to you that Vasilia knows these strange feelings you have in connection with Gladia?"

Gremionis stiffened. "I've never told her. —I mean in so many words."

"Isn't it possible that she understands your feelings without having to ask? Is she aware that you have repeatedly offered yourself to Gladia?"

"Well— She would ask how I was getting along. In the way of long-standing acquaintanceship, you know. I would say certain things. Nothing intimate."

"Are you sure that it was never anything intimate? Surely she encouraged you to continue to offer."

"You know—now that you mention it, I seem to see it all in a new way. I don't see quite how you managed to put it into my head. It's the questions you ask, I suppose, but it seems to me now that she did continue to encourage my friendship with Gladia. She actively supported it." He looked very uneasy. "This never occurred to me before. I never really thought about it."

"Why do you think she encouraged you to make repeated offers to Gladia?"

Gremionis twitched his eyebrows ruefully and his finger went to his mustache. "I suppose some might guess she was trying to get rid of me. Trying to make sure I wouldn't want to bother *her*." He made a small laughing sound. "That's not very complimentary to me, is it?"

"Did Dr. Vasilia cease being friendly with you?"

"Not at all. She was more friendly—if anything."

"Did she try to tell you how to be more successful with Gladia? To show a greater interest in Gladia's work, for example?"

"She didn't have to do that. Gladia's work and mine are very similar. I work with human beings and she with robots, but we're both design-ers—artists— That does make for closeness, you know. We even help each other at times. When I'm not offering and being rejected, we're good friends. —That's a lot, when you come to think of it."

"Did Dr. Vasilia suggest you show a greater interest in Dr. Fastolfe's work?"

"Why should she suggest that? I don't know anything about Dr. Fastolfe's work."

"Gladia might be interested in her benefactor's work and it might be a way for you to ingratiate yourself with her."

Gremionis' eyes narrowed. He rose with almost explosive force, walked to the other end of the room, came back, stood in front of Baley, and said, "*Now—you—look—here!* I'm not the biggest brain on the planet, not even the second-biggest, but I'm not a blithering idiot. I see what you're getting at, you know."

"Oh?"

"All your questions have served to sort of wriggle me into saying that Dr. Vasilia got me to fall in love—That's it"—he stopped in sud-den surprise—"I'm in love, like in the historical novels." He thought about that with the light of wonder in his eyes. Then the anger re-turned. "That she got me to fall in love and to stay in love, so that I could find out things from Dr. Fastolfe and learn how to immobilize that robot, Jander."

"You don't think that's so?"

"No, it's not!" shouted Gremionis. "I don't know anything about robotics. *Anything*. No matter how carefully anything about robotics were explained to me, I wouldn't understand it. And I don't think Gladia would either. Besides, I never asked anyone about robotics. I was never told—by Dr. Fastolfe or anyone—anything about robotics. No one ever suggested I get involved with robotics. Dr. Vasilia never suggested it. Your whole rotten theory doesn't work." He shot his arms out to either side. "It doesn't work. Forget it."

He sat back, folded his arms rigidly across his chest, and forced his lips together in a thin line, making his small mustache bristle.

Baley looked up at the unsegmented orange, which was still humming its low, pleasantly varying tune and displaying a gentle change of color as it swayed hypnotically through a small, slow arc.

If Gremionis' outburst had upset his line of attack, he showed no sign of it. He said, "I understand what you're saying, but it's still true that you see much of Gladia, isn't it?"

"Yes, I do."

"Your repeated offers do not offend her—and her repeated rejections do not offend you?"

Gremionis shrugged. "My offers are polite. Her refusals are gentle. Why should we be offended?"

"But how do you spend time together? Sex is out, obviously, and you don't talk robotics. What do you do?"

"Is that all there is to companionship—sex and robotics? We do a great deal together. We talk, for one thing. She is very curious about Aurora and I spend hours describing the planet. She's seen very little of it, you know. And she spends hours telling me about Solaria and what a hellhole it is. I'd rather live on Earth—no offense intended. And there's her dead husband. What a miserable character *he* was. Gladia's had a hard life, poor woman.

"We go to concerts, I took her to the Art Institute a few times, and we *work* together. I told you that. We go over my designs—or her designs—together. To be perfectly honest, I don't see that working on robots is very rewarding, but we all have our own notions, you know. For that matter, she seemed to be amused when I explained why it was so important to cut hair correctly—her own hair isn't *quite* right, you know. But mostly, we go for walks."

"Walks? Where?"

"Nowhere particularly. Just walks. That is her habit—because of the way she was brought up on Solaria. Have you ever been on Solaria? —Yes, you have been, of course. I'm sorry. —On Solaria, there are these huge estates with only one or two human beings on them, just robots otherwise. You can walk for miles and be completely alone and Gladia says that it makes you feel as though you owned the entire planet. The robots are always there, of course, keeping an eye on you and taking care of you, but, of course, they keep out of sight. Gladia misses that feeling of world ownership here on Aurora."

"Do you mean that she wants world ownership?"

"You mean a kind of lust for power? Gladia? That's crazy. All she means is that she misses the feeling of being alone with nature. I don't see it myself, you understand, but I like humoring her. Of course, you can't quite get the Solarian feeling in Aurora. There are bound to be people about, especially in the Eos metropolitan area, and robots haven't been programmed to keep out of sight. In fact, Aurorans generally walk *with* robots. —Still, I know some routes that are pleasant and not very crowded and Gladia enjoys them."

"Do you enjoy them, too?"

"Well, only because I would be with Gladia. Aurorans are walkers, too, by and large, but I must admit I'm not. I had protesting muscles at first and Vasilia laughed at me."

"She knew you went on walks, did she?"

"Well, I came in limping one day and creaking at the thighs, so I had to explain. She laughed and said it was a good idea and the best way to get a walker to accept an offer was to walk with them. 'Keep it up,' she said, 'and she'll cancel her rejection before you get a chance to offer again. She'll make the offer herself.' As it happened, Gladia didn't, but eventually I grew to like the walks very much, just the same."

He seemed to have gotten over his flash of anger and was now very much at his ease. He might have been thinking of the walks, Baley thought, for there was a half-smile on his face. He looked rather likable—and vulnerable—with his mind back on who-knew-what conversational passage on a walk that had taken them who-knew-where. Baley almost smiled in response.

"Vasilia knew, then, that you continued the walks."

"I suppose so. I began to take Wednesdays and Saturdays off because that fit in with Gladia's schedule choice—and Vasilia would sometimes joke about my 'WS walks' when I brought in some sketches."

"Did Dr. Vasilia ever join the walks?"

"Certainly not."

Baley shifted in his seat and stared intently at his fingertips as he said, "I presume you had robots accompanying you on your walks."

"Absolutely. One of mine, one of hers. They kept rather out of the way, though. They didn't tag along in what Gladia called Aurora fashion. She wanted Solarian solitude, she said. So I obliged, though at first I got a crick in my neck looking around to see if Brundij was with me."

"And which robot accompanied Gladia?"

"It wasn't always the same one. Whichever he was, he held off, too. I didn't get to talk to him."

"What about Jander?"

Some of the sunniness left Gremionis' expression at once.

"What about him?" he asked.

"Did he ever come along? If he did, you would know, wouldn't you?"

"A humaniform robot? I certainly would. And he did not accompany us—not ever."

"Are you certain?"

"Completely certain." Gremionis scowled. "I imagine she thought him far too valuable to waste on duties any ordinary robot could perform."

"You seem annoyed. Did you think so, too?"

"He was her robot. I didn't worry about it."

"And you never saw him when you were at Gladia's establishment?"

"Never."

"Did she ever say anything about him? Discuss him?"

"Not that I recall."

"Didn't you consider that strange?"

Gremionis shook his head. "No. Why talk about robots?"

Baley's somber eyes fixed on the other's face. "Did you have any idea of the relationship between Gladia and Jander?"

Gremionis said, "Are you going to tell me that there was sex between them?"

Baley said, "Would you be surprised if I did?"

Gremionis said stolidly, "It happens. It's not unusual. You can use a robot sometimes, if you feel like it. And a humaniform robot—completely humaniform, I believe—"

"Completely," said Baley with an appropriate gesture.

Gremionis' lips curved downward. "Well, then, it would be hard for a woman to resist."

"She resisted *you*. Doesn't it bother you that Gladia would prefer a robot to you?"

"Well, if it comes to that, I'm not sure that I believe this is true—but if it is, it's nothing to worry about. A robot is just a robot. A woman and a robot—or a man and a robot—it's just masturbation."

"You honestly never knew of the relationship, Mr. Gremionis? You never suspected?"

"I never gave it any thought," insisted Gremionis.

"Didn't know? Or did know, but paid it no mind?"

Gremionis scowled. "You're pushing again. What do you want me to say? Now that you put it into my head and push, it seems to me, if I look back, that maybe I was wondering about something like that. Just the same, I never felt anything was happening before you started asking questions."

"Are you sure?"

"Yes, I'm sure. Don't badger me."

"I'm not badgering you. I'm just wondering if it were possible that you did know that Gladia was regularly engaging in sex with Jander, that you

knew that you would never be accepted as her lover as long as that was
so, that you wanted her so much that you would stop at nothing to eliminate Jander, that, in short, you were so jealous that you—"

And at that moment, Gremionis—as though some tightly coiled
spring, held back with difficulty for some minutes, had suddenly
twitched loose—hurled himself at Baley with a loud and incoherent
cry. Baley, taken completely by surprise, pushed backward instinc-
tively and his chair went over.

51

There were strong arms upon him at once. Baley felt himself lifted,
the chair righted, and was aware that he was in the grip of a robot.
How easy it was to forget they were in the room when they stood
silent and motionless in their niches.

It was neither Daneel nor Giskard who had come to his rescue,
however. It was Gremionis' robot, Brundij.

"Sir," said Brundij, his voice just a bit unnatural, "I hope you are
not hurt."

Where were Daneel and Giskard?

The question answered itself at once. The robots had divided the
labor neatly and quickly. Daneel and Giskard, estimating instantly that
an overturned chair offered less chance of harm to Baley than a maddened Gremionis, had launched themselves at the host. Brundij, seeing at once that he was not needed in that direction, saw to the welfare
of the guest.

Gremionis—still standing, his breath heaving—was completely immobilized in the careful double-grasp of Baley's robots.

Gremionis said, in very little above a whisper, "Release me. I am in
control of myself."

"Yes, sir," said Giskard.

"Of course, Mr. Gremionis," said Daneel with what was almost
suavity.

But although their arms released their hold, neither moved back for
a period of time. Gremionis looked right and left, adjusted the smoothness of his clothing, and then, deliberately, sat down. His breathing
was still rapid and his hair was, to a small extent, in disarray.

Baley now stood, one hand on the back of the chair on which he
had been sitting.

Gremionis said, "I am sorry, Mr. Baley, for losing control. It is something I have not done in my adult life. You accused me of being
j-jealous. It is a word no respectable Auroran would use of another, but
I should have remembered you are an Earthman. It is a word *we* en-

counter only in historical romances and even then the word is usually spelled with a 'j,' followed by a dash. Of course, that is not so on your world. I understand that."

"I am sorry, too, Mr. Gremionis," said Baley gravely, "that my forgetfulness of Auroran custom led me astray in this instance. I assure you that such a lapse will not happen again." He seated himself and said, "I don't know that there is much more to discuss—"

Gremionis did not seem to be listening. "When I was a child," he said, "I would sometimes push against another, and be pushed, and it would be awhile before the robots would take the trouble to separate us, of course—"

Daneel said, "If I may explain, Partner Elijah. It has been well-established that total suppression of aggression in the very young has undesirable consequences. A certain amount of youthful play involving physical competition is permitted—even encouraged—provided no real hurt is involved. Robots in charge of the young are carefully programmed to be able to distinguish the chances and level of harm that may take place. I, for instance, am not properly programmed in this respect and would not qualify as a guardian of the young except under emergency conditions for brief periods. —Nor would Giskard."

Baley said, "Such aggressive behavior is stopped during adolescence, I suppose."

"Gradually," said Daneel, "as the level of harm that may be inflicted increases and as the desirability of self-control becomes more pronounced."

Gremionis said, "By the time I was ready for higher schooling, I, like all Aurorans, knew quite well that all competition rested on the comparison of mental capacity and talent—"

"No physical competition?" said Baley.

"Certainly, but only in fashions that do not involve deliberate physical contact with intent to injure."

"But since you've been an adolescent—"

"I've attacked no one. Of course I haven't. I've had the urge to do so on a number of occasions, to be sure. I suppose I wouldn't be entirely normal if I hadn't, but until this moment, I've been able to control it. But then, no one ever called me— *that* before."

Baley said, "It would do no good to attack, in any case, if you are going to be stopped by robots, would it? I presume there is always a robot within reach on both sides of both the attacker and the attacked."

"Certainly. —All the more reason for me to be ashamed of having lost my self-control. I trust that this won't have to go into your report."

"I assure you I will tell no one of this. It has nothing to do with the case."

"Thank you. Did you say that the interview is over?"

"I think it is."

"In that case, will you do as I have asked you to do?"

"What is that?"

"To tell Gladia I had nothing to do with Jander's immobilization."

Baley hesitated. "I will tell her that that is my opinion."

Gremionis said, "Please make it stronger than that. I want her to be absolutely certain that I had nothing to do with it; all the more so if she was fond of the robot from a sexual standpoint. I couldn't bear to have her think I was j-j— Being a Solarian, she might think that."

"Yes, she might," said Baley thoughtfully.

"But look," said Gremionis, speaking quickly and earnestly. "I don't know anything about robots and no one—Dr. Vasilia or anyone else— has told me anything about them—how they work, I mean. There is just no way in which I could have destroyed Jander."

Baley seemed, for a moment, to be deep in thought. Then he said, with clear reluctance, "I can't help but believe you. To be sure, I don't know everything. And it is possible—I say this without meaning offense—that either you or Dr. Vasilia—or both—are lying. I know surprisingly little about the intimate nature of Auroran society and I can perhaps be easily fooled. And yet, I can't help but believe you. Nevertheless, I can't do more than tell Gladia that, in my opinion, you are completely innocent. I must say 'in my opinion,' however. I am sure she will find that strong enough."

Gremionis said gloomily, "Then I will have to be satisfied with that. —If it will help, though, I assure you, on the word of an Auroran citizen, that I am innocent."

Baley smiled slightly. "I wouldn't dream of doubting your word, but my training forces me to rely on objective evidence alone."

He stood up, stared solemnly at Gremionis for a moment, then said, "What I am about to say should not be taken amiss, Mr. Gremionis. I take it that you are interested in having me give Gladia this reassurance because you want to retain her friendship."

"I want that very much, Mr. Baley."

"And you intend, on some suitable occasion, to offer yourself again?"

Gremionis flushed, swallowed visibly, then said, "Yes, I do."

"May I then give you a word of advice, sir? Don't do it."

"You may keep your advice, if that's what you're going to tell me. I don't intend ever to give up."

"I mean do not go through the usual formal procedure. You might consider simply"—Baley looked away, feeling unaccountably embarrassed—"putting your arms around her and kissing her."

"No," said Gremionis earnestly. "*Please.* An Auroran woman would not endure that. Nor an Auroran man."

"Mr. Gremionis, won't you remember that Gladia is *not* Auroran? She is Solarian and has other customs, other traditions. I would try it if I were you."

Baley's level gaze masked a sudden internal fury. What was Gremionis to him that he should give such advice? Why tell another to do that which he himself longed to do?

13.

Amadiro

52

Baley got back to business, with a somewhat deeper baritone to his voice than was usual. He said, "Mr. Gremionis, you mentioned the name of the head of the Robotics Institute earlier. Could you give me that name again?"

"Kelden Amadiro."

"And would there be some way of reaching him from here?"

Gremionis said, "Well, yes and no. You can reach his receptionist or his assistant. I doubt that you'll reach him. He's a rather standoffish person, I'm told. I don't know him personally, of course. I've seen him now and then, but I've never talked to him."

"I take it, then, he doesn't use you as a clothes designer or for personal grooming?"

"I don't know that he uses anyone and, from the few occasions when I've seen him, I can tell you he looks it, though I'd rather you didn't repeat that remark."

"I'm sure you're right, but I'll keep the confidence," said Baley gravely. "I would like to try to reach him, despite his standoffish reputation. If you have a trimensic outlet, would you mind my making use of it for that purpose?"

"Brundij can make the call for you."

"No, I think my partner, Daneel, should—that is, if you don't mind."

"I don't mind at all," said Gremionis. "The outlet is in there, so just follow me, Daneel. The pattern you must use is 75-30-up-20."

Daneel bowed his head. "Thank you, sir."

The room with the trimensic outlet was quite empty, except for a thin pillar toward one side of the room. It ended waist-high in a flat surface on which there was a rather complicated console. The pillar stood in the center of a circle marked off on the light green floor in a neutral gray. Near it was an identical circle in size and color, but on the second one there stood no pillar.

Daneel stepped to the pillar and, as he did so, the circle on which it stood glowed with a faint white radiance. His hand moved over the console, his fingers flicking too quickly for Baley to make out clearly what it was they did. It only took a second and then the other circle glowed in precisely the same way. A robot appeared on it, three-dimensional in appearance but with a very faint flicker that gave away the fact that it was a holographic image. Next to him was a console like that next to which Daneel stood, but the robot's console also flickered and was also an image.

Daneel said, "I am R. Daneel Olivaw"—he faintly emphasized the "R." so the robot would not mistake him for a human being—"and I represent my partner, Elijah Baley, a plainclothesman from Earth. My partner would like to speak with Master Roboticist Kelden Amadiro."

The robot said, "Master Roboticist Amadiro is in conference. Would it be sufficient to speak to Roboticist Cicis?"

Daneel looked quickly in Baley's direction. Baley nodded and Daneel said, "That will be quite satisfactory."

The robot said, "If you will ask Plainclothesman Baley to take your place, I will try to locate Roboticist Cicis."

Daneel said smoothly, "It would perhaps be better if you were first to—"

But Baley called out, "It's all right, Daneel. I don't mind waiting."

Daneel said, "Partner Elijah, as the personal representative of Master Roboticist Han Fastolfe, you have assimilated his social status, at least temporarily. It is not your place to have to wait for—"

"It's all *right*, Daneel," said Baley, with enough emphasis to preclude further discussion. "I don't wish to create delay by a dispute over social etiquette."

Daneel stepped off the circle and Baley stepped on. He felt a slight tingle as he did so (perhaps a purely imaginary one), but it quickly passed.

The robot's image, standing on the other circle, faded and disappeared. Baley waited patiently and eventually another image darkened and took on apparent three-dimensionality.

"Roboticist Maloon Cicis here," said the figure in a rather sharp, clear voice. He had the close-cut bronze hair that alone sufficed to give him what Baley thought of as a typical Spacer look, though there was a certain un-Spacerlike asymmetry to the line of his nose.

Baley said quietly, "I am Plainclothesman Elijah Baley from Earth. I would like to speak with Master Roboticist Kelden Amadiro."

"Do you have an appointment, Plainclothesman?"

"No, sir."

"You will have to make one if you wish to see him—and there's no time slot available for this week or next."

"I am Plainclothesman Elijah Baley of Earth—"

"So I have been given to understand. It doesn't alter the facts."

Baley said, "At the request of Dr. Han Fastolfe and with the permission of the World Legislature of Aurora, I am investigating the murder of Robot Jander Panell—"

"The *murder* of Robot Jander Panell?" asked Cicis so politely as to indicate contempt.

"Roboticide, if you prefer, then. On Earth, the destruction of a robot would not be so great a matter, but on Aurora, where robots are treated more or less as human beings, it seemed to me that the word 'murder' might be used."

Cicis said, "Nevertheless, whether murder, roboticide, or nothing at all, it is still impossible to see Master Roboticist Amadiro."

"May I leave a message for him?"

"You may."

"Will it be delivered to him instantly? Now?"

"I can try, but obviously I can make no guarantee."

"Good enough. I will make several points and I will number them. Perhaps you would like to make notes."

Cicis smiled faintly. "I think I will be able to remember."

"First, where there is a murder, there is a murderer, and I would like to give Dr. Amadiro a chance to speak in his own defense—"

"What!" said Cicis.

(And Gremionis, watching from the other side of the room, let his jaw drop.)

Baley managed to imitate the faint smile that had suddenly disappeared from the other's lips. "Am I too fast for you, sir? Would you like to make notes after all?"

"Are you accusing the Master Roboticist of having had anything to do with this Jander Panell business?"

"On the contrary, Roboticist. It is because I *don't* want to accuse him that I must see him. I would hate to imply any connection between the Master Roboticist and the immobilized robot on the basis of incomplete information, when a word from him might make everything clear."

"You are mad!"

"Very well. Then tell the Master Roboticist that a madman wants a word with him in order to avoid accusing him of murder. That's my first point. I have a second. Could you tell him that the same madman has just completed a detailed interrogation of Personnel Artist Santirix Gremionis and is calling from Gremionis' establishment. And the third point—am I going too fast for you?"

"No! Finish!"

"The third point is this. It may be that the Master Roboticist, who surely has a great deal on his mind that is of much moment, does not remember who Personnel Artist Santirix Gremionis is. In that case, please identify him as someone living on the Institute grounds who has, in the last year, taken many long walks with Gladia, a woman from Solaria who now lives on Aurora."

"I cannot deliver a message so ridiculous and offensive, Earthman."

"In that case, would you tell him I will go straight to the Legislature and I will announce that I cannot continue with my investigation because one Maloon Cicis takes it upon himself to assure me that Master

Roboticist Kelden Amadiro will not assist me in the investigation of
the destruction of Robot Jander Panell and will not defend himself
against accusations of being responsible for that destruction?"

Cicis reddened. "You wouldn't *dare* say anything of the sort."

"Wouldn't I? What would I have to lose? On the other hand, how
will it sound to the general public? After all, Aurorans are perfectly
aware that Dr. Amadiro is second only to Dr. Fastolfe himself in expertise in robotics and that, if Fastolfe himself is not responsible for
the roboticide— Is it necessary to continue?"

"You will find, Earthman, that the laws of Aurora against slander
are strict."

"Undoubtedly, but if Dr. Amadiro is effectively slandered, his punishment is likely to be greater than mine. But why don't you simply
deliver my message *now*? Then, if he explains just a few minor points,
we can avoid all question of slander or accusation or anything of the
sort."

Cicis scowled and said stiffly, "I will tell Dr. Amadiro this and I will
strongly advise him to refuse to see you." He disappeared.

Again, Baley waited patiently, while Gremionis gestured fiercely and
said in a loud whisper, "You can't do that, Baley. You can't do it."
Baley waved him quiet.

After some five minutes (it seemed much longer to Baley), Cicis
reappeared, looking enormously angry. He said, "Dr. Amadiro will take
my place here in a few minutes and will talk to you. Wait!"

And Baley said at once, "There is no point in waiting. I will come
directly to Dr. Amadiro's office and I will see him there."

He stepped off the gray circle and made a cutting gesture to Daneel,
who promptly broke the connection.

Gremionis said, with a kind of strangled gasp, "You can't talk to Dr.
Amadiro's people that way, Earthman."

"I just have," said Baley.

"He'll have you thrown off the planet within twelve hours."

"If I don't make progress in straightening out this mess, I may in
any case be thrown off the planet within twelve hours."

Daneel said, "Partner Elijah, I fear that Mr. Gremionis is justified
in his alarm. The Auroran World Legislature cannot do more than
evict you, since you are not an Auroran citizen. Nevertheless, they
can insist that the Earth authorities punish you severely and Earth
will do so. They could not resist an Auroran demand, in this case. I
would not wish you to be punished in this way, Partner Elijah."

Baley said heavily, "Nor do I wish the punishment, Daneel, but I
must take the chance. —Mr. Gremionis, I am sorry that I had to tell
him I was calling from your establishment. I had to do something to
persuade him to see me and I felt he might attach importance to that
fact. What I said was, after all, the truth."

Gremionis shook his head. "If I had known what you were going to do, Mr. Baley, I would not have permitted you to call from my establishment. I feel sure that I'm going to lose my position here and"— with bitterness—"what are you going to do for me that will make up for that?"

"I will do my best, Mr. Gremionis, to see that you do not lose your position. I feel confident that you will be in no trouble. If I fail, however, you are free to describe me as a madman who made wild accusations against you and frightened you with threats of slander, so that you had to let me use your viewer. I'm sure Dr. Amadiro will believe you. After all, you have already sent him a memo complaining that I have been slandering you, have you not?"

Baley lifted his hand in farewell. "Good-bye, Mr. Gremionis. Thank you again. Don't worry and—remember what I said about Gladia."

With Daneel and Giskard sandwiching him fore and aft, Baley stepped out of Gremionis' establishment, scarcely conscious of the fact that he was moving out into the open once more.

53

Once out in the open, it was a different matter. Baley stopped and looked up.

"Odd," he said. "I didn't think that that much time had passed, even allowing for the fact that the Auroran day is a little shorter than standard."

"What is it, Partner Elijah?" asked Daneel solicitously.

"The sun has set. I wouldn't have thought it."

"The sun has not yet set, sir," put in Giskard. "It is about two hours before sunset."

Daneel said, "It is the gathering storm, Partner Elijah. The clouds are thickening, but the storm will not actually break for some time yet."

Baley shivered. Dark, in itself, did not disturb him. In fact, when Outside, night, with its suggestion of enclosing walls, was far more soothing than the day, which broadened the horizons and opened space in every direction.

The trouble was that this was neither day nor night.

Again, he tried to remember what it had been like that time it had rained when he had been Outside.

It suddenly occurred to him that he had never been out when it snowed and that he wasn't even sure what the rain of crystalline solid water was like. Descriptions in words were surely insufficient. The younger ones sometimes went out to go sliding or sledding—or whatever—and returned shrieking with excitement—but always glad to get within the City walls. Ben had once tried to make a pair of skis, according to directions in some ancient book or other, and had gotten himself half-buried in a drift of the white stuff. And even Ben's descriptions of what it was like to see and feel snow were distressingly vague and unsatisfying.

Then, too, no one went out when it was actually snowing, as opposed to having the material merely lying about on the ground. Baley told himself, at this point, that the one thing everyone agreed on was that it only snowed when it was very cold. It was not very cold now; it was merely cool. Those clouds did *not* mean it was going to snow. —Somehow, he felt only minimally consoled.

This was not like the cloudy days on Earth, which he *had* seen. On Earth, the clouds were lighter; he was sure of that. They were grayish-white, even when they covered the sky solidly. Here, the light—what there was of it—was rather bilious, a ghastly yellowish-slate.

Was that because Aurora's sun was more orange than Earth's was?

He said, "Is the color of the sky—unusual?"

Daneel looked up at the sky. "No, Partner Elijah. It is a storm."

"Do you often have storms like this?"

"At this time of year, yes. Occasional thunderstorms. This is no surprise. It was predicted in the weather forecast yesterday and again this morning. It will be over well before daybreak and the fields can use the water. We've been a bit subnormal in rainfall lately."

"And it gets this cold, too? Is that normal, too?"

"Oh yes. —But let us get into the airfoil, Partner Elijah. It can be heated."

Baley nodded and walked toward the airfoil, which lay on the grassy plot where it had been brought to rest before lunch. He paused.

"Wait. I did not ask Gremionis for directions to Amadiro's establishment—or office."

"No need, Partner Elijah," said Daneel immediately, his hand in the crook of Baley's elbow, propelling him gently but unmistakably onward. "Friend Giskard has the map of the Institute clearly in his memory banks and he will take us to the Administration Building. It is very likely that Dr. Amadiro has his office there."

Giskard said, "My information is to the effect that Dr. Amadiro's office *is* in the Administration Building. If, by some chance, he is not at his office but is in his establishment, that is nearby."

Again, Baley found himself crammed into the front seat between the two robots. He welcomed Daneel particularly, with his humanlike body warmth. Although Giskard's textilelike outermost layer was insulating and not as cold to the touch as bare metal would have been, he was the less attractive of the two in Baley's current chilly state.

Baley caught himself on the verge of putting an arm around Da-neel's shoulder, with the intention of finding comfort by drawing him even closer. He brought his arm down to his lap in confusion.

He said, "I don't like the way it looks out there."

Daneel, perhaps in an effort to take Baley's mind off the appearance Outside, said, "Partner Elijah, how is it you knew that Dr. Vasilia had encouraged Mr. Gremionis' interest in Miss Gladia? I did not see that you had received any evidence to that effect."

"I didn't," said Baley. "I've been desperate enough to play long shots—that is, to gamble on events of low probability. Gladia told me that Gremionis was the one person sufficiently interested in her to offer himself repeatedly. I thought he might have killed Jander out of jealousy. I didn't think he could possibly know enough about robotics to do it, but then I heard that Fastolfe's daughter Vasilia was a robo-ticist and resembled Gladia physically. I wondered if Gremionis, hav-ing been fascinated by Gladia, might not have been fascinated by Vasilia earlier—and if the killing might possibly have been the result of a conspiracy between the two. It was by hinting obscurely at the existence of such a conspiracy that I was able to persuade Vasilia to see me."

Daneel said, "But there was no conspiracy, Partner Elijah—at least as far as the destruction of Jander was concerned. Vasilia and Gre-mionis could not have engineered that destruction, even if they had worked together."

"Granted—and yet Vasilia had been made nervous by the sugges-tion of having had a connection with Gremionis. Why? When Gre-mionis told us of having been attracted to Vasilia first, and then to Gladia, I wondered if the connection between the two had been more indirect, if Vasilia might have encouraged the transfer for some reason more distantly connected—but connected nevertheless—to Jander's death. After all, there had to be some connection between the two; Vasilia's reaction to the original suggestion showed that.

"My suspicion was correct. Vasilia had engineered Gremionis' switch from one woman to the other. Gremionis was astonished at my know-ing this and that, too, was useful, for if the matter were something completely innocent, there would have been no reason to make a se-cret of it—and a secret it obviously was. You remember that Vasilia mentioned nothing of urging Gremionis to turn to Gladia. When I told her that Gremionis had offered himself to Gladia, she acted as though that was the first time she had heard of it."

"But, Partner Elijah, of what importance is this?"

"We may find out. It seemed to me that there was no importance in it to either Gremionis or Vasilia. Therefore, if it had any importance at all, it might be that a third person was involved. If it had anything to do with the Jander affair, then it ought to be a roboticist still more skillful than Vasilia—and that might be Amadiro. So I hinted to him of the existence of a conspiracy by deliberately pointing out I had been questioning Gremionis and was calling from his establishment—and that worked, too."

"Yet I still don't know what it all means, Partner Elijah."

"Nor I—except for some speculations. But perhaps we'll find out at Amadiro's. Our situation is so bad, you see, we have nothing to lose by guessing and gambling."

During this exchange, the airfoil had risen on its air-jets, and had moved to a moderate height. It cleared a line of bushes and was now once again speeding along over grassy areas and graveled roads. Baley noticed that, where the grass was taller, it was swept to one side by the wind as though an invisible—and much larger—airfoil were passing over it.

Baley said, "Giskard, you have been recording the conversations which have taken place in your presence, haven't you?"

"Yes, sir."

"And can reproduce them at need?"

"Yes, sir."

"And can easily locate—and reproduce—some particular statement made by some given person?"

"Yes, sir. You would not have to listen to the entire recording."

"And could you, at need, serve as a witness in a courtroom?"

"I, sir? No, sir." Giskard's eyes were fixed firmly on the road. "Since a robot can be directed to lie by a skillful enough command and not all the exhortations or threats of a judge might help, the law wisely considers a robot an incompetent witness."

"But, in that case, of what use are your recordings?"

"That, sir, is a different thing. A recording, once made, cannot be altered on simple command, though it might be erased. Such a recording can, therefore, be admitted as evidence. There are no firm precedents, however, and whether it is—or is not—admitted depends on the individual case and on the individual judge."

Baley could not tell whether that statement was depressing in itself or whether he was influenced by the unpleasant livid light that bathed the landscape. He said, "Can you see well enough to drive, Giskard?"

"Certainly, sir, but I do not need to. The airfoil is equipped with a computerized radar that would enable it to avoid obstacles on its own, even if I were, unaccountably, to fail in my task. It was this that was in operation yesterday morning when we traveled comfortably though all the windows were opacified."

"Partner Elijah," said Daneel, again veering the conversation away from Baley's uncomfortable awareness of the coming storm, "do you have hope that Dr. Amadiro might indeed be helpful?"

Giskard brought the airfoil to rest on a wide lawn before a broad but not very high building, with an intricately carved façade that was clearly new and yet gave the impression of imitating something quite old.

Baley knew it was the Administration Building without being told. He said, "No, Daneel, I suspect that Amadiro may be far too intelligent to give us the least handle to grasp him by."

"And if that is so, what do you plan to do next?"

"I don't know," said Baley, with a grim feeling of *déjà vu* , "but I'll try to think of something."

54

When Baley entered the Administration Building, his first feeling was one of relief at removing himself from the unnatural lighting Outside. The second was one of wry amusement.

Here on Aurora, the establishments—the private dwelling places— were all strictly Auroran. He couldn't, for a moment, while sitting in Gladia's living room, or breakfasting in Fastolfe's dining room, or talking in Vasilia's work room, or making use of Gremionis' trimensional viewing device, have thought himself on Earth. All four were distinct from each other, but all fell within a certain genus, widely different from that of the underground apartments on Earth.

The Administration Building, however, breathed officialdom and that, apparently, transcended ordinary human variety. It did not belong to the same genus as the dwelling places on Aurora, any more than an official building in Baley's home City resembled an apartment in the dwelling Sectors—but the two official buildings on the two worlds of such widely different natures strangely resembled each other.

This was the first place on Aurora where, for an instant, Baley might have imagined himself on Earth. Here were the same long cold bare corridors, the same lowest common denominator of design and decoration, with every light source designed so as to irritate as few people as possible and to please just as few.

There were some touches here that would have been absent on Earth—the occasional suspended pots of plants, for instance, flourishing in the light and outfitted with devices (Baley guessed) for controlled and automatic watering. That natural touch was absent on Earth and its presence did not delight him. Might such pots not sometimes fall? Might they not attract insects? Might not the water drip?

There were some things missing here, too. On Earth, when one was within a City, there was always the vast, warm hum of people and machinery—even in the most coldly official of administrative structures. It was the "Busy Buzz of Brotherhood," to use the phrase popular among Earth's politicians and journalists.

Here, on the other hand, it was quiet. Baley had not particularly noticed the quiet in the establishments he had visited that day and the day before, since everything had seemed so unnatural there that one more oddity escaped his notice. Indeed, he had been more aware of the soft susurration of insect life outside or of the wind through the vegetation than of the absence of the steady "Hum of Humanity" (another popular phrase).

Here, however, where there seemed a touch of Earth, the absence of the "Hum" was as disconcerting as was the distinct orange touch to the artificial light—which was far more noticeable against the blank off-white of the walls here than among the busy decoration that marked the Auroran establishments.

Baley's reverie did not last long. They were standing just inside the main entrance and Daneel had held out his arm to stop the other two. Some thirty seconds passed before Baley, speaking in an automatic whisper in view of the silence everywhere, said, "Why are we waiting?"

"Because it is advisable to do so, Partner Elijah," said Daneel. "There is a tingle field ahead."

"A what?"

"A tingle field, Partner Elijah. Actually, the name is a euphemism. It stimulates the nerve endings and produces a rather sharp pain. Robots can pass, but human beings cannot. Any breach, of course, whether by human or robot, will set off an alarm."

Baley said, "How can you tell there's a tingle field?"

"It can be seen, Partner Elijah, if you know what to look for. The air seems to twinkle a bit and the wall beyond that region has a faint greenish tinge as compared to the wall in front of it."

"I'm not at all sure I see it," said Baley indignantly. "What's to prevent me—or any innocent outsider—from walking into it and experiencing agony?"

Daneel said, "Those who are members of the Institute carry a neutralizing device; those who are visitors are almost always attended by one or more robots who will surely detect the tingle field."

A robot was approaching down the corridor on the other side of the field. (The twinkling of the field was more easily noted against the muted smoothness of his metallic surface.) He seemed to ignore Giskard, but, for a moment, he hesitated as he looked from Baley to Daneel and back. And then, having made a decision, he addressed Baley. (Perhaps, thought Baley, Daneel looks too human to be human.)

The robot said, "Your name, sir?"

Baley said, "I am Plainclothesman Elijah Baley from Earth. I am accompanied by two robots of the establishment of Dr. Han Fastolfe—Daneel Olivaw and Giskard Reventlov."

"Identification, sir?"

Giskard's serial number flared out in soft phosphorescence on the left side of his chest. "I vouch for the other two, friend," he said.

The robot studied the number a moment, as though comparing it with a file in his memory banks. Then he nodded and said, "Serial number accepted. You may pass."

Daneel and Giskard moved forward at once, but Baley found himself edging ahead slowly. He put out one arm as a way of testing the coming of pain.

Daneel said, "The field is gone, Partner Elijah. It will be restored after we have passed through."

Better safe than sorry, thought Baley, and continued his shuffle till he was well past the point where the barrier of the field might have existed.

The robots, showing no sign of impatience or condemnation, waited for Baley's reluctant steps to catch up with them.

They then stepped onto a helical ramp that was only two people wide. The robot was first, by himself; Baley and Daneel stood side by side behind him (Daneel's hand rested lightly, but almost possessively, on Baley's elbow); and Giskard brought up the rear.

Baley was conscious of his shoes pointing upward just a bit uncomfortably and felt vaguely that it would be a little tiresome mounting this too-steep ramp and having to lean forward in order to avoid a clumsy slip. Either the soles of his shoes or the surface of the ramp— or both—ought to be ridged. In fact, neither was.

The robot in the lead said, "Mr. Baley," as though warning of something, and the robot's hand then visibly tightened on the railing that it held.

At once, the ramp divided into sections that slid against each other to form steps. Immediately thereafter, the whole ramp began to move upward. It made a complete turn, passing up through the ceiling, a section of which had retracted, and, when it came to a halt, they were on what was (presumably) the second floor. The steps disappeared and the four stepped off.

Baley looked back curiously. "I suppose it will service those who want to go down as well, but what if there is a period where more people want to go up than down? It would end up sticking half a kilometer into the sky—or into the ground, in reverse."

"That is an up-helix," said Daneel in a low voice. "There are separate down-helices."

"But it has to get down again, doesn't it?"

"It collapses at the top—or the bottom—depending on which we're speaking of, Partner Elijah, and, in periods of nonuse, it unwinds, so to speak. This up-helix is descending now."

Baley looked back. The smooth surface might be sliding downward, but it showed no irregularity or mark whose motion he could notice.

"And if someone should want to use it when it has moved up as far as it can?"

"Then one must wait for the unwinding, which would take less than a minute. —There are ordinary flights of stairs as well, Partner Elijah, and most Aurorans are not reluctant to use them. Robots almost always use the stairs. Since you are a visitor, you are being offered the courtesy of the helix."

They were walking down a corridor again, toward a door more ornate than the others. "They are offering me courtesy, then," said Baley. "A hopeful sign."

It was perhaps another hopeful sign that an Auroran now appeared in the ornate doorway. He was tall, at least eight centimeters taller than Daneel, who was some five centimeters taller than Baley. The man in the doorway was broad as well, somewhat heavyset, with a round face, a somewhat bulbous nose, curly dark hair, a swarthy complexion, and a smile.

It was the smile that was most noticeable. Wide and apparently unforced, it revealed prominent teeth that were white and well-shaped.

He said, "Ah, it is Mr. Baley, the famous investigator from Earth, who has come to our little planet to show that I am a dreadful villain. Come in, come in. You are welcome. I am sorry if my able aide, Roboticist Maloon Cicis, gave you the impression that I would be unavailable, but he is a cautious fellow and is a great deal more concerned about my time than I myself am."

He stepped to one side as Baley walked in and tapped him lightly with the flat of his hand on the shoulder blade as he passed. It seemed to be a gesture of friendship of a kind that Baley had not yet experienced on Aurora.

Baley said, cautiously (was he assuming too much?), "I take it you are Master Roboticist Kelden Amadiro?"

"Exactly. Exactly. The man who intends to destroy Dr. Han Fastolfe as a political force upon this planet—but that, as I hope to persuade you, does not really make me a villain. After all, I am not trying to prove that it is Fastolfe who is a villain simply because of the foolish vandalism he committed on the structure of his own creation—poor Jander. Let us say only that I will demonstrate that Fastolfe is—mistaken."

He gestured lightly and the robot who had guided them in stepped forward and into a niche.

As the door closed, Amadiro gestured Baley jovially to a well-upholstered armchair and, with admirable economy, indicated, with his other arm, wall niches for Daneel and Giskard as well.

Baley noticed that Amadiro stared with a moment's hunger at Daneel and that, for that moment, his smile disappeared and a look that was almost predatory appeared on his face. It was gone quickly and he was smiling again. Baley was left to wonder if, perhaps, that momentary change of expression was an invention of his own imagination.

Amadiro said, "Since it looks as though we're in for some mildly nasty weather, let's do without the ineffective daylight we are now dubiously blessed with."

Somehow (Baley did not follow exactly what it was that Amadiro did on the control-panel of his desk) the windows opacified and the walls glowed with gentle daylight.

Amadiro's smile seemed to broaden. "We do not really have much to talk about, you and I, Mr. Baley. I took the precaution of speaking to Mr. Gremionis while you were coming here. From what he said, I decided to call Dr. Vasilia as well. Apparently, Mr. Baley, you have more or less accused both of complicity in the destruction of Jander and, if I can understand the language, you have also accused me."

"I merely asked questions, Dr. Amadiro, as I intend to do now."

"No doubt, but you are an Earthman, so you are not aware of the enormity of your actions and I am really sorry that you must nonetheless suffer the consequences of them. —You know perhaps that Gremionis sent me a memo concerning your slander of him."

"He told me he had, but he misinterpreted my action. It was not slander."

Amadiro pursed his lips as though considering the statement. "I dare say you are right from your standpoint, Mr. Baley, but you don't understand the Auroran definition of the word. I was forced to send Gremionis' memo on to the Chairman and, as a result, it is very likely that you'll be ordered off the planet by tomorrow morning. I regret this, of course, but I fear that your investigation is about to come to an end."

Again Amadiro

55

Baley was taken aback. He did not know what to make of Amadiro and he had not expected this confusion within himself. Gremionis had described him as "standoffish." From what Cicis had said, he expected Amadiro to be autocratic. In person, however, Amadiro seemed jovial, outgoing, even friendly. Yet if his words were to be trusted, Amadiro was calmly moving to end the investigation. He was doing it pitilessly—and yet with what seemed to be a commiserating smile.

What was he?

Automatically, Baley glanced toward the niches where Giskard and Daneel were standing, the primitive Giskard of course without expression, the advanced Daneel calm and quiet. That Daneel had ever met Amadiro in his short existence was, on the face of it, unlikely. Giskard, on the other hand, in his—how many?—decades of life might very well have met him.

Baley's lips tightened as he thought he might have asked Giskard in advance what Amadiro might be like. He might, in that case, be now better able to judge how much of this roboticist's present persona was real and how much was cleverly calculated.

Why on Earth—or off it, Baley wondered, didn't he use these robotic resources of his more intelligently? Or why didn't Giskard volunteer information—but no, that was unfair. Giskard clearly lacked the capacity for independent activity of that sort. He would yield information on request, Baley thought, but would produce none on his own initiative.

Amadiro followed the brief flicking of Baley's eyes and said, "I'm one against three, I think. As you see, I have none of my robots here in my office—although any number are on instant call, I admit—while you have two of Fastolfe's robots: the old reliable Giskard and that marvel of design, Daneel."

"You know them both, I see," said Baley.

"By reputation only. I actually see them—I, a roboticist, was about to say 'in the flesh'—I actually see them physically for the first time now, although I saw Daneel portrayed by an actor in that hyperwave show."

"Everyone in all the worlds has apparently seen that hyperwave show," said Baley glumly. "It makes my life—as a real and limited individual—difficult."

571

"Not with me," said Amadiro, his smile broadening. "I assure you I did not take your fictional representation with any seriousness whatever. I assumed you were limited in real life. And so you are—or you would not have indulged so freely in unwarranted accusations on Aurora."

"Dr. Amadiro," said Baley, "I assure you I was making no formal accusations. I was merely pursuing an investigation and considering possibilities."

"Don't misunderstand me," said Amadiro with sudden earnestness. "I don't blame you. I am sure that you were behaving perfectly by Earth standards. It is just that you are up against Auroran standards now. We treasure reputation with unbelievable intensity."

"If that were so, Dr. Amadiro, then haven't you and other Globalists been slandering Dr. Fastolfe with suspicion, to a far greater extent than any small thing I have done?"

"Quite true," agreed Amadiro, "but I am an eminent Auroran and have a certain influence, while you are an Earthman and have no influence whatever. That is most unfair, I admit, and I deplore it, but that is the way the worlds are. What can we do? Besides, the accusation against Fastolfe can be maintained—and *will* be maintained—and slander isn't slander when it is the truth. Your mistake was to make accusations that simply can't be maintained. I'm sure you must admit that neither Mr. Gremionis nor Dr. Vasilia Aliena—nor both together—could possibly have disabled poor Jander."

"I did not formally accuse either."

"Perhaps not, but you can't hide behind the word 'formally' on Aurora. It's too bad Fastolfe didn't warn you of this when he brought you in to take up this investigation, this—as it now is, I'm afraid—ill-fated investigation."

Baley felt the corner of his mouth twitch as he thought that Fastolfe might indeed have warned him.

He said, "Am I to get a hearing in the matter or is it all settled?"

"Of course you will get a hearing before being condemned. We are not barbarians here on Aurora. The Chairman will consider the memo I have sent him, together with my own suggestions in the matter. He will probably consult Fastolfe as the other party intimately concerned and then arrange to meet with all three of us, perhaps tomorrow. Some decision might be reached then—or later—and it would be ratified by the full Legislature. All due process of law will be followed, I assure you."

"The letter of the law will be followed, no doubt, but what if the Chairman has already made up his mind, what if nothing I say will be accepted, and what if the Legislature simply rubber-stamps a foregone decision? Is that possible?"

Amadiro did not exactly smile at that, but he seemed subtly amused.

"You are a realist, Mr. Baley. I am pleased with that. People who dream of justice are so apt to be disappointed—and they are usually such wonderful people that one hates to see that happen."

Amadiro's glance fixed itself on Daneel again. "A remarkable job, this humaniform robot," he said. "It is astonishing how close to his vest Fastolfe has kept things. And it is a shame that Jander was lost. There Fastolfe did the unforgivable."

"Dr. Fastolfe, sir, denies that he was in any way implicated."

"Yes, Mr. Baley, of course he would. Does he say that I am implicated? Or is my implication entirely your own idea?"

Baley said deliberately, "I have no such idea. I merely wish to question you on the matter. As for Dr. Fastolfe, he is not a candidate for one of your accusations of slander. He is certain you have had nothing to do with what happened to Jander because he is quite certain you lack the knowledge and capacity to immobilize a humaniform robot."

If Baley hoped to stir things up in that manner, he failed. Amadiro accepted the slur with no loss of good humor and said, "In that he is right, Mr. Baley. Sufficient ability is not to be found in any roboticist—alive or dead—except for Fastolfe himself. Isn't that what he says, our modest master of masters?"

"Yes, he does."

"Then whatever does he say happened to Jander, I wonder?"

"A random event. Purely chance."

Amadiro laughed. "Has he calculated the probability of such a random event?"

"Yes, Master Roboticist. Yet even an extremely unlikely chance might happen, especially if there were incidents that bettered the odds."

"Such as what?"

"That is what I am hoping to find out. Since you have already arranged to have me thrown off the planet, do you now intend to forestall any questioning of yourself—or may I continue my investigation until such time as my activity in that respect is legally ended?—Before you answer, Dr. Amadiro, please consider that the investigation has *not* yet been legally ended and, in any hearing that may come up, whether tomorrow or later, I will be able to accuse you of refusing to answer my questions if you should insist on now ending this interview. That might influence the Chairman in his decision."

"It would not, my dear Mr. Baley. Don't imagine you can in any way interfere with me.—However, you may interview me for as long as you wish. I will cooperate fully with you, if only to enjoy the spectacle of the good Fastolfe trying uselessly to disentangle himself from his unfortunate deed. I am not extraordinarily vindictive, Mr. Baley, but the fact that Jander was Fastolfe's own creation does not give him the right to destroy it."

Baley said, "It is not legally established that this is what he has done, so that what you have just said is, at least potentially, slander. Let us put that to one side, therefore, and get on with this interview. I need information. I will ask my questions briefly and directly and, if you answer in the same way, this interview may be completed quickly."

"No, Mr. Baley. It is not you who will set the conditions for this interview," said Amadiro. "I take it that one or both of your robots is equipped to record our conversation in full."

"I believe so."

"I know so. I have a recording device of my own as well. Don't think, my good Mr. Baley, that you will lead me through a jungle of short answers to something that will serve Fastolfe's purpose. I will answer as I choose and make certain that I am not misinterpreted. And my own recording will help me make it certain that I am not misinterpreted." Now, for the first time, there was the suggestion of the wolf behind Amadiro's attitude of friendliness.

"Very well, then, but if your answers are deliberately long-winded and evasive, that, too, will show up in the recording."

"Obviously."

"With that understood, may I have a glass of water, to begin with?"

"Absolutely.—Giskard, will you oblige Mr. Baley?"

Giskard was out of his niche at once. There was the inevitable tinkle of ice at the bar at one end of the room and a tall glass of water was on the desk immediately before Baley.

Baley said, "Thank you, Giskard," and waited for him to move back onto his niche.

He said, "Dr. Amadiro, am I correct in considering you the head of the Robotics Institute?"

"Yes, you are."

"And its founder?"

"Correct. —You see, I answer briefly."

"How long has it been in existence?"

"As a concept—decades. I have been gathering like-minded people for at least fifteen years. Permission was obtained from the Legislature twelve years ago. Building began nine years ago and active work began six years ago. In its present completed form, the Institute is two years old and there are long-range plans for further expansion, eventually. —There you have a long answer, sir, but presented reasonably concisely."

"Why did you find it necessary to set up the Institute?"

"Ah, Mr. Baley. Here you surely expect nothing but a long-winded answer."

"As you please, sir."

At this point, a robot brought in a tray of small sandwiches and still smaller pastries, none of which were familiar to Baley. He tried a sand-

wich and found it crunchy and not exactly unpleasant but odd enough
for him to finish it only with an effort. He washed it down with what
was left of his water.

Amadiro watched with a kind of gentle amusement and said, "You
must understand, Mr. Baley, that we Aurorans are unusual people. So
are Spacers generally, but I speak of Aurorans in particular now. We
are descended from Earthpeople—something most of us do not willingly think about—but we are self-selected."

"What does that mean, sir?"

"Earthpeople have long lived on an increasingly crowded planet and
have drawn together into still more crowded cities that finally became
the beehives and anthills you call Cities with a capital 'C.' What kind
of Earthpeople, then, would leave Earth and go to other worlds that
are empty and hostile so that they might build new societies from
nothing, societies that they could not enjoy in completed form in their
own lifetime—trees that would still be saplings when they died, so to
speak."

"Rather unusual people, I suppose."

"Quite unusual. Specifically, people who are not so dependent on
crowds of their fellows as to lack the ability to face emptiness. People
who even prefer emptiness, who would like to work on their own and
face problems by themselves, rather than hide in the herd and share
the burden so that their own load is virtually nothing. Individualists,
Mr. Baley. Individualists!"

"I see that."

"And our society is founded on that. Every direction in which the
Spacer worlds have developed further emphasizes our individuality.
We are proudly human on Aurora, rather than being huddled sheep
on Earth. —Mind you, Mr. Baley, I use the metaphor not as a way of
deriding Earth. It is simply a different society which I find unadmir-
able but which you, I suppose, find comforting and ideal."

"What has this to do with the founding of the Institute, Dr. Amadiro?"

"Even proud and healthy individualism has its drawbacks. The
greatest minds—working singly, even for centuries—cannot progress
rapidly if they refuse to communicate their findings. A knotty puzzle
may hold up a scientist for a century, when it may be that a colleague
has the solution already and is not even aware of the puzzle that it
might solve. —The Institute is an attempt, in the narrow field of robotics at least, to introduce a certain community of thought."

"Is it possible that the particular knotty puzzle you are attacking is
that of the construction of a humaniform robot?"

Amadiro's eyes twinkled. "Yes, that is obvious, isn't it? It was twenty-
six years ago that Fastolfe's new mathematical system, which he calls
'intersectional analysis,' made it possible to design humaniform ro-

bots—but he kept the system to himself. Years afterward, when all the difficult technical details were worked out, he and Dr. Sarton applied the theory to the design of Daneel. Then Fastolfe alone completed Jander. But all of those details were kept secret, also.

"Most roboticists shrugged and felt that this was natural. They could only try, individually, to work out the details for themselves. I, on the other hand, was struck by the possibility of an Institute in which efforts would be pooled. It wasn't easy to persuade other roboticists of the usefulness of the plan, or to persuade the Legislature to fund it against Fastolfe's formidable opposition, or to persevere through the years of effort, but here we are."

Baley said, "Why was Dr. Fastolfe opposed?"

"Ordinary self-love, to begin with—and I have no fault to find with that, you understand. All of us have a very natural self-love. It comes with the territory of individualism. The point is that Fastolfe considers himself the greatest roboticist in history and also considers the humaniform robot his own particular achievement. He doesn't want that achievement duplicated by a group of roboticists, individually faceless compared to himself. I imagine he viewed it as a conspiracy of inferiors to dilute and deface his own great victory."

"You say that was his motive for opposition 'to begin with.' That means there were other motives. What were they?"

"He also objects to the uses to which we plan to put the humaniform robots."

"What uses are these, Dr. Amadiro?"

"Now now. Let's not be ingenuous. Surely Dr. Fastolfe has told you of the Globalist plans for settling the Galaxy?"

"That he has and, for that matter, Dr. Vasilia has spoken to me of the difficulties of scientific advance among individualists. However, that does not stop me from wanting to hear your views on these matters. Nor should it stop you from wanting to tell me. For instance, do you want me to accept Dr. Fastolfe's interpretation of Globalist plans as unbiased and impartial—and would you state that for the record? Or would you prefer to describe your plans in your own words?"

"Put that way, Mr. Baley, you intend to give me no choice."

"None, Dr. Amadiro."

"Very well. I—we, I should say, for the people at the Institute are like-minded in this—look into the future and wish to see humanity opening ever more and ever newer planets to settlement. We do not, however, want the process of self-selection to destroy the older planets or to reduce them to moribundity, as in the case—pardon me—of Earth. We don't want the new planets to take the best of us and to leave behind the dregs. You see that, don't you?"

"Please go on."

"In any robot-oriented society, as in the case of our own, the easy solution is to send out robots as settlers. The robots will build the society and the world and we can then all follow later without selection, for the new world will be as comfortable and as adjusted to ourselves as the old worlds were, so that we can go on to new worlds without leaving home, so to speak."

"Won't the robots create robot worlds rather than human worlds?"

"Exactly, if we send out robots that are nothing but robots. We have, however, the opportunity of sending out humaniform robots like Daneel here, who, in creating worlds for themselves, would automatically create worlds for us. Dr. Fastolfe, however, objects to this. He finds some virtue in the thought of human beings carving a new world out of a strange and forbidding planet and does not see that the effort to do so would not only cost enormously in human life, but would also create a world molded by catastrophic events into something not at all like the worlds we know."

"As the Spacer worlds today are different from Earth and from each other?"

Amadiro, for a moment, lost his joviality and looked thoughtful. "Actually, Mr. Baley, you touch an important point. I am discussing Aurora only. The Spacer worlds do indeed differ among themselves and I am not overly fond of most of them. It is clear to me—though I may be prejudiced—that Aurora, the oldest among them, is also the best and most successful. I don't want a variety of new worlds of which only a few might be really valuable. I want many Auroras—uncounted millions of Auroras—and for that reason I want new worlds carved into Auroras *before* human beings go there. That's why we call ourselves 'Globalists' by the way. We are concerned with *this* globe of ours—Aurora—and no other."

"Do you see no value in variety, Dr. Amadiro?"

"If the varieties were equally good, perhaps there would be value, but if some—or most—are inferior, how would that benefit humanity?"

"When do you start this work?"

"When we have the humaniform robots with which to do it. So far there were Fastolfe's two, of which he destroyed one, leaving Daneel the only specimen." His eyes strayed briefly to Daneel as he spoke.

"When will you have humaniform robots?"

"That is difficult to say. We have not yet caught up with Dr. Fastolfe."

"Even though he is one and you are many, Dr. Amadiro?"

Amadiro twitched his shoulders slightly. "You waste your sarcasm, Mr. Baley. Fastolfe was well ahead of us to begin with and, though the Institute has been in embryo for a long time, we have been fully at work for only two years. Besides, it will be necessary for us not only to catch up with Fastolfe but to move ahead of him. Daneel is a good product, but he is only a prototype and is not good enough."

"In what way must the humaniform robots be improved beyond Daneel's mark?"

"They must be even more human, obviously. They must exist in both sexes and there must be the equivalent of children. We must have a generational spread if a sufficiently human society is to be built up on the planets."

"I think I see difficulties, Dr. Amadiro."

"No doubt. There are many. Which difficulties do you foresee, Mr. Baley?"

"If you produce humaniform robots who are so humaniform they can produce a human society, and if they are produced with a generational spread in both sexes, how will you be able to distinguish them from human beings?"

"Will that matter?"

"It might. If such robots are too human, they might melt into Auroran society and become part of human family groups—and might not be suitable for service as pioneers."

Amadiro laughed. "That thought clearly entered your head because of Gladia Delmarre's attachment to Jander. You see, I know something of your interview with that woman from my conversations with Gremionis and with Dr. Vasilia. I remind you that Gladia is from Solaria and her notion of what constitutes a husband is not necessarily Auroran in nature."

"I was not thinking of her in particular. I was thinking that sex on Aurora is broadly interpreted and that robots as sex partners are tolerated even now, with robots who are only approximately humaniform. If you really cannot tell a robot from a human being—"

"There's the question of children. Robots can neither father nor mother children."

"But that brings up another point. The robots will be long-lived, since the proper building of the society may take centuries."

"They would, in any case, have to be long-lived if they are to resemble Aurorans."

"And the children—also long-lived?"

Amadiro did not speak.

Baley said, "These will be artificial robot children and will never grow older—they will not age and mature. Surely this will create an element sufficiently nonhuman to cast the nature of the society into doubt."

Amadiro sighed. "You are penetrating, Mr. Baley. It is indeed our thought to devise some scheme whereby robots can produce babies who can in some fashion grow and mature—at least long enough to establish the society we want."

"And then, when human beings arrive, the robots can be restored to more robotic schemes of behavior."

"Perhaps—if that seems advisable."

"And this production of babies? Clearly, it would be best if the system used were as close to the human as possible, wouldn't it?"

"Possibly."

"Sex, fertilization, birth?"

"Possibly."

"And if these robots form a society so human that they cannot be differentiated from human, then, when true human beings arrive, might it not be that the robots would resent the immigrants and try to keep them off? Might the robots not react to Aurorans as you react to Earthpeople?"

"Mr. Baley, the robots would still be bound by the Three Laws."

"The Three Laws speak of refraining from injuring human beings and of obeying human beings."

"Exactly."

"And what if the robots are so close to human beings that they regard *themselves* as the human beings they should protect and obey? They might, very rightly, place themselves above the immigrants."

"My good Mr. Baley, why are you so concerned with all these things? They are for the far future. There will be solutions, as we progress in time and as we understand, by observation, what the problems really are."

"It may be, Dr. Amadiro, that Aurorans may not very much approve what you are planning, once they understand what it is. They may prefer Dr. Fastolfe's views."

"Indeed? Fastolfe thinks that, if Aurorans cannot settle new planets directly and without the help of robots, then Earthpeople should be encouraged to do so."

Baley said, "It seems to me that that makes good sense."

"Because you are an Earthman, my good Baley. I assure you that Aurorans would not find it pleasant to have Earthpeople swarming over the new worlds, building new beehives and forming some sort of Galactic Empire in their trillions and quadrillions and reducing the Spacer worlds to what? To insignificance at best and to extinction at worst."

"But the alternative to that is worlds of humaniform robots, building quasi-human societies and allowing no true human beings among themselves. There would gradually develop a robotic Galactic Empire, reducing the Spacer worlds to insignificance at best and to extinction at worst. Surely Aurorans would prefer a human Galactic Empire to a robotic one."

"What makes you so sure of that, Mr. Baley?"

"The form your society takes now makes me sure. I was told, on my way to Aurora, that no distinctions are made between robots and human beings on Aurora, but that is clearly wrong. It may be a wished-for ideal that Aurorans flatter themselves truly exists, but it does not."

"You've been here—what?—less than two days and you can already tell?"

"Yes, Dr. Amadiro. It may be precisely because I'm a stranger that I can see clearly. I am not blinded by custom and ideals. Robots are not permitted to enter Personals and that's one distinction that is clearly made. It permits human beings to find one place where they can be alone. You and I sit at our ease, while robots remain standing in their niches, as you see"—Baley waved his arm toward Daneel—"which is another distinction. I think that human beings—even Aurorans—will always be eager to make distinctions and to preserve their own humanity."

"Astonishing, Mr. Baley."

"Not astonishing at all, Dr. Amadiro. You have lost. Even if you manage to foist your belief that Dr. Fastolfe destroyed Jander upon Aurorans generally, even if you reduce Dr. Fastolfe to political impotence, even if you get the Legislature and the Auroran people to approve your plan of robot settlement, you will only have gained time. As soon as the Aurorans see the implications of your plan, they will turn against you. It might be better, then, if you put an end to your campaign against Dr. Fastolfe and meet with him to work out some compromise whereby the settlement of new worlds by Earthmen can be so arranged as to represent no threat to Aurora or to the Spacer worlds in general."

"Astonishing, Mr. Baley," said Amadiro a second time.

"You have no choice," said Baley flatly.

But Amadiro answered, in a leisurely and amused tone, "When I say your remarks are astonishing, I do not refer to the content of your statements but only to the fact that you make them at all—and that you think they are worth something."

56

Baley watched Amadiro forage for one last piece of pastry and put half of it into his mouth, clearly enjoying it.

"Very good," said Amadiro, "but I am a little too fond of eating. What was I saying?—Oh yes. Mr. Baley, do you think you have discovered a secret? That I have told you something that our world does not already know? That my plans are dangerous, but that I blab them to every newcomer? I imagine you may think that, if I talk to you long

enough, I will surely produce some verbal folly that you will be able
to make use of. Be assured that I am not likely to. My plans for ever
more humaniform robots, for robot families, and for as human a culture as possible are all on record. They are available to the Legislature
and to anyone who is interested."

Baley said, "Does the general public know?"

"Probably not. The general public has its own priorities and is more
interested in the next meal, the next hyperwave show, the next space-
soccer contest than in the next century and the next millennium. Still,
the general public will be as glad to accept my plans, as are the intellectually minded who already know. Those who object will not be
numerous enough to matter."

"Can you be certain of that?"

"Oddly enough, I can be. You don't understand, I'm afraid, the
intensity of the feelings that Aurorans—and Spacers generally—have
toward Earthpeople. I don't share those feelings, mind you, and I am,
for instance, quite at ease with you. I don't have that primitive fear
of infection, I don't imagine that you smell bad, I don't attribute to
you all sorts of personality traits that I find offensive, I don't think
that you and yours are plotting to take our lives or steal our property—
but the large majority of Aurorans have all these attitudes. It may not
be very close to the surface and Aurorans may bring themselves to be
very polite to individual Earthpeople who seem harmless, but put them
to the test and all their hatred and suspicion will emerge. Tell them
that Earthpeople are swarming over new worlds and will preempt the
Galaxy and they will howl for Earth's destruction before such a thing
can happen."

"Even if the alternative was a robot society?"

"Certainly. You don't understand how we feel about robots, either.
We are familiar with them. We are at home with them."

"No. They are your servants. You feel superior to them and are at
home with them only while that superiority is maintained. If you are
threatened by an overturn, by having *them* become your superiors,
you will react with horror."

"You say that only because that is how Earthpeople would react."

"No. You keep them out of the Personals. It is a symptom."

"They have no use for those rooms. They have their own facilities
for washing and they do not excrete. —Of course, they are not truly
humaniform. If they were, we might not make that distinction."

"You would fear them the more."

"Truly?" said Amadiro. "That's foolish. Do you fear Daneel? If I
can trust that hyperwave show—and I admit I do not think I can—
you developed a considerable affection for Daneel. You feel it now,
don't you?"

Baley's silence was eloquent and Amadiro pursued his advantage.

"Right now," he said, "you are unmoved by the fact that Giskard is standing, silent and unresponsive, in an alcove, but I can tell by small examples of body language that you are uneasy over the fact that Daneel is doing so, too. You feel he is too human in appearance to be treated as a robot. You don't fear him the more because he looks human."

"I am an Earthman. We have robots," said Baley, "but not a robot culture. You cannot judge from my case."

"And Gladia, who preferred Jander to human beings—"

"She is a Solarian. You cannot judge from her case, either."

"What case can you judge from, then? You are only guessing. To me, it seems obvious that, if a robot is human enough, he would be accepted as human. Do you demand proof that *I* am not a robot? The fact that I *seem* human is enough. In the end, we will not worry whether a new world is settled by Aurorans who are human in fact or in appearance, if no one can tell the difference. But—human or robot—the settlers will be *Aurorans* either way, not Earthpeople."

Baley's assurance faltered. He said unconvincingly, "What if you never learn how to construct a humaniform robot?"

"Why would you expect we would not? Notice that I say 'we.' There are many of us involved here."

"It may be that any number of mediocrities do not add up to one genius."

Amadiro said shortly, "We are not mediocrities. Fastolfe may yet find it profitable to come in with us."

"I don't think so."

"I do. He will not enjoy being without power in the Legislature and, when our plans for settling the Galaxy move ahead and he sees that his opposition does not stop us, he will join us. It will be only human of him to do so."

"I don't think you will win out," said Baley.

"Because you think that somehow this investigation of yours will exonerate Fastolfe and implicate me, perhaps, or someone else."

"Perhaps," said Baley desperately.

Amadiro shook his head. "My friend, if I thought that anything you could do would spoil my plans, would I be sitting still and waiting for destruction?"

"You are not. You are doing everything you can to have this investigation aborted. Why would you do that if you were confident that nothing I could do would get in your way?"

"Well," said Amadiro, "you *can* get in my way by demoralizing some of the members of the Institute. You can't be dangerous, but you can be annoying—and I don't want that either. So, if I can, I'll put an end to the annoyance—but I'll do that in reasonable fashion, in gentle fashion, even. If you were actually *dangerous*—"

"What could you do, Dr. Amadiro, in that case?"

"I could have you seized and imprisoned until you were evicted. I don't think Aurorans generally would worry overmuch about what I might do to an Earthman."

Baley said, "You are trying to browbeat me and that won't work. You know very well you could not lay a hand on me with my robots present."

Amadiro said, "Does it occur to you that I have a hundred robots within call? What would yours do against *them*?"

"All hundred could not harm me. They cannot distinguish between Earthmen and Aurorans. I am human within the meaning of the Three Laws."

"They could hold you quite immobilized—without harming you—while your robots were destroyed."

"Not so," said Baley. "Giskard can hear you and, if you make a move to summon your robots, Giskard will have *you* immobilized. He moves very quickly and, once that happens, your robots will be helpless, even if you manage to call them. They will understand that any move against me will result in harm to you."

"You mean that Giskard will hurt me?"

"To protect me from harm? Certainly. He will kill you, if absolutely necessary."

"Surely you don't mean that."

"I do," said Bailey. "Daneel and Giskard have orders to protect me. The First Law, in this respect, has been strengthened with all the skill Dr. Fastolfe can bring to the job—and with respect to me, specifically. I haven't been told this in so many words, but I'm quite sure it's true. If my robots must choose between harm to you and harm to me, Earthman though I am, it will be easy for them to choose harm to you. I imagine you are well aware that Dr. Fastolfe is not very eager to ensure *your* well-being."

Amadiro chuckled and a grin wreathed his face. "I'm sure you're right in every respect, Mr. Baley, but it *is* good to have you say so. You know, my good sir, that I am recording this conversation also—I told you so at the start—and I'm glad of it. It is possible that Dr. Fastolfe will erase the last part of this conversation, but I assure you I won't. It is clear from what you have said that he is quite prepared to devise a robotic way of doing harm to me—even kill me, if he can manage that—whereas it cannot be said from anything in this conversation—or any other—that I plan any physical harm to him whatever or even to you. Which of us is the villain, Mr. Baley?—I think you have established that and I think, then, that this is a good place at which to end the interview."

He rose, still smiling, and Baley, swallowing hard, stood up as well, almost automatically.

Amadiro said, "I still have one thing to say, however. It has nothing to do with our little contretemps here on Aurora—Fastolfe's and mine. Rather, with your own problem, Mr. Baley."

"My problem?"

"Perhaps I should say Earth's problem. I imagine that you feel very anxious to save poor Fastolfe from his own folly because you think that will give your planet a chance for expansion. —Don't think so, Mr. Baley. You are quite wrong, rather arsyvarsy, to use a vulgar expression I've come across in some of your planet's historical novels."

"I'm not familiar with that phrase," said Baley stiffly.

"I mean you have the situation reversed. You see, when my view wins out in the Legislature—and note that I say 'when' and not 'if'— Earth will be forced to remain in her own planetary system, I admit, but that will actually be to her benefit. Aurora will have the prospect of expansion and of establishing an endless empire. If we then know that Earth will merely be Earth and never anything more, of what concern will she be to us? With the Galaxy at our disposal, we will not begrudge Earthpeople their one world. We would even be disposed to make Earth as comfortable a world for her people as would be practical.

"On the other hand, Mr. Baley, if Aurorans do what Fastolfe asks and allow Earth to send out settling parties, then it won't be long before it will occur to an increasing number of us that Earth will take over the Galaxy and that we will be encircled and hemmed in, that we will be doomed to decay and death. After that, there will be nothing I can do. My own quite kindly feeling toward Earthmen will not be able to withstand the general kindling of Auroran suspicion and prejudice and it will then be *very* bad for Earth.

"So if, Mr. Baley, you are truly concerned for your own people, you should be very anxious indeed for Fastolfe *not* to succeed in foisting upon this planet his very misguided plan. You should be a strong ally of mine. Think about it. I tell you this, I assure you, out of a sincere friendship and liking for you and for your planet."

Amadiro was smiling as broadly as ever, but it was all wolf now.

57

Baley and his robots followed Amadiro out the room and along the corridor.

Amadiro stopped at one inconspicuous door and said, "Would you care to use the facilities before leaving?"

For a moment, Baley frowned in confusion, for he did not understand. Then he remembered the antiquated phrase Amadiro had used, thanks to his own reading of historical novels.

He said, "There was an ancient general, whose name I have forgotten, who, mindful of the exigencies of sudden absorption in military affairs, once said, 'Never turn down a chance to piss.' "

Amadiro smiled broadly and said, "Excellent advice. Quite as good as my advice to think seriously about what I have said.—But I notice that you hesitate, even so. Surely you don't think I am laying a trap for you. Believe me, I am not a barbarian. You are my guest in this building and, for that reason alone, you are perfectly safe "

Baley said cautiously, "If I hesitate, it is because I am considering the propriety of using your—uh—facilities, considering that I am not an Auroran."

"Nonsense, my dear Baley. What is your alternative? Needs must. Please make use of it. Let that be a symbol that I myself am not subject to the general Auroran prejudices and wish you and Earth well."

"Could you go a step further?"

"In what way, Mr. Baley?"

"Could you show me that you are also superior to this planet's prejudice against robots—"

"There is no prejudice against robots," said Amadiro quickly.

Baley nodded his head solemnly in apparent acceptance of the remark and completed his sentence. "—by allowing them to enter the Personal with me. I have grown to feel uncomfortable without them."

For one moment, Amadiro seemed shaken. He recovered almost at once and said, with what was almost a scowl, "By all means, Mr. Baley."

"Yet whoever is now inside might object strenuously. I would not want to create scandal."

"No one is in there. It is a one-person Personal and, if someone were making use of it, the in-use signal would indicate that."

"Thank you, Dr. Amadiro," said Baley. He opened the door and said, "Giskard, please enter."

Giskard clearly hesitated, but said nothing in objection and entered. At a gesture from Baley, Daneel followed, but as he passed through the door, he took Baley's elbow and pulled him in as well.

Baley said, as the door closed behind him, "I'll be out again soon. Thank you for allowing this."

He entered the room with as much unconcern as he could manage and yet he felt a tightness in the pit of his abdomen. Might it contain some unpleasant surprise?

58

Baley found the Personal empty, however. There was not even much to search. It was smaller than the one in Fastolfe's establishment.

Eventually, he noticed Daneel and Giskard standing silently side by side, backs against the door, as though endeavoring to have entered the room by the least amount possible.

Baley tried to speak normally, but what came out was a dim croak. He cleared his throat with unnecessary noise and said, "You can come farther into the room—and you needn't remain silent, Daneel." (Daneel had been on Earth. He knew the Earthly taboo against speech in the Personal.)

Daneel displayed that knowledge at once. He put his forefinger to his lips.

Baley said, "I know, I know, but forget it. If Amadiro can forget the Auroran taboo about robots in Personals, I can forget the Earthly taboo about speech there."

"Will it not make you uncomfortable, Partner Elijah?" asked Daneel in a low voice.

"Not a bit," said Baley in an ordinary one. (Actually, speech felt different with Daneel—a robot. The sound of speech in a room such as this when, actually, no *human being* was present was not as horrifying as it might be. In fact, it was not horrifying at all when only robots were present, however humaniform one of them might be. Baley could not say so, of course. Though Daneel had no feelings a human being could hurt, Baley had feelings on his behalf.)

And then Baley thought of something else and felt, quite intensely, the sensation of being a thoroughgoing fool.

"Or," he said to Daneel, in a voice that was suddenly very low indeed, "are you suggesting silence because this room is bugged?" The last word came out merely as a shaping of the mouth.

"If you mean, Partner Elijah, that people outside this room can detect what is spoken inside this room through some sort of eavesdropping device, that is quite impossible."

"Why impossible?"

The toilet device flushed itself with quick and silent efficiency and Baley advanced toward the washbasin.

Daneel said, "On Earth, the dense packing of the Cities makes privacy impossible. Overhearing is taken for granted and to use a device to make overhearing more efficient might seem natural. If an Earthman wishes not to be overheard, he simply doesn't speak, which may be why silence is so mandatory in places where there is a pretense of privacy, as in the very rooms you call Personals.

"On Aurora, on the other hand, as on all the Spacer worlds, privacy

is a true fact of life and is greatly valued. You remember Solaria and
the diseased extremes to which it was carried there. But even on Aurora, which is no Solaria, every human being is insulated from every
other human being by the kind of space extension unthinkable on
Earth and by a wall of robots, in addition. To break down that privacy
would be an unthinkable act."

Baley said, "Do you mean it would be a crime to bug this room?"

"Much worse, Partner Elijah. It would not be the act of a civilized
Auroran gentleman."

Baley looked about. Daneel, mistaking the gesture, plucked a towel
out of the dispenser, which might not have been instantly apparent
to the other's unaccustomed eyes, and offered it to Baley.

Baley accepted the towel, but that was not the object of his questing
glance. It was a bug for which his eyes searched, for he found it difficult to believe that someone would forego an easy advantage on the
ground that it would not be civilized behavior. It was, however, useless
and Baley, rather despondently, knew it would be. He would not be
able to detect an Auroran bug, even if one were there. He wouldn't
know what to look for in a strange culture.

Whereupon he followed the course of another strand of suspicion
in his mind. "Tell me, Daneel, since you know Aurorans better than
I do, why do you suppose Amadiro is taking all this trouble with me?
He talks to me at his leisure. He sees me out. He offers me the use of
this room—something Vasilia would not have done. He seems to have
all the time in the world to spend on me. Politeness?"

"Many Aurorans pride themselves on their politeness. It may be
that Amadiro does. He has several times stressed that he is not a barbarian."

"Another question. Why do you think he was willing to have me
bring you and Giskard into this room?"

"It seemed to me that that was to remove your suspicions that the
offer of this room might conceal a trap."

"Why should he bother? Because he was concerned over the possibility of my experiencing unnecessary anxiety?"

"Another gesture of a civilized Auroran gentleman, I should imagine."

Baley shook his head. "Well, if this room is bugged and Amadiro can
hear me, let him hear me. I don't consider him a civilized Auroran gentleman. He made it quite clear that, if I did not abandon my investigation,
he would see to it that Earth as a whole would suffer. Is that the act of a
civilized gentleman? Or of an incredibly brutal blackmailer?"

Daneel said, "An Auroran gentleman may find it necessary to utter
threats, but if so, he would do it in a gentlemanly manner."

"As Amadiro did. It is, then, the manner and not the content of speech that marks the gentleman. But then, Daneel, you are a robot and therefore can not really criticize a human being, can you?"

Daneel said, "It would be difficult for me to do so. But may I ask a question, Partner Elijah? Why did you ask permission to bring friend Giskard and me into this room? It had seemed to me that you were reluctant, earlier, to believe you were in danger. Have you now decided that you are not safe except in our presence?"

"No, not at all, Daneel. I am now quite convinced that I am not in danger and have not been."

"Yet there was a distinctly suspicious cast about your actions when you entered this room, Partner Elijah. You searched it."

Baley said, "Of course! I said I am not in danger, but I do not say there is no danger."

"I do not think I see the distinction, Partner Elijah," said Daneel.

"We will discuss it later, Daneel. I am still not certain as to whether this room is bugged or not."

Baley was by now quite done. He said, "Well, Daneel, I've been leisurely about this; I haven't rushed at all. Now I'm ready to go out again and I wonder if Amadiro is still waiting for us after all this time or whether he has delegated an underling to do the rest of the job of showing us out. After all, Amadiro is a busy man and cannot spend all day with me. What do you think, Daneel?"

"It would be more logical if Dr. Amadiro had delegated the task."

"And you, Giskard? What do you think?"

"I agree with friend Daneel, though it is my experience that human beings do not always make what would seem the logical response."

Baley said, "For my part, I suspect Amadiro is waiting for us quite patiently. If something has driven him to waste this much time on us, I rather think that the driving force—whatever it might be—has not yet weakened."

"I do not know what might be the driving force you speak of, Partner Elijah," said Daneel.

"Nor I, Daneel," said Baley, "which bothers me a great deal. But let us open the door now and see."

59

Amadiro was waiting outside the door for them, precisely where Baley had left him. He smiled at them, showing no sign of impatience. Baley could not resist shooting a quiet I-told-you-so glance at Daneel, who responded with bland impassivity.

Amadiro said, "I rather regretted, Mr. Baley, that you had not left Giskard outside when you entered the Personal. I might have known

him in times past, when Fastolfe and I were on better terms, but
somehow never did. Fastolfe was my teacher once, you know."

"Was he?" said Baley. "I didn't know that, as a matter of fact."

"No reason you should, unless you had been told—and, in the short
time you've been on the planet, you can scarcely have had time to
learn much in the way of this sort of trivia, I suppose. —Come now, it
has occurred to me that you can scarcely think me hospitable if I do
not take advantage of your being at the Institute to show you around."

"Really," said Baley, stiffening a bit. "I must—"

"I insist," said Amadiro, with something of a note of the imperious
entering his voice. "You arrived on Aurora yesterday morning and I
doubt that you will be staying on the planet much longer. This may
be the only chance you will ever have of getting a glimpse of a modern
laboratory doing research work on robotics."

He linked arms with Baley and continued to speak in familiar terms.
("Prattled" was the term that occurred to the astonished Baley.)

"You've washed," said Amadiro. "You've taken care of your needs.
There may be other roboticists here whom you will wish to question
and I would welcome that, since I am determined to show I have put
no barriers in your way during the short time in which you will yet be
permitted to conduct your investigation. In fact, there is no reason
you can't have dinner with us."

Giskard said, "If I may interrupt, sir—"

"You may not!" said Amadiro with unmistakable firmness and the
robot fell silent.

Amadiro said, "My dear Mr. Baley, I understand these robots. Who
should know them better? —Except for the unfortunate Fastolfe, of
course. Giskard, I am sure, was going to remind you of some appointment, some promise, some business—and there is no point in any of
that. Since the investigation is about over, I promise you, none of what
he was going to remind you of will have any significance. Let us forget
all such nonsense and, for a brief time, be friends.

"You must understand, my good Mr. Baley," he went on, 'that I
am quite an aficionado of Earth and its culture. It is not the most
popular of subjects on Aurora, but I find it fascinating. I am particularly interested in Earth's past history, the days when it had a hundred
languages and Interstellar Standard had not yet been developed.
—May I compliment you, by the way, on your own handling of Interstellar?

"This way, this way," he said, turning a corner. "We'll be coming
to the pathway-simulation room, which has its own weird beauty, and
we may have a mock-up in operation. Quite symphonic, actually.
—But I was talking about your handling of Interstellar. It is one of the
many Auroran superstitions concerning Earth, that Earthpeople speak

an all-but-incomprehensible version of Interstellar. When the show about you was produced, there were many who said that the actors could not be Earthpeople because they could be understood, yet I can understand you." He smiled as he said that.

"I've tried reading Shakespeare," he continued with a confidential air, "but I can't read him in the original, of course, and the translation is curiously flat. I can't help but believe that the fault lies with the translation and not with Shakespeare. I do better with Dickens and Tolstoy, perhaps because that is prose, although the names of the characters are, in both cases, virtually unpronounceable to me.

"What I'm trying to say, Mr. Baley, is that I'm a friend of Earth. I really am. I want what is best for it. Do you understand?" He looked at Baley and again the wolf showed in his twinkling eyes.

Baley raised his voice, forcing it between the softly running sentences of the other. "I'm afraid I *cannot* oblige you, Dr. Amadiro. I must be about my business and I have no further questions to ask of either you or anyone else here. If you—"

Baley paused. There was a faint and curious rumble of sound in the air. He looked up, startled. "What is that?"

"What is what?" asked Amadiro. "I sense nothing." He looked at the robots, who had been following the two human beings in grave silence. "Nothing!" he said forcefully. "Nothing."

Baley recognized that as the equivalent of an order. Neither robot could now claim to have heard the rumble in direct contradiction to a human being, unless Bailey himself applied a counter-pressure—and he was sure he could not manage to do it skillfully enough in the face of Amadiro's professionalism.

Nevertheless, it didn't matter. He had heard something and he was not a robot; he would not be talked out of it. He said, "By your own statement, Dr. Amadiro, I have little time left me. That is all the more reason that I must—"

The rumble again. Louder.

Baley said, with a sharp, cutting edge to his voice, "That, I suppose, is precisely what you didn't hear before and what you don't hear now. Let me go, sir, or I will ask my robots for help."

Amadiro loosened his grip on Baley's upper arm at once. "My friend, you had but to express the wish. Come! I will take you to the nearest exit and, if ever you are on Aurora again, which seems unlikely in the extreme, please return and you may have the tour I promised you."

They were walking faster. They moved down the spiral ramp, out along a corridor to the commodious and now empty anteroom and the door by which they had entered.

The windows in the anteroom showed utterly dark. Could it be night already?

It wasn't. Amadiro muttered to himself, "Rotten weather! They've opacified the windows."

He turned to Baley. "I imagine it's raining. They predicted it and the forecasts can usually be relied on—always, when they're unpleasant."

The door opened and Baley jumped backward with a gasp. A cold wind gusted inward and against the sky—not black but a dull, dark gray—the tops of trees were whipping back and forth.

There was water pouring from the sky—descending in streams. And as Baley watched, appalled, a streak of light flashed across the sky with blinding brilliance and then the rumble came again, this time with a cracking report, as though the light-streak had split the sky and the rumble was the noise it had made.

Baley turned and fled back the way he had come, whimpering.

15.

Again Daneel and Giskard

60

Baley felt Daneel's strong grip on his arms, just beneath his shoulders. He halted and forced himself to stop making that infantile sound. He could feel himself trembling.

Daneel said with infinite respect, "Partner Elijah, it is a thunderstorm—expected—predicted—normal."

"I know that," whispered Baley.

He did know it. Thunderstorms had been described innumerable times in the books he had read, whether fiction or nonfiction. He had seen them in holographs and on hyperwave shows—sound, sight, and all.

The real thing, however, the actual sound and sight, had never penetrated into the bowels of the City and he had never in his life actually experienced such a thing.

With all he knew—intellectually—about thunderstorms, he could not face—viscerally—the actuality. Despite the descriptions, the collections of words, the sight in small pictures and on small screens, the sounds captured in recordings; despite all that, he had no idea the flashes were so bright and streaked so across the sky; that the sound was so vibratorily bass in sound when it rattled across a hollow world; that both were so *sudden*; and that rain could be so like an inverted bowl of water, endlessly pouring.

He muttered in despair, "I can't go out in that."

"You won't have to," said Daneel urgently. "Giskard will get the airfoil. It will be brought right to the door for you. Not a drop of rain will fall on you."

"Why not wait until it's over?"

"Surely that would not be advisable, Partner Elijah. Some rain, at least, will continue past midnight and if the Chairman arrives tomorrow morning, as Dr. Amadiro implied he might, it might be wise to spend the evening in consultation with Dr. Fastolfe."

Baley forced himself to turn around, face in the direction from which he wanted to flee, and look into Daneel's eyes. They seemed deeply concerned, but Baley thought dismally that that was merely the result of his own interpretation of the appearance of those eyes. The robot had no feelings, only positronic surges that mimicked those feelings. (And perhaps human beings had no feelings, only neuronic surges that were interpreted as feelings.)

He was somehow aware that Amadiro was gone. He said, "Amadiro delayed me deliberately—by ushering me into the Personal, by his senseless talk, by his preventing you or Giskard from interrupting and warning me about the storm. He would even have tried to persuade me to tour the building or dine with him. He desisted only at the sound of the storm. That was what he was waiting for."

"It would seem so. If the storm now keeps you here, *that* may be what he was waiting for."

Baley drew a deep breath. "You are right. I must leave—somehow."

Reluctantly, he took a step toward the door, which was still open, still filled with a dark gray vista of whipping rain. Another step. And still another—leaning heavily on Daneel.

Giskard was waiting quietly at the door.

Baley paused and closed his eyes for a moment. Then he said in a low voice, to himself rather than to Daneel, "I must do it," and moved forward again.

61

"Are you well, sir?" asked Giskard.

It was a foolish question, dictated by the programming of the robot, thought Baley, though, at that, it was no worse than the questions asked by human beings, sometimes with wild inappropriateness, out of the programming of etiquette.

"Yes," said Baley in a voice he tried—and failed—to raise above a husky whisper. It was a useless answer to the foolish question, for Giskard, robot though he was, could surely see that Baley was unwell and that Baley's answer was a palpable lie.

The answer was, however, given and accepted and that freed Giskard for the next step. He said, "I will now leave to get the airfoil and bring it to the door."

"Will it work—in all this—this water, Giskard?"

"Yes, sir. This is not an uncommon rain."

He left, moving steadily into the downpour. The lightning was flickering almost continuously and the thunder was a muted growl that rose to a louder crescendo every few minutes.

For the first time in his life, Baley found himself envying a robot. Imagine being able to walk through *that*; to be indifferent to water, to sight, to sound; to be able to ignore surroundings and to have a pseudo-life that was absolutely courageous; to know no fear of pain or of death, because there was no pain or death.

And yet to be incapable of originality of thought, to be incapable of unpredictable leaps of intuition—

Were such gifts worth what humanity paid for them?

At the moment, Baley could not say. He knew that, once he no longer felt terror, he would know that no price was too high to pay for being human. But now that he experienced nothing but the pounding of his heart and the collapse of his will, he could not help but wonder of what use it might be to be a human being if one could not overcome these deep-seated terrors, this intense agoraphobia.

Yet he had been in the open for much of two days and had managed to be almost comfortable.

But the fear had not been conquered. He knew that now. He had suppressed it by thinking intensely of other things, but the storm overrode all intensity of thought.

He could not allow this. If all else failed—thought, pride, will—then he would have to fall back on shame. He could not collapse under the impersonal, superior gaze of the robots. Shame would have to be stronger than fear.

He felt Daneel's steady arm about his waist and shame prevented him from doing what, at the moment, he most wanted to do—to turn and hide his face against the robotic chest. He might have been unable to resist if Daneel had been human—

He had lost contact with reality, for he was becoming aware of Daneel's voice as though it were reaching him from a long distance. It sounded as though Daneel was feeling something akin to panic.

"Partner Elijah, do you hear me?"

Giskard's voice, from an equal distance, said, "We must carry him."

"No," mumbled Baley. "Let me walk."

Perhaps they did not hear him. Perhaps he did not really speak, but merely thought he did. He felt himself lifted from the ground. His left arm dangled helplessly and he strove to lift it, to push it against someone's shoulder, to lift himself upright again from the waist, to grope for the floor with his feet and stand upright.

But his left arm continued to dangle helplessly and his striving went for nothing.

He was somehow aware that he was moving through the air and he felt a wash of spray against his face. Not actually water but the sifting of damp air. Then there was the pressure of a hard surface against his left side, a more resilient one against his right side.

He was in the airfoil, wedged in once more between Giskard and Daneel. What he was most conscious of was that Giskard was very wet.

He felt a jet of warm air cascading over him. Between the near-darkness outside and the film of trickling water upon the glass, they might as well have been opacified—or so Baley thought till opacification actually took place and total darkness descended. The soft noise of the jet, as the airfoil rose above the grass and swayed, muted the thunder and seemed to draw its teeth.

Giskard said, "I regret the discomfort of my wet surface, sir. I will dry quickly. We will wait here a short while till you recover."

Baley was breathing more easily. He felt wonderfully and comfortably enclosed. He thought: Give me back my City. Wipe out all the Universe and let the Spacers colonize it. Earth is all we need.

And even as he thought it, he knew it was his madness that believed it, not he.

He felt the need to keep his mind busy.

He said weakly, "Daneel."

"Yes, Partner Elijah?"

"About the Chairman. Is it your opinion that Amadiro was judging the situation correctly in supposing that the Chairman would put an end to the investigation or was he perhaps allowing his wishes to do his thinking for him?"

"It may be, Partner Elijah, that the Chairman will indeed interview Dr. Fastolfe and Amadiro on the matter. It would be a standard procedure for settling a dispute of this nature. There are ample precedents."

"But why?" asked Baley weakly. "If Amadiro was so persuasive, why should not the Chairman simply order the investigation stopped?"

"The Chairman," said Daneel, "is in a difficult political situation. He agreed originally to allow you to be brought to Aurora at Dr. Fastolfe's urging and he cannot so sharply reverse himself so soon without making himself look weak and irresolute—and without angering Dr. Fastolfe, who is still a very influential figure in the Legislature."

"Then why did he not simply turn down Amadiro's request?"

"Dr. Amadiro is also influential, Partner Elijah, and likely to grow even more so. The Chairman must temporize by hearing both sides and by giving at least the appearance of deliberation before coming to a decision."

"Based on what?"

"On the merits of the case, we must presume."

"Then by tomorrow morning, I must come up with something that will persuade the Chairman to side with Fastolfe, rather than against him. If I do that, will that mean victory?"

Daneel said, "The Chairman is not all-powerful, but his influence is great. If he comes out strongly on Dr. Fastolfe's side, then, under the present political conditions, Dr. Fastolfe will probably win the backing of the Legislature."

Baley found himself beginning to think clearly again. "That would seem explanation enough for Amadiro's attempt to delay us. He might have reasoned that I had nothing yet to offer the Chairman and he needed only to delay to keep me from getting anything in the time that remained to me."

"So it would seem, Partner Elijah."

"And he let me go only when he thought he could rely on the storm continuing to keep me."

"Perhaps so, Partner Elijah."

"In that case, we cannot allow the storm to stop us."

Giskard said calmly, "Where do you wish to be taken, sir?"

"Back to the establishment of Dr. Fastolfe."

Daneel said, "May we have one moment's more pause, Partner Elijah? Do you plan to tell Dr. Fastolfe that you cannot continue the investigation?"

Baley said sharply, "Why do you say that?" It was a measure of his recovery that his voice was loud and angry.

Daneel said, "It is merely that I fear you might have forgotten for a moment that Dr. Amadiro urged you to do so for the sake of Earth's welfare."

"I have not forgotten," said Baley grimly, "and I am surprised, Daneel, that you should think that that would influence me. Fastolfe must be exonerated and Earth must send its settlers outward into the Galaxy. If there is danger in that from the Globalists, that danger must be chanced."

"But, in that case, Partner Elijah, why go back to Dr. Fastolfe? It doesn't seem to me that we have anything of moment to report to him. Is there no direction in which we can further continue our investigation *before* reporting to Dr. Fastolfe?"

Baley sat up in his seat and placed his hand on Giskard, who was now entirely dry. He said, in quite a normal voice, "I am satisfied with the progress I have already made, Daneel. Let's get moving, Giskard. Proceed to Fastolfe's establishment."

And then, tightening his fists and stiffening his body, Baley added, "What's more, Giskard, clear the windows. I want to look out into the face of the storm."

62

Baley held his breath in preparation for transparency. The small box of the airfoil would no longer be entirely enclosed; it would no longer have unbroken walls.

As the windows clarified, there was a flash of light that came and went too quickly to do anything but darken the world by contrast.

Baley could not prevent his cringe as he tried to steel himself for the thunder which, after a moment or two, rolled and grumbled.

Daneel said pacifyingly, "The storm will get no worse and soon enough it will recede."

"I don't care whether it recedes or not," said Baley through trembling lips. "Come on. Let's go." He was trying, for his own sake, to maintain the illusion of a human being in charge of robots.

The airfoil rose slightly in the air and at once underwent a sideways movement that tilted it so that Baley felt himself pushing hard against Giskard.

Baley cried out (gasped out, rather), "Straighten the vehicle, Giskard!"

Daneel placed his arm around Baley's shoulder and pulled him gently back. His other arm was braced about a hand-grip attached to the frame of the airfoil.

"That cannot be done, Partner Elijah," Daneel said. "There is a fairly strong wind."

Baley felt his hair bristle. "You mean—we're going to be blown away?"

"No, of course not," said Daneel. "If the car were antigrav—a form of technology that does not, of course, exist—and if its mass and inertia were eliminated, then it would be blown like a feather high into the air. However, we retain our full mass even when our jets lift us and poise us in the air, so our inertia resists the wind. Nevertheless, the wind makes us sway, even though the car remains completely under Giskard's control."

"It doesn't feel like it." Baley was conscious of a thin whine, which he imagined to be the wind curling around the body of the airfoil as it cut its way through the protesting atmosphere. Then the airfoil lurched and Baley, who could not for his life have helped it. seized Daneel in a desperate grip around the neck.

Daneel waited a moment. When Baley had caught his breath and his grip grew less rigid, Daneel released himself easily from the other's embrace, while somewhat tightening the pressure of his own arm around Baley.

He said, "In order to maintain course, Partner Elijah, Giskard must counter the wind by an asymmetric ordering of the airfoil's jets. They are sent to one side so as to cause the airfoil to lean into the wind and these jets have to be adjusted in force and direction as the wind itself changes force and direction. There are none better at this than Giskard, but, even so, there are occasional jiggles and lurches. You must excuse Giskard, then, if he does not participate in our conversation. His attention is fully on the airfoil."

"Is it—it safe?" Baley felt his stomach contract at the thought of playing with the wind in this fashion. He was devoutly glad he had not eaten for some hours. He could not—dared not—be sick in the close confines of the airfoil. The very thought unsettled him further and he tried to concentrate on something else.

He thought of running the strips back on Earth, of racing from one moving strip to its neighboring faster strip, and then to its neighboring still faster strip, and then back down into the slower regions, leaning expertly into the wind either way; in one direction as one fastered (an odd word used by no one but strip-racers) and in the other direction, as one slowered. In his younger days, Baley could do it without pause and without error.

Daneel had adjusted to the need without trouble and, the one time they had run the strips together, Daneel had done it perfectly. Well, this was just the same! The airfoil was running strips. Absolutely! It was the same!

Not quite the same, to be sure. In the City, the speed of the strips was a fixed quantity. What wind there was blew in absolutely predictable fashion, since it was only the result of the movement of the strips. Here in the storm, however, the wind had a mind of its own or, rather, it depended on so many variables (Baley was deliberately striving for rationality) that it seemed to have a mind of its own—and Giskard had to allow for that. That was all. Otherwise, it was just running the strips with an added complication. The strips were moving at variable—and sharply changing—speeds.

Baley muttered, "What if we blow into a tree?"

"Very unlikely, Partner Elijah. Giskard is far too skillful for that. And we are only very slightly above the ground, so that the jets are particularly powerful."

"Then we'll hit a rock. It will cave us in underneath."

"We will not hit a rock, Partner Elijah."

"Why not? How on Earth can Giskard see where he's going, anyway?" Baley stared at the darkness ahead.

"It is just about sunset," said Daneel, "and some light is making its way through the clouds. It is enough for us to see by with the help of our headlights. And as it grows darker, Giskard will brighten the headlights."

"What headlights?" asked Baley rebelliously.

"You do not see them very well because they have a strong infrared component, to which Giskard's eyes are sensitive but yours are not. What's more, the infrared is more penetrating than shorter wave light is and, for that reason, is more effective in rain, mist, and fog."

Baley managed to feel some curiosity, even amid his uneasiness. "And *your* eyes, Daneel?"

"My eyes, Partner Elijah, are designed to be as similar to those of human beings as possible. That is regrettable, perhaps, at this moment."

The airfoil trembled and Baley found himself holding his breath again. He said in a whisper, "Spacer eyes are still adapted to Earth's sun, even if robot eyes aren't. A good thing, too, if it helps remind them they're descended from Earthpeople."

His voice faded out. It was getting darker. He could see nothing at all now and the intermittent flashes lighted nothing, either. They were merely blinding. He closed his eyes and that didn't help. He was the more conscious of the angry, threatening thunder.

Should they not stop? Should they not wait for the worst of the storm to pass?

Giskard suddenly said, "The vehicle is not reacting properly."

Baley felt the ride become ragged as though the machine was on wheels and was rolling over ridges.

Daneel said, "Can it be storm damage, friend Giskard?"

"It does not have the feel of that, friend Daneel. Nor does it seem likely that this machine would suffer from this kind of damage in this or any other storm."

Baley absorbed the exchange with difficulty. "Damage?" he muttered. "What kind of damage?"

Giskard said, "I should judge the compressor to be leaking, sir, but slowly. It's not the result of an ordinary puncture."

"How did it happen, then?" Baley asked.

"Deliberate damage, perhaps, while it was outside the Administration Building. I have known, now, for some little time that we are being followed and carefully not being overtaken."

"Why, Giskard?"

"A possibility, sir, is that they are waiting for us to break down completely." The airfoil's motion was becoming more ragged.

"Can you make it to Dr. Fastolfe's?"

"It would not seem so, sir."

Baley tried to fling his reeling mind into action. "In that case, I've completely misjudged Amadiro's reason for delaying us. He was keeping us there to have one or more of his robots damage the airfoil in such a way as to bring us down in the midst of desolation and lightning."

"But why should he do that?" said Daneel, sounding shocked. "To get you?—In a way, he already had you."

"He doesn't want me. No one wants *me*," said Baley with a somewhat feeble anger. "The danger is to you, Daneel."

"To me, Partner Elijah?"

"Yes, *you!* Daneel. —Giskard, choose a safe place to come down and, as soon as you do, Daneel must get out of the car and be off to a place of safety."

Daneel said, "That is impossible, Partner Elijah. I could not leave you when you are feeling ill—and most especially if there are those who pursue us and might do you harm."

Baley said, "Daneel, they're pursuing *you*. You *must* leave. As for me, I will stay in the airfoil. I am in no danger."

"How can I believe that?"

"Please! Please! How can I explain the whole thing with everything spinning—Daneel"—Baley's voice grew desperately calm—"you are the most important individual here, far more important than Giskard and I put together. It's not just that I care for you and want no harm to come to you. All of humanity depends on you. Don't worry about me; I'm one man; worry about *billions*. Daneel—please—"

63

Baley could feel himself rocking back and forth. Or was it the airfoil? Was it breaking up altogether? Or was Giskard losing control? Or was he taking evasive action?

Baley didn't care. He didn't *care*! Let the airfoil crash. Let it smash to bits. He would welcome oblivion. Anything to get rid of this terrible fright, this total inability to come to terms with the Universe.

Except that he had to make sure that Daneel got away—safely away. But how?

Everything was unreal and he was not going to be able to explain anything to these robots. The situation was so clear to him, but how was he to transfer this understanding to these robots, to these non-men, who understood nothing but their Three Laws and who would let all of Earth and, in the long run, all of humanity go to hell because they could only be concerned with the one man under their noses?

Why had robots ever been invented?

And then, oddly enough, Giskard, the lesser of the two, came to his aid.

He said in his contentless voice, "Friend Daneel, I cannot keep this airfoil in motion much longer. Perhaps it will be more suitable to do as Mr. Baley suggests. He has given you a very strong order."

"Can I leave him when he is unwell, friend Giskard?" said Daneel, perplexed.

"You cannot take him out into the storm with you, friend Daneel. Moreover, he seems so anxious for you to leave that it may do him harm for you to stay."

Baley felt himself reviving. "Yes—yes—" he managed to croak out. "As Giskard says. Giskard, you go with him, hide him, make sure he doesn't return—then come back for me."

Daneel said forcefully, "That cannot be, Partner Elijah. We cannot leave you alone, untended, unguarded."

"No danger—I am in no danger. Do as I say—"

Giskard said, "Those following are probably robots. Human beings would hesitate to come out in the storm. And robots would not harm Mr. Baley."

Daneel said, "They might take him away."

"Not into the storm, friend Daneel, since that would work obvious harm to him. I will bring the airfoil to a halt now, friend Daneel. You must be ready to do as Mr. Baley orders. I, too."

"Good!" whispered Baley. "Good!" He was grateful for the simpler brain that could more easily be impressed and that lacked the ability to get lost and uncertain in ever-expanding refinements.

Vaguely, he thought of Daneel trapped between his perception of Baley's ill-being and the urgency of the order—and of his brain snapping under the conflict.

Baley thought: No no, Daneel. Just do as I say and don't question it.

He lacked the strength, almost the will, to articulate it and he let the order remain a thought.

The airfoil came down with a bump and a short, harsh, scraping noise.

The doors flew open, one on either side, and then closed with a soft, sighing noise. At once, the robots were gone. Having come to their decision, there was no hesitation and they moved with a speed that human beings could not duplicate.

Baley took a deep breath and shuddered. The airfoil was rock-steady now. It was part of the ground.

He was suddenly aware of how much of his misery had been the result of the swaying and bucking of the vehicle, the feeling of insubstantiality, of not being connected to the Universe but of being at the mercy of inanimate, uncaring forces.

Now, however, it was still and he opened his eyes.

He had not been aware that they had been closed.

There was still lightning on the horizon and the thunder was a subdued mutter, while the wind, meeting a more resistant and less yielding object now than it had hitherto, keened a higher note than before.

It was dark. Baley's eyes were no more than human and he saw no light of any kind, other than the occasional blip of lightning. The sun must surely have set and the clouds were thick.

And for the first time since Baley had left Earth, he was alone!

64

Alone!

He had been too ill, too beside himself, to make proper sense. Even now, he found himself struggling to understand what it was he should have done and would have done—if he had had room in his tottering mind for more than the one thought that Daneel must leave.

For instance, he had not asked where he now was, what he was near, where Daneel and Giskard were planning to go. He did not know how any portion of the grounded airfoil worked. He could not, of course, make it move, but he might have had it supply heat if he felt cold or turn off the heat if there were too much—except that he did not know how to direct the machine to do either.

He did not know how to opacify the windows if he wanted to be enclosed or how to open a door if he wanted to leave.

The only thing he could do now was to wait for Giskard to come back for him. Surely that was what Giskard would expect him to do. The orders to him had simply been: Come back for me.

There had been no indication that Baley would change position in any way and Giskard's clear and uncluttered mind would surely interpret the "Come back" with the assumption that he was to come back to the airfoil.

Baley tried to adjust himself to that. In a way, it was a relief merely to wait, to have to make no decisions for a while, because there were no decisions he could possibly make. It was a relief to be steady and to feel at rest and to be rid of the terrible light flashes and the disturbing crashes of sound.

Perhaps he might even allow himself to go to sleep.

And then he stiffened. —Dare he do that?

They were being pursued. They were under observation. The airfoil, while parked and waiting for them outside the Administration Building of the Robotics Institute, had been tampered with and no doubt the tamperers would soon be upon him.

He was waiting for them, too, and not for Giskard only.

Had he thought it out clearly in the midst of his misery? The machine had been tampered with outside the Administration Building. That might have been done by anyone, but most likely by someone who knew it was there—and who would know that better than Amadiro?

Amadiro had intended delay until the storm. That was obvious. He was to travel in the storm and he was to break down in the storm. Amadiro had studied Earth and its population; he boasted of that. He would know quite clearly just what difficulty Earthpeople would have with the Outside generally and with a thunderstorm in particular.

He would be quite certain that Baley would be reduced to complete helplessness.

But why should he want that?

To bring Baley back to the Institute? He had already had him, but he had had a Baley in the full possession of his faculties and along with him he had had two robots perfectly capable of defending Baley physically. It would be different now!

If the airfoil were disabled in a storm, Baley would be disabled emotionally. He would even be unconscious, perhaps, and would certainly not be able to resist being brought back. Nor would the two robots

object. With Baley clearly ill, their only appropriate reaction would be
to assist Amadiro's robots in rescuing him.

In fact, the two robots would have to come along with Baley and
would do so helplessly.

And if anyone ever questioned Amadiro's action, he could say that
he had feared for Baley in the storm; that he had tried to keep him at
the Institute and failed; that he had sent his robots to trail him and
assure his safety; and that, when the airfoil came to grief in the storm,
those robots brought Baley back to haven. Unless people understood
that it had been Amadiro who had ordered the airfoil tampered with
(and who would believe that—and how could one prove it?), the only
possible public reaction would be to praise Amadiro for his humani-
tarian feelings—all the more astonishing for having been expressed
toward a subhuman Earthman.

And what would Amadiro do with Baley then?

Nothing, except to keep him quiet and helpless for a time. Baley
was not himself the quarry. That was the point.

Amadiro would also have two robots and they would now be helpless. Their instructions forced them, in the strongest manner, to guard
Baley and, if Baley were ill and being cared for, they could only follow
Amadiro's orders if those orders were clearly and apparently for Baley's benefit. Nor would Baley be (perhaps) sufficiently himself to protect them with further orders—certainly not if he were kept under
sedation.

It was clear! It was clear! Amadiro had had Baley, Daneel, and Giskard—but in unusable fashion. He had sent them out into the storm
in order to bring them back and have them again—in usable fashion.
Especially Daneel! It was Daneel who was the key.

To be sure, Fastolfe would be searching for them eventually and
would find them, too, and retrieve them, but by then it would be too
late, wouldn't it?

And what did Amadiro want with Daneel?

Baley, his head aching, was sure he knew—but how could he possibly prove it?

He could think no more. —If he could opacify the windows, he
could make a little interior world again, enclosed and motionless, and
then maybe he could continue his thoughts.

But he did not know how to opacify the windows. He could only sit
there and look at the flagging storm beyond those windows, hear the
whip of rain against the windows, watch the fading lightning, and
listen to the muttering thunder.

He closed his eyes tightly. The eyelids made a wall, too, but he dared
not sleep.

The car door on his right opened. He heard the sighing noise it
made. He felt the cool, damp breeze enter, the temperature drop, the

sharp smell of things green and wet enter and drown out the faint and friendly smell of oil and upholstery that reminded him somehow of the City that he wondered if he would ever see again.

He opened his eyes and there was the odd sensation of a robotic face staring at him—and drifting sideways, yet not really moving. Baley felt dizzy.

The robot, seen as a darker shadow against the darkness, seemed a large one. He had, somehow, an air of capability about him. He said, "Your pardon, sir. Did you not have the company of two robots?"

"Gone," muttered Baley, acting as ill as he could and aware that it did not require acting. A brighter flash of the heavens made its way through the eyelids that were now half-open.

"Gone! Gone where, sir?" And then, as he waited for an answer, he said, "Are you ill, sir?"

Baley felt a distant twinge of satisfaction within the inner scrap of himself that was still capable of thinking. If the robot had been without special instruction, he would have responded to Baley's clear signs of illness before doing anything else. To have asked first about the robots implied hard and close-pressed directions as to their importance.

It fit.

He tried to assume a strength and normality he did not possess and said, "I am well. Don't concern yourself with me."

It could not possibly have convinced an ordinary robot, but this one had been so intensified in connection with Daneel (obviously) that he accepted it. He said, "Where have the robots gone, sir?"

"Back to the Robotics Institute."

"To the Institute? Why, sir?"

"They were called by Master Roboticist Amadiro and he ordered them to return. I am waiting for them."

"But why did you not go with them, sir?"

"Master Roboticist Amadiro did not wish me to be exposed to the storm. He ordered me to wait here. I am following Master Roboticist Amadiro's orders."

He hoped the repetition of the prestige-filled name with the inclusion of the honorific, together with the repetition of the word "order" would have its effect on the robot and persuade him to leave Baley where he was.

On the other hand, if they had been instructed, with particular care, to bring back Daneel, and if they were convinced that Daneel was already on his way back to the Institute, there would be a decline in the intensity of their need in connection with that robot. They would have time to think of Baley again. They would say—

The robot said, "But it appears you are not well, sir."

Baley felt another twinge of satisfaction. He said, "I am well."

Behind the robot, he could vaguely see a crowding of several other robots—he could not count them—with their faces gleaming in the occasional lightning flash. As Baley's eyes adapted to the return of darkness, he could see the dim shine of *their* eyes.

He turned his head. There were robots at the left door, too though that remained closed.

How many had Amadiro sent? Were they to have been returned by force, if necessary?

He said, "Master Roboticist Amadiro's orders were that my robots were to return to the Institute and I was to wait. You see that they are returning and that I am waiting. If you were sent to help, if you have a vehicle, find the robots, who are on their way back, and transport them. This airfoil is no longer operative." He tried to say it all without hesitation and firmly, as a well man would. He did not entirely succeed.

"They have returned on foot, sir?"

Baley said, "Find them. Your orders are clear."

There was hesitation. Clear hesitation.

Baley finally remembered to move his right foot—he hoped properly. He should have done it before, but his physical body was not responding properly to his thoughts.

Still the robots hesitated and Baley grieved over that. He was not a Spacer. He did not know the proper words, the proper tone, the proper air with which to handle robots with the proper efficiency. A skilled roboticist could, with a gesture, a lift of an eyebrow, direct a robot as though it were a marionette of which he held the strings. —Especially if the robot were of his own design.

But Baley was only an Earthman.

He frowned—that was easy to do in his misery—and whispered a weary "Go!" and motioned with his hands.

Perhaps that added the last small and necessary quantity of weight to his order—or perhaps an end had simply been reached to the time it took for the robots' positronic pathways to determine, by voltage and counter-voltage, how to sort out their instructions according to the Three Laws.

Either way, they had made up their minds and, after that, there was no further hesitation. They moved back to their vehicle, whatever and wherever it was, with such determined speed that they seemed simply to disappear.

The door the robot had held open now closed of its own accord. Baley had moved his foot in order to place it in the pathway of the closing door. He wondered distantly if his foot would be cut off cleanly or if its bones would be crushed, but he didn't move it. Surely no vehicle would be designed to make such a misadventure possible.

He was alone again. He had forced robots to leave a patently unwell human being by playing on the force of the orders given them by a competent robot master who had been intent on strengthening the Second Law for his own purposes—and had done it to the point where Baley's own quite apparent lies had subordinated the First Law to it.

How well he had done it, Baley thought with distant self-satisfaction—and became aware that the door which had swung shut was still ajar, held so by his foot, and that that foot had not been the least bit damaged as a result.

65

Baley felt cool air curling about his foot and a sprinkle of cool water. It was a frighteningly abnormal thing to sense, yet he could not allow the door to close, for he would then not know how to open it. (How did the robots open those doors? Undoubtedly, it was no puzzle to members of the culture, but in his reading on Auroran life, there was no careful instruction of just how one opens the door of a standard airfoil. Everything of importance is taken for granted. You're supposed to *know*, even though you are, in theory, being informed.)

He was groping in his pockets as he thought this and even the pockets were not easy to find. They were not in the right places and they were sealed, so that they had to be opened by fumbles till he found the precise motion that caused the seal to part. He pulled out a handkerchief, balled it, and placed it between the door and jamb so that the door would not entirely close. He then removed his foot.

Now to think—if he could. There was no point to keeping the door open unless he meant to get out. Was there, however, any purpose in getting out?

If he waited where he was, Giskard would eventually come back for him and, presumably, lead him to safety.

Dare he wait?

He did not know how long it would take Giskard to see Daneel to safety and then return.

But neither did he know how long it would take the pursuing robots to decide they would not find Daneel and Giskard on any road leading back to the Institute. (Surely it was impossible that Daneel and Giskard had actually moved backward toward the Institute in search of sanctuary. Baley had not actually ordered them not to—but what if that were the only feasible route? —No! Impossible!)

Baley shook his head in silent denial of the possibility and felt it ache in response. He put his hands to it and gritted his teeth.

How long would the pursuing robots continue to search before they would decide that Baley had misled them—or had been himself misled? Would they then return and take him in custody, very politely

and with great care not to harm him? Could he hold them off by
telling them he would die if exposed to the storm?

Would they believe that? Would they call the Institute to report?
Surely they would do *that*. And would human beings then arrive? *They*
would not be overly concerned about his welfare.

If Baley got out of the car and found some hiding place in the
surrounding trees, it would be that much harder for the pursuing robots to locate him—and that would gain him time.

It would also be harder for Giskard to locate him, but Giskard would
be under a much more intense instruction to guard Baley than the
pursuing robots were to find him. The primary task of the former
would be to locate Baley—and of the latter, to locate Daneel.

Besides, Giskard was programmed by Fastolfe himself and Amadiro,
however skillful, was no match for Fastolfe.

Surely, then, all things being equal, Giskard would be back before
the other robots could possibly be.

But would all things be equal? With a faint attempt at cynicism,
Baley thought: I'm worn-out and can't really think. I'm merely seizing
desperately at whatever will console me.

Still, what could he do but play the odds, as he conceived the odds
to be?

He leaned against the door and was out into the open. The handkerchief fell out into the wet, rank grass and he automatically bent
down to pick it up, holding it in his hands as he staggered away from
the car.

He was overwhelmed by the gusts of rain that soaked his face and
hands. After a short while, his wet clothes were clinging to his body
and he was shivering with cold.

There was a piercing splitting of the sky—too quick for him to close
his eyes against—and then a sharp hammering that stiffened him in
terror and made him clap his hands over his ears.

Had the storm returned? Or did it sound louder only because he
was out in the open?

He had to move. He had to move away from the car, so that the
pursuers would not find him too easily. He must not waver and remain
in its vicinity or he might as well have stayed inside—and dry.

He tried to wipe his face with the handkerchief, but it was as wet
as his face was and he let it go. It was useless.

He moved on, hands outstretched. Was there a moon that circled
Aurora? He seemed to recall there had been mention of such a thing
and he would have welcomed its light. —But what did it matter? Even
if it existed and were in the sky now, the clouds would obscure it.

He felt something. He could not see what it was, but he knew it to
be the rough bark of a tree. Undoubtedly a tree. Even a City man
would know that much.

And then he remembered that lightning might hit trees and might kill people. He could not remember that he had ever read a description of how it felt to be hit by lightning or if there were any measures to prevent it. He knew of no one on Earth who had been hit by lightning.

He felt his way about the tree and was in an agony of apprehension and fear. How much was halfway around, so that he would end up moving in the same direction?

Onward!

The underbrush was thick now and hard to get through. It was like bony, clutching fingers holding him. He pulled petulantly and he heard the tearing of cloth.

Onward!

His teeth were chattering and he was trembling.

Another flash. Not a bad one. For a moment, he caught a glimpse of his surroundings.

Trees! A number of them. He was in a grove of trees. Were many trees more dangerous than one tree where lightning was concerned?

He didn't know.

Would it help if he didn't actually touch a tree?

He didn't know that, either. Death by lightning simply wasn't a factor in the Cities and the historical novels (and sometimes histories) that mentioned it never went into detail.

He looked up at the dark sky and felt the wetness coming down. He wiped at his wet eyes with his wet hands.

He stumbled onward, trying to step high. At one point, he splashed through a narrow stream of water, sliding over the pebbles underlaying it.

How strange! It made him no wetter than he was.

He went on again. The robots would not find him. Would Giskard?

He didn't know where he was. Or where he was going. Or how far he was from anything.

If he wanted to return to the car, he couldn't.

If he was trying to find himself, he couldn't.

And the storm would continue forever and he would finally dissolve and pour down in a little stream of Baley and no one would ever find him again.

And his dissolved molecules would float down to the ocean.

Was there an ocean on Aurora?

Of course there was! It was larger than Earth's, but there was more ice at the Auroran poles.

Ah, he would float to the ice and freeze there, glistening in the cold orange sun.

His hands were touching a tree again—wet hands—wet tree—rumble of thunder—funny he didn't see the flash of lightning—lightning came first—was he hit?

.He didn't feel anything—except the ground.

The ground was under him because his fingers were scrabbling into cold mud. He turned his head so he could breathe. It was rather comfortable. He didn't have to walk anymore. He could wait. Giskard would find him.

He was suddenly very sure of it. Giskard would have to find him because—

No, he had forgotten the because. It was the second time he had forgotten something. Before he went to sleep —Was it the same thing he had forgotten each time?— The same thing?—

It didn't matter.

It would be all right—all—

And he lay there, alone and unconscious, in the rain at the base of a tree, while the storm beat on.

16.

66

Afterward, looking back and estimating times, it would appear that Baley had remained unconscious not less than ten minutes and not more than twenty.

At the time, though, it might have been anything from zero to infinity. He was conscious of a voice. He could not hear the words it spoke, just a voice. He puzzled over the fact that it sounded odd and solved the matter to his satisfaction by recognizing it as a woman's voice.

There were arms around him, lifting him, heaving him. One arm—his arm—dangled. His head lolled.

He tried feebly to straighten out, but nothing happened. The woman's voice again.

He opened his eyes wearily. He was aware of being cold and wet and suddenly realized that water was not striking him. And it was not dark, not entirely. There was a dim suffusing light and, by it, he saw a robot's face.

He recognized it. "Giskard," he whispered and with that he remembered the storm and the flight. And Giskard had reached him first; he had found him before the other robots had.

Baley thought contentedly: I knew he would.

He let his eyes close again and felt himself moving rapidly but with the slight—yet definite—unevenness that meant he was being carried by someone who was walking. Then a stop and a slow adjustment until he was resting on something quite warm and comfortable. He knew it was the seat of a car covered, perhaps, with toweling, but did not question how he knew.

Then there was the sensation of smooth motion through the air and the feeling of soft absorbent fabric over his face and hands, the tearing open of his blouse, cold air upon his chest, and then the drying and blotting again.

After that, the sensations crowded in upon him.

He was in an establishment. There were flashes of walls, of illumination, of objects (miscellaneous shapes of furnishings) which he saw now and then when he opened his eyes.

He felt his clothes being stripped off methodically and made a few feeble and useless attempts to cooperate, then he felt warm water and vigorous scrubbing. It went on and on and he didn't want it to stop.

At one point, a thought occurred to him and he seized the arm that was holding him. "Giskard! Giskard!"

He heard Giskard's voice. "I am here, sir."

"Giskard, is Daneel safe?"

"He is quite safe, sir."

"Good." Baley closed his eyes again and made no effort whatever in connection with the drying. He felt himself turned over and over in the stream of dry air and then he was being dressed again in something like a warm robe.

Luxury! Nothing like this had happened to him since he was an infant and he was suddenly sorry for the babies for whom everything was done and who were not sufficiently conscious of it to enjoy it.

Or did they? Was the hidden memory of that infant luxury a determinant of adult behavior? Was his own feeling now just an expression of the delight of being an infant again?

And he had heard a woman's voice. Mother?

No, that couldn't possibly be.

—Mamma?

He was sitting in a chair now. He could sense as much and he could also feel, somehow, that the short, happy period of renewed infancy was coming to an end. He had to return to the sad world of self-consciousness and self-help.

But there had been a woman's voice. —What woman?

Baley opened his eyes. "Gladia?"

67

It was a question, a surprised question, but deep within himself he was not really surprised. Thinking back, he had, of course, recognized her voice.

He looked around. Giskard was standing in his alcove, but he ignored him. First things first.

He said, "Where's Daneel?"

Gladia said, "He has cleaned and dried himself in the robot's quarters and he has dry clothing. He is surrounded by my household staff and they have their instructions. I can tell you that no outsider will approach within fifty meters of my establishment in any direction without our all knowing it at once.—Giskard is cleaned and dried as well."

"Yes, I can see that," said Baley. He was not concerned with Giskard, only with Daneel. He was relieved that Gladia seemed to accept the necessity of guarding Daneel and that he would not have to face the complications of explaining the matter.

Yet there was one breach in the wall of security and a note of querulousness entered in his voice as he said, "Why did you leave him, Gladia? With you gone, there was no human being in the house to stop the approach of a band of outside robots. Daneel could have been taken by force."

"Nonsense," said Gladia with spirit. "We were not gone long and Dr. Fastolfe had been informed. Many of his robots had joined mine and he could be on the spot in minutes if needed—and I'd like to see any band of outside robots withstand *him*."

"Have you seen Daneel since you returned, Gladia?"

"Of course! He's safe, I tell you."

"Thank you!" Baley relaxed and closed his eyes. Oddly enough, he thought: It wasn't so bad.

Of course it wasn't. He had survived, hadn't he? When he thought that, something inside himself grinned and was happy.

He had survived, hadn't he?

He opened his eyes and said, "How did you find me, Gladia?"

"It was Giskard. They had come here—both of them—and Giskard explained the situation to me quickly. I set right about securing Daneel, but he wouldn't budge until I had promised to order Giskard out after you. He was very eloquent. His responses with respect to you are very intense, Elijah.

"Daneel remained behind, of course. It made him very unhappy, but Giskard insisted that I order him to stay at the very top of my voice. You must have given Giskard some mighty strict orders. Then we got in touch with Dr. Fastolfe and, after that, we took my personal airfoil."

Baley shook his head wearily. "You should not have come along, Gladia. Your place was here, making sure Daneel was safe."

Gladia's face twisted into scorn. "And leave you dying in the storm, for all we knew? Or being taken up by Dr. Fastolfe's enemies? I have a little holograph of myself letting that happen. No, Elijah. I might have been needed to keep the other robots away from you if they had gotten to you first. I may not be much good in most ways, but any Solarian can handle a mob of robots, let me tell you. We're used to it."

"But how did you find me?"

"It wasn't so terribly hard. Actually, your airfoil wasn't far away, so that we could have walked it, except for the storm. We—"

Baley said, "You mean we had almost made it to Fastolfe's?"

"Yes," said Gladia. "Either your airfoil, in being damaged, wasn't damaged sufficiently to force you to a standstill sooner or Giskard's skill kept it going for longer than the vandals had anticipated. Which is a good thing. If you had come down closer to the Institute, they might have gotten you all. Anyway, we took my airfoil to where yours had come down. Giskard knew where it was, of course, and we got out—"

"And you got all wet, didn't you, Gladia?"

"Not a bit," she replied. "I had a large rain shade and a light sphere, too. My shoes got muddy and my feet got a little damp because I didn't have time to spray on Latex, but there's no harm in that. —Anyway, we were back at your airfoil less than half an hour after Giskard and Daneel had left you and, of course, you weren't there."

"I had tried—" began Baley.

"Yes, we know. I thought they—the others—had taken you away because Giskard said you were being followed. But Giskard found your handkerchief about fifty meters from the airfoil and he said that you must have wandered off in that direction. Giskard said it was an illogical thing to do, but that human beings were often illogical, so that we should search for you.—So we looked—both of us—using the light sphere, but it was he who found you. He said he saw the infrared glimmer of your body heat at the base of the tree and we brought you back."

Baley said, with a spark of annoyance, "Why was my leaving an illogical thing to do?"

"He didn't say, Elijah. Do you wish to ask him?" She gestured toward Giskard.

Baley said, "Giskard, what's this?"

Giskard's impassivity was disrupted at once and his eyes focused on Baley. He said, "I felt that you had exposed yourself to the storm unnecessarily. If you had waited, we would have brought you here sooner."

"The other robots might have gotten to me first."

"They did—but you had sent them away, sir."

"How do you know that?"

"There were many robotic footprints around the doors on either side, sir, but there was no sign of dampness within the airfoil, as there would have been if wet arms had reached in to lift you out. I judged you would not have gotten out of the airfoil of your own accord in order to join them, sir. And, having sent them away, you need not have feared they would return very quickly, since it was Daneel they were after—by your own estimate of the situation—and not you. In addition, you might have been certain that I would have been back quickly."

Baley muttered, "I reasoned precisely in that manner but I felt that confusing the issue might help further. I did what seemed best to me and you did find me, even so."

"Yes, sir."

Baley said, "But why bring me here? If we were close to Gladia's establishment, we were just as close, perhaps closer, to Dr. Fastolfe's."

"Not quite, sir. This residence was somewhat closer and I judged, from the urgency of your orders, that every moment counted in securing Daneel's safety. Daneel concurred in this, though he was most reluctant to leave you. Once he was here, I felt you would want to be here, too, so that you could, if you desired, assure yourself of his safety firsthand."

Baley nodded and said grumpily (he was still annoyed at that remark concerning his illogicality), "You did well, Giskard."

Gladia said, "Is it important that you see Dr. Fastolfe, Elijah? I can have him summoned here. Or you can view him trimensionally."

Baley leaned back in his chair again. He had leisure to realize that his thought processes were blunted and that he was very tired. It would do him no good to face Fastolfe now. He said, "No. I'll see him tomorrow after breakfast. Time enough. And then I think I'll be seeing this man, Kelden Amadiro, the head of the Robotics Institute. And a high official—what d'you call him?—the Chairman. *He* will be there, too, I suppose."

"You look terribly tired, Elijah," said Gladia. "Of course, we don't have those microorganisms—those germs and viruses—that you have on Earth and you've been cleaned out, so you won't get any of the diseases they have all over your planet, but you're clearly tired."

Baley thought: After all that, no cold? No flu? No pneumonia?—There was something to being on a Spacer world at that.

He said, "I admit I'm tired, but that can be cured by a bit of rest."

"Are you hungry? It's dinnertime."

Baley made a face. "I don't feel like eating."

"I'm not sure that's wise. You don't want a heavy meal, perhaps, but how about some hot soup. It will do you good."

Baley felt the urge to smile. She might be Solarian, but given the proper circumstances she sounded exactly like an Earth-woman. He suspected that this would be true of Aurorans as well. There are some things that differences in culture don't touch.

He said, "Do you have soup available? I don't want to be a problem."

"How can you be a problem? I have a staff—not a large one, as on Solaria, but enough to prepare any reasonable item of food on short order. —Now you just sit there and tell me what kind of soup you would like. It will all be taken care of."

Baley couldn't resist. "Chicken soup?"

"Of course." Then innocently, "Just what I would have suggested—and with lumps of chicken, so that it will be substantial."

The bowl was put before him with surprising speed. He said, "Aren't you going to eat, Gladia?"

"I've eaten already, while you were being bathed and treated."

"Treated?"

"Only routine biochemical adjustment, Elijah. You had been rather psychic-damaged and we wanted no repercussions.—Do eat!'

Baley lifted an experimental spoonful to his lips. It was not bad chicken soup, though it had the queer tendency of Auroran food to be rather spicier than Baley would prefer. Or perhaps it was prepared with different spices than those he was used to.

He remembered his mother suddenly—a sharp thrust of memory that made her appear younger than he himself was right now. He remembered her standing over him when he rebelled at eating his "nice soup."

She would say to him, "Come, Lije. This is real chicken and very expensive. Even the Spacers don't have anything better."

They didn't. He called to her in his mind across the years: They don't, Mom!

Really! If he could trust memory and allow for the power of youthful taste buds, his mother's chicken soup, when it wasn't dulled by repetition, was far superior.

He sipped again and again—and when he finished, he muttered in a shamefaced way, "Would there be a little more?"

"As much as you want, Elijah."

"Just a little more."

Gladia said to him, as he was finishing, "Elijah, this meeting tomorrow morning—"

"Yes, Gladia?"

"Does it mean that your investigation is over? Do you know what happened to Jander?"

Baley said judiciously, "I have an idea as to what might have happened to Jander. I don't think I can necessarily persuade anyone that I am right."

"Then why are you having the conference?"

"It's not my idea, Gladia. It's Master Roboticist Amadiro's idea. He objects to the investigation and he's going to try to have me sent back to Earth."

"Is he the one who tampered with your airfoil and tried to have his robots take Daneel?"

"I think he is."

"Well, can't he be tried and convicted and punished for that?"

"He certainly could," said Baley feelingly, "except for the very small problem that I can't prove it."

"And can he do all that and get away with it—and stop the investigation, too?"

"I'm afraid he has a good chance of being able to do so. As he himself says, people who don't expect justice don't have to suffer disappointment."

"But he mustn't. You mustn't let him. You've got to complete your investigation and find out the truth."

Baley sighed. "What if I can't find out the truth? Or what if I can—but can't make people listen to me?"

"You *can* find out the truth. And you *can* make people listen to you."

"You have a touching faith in me, Gladia. Still, if the Auroran World Legislature wants to send me back and orders the investigation ended, there's nothing I'm going to be able to do about it."

"Surely you won't be willing to go back with nothing accomplished."

"Of course I won't. It's worse than just accomplishing nothing, Gladia. I'll go back with my career ruined and with Earth's future destroyed."

"Then don't let them do that, Elijah."

And he said, "Jehoshaphat, Gladia, I'm going to try not to, but I can't lift a planet with my bare hands. You can't ask me for miracles."

Gladia nodded and, eyes downcast, put her fist to her mouth, sitting there motionlessly, as though in thought. It took a while for Baley to realize that she was weeping soundlessly.

68

Baley stood up quickly and walked around the table to her. He noted absently—and with some annoyance—that his legs were trembling and that there was a tic in the muscle of his right thigh.

"Gladia," he said urgently, "don't cry."

"Don't bother, Elijah," she whispered. "It will pass."

He stood helplessly at her side, reaching out to her yet hesitating. "I'm not touching you," he said. "I don't think I had better do so, but—"

"Oh, touch me. Touch me. I'm not all that fond of my body and I won't catch anything from you. I'm not—what I used to be."

So Baley reached out and touched her elbow and stroked it very slightly and clumsily with his fingertips. "I'll do what I can tomorrow, Gladia," he said. "I'll give it my very best try."

She rose at that, turned toward him, and said, "Oh, Elijah."

Automatically, scarcely knowing what he was doing, Baley held out his arms. And, just as automatically, she walked into them and he was holding her while her head cradled against his chest.

He held her as lightly as he could, waiting for her to realize that she was embracing an Earthman. (She had undoubtedly embraced a humaniform robot, but he had been no Earthman.)

She sniffed loudly and spoke while her mouth was half-obscured in Baley's shirt.

She said, "It isn't fair. It's because I'm a Solarian. No one really cares what happened to Jander and they would if I were an Auroran. It just boils down to prejudice and politics."

Baley thought: Spacers are *people*. This is exactly what Jessie would say in a similar situation. And if it were Gremionis who was holding Gladia, he'd say exactly what I'll say—if I knew what I would say.

And then he said, "That's not entirely so. I'm sure Dr. Fastolfe cares what happened to Jander."

"No, he doesn't. Not really. He just wants to have his way in the Legislature, and that Amadiro wants to have *his* way, and either one would trade Jander for his way."

"I promise you, Gladia, I won't trade Jander for anything."

"No? If they tell you that you can go back to Earth with your career saved and no penalty for your world, provided you forget all about Jander, what would you do?"

"There's no use setting up hypothetical situations that can't possibly come to pass. They're not going to give me anything in return for abandoning Jander. They're just going to try to send me back with nothing at all except ruin for me and my world. But, if they were to let me, I would get the man who destroyed Jander and see to it that he was adequately punished."

"What do you mean *if* they were to let you? *Make* them let you!"

Baley smiled bitterly. "If you think Aurorans pay no attention to you because you're a Solarian, imagine how little you would get if you were from Earth, as I am."

He held her closer, forgetting he was from Earth, even as he said the word. "But I'll try, Gladia. It's no use raising hopes, but I don't have a completely empty hand. I'll try—" His voice trailed off.

"You keep saying you'll try. —But *how*?" She pushed away from him a bit to look up into his face.

Baley said, bewildered, "Why, I may—"

"Find the murderer?"

"Whatever. —Gladia, please, I must sit down."

He reached out for the table, leaning on it.

She said, "What is it, Elijah?"

"I've had a difficult day, obviously, and I haven't quite recovered, I think."

"You'd better go to bed, then."

"To tell you the truth, Gladia, I would like to."

She released him, her face full of concern and with no further room in it for tears. She lifted her arm and made a rapid motion and he was (it seemed to him) surrounded by robots at once.

And when he was in bed eventually and the last robot had left him, he found himself staring up at darkness.

He could not tell whether it was still raining Outside or whether some feeble lightning flashes were still making their last sleepy sparks, but he knew he heard no thunder.

He drew a deep breath and thought: Now what is it I have promised Gladia? What will happen tomorrow?

Last act: Failure?

And as Baley drifted into the borderland of sleep, he thought of that unbelievable flash of illumination that had come before sleep.

Twice before, it had happened. Once the night before when, as now, he was falling asleep and once earlier this evening when he had slipped into unconsciousness beneath the tree in the storm. Each time, something had occurred to him, some enlightenment that had unmystified the problem as the lightning had undarkened the night.

And it had stayed with him as briefly as the lightning had.

What was it?

Would it come to him again?

This time, he tried consciously to seize it, to catch the elusive truth. —Or was it the elusive illusion? Was it the slipping away of conscious reason and the coming of attractive nonsense that one couldn't analyze properly in the absence of a properly thinking brain?

The search for whatever it was, however, slid slowly away. It would no more come on call than a unicorn would in a world in which unicorns did not exist.

It was easier to think of Gladia and of how she had felt. There had been the direct touch of the silkiness of her blouse, but beneath it were the small and delicate arms, the smooth back.

Would he have dared to kiss her if his legs had not begun to buckle beneath him? Or would that have been going too far?

He heard his breath exhale in a soft snore and, as always, that embarrassed him. He flogged himself awake and thought of Gladia again. Before he left, surely—but not if he could gain nothing for her in ret— Would that be payment for services ren—He heard the soft snore again and cared less this time.

Gladia— He had never thought he would see her again—let alone touch her—let alone hold her—hold her—

And he had no way of telling at what point he passed from thought to dream.

He was holding her again, as before— But there was no blouse— and her skin was warm and soft—and his hand moved slowly down

the slope of her shoulder blade and down the hidden ridges of her
ribs—

There was a total aura of reality about it. All of his senses were
engaged. He smelled her hair and his lips tasted the faint, faint salt of
her skin—and now somehow they were no longer standing. Had they
lain down or were they lying down from the start? And what had
happened to the light?

He felt the mattress beneath him and the cover over him—darkness—and she was still in his arms and her body was bare.

He was shocked awake. "Gladia?"

Rising inflection—disbelieving—

"Shh. Elijah." She placed the fingers of one hand gently on his lips.
"Don't say anything."

She might as well have asked him to stop the current of his blood.

He said, "What are you *doing*?"

She said, "Don't you *know* what I'm doing? I'm in bed with you."

"But why?"

"Because I want to." Her body moved against his.

She pinched the top of his night garment and the seam that held it
together fell apart.

"Don't move, Elijah. You're tired and I don't want you to wear
yourself out further."

Elijah felt a warmth stirring within him. He decided not to protect
Gladia against herself. He said, "I'm not *that* tired, Gladia."

"No," she said sharply. "Rest! I want you to rest. Don't move."

Her mouth was on his as though intent on forcing him to keep
quiet. He relaxed and the small thought flitted past him that he was
following orders, that he *was* tired and was willing to be done to
rather than to do. And, tinged with shame, it occurred to him that
it rather diluted his guilt. (I couldn't help it, he heard himself say.
She made me.) Jehoshaphat, how cowardly! How unbearably demeaning!

But those thoughts washed away, too. Somehow there was soft music in the air and the temperature had risen a bit. The cover had
vanished and so had his nightclothes. He felt his head moved into the
cradle of her arms and pressed against softness.

With a detached surprise, he knew, from her position, that the softness was her left breast and that it was centered, contrastingly, with
its nipple hard against his lips.

Softly, she was singing to the music, a sleepily joyful tune he did
not recognize.

She rocked gently back and forth and her fingertips grazed his chin
and neck. He relaxed, content to do nothing, to let her initiate and
carry through every activity. When she moved his arms, he did not
resist and let them rest wherever she placed them.

He did not help and, when he did respond with heightened excitement and climax, it was only out of helplessness to do otherwise.

She seemed tireless and he did not want her to stop. Aside from the sensuality of sexual response, he felt again what he had felt earlier, the total luxury of the infant's passivity.

And, finally, he could respond no more and, it seemed, she could do no more and she lay with her head in the hollow where his left shoulder met his chest and her left arm lay across his ribs, her fingers stroking the short, curling hairs tenderly.

He seemed to hear her murmuring, "Thank you— Thank you—"

For what? he wondered.

He was scarcely conscious of her now, for this utterly soft end of a hard day was as soporific as the fabled nepenthe and he could feel himself slipping away, as though his fingertips were relaxing from the edge of the cliff of harsh reality in order that he might drop—drop—through the soft clouds of gathering sleep into the slowly swaying ocean of dreams.

And as he did so, what had not come on call came of itself. For the third time, the curtain was lifted and all the events since he had left Earth shuffled once more into hard focus. Again, it was all clear. He struggled to speak, to hear the words he needed to hear, to fix them and make them part of his thought processes, but though he clutched at them with every tendril of his mind, they slipped past and through and were gone.

So that, in this respect, Baley's second day on Aurora ended very much as his first had.

17.

The
Chairman

70

When Baley opened his eyes, it was to find sunlight streaming through the window and he welcomed it. To his still-sleepy surprise, he welcomed it.

It meant the storm was over and it was as though the storm had never happened. Sunlight—when viewed only as an alternative to the smooth, soft, warm, controlled light of the Cities—could only be considered harsh and uncertain. But compare it with the storm and it was the promise of peace itself. Everything, Baley thought, is relative and he knew he would never think of sunshine as entirely evil again.

"Partner Elijah?" Daneel was standing at the side of the bed. A little behind him stood Giskard.

Baley's long face dissolved in a rare smile of pure pleasure. He held out his hands, one to each. "Jehoshaphat, men"—and he was totally unaware, at the moment, of any inappropriateness in the word—"when I last saw you two together, I wasn't in the least sure I would ever see either of you again."

"Surely," said Daneel softly, "none of us would have been harmed under any circumstances."

"With the sunlight coming in, I see that," said Baley. "But last night, I felt as though the storm would kill me and I was certain you were in deadly danger, Daneel. It even seemed possible that Giskard might be damaged in some way, trying to defend me against overwhelming odds. Melodramatic, I admit, but I wasn't quite myself, you know."

"We were aware of that, sir," said Giskard. "That was what made it difficult for us to leave you, despite your urgent order. We trust that this is not a source of displeasure for you at present."

"Not at all, Giskard."

"And," said Daneel, "we also know that you have been well cared for since we left you."

It was only then that Baley remembered the events of the night before.

Gladia!

He looked about in sudden astonishment. She was not anywhere in the room. Had he imagined—

No, of course not. That would be impossible.

And then he looked at Daneel with a frown, as though suspecting his remark to bear a libidinous character.

But no, that would be impossible, too. A robot, however humaniform, would not be designed to take lubricious delight in innuendo.

He said, "*Quite* well cared for. But what I need at the moment is to be shown to the Personal."

"We are here, sir," said Giskard, "to direct you and help you through the morning. Miss Gladia felt you would be more comfortable with us than with any of her own staff and she stressed that we were to leave nothing wanting for your comfort."

Baley looked doubtful. "How far did she instruct you to go? I feel pretty well now, so I don't have to have anyone wash and dry me. I can take care of myself. She does understand that, I hope."

"You need fear no embarrassment, Partner Elijah," said Daneel, with the small smile that (it seemed to Baley) came at those moments when, in a human being, it might be judged that a feeling of affection would have arisen. "We are merely to see to your comfort. If, at any time, you are most comfortable in privacy, we will wait at some distance."

"In that case, Daneel, we're all set." Baley scrambled out of bed. It pleased him to see that he felt quite steady on his legs. The night's rest and the treatment when he was brought back (whatever it might have been) had done marvels. —And Gladia, too.

71

Still nude and just damp enough from his shower to feel thoroughly fresh, Baley, having brushed his hair, studied the result critically. It seemed natural that he would have breakfast with Gladia and he wasn't certain how he might be received. It might be best, perhaps, to take the attitude that nothing had happened and to be guided by her attitude. And somehow, he thought, it might help if he looked reasonably good—provided that was within the realm of the possible. He made a dissatisfied face at his reflection in the mirror.

"Daneel!" he called.

"Yes, Partner Elijah."

Speaking through and around toothpaste, Baley said, "Those are new clothes you are wearing, it seems."

"Not mine originally, Partner Elijah. They had been friend Jander's."

Baley's eyebrows climbed. "She let you have Jander's?"

"Miss Gladia did not wish me to be unclothed while waiting for my storm-drenched items to be washed and to dry. Those are ready now, but Miss Gladia says I may keep these."

"When did she say that?"

"This morning, Partner Elijah."

"She's awake, then?"

"Indeed. And you will be joining her at breakfast when you are ready."

Baley's lips tightened. It was odd that, at the moment, he was more concerned with having to face Gladia than, a little later on, the Chairman. The matter of the Chairman was, after all, in the lap of the Fates. He had decided on his strategy and it would either work or it would not work. As for Gladia—he simply had no strategy.

Well, he would have to face her.

He said, with as careful an air of indifference as he might manage, "And how is Miss Gladia this morning?"

Daneel said, "She seems well."

"Cheerful? Depressed?"

Daneel hesitated. "It is difficult to judge the inner attitude of a human being. There is nothing in her behavior to indicate internal turmoil."

Baley cast a quick eye on Daneel and again he wondered if he were referring to the events of last night. —And again he dismissed the possibility.

Nor did it do any good to study Daneel's face. One could not stare at a robot to guess thoughts from expression, for there were no thoughts in the human sense.

He stepped out into the bedroom and looked at the clothes that had been laid out for him, considering them thoughtfully and wondering if he could put them on without error and without requiring robotic help. The storm and the night were over and he wanted to assume the mantle of adulthood and independence once again.

He said, "What is this?" He held up a long sash covered with an intricately colored arabesque.

"It is a pajama sash," said Daneel. "It is purely ornamental. It passes over the left shoulder and is tied at the right side of the waist. It is traditionally worn at breakfast on some Spacer worlds but is not very popular on Aurora."

"Then why should I wear it?"

"Miss Gladia thought it would become you, Partner Elijah. The method of tieing is rather intricate and I will be glad to help you."

Jehoshaphat, thought Baley ruefully, she wants me to be pretty. What does she have in mind?

Don't think about it!

Baley said, "Never mind. I'll manage with a simple bowknot. —But listen, Daneel, after breakfast I will be going over to Fastolfe's, where I will meet with him, with Amadiro, and with the Chairman of the Legislature. I don't know if there will be any others present."

"Yes, Partner Elijah. I am aware of that. I don't think there will be others present."

"Well, then," said Baley, beginning to put on his undergarments and doing it slowly so as to make no mistake and thus find it unnecessary to appeal for help to Daneel, "tell me about the Chairman. I know from my reading that he is the nearest thing to an executive officer that there is on Aurora, but I gathered from that same reading that the position is purely honorary. He has no power, I take it."

Daneel said, "I am afraid, Partner Elijah—"

Giskard interrupted. "Sir, I am more aware of the political situation on Aurora than friend Daneel is. I have been in operation for much longer. Would you be willing to have me answer the question?"

"Why, certainly, Giskard. Go ahead."

"When the government of Aurora was first set up, sir," began Giskard in a didactic way, as though an information reel within him were methodically spinning, "it was intended that the executive officer fulfill only ceremonial duties. He was to greet dignitaries from other worlds, open all meetings of the Legislature, preside over its deliberations, and vote only to break a tie. After the River Controversy, however—"

"Yes, I read about that," said Baley. It had been a particularly dull episode in Auroran history, in which impenetrable arguments over the proper division of hydroelectric power had led to the nearest approach to civil war the planet had ever seen. "You needn't go into details."

"No, sir," said Giskard. "After the River Controversy, however, there was a general determination never to allow controversy to endanger Auroran society again. It has become customary, therefore, to settle all disputes in a private and peaceable manner outside the Legislature. When the legislators finally vote, it is in an agreed-upon fashion, so that there is always a large majority on one side or the other.

"The key figure in the settlement of disputes is the Chairman of the Legislature. He is held to be above the struggle and his power— which, although nil in theory, is considerable in practice—only holds as long as he is seen to be so. The Chairman therefore jealously guards his objectivity and, as long as he succeeds in this, it is he who usually makes the decision that settles any controversy in one direction or another."

Baley said, "You mean that the Chairman will listen to me, to Fastolfe, and to Amadiro, and then come to a decision?"

"Possibly. On the other hand, sir, he may remain uncertain and require further testimony, further thought—or both."

"And if the Chairman does come to a decision, will Amadiro bow to it if it is against him—or will Fastolfe bow if it is against *him?*"

"That is not an absolute necessity. There are almost always some who will not accept the Chairman's decision and both Dr. Amadiro and Dr. Fastolfe are headstrong and obstinate individuals—if one may

judge from their actions. Most of the legislators, however, will go along
with the Chairman's decision, whatever that might be. Dr. Fastolfe or
Dr. Amadiro—whichever it may be who will be decided against by the
Chairman—will then be sure to find himself in a small minority when
the vote is taken."

"How sure, Giskard?"

"Almost sure. The Chairman's term of office is ordinarily thirty
years, with the opportunity for reelection by the Legislature for another thirty years. If, however, a vote were to go against the Chairman's recommendation, the Chairman would be forced to resign
forthwith and there would be a governmental crisis while the Legislature tried to find another Chairman under conditions of bitter dispute. Few legislators are willing to risk that and the chance of getting
a majority to vote against the Chairman, when that is the consequence, is almost nil."

"Then," said Baley ruefully, "everything depends on this morning's
conference."

"That is very likely."

"Thank you, Giskard."

Gloomily, Baley arranged and rearranged his line of thought. It
seemed hopeful to him, but he did not have any idea what Amadiro
might say or what the Chairman might be like. It was Amadiro who
had initiated the meeting and *he* must feel confident, sure of himself.

It was then that Baley remembered that once again, when he was
falling asleep, with Gladia in his arms, he had seen—or thought he
had seen—or imagined he had seen—the meaning of all the events on
Aurora. Everything had seemed clear—obvious—certain. And once
more, for the third time, it was gone as though it had never been.

And with that thought, his hopes seemed to go, too.

72

Daneel led Baley into the room where breakfast was being served—
it seemed more intimate than an ordinary dining room. It was small
and plain, with no more in the way of furnishings than a table and
two chairs, and when Daneel retired, he did not move into a niche.
In fact, there were no niches and, for a moment, Baley found himself
alone—entirely alone—in the room.

That he was not really alone, he was certain. There would be robots
on instant call. Still, it was a room for two—a no-robots room—a room
(Baley hesitated at the thought) for lovers.

On the table there were two stacks of pancakelike objects that did
not smell like pancakes but smelled good. Two containers of what

looked like melted butter (but might not be) flanked them. There was
a pot of the hot drink (which Baley had tried and had not liked very
much) that substituted for coffee.

Gladia walked in, dressed in rather prim fashion and with her hair
glistening, as though freshly conditioned. She paused a moment, her
face wearing a half-smile. "Elijah?"

Baley, caught a little by surprise at the sudden appearance, jumped
to his feet. "How are you, Gladia?" He stuttered a bit.

She ignored that. She seemed cheerful, carefree. She said, "If you're
worried about Daneel not being in sight, don't be. He's completely
safe and he'll stay so. As for us—" She came to him, standing close,
and put a hand slowly to his cheek, as once, long ago, she had done
in Solaria.

She laughed lightly. "That was all I did then, Elijah. Do you remember?"

Elijah nodded silently.

"Did you sleep well, Elijah? —Sit down, dear."

He sat down. "Very well. —Thank you, Gladia." He hesitated before
deciding not to return the endearment in kind.

She said, "Don't thank me. I've had my best night's sleep in weeks
and I wouldn't have if I hadn't gotten out of bed after I was sure you
were sleeping soundly. If I had stayed—as I wanted to—I would have
been annoying you before the night was over and you would not have
gotten your rest."

He recognized the need for gallantry. "There are some things more
important than r-rest, Gladia," he said, but with such formality that
she laughed again.

"Poor Elijah," she said. "You're embarrassed."

The fact that she recognized that embarrassed him even more. Baley
had been prepared for contrition, disgust, shame, affected indifference, tears—everything but the frankly erotic attitude she had assumed.

She said, "Well, don't suffer so. You're hungry. You hardly ate last
night. Get some calories inside you and you'll feel more carnal."

Baley looked doubtfully at the pancakes that weren't.

Gladia said, "Oh! You've probably never seen these. They're Solarian delicacies. Pachinkas! I had to reprogram my chef before he could
make them properly. In the first place, you have to use imported Solarian grain. It won't work with the Auroran varieties. And they're
stuffed. Actually, there are a thousand stuffings you can use, but this
is my favorite and I know you'll like it, too. I won't tell you what's in
it, except for chestnut puree and a touch of honey, but try it and tell
me what you think. You can eat it with your fingers, but be careful
how you bite into it."

She picked one up, holding it daintily between the thumb and middle finger of each hand, then took a small bite, slowly, and licked at the golden, semiliquid filling that flowed out.

Baley imitated her action. The pachinka was hard to the touch and not too hot to hold. He put one end cautiously in his mouth and found it resisted biting. He put more muscle into it and the pachinka cracked and he found the contents flowing over his hands.

"The bite was too large and too forceful," said Gladia, rushing to him with a napkin. "Now lick at it. No one eats a pachinka neatly. There's no such thing. You're supposed to wallow in it. Ideally you're supposed to eat it in the nude, then take a shower."

Baley tried a hesitant lick and his expression was clear enough.

"You like it, don't you?" said Gladia.

"It's delicious," said Baley and he bit away at it slowly and gently. It wasn't too sweet and it seemed to soften and melt in the mouth. It scarcely required swallowing.

He ate three pachinkas and it was only shame that kept him from asking for more. He licked at his fingers without urging and eschewed the use of napkins, for he wanted none of it to be wasted on an inanimate object.

"Dip your fingers and hands in the cleanser, Elijah," and she showed him. The "melted butter" was a finger bowl, obviously.

Baley did as he was shown and then dried his hands. He sniffed at them and there was no odor whatever.

She said, "*Are* you embarrassed about last night, Elijah? Is that all you feel?"

What did one say? Baley wondered.

Finally, he nodded. "I'm afraid I am, Gladia. It's not all I feel, by twenty kilometers or more, but I *am* embarrassed. Stop and think. I'm an Earthman and you know that, but for the time being you're repressing it and 'Earthman' is only a meaningless disyllabic sound to you. Last night you were sorry for me, concerned over my problem with the storm, feeling toward me as you would toward a child, and—sympathizing with me, perhaps, out of the vulnerability produced in you by your own loss—you came to me. But that feeling will pass—I'm surprised it hasn't passed already—and then you will remember that I am an Earthman and you will feel ashamed, demeaned, and dirtied. You will hate me for what I have done for you and I don't want to be hated. —I don't want to be hated, Gladia." (If he looked as unhappy as he felt, he looked unhappy indeed.)

She must have thought so, for she reached out to him and stroked his hand. "I won't hate you, Elijah. Why should I? You did nothing to me that I can object to. I did it to you and I'll be glad for the rest of my life that I did. You freed me by a touch two years ago, Elijah, and last night you freed me again. I needed to know, two years ago, that I could feel desire—and last night I needed to know that I could feel desire *again* after Jander. Elijah—stay with me. It would be—"

He cut her off earnestly. "How can that be, Gladia? I must go back to my own world. I have duties and goals there and you cannot come with me. You could not live the kind of life that is lived on Earth. You would die of Earthly diseases—if the crowds and enclosure did not kill you first. Surely you understand."

"I understand about Earth," said Gladia with a sigh, "but surely you needn't leave immediately."

"Before the morning is over, I may be ordered off the planet by the Chairman."

"You won't be," said Gladia energetically. "You won't let yourself be. —And if you are, we can go to another Spacer world. There are dozens we can choose from. Does Earth mean so much to you that you wouldn't live on a Spacer world?"

Baley said, "I could be evasive, Gladia, and point out that no other Spacer world would let me make my home there permanently—and you know that's so. The greater truth is, though, that even if some Spacer world *would* accept me, Earth means so much to me that I would have to return. —Even if it meant leaving you."

"And never visiting Aurora again? Never seeing me again?"

"If I could see you again, I would," Baley said, wishing. "Over and over again, believe me. But what's the use of saying so? You know I'm not likely to be invited back. And you know I can't return without an invitation."

Gladia said in a low voice, "I don't want to believe that, Elijah."

Baley said, "Gladia, don't make yourself unhappy. Something wonderful happened between us, but there are other wonderful things that will happen to you, too—many of them, of all kinds, but not the *same* wonderful thing. Look forward to the others."

She was silent.

"Gladia," he said urgently, "need anyone know what has happened between us?"

She looked up at him, a pained expression on her face. "Are you *that* ashamed?"

"Of what happened, certainly not. But even though I am not ashamed, there could be consequences that would be discomforting. The matter would be talked about. Thanks to that hateful hyperwave drama, which included a distorted view of our relationship, we are news. The Earthman and the Solarian woman. If there is the slightest reason to suspect that there is—love between us, it will get back to Earth at the speed of hyperspatial drive."

Gladia lifted her eyebrows with a touch of hauteur. "And Earth will consider you demeaned? You will have indulged in sex with someone beneath your station?"

"No, of course not," said Baley uneasily, for he knew that that would certainly be the view of billions of Earthpeople. "Has it occurred to you that my wife would hear of it? I'm married."

"And if she does? What of it?"

Baley took a deep breath. "You don't understand. Earth ways are not Spacer ways. We have had times in our history when sexual mores were fairly loose, at least in some places and for some classes. This is not one of those times. Earthmen live crowded together and it takes a puritan ethic to keep the family system stable under such conditions."

"Everyone has one partner, you mean, and no other?"

"No," said Baley. "To be honest, that's not so. But care is taken to keep irregularities sufficiently quiet, so that everyone can—can—"

"Pretend they don't know?"

"Well, yes, but in this case—"

"It will all be so public that no one could pretend not to know—and your wife will be angry with you and will strike you."

"No, she won't strike me, but she will be shamed, which is worse. I will be shamed as well and so will my son. My social position will suffer and— Gladia, if you don't understand, you don't understand, but tell me that you will not speak freely of this thing as Aurorans do." He was conscious of making a rather miserable show of himself.

Gladia said thoughtfully, "I do not mean to tease you, Elijah. You have been kind to me and I would not be unkind to you, but" —she threw her arms up hopelessly—"your Earth ways are so nonsensical."

"Undoubtedly. Yet I must live with them—as you have lived with Solarian ways."

"Yes." Her expression darkened with memory. Then, "Forgive me, Elijah. Really and honestly, I apologize. I want what I can't have and I take it out on you."

"It's all right."

"No, it's not all right. Please, Elijah, I must explain something to you. I don't think you understand what happened last night. Will you be all the more embarrassed if I do?"

Baley wondered how Jessie would feel and what she would do if she could hear this conversation. Baley was quite aware that his mind should be on the confrontation with the Chairman that was looming immediately up ahead and not on his own personal marital dilemma. He should be thinking of Earth's danger and not of his wife's, but, in actual fact, he was thinking of Jessie.

He said, "I'll probably be embarrassed, but explain it anyway."

Gladia moved her chair, refraining from calling one of her robotic staff to do it for her. He waited for her nervously, not offering to move it himself.

She put her chair immediately next to his, facing it in the other direction, so that she was looking at him directly when she sat down. And as she did so, she put out her small hand and placed it in his and he felt his own hand press it.

"You see," she said, "I no longer fear contact. I'm no longer at the stage where all I can do is brush your cheek for an instant."

"That may be, but this does not affect you, Gladia, does it, as that bare touch did then?"

She nodded. "No, it doesn't affect me that way, but I like it anyway. I think that's an advance, actually. To be turned inside out just by a single moment of touch shows how abnormally I had lived and for how long. Now it is better. May I tell you how? What I have just said is actually prologue."

"Tell me."

"I wish we were in bed and it was dark. I could talk more freely."

"We are sitting up and it is light, Gladia, but I am listening."

"Yes. —On Solaria, Elijah, there was no sex to speak of. You know that."

"Yes, I do."

"I experienced none, in any real sense. On a few occasions—only a few—my husband approached me out of duty. I won't even describe how that was, but you will believe me when I tell you that, looking back on it, it was worse than none."

"I believe you."

"But I knew about sex. I read about it. I discussed it with other women sometimes, all of whom pretended it was a hateful duty that Solarians must undergo. If they had children to the limit of their quota, they always said they were delighted they would never have to deal with sex again."

"Did you believe them?"

"Of course I did. I had never heard anything else and the few non-Solarian accounts I read were denounced as false distortions. I believed that, too. My husband found some books I had, called them pornography, and had them destroyed. Then, too, you know, people can make themselves believe anything. I think Solarian women believed what they said and really *did* despise sex. They certainly sounded sincere enough and it made me feel there was something terribly wrong with me because I had a kind of curiosity about it—and odd feelings I could not understand."

"You did not, at that time, use robots for relief in any way?"

"No, it didn't occur to me. Or any inanimate object. There were occasional whispers of such things, but with such horror—or pretended horror—that I would never *dream* of doing anything like that.

Of course, I had dreams and sometimes something that, as I look back on it, must have been incipient orgasms, would wake me. I never understood them, of course, or dared talk of it. I was bitterly ashamed of it, in fact. Worse, I was frightened of the pleasure they brought me. And then, of course, I came to Aurora."

"You told me of that. Sex with Aurorans was unsatisfactory."

"Yes. It made me think that Solarians were right after all. Sex was not like my dreams at all. It was not until Jander that I understood. It is not sex that they have on Aurora; it is, it is—choreography. Every step of it is dictated by fashion, from the method of approach to the moment of departure. There is nothing unexpected, nothing spontaneous. On Solaria, since there was so little sex, nothing was given or taken. And on Aurora, sex was so stylized that, in the end. nothing was given or taken either. Do you understand?"

"I'm not sure, Gladia, never having experienced sex with an Auroran woman or, for that matter, never having been an Auroran man. But it's not necessary to explain. I have a dim notion of what you mean."

"You're terribly embarrassed, aren't you?"

"Not to the point of being unable to listen."

"But then I met Jander and learned to use him. He was not an Auroran man. His only aim, his *only* possible aim, was to please me. He gave and I took and, for the first time, I experienced sex as it should be experienced. Do you understand *that*? Can you imagine what it must be like suddenly to know that you are not mad, or distorted, or perverted, or even simply wrong—but to know that you are a woman and have a satisfying sex partner?"

"I think I can imagine that."

"And then, after so short a time, to have it all taken away from me. I thought—I thought—that that was the end. I was doomed. I was never again, through centuries of life, to have a good sexual relationship again. Not to have had it to start with—and then never to have had it at all—was bad enough. But to get it against all expectation and to have it, then suddenly to *lose* it and go back to nothing—*that* was unbearable. —You see how important, therefore, last night was."

"But why me, Gladia? Why not someone else?"

"No, Elijah, it *had* to be you. We came and found you, Giskard and I, and you were helpless. Truly helpless. You were not unconscious, but you did not rule your body. You had to be lifted and carried and placed in the car. I was there when you were warmed and treated, bathed and dried, helpless throughout. The robots did it all with marvelous efficiency, intent on caring for you and preventing harm from coming to you but totally without actual feeling. I, on the other hand, watched and I *felt*."

Baley bent his head, gritting his teeth at the thought of his public helplessness. He had luxuriated in it when it had happened, but now he could only feel the disgrace of being observed under such conditions.

She went on. "I wanted to do it all for you. I resented the robots for reserving for themselves the right to be kind to you—and to give. And as I thought of myself doing it, I felt a growing sexual excitement, something I hadn't felt since Jander's death.—And it occurred to me then that, in my only successful sex, what I had done was to take. Jander gave whatever I wished, but he never took. He was incapable of taking, since his only pleasure lay in pleasing me. And it never occurred to me to give because I was brought up with robots and knew they couldn't take.

"And as I watched, it came to me that I knew only half of sex and I desperately wanted to experience the other half. But then, at the dinner table with me afterward, when you were eating your hot soup, you seemed recovered, you seemed strong. You were strong enough to console me and because I had had that feeling for you, when you were being cared for, I no longer feared your being from Earth and I was willing to move into your embrace. I *wanted* it. But even as you held me, I felt a sense of loss, for I was taking again and not giving.

"And you said to me, 'Gladia, please, I must sit down.' Oh, Elijah, it was the most wonderful thing you could have said to me."

Baley felt himself flush. "It embarrassed me hideously at the time. Such a confession of weakness."

"It was just what I wanted. It drove me wild with desire. I forced you to bed and came to you and, for the first time in my life, I gave. I took nothing. And the spell of Jander passed, for I knew that he had not been enough, either. It must be possible to take and give, *both*. —Elijah, stay with me."

Baley shook his head. "Gladia, if I tore my heart in two, it wouldn't change the facts. I cannot remain on Aurora. I must return to Earth. You cannot come to Earth."

"Elijah, what if I *can* come to Earth?"

"Why do you say such a foolish thing? Even if you could, I would age quickly and soon be useless to you. In twenty years, thirty at the most, I will be an old man, probably dead, while you will stay as you are for centuries."

"But that is what I mean, Elijah. On Earth, I will catch your infections and I will grow old quickly, too."

"You wouldn't want that. Besides, old age isn't an infection. You will merely grow sick, very quickly, and die. Gladia, you can find another man."

"An Auroran?" She said it with contempt.

"You can teach. Now that you know how to take and to give, teach them how to do both as well."

"If I teach, will they learn?"

"Some will. Surely some will. You have so much time to find the one who will. There is—" (No, he thought, it is not wise to mention Gremionis now, but perhaps if he comes to her—less politely and with a little more determination—)

She seemed thoughtful. "Is it possible?" Then, looking at Baley, with her gray-blue eyes moist, "Oh, Elijah, do you remember anything at all of what happened last night?"

"I must admit," said Baley a little sadly, "that some of it is distressingly hazy."

"If you remembered, you would not want to leave me."

"I don't want to leave you as it is, Gladia. It is just that I must."

"And afterward," she said, "you seemed so quietly happy, so rested. I lay nestled on your shoulder and felt your heart beat rapidly at first, then more and more slowly, except when you sat up so suddenly. Do you remember that?"

Baley started and leaned a little away from her, gazing into her eyes wildly. "No, I don't remember that. What do you mean? What did I do?"

"I told you. You sat up suddenly."

"Yes, but what else?" His heart was beating rapidly now, as rapidly as it must have in the wake of last night's sex. Three times, something that had seemed the truth had come to him, but the first two times he had been entirely alone. The third time, last night, however, Gladia had been with him. He had had a witness.

Gladia said, "Nothing else, really. I said, 'What is it, Elijah?' but you paid no attention to me. You said, 'I have it. I have it.' You didn't speak clearly and your eyes were unfocused. It was a little frightening."

"Is that all I said? Jehoshaphat, Gladia! Didn't I say anything more?"

Gladia frowned. "I don't remember. But then you lay back and I said, 'Don't be frightened, Elijah. Don't be frightened. You're safe now.' And I stroked you and you settled back and fell asleep—and *snored*. —I never heard anyone snore before, but that's what it must have been—from the descriptions." The thought clearly amused her.

Baley said, "Listen to me, Gladia. What did I say? 'I have it. I have it.' Did I say what it was I had?"

She frowned again. "No. I don't remember— Wait, you did say one thing in a very low voice. You said, 'He was there first.'"

" 'He was there first.' That's what I said?"

"Yes. I took it for granted that you meant Giskard was there before the other robots, that you were trying to overcome your fears of being taken away, that you were reliving that time in the storm. Yes! That's why I stroked you and said, 'Don't be frightened, Elijah. You're safe now,' till you relaxed."

" 'He was there first.' 'He was there first.' —I won't forget it now. Gladia, thanks for last night. Thanks for talking to me now."

Gladia said, "Is there something important about you saying that Giskard found you first? He *did*. You know that."

"It can't be that, Gladia. It must be something I *don't* know but manage to discover only when my mind is totally relaxed."

"But what does it mean, then?"

"I'm not sure, but if that's what I said, it must mean something. And I have an hour or so to figure it out." He stood up. "I must leave now."

He had taken a few steps toward the door, but Gladia flew to him and put her arms around him. "Wait, Elijah."

Baley hesitated, then lowered his head to kiss her. For a long moment, they clung together.

"Will I see you again, Elijah?"

Baley said sadly, "I can't say. I hope so."

And he went off to find Daneel and Giskard, so that he could make the necessary preparations for the confrontation about to come.

73

Baley's sadness persisted as he walked across the long lawn to Fastolfe's establishment.

The robots walked on either side. Daneel seemed at his ease, but Giskard, faithful to his programming and apparently unable to relax it, maintained his close watch on the surroundings.

Baley said, "What is the name of the Chairman of the Legislature, Daneel?"

"I cannot say, Partner Elijah. On the occasions when he has been referred to in my hearing, he has been referred to only as 'the Chairman.' He is addressed as 'Mr. Chairman.' "

Giskard said, "His name is Rutilan Horder, sir, but it is never mentioned officially. The title alone is used. That serves to impress continuity on the government. Human holders of the position have, individually, fixed terms, but 'the Chairman' always exists."

"And this particular individual Chairman—how old is he?"

"Quite old, sir. Three hundred and thirty-one," said Giskard, who typically had statistics on tap.

"In good health?"

"I know nothing to the contrary, sir."

"Any outstanding personal characteristics it might be well for me to be prepared for?"

That seemed to stop Giskard. He said, after a pause, "That is difficult for me to say, sir. He is in his second term. He is considered an efficient Chairman who works hard and gets results."

"Is he short-tempered? Patient? Domineering? Understanding?"

Giskard said, "You must judge such things for yourself, sir."

Daneel said, "Partner Elijah, the Chairman is above partisanship. He is just and evenhanded, by definition."

"I'm sure of that," muttered Baley, "but definitions are abstract, as is 'the Chairman,' while individual Chairmen—with names—are concrete and may have minds to match."

He shook his head. His own mind, he would swear, had a strong measure of concrete itself. Having three times thought of something and three times lost it, he was now presented with his own comment at the time of having the thought and it *still* didn't help.

"He was there first."

Who was there first? When?

Baley had no answer.

74

Baley found Fastolfe waiting for him at the door of his establishment, with a robot behind him who seemed most unrobotically restless, as though unable to perform his proper function of greeting a visitor and upset by the fact.

(But then, one was always reading human motivations and responses into robots. What was more likely true was no upsettedness—no feeling of any kind—merely a slight oscillation of positronic potentials resulting from the fact that his orders were to greet and inspect all visitors and he could not quite perform the task without pushing past Fastolfe, which he also could not do, in the absence of overriding necessity. So he made false starts, one after the other, and that made him seem restless.)

Baley found himself staring at the robot absently and only with difficulty managing to bring his eyes back to Fastolfe. (He was thinking of robots, but he didn't know why.)

"I'm glad to see you again, Dr. Fastolfe," he said and thrust his hand forward. After his encounter with Gladia, it was rather difficult to remember that Spacers were reluctant to make physical contact with an Earthman.

Fastolfe hesitated a moment and then, as manners triumphed over prudence, he took the hand offered him, held it lightly and briefly, and let it go. He said, "I am even more delighted to see you, Mr. Baley. I was quite alarmed over your experience last evening. It was not a particularly bad storm, but to an Earthman it must have seemed overwhelming."

"You know about what happened, then?"

"Daneel and Giskard have brought me fully up to date in that respect. I would have felt better if they had come here directly and, eventually, brought you here with them, but their decision was based on the fact that Gladia's establishment was closer to the breakdown point of the airfoil and that your orders had been extremely intense and had placed Daneel's safety ahead of your own. They did not misinterpret you?"

"They did not. I forced them to leave me."

"Was that wise?" Fastolfe led the way indoors and pointed to a chair.

Baley sat down. "It seemed the proper thing to do. We were being pursued."

"So Giskard reported. He also reported that—"

Baley intervened. "Dr. Fastolfe, please. I have very little time and I have questions that I must ask you."

"Go ahead, please," said Fastolfe at once, with his usual air of unfailing politeness.

"It has been suggested that you place your work on brain function above everything else, that you—"

"Let me finish, Mr. Baley. That I will let nothing stand in my way, that I am totally ruthless, oblivious to any consideration of immorality or evil, would stop at nothing, would excuse everything, all in the name of the importance of my work."

"Yes."

"Who told you this, Mr. Baley?" asked Fastolfe.

"Does it matter?"

"Perhaps not. Besides, it's not difficult to guess. It was my daughter Vasilia. I'm sure of that."

Baley said, "Perhaps. What I want to know is whether this estimate of your character is correct."

Fastolfe smiled sadly. "Do you expect an honest answer from me about my own character? In some ways, the accusations against me are true. I *do* consider my work the most important matter there is and I *do* have the impulse to sacrifice anything and everything to it. I *would* ignore conventional notions of evil and immorality if these got in my way. —The thing is, however, that I don't. I can't bring myself to. And, in particular, if I have been accused of killing Jander because that would in some way advance my study of the human brain, I deny it. It is not so. I did not kill Jander."

Baley said, "You suggested I submit to a Psychic Probe to get some information that I can't reach otherwise out of my brain. Has it occurred to you that, if *you* submitted to a Psychic Probe, your innocence could be demonstrated?"

Fastolfe nodded his head thoughtfully. "I imagine Vasilia suggested that my failure to offer to submit to one was proof of my guilt. Not so. A Psychic Probe is dangerous and I am as nervous about submitting myself to one as you are. Still, I would have done so, despite my fears, were it not for the fact that that is what my opponents would most like to have me do. They would argue against any evidence to my innocence and the Psychic Probe is not delicate enough an instrument to demonstrate innocence beyond argument. But what they *would* get by use of the Probe is information about the theory and design of humaniform robots. *That* is what they are after and *that* is what I am not going to give them."

Baley said, "Very well. Thank you, Dr. Fastolfe."

Fastolfe said, "You are welcome. And now, if I may get back to what I was saying, Giskard reported that, after you were left alone in the airfoil, you were accosted by strange robots. At least, you spoke of strange robots, rather disjointedly, after you were found unconscious and exposed to the storm."

"The strange robots *did* accost me, Dr. Fastolfe. I managed to deflect them and send them away, but I thought it wise to leave the airfoil rather than await their return. I may not have been thinking clearly when I reached that decision. Giskard said I was not."

Fastolfe smiled. "Giskard has a simplistic view of the Universe. Have you any idea whose robots they were?"

Baley moved about restlessly and seemed to find no way of adjusting himself to the seat in a comfortable manner. He said, "Has the Chairman arrived yet?"

"No, but he will be here momentarily. So will Amadiro, the head of the Institute, whom, the robots told me, you met yesterday. I am not sure that was wise. You irritated him."

"I had to see him, Dr. Fastolfe, and he did not seem irritated."

"That is no guide with Amadiro. As a result of what he calls your slanders and your unbearable sullying of professional reputation, he has forced the Chairman's hand."

"In what way?"

"It is the Chairman's job to encourage the meeting of contending parties and to work for a compromise. If Amadiro wishes to meet with me, the Chairman could not, by definition, discourage it, much less forbid it. He must hold the meeting and, if Amadiro can find enough evidence against you—and it is easy to find evidence against an Earthman—that will end the investigation."

"Perhaps, Dr. Fastolfe, you should not have called on an Earthman to help, considering how vulnerable we are."

"Perhaps not, Mr. Baley, but I could think of nothing else to do. I still can't, so I must leave it up to you to persuade the Chairman to our point of view—if you can."

"The responsibility is mine?" said Baley glumly.

"Entirely yours," said Fastolfe smoothly.

Baley said, "Are we four to be the only ones present?"

Fastolfe said, "Actually, we three: the Chairman, Amadiro, and myself. We are the two principals and the compromising agent, so to speak. You will be there as a fourth party, Mr. Baley, only on sufferance. The Chairman can order you to leave at will, so I hope you will not do anything to upset him."

"I'll try not to, Dr. Fastolfe."

"For instance, Mr. Baley, do not offer him your hand—if you will forgive my rudeness."

Baley felt himself grow warm with retroactive embarrassment at his earlier gesture. "I will not."

"And be unfailingly polite. Make no angry accusations. Do not insist on statements for which there is no support—"

"You mean don't try to stampede anyone into betraying himself. Amadiro, for instance."

"Yes, do not do so. You will be committing slander and it will be counterproductive. Therefore, be polite! If the politeness masks an attack, we won't quarrel with that. And try not to speak unless you are spoken to."

Baley said, "How is it, Dr. Fastolfe, that you are so full of careful advice now and yet you never warned me about the dangers of slander earlier."

"The fault is indeed mine," said Dr. Fastolfe. "It was a matter of such basic knowledge to me that it never occurred to me that it had to be explained."

Baley grunted. "Yes, I thought so."

Fastolfe raised his head suddenly. "I hear an airfoil outside. More than that, I can hear the steps of one of my staff, heading for the entrance. I presume the Chairman and Amadiro are at hand."

"Together?" asked Baley.

"Undoubtedly. You see, Amadiro suggested my establishment as the meeting place, thus granting me the advantage of home ground. He will therefore have the chance of offering, out of apparent politeness, to call for the Chairman and bring him here. After all, they must both come here. This will give him a few minutes to talk privately with the Chairman and push his point of view."

"That is scarcely fair," said Baley. "Could you have stopped that?"

"I didn't want to. Amadiro takes a calculated risk. He may say something that will irritate the Chairman."

"Is the Chairman particularly irritable by nature?"

"No. No more so than any Chairman in the fifth decade of his term of office. Still, the necessity of strict adherence to protocol, the further necessity of never taking sides, and the actuality of arbitrary power all combine toward making a certain irritability inevitable. And Amadiro is not always wise. His jovial smile, his white teeth, his exuding bonhomie can be extremely irritating when those upon whom he lavishes it are not in a good mood, for some reason. —But I must go meet them, Mr. Baley, and supply what I hope will be a more substantial version of charm. Please stay here and don't move from that chair."

Baley could do nothing but wait now. He thought, irrelevantly, that he had been on Aurora for just a bit short of fifty standard hours.

 **18.** **Again the Chairman**

75

The Chairman was short, surprisingly short. Amadiro towered over him by nearly thirty centimeters.

However, since most of his shortness was in his thighs, the Chairman, when all were seated, was not noticeably inferior in height to the others. Indeed, he was thickset, with a massive chest and shoulders, and looked almost overpowering under those conditions.

His head was large, too, but his face was lined and marked by age. Nor were its wrinkles the kindly type carved by laughter. They were impressed into his cheeks and forehead, one felt, by the exercise of power. His hair was white and sparse and he was bald in the spot where the hairs would have met in a whorl.

His voice suited him—deep and decisive. Age had robbed it of some of its timbre, perhaps, and lent it a bit of harshness, but in a Chairman (Baley thought) that might help rather than hinder.

Fastolfe went through the full ritual of greeting, exchanged stroking remarks without meaning, and offered food and drink. Through all of this, no mention was made of the outsider and no notice was taken of him.

It was only when the preliminaries were finished and when all were seated that Baley (a little farther from the center than the others) was introduced.

He said, "Mr. Chairman," without holding out his hand. Then, with an offhand nod, he said, "And, of course, I have met Dr. Amadiro."

Amadiro's smile did not waver at the touch of insolence in Baley's voice.

The Chairman, who had not acknowledged Baley's greeting, placed his hands on each knee, fingers spread apart, and said, "Let us get started and let us see if we can't make this as brief and as productive as possible.

"Let me stress first that I wish to get past this matter of the misbehavior—or possible misbehavior—of an Earthman and strike instantly to the heart of the matter. Nor, in dealing with the heart of the matter, are we speaking of this overblown matter of the robot. Disrupting the activity of a robot is a matter for the civil courts; it can result in a judgment of the infringement of property rights and the inflicting of a penalty of costs but nothing more than that. What's more, if it should be proved that Dr. Fastolfe had rendered the robot,

Jander Panell, inoperable, it is a robot who, after all, he helped design, whose construction he supervised, and the ownership of whom he held at the time of the inoperability. No penalty is likely to apply, since a person may do what he likes with his own.

"What is really at issue is the matter of the exploration and settlement of the Galaxy: whether we of Aurora carry it through alone, whether we do it in collaboration with the other Spacer worlds, or whether we leave it to Earth. Dr. Amadiro and the Globalists favor having Aurora shoulder the burden alone; Dr. Fastolfe wishes to leave it to Earth.

"If we can settle this matter, then the affair of the robot can be left to the civil courts, and the question of the Earthman's behavior will probably become moot, and we can simply get rid of him.

"Therefore, let me begin by asking whether Dr. Amadiro is prepared to accept Dr. Fastolfe's position in order to achieve unity of decision or whether Dr. Fastolfe is prepared to accept Dr. Amadiro's position with the same end in view."

He paused and waited.

Amadiro said, "I am sorry, Mr. Chairman, but I must insist that Earthmen be confined to their planet and that the Galaxy be settled by Aurorans only. I would be willing to compromise, however, to the extent of allowing other Spacer worlds to share in the settlement if that would prevent needless strife among us."

"I see," said the Chairman. "Will you, Dr. Fastolfe, in view of this statement, abandon your position?"

Fastolfe said, "Dr. Amadiro's compromise has scarcely anything of substance in it, Mr. Chairman. I am willing to offer a compromise of greater significance. Why should not the worlds of the Galaxy be thrown open to Spacers and Earthpeople alike? The Galaxy is large and there would be room for both. I would be willing to accept such an arrangement."

"No doubt," said Amadiro quickly, "for it is no compromise. The over eight billion population of Earth is more than half again the population of all the Spacer worlds combined. Earth's people are short-lived and are used to replacing their losses quickly. They lack our regard for individual human life. They will swarm over the new worlds at any cost, multiplying like insects, and will preempt the Galaxy even while we are making a bare beginning. To offer Earth a supposedly equal chance at the Galaxy is to *give* them the Galaxy—and that is not equality. Earthpeople must be confined to Earth."

"And what have you to say to that, Dr. Fastolfe?" asked the Chairman.

Fastolfe sighed. "My views are on record. I'm sure I don't need to repeat them. Dr. Amadiro plans to use humaniform robots to build the settled worlds that human Aurorans will then enter, ready-made, yet he doesn't even have humaniform robots. He cannot construct them and the project would not work, even if he did have them. No compromise is possible unless Dr. Amadiro consents to the principle that Earthpeople may at least share in the task of the settlement of new worlds."

"Then no compromise is possible," said Amadiro.

The Chairman looked displeased. "I'm afraid that one of you two *must* give in. I do not intend Aurora to be torn apart in an emotional orgy on a question this important."

He looked at Amadiro blankly, his expression carefully signifying neither favor nor disfavor. "You intend to use the inoperability of the robot, Jander, as an argument against Fastolfe's view, do you not?"

"I do," said Amadiro.

"A purely emotional argument. You are going to claim that Fastolfe is trying to destroy your view by falsely making humaniform robots appear less useful than they, in effect, are."

"That is exactly what he *is* trying to do—"

"Slander!" put in Fastolfe in a low voice.

"Not if I can prove it, which I can," said Amadiro. "The argument may be an emotional one, but it will be effective. You see that, Mr. Chairman, don't you? My view will surely win, but left to itself it will be messy. I would suggest that you persuade Dr. Fastolfe to accept inevitable defeat and spare Aurora the enormous sadness of a spectacle that will weaken our position among the Spacer worlds and shake our own belief in ourselves."

"How can you prove that Dr. Fastolfe rendered the robot inoperative?"

"He himself admits he is the only human being who could have done so. You know this."

"I know," said the Chairman, "but I wanted to hear you say this, not to your constituency, not to the media, but to me—in private. And you have done so."

He turned to Fastolfe. "And what do you say, Dr. Fastolfe? Are you the only man who could have destroyed the robot?"

"Without leaving physical marks? I am, as far as I know. I don't believe that Dr. Amadiro has the skill in robotics to do so and I am constantly amazed that, after having founded his Robotics Institute, he is so eager to proclaim his own incapacity, even with all his associates at his back—and to do so publicly." He smiled at Amadiro, not entirely without malice.

The Chairman sighed. "No, Dr. Fastolfe. No rhetorical tricks now. Let us dispense with sarcasm and clever thrusts. What is your defense?"

"Why, only that I did no harm to Jander. I do not say anyone did.

It was chance—the uncertainty principle at work on the positronic pathways. It can happen every so often. Let Dr. Amadiro merely admit that it was chance, that no one be accused without evidence, and we can then argue the competing proposals about settlement on their own merits."

"No," said Amadiro. "The chance of accidental destruction is too small to be considered, far smaller than the chance that Dr. Fastolfe is responsible—so much smaller that to ignore Dr. Fastolfe's guilt is irresponsible. I will not back down and I will win. Mr. Chairman, you know I will win and it seems to me that the only rational step to be taken is to force Dr. Fastolfe to accept his defeat in the interest of global unity."

Fastolfe said quickly, "And that brings me to the matter of the investigation I have asked Mr. Baley of Earth to undertake."

And Amadiro said, just as quickly, "A move I opposed when it was first suggested. The Earthman may be a clever investigator, but he is unfamiliar with Aurora and can accomplish nothing here. Nothing, that is, except to strew slander and to hold Aurora up to the Spacer worlds in an undignified and ridiculous light. There have been satirical pieces on the matter in half a dozen important Spacer hyperwave news programs on as many different worlds. Recordings of these have been sent to your office."

"And have been brought to my attention," said the Chairman.

"And there has been murmuring here on Aurora," Amadiro drove on. "It would be to my selfish interest to allow the investigation to continue. It is costing Fastolfe support among the populace and votes among the legislators. The longer it continues, the more certain I am of victory, but it is damaging Aurora and I do not wish to add to my certainty at the cost of harm to my world. I suggest—with respect—that you end the investigation, Mr. Chairman, and persuade Dr. Fastolfe to submit gracefully now to what he will eventually have to accept—at much greater cost."

The Chairman said, "I agree that to have permitted Dr. Fastolfe to set up this investigation *may* have been unwise. I say '*may.*' I admit I am tempted to end it. And yet the Earthman"—he gave no indication of knowing that Baley was in the room—"has already been here for some time—"

He paused, as though to give Fastolfe a chance for corroboration, and Fastolfe took it, saying, "This is the third day of his investigation, Mr. Chairman."

"In that case," said the Chairman, "before I end that investigation, it would be fair, I believe, to ask if there have been any significant findings so far."

He paused again. Fastolfe glanced quickly at Baley and made a small motion of his head.

Baley said in a low voice, "I do not wish, Mr. Chairman, to obtrude, unasked, any observations. Am I being asked a question?"

The Chairman frowned. Without looking at Baley, he said, "I am asking Mr. Baley of Earth to tell us whether he has any findings of significance."

Baley took a deep breath. This was it.

76

"Mr. Chairman," he began. "Yesterday afternoon, I was interrogating Dr. Amadiro, who was most cooperative and useful to me. When my staff and I left—"

"Your staff?" asked the Chairman.

"I was accompanied by two robots on all phases of my investigation, Mr. Chairman," said Baley.

"Robots who belong to Dr. Fastolfe?" asked Amadiro. "I ask this for the record."

"For the record, they do," said Baley. "One is Daneel Olivaw, a humaniform robot, and the other is Giskard Reventlov, an older non-humaniform robot."

"Thank you," said the Chairman. "Continue."

"When we left the Institute grounds, we found that the airfoil we used had been tampered with."

"Tampered with?" asked the Chairman, startled. "By whom?"

"We don't know, but it happened on Institute grounds. We were there by invitation, so it was known by the Institute personnel that we would be there. Moreover, no one else would be likely to be there without the invitation and knowledge of the Institute staff. If it were at all thinkable, it would be necessary to conclude that the tampering could only have been done by someone on the Institute staff and that would, in any case, be impossible—except at the direction of Dr. Amadiro himself, which would also be unthinkable."

Amadiro said, "You seem to think a great deal about the unthinkable. Has the airfoil been examined by a qualified technician to see if it has indeed been tampered with? Might there not have been a natural failing?" asked Amadiro.

"No, sir," said Baley, "But Giskard, who is qualified to drive an airfoil and who has frequently driven that particular one, maintains that it was tampered with."

"And he is one of Dr. Fastolfe's staff and is programmed by him and receives his daily orders from him," said Amadiro.

"Are you suggesting—" began Fastolfe.

"I am suggesting nothing." Amadiro held up his hand in a benign gesture. "I am merely making a statement—for the record."

The Chairman stirred. "Will Mr. Baley of Earth please continue?"

Baley said, "When the airfoil broke down, there were others in pursuit."

"Others?" asked the Chairman.

"Other robots. They arrived and, by that time, my robots were gone."

"One moment," said Amadiro. "What was your condition at the time, Mr. Baley?"

"I was not entirely well."

"Not entirely well? You are an Earthman and unaccustomed to life except in the artificial setting of your Cities. You are uneasy in the open. Is that not so, Mr. Baley?" asked Amadiro.

"Yes, sir."

"And there was a severe thunderstorm in progress last evening, as I am sure the Chairman recalls. Would it not be accurate to say that you were quite ill? Semiconscious, if not worse?"

"I was quite ill," said Baley reluctantly.

"Then how is it your robots were gone?" asked the Chairman sharply. "Should they not have been with you in your illness?"

"I ordered them away, Mr. Chairman."

"Why?"

"I thought it best," said Baley, "and I will explain—if I may be allowed to continue."

"Continue."

"We were indeed being pursued, for the pursuing robots arrived shortly after my robots had left. The pursuers asked me where my robots were and I told them I had sent them away. It was only after that that they asked if I were ill. I said I wasn't ill and they left me in order to continue a search for my robots."

"In search of Daneel and Giskard?" asked the Chairman.

"Yes, Mr. Chairman. It was clear to me that they were under intense orders to find the robots."

"In what way was that clear?"

"Although I was obviously ill, they asked about the robots before they asked about me. Then, later, they abandoned me in my illness to search for my robots. They must have received enormously intense orders to find those robots or it would not have been possible for them to disregard a patently ill human being. As a matter of fact, I had anticipated this search for my robots and that was why I had sent them away. I felt it all-important to keep them out of unauthorized hands."

Amadiro said, "Mr. Chairman, may I continue to question Mr. Baley on this point, in order to show the worthlessness of this statement?"

"You may."

Amadiro said, "Mr. Baley. You were alone after your robots had left, were you not?"

"Yes, sir."

"Therefore you have no recording of events? You are not yourself equipped to record them? You have no recording device?"

"No to all three, sir."

"And you were ill?"

"Yes, sir."

"Distraught? Possibly too ill to remember clearly?"

"No, sir. I remember quite clearly."

"You would think so, I suppose, but you may well have been delirious and hallucinating. Under those conditions, it seems clear that what the robots said or, indeed, whether robots appeared at all would seem highly dubious."

The Chairman said thoughtfully, "I agree. Mr. Baley of Earth, assuming that what you remember—or claim to remember—is accurate, what is your interpretation of the events you are describing?"

"I hesitate to give you my thoughts on the matter, Mr. Chairman," said Baley, "lest I slander the worthy Dr. Amadiro."

"Since you speak at my request and since your remarks are confined to this room"—the Chairman looked around; the wall niches were empty of robots—"there is no question of slander, unless it seems to me you speak with malice."

"In that case, Mr. Chairman," said Baley, "I had thought it possible that Dr. Amadiro detained me in his office by discussing matters with me at greater length than was perhaps necessary, so that there would be time for the damaging of my machine, then detained me further in order that I might leave after the thunderstorm had begun, thus making sure that I would be ill in transit. He had studied Earth's social conditions, as he told me several times, so he would know what my reaction to the storm might be. It seemed to me that it was his plan to send his robots after us and, when they came upon our stalled airfoil, to have them take us all back to the Institute grounds, presumably so that I might be treated for my illness but actually so that he might have Dr. Fastolfe's robots."

Amadiro laughed gently. "What motive am I supposed to have for all this. You see, Mr. Chairman, that this is supposition joined to supposition and would be judged slander in any court on Aurora."

The Chairman said severely, "Has Mr. Baley of Earth anything to support these hypotheses?"

"A line of reasoning, Mr. Chairman."

The Chairman stood up, at once losing some of his presence, since he scarcely unfolded to a greater than sitting height. "Let me take a short walk, so that I might consider what I have heard so far. I will be right back." He left for the Personal.

Fastolfe leaned in the direction of Baley and Baley met him halfway. (Amadiro looked on in casual unconcern, as though it scarcely mattered to him what they might have to say to each other.)

Fastolfe whispered, "Have you anything better to say?"

Baley said, "I think so, if I get the proper chance to say it. but the Chairman does not seem to be sympathetic."

"He is not. So far you have merely made things worse and I would not be surprised if, when he comes back, he calls these proceedings to a halt."

Baley shook his head and stared at his shoes.

77

Baley was still staring at his shoes when the Chairman returned, reseated himself, and turned a hard and rather baleful glance at the Earthman.

He said, "Mr. Baley of Earth?"

"Yes, Mr. Chairman."

"I think you are wasting my time, but I do not want it said that I did not give either side a full hearing, *even* when it seemed to be wasting my time. Can you offer me a motive that would account for Dr. Amadiro acting in the mad way in which you accuse him of acting?"

"Mr. Chairman," said Baley in a tone approaching desperation, "there is indeed a motive—a very good one. It rests on the fact that Dr. Amadiro's plan for settling the Galaxy will come to nothing if he and his Institute cannot produce humaniform robots. So far he has produced none and can produce none. Ask him if he is willing to have a legislative committee examine his Institute for any indication that successful humaniform robots are being produced or designed. If he is willing to maintain that successful humaniforms are on the assembly lines or even on the drawing boards—or even in adequate theoretical formulation—and if he is prepared to demonstrate that fact to a qualified committee, I will say nothing more and admit that my investigation has achieved nothing." He held his breath.

The Chairman looked at Amadiro, whose smile had faded.

Amadiro said, "I will admit that we have no humaniform robots in prospect at the moment."

"Then I will continue," said Baley, resuming his interrupted breathing with something very much like a gasp. "Dr. Amadiro can, of course, find all the information he needs for his project if he turns to Dr. Fastolfe, who has the information in his head, but Dr. Fastolfe will not cooperate in this matter."

"No, I will not," murmured Fastolfe, "under any conditions."

"But, Mr. Chairman," Baley continued, "Dr. Fastolfe is *not* the only individual who has the secret of the design and construction of humaniform robots."

"No?" said the Chairman. "Who else would know? Dr. Fastolfe himself looks astonished at your comment, Mr. Baley." (For the first time, he did not add "of Earth.")

"I am indeed astonished," said Fastolfe. "To my knowledge, I am certainly the only one. I don't know what Mr. Baley means."

Amadiro said, with a small curling of the lip, "I suspect Mr. Baley doesn't know, either."

Baley felt hemmed in. He looked from one to the other and felt that not one of them—not one—was on his side.

He said, "Isn't it true that any humaniform robot would know? Not consciously perhaps, not in such a way as to be able to give instructions in the matter—but the information would surely be there within him, wouldn't it? If a humaniform robot was properly questioned, his answers and responses would betray his design and construction. Eventually, given enough time and given questions properly framed, a humaniform robot would yield information that would make it possible to plan the design of other humaniform robots. —To put it briefly, no machine can be of secret design if the machine itself is available for sufficiently intense study."

Fastolfe seemed struck. "I see what you mean, Mr. Baley, and you are right. I had never thought of that."

"With respect, Dr. Fastolfe," said Baley, "I must tell you that, like all Aurorans, you have a peculiarly individualistic pride. You are entirely too satisfied with being the best roboticist, the *only* roboticist who can construct humaniforms—so you blind yourself to the obvious."

The Chairman relaxed into a smile. "He has you there, Dr. Fastolfe. I have wondered why you were so eager to maintain that you were the only one with the know-how to destroy Jander when that so weakened your political case. I see clearly now that you would rather have your political case go down than your uniqueness."

Fastolfe chafed visibly.

As for Amadiro, he frowned and said, "Has this anything to do with the problem under discussion?"

"Yes, it does," said Baley, his confidence rising. "You cannot force any information from Dr. Fastolfe directly. Your robots cannot be ordered to do him harm, to torture him into revealing his secrets, for instance. You can't harm him directly yourself against the protection of Dr. Fastolfe by his staff. However, you can isolate a robot and have it taken by other robots when the human being present is too ill to take the necessary action to prevent you. All the events of yesterday afternoon were part of a quickly improvised plan to get your hands on

Daneel. You saw your opportunity as soon as I insisted on seeing you at the Institute. If I had not sent my robots away, if I had not been just well enough to insist I was well and to send your robots in the wrong direction, you would have had him. And eventually you might have worked out the secret of humaniform robots by some long-sustained analysis of Daneel's behavior and responses."

Amadiro said, "Mr. Chairman, I protest. I have never heard slander so viciously expressed. This is all based on the fancies of an ill man. We don't know—and perhaps can't ever know—whether the airfoil was really damaged; and if it was, by whom; whether robots really pursued the airfoil and really spoke to Mr. Baley or not. He is merely piling inference on inference, all based on dubious testimony concerning events of which he is the only witness—and that at a time when he was half-mad with fear and may have been hallucinating. None of this can stand up for one moment in a courtroom."

"This is not a courtroom, Dr. Amadiro," said the Chairman, "and it is my duty to listen to everything that may be germane to a question under dispute."

"This is not germane, Mr. Chairman. It is a cobweb."

"Yet it hangs together, somehow. I do not seem to catch Mr. Baley in a clear-cut illogicality. If one admits what he claims to have experienced, then his conclusions make a kind of sense. Do you deny all this, Dr. Amadiro? The airfoil damage, the pursuit, the intention to appropriate the humaniform robot?"

"I do! Absolutely! None of it is true!" said Amadiro. It had been a noticeable while since he had smiled. "The Earthman can produce a recording of our entire conversation and no doubt he will point out that I was delaying him by speaking at length, by inviting him to tour the Institute, by inviting him to have dinner—but all that can equally well be interpreted as my stretching a point to be courteous and hospitable. I was misled by a certain sympathy I have for Earthmen, perhaps, and that's all there is to that. I deny his inferences and nothing of what he says can stand up against my denial. My reputation is not such that a mere speculation can persuade anyone that I am the kind of devious plotter this Earthman says I am."

The Chairman scratched at his chin thoughtfully and said, "Certainly, I am not of a mind to accuse you on the basis of what the Earthman has said so far. —Mr. Baley, if this is all you have, it is interesting but insufficient. Is there anything more you have to say of substance? I warn you that, if not, I have now spent all the time on this that I can afford to."

78

Baley said, "There is but one more subject I wish to bring up, Mr. Chairman. You have perhaps heard of Gladia Delmarre—or Gladia Solaria. She calls herself simply Gladia."

"Yes, Mr. Baley," said the Chairman with a testy edge to his voice. "I have heard of her. I have seen the hyperwave show in which you and she play such remarkable parts."

"She was associated with the robot, Jander, for many months. In fact, toward the end, he was her husband."

The Chairman's unfavorable stare at Baley became a hard glare. "Her *what*?"

"Husband, Mr. Chairman."

Fastolfe, who half-rose, sat down again, looking perturbed.

The Chairman said harshly, "That is illegal. Worse, it is ridiculous. A robot could not impregnate her. There could be no children. The status of a husband—or of a wife—is never granted without some statement as to willingness to have a child if permitted. Even an Earthman, I should think, would know that."

Baley said, "I am aware of this, Mr. Chairman. So, I am certain, was Gladia. She did not use the word 'husband' in its legal sense but in an emotional one. She considered Jander the equivalent of a husband. She felt toward him as though he were a husband."

The Chairman turned to Fastolfe. "Did you know of this, Dr. Fastolfe? He was a robot on your staff."

Fastolfe, clearly embarrassed, said, "I knew she was fond of him. I suspected she made use of him sexually. I knew nothing of this illegal charade, however, until Mr. Baley told me of it."

Baley said, "She was a Solarian. Her concept of 'husband' was not Auroran."

"Obviously not," said the Chairman.

"But she did have enough of a sense of reality to keep it to herself, Mr. Chairman. She never told of this charade, as Dr. Fastolfe calls it, to any Auroran. She told me the day before yesterday because she wanted to urge me on in the investigation of something that meant so much to her. Yet even so, I imagine she would not have used the word if she had not known I was an Earthman and would understand it in her sense—and not in an Auroran's."

"Very well," said the Chairman. "I'll grant her a bare minimum of good sense—for a Solarian. Is that the one more subject you wanted to bring up?"

"Yes, Mr. Chairman."

"In that case, it is totally irrelevant and can play no part in our deliberations."

"Mr. Chairman, there is one question I must still ask. One question. A dozen words, sir, and then I will be through." He said it as earnestly as he could, for everything depended on this.

The Chairman hesitated. "Agreed. One last question."

"Yes, Mr. Chairman." Baley would have liked to bark out the words, but he refrained. Nor did he raise his voice. Nor did he even point his finger. Everything depended on this. Everything had led up to this and yet he remembered Fastolfe's warning and said it almost casually. "How is it that Dr. Amadiro knew that Jander was Gladia's husband?"

"*What?*" The Chairman's white and bushy eyebrows raised themselves in surprise. "Who said he knew anything of this?"

Asked a direct question, Baley could continue. "Ask him, Mr. Chairman."

And he merely nodded in the direction of Amadiro, who had risen from his seat and was staring at Baley in obvious horror.

79

Baley said again, very softly, reluctant to draw attention away from Amadiro, "Ask him, Mr. Chairman. He seems upset."

The Chairman said, "What is this, Dr. Amadiro? Did you know anything about the robot as supposed husband of this Solarian woman?"

Amadiro stuttered, then pressed his lips together for a moment and tried again. The paleness which had struck him had vanished and was replaced by a dull flush. He said, "I am caught by surprise at this meaningless accusation, Mr. Chairman. I do not know what it is all about."

"May I explain, Mr. Chairman? Very briefly?" said Baley. (Would he be cut off?)

"You had better," said the Chairman grimly. "If you have any explanation, I would certainly like to hear it."

"Mr. Chairman," said Baley. "I had a conversation with Dr. Amadiro yesterday afternoon. Because it was his intention to keep me until the storm broke, he spoke more lengthily than he intended and, apparently, more carelessly. In referring to Gladia, he casually referred to the robot, Jander, as her husband. I'm curious as to how he knew that fact."

"Is this true, Dr. Amadiro?" asked the Chairman.

Amadiro was still standing, bearing almost the appearance of a prisoner before a judge. He said, "Whether it is true or not has no bearing on the question under discussion."

"Perhaps not," said the Chairman, "but I was astonished at your reaction to the question when it was put. It occurs to me that there is a meaning to this that Mr. Baley and you both understand and that I do not. I therefore want to understand also. Did you or did you not know of this impossible relationship between Jander and the Solarian woman?"

Amadiro said in a choking voice, "I could not possibly have."

"That is no answer," said the Chairman. "That is an equivocation. You are making a judgment when I am asking you to hand me a memory. Did you or did you not make the statement imputed to you?"

"Before he answers," said Baley, feeling more certain of his ground now that the Chairman was governed by moral outrage, "it is only fair to Dr. Amadiro for me to remind him that Giskard, a robot who was also present at the meeting, can, if asked to do so, repeat the entire conversation, word for word, using the voice and intonation of both parties. In short, the conversation is recorded."

Amadiro burst into a kind of rage. "Mr. Chairman, the robot, Giskard, was designed, constructed, and programmed by Dr. Fastolfe, who announced himself to be the best roboticist who exists and who is bitterly opposed to me. Can we trust a recording produced by such a robot?"

Baley said, "Perhaps you ought to hear the recording and come to your own decision, Mr. Chairman."

"Perhaps I ought," said the Chairman. "I am not here, Dr. Amadiro, to have my decisions made for me. But let us put that aside for a moment. Regardless of what the recording says, Dr. Amadiro, do you wish to state for the record that you did not know that the Solarian woman considered her robot to be her husband and that you never referred to him as her husband? Please remember (as you both, being legislators, should) that, although no robot is present, this entire conversation is being recorded in my own device." He tapped a small bulge at his breast pocket. "Flatly, then, Dr. Amadiro. Yes or no."

Amadiro said, with an edge of desperation in his voice, "Mr. Chairman, I honestly cannot remember what I said in casual conversation. If I did mention the word—and I don't admit I did—it may have been the result of some other casual conversation in which someone mentioned the fact that Gladia acted as love-struck toward her robot as though he were her husband."

The Chairman said, "And with whom did you have this other casual conversation? Who made this statement to you?"

"At the moment, I cannot say."

Baley said, "Mr. Chairman, if Dr. Amadiro will be so kind as to list anyone and everyone who *might* have used the word to him, we can question every one of them to discover which one can remember making such a remark."

Amadiro said, "I hope, Mr. Chairman, you will consider the effect on the morale of the Institute if anything of this sort is done."

The Chairman said, "I hope you will consider it, too, Dr. Amadiro, and come up with a better answer to our question, so that we are not forced to extremes."

"One moment, Mr. Chairman," said Baley, as obsequiously as he could manage, "there remains a question."

"Again? Another one?" The Chairman looked at Baley without favor. "What is it?"

"Why is Dr. Amadiro struggling so to avoid admitting he knew of Jander's relation to Gladia? He says it is irrelevant. In that case, why not say he knew of the relationship and be done with it? I say it is relevant and that Dr. Amadiro knows that his admission could be used to demonstrate criminal activity on his part."

Amadiro thundered, "I resent the expression and I demand an apology!"

Fastolfe smiled thinly and Baley's lips pressed together grimly. He had forced Amadiro over the edge.

The Chairman turned an almost alarming red and said with passion, "You demand? You *demand*? To whom do you demand? I am the Chairman. I hear all views before deciding what to suggest as best to be done. Let me hear what the Earthman has to say about his interpretation of your action. If he is slandering you, he shall be punished, you may be sure, and I will take the broadest view of the slander statutes, too, you may be sure. But *you*, Amadiro, may make no demands upon me. Go on, Earthman. Say what you have to say, but be extraordinarily careful."

Baley said, "Thank you, Mr. Chairman. Actually, there is one Auroran to whom Gladia *did* tell the secret of her relationship with Jander."

The Chairman interrupted. "Well, who is that? Do not play your hyperwave tricks on me."

Baley said, "I have no intention of anything but a straightforward statement, Mr. Chairman. The one Auroran is, of course, Jander himself. He may have been a robot, but he is an inhabitant of Aurora and might be viewed as an Auroran. Gladia must surely, in her passion, have addressed him as 'my husband.' Since Dr. Amadiro has admitted he might possibly have heard from someone else some statement to the effect of Jander's husbandly relationship to Gladia, isn't it logical to suppose that he heard of the matter from Jander? Would Dr. Amadiro be willing, right now, to state for the record that he never spoke to Jander during the period when Jander formed part of Gladia's staff?"

Twice Amadiro's mouth opened as though he would speak. Twice he did not utter a sound.

"Well," said the Chairman, "did you speak to Jander during that period, Dr. Amadiro?"

There was still no answer.

Baley said softly, "If he did, it is entirely relevant to the matter at hand."

"I'm beginning to see that it must be, Mr. Baley. Well, Dr. Amadiro, once again—yes or no."

And Amadiro burst forth, "What evidence does this Earthman have against me in this matter? Does he have a recording of any conversation I have had with Jander? Does he have witnesses who are willing to say they have seen me with Jander? Does he have anything at all besides mere self-serving statements?"

The Chairman turned to look at Baley and Baley said, "Mr. Chairman, if I have nothing at all, then Dr. Amadiro should not hesitate to deny, for the record, any contact with Jander—but he does not do so. As it happens, in the course of my investigation, I spoke to Dr. Vasilia Aliena, the daughter of Dr. Fastolfe. I spoke also to a young Auroran named Santirix Gremionis. In the recordings of both interviews, it will be plain that Dr. Vasilia encouraged Gremionis to pay court to Gladia. You may question Dr. Vasilia as to her purpose in so doing and as to whether this course of action had been suggested to her by Dr. Amadiro. It also appears that it was Gremionis' custom to take long walks with Gladia, which both enjoyed, and on which they were not accompanied by the robot, Jander. You might check on this, if you wish, sir."

The Chairman said dryly, "I may do so, but if all is as you say, what does this show?"

Baley said, "I have stated that, failing Dr. Fastolfe himself, the secret of the humaniform robot could be obtained only from Daneel. Before Jander's death, it could, with equal facility, have been obtained from Jander. Whereas Daneel was part of Dr. Fastolfe's establishment and could not easily be reached, Jander was part of Gladia's establishment and she was not as sophisticated as Dr. Fastolfe in seeing to a robot's protection.

"Isn't it likely that Dr. Amadiro took the occasion of Gladia's periodic absences from her establishment, when she was walking with Gremionis, to converse with Jander, perhaps by trimensional viewing, to study his responses, to subject him to various tests, and then to erase any sign of his visit with Jander, so that he could never inform Gladia of it? It may be that he came close to finding what he wanted to know—before the attempt ended when Jander went out of action. His concentration then shifted to Daneel. He felt perhaps that he had only a few tests and observations left to make and so he set up the trap of yesterday evening, as I said earlier in my—my testimony."

The Chairman said, in what was almost a whisper, "Now it all hangs together. I am almost forced to believe."

"Plus one final point and then I will truly have nothing more to say," said Baley. "In his examination and testing of Jander, it is entirely possible that Dr. Amadiro accidentally —and without any deliberate intention whatever—immobilized Jander and thus committed roboticide."

And Amadiro, maddened, shouted, "No! Never! Nothing I did to that robot could possibly have immobilized him!"

Fastolfe interposed. "I agree. Mr. Chairman, I, too, think that Dr. Amadiro did not immobilize Jander. However, Mr. Chairman, Dr. Amadiro's statement just now would seem an implicit admission that he was working with Jander—and that Mr. Baley's analysis of the situation is essentially accurate."

The Chairman nodded. "I am forced to agree with you, Dr. Fastolfe. —Dr. Amadiro, you may insist on a formal denial of all this and that may force me into a full-fledged investigation, which could do you a great deal of damage, however it turned out—and I rather suspect, at this stage, it is likely to turn out to your great disadvantage. My suggestion is that you do not force this—that you do not cripple your own position in the Legislature and, perhaps, cripple Aurora's ability to continue along a smooth political course.

"As I see it, before the matter of Jander's immobilization came up, Dr. Fastolfe had a majority of the legislators—not a large majority, admittedly—on his side in the matter of Galactic settlement. You would have swung enough legislators to your side by pushing the matter of Dr. Fastolfe's supposed responsibility for Jander's immobilization and thus have gained the majority. But now Dr. Fastolfe, if he wishes, can turn the tables by accusing you of the immobilization and, moreover, of having tried to hang a false accusation upon your opponent as well—and you would lose.

"If I do not interfere, then it may be that you, Dr. Amadiro, and you, Dr. Fastolfe, actuated by stubbornness or even vindictiveness, will both marshal your forces and accuse each other of all sorts of things. Our political forces and public opinion, too, will be hopelessly divided—even fragmented—to our infinite harm.

"I believe that, in that case, Fastolfe's victory, while inevitable, would be a very costly one, so that it would be my task as the Chairman to swing the votes in his direction to begin with, and to place pressure upon you and your faction, Dr. Amadiro, to accept Fastolfe's victory with as much grace as you can manage, and to do it right now—for the good of Aurora."

Fastolfe said, "I am not interested in a crushing victory, Mr. Chairman. I propose again a compromise whereby Aurora, the other Spacer worlds, and Earth, too, all have the freedom of settlement in the Galaxy. In return, I will be glad to join the Robotics Institute, put my knowledge of humaniform robots at its disposal, and thus facilitate Dr.

Amadiro's plan, in return for his solemn agreement to abandon all
thought of retaliation against Earth at any time in the future and to
put this into treaty form, with ourselves and Earth as signatories."

The Chairman nodded. "A wise and statesmanlike suggestion. May
I have your acceptance of this, Dr. Amadiro?"

Amadiro now sat down. His face was a study in defeat. He said, "I
have not wanted personal power or the satisfaction of victory. I wanted
what I know to be best for Aurora and I am convinced that this plan
of Dr. Fastolfe's means an end to Aurora someday. However, I recognize that I am now helpless against the work of this Earthman"—
he shot a quick venomous glance toward Baley—"and I am forced to
accept Dr. Fastolfe's suggestion—though I will ask for permission to
address the Legislature on the subject and to state, for the record, my
fears of the consequences."

"We will, of course, allow that," said the Chairman. "And if you'll
be guided by me, Dr. Fastolfe, you'll get this Earthman off our world
as fast as possible. He has won your viewpoint for you, but it will not
be a very popular one if Aurorans have too long a time to brood over
it as an Earthly victory over Aurorans."

"You are quite right, Mr. Chairman, and Mr. Baley will be gone
quickly—with my thanks and, I trust, with yours as well."

"Well," said the Chairman, not with the best of grace, "since his
ingenuity has saved us from a bruising political battle, he has my
thanks. —Thank you, Mr. Baley."

**19.** **Again Baley**

80

Baley watched them leave from a distance. Though Amadiro and the Chairman had come together, they now left separately.

Fastolfe came back from seeing them off, making no attempt to hide his intense relief.

"Come, Mr. Baley," he said, "you will have lunch with me and then, as soon after that as possible, you will leave for Earth again."

His robotic staff was clearly in action with that in mind.

Baley nodded and said sardonically, "The Chairman managed to thank me, but it seemed to stick in his throat."

Fastolfe said, "You have no idea how you have been honored. The Chairman rarely thanks anyone, but then no one ever thanks the Chairman. It is always left to history to praise Chairmen and this one has served for over forty years. He has grown cranky and ill-tempered, as Chairmen always do in their final decades.

"However, Mr. Baley, once again I thank you and, through me, Aurora will thank you. You will live to see Earthmen move outward into space, even in your short lifetime, and we will help you with our technology.

"How you have managed to untie this knot of ours, Mr. Baley, in two and a half days—less—I can't imagine. You are a wonder. —But, come, you will want to wash and freshen up. I know I do."

For the first time since the Chairman arrived, Baley had time to think of something besides his next sentence.

He still didn't know what it was that had come to him three times, first on the point of sleep, then on the point of unconsciousness, and finally in postcoital relaxation.

"He was there first!"

It was still meaningless, yet he had made his point to the Chairman and carried all before him without it. Could it have any meaning at all, then, if it was a part of a mechanism that didn't fit and didn't seem needed? Was it nonsense?

It chafed at the corner of his mind and he came to lunch a victor without the proper sensation of victory. Somehow, he felt as though he had missed the point.

For one thing, would the Chairman stick to his resolve? Amadiro had lost the battle, but he didn't seem the kind of person who would give up altogether under any circumstances. Give him credit and assume he meant what he said, that he was driven not by personal vain-glory but by his concept of Auroran patriotism. If that were so, he *could not* give up.

Baley felt it necessary to warn Fastolfe.

"Dr. Fastolfe," he said, "I don't think it's over. Dr. Amadiro will continue to fight to exclude Earth."

Fastolfe nodded as the dishes were served. "I know he will. I expect him to. However, I have no fear as long as the matter of Jander's immobilization is set to rest. With that aside, I'm sure I can always outmaneuver him in the Legislature. Fear not, Mr. Baley, Earth will move along. Nor need you fear personal danger from a vengeful Ama-diro. You will be off this planet and on your way back to Earth before sunset—and Daneel will escort you, of course. What's more, the report we'll send with you will ensure, once more, a healthy promotion for you."

"I am eager to go," said Baley, "but I hope I will have time to say my good-byes. I would like to—to see Gladia once more and I would like to say good-bye to Giskard, who may have saved my life last night."

"No question of that, Mr. Baley. But please eat, won't you?"

Baley went through the motions of eating, but didn't enjoy it. Like the confrontation with the Chairman and the victory that ensued, the food was oddly flavorless.

He should not have won. The Chairman should have cut him off. Amadiro, if necessary, should have made a flat denial. It would have been accepted over the word—or the reasoning—of an Earthman.

But Fastolfe was jubilant. He said, "I had feared the worst, Mr. Baley. I feared the meeting with the Chairman was premature and that nothing you could say would help the situation. Yet you managed it so well. I was lost in admiration, listening to you. At any moment, I expected Amadiro to demand that his word be taken against an Earth-man who, after all, was in a constant state of semimadness at finding himself on a strange planet in the open—"

Baley said frigidly, "With all respect, Dr. Fastolfe, I was not in a constant state of semimadness. Last night was exceptional, but it was the only time I lost control. For the rest of my stay on Aurora, I may have been uncomfortable from time to time, but I was always in my perfect mind." Some of the anger he had suppressed at considerable cost to himself in the confrontation with the Chairman was expressing itself now. "Only during the storm, sir—except, of course"—recollect-ing—"for a moment or two on the approaching spaceship—"

He was not conscious of the manner in which the thought—the memory, the interpretation—came to him or at what speed. One mo-ment it did not exist, the next moment it was full-blown in his mind, as though it had been there all the time and needed only the bursting of a soap-bubble veil to show it.

"Jehoshaphat!" he said in an awed whisper. Then, with his fist coming down on the table and rattling the dishes, "*Jehoshaphat!*"

"What is it, Mr. Baley?" asked Fastolfe, startled.

Baley stared at him and heard the question only belatedly. "Nothing, Dr. Fastolfe. I was just thinking of Dr. Amadiro's infernal gall in doing the damage to Jander and then laboring to fix the blame on you, in arranging to have me go half-mad in the storm last night and then using that as a way of casting doubt on my statements. I was just—momentarily—angry."

"Well, no need to be, Mr. Baley. And actually, it is quite impossible for Amadiro to have immobilized Jander. It remains purely a chance event. —To be sure, it is possible that Amadiro's investigation may have increased the odds of such a chance event taking place, but I would not argue the matter."

Baley heard the statement with half of one ear. What he had just said to Fastolfe was fiction and what Fastolfe was saying didn't matter. It was (as the Chairman would have said) irrelevant. In fact, everything that had happened—everything that Baley had explained—was irrelevant. —But nothing had to be changed because of that.

Except one thing—after a while.

Jehoshaphat! he whispered in the silence of his mind and turned suddenly to the lunch, eating with gusto and with joy.

81

Once again, Baley crossed the lawn between Fastolfe's establishment and Gladia's. He would be seeing Gladia for the fourth time in three days—and (his heart seemed to compress into a hard knot in his chest) now for the last time.

Giskard was with him but at a distance, more intent than ever on the surroundings. Surely, with the Chairman in full possession of the facts, there should be a relaxation of any concern for Baley's safety—if there ever had been any, by rights, when it was Daneel who had been in danger. Presumably, Giskard had not yet been reinstructed in the matter.

Only once did he approach Baley and that was when the latter called out, "Giskard, where's Daneel?"

Swiftly, Giskard covered the ground between them, as though reluctant to speak in anything but a quiet tone. "Daneel is on his way to the spaceport, sir, in the company of several others of the staff, in order to make arrangements for your transportation to Earth. When you are taken to the spaceport, he will meet you there and be on the ship with you, taking his final leave of you at Earth."

"Good news. I treasure every day of companionship with Daneel. And you, Giskard? Will you accompany us?"

"No, sir. I am instructed to remain on Aurora. However, Daneel will serve you well, even in my absence."

"I am sure of that, Giskard, but I will miss you."

"Thank you, sir," said Giskard and retreated as rapidly as he had come. Baley gazed after him speculatively for a moment or so. —No, first things first. He had to see Gladia.

82

She advanced to greet him—and what a world of change had taken place in two days. She was not joyous, she was not dancing, she was not bubbling; there was still the grave look of one who had suffered a shock and a loss—but the troubled aura around her was gone. There was a kind of serenity now, as though she had grown aware of the fact that life continued after all and might even, on occasion, be sweet.

She managed a smile, warm and friendly, as she advanced to him and held out her hand.

"Oh, take it, take it, Elijah," she said when he hesitated. "It's ridiculous for you to hang back and pretend you don't want to touch me after last night. You see, I still remember it and I haven't come to regret it. Quite the contrary."

Baley performed the unusual operation (for him) of smiling in return. "I remember it, too, Gladia, and I don't regret it either. I would even like to do it again, but I have come to say good-bye."

A shade fell across her face. "Then you'll be going back to Earth. Yet the report I got by way of the robot network that always operates between Fastolfe's establishment and my own is that all went well. You *can't* have failed."

"I did not fail. Dr. Fastolfe, has, in fact, won completely. I don't believe there will be any suggestion at all that he was in any way involved in Jander's death."

"Because of what you had to say, Elijah?"

"I believe so."

"I knew it." There was a tinge of self-satisfaction to that. "I knew you would do it when I told them to get you on the case. —But then why are you being sent home?"

"Precisely because the case is solved. If I remain here longer, I will be a foreign irritant in the body politic, apparently."

She looked at him dubiously for a moment and said, "I'm not sure what you mean by that. It sounds like an Earth expression to me. But never mind. Were you able to find out who killed Jander? That is the important part."

Baley looked around. Giskard was standing in one niche, one of Gladia's robots in another.

Gladia interpreted the look without trouble. She said, "Now, Elijah, you must learn to stop worrying about robots. You don't worry about the presence of the chair, do you, or of these drapes?"

Baley nodded. "Well, then, Gladia, I'm sorry—I'm terribly sorry— but I had to tell them of the fact that Jander was your husband."

Her eyes opened wide and he hastened on. "I *had* to. It was essential to the case, but I promise it won't affect your status on Aurora." As briefly as he might, he summarized the events of the confrontation and concluded, "So, you see, no one killed Jander. The immobilization was the result of a chance change in his positronic pathways, though the probabilities of that chance change may have been enhanced by what had been going on."

"And I never knew," she moaned, "I never knew. I *connived* at this Amadiro's foul plan. —And he is the one responsible just as much, as though he had deliberately hacked away at him with a sledgehammer."

"Gladia," said Baley earnestly, "that is uncharitable. He had no intention of doing harm to Jander and what he was doing was, in his own eyes, for the good of Aurora. As it is, he is punished. He is defeated, his plans are in shambles, and the Robotics Institute will come under the domination of Dr. Fastolfe. You yourself could not work out a more suitable punishment, no matter how you tried."

She said, "I'll think about that. —But what do I do with Santirix Gremionis, this good-looking young lackey whose job it was to lure me away? No wonder he appeared to cling to hope despite my repeated refusal. Well, he'll come here again and I will have the pleasure of—"

Baley shook his head violently. "Gladia, *no*. I have interviewed him and I *assure* you he had no knowledge of what was going on. He was as much deceived as you were. In fact, you have it reversed. He was not persistent because it was important to lure you away. He was useful to Amadiro *because* he was so persistent—and that persistence was out of regard for you. Out of love, if the word means on Aurora what it means on Earth."

"On Aurora, it is choreography. Jander was a robot and you are an Earthman. It is different with the Aurorans."

"So you have explained. But Gladia, you learned from Jander to take; you learned from me—not that I meant it—to give. If you benefit by learning, is it not only right and fair that you should teach in your turn? Gremionis is sufficiently attracted to you to be willing to learn. He already defies Auroran convention by persisting in the face of your refusal. He will defy more. You can teach him to give and take and you will learn to do both in alternation or together, in company with him."

Gladia looked searchingly into his eyes. "Elijah, are you trying to get rid of me?"

Slowly, Baley nodded. "Yes, Gladia, I am. It's your happiness I want at this moment, more than I have ever wanted anything for myself or for Earth. I can't give you happiness, but if Gremionis can give it to you, I will be as happy—*almost* as happy as if it were I myself who were making the gift.

"Gladia, he may surprise you with how eagerly he will break through the choreography when you show him how. And the word will somehow spread, so that others will come to swoon at your feet—and Gremionis may find it possible to teach other women. Gladia, it may be that you will revolutionize Auroran sex before you are through. You will have three centuries in which to do so."

Gladia stared at him and then broke into a laugh. "You are teasing. You are being deliberately foolish. I wouldn't have thought it of you, Elijah. You always look so long-faced and grave. Jehoshaphat!" (And, with the last word, she tried to imitate his somber baritone.)

Baley said, "Perhaps I'm teasing a little, but I mean it in essence. Promise me that you will give Gremionis his chance."

She came closer to him and, without hesitation, he put his arm around her. She placed her finger on his lips and he made a small kissing motion. She said softly, "Wouldn't you rather have me for yourself, Elijah?"

He said, just as softly (and unable to become unaware of the robots in the room), "Yes, I would, Gladia. I am ashamed to say that at this moment I would be content to have the Earth fall to pieces if I could have you—but I can't. In a few hours, I'll be off Aurora and there's no way you will be allowed to go with me. Nor do I think I will ever be allowed to come back to Aurora, nor is it possible that you will ever visit Earth.

"I will never see you again, Gladia, but I will never forget you, either. I will die in a few decades and when I do you will be as young as you are now, so we would have to say good-bye soon whatever we could imagine as happening."

She put her head against his chest. "Oh, Elijah, twice you came into my life, each time for just a few hours. Twice you've done so much for me and then said good-bye. The first time all I could do was touch your face, but what a difference that made. The second time, I did so much more—and again what a difference that made. I'll never forget you, Elijah, if I live more centuries than I can count."

Baley said, "Then let it not be the kind of memory that cuts you off from happiness. Accept Gremionis and make *him* happy—and let him make you happy as well. And, remember, there is nothing to prevent you from sending me letters. The hyperpost between Aurora and Earth exists."

"I will, Elijah. And you will write to me as well?"

"I will, Gladia."

Then there was silence and, reluctantly, they moved apart. She remained standing in the middle of the room and when he went to the door and turned back, she was still standing there with a little smile. His lips shaped: *Good-bye.* And then because there was no sound—he could not have done it with sound—he added, *my love.*

And her lips moved too. *Good-bye, my dearest love.*

And he turned and walked out and knew he would never see her in tangible form, never touch her again.

83

It was a while before Elijah could bring himself to consider the task that still lay before him. He had walked in silence perhaps half the distance back to Fastolfe's establishment before he stopped and lifted his arm.

The observant Giskard was at his side in a moment.

Baley said, "How much time before I must leave for the spaceport, Giskard?"

"Three hours and ten minutes, sir."

Baley thought a moment. "I would like to walk over to that tree there and sit down with my back against the trunk and spend some time there alone. With you, of course, but away from other human beings."

"In the open, sir?" The robot's voice was unable to express surprise and shock, but somehow Baley had the feeling that, if Giskard were human, those words would express those feelings.

"Yes," said Baley, "I have to think and, after last night, a calm day like this—sunny, cloudless, mild—scarcely seems dangerous. I'll go indoors if I get agoraphobic. I promise. So will you join me?"

"Yes, sir."

"Good." Baley led the way. They reached the tree and Baley touched the trunk gingerly and then stared at his finger, which remained perfectly clean. Reassured that leaning against the trunk would not dirty him, he inspected the ground and then sat down carefully and rested his back against the tree.

It was not nearly as comfortable as the back of a chair would have been, but there was a feeling of peace (oddly enough) that perhaps he would not have had inside a room.

Giskard remained standing and Baley said, "Won't you sit down, too?"

"I am as comfortable standing, sir."

"I know that, Giskard, but I will think better if I don't have to look up at you."

"I could not guard you against possible harm as efficiently if I were seated, sir."

"I know that, too, Giskard, but there is no reasonable danger at the moment. My mission is over, the case is solved, Dr. Fastolfe's position is secure. You can risk being seated and I order you to sit down."

Giskard at once sat down, facing Baley, but his eyes continued to wander in this direction and that and were ever alert.

Baley looked at the sky, through the leaves of the tree, green against blue, listened to the susurration of insects and to the sudden call of a bird, noted a disturbance of grass nearby that might have meant a small animal passing by, and again thought how oddly peaceful it all was and how different this peacefulness was from the clamor of the City. This was a quiet peace, an unhurried peace, a removed peace.

For the first time, Baley caught a faint suggestion of how it might be to prefer Outside to the City. He caught himself being thankful to his experiences on Aurora, to the storm most of all—for he knew now that he would be able to leave Earth and face the conditions of whatever new world he might settle on, he and Ben—and perhaps Jessie.

He said, "Last night, in the darkness of the storm, I wondered if I might have seen Aurora's satellite were it not for the clouds. It has a satellite, if I recall my reading correctly."

"Two, actually, sir. The larger is Tithonus, but it is still so small that it appears only as a moderately bright star. The smaller is not visible at all to the unaided eye and is simply called Tithonus II, when it is referred to at all."

"Thank you. —And thank you, Giskard, for rescuing me last night." He looked at the robot. "I don't know the proper way of thanking you."

"It is not necessary to thank me at all. I was merely following the dictates of the First Law. I had no choice in the matter."

"Nevertheless, I may even owe you my life and it is important that you know I understand this. —And now, Giskard, what ought I to do?"

"Concerning what matter, sir?"

"My mission is over. Dr. Fastolfe's views are secure. Earth's future may be assured. It would seem I have nothing more to do and yet there is the matter of Jander."

"I do not understand, sir."

"Well, it seems settled that he died by a chance shift of positronic potential in his brain, but Fastolfe admits the chance of that is infinitesimally small. Even with Amadiro's activities, the chance, though possibly greater, would remain infinitesimally small. At least, so Fastolfe thinks. It continues to seem to me, then, that Jander's death was one of deliberate roboticide. Yet I don't dare raise this point now. I don't want to unsettle matters that have been brought to such a satisfactory conclusion. I don't want to put Fastolfe in jeopardy again. I don't want to make Gladia unhappy. I don't know what to do. I can't talk to a human being about this, so I'm talking to you, Giskard."

"Yes, sir."

"I can always order you to erase whatever I have said and to remember it no more."

"Yes, sir."

"In your opinion, what ought I to do?"

Giskard said, "If there is a roboticide, sir, there must be someone capable of committing the act. Only Dr. Fastolfe is capable of committing it and he says he did not do it."

"Yes, we started with that situation. I believe Dr. Fastolfe and am quite certain he did not do it."

"Then how could there have been a roboticide, sir?"

"Suppose that someone else knew as much about robots as Dr. Fastolfe does, Giskard."

Baley drew up his knees and clasped his hands around them. He did not look at Giskard and seemed lost in thought.

"Who might that be, sir?" asked Giskard.

And finally, Baley reached the crucial point.

He said, "You, Giskard."

84

If Giskard had been human, he might have simply stared, silent and stunned; or he might have raged angrily; or shrunk back in terror; or had any of a dozen responses. Because he was a robot, he showed no sign of any emotion whatever and simply said, "Why do you say so, sir?"

Baley said, "I am quite certain, Giskard, that you know exactly how I have come to this conclusion, but you will do me a favor if you allow me, in this quiet place and in this bit of time before I must leave, to explain the matter for my own benefit. I would like to hear myself talk about it. And I would like you to correct me where I am wrong."

"By all means, sir."

"I suppose my initial mistake was to suppose that you are a less complicated and more primitive robot than Daneel is, simply because you look less human. A human being will always suppose that, the more human a robot is, the more advanced, complicated, and intelligent he will be. To be sure, a robot like you is easily designed and one like Daneel is a great problem for men like Amadiro and can be handled only by a robotics genius such as Fastolfe. However, the difficulty in designing Daneel lies, I suspect, in reproducing all the human aspects such as facial expression, intonation of voice, gestures and movements that are extraordinarily intricate but have nothing really to do with complexity of mind. Am I right?"

"Quite right, sir."

"So I automatically underestimated you, as does everyone. Yet you gave yourself away even before we landed on Aurora. You remember, perhaps, that during the landing, I was overcome by an agoraphobic spasm and was, for a moment, even more helpless than I was last night in the storm."

"I do, sir."

"At the time, Daneel was in the cabin with me, while you were outside the door. I was falling into a kind of catatonic state, noiselessly, and he was, perhaps, not looking at me and so knew nothing of it. You were outside the cabin and yet it was you who dashed in and turned off the vewier I was holding. You got there first, ahead of Daneel, though his reflexes are as fast as yours, I'm sure—as he demonstrated when he prevented Dr. Fastolfe from striking me."

"Surely it cannot be that Dr. Fastolfe was striking you."

"He wasn't. He was merely demonstrating Daneel's reflexes. —And yet, as I say, in the cabin you got there first. I was scarcely in condition to observe that fact, but have been trained to observe and I am not put entirely out of action even by agoraphobic terror, as I showed last night. I did notice you were there first, though I tended to forget the fact. There is, of course, only one logical solution."

Baley paused, as though expecting Giskard to agree, but the robot said nothing.

(In later years, this was what Baley pictured first when thinking of his stay on Aurora. Not the storm. Not even Gladia. It was, rather, the quiet time under the tree, with the green leaves against the blue sky, the mild breeze, the soft sound of animals, and Giskard opposite him with faintly glowing eyes.)

Baley said, "It would seem that you could somehow detect my state of mind and, even through the closed door, tell that I was having a seizure of some sort. Or, to put it briefly and perhaps simplistically, you can read minds."

"Yes, sir," said Giskard quietly.

"And you can somehow influence minds, too. I believe you noted that I had detected this and you obscured it in my mind, so that I somehow did not remember or did not see the significance—if I did casually recall the situation. Yet you did not do that entirely efficiently, perhaps because your powers are limited—"

Giskard said, "Sir, the First Law is paramount. I had to come to your rescue, although I quite realized that would give me away. And

I had to obscure your mind minimally, in order not to damage it in any way."

Baley nodded. "You have your difficulties, I see. Obscured minimally—so I did remember it when my mind was sufficiently relaxed and could think by free association. Just before I lost consciousness in the storm. I knew you would find me first, as you had on the ship. You may have found me by infrared radiation, but every mammal and bird was radiating as well and that might be confusing—but you could also detect mental activity, even if I were unconscious, and that would help you to find me."

"It certainly helped," said Giskard.

"When I did remember, close to sleep or unconsciousness, I would forget again when fully conscious. Last night, however, I remembered for the third time and I was not alone. Gladia was with me and could repeat what I had said, which was 'He was there first.' And even *then* I could not remember the meaning, until a chance remark of Dr. Fastolfe's led to a thought that worked its way past the obscuration. Then, once it dawned on me, I remembered other things. Thus, when I was wondering if I were really landing on Aurora, you assured me that our destination was Aurora before I actually asked. —I presume you allow no one to know of your mind-reading ability."

"That is true, sir."

"Why is that?"

"My mind reading gives me a unique ability to obey the First Law, sir, so I value its existence. I can prevent harm to human beings far more efficiently. It seemed to me, however, that neither Dr. Fastolfe— nor any other human being—would long tolerate a mind-reading robot, so I keep the ability secret. Dr. Fastolfe loves to tell the legend of the mind-reading robot who was destroyed by Susan Calvin and I would not want him to duplicate Dr. Calvin's feat."

"Yes, he told the legend to me. I suspect that he knows, subliminally, that you read minds or he wouldn't harp on the legend so. And it is dangerous for him to do so, as far as you are concerned, I should think. Certainly, it helped put the matter in my mind."

"I do what I can to neutralize the danger without unduly tampering with Dr. Fastolfe's mind. Dr. Fastolfe invariably stresses the legendary and impossible nature of the story when he tells it."

"Yes, I remember that, too. But if Fastolfe does not know you can read minds, it must be that you were not designed originally with these powers. How, then, do you come to have them? —No, don't tell me, Giskard. Let me suggest something. Miss Vasilia was particularly fascinated with you when she was a young woman first becoming interested in robotics. She told me that she had experimented by programming you under Fastolfe's distant supervision. Could it be that, at one time, quite by accident, she did something that gave you the power? Is that correct?"

"That is correct, sir."

"And do you know what that something is?"

"Yes, sir."

"Are you the only mind-reading robot that exists?"

"So far, yes, sir. There will be others."

"If I asked you what it was that Dr. Vasilia did to you to give you such powers—or if Dr. Fastolfe did—would you tell us by virtue of the Second Law?"

"No, sir, for it is my judgment that it would do you harm to know and my refusal to tell you under the First Law would take precedence. The problem would not arise, however, for I would know that someone was going to ask the question and give the order and I would remove the impulse to do so from the mind before it could be done."

"Yes," said Baley. "Evening before last, as we were walking from Gladia's to Fastolfe's, I asked Daneel if he had had any contact with Jander during the latter's stay with Gladia and he answered quite simply that he had not. I then turned to ask you the same question and, somehow, I never did. You quashed the impulse for me to do so, I take it."

"Yes, sir."

"Because if I had asked, you would have had to say that you knew him at that time and you were not prepared to have me know that."

"I was not, sir."

"But during this period of contact with Jander, you knew he was being tested by Amadiro because, I presume, you could read Jander's mind or detect his positronic potentials—"

"Yes, sir, the same ability covers both robotic and human mental activity. Robots are far easier to understand."

"You disapproved of Amadiro's activities because you agreed with Fastolfe on the matter of settling the Galaxy."

"Yes, sir."

"Why did you not stop Amadiro? Why did you not remove from his mind the impulse to test Jander?"

Giskard said, "Sir, I do not lightly tamper with minds. Amadiro's resolve was so deep and complex that, to remove it, I would have had to do much—and his mind is an advanced and important one that I would be reluctant to damage. I let the matter continue for a great while, during which I pondered on which action would best fulfill my First Law needs. Finally, I decided on the proper manner to correct the situation. It was not an easy decision."

"You decided to immobilize Jander before Amadiro could work out the method for designing a true humaniform robot. You knew how to do so, since you had, over the years, gained a perfect understanding of Fastolfe's theories from Fastolfe's mind. Is that right?"

"Exactly, sir."

"So that Fastolfe was not the only one, after all, expert enough to immobilize Jander."

"In a sense, he was, sir. My own ability is merely the reflection—or the extension—of his."

"But it will do. Did you not see that this immobilization would place Fastolfe in great danger? That he would be the natural suspect? Did you plan on admitting your action and revealing your abilities if that were necessary to save him?"

Giskard said, "I did indeed see that Dr. Fastolfe would be in a painful situation, but I did not intend to admit my guilt. I had hoped to utilize the situation as a wedge for getting you to Aurora."

"Getting *me* here? Was that *your* idea?" Baley felt rather stupefied.

"Yes, sir. With your permission, I would like to explain."

Baley said, "Please do."

Giskard said, "I knew of you from Miss Gladia and from Dr. Fastolfe, not only from what they said but from what was in their minds. I learned of the situation on Earth. Earthmen, it was clear, live behind walls, which they find difficult to escape from, but it was just as clear to me that Aurorans live behind walls, too.

"Aurorans live behind walls made of robots, who shield them from all the vicissitudes of life and who, in Amadiro's plans, would build up shielded societies to wall up Aurorans settling new worlds. Aurorans also live behind walls made up of their own extended lives, which forces them to overvalue individuality and keeps them from pooling their scientific resources. Nor do they indulge in the rough-and-tumble of controversy, but, through their Chairman, demand a short-circuiting of all uncertainty and that decisions on solutions be reached before problems are aired. They could not be bothered with actually thrashing out best solutions. What they wanted were *quiet* solutions.

"The Earthman's walls are crude and literal, so that their existence is obtrusive and obvious—and there are always some who long to escape. The Aurorans' walls are immaterial and aren't even seen as walls, so that none can even conceive of escaping. It seemed to me, then, that it must be Earthmen and not Aurorans—or any other Spacers—who must settle the Galaxy and establish what will someday become a Galactic Empire.

"All this was Dr. Fastolfe's reasoning and I agreed with it. Dr. Fastolfe was, however, satisfied with the reasoning, while I, given my own abilities, could not be. I had to examine the mind of at least one Earthman directly, in order that I might check my conclusions, and you were the Earthman I thought I could bring to Aurora. The immobilization of Jander served both to stop Amadiro and to be the occasion for your visit. I pushed Miss Gladia very slightly to have her suggest your coming to Dr. Fastolfe; I pushed him in turn, very slightly, to have him suggest it to the Chairman; and I pushed the Chairman, very slightly, to have him agree. Once you arrived, I studied you and was pleased with what I found."

Giskard stopped speaking and became robotically impassive again.

Baley frowned. "It occurs to me that I have earned no credit in what I have done here. You must have seen to it that I found my way to the truth."

"No, sir. On the contrary. I placed barriers in your way—reasonable ones, of course. I refused to let you recognize my abilities, even though I was forced to give myself away. I made sure that you felt dejection and despair at odd times. I encouraged you to risk the open, in order to study your responses. Yet you found your way through and over all these obstacles and I was pleased.

"I found that you longed for the walls of your City but recognized that you must learn to do without them. I found that you suffered from the view of Aurora from space and from your exposure to the storm, but that neither prevented you from thinking nor drove you from your problem. I found that you accept your shortcomings and your brief life—and that you do not dodge controversy."

Baley said, "How do you know I am representative of Earthpeople generally?"

"I know you are not. But from your mind, I know there are some like you and we will build with those. I will see to it—and now that I know clearly the path that must be followed, I will prepare other robots like myself—and they will see to it, too."

Baley said suddenly, "You mean that mind-reading robots will come to Earth?"

"No, I do not. And you are right to be alarmed. Involving robots directly will mean the construction of the very walls that are dooming Aurora and the Spacer worlds to paralysis. Earthmen will have to settle the Galaxy without robots of any kind. It will mean difficulties, dangers, and harm without measure—events that robots would labor to prevent if they were present—but, in the end, human beings will be better off for having worked on their own. And perhaps someday— some long-away day in the future—robots can intervene once more. Who can tell?"

Baley said curiously, "Do you see the future?"

"No, sir, but studying minds as I do, I can tell dimly that there are laws that govern human behavior as the Three Laws of Robotics govern robotic behavior; and with these it may be that the future will be dealt with, after a fashion—someday. The human laws are far more complicated than the Laws of Robotics are and I do not have any idea as to how they may be organized. They may be statistical in nature, so that they might be fruitfully expressed except when dealing with huge populations. They may be very loosely binding, so that they might not make sense unless those huge populations are unaware of the operation of those laws."

"Tell me, Giskard, is this what Dr. Fastolfe refers to as the future science of 'psychohistory'?"

"Yes, sir. I have gently inserted it into his mind, in order that the process of working it out begin. It will be needed someday, now that the existence of the Spacer worlds as a long-lived robotized culture is coming to an end and a new wave of human expansion by short-lived human beings—without robots—will be beginning.

"And now"—Giskard rose to his feet—"I think, sir, that we must go to Dr. Fastolfe's establishment and prepare for your leavetaking. All that we have said here will not be repeated, of course."

"It is strictly confidential, I assure you," said Baley.

"Indeed," said Giskard calmly. "But you need not fear the responsibility of having to remain silent. I will allow you to remember, but you will never have the urge to repeat the matter—not the slightest."

Baley lifted his eyebrows in resignation over that and said, "One thing, though, Giskard, before you clamp down on me. Will you see to it that Gladia is not disturbed on this planet, that she is not treated unkindly because she is a Solarian and has accepted a robot as her husband, and—and that she will accept the offers of Gremionis?"

"I heard your final conversation with Miss Gladia, sir, and I understand. It will be taken care of. Now, sir, may I take my leave of you while no other is watching?" Giskard thrust out his hand in the most human gesture Baley had ever seen him make.

Baley took it. The fingers were hard and cool in his grip. "Good-bye—friend Giskard."

Giskard said, "Good-bye, friend Elijah, and remember that, although people apply the phrase to Aurora, it is, from this point on, Earth itself that is the true World of the Dawn."

About the Author

Isaac Asimov was born in the Soviet Union to his great surprise. He moved quickly to correct the situation. When his parents emigrated to the United States, Isaac (three years old at the time) stowed away in their baggage. He has been an American citizen since the age of eight.

Brought up in Brooklyn, and educated in its public schools, he eventually found his way to Columbia University and, over the protests of the school administration, managed to annex a series of degrees in chemistry, up to and including a Ph.D. He then infiltrated Boston University and climbed the academic ladder, ignoring all cries of outrage, until he found himself Professor of Biochemistry.

Meanwhile, at the age of nine, he found the love of his life (in the inanimate sense) when he discovered his first science-fiction magazine. By the time he was eleven, he began to write stories, and at eighteen, he actually worked up the nerve to submit one. It was rejected. After four long months of tribulation and suffering, he sold his first story and, thereafter, he never looked back.

In 1941, when he was twenty-one years old, he wrote the classic short story "Nightfall" and his future was assured. Shortly before that he had begun writing his robot stories, and shortly after that he had begun his Foundation series.

What was left except quantity? At the present time, he has published over 300 books, distributed through every major division of the Dewey system of library classification, and shows no signs of slowing up. He remains as youthful, as lively, and as lovable as ever, and grows more handsome with each year. You can be sure that this is so since he has written this little essay himself and his devotion to absolute objectivity is notorious.

He is married to Janet Jeppson, psychiatrist and writer, has two children by a previous marriage, and lives in New York City.